JINX

Also by P. C. Cast and Kristin Cast

THE DYSASTERS

The Dysasters: The Graphic Novel

HOUSE OF NIGHT

Marked

Betrayed

Chosen

Untamed

Hunted

Tempted

Burned

Awakened

Destined

Hidden

Revealed

Redeemed

The Fledgling Handbook 101

Dragon's Oath

Lenobia's Vow

Neferet's Curse

Kalona's Fall

A 2-in-1 Sisters of Salem Collection

JINX

P. C. Cast

Kristin Cast

WEDNESDAY BOOKS
NEW YORK

This is a work of fiction. All of the characters, organizations, and events portrayed in this novel are either products of the authors' imaginations or are used fictitiously.

Published in the United States by Wednesday Books, an imprint of St. Martin's Publishing Group

www.wednesdaybooks.com

Design by Jonathan Bennett

Map by Sabine Stangenberg

The Library of Congress Cataloging-in-Publication Data is available upon request.

ISBN 978-1-250-85602-9 (trade paperback)

First Wednesday Books Trade Paperback Edition: 2023

10 9 8 7 6 5 4 3 2 1

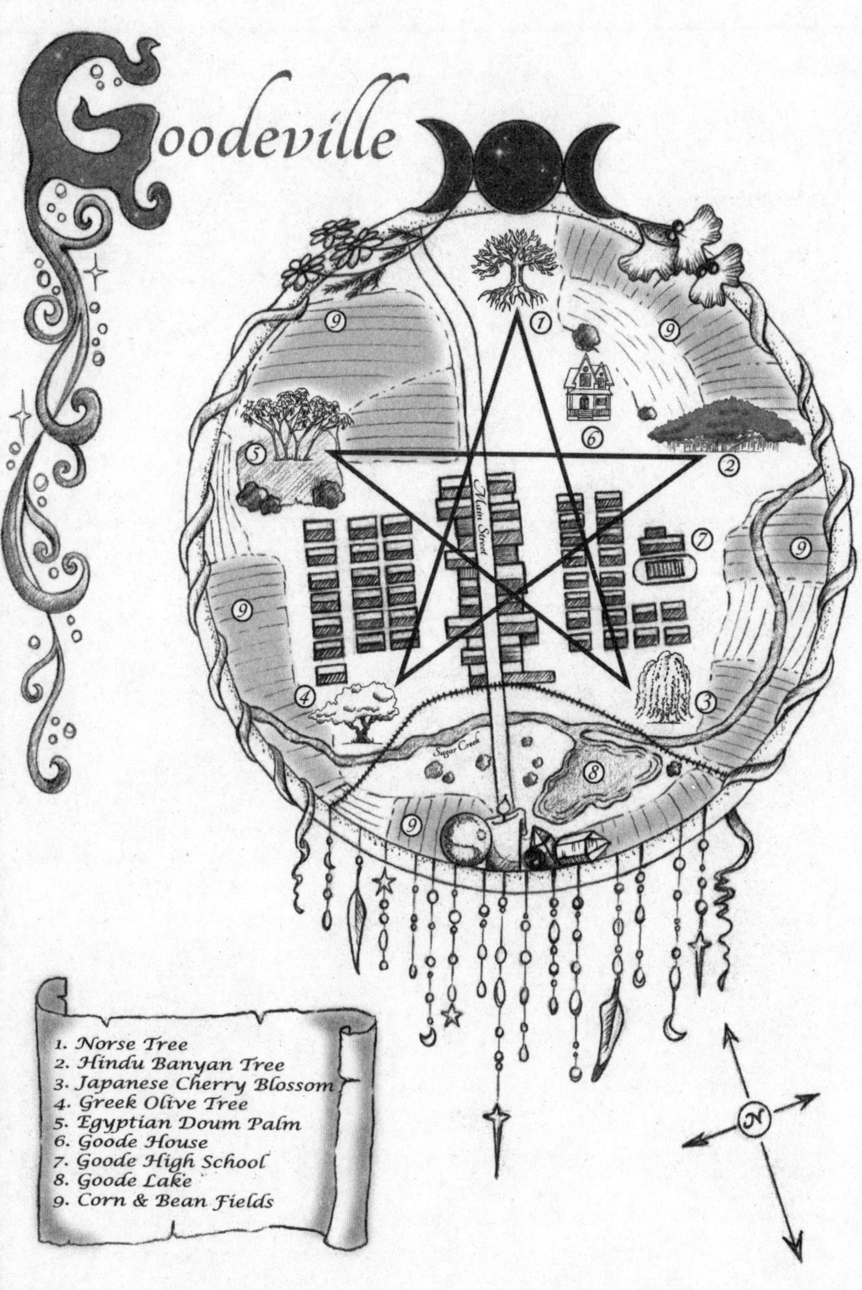

1. Norse Tree
2. Hindu Banyan Tree
3. Japanese Cherry Blossom
4. Greek Olive Tree
5. Egyptian Doum Palm
6. Goode House
7. Goode High School
8. Goode Lake
9. Corn & Bean Fields

SPELLS TROUBLE

To Monique Patterson, our longtime editor.
Thank you for being our champion. This one's for you!

Prologue

JULY 19, 1692

Salem, Massachusetts

Sarah Goode didn't open her eyes when they began to test the gallows. Though Procter's Ledge was a goodly walk from the courthouse where Sarah was jailed, the breeze carried the sound through the bars of the glassless window above her head. It was ghastly. The metallic *creeeeak—snap* of the lever that opened the trapdoor splintered the night followed closely by the *thunk* of the burlap bag of sand they used in place of a falling body. The sarcastic guffaws and muffled comments from the men who witnessed the test flitted wasp-like to her through the otherwise silent night.

Beside her mother, little Dorothy stirred on the narrow cot and Sarah stroked the child's thin back comfortingly. She drew a deep breath, and the taste of rosemary filled her. She held in check the anger she felt at *them*. Bad enough that they had fabricated a reason to arrest her for witchcraft, but they'd jailed her four-year-old daughter as well because they'd found a fleabite on her little finger—*a fleabite!*

Sarah had paid attention to omens that warned she was in danger—the raven that had called through her window three mornings in a row—the mandrake roots she'd unearthed that were filled with rot—and especially the rabbit she'd found dead on her doorstep. Sarah had heeded their warning and she had prepared, though she had underestimated how swiftly the town would move against her, or how her own husband would add to the accusations.

Still, she hadn't panicked until the day Constable Locker appeared at the close-set bars of her jail cell with Dorothy's small hand in his—and then opened the door and pushed the child in to her mother, saying, "Aye, well, 'tis true. The child confessed to witchery like her mother and showed Satan's mark as well. So she will abide with ye." That was the day Sarah knew the town would not overcome the hysteria that gripped it. They would not see reason and allow her or her precious child to go free—and if they did, where would her daughter go? Back to her treacherous father?

Sarah had to get her away.

Creeeeak—snap! Thunk! This time the men's laughter was punctuated by a smattering of applause.

Dorothy murmured restlessly against her mother's side, and Sarah hummed a familiar lullaby under her breath while she stroked her back. Normally she would sing to her daughter, but not that night. That night Sarah soothed the child just enough to keep her silent and sleeping. Her main focus—her true intention—was on the sprig of fresh rosemary she chewed slowly, carefully, into a fragrant pulp.

The time was nigh. The testing of the gallows confirmed that it was the night before she, along with four others—Goodwifes Martin, Howe, Nurse, and Wilde—were to be hung at dawn.

Why test the gallows in the deep of the night?

Sarah's full lips tilted up as the answer filled her mind. *'Tis because of cruelty mixed with their fear.* The small-minded men who ruled Salem called midnight The Witch's Hour—but they knew little else. Their show of bravado was meant to frighten away Satan should he stride into town, forked tongue flashing, to rescue the women Reverend Noyes called Satan's handmaids. They'd jailed each woman in different parts of the courthouse—to keep them from joining to call their master.

Sarah snorted. Fools—every one of them.

The other four women meant to hang that day were no more witches than Reverend Noyes was a warlock. *May that monstrous man's God give him only blood to drink for the misery he has caused,* Sarah thought. *And me? If I be a handmaid, it is for the Earth Mother Gaia.* Sarah Goode no more believed in Satan than she did in fairies.

Creeeeak—snap! Thunk!

Dorothy reacted less to the sound each time it came. She snored softly, her restlessness abating, which left Sarah to focus completely on the spell. She had surreptitiously palmed a sprig of rosemary during the brief trip she and Dorothy had taken to the outhouse to relieve themselves. Sarah continued to silently recite her intent, over and over as she chewed the rosemary.

Unaltered the fragrance aids memory
I muddle—I chew—I alter thee three by three by three
So that befuddled with sleep he shall be . . .

"Yowl!"

The cat's cry sounded just outside the door to the courthouse jail, eerie accompaniment to the macabre gallows music, though to Sarah's ears the cat's lament was water to a parched desert. Gently, she shook her daughter's shoulders.

The child opened her moss green eyes immediately.

Sarah pressed her finger to her lips and Dorothy nodded, her eyes bright with intelligence. The child didn't move. She didn't speak. She also didn't go back to sleep.

"Yoooowl!"

"God's teeth!" Constable Grant, the junior guard, who went from room to room throughout the night to watch over the condemned, stood at his great oak desk. He set his cheap cigar on the fireplace ledge and closed his Bible abruptly, holding it in his bony hands as he stared at the door.

"Yowl!"

The constable jammed the cigar between his teeth and strode to the entrance of the courthouse's jail, which held three small cells along the rear wall, though only one was occupied. "Begone, foul beast of Satan!" he said around the cigar as he threw open the door and waved the Bible into the night.

The huge cat slipped lithely around him, ear tufts bobbing as the feline padded directly to the cell that held Sarah and her daughter. Constable Grant slammed the door and turned, only then seeing that the cat had snuck inside. He spat out the cigar, dropped the Bible, and stared incredulously as the large black-and-tan-striped feline rubbed itself languidly along the bars of the cell and purred riotously.

Sarah squeezed her daughter's shoulder. It was time.

Immediately Dorothy sat, holding her arms out and saying, "Mommy! Odysseus! 'Tis Odysseus!" Then, just as they'd practiced earlier, the child trotted to the edge of their cell where she sat and reached through the bars with both hands to caress the cat who was so unusually large he dwarfed—and intimidated—many of the village dogs.

"Get the child back! Back, I say Mistress Goode! I shall not abide Satan's beast!" Constable Grant grabbed an iron fireplace poker and held it menacingly aloft as he threatened the purring cat and grinning child.

Sarah squeaked a sound of motherly distress through the ball of masticated rosemary she held in her mouth and rushed to her child—and as the constable loomed over the massive cat, Odysseus met Sarah's gaze. She nodded. The feline familiar drew a deep breath and then squeezed between two bars until, like a cork freed from underwater, he popped into their cell to curl up contentedly in Dorothy's lap.

Constable Grant banged the poker against the bars, red-faced and repeating, "I shall not abide Satan's beast!"

At the same moment Sarah reached the bars. She looked up at the florid young man who was only a handspan away from her and then spat the mouthful of rosemary—filled with intention and saliva—directly into his face.

He dropped the poker. It clanged against the stone floor as he made odd squeaking noises while wiping frantically at the green goo that bespeckled his face and filled his watering eyes.

Sarah lifted her hands and grounded herself. With all of her being she reached down, down, down through the stone floor to the fertile earth below and drew to her the power that rested there as surely as the moon drew the tide. She felt the heat of the earth warm her skin and raise the small hairs on her arms and then Sarah Goode spoke urgently, her voice filled with the confidence and authority that had so intimidated the men of Salem that they had felt the need to hang her.

Rosemary muddled through the mid of night,
Shall now make thee fumble—make thee lose sight.

Grant gasped as she began the spell. His face blanched to milk while he staggered and wiped frantically at his eyes. Blindly, he stumbled back. His gait was awkward—as if he could not quite make himself awaken from a nightmare. He dropped heavily to his knees while he continued to wipe at his face.

Heavy are thy thoughts
Upon waking you shall remember naught.

"Satan's whore!" he slurred, and lurched to his feet.

Undaunted, Sarah continued her spell.

Deep shall be thy sleep
But first thrice I say to thee—drop the key, drop the key, drop the key!

"I shall not succumb to you!" Constable Grant reached blindly into his pocket for the iron key ring as he stumbled backward, toward the door. "Witch! You shall never get—" His words broke off as his feet tripped over the Bible he'd dropped. He fell, arms windmilling. Grant's head hit the corner of his desk and he collapsed unmoving to the floor. The constable's hand opened and with a musical jingle the keys dropped against the stone.

"Hurry, Odysseus!" Sarah spoke to the feline, who bounded off Dorothy's lap, drew in another deep breath, and squeezed back through the narrow bars. He padded to the ring of keys and picked them up with his mouth, carrying them to the jail cell.

It took only moments for Sarah to open the door. She and Dorothy rushed out and Sarah locked the door again before returning the keys to the constable's deep pocket.

Odysseus growled softly.

Sarah nodded. "Yes, yes, I know. But he will awake with no memory of what happened and an empty jail cell. He shall spread the story of how the Goode witch and her spawn magically flew through iron bars and disappeared into the night—likely on the back of Satan's steed—which would be you, my Odysseus."

The huge cat purred as he wound around her legs.

"His tall tale will do more to make the townsfolk pause before tracking me than if I tied him and locked him away."

Odysseus chirped contentedly as Sarah took Dorothy's little hand and cracked open the door.

The night was dark and still and filled with the scent of rosemary. Sarah waited impatiently for the next ghastly *creeeeak—snap! Thunk!* of the gallows. Predictably, the men's laughter and applause followed, covering any sound she, her child, and their faithful familiar might make as they darted from the jail. They hugged the side of the courthouse, then dashed from shadow to shadow, making their way from the center of town.

"Mamma! Mamma!" Dorothy whispered urgently and tugged on her mother's hand.

Barely pausing, Sarah bent and picked up her daughter. "What is it, little love?"

"You are going the wrong way."

Sarah jogged across another dark dirt road and past two clapboard houses before she answered. "We are going to a new home—one that is far, far away."

"Is Father not coming with us?"

Sarah's jaw set. She caressed her daughter's matted curls and reined in her anger. "No, love. Your father did not keep us safe. So forevermore that will be my job."

Beside them Odysseus chirruped up at Sarah. She smiled and corrected, "My job and Odysseus's."

Dorothy's expression was somber and she suddenly appeared much older than her four years. "We shall keep each other safe."

"Indeed we will, little love. Indeed we will."

The predawn gloaming had begun to turn the sky the gray of a dove's breast when the three fugitives finally made their way to the apple grove that divided the west side of Salem from the farmlands and forests beyond. Sarah slowed, then, and allowed Dorothy to walk beside her while Odysseus trotted with them, weaving between the fruit-laden trees as she made her way to the oldest of the apple trees.

At the heart of the grove Sarah approached the ancient tree respectfully. She placed her hand against the rough bark and whispered, "Merry meet, old friend. I give thanks for you to our great goddess, Gaia." Sarah smiled up as the leaves above her quivered in response, though the lazy night breeze had completely died. She walked to the north side of the tree, where two massive roots had broken through the surface to form the V of a divining rod. There she dropped to her knees and, using a sharp stone, began to dig.

It didn't take long for her fingers to touch the wooden box. Sarah didn't bother to pull it free. Instead she cleared the dirt from it, opened the lid, and pulled out the cloth satchel she had buried the day before they'd come for her. It held her treasures—the means to a new future: travel cloaks for herself and Dorothy as well as a change of clothes, a leather purse filled with every coin she had saved, and her grimoire disguised as a prayer book. Beneath the book was a piece of cloth, carefully dyed the deep green of moss and of her daughter's eyes. Within it was wrapped a tin of salt and a precious walnut-sized opal that glimmered lazily in the wan predawn light.

"Sit here at the base, little love," Sarah told her daughter as she poured a circle of salt around the ancient tree. Then, with Dorothy by her feet and Odysseus beside her, Sarah drew three deep breaths and held the opal to the center of her forehead as she invoked.

By stone and salt I call to thee,
Guide mine steps from this fair tree.
Gaia, goddess good and kind and just—
In you I have always placed my trust.
Now I beseech, show me thy way
I am yours to command—yesterday, tomorrow, today.
Lead me to a place of power
Where never again will your daughters fear and cower!

With the last word of her spell Sarah closed her eyes and imagined that she peered out through her own forehead, into the flaming opal, and past it—to the magic it revealed.

"Oh, goddess be blessed! Thank you, Gaia! Thank you!" The words rushed from Sarah as green light lifted from the floor of the grove. Under her feet a ribbon of emerald pointed westward. As Gaia's power channeled through the opal to enhance her sight, the path blazed and pulsed with energy, building in intensity in the distance. She felt its pull as if she had been tethered to it.

Sarah opened her eyes then and bowed her head reverently. "I shall follow your path—now and always. Blessed be, Earth Mother." She kissed the center of the opal and then turned to the ancient oak. On tiptoes Sarah reached up to press the stone into a niche in the bark. "Thank you, Mother Apple. I shall always remember how you stood sentry over my future." Again, the leaves above her shivered in response.

Only then did she gather their supplies, rebury the now empty box, and—with her daughter's hand in hers and the feline familiar at their side—Sarah Goode broke the salt circle and headed west, following the ley line of power that thrummed like a heartbeat beneath her feet.

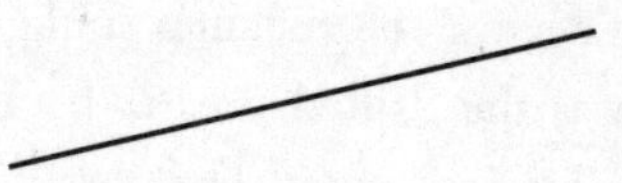

Present Day

GOODEVILLE, ILLINOIS – SALEM COUNTY

One

Goode Lake was postcard perfect with its tree-lined banks and sandy shores that gradually sloped into the crystal blue water. The lake always looked good, but somehow today it looked better. Maybe it was because today was Hunter Goode's sixteenth birthday. Or maybe it was because Hunter was looking for a reason to procrastinate. Either way, she had charged down to the edge of the water, towel in hand, shimmied out of her T-shirt and shorts, and now waded into the calm blue.

Goose bumps crested against her skin and she stared down at her feet as the gentle waves consumed more of her. The water reached the high neck of her swimsuit top and she could still see her toes, blurry pale orbs against the camel-colored sand. Another few steps and they were gone, swallowed by the rich navy of the deep water, and Hunter was floating.

She lifted her legs, stretched out her arms, tipped her head back, and closed her eyes against the piercing sunlight. Her ears plunged beneath the surface as she drifted on her back. The dull *whoosh* of water was an active kind of quiet. The sort of roaring silence that made drifting off to sleep more of a command than a choice. And, for Hunter, this forceful silence was always welcome. It kept her from her thoughts. Better yet, it kept her from her memories.

A boat motor stirred the water and roared through Hunter's reverie. She shielded her eyes and let her legs sink back into the water. The red-and-black boat circled the far side of the lake before it returned to the center. Its belly smacked the water as it jumped its own white-capped wake. A chorus of whoops and cheers erupted as the boat slowed and bobbed on top of the surging water.

A wave slapped Hunter in the face, and she wiped her eyes before squinting at the boat and its passengers. Its *five* passengers. Hunter blinked more water from her eyes. Five *male* passengers. And one of them was waving at—

"Hey!" The only shirtless member stood on the row of seats flapping his arms like a goose. "You go to Goode High, right? You're a Mustang."

The boat drifted closer to Hunter. She stared back at the five young men who looked at her expectantly. She opened her mouth to speak, but no words came out. Her heart was lodged inside her throat and her pulse hammered against her eardrums. She dove under the water and swam back to the safety of the sand and her towel and the clothes she'd stripped off when she knew no one was watching. Her chest ached for oxygen, but she kept swimming. She could hear them laughing. It rang louder than her pulse and the roaring silence. In middle school, she'd been everyone's favorite joke. Two years later, she still expected to be.

Hunter's lungs forced her above water. She gasped for air and crawled from the lake, nearly collapsing onto her neatly folded towel and pile of clothes. She didn't want to look back at the boat, at the boys, and see them pointing and staring, but she had to. The joke wasn't complete until she did.

Hunter's eyes burned. She shook away the tears. Crying only made things worse. She plucked her thin rope cord from the pile and squeezed the T-shaped opalescent pendant in her fist as she swept her gaze over the settling waves and back to the boat. The guys were dancing. Another had removed his shirt and was twirling it over his head. They turned up the volume and a fast, staccato beat reached Hunter as the motor roared and they took off.

Hunter's pent-up breath came out in staggered wheezes, and she dropped to her knees. They hadn't been laughing. Not at her, at least. The tears came then, and she let them. They splattered against the shore, painting the sand a deeper shade of tan. Maybe this next phase of her life would be different.

She dried her eyes, wrapped her hair in her towel, and tugged her shorts on over her swimsuit bottoms. Her necklace dangled from her fingertips as she threw her T-shirt over her shoulder and headed toward the dock. She was alone again, and it was perfect.

The weathered boards of the dock creaked as she shuffled to the row of three chaise lounge chairs and the faux leather–bound journal she'd abandoned for the blue waters of Goode Lake. Hunter shook out her towel-dried hair and pulled it back into the high ponytail she always wore before tugging on her T-shirt and collapsing into her chair. She opened her journal and fastened her necklace around her neck. She smoothed her fingers over the pendant and stared down at the blank unlined pages, unnervingly white under the bright April sun. She slid her pen from its holder and clicked and unclicked the retractable top. In the three weeks she'd owned the faux leather–bound book, all she'd managed to write was one sentence underneath her name, which she'd erased, written again, erased again and finally written it, ***HUNTER GOODE,*** in black marker on the worn page. She hadn't written her name incorrectly, it just wasn't . . . *right.*

That's what held Hunter back now, the not *rightness* of everything she wanted to say. She was supposed to author the next great American novel and, until she'd purchased the journal from the cute paper and craft store on Main Street, she'd thought she'd be at least halfway finished doing exactly that. She had already chosen a title and character names. Weren't those the most difficult parts?

Hunter rubbed the opalescent jewel hanging from the thin rope cord around her neck. The dip in Goode Lake was supposed to clear her head, but it'd only managed to stir up feelings she so desperately tried to keep tamped down. The deep purplish-pink core of the pendant spun like a top. It always did when she was this perplexed, like her confusion was a blender, her body the power source, and her budding magic a milky purple-pink smoothie.

She pressed the swirling gem against her palm and gazed up at the sky. Puffy white clouds floated above the lake. There were too many for her to see the moon's ghostly imprint against the pale blue. Without the moon, *her* moon, daytime often felt like Hunter's nemesis. She never should have left her tarot cards at home.

Hunter sighed and let her necklace drop against her chest. It stopped churning as soon as it left her fingers. It was weird how it couldn't sense her magic through a simple layer of cotton. Perhaps there wasn't enough of it. She smoothed down a few frayed strands of rope. After tonight, she'd be practically overflowing with enough magic no T-shirt would be able to get in its way.

A sharp, chittering meow lifted the hairs on the back of Hunter's neck. Seconds later, a brown, black, and white Maine coon pounced on the end of Hunter's chaise. She curled up next to Hunter's feet and yawned, the points of her sharp teeth glistening in the sunlight as she stretched her large paws and kneaded Hunter's shin. Xena was always popping up around town to check on Hunter. It was as comforting as it was stalkerish.

"Thanks for getting me back on track, Xena." Hunter set the point of her pen against the white page. After all these weeks she was finally doing it. She wrote the word *title* in loopy cursive and dotted the *i* with a perfectly drawn star.

When Darkness Rises.

She wrote that in block letters and didn't dot the *i* with anything. From here on out, it was serious author business only. And now her title was final. She nodded to herself and underlined the three words. Yep, it was set in stone forever.

She tapped the end of the pen against her round chin and leaned forward and combed her fingers through the cat's soft fur. "And then there are my main characters, Maisie and Mitchell, who will overcome all odds and fall deeply and madly in love with each other . . ." Hunter stared out past the end of the dock at the rippling blue surface of Goode Lake as she continued to scratch Xena. "Maybe they're causing my writer's block . . ." she mused. "Maisie and Mitchell . . ."

Hunter's fingers tingled as her thoughts shifted. Maisie and Mitchell weren't really the problem. Tonight was the problem. Tonight topped her list of *things not to think about.* It had for the past three weeks. The dedication ceremony and the gate . . . It was all *so much.* Her life was about to change, in an amazing and magical way, but still. Change was big. Change was difficult. And Hunter wasn't sure if she was ready.

Xena chattered her displeasure as Hunter's fingers stilled on the cat's back.

Hunter shook her head, clearing away the doubt to focus on the task at hand. "What if I change Maisie and Mitchell to Maisie and *Madison*?" Hunter wrote the names below the title and underlined each twice before turning her attention back to the disgruntled cat. "After all, don't they say to *write what you know*?"

The dock groaned and Xena's ears pinned flat against her head as the *slap, slap* of flip-flops drew near. Emily Parrott waved as the breeze caught the flowing skirt of her sunflower yellow dress and tangled around her legs. "Damn nature!" she hissed, and pushed her sunglasses on top of her head before gathering the silky lengths. "You

Goodes and your *always wanting to be outside* weirdness." She paused and adjusted the shoulder strap of her oversized neon pink bag before continuing. "There are perfectly good venues *in* town where you could've thrown *the best* birthday bash. Venues that have a/c and free Wi-Fi that would make your ridiculous midnight curfew more bearable." She wrinkled her nose and cocked her pointed chin. "More bearable for me, at least."

Hunter closed her journal and fastened it shut with the buckle she'd found in her mother's basket of Kitchen Witch Accoutrements. "It'll still be *the best,* Em. Even without air-conditioning and Wi-Fi and with us leaving at midnight." Hunter's throat tightened and she scrubbed her fingers along the thick trunk of her pendant.

Before Hunter could wrangle the giant Maine coon, Xena jumped off the lounger and stalked toward Emily.

The contents of Emily's bag clanked as she thrust it in the cat's direction. "If you don't move out of my way, I'm going to skin you and make you into a scarf."

The tabby arched her back and hissed. Her puffy black-and-brown-striped tail twitched in the air like a fly-fishing line.

Hunter tossed her journal and pen onto her empty seat as she stood and scooped up the mound of irritated fluffiness. "It's okay, Xena," she murmured, and rubbed the tufts of fur sprouting from the ends of the cat's pointed ears. "It's just mean ol' Emily Parrott. And she would never make you into a scarf."

Emily sneezed into her balled-up dress and rubbed her watering eyes. "I would, cat. Just try me." Another sneeze. "She knows I'm allergic and is trying to kill me." She wiped her nose on her dress and frowned. *"See?"* She held out the fabric as evidence. "That cat is making me leak!"

Xena melted against Hunter's fingertips as she scratched under the cat's chin. The Maine coon had been slinking around Goodeville, monitoring the town of five thousand Illinoisans, since before Hunter was born. Xena had even been there on the very day Hunter arrived in the world—quiet and doe-eyed (so her mother said), fifteen years, three hundred and sixty-four days and nineteen and a half hours ago. But who was counting?

The Maine coon's long body vibrated with a round of purrs while Hunter stroked her long back. "You should go, Xena." Hunter kissed the top of the cat's brown-and-white head. "Thanks for checking in."

Xena nuzzled Hunter's chin a final time and leapt from her arms. She landed at Emily's flip-flop clad feet, glared up at the tall, lanky brunette, and hissed before padding away toward the end of the dock.

"Begone, cat!" Emily shouted as Xena jumped onto land and twined herself through the wildflowers rimming the shoreline. "That cat is practically a dog, following you and your sister around all the time."

Hunter gathered her journal and pen before plopping back down into the chaise. "She really wouldn't like that you said that."

"She's a cat. Unless your mom has some kind of *cat-talking* spell, Xena has no idea what I'm saying." Emily dropped her bag and it landed on the dock with a clatter. "Not that I'd be surprised if your mom *did* have a cat-talking spell. I mean, that cat *has* been alive for a million years . . ."

Hunter picked at her fingernail. There were some things even Emily shouldn't know.

"Oh my god, your mom has a cat-talking spell!" Emily kicked off her flips and pushed them under the empty chaise next to Hunter. "I can't believe you've been holding out on me! Spill!"

The blaring speakers of a nearing ski boat saved Hunter from having to tell a lie Emily would have seen through before it left Hunter's lips.

Emily's back stiffened and she craned her long neck to get a better view at the boat's passengers. "Well, well, well, would you look at that."

Hunter tucked her chin into her shirt and followed Emily's gaze. The black-and-red boat was back. The five guys stood in the center, bobbing in time to the pulsing music. One of the shirtless members crouched down. Silver cans glinted in the sunlight as he tossed one to each of his friends.

Emily rose to her tiptoes and slid the thin straps of her dress down her russet brown shoulders. When she turned on the charm, appeal poured from Emily like a tapped tree poured sap.

Hunter chewed the tip of her fingernail and watched as, one at a time, each guy stopped bouncing and turned like a mob of meerkats to face the dock. The lump returned to the back of her throat and she sank farther down into her seat.

Emily continued her show, adjusting her strapless bikini top before smoothing the dress down her narrow hips and letting it pool around her feet. Not once did she look at the boat or the guys or even Hunter. She was alone. An island enjoying its own beauty. She didn't bother picking up her discarded dress. Instead, she stepped out of it and settled into the lounger. "I just love a good view, don't you?" She slid her sunglasses down to the rounded tip of her nose and stared out at the boat.

Hunter smoothed her fingers over her pendant. "I'm Hunter, not Mercy." She said the words without thinking. It was a line she'd spoken more than any other. It was a line that usually ended a conversation.

With a sigh, Emily eyed Hunter. "Well, yeah." Emily's golden eyes swept over Hunter's damp ponytail, closed journal, plain white tee, and plain jean shorts. "You two may be identical to most, but I've known you since second grade. Plus, there's no way Mercy would be caught dead without some sort of . . ." Emily waved her hand in front of Hunter, her gesture taking in every bit of the twin. "Bedazzlement. Your sister also wouldn't arrive half an hour before her party even started." She twirled a long curl around her finger. "I mean, Mercy practically *is* the party, so I guess it won't officially start until she gets here anyway."

Hunter tugged her shirt from her chin and clutched her journal against her chest. It pressed against the pendant of Tyr hidden under her shirt as she resumed chewing her nail and stared past the boat at the sunlight glinting off the lake's gently pulsing waves. "Why are *you* here so early, Em?"

Emily hefted her bag onto her lap and pulled out a stack of red cups. "My mom just flew back from her trip to DC and my dad doesn't leave for some gross embalming conference in LA for a couple days." She plucked a cup off for herself and offered the stack to Hunter. "So, both of my parents are home. Occupying the same space at the same time. And we all know how well they do that."

Hunter stared at the stop sign–red plastic cups and swallowed. She didn't want one. She also didn't want to be rude. "I'm sorry, Em," she said and took a cup.

"Don't be. They did it to themselves." Emily shook her head and set the tower of cups on the deck before reaching back into her bag. She wiggled her shoulders as she pulled out a glass bottle and unscrewed the cap. "Let's toast to divorce."

Hunter grimaced. "Is that vodka?"

Emily's brow furrowed. "I brought mixers, too. I'm not a savage." The clear liquid whooshed as Emily poured some into Hunter's cup and even more into her own. "I have OJ, tonic, cranberry, something called lemonberry spritz that I took from my mom's minifridge . . ." She shrugged. "Pick your poison, Miss Goode."

Hunter's stomach twisted. "I'm fine. I'll just hold on to this until you need another drink."

"Unclench, H. You know, live a little." Emily took out a plastic bottle of orange juice and poured far less juice into her cup than she had vodka before doing the same to Hunter's. "As someone who's been sixteen for, like, six months now, I'm going to give you some advice." She took a drink, grimaced, and took another. "Guys, girls, *whoever,* want to be with a girl who's free and relaxed, not rigid and uptight. Look at Mercy. She got Kirk because she's wild and breezy and weird, but in the best sort of way, like a kite, or a unicorn." She took another drink, motioned for Hunter to do the same, and settled against the chaise.

"Whether or not any of us *really* dig Kirk doesn't change the fact that all that stuff is what people want."

Hunter ran the edge of her ragged nail against her shorts. "People want a unicorn kite?"

"Exactly." Emily grimaced and downed the rest of her drink before she reached out and tapped Hunter's. The orange-tinged contents sloshed over the side of the cup and onto Hunter's fingers. "I'll also add some cran. It'll make it a smidge less brutal," Emily said, too busy rummaging through her bag for the mixer to notice the mess.

Hunter dried her hand on the bottom of her shirt. Just because it was simple white cotton and not covered in splashes of color or fringe or sparkles didn't mean she was devoid of personality. It meant she was different from her sister. And she liked being different than Mercy. It meant she could be there for her impulsive, trouble-making sister. If they were both irresponsible and spontaneous, the entire town would end up in flames. She was Mercy's counterbalance, and Mercy hers. They were perfect together, perfect for each other. Jax understood that about the twins. Sometimes it felt like he was the only one of their friends who did.

Emily poured a splash of scarlet juice into Hunter's cup and stared at her expectantly. Hunter brought the cup to her lips and closed her eyes. It smelled like rubbing alcohol and brunch. She tilted the cup back and swallowed. The liquid burned her throat and slid, fiery and hot into her stomach. Her eyelids flew open and she thrust the cup at Emily. "It's—terrible," she said between coughs.

"Well, yeah." Emily shrugged, took a sip, and refocused on the boat full of boys. She whooped as another peeled off his shirt and shook out his dark hair. "Don't you just love watching animals in the wild?" she asked, leaning into Hunter.

He performed an exaggerated bow before walking to the edge of the boat and jumping into the water.

"They're not there for you to ogle, Em. They're people." Hunter brought her nail to her lips and grimaced. Her fingers smelled like alcohol.

Emily blinked at Hunter from above the rim of her cup as if waiting for the punch line.

Hunter sighed. "They're people out here enjoying the lake just like *we're* out here enjoying the lake."

Emily pooched out her glossed lips and adjusted her long legs until she was stretched across the chaise like a cat. "And I expect to be ogled." She pushed her sunglasses back up her nose and readjusted her pout until it was duck lip perfection.

Hunter's chest warmed in the comforting way it did when her sister was near. Like she'd just taken the first drink of hot chocolate on a snowy winter day. It was one of the best feelings in the world.

"Mercy's here," Hunter said as she clipped her pen to the cover of her journal. Another writing day gone with nothing to show. At least tonight, if she could muster the courage to get through the midnight ceremony, would more than make up for it.

Emily lifted her cup to the sky and tipped her chin toward the sun. "Let's get this party started!"

Two

Let's get this par-tay started!" Mercy danced her way down the dock to where her bestie and her sister were stretched out in the chaise lounges. She raised her hands over her head and rolled her hips back and forth in a classic belly-dancing move that had the fringe belt she'd made and slung low on her hips rippling like water over the boyfriend jeans she's spent *months* freehand embroidering vines and flowers all over. Her shirt was a retro halter top—the same pink as the fringe around her waist, and her long, dark hair was thick and loose around her shoulders—her fav way to wear it. The big, worn leather boho purse she always carried was over her shoulder and her hip bumped it like a tambourine. Mercy felt as good as she looked, and she knew how good she looked because Kirk Whitfield—and most of the football team that'd followed them to the dock—couldn't keep their eyes off her.

"Going to get some red Solo!" Kirk yelled as he trooped off with the guys to find the keg.

"Okie dokie!" Mercy said as she blew him a kiss and dropped her purse with a seismic *plop* into an empty chair.

"Girlfriend, those jeans *slay*!" Emily said as she unfolded herself from the lounger she'd been sunning on and bent to mix Mercy a drink, displaying a whole lot of firm round ass, which had the football players who hadn't already followed their quarterback to the keg crowding the dock behind Mercy and cheering.

Mercy turned and narrowed her eyes at the herd of football sheeples. "Bloody buggering hell! It's just a girl in a bikini. Pick your tongues up off the dock. The keg is over there by the bonfire, which needs to be lit so we can toast wieners and marshmallows. So, light it or I'll do a little bibbity-bobbity-bitch and the veggie wieners will be replaced by a meatier variety." Mercy raised her hands and flicked her fingers at the football team, aiming for just below their belts.

As expected, the players backed off fast—heading to the keg and the heap of kindling and firewood as they rearranged their personal non-vegan wieners and sent her suspicious glances like they weren't entirely sure she was kidding.

"You know Mom would lecture you about teasing them like that. She'd say, *'What you put out into the world returns to you, and that goes for thoughts, acts, and energy.'*"

Mercy grinned impishly as she turned to face her twin. "True, but Abigail's *not here.*" She threw her arms around her sister—her favorite person in the world, though their mom was a close second. "Happy birthday, little sis!"

"I seriously don't think being three minutes older makes me your *little* sister." Hunter repeated the line she'd been saying for as long as both twins could remember, though she hugged her sister back and whispered, "Happy birthday."

"Aww, twin love." From a few feet behind them on the dock, a tall raven-haired player grinned a familiar crooked-toothed smile at the sisters.

Hunter broke the hug instantly and hurled herself into her best friend's arms like she hadn't just seen him at school a few hours ago.

"Jax! Finally! I thought you'd never get here."

"Sorry. Meant to be here earlier, H, but football practice was hell, and then I was stalking my mailbox for your—" Jax paused and dramatically lifted a smallish rectangular box from behind his back. It was wrapped in swirly blue paper that had stars all over it and tied with a silver bow. "Birthday present! Ta-da!"

"Ooooh! You shouldn't have, but I'm glad you did!" Hunter squealed and bounced on her toes.

Emily bumped Mercy's shoulder. "I will forever think it's weird that your sister's bestie is a dude."

Mercy shrugged. "Well, as *my* bestie, I'm expecting you to gift me an awesome birthday pressie with tons of girl power that will put Jax's to shame."

Both girls watched while Hunter tore open the box and then shrieked in pleasure as she held up a gorgeous fountain pen made of something that seemed to glow.

"Ohmygod! It's opal! You got me a pen made of my favorite stone! You're the *best,* Jax!"

Mercy looked at Emily and held out her hands expectantly. "Gift me."

Emily shrugged and handed her the red plastic cup she'd just filled. "Happy birthday."

Mercy took the cup, sniffed it, and sipped it. "It's vodka and cranberry."

"I know, right?" Emily said. "Your fav!"

"Em," Mercy sighed. "You're gonna have to do better at Yule. You can't keep letting a dude out-gift you."

Emily's full bottom lip stuck out as she pouted. "But it *is* your fav."

"True, so you do get some bestie points for knowing that." Mercy handed the cup back to Em. "Which you immediately lose 'cause I cannot drink this—not tonight. You know H and I have to meet Mom in just a few hours for our special fam celebration thing—and I cannot be toasted for that. Gotta stick to beer—and just a little."

"Well, shit. Sorry," said Em. "Good thing my sparkling personality is a gift itself."

"It's something, that's for sure."

"Mercy, isn't it perfect?" Hunter waved her new pen around.

Mercy grinned at her sister. "Yep." She looked up at the guy who had been her sister's best friend since second grade and shared the grin with him. "Way to go, Jax. You #nailedit."

"And I got you this." Jax ran his fingers through his black hair and tossed a tiny plastic baggie to her.

Mercy opened it and out slid a button that quoted, "I ask no favor for my sex. All I ask of our brethren is that they take their feet off our necks."—RBG. She looked up at Jax. "I love it. Seriously. Thanks, Jax!" Mercy pinned the button to her giant purse and then hugged her sister's broad-shouldered bestie tightly, enveloping him in her signature scent of spring lilacs as he grinned and patted her back affectionately.

A deep voice boomed with mock heartbreak down the dock at them. "Hey, whoa! I'm gone for, like, two minutes and I've been replaced?"

Mercy moved out of Jax's hug and turned to grin at Kirk. He carried two full cups of beer. Somewhere between the keg and the dock he'd taken off his shirt and the waning light of the setting sun caught the chiseled ridges of his pecs and biceps. His blond hair was shaggy and thick, and a lock had fallen over his face to obscure one of his perfect cerulean eyes.

"Oh, please Kirk. It's *Jax*." Mercy met him and tiptoed for a kiss before she took the beer he offered her.

"Who has been our friend for literally years before you managed to acknowledge Mercy even existed," said Hunter with an eye roll.

Kirk lifted the hand not holding his beer in surrender. "Ow!! I was just kidding around. Right, Jaxie?" Kirk leaned over and punched Jax in his shoulder, which had Hunter frowning and putting her hands on her hips. Jax let out an awkward laugh and furrowed his thick eyebrows.

"Of course Kirk was kidding!" Before her sister could start *another* argument with Kirk, Mercy stepped between them. "Guys, check out what Kirk gave me for my birthday." Mercy fished the cheap stainless steel ball chain out from under her shirt—making a mental note to swap it for something nicer when she got home—and lifted the ring that dangled from it. "As of this afternoon I am wearing his class ring."

"That's right, babe. You and I are official!"

"I'm your girlfriend, not your property. Remember? We talked about how saying that makes you sound douchey," Mercy said.

"That's why I don't." Kirk opened his arms while his blue eyes sparkled mischievously. "Come here, beautiful."

As Mercy melted against the quarterback's perfect body she heard her sister mutter, "Nice. A present that cost him nothing, but gets him everything."

Mercy ignored her sister's typical grumble—wishing that for once she could just get along with her boyfriend without constantly picking at him. Over Kirk's shoulder she saw a flash of orange and yellow. She unwound herself from him. "Hey, the bonfire's lit!"

"Oooh! Yeah!" Emily said. "Let's start roasting some of those wieners!"

"Good idea. Football practice made me puke, which means I'm starving," said Jax.

"Eww," said Hunter. "I don't understand why you'd play something that makes you hurl."

"What doesn't kill you makes you stronger!" said Kirk. He wrapped his arm around Mercy, barely giving her time to snag her giant purse before he led her from the dock. As the large group followed him to the picnic grounds that overlooked the placid lake, Kirk said, "Hey, babe, I got your wiener right here."

Mercy giggled and elbowed him. "Stop! And you know I'm a vegan."

"I'm hoping I can add a little more protein to your diet." He pretended to whisper, but his comment easily carried behind them to Emily, Hunter, and Jax.

Emily made retching sounds. Hunter didn't say anything, but Mercy knew she'd hear about Kirk's silly comment later and made a second mental note to remind Kirk—again—to watch his mouth. He didn't pose and bluster when it was just the two of them. He was sweet and sensitive and funny, but add a few people and his insecurities crept out in the stupidest ways.

It's okay, Mercy told herself. *He'll be better after we've been together for a while and he knows I'm not gonna take off like his mom did.*

"Happy birthday, Mercy and Hunter!" The growing group that was congregating around the bonfire greeted the twins with a planned shout.

"Veggie wieners, chips, and marshmallows for everyone!" Mercy shouted. "Let the music play!" She pointed at Emily.

"Syncing!" Emily pulled out her phone and then shouted victoriously when Taylor Swift's latest blasted from the Bluetooth speaker perched amongst the bags of chips.

"Ooooh, Come on, H! Let's dance!" Mercy grabbed her sister's wrist, but Hunter shook her off, laughing.

"Um, no. I will not dance with you because you stripper dance."

Mercy backed toward the bonfire where football players coupled up with cheerleaders and the pom squad, who'd just arrived amidst a lot of squeals and whoops.

"I do *not* stripper dance," Mercy said as she gyrated her hips and flung her hair around—like a stripper. "Plus, it's our birthday! Dance with me, woman!"

"She's definitely stripper dancing," said Jax, smiling crooked teeth at Hunter.

"As always," laughed Hunter, and she looked up at her tall best friend. "There's no way I'm going out there."

Jax leaned into Hunter. "Stop turtling and go and birthday dance with your sister!"

Hunter frowned and stared down at her feet as if the earth below would supply her with answers. She shook her head and sighed, the corner of her mouth lifting a little as her hips began to twitch. As

Hunter started to dance her way toward Mercy the music abruptly changed and "Witchy Woman" blasted across the campground.

"Yaaasss! That's my song!" Mercy twirled around, getting closer to the fire.

"That's right, it is, babe! That's why I played it." Fireside, Kirk crooked a finger at her.

As Mercy danced to him she surreptitiously stuck her hand into an outer pocket of her purse and spun her way closer to the fire. She flicked a handful of club moss quickly into the blaze as she raised her hands over her head and moved liquidly with the music, whispering to the fire, "By tree and leaf—wood and fire—burn bright, burn brilliant then fade to ghostly wisps of what you once were and what you shall be again." Mercy felt earth energy lift around her, like fireflies darting into the night sky.

There was a big flash and a fireball shot up, making everyone—except Mercy and Hunter—gasp.

"Come here, my little witch!" Kirk danced with her as the fireball gave way to white smoke that billowed up from the bonfire, forming the outline of the big oak that the logs had once been.

"Hey, that's cool! Doesn't it look like a tree?" someone shouted over the music.

Mercy smiled to herself as she let Kirk run his hands down her hips to cup her ass. Gracefully, she spun away from him, and as she did she caught a glimpse of her sister's face. Hunter had been watching the smoke with a knowing smile, but that smile suddenly changed to openmouthed shock. Her eye found Mercy and she jerked her chin at the bonfire as several of the kids shouted.

Mercy turned to the fire in time to see that the smoky outline of the oak had changed to become a nightmarish face that looked like a slavering wolf—or worse. Something with impossibly long teeth that shouldn't exist in this world. Quickly, Mercy plunged her hand back into the outside pouch of her purse and snagged the little bag of copper chloride she'd prepared for later. While everyone was gaping at the fanged thing in the smoke, Mercy threw the bag into the fire. Instantly the flames changed from yellow to blue, dissipating the smoke and sending the creature back to whatever hell it came from.

Mercy spun around, meeting her sister's gaze again. Hunter gestured for her to *come here,* but Kirk was there again. He pulled her against him and nuzzled her neck while he sang, *"Oooh, oooh, witchy woman,"* out of key into her ear. Over Kirk's shoulder she mouthed to Hunter, *I don't know what that was! Hang on—be there in a sec!*

Hunter rolled her eyes and mouthed, *never mind.* Before she turned her back on Mercy to take a hot dog from Jax she pulled Tyr's pendant out from under the collar of her tee and let it fall against her chest like it was a shield.

Well, she's pissed, but how am I supposed to know what that was? Mercy stewed as Kirk moved her around the bonfire. *Probably something to do with what's happening with our powers tonight, but I don't know any more than Hunter about it. Goddess! She's such a worrier. I really wish she'd learn to loosen up.* Instantly Mercy felt crappy about being frustrated with her sister. Of course Hunter worried—that's what happened when girls got bullied. Even when they weren't so little anymore they still had to deal with the emotional garbage left by jerks and assholes. Mercy sighed. *I tried to protect her, but I was only a kid, too . . .*

"Hey, are you not into dancing?" Kirk asked as he pulled a little away from her.

"I am. It's just . . ." Mercy's gaze automatically found her sister.

Kirk took her chin in his hand and gently turned her face up. "Don't let Hunter stress you out. I'll try harder to make her like me. Promise. And you know how charming I am." He kissed her then, softly—sweetly.

"I absolutely do and you absolutely are."

"Sorry I was kinda douchey before," he whispered as they swayed together. "I'm a dick when I'm nervous."

She pulled back to look into his eyes. "You were nervous?"

His blue eyes pulled her in and trapped her. "Yeah, of course. I know I'm not your sister's favorite person and I wanted everything to be perfect for you tonight. I shoulda gotten you something besides my ring. It was stupid of me to think that—"

"Shh." Mercy cut his words off by pressing her finger against his lips. "I *love* that you gave me your ring. Best present *ever.* And don't worry about H. She'll come around. Now I need a wiener!" He opened his mouth to say something she was sure would be douchey—again—and she pressed her finger back against his lips. "This is one of those learning experiences we talked about. Every time I say wiener you don't have to make a dick joke."

He laughed. "Got it! Now let's go get you some sausage!"

Mercy decided that was an improvement, albeit small. She searched for Hunter as she and Kirk made their way to the grills and the hot-dog dressing station, but her sister had her head together with Jax and didn't look her way. Mercy squelched a sigh. *It's going to be okay. Hunter will get used to Kirk and Kirk will get used to Hunter, and I'll get my happily ever after.*

Three

Mercy finally spotted her bestie coming from the direction of the porta potties and hurried to intercept her. "Hey Em, have you seen Hunter?"

"God those things are *so fucking gross.*" Emily grimaced and wiped her hands delicately on her jeans. "Sorry, what'd you say?"

Mercy sighed. "Hunter. Have you seen her?"

"Oh, yeah, she's been with Jax all night." She fluttered her fingers at the lake. "I think they're taking pics of the moon over by the dock, which is weird, but definitely the norm for your sis."

"Mom's present to her was a bunch of attachments for her phone so Hunter can take night sky pictures." Mercy dug into her bottomless bag and checked her phone. "Sod it! It's eleven thirty! We gotta get outta here now so we can be home before midnight." Quickly, she texted:

WHERE R U?!

Then Mercy looked around the groups of semi-drunk kids. Some danced by the fire—some made out in the shadows—and a big group of the pom squad was skinny-dipping—or whatever it was called when you left your panties and bra on and jumped, squealing, into the lake from the dock. "Oh, bloody buggering hell! Is that Hunter over at the edge of the dock? She's not skinny-dipping, is she? She'll never dry before Abigail sees her!" Mercy started to rush toward the water, but Kirk's big hand on her shoulder stopped her.

"Did I hear you sssay those two magic words—sssskinny-dipping?" He leaned heavily on her and slurred his words.

Mercy turned to frown up at him. "Not tonight." *I asked him not to get wasted!* She shrugged his hand off her shoulder. "I gotta get Hunter and go. You know Mom wants us home before midnight."

He bent and booze-scented breath wafted over her. "Can't you be a little late?"

"No." Emily stepped between them and put her fists on her hips like Wonder Woman. "They can't. Abigail is cool, but when it comes to family traditions she does not play—just like she doesn't play about dudes who drink too much when they're out with her daughter. Go away, Kirk. Sober up. Byyyye." She hooked her arm through Mercy's and pulled her around Kirk.

"I'll text you tomorrow. Be sure you don't drive home." Mercy blew him a kiss and waved.

"Hey! I thought I was taking you home!"

"Not drunk you're not," Mercy said, but she smiled at him. "It's cool, though. Stay. Have fun. Just don't drive. Later!"

Emily didn't say anything, which made Mercy sigh. "You hate him, too, don't you?"

"Nope. He's tall and hot and captain of the football team. Nothing to hate about that."

Mercy waited and when that's all Em said she prompted. "But?"

"No buts. I'm your bestie. If you want him I've got your back. I've also got your back if he tries to do something stupid like drink and drive with you in the car—I mean, I knew I was driving you two home before midnight so I switched to water hours ago. If he can't figure out how to be responsible, too, then you don't get in the car with him. That's all."

"I wish Hunter felt like you do. I hate that she's such a bitch to Kirk."

Emily stopped and faced her. "Hunter is your twin. She's just protecting you—like you've always done for her. That's what you two do. You're there for each other. I know. I've been jelly of it since the first day of second grade when we met. Stop being so hard on her about it and start working on Kirk making a better impression."

Mercy chewed her lip. "That's what I tried to do tonight."

Emily snorted. "Girl, try harder. I could see that Kirk was being super sweet with you, but with the rest of us? Not so much."

"Okay, I get it. And you're right. I just—"

Hunter hurried up. "There you are. Let's go! We're gonna be late."

"H, I've been looking for you all night," Mercy said.

"Be serious. Your face has been smooshed against Kirk's all night." Hunter strode past them, heading to the grassy lot where Emily's car was parked and waiting for them.

Mercy didn't say anything. The fact that Hunter was right didn't help, but she wasn't sure *why* it didn't help. She wrenched open the front door and started to toss her boho bag to the floorboard, but Em reached around her, pulled the passenger's seat forward, and then pointed at the empty backseat of the 1966 Thunderbird convertible that had been Emily's sixteenth birthday guilt gift from her parents three months after her actual birthday, which they had both forgotten.

"Nope. You two sit back there. Together. Now," Emily said firmly.

Mercy and Hunter climbed into the backseat and remained silent as Em took the windy road that followed Goode Lake around to the two-lane blacktop that led to downtown Goodeville.

"Okay. I'm so over this." Emily glanced in the rearview mirror at the twins. "Mercy—Hunter, I hate it when you two fight. Do you know why?"

"Uh-uh," Mercy said softly.

"I hate it because you two almost never fight, and when you do it's like the fucking earth shifts on its axis and shit is not right. So, fix this right now and stop it. Jesus! It's your birthday."

Mercy gave Hunter a sideways glance. She was picking at her fingernails, her tell for being upset.

"H, I wish you'd give Kirk a chance," Mercy said.

"And I wish you'd get over your hormones. He's a douchebag," Hunter shot back.

Mercy slid to the side so she could face her sister. "He's only like that around you guys because you make him nervous."

"Riiiiight. I make him nervous. He told you that?"

"Yes. H, underneath all that—"

"Toxic masculinity."

"*No,* under all that pretend macho act is a really sweet boy who misses his mom. A lot." Mercy sighed. "Plus, now that I'm with Kirk we've totally made it! H, we get invited to all the cool parties and have lots more friends."

Hunter rolled her eyes. "You mean *you* get invited to all the cool parties and *you* have lots of new friends."

Mercy threw her hands up in frustration. "Oh my goddess! All you'd have to do is actually *participate* and you'd be included, too."

"I don't know if I want to participate." Hunter shook her head. "Not with them."

Mercy chewed her lip. *Why couldn't Hunter just leave the past in the past? She hadn't been bullied in ages. Can't she just get over it?* Mercy sighed again. "Look, I don't want to fight with you, especially not today."

Hunter's sigh was a mirror of her sister's. "Yeah, me, either. Sorry. I just don't like how Kirk talks to you."

"He *doesn't* talk to me like that when we're alone. Do you trust me?"

Hunter's gaze snapped to hers. "Of course I trust you."

"Then trust that I'm right about him."

Hunter picked at her fingernails some more. "I'll work on it. Promise. And I'm sorry I avoided you tonight."

"I'm sorry I let some guy come between us. I promise not to let that happen again. And if Kirk really is a douchebag, I promise I'll dump him faster than Xena makes Em sneeze—Goode guarantee?" Mercy lifted her hand.

"Goode guarantee!" Hunter's ponytail bobbed as she nodded and extended her pinky, which Mercy caught with her own—pinkies still hooked, the twins tapped their knuckles together before their hands separated, fingers fluttering like birds as they shouted, "Sisters of Salem!"

"Hugsees?" Hunter said.

"Total hugsees." Mercy grabbed her sister and squeezed her tightly.

"Yaaasss! Now *those* are my twins!" Emily grinned at them in the rearview mirror. "And it was a super fun party, though I don't know what the hell happened with that scary beast thing in the smoke. And Mercy Anne Goode, I'm talking to you."

"Hey, I don't know, either! I just did a little witchy stuff to the wood. You shoulda just seen the cool oak tree. No clue what happened."

"Wait, I think I know what went wrong," Hunter said. "You only called on oak?"

Mercy nodded. "Yeah, I checked out the woodpile before they lit it—well, from a distance—but it all looked like that old oak that split from lightning last spring. They cut it up and left it at the campgrounds for people making campfires."

"It wasn't all oak. Remember the apple grove just after you turn in to the lake drive?"

"I know what you're talking about. That's Mr. Caldwell's grove," Emily said. "Mercy and I got super sick the summer we were thirteen from eating too many green apples from there. Remember, Mercy?"

Mercy shuddered. "I'll never forget."

"Last winter that ice storm killed the oldest tree out there." Hunter tightened her ponytail as she explained. "Mom told us about it. Mr. Caldwell called her to see if she could save it, but it was too late. I remember she said that the apple wood was being chopped up and given to the campsite."

"Huh. I got the wood wrong. Still weird," said Mercy.

"And *super* weird that it was *apple* wood." Hunter touched her T-shaped pendant and shared a *look* with her sister. Neither needed words to understand the significance of that particular type of tree this particular night.

Emily waved her hand around, redirecting the twins' attention. "Hey, did you two ever consider that what happened might have just been a fluke and more about the weird smoke caused by your exploding moss fire bomb than anything remotely witchy? I mean, no offense, but that makes way more sense than saying that you actually *conjured* something from smoke."

Mercy and Hunter locked their gazes and smiled knowingly.

"You're right, Em," said Mercy.

"Makes *way* more sense," added Hunter.

"Well, anyway, it was a super cool party! And now that you two are back to your normal psychic-level closeness, all is right in the world."

"Oh, sod it! I'm a wanker! I didn't give you—" Mercy began.

"Your pressie!" Hunter finished.

"Mercy, you're *not* British." Emily tossed her mass of tight, dark curls back from her face as she glanced in the rearview mirror at her bestie.

"Neither are you!" Mercy giggled. "Me first!" She fished into her bag until she caught the little box she'd wrapped in silver foil and handed it to her sister.

Hunter shook it and then tore into it. She opened the box and her eyes went huge. "Holy Tyr! They're unbelievably gorgeous! Mag, you shouldn't have. They're way expensive." The moonlight that came in through the car's windows glistened off the moonstone studs that were set in white gold and circled by little diamonds.

"The look on your face was worth every second of the six months of babysitting I had to do to pay for them."

"Seriously? *That's* why you've been so cheap for the past six months?" Em said. "Why didn't you tell me?"

"Because you suck at keeping presents secret!" said the twins together. Then they laughed and, at the same moment, said, "Jinx!"

"I am so good at keeping secrets," Emily grumbled.

"Yeah, you are—as long as they're not about presents," said Mercy. "But don't worry. We love you anyway." She held out her hands to her sister. "Okay, now me!"

"You're super sure I got you something and I have it with me."

"Of course you did and of course you do. It's probably something little that you can fit into that ridiculously small cross-body you carry."

"Oh, please. What's ridiculous is that suitcase you lug with you everywhere." Hunter bent and felt around under the bucket seat in front of her.

"Yeah, but if the zombie apocalypse happens I'm set." Mercy patted the bulging bag at her side.

"Do not tell me that you hid her pressie in my car and *did not tell me about it,*" Emily squeaked.

"Okay, we won't tell you," Hunter and Mercy said together.

"Stop with the creepy twin speak," Emily said, and added, "and I can *so* keep a secret."

"Happy birthday." Hunter handed a narrow box to Mercy. She'd wrapped it with green paper covered in vines.

"Ooooh, the paper is awesome!" Unlike her sister, Mercy carefully peeled every piece of tape off and then smoothed the paper as she freed the box. She opened the lid and gasped. "Hunter! It's perfect!" Mercy caressed the slim stack of squares of vintage lace, then lifted each to study their unique beauty. "Ohmygoddess! I'll make such cool stuff with these!"

"I can't wait to see what you come up with," said Hunter. "Happy birthday. Love you twin."

"Happy birthday, love you, too, twin."

In the rearview mirror Emily smiled at them all the rest of the way home.

Mercy loved everything about the old Victorian home that had housed Goodes since the mid-1800s. It was the last house at the northern most edge of Main Street, backing onto acres and acres of cornfields or, depending on the year, bean fields. This was a corn year and the stalks were already as tall as the twins. Mercy loved it when the mature corn secluded their house and the expansive gardens that filled their five acres, which included a koi pond with a fountain of Athena, their mother's patron goddess, complete with plumed helmet, an owl on her shoulder, and a dolphin beside her spouting water from its mouth. And, of course, in one corner, surrounded by lilacs and framed by a wrought-iron fence covered with wisteria, was the meticulously tended Goode family cemetery.

It was over the top, but the entire Victorian house was gloriously over the top. The majority of the house was butter yellow, with its ornate trim painted highlights of purple, fuchsia, and dark green. The double front doors were the same bull's blood red as the wraparound porch. *Literally* bull's blood red, as their mom liked to remind them. Every time the house had been repainted, actual bull's blood, as well as protective spells, were mixed into the paint.

"There are my birthday girls! And right on time. Was the party fun?" Abigail Goode hugged each daughter in turn as they came inside. Without giving them a chance to respond she hurried on. "You need to get upstairs and change. Quickly. Then meet me in the kitchen and we'll gather the rest of the supplies together for the ritual." Abigail pushed them gently toward the stairs when they didn't move fast enough. "Quickly! Tonight is too important to chance being even a minute late."

The twins sprinted up the winding staircase to their side-by-side rooms. Mercy rushed to her closet. She'd hooked the hanger on which her ceremonial dress hung on the outside of her closet closet door, and she couldn't help taking a moment to reverently run her fingers over the intricate design of vines, flowers, and falcon feathers—one of the goddess Freya's favorite symbols. It had taken Mercy an entire year to finish the embroidering. The cut of the dress was simple—cream-colored hemp jersey flowed long and free from a teardrop neckline. Mercy stroked the material. "Soft as silk, but a lot easier to embroider," she murmured to herself. It was her artistic hand at embroidery that made the dress special and Mercy had meticulously decorated the neckline, sleeves, and the hem of the full skirt with symbols that celebrated the earth and her chosen goddess. She didn't wear an amulet that represented her goddess, like Hunter did her god. Instead Mercy imagined Freya as part of the earth itself, so every flower and tree, even every blade of grass symbolized her goddess.

Mercy hurried out of her clothes and then sighed happily as the dress slid over her head and down her body with the smoothness of water. Quickly, she brushed out her hair, put on big silver hoop earrings she'd saved for this night, dabbed more of the homemade lilac scent she loved so much behind each ear, and then slathered on her favorite pink lip gloss. Mercy blew her reflection a cheeky kiss, hefted her bag over her shoulder, and almost ran into Hunter as she bolted out the door.

"Sheesh, Mag, be careful!" But Hunter's annoyed frown turned into a soft smile. "Wow. I haven't seen it since you finished it."

"Do you like it?" Mercy twirled so that the full skirt of the dress swirled around her long legs.

"Yeah, I really do." Hunter cleared her throat and nervously smoothed her hands down her dress. "What do you think? Too plain?"

Mercy cocked her head and studied her twin. Hunter had chosen a short-sleeved tunic dress that looked like a long T-shirt. The color of the fabric was unusual. It brought to mind newly blooming purple pansies washed with the silver of a full moon. Her legs looked slim and strong—and appealingly cute, especially because she was wearing simple high-top canvas sneakers. The dress had no embellishment, which only served to highlight the T-shaped amulet that was her only jewelry.

Mercy touched Hunter's sleeve gently. "This color is absolutely perfect, H. Seriously. It's exactly like the very center of your amulet."

Hunter's smile was a beam of sunshine. "You really think so?"

Mercy nodded. "Yep. Totally. We look fantastic! Abigail is going to be so happy! Come on." She grabbed her sister's hand and together they raced downstairs to the kitchen. Before they walked in, Mercy pulled Hunter back and whispered, "Wait. Don't you love watching her putter around in the kitchen?"

"Yep. She's beautiful, isn't she?" Hunter said, keeping her voice low.

"Like a goddess," Mercy agreed.

The sisters stood, hand in hand, and watched their mom as she hummed a tune and collected supplies from her expansive pantry, placing each carefully in the basket that never seemed far from her. Mercy used to think her mother was an actual goddess, and then as she got older she understood that she was a mortal who worshipped a goddess, but that didn't diminish her beauty or the magic aura that hovered around her like the scents of cinnamon and spice she cooked with so often.

Abigail Goode had just turned forty-six, but she could easily have passed for a decade younger, especially dressed as she was that night in her favorite ritual garb—a dove gray floor-length silk dress that was as simple as it was flattering. Over her left breast was the only adornment on the dress—an owl that Abigail had painstakingly painted on the silk. Her long, brunette hair was usually pulled back in a cute French knot, with only a few tendrils allowed to escape. But tonight, as every ritual night, it drifted free around her waist—dark and wavy.

Without turning around she shouted, "Girls! We must go!"

"Jeeze, Abigail, you don't need to shout," said Mercy.

Their mom startled and pressed her hand over her heart. "Athena's shield! You're going to give your old mother a heart attack!"

Hunter snorted. "*Old?* You did not just call yourself old."

Mercy shoved a gingersnap cookie in her mouth and around it said, "Abigail, you won't be old until you start wearing a bra."

Their mother looked down at her perky though ample breasts. "Well, then, I'll never be old." When her gaze returned to her girls a smile blossomed across her face. "You two look perfect. Absolutely perfect. Hunter, the dye job on your dress is exquisite, and a wonderful match for Tyr's amulet. Mercy, I was worried your dress would be too plain because it's just an off-white flowy thing, but your embroidery is lovely. I particularly like the addition of your goddess's falcon feathers. Both deities will be well pleased tonight by my magnificent daughters." Then she turned all business. "Mercy, your apple pie has cooled nicely. It's still on the rack there by the window. You'll need to collect it and your candles quickly. Your basket is on the counter." Abigail fired instructions at the girls as she continued to gather items from her spacious pantry. "Hunter, your beer is on ice in the sink. It's going to be so interesting to invoke a god. I've been rereading our ancestors' grimoires and I couldn't find one instance where any of them chose a god. Huh. It's actually surprising that's never happened before."

Hunter picked at her fingernail. "Are you sure it's okay?"

"Sweetheart, as I told you three years ago when you chose Tyr as your deity—it is *your* choice. There is no wrong answer. And today I'll add to that by saying that it's about time a Goode chose a god instead of a goddess. It'll keep things interesting." Abigail paused and brushed a long, thick lock of hair from her face. "Now, stop worrying and get your candles together. And don't forget the opener for the beer bottle." She tapped her foot as she stared into the pantry. "Ah! Matches! That's what I was forgetting." Abigail looked over her shoulder at her daughters. "Go on! We need to leave in the next five minutes to make it to the tree in time. Shoo, my little chickies! Shoo!"

Mercy and Hunter grinned at each other.

"That's what we were waiting for," said Mercy.

Hunter nodded. "Yep, to be called your chickies and shooed."

"Are you making fun of your mother?" Abigail put her fists on her curvy waist and tossed back her thick hair that was artistically streaked with a blaze of silver gray that looked professionally created, but was actually as natural as their mother's sweet smile and brilliant green eyes.

"Us?" Hunter said with mock surprise.

"Perish the thought, Abigail!" Mercy added, clutching her pearls.

"Xena! The girls are making fun of me again," Abigail called.

In a heartbeat the huge Maine coon padded into the kitchen to wind around their mother's legs as she chirped and mewed accusatorily at the twins.

"Okay! Okay! We're getting our stuff together." Mercy backed away like the cat might explode all over them.

"Yeah, call her off! Call her off!" Hunter tried to keep up the pretense of horror, but when Xena plopped her fluffy butt down and began berating them in earnest, she dissolved into giggles.

"I know, they don't always respect their elders properly," Abigail soothed the big cat while she stroked her from her black-tufted ears to the tip of her bushy tail. "Yes, I'm not surprised by that, Xena sweetheart."

As Mercy packed her basket she asked, "What'd she say?"

"Not important," said Abigail, taking a white candle poured into a tall, clear glass from the pantry and adding it to her basket. "What is important is that she told me half the school showed up for your party—which means it was a success. Oh, and it seems one of my daughters is now going steady." Xena and Abigail sent Mercy pointed looks.

"I swear that cat spies on us," muttered Mercy.

"For sure," said Hunter.

"Well?" asked their mother.

"Abigail, it hasn't been called *going steady* for decades. Literally," said Mercy.

"Oh, I don't care about your hip teenage talk. When a boy gives you his class ring you're going steady. Let me see!"

With a grin Mercy lifted the class ring that dangled from its chain. "Kirk gave it to me tonight right before the party."

"Mag!" Her mom used the nickname she'd been shackled with since first grade when Hunter had figured out what her initials, Mercy Anne Goode, spelled out. "That's adorable of Kirk." Abigail studied the ring and then smiled slyly. "Ooooh, what big fingers he has. Which reminds me. There are condoms in the pantry. Be sure some of them make their way into that suitcase you schlep around with you—and also make their way onto Kirk's penis."

"Yes, Abigail, I know."

"Do I need to schedule a gynecological appointment with our naturopath?"

"No, Abigail." Mercy tried to breathe through the heat spreading across her face as she stoically packed brown and green candles in her basket beside the apple pie.

"Sweetheart, would you like to discuss your clitoris—again?" her mother asked.

Hunter tapped her chin contemplatively. "Yes, Mag, would you?"

"No. Thank you. One clitoris discussion is all I needed."

Her mother sighed. "Well, if you have any questions you know I'm here with answers. Your pleasure is just as important as his. Do *not* forget that. Oh, and you're welcome for your multiple orgasms. They're familial, you know."

Mercy buried her burning face in her basket. "I do now."

"Thanks, Mom!" Hunter said cheerfully.

"You're most welcome sweetheart," said their mom happily. "Oh, I need to get those quilts. Now, Xena, where did I put them after the Yule ritual?" Chirping nonstop, the Maine coon trotted from the room with Abigail following.

"If you encourage her to talk about my clitoris again I am going to cut off all your hair while you sleep."

Hunter grinned. "But you know how she likes to feel helpful."

"I do *not* need clitoris help!" She almost hissed the words at her sister.

"Mag, if you're *going steady* with Kirk, I'm pretty sure you do."

Abigail hurried back into the kitchen, carrying a slender pile of three vintage quilts—each the perfect size to wrap around their shoulders. "Xena knew where they were. Now, where were we? Did I hear you say you needed help with Kirk?"

Hunter was still grinning, but she came to her sister's rescue. "No, Mom, we were talking about the ritual."

Mercy grasped onto the change in subject like a lifeline. "Yeah, shouldn't we be setting our intention?"

"Oh, yes. Absolutely." Abigail hooked her laden basket in the crook of her arm. "But let's do that as we walk to the tree. Come, girls! Carry your baskets and let's go write another page of Goode history!"

Four

Mercy and Hunter, with Xena padding along somewhere beside them, followed their mother through their backyard and to the little iron gate that opened to a hedgerow that divided two massive cornfields. The family of four slipped through the gate and began walking along the hedgerow. It was late—almost midnight—but the full Pink Moon, named by settlers hundreds of years ago after early blooming wild phlox—made it easy for them to find their way.

"To set our intention let us begin by remembering the past. On July 29th, 1692, our ancestress, Sarah Goode, was convicted of witchcraft and sentenced to hang in Salem. Thankfully, unlike many of those poor, persecuted women, Sarah was, indeed, a powerful witch. Hunter, how did she escape?"

"She bespelled the jail guard so that he fell asleep. Then Sarah's familiar, a cat named Odysseus—" She paused as Xena meowed loudly, causing them all to laugh, before continuing, "brought her the keys to her cell so she and her daughter, Dorothy, could escape."

"Excellent. Mercy, how did Sarah and her daughter find their way to what would become Goodeville?"

Mercy and Hunter knew every word of their history. They also knew how to set their intention for a successful ritual, but they loved telling the story of their ancestress, especially because the telling of it made their mother so happy.

As Mercy answered she spread one arm wide and let her fingertips touch the slick, green edges of the nearby corn leaves that were already damp with dew. "Well, because Sarah had listened to omens of warning sent to her by her goddess, Gaia, she had buried money, clothes, and spellwork things outside town. The night she escaped Sarah made her way to her buried stash and, using a large opal, Gaia illuminated a path for her. So, she, her daughter, and her familiar started walking southwest, following a strong ley line of earth power. Eventually, they joined a wagon train that was happy to have a healer ride with them. The journey was long and dangerous, but Sarah kept heading west, following the ley line, and it kept getting stronger, until it brought her here, to what would eventually become central Illinois."

"Well told, Mercy." Her mother nodded appreciatively. "Sarah Goode stopped here, along with several families she'd become close with during the journey, because Gaia revealed that this was a site where five power-filled ley lines converged. Hunter, why was this beautiful, fertile land unsettled and avoided even by the aboriginal peoples?"

"Because they were freaked out by the monsters that roamed around here, slaughtering anyone who got too close to where the ley lines converged."

Abigail smiled over her shoulder at her youngest daughter. "You are an excellent storyteller, Hunter. Mercy, why were there literal monsters loose here?"

"Because at the apex of each ley line was the entrance to what we describe as a different mythological Underworld, though that never made sense to me."

"Why not?" her mother asked.

"Well, Abigail, if the Underworlds were mythological, the oogly-booglies"—she winked at Hunter—"wouldn't be real. And they definitely were."

"Are," her mom corrected her. "We must never forget that what is on the other side of each of the Underworld gates is all too real."

"Good point, Abigail. It also supports my point about those places not being myths," said Mercy.

"I agree," said her mother. "Hunter, what did Sarah do then?"

"Sarah used her witchy wisdom and figured out how to close each of the entrances with a kind of a gate. Each gate is marked by a tree she planted, and each tree is from the area of the world the oogly-booglies were from," said Hunter.

"Correct," Abigail said. "But never forget that the trees were steeped in magic from their inception. Sarah was a Green Witch." She smiled at Mercy who grinned proudly back at her. "So first Sarah called forth the saplings magically. They were formed from the fertile earth below our feet mixed with her powerful magic. At the Norse gate the sapling that grew from her invocation spell was an apple tree. At the Greek gate an olive tree sprouted. For the Egyptian gate the magic chose a doum palm tree, and for the Japanese gate there appeared a very young, very supple weeping cherry tree. For the final gate, the Hindu one, a banyan tree lifted from the verdant ground. And when she was done calling forth the trees and casting the spell that sealed the gates with them, what did she discover, girls?"

Together the twins said, "That the trees created a giant pentagram!"

"Exactly! So she and the families that had stopped with her founded our town within the pentagram, and, in honor of their beloved healer, named it Goodeville. And every High Feast Day Sarah returned to one of the trees and performed a powerful protection ritual to be sure the gate remained sealed. During the rest of the year, what did she do, Hunter?"

"Exactly what you do, Mom. Sarah tended the trees to be sure they thrived and grew," said Hunter.

"Yes. Then Sarah settled here and worked as a midwife and healer, and she lived a full life to a very old age. She trained her daughter, Dorothy, to take her place after her own body returned to the earth, tasking her and each female from the Goode line that followed with tending to the trees, which close the gateways to the Underworlds beyond. So, as Sarah did all those generations ago, we also do. Our intention for tonight has not changed. We shall use the energy carried through the ley lines in the earth to strengthen the apple tree that guards the Norse gate. As we do that we imagine that the tree *is* a gate, and its strength is what keeps the Underworld gate closed.

"In addition, tonight my beloved daughters will speak aloud the type of witchcraft they have decided to practice in the name of their goddess—and god." Abigail smiled over her shoulder at Hunter. "Ah, and here we are! Right on time."

The hedgerow had ended in a grassy meadow where four fields converged. In the center of the meadow stood a thick-trunk apple tree whose gnarled branches spread like an enormous spiderweb. Some of the boughs were so huge and heavy that Abigail had placed wooden posts with padded Ys beneath them for support. Spring had been unusually warm, and the tree had bloomed early this year, but even though most of the blossoms were already turning into hard little green balls, the air around the tree was still fragrant and sweet.

"Daughters, place your baskets in the center of the pentagram along with your shoes, and then put your offerings at the feet of the gatekeeper."

The apple tree, like each of the other four magical gatekeepers, was positioned on one of the points of a pentagram. The Norse apple tree also happened to be the northernmost gatekeeper—spreading out from it, the other trees formed the rest of the points of a huge pentagram that encased Goodeville.

Before the trees were subtle markers that Sarah, and the generations of witches that had come after her, tended. They symbolized the invisible points of the pentagrams around the individual trees. At the Norse tree the markers were four large rocks, smoothed over by time and the elements. They were meaningless to anyone except Goode witches, who recognized them for what they were—symbols of the points of a pentagram.

Abigail's graceful gesture took in the rocks and the tree. "And why do we use the pentagram as our magical symbol?"

"Because each point symbolizes one of the five elements, which is powerful magic," said Mercy.

"Yeah, and our circle is traced around the points of the pentagram and includes everything inside it," finished Hunter.

"Well done, my beautiful girls. Now, let us begin," said Abigail.

The three women stepped within the pentagram and bared their feet. Then Mercy took the apple pie she'd baked for her goddess from her basket and placed it amidst the roots of the huge tree as Hunter opened her bottle of beer and poured it in a circle over the hard-packed ground. Then they returned to where their mother waited.

"Now we shall set our candles." Abigail's voice had become appropriately solemn as they were about to perform a powerful ritual that guarded all of them, and their cherished town, from unspeakable horrors.

When the girls had their candles in hand, their mother took out a long box of ritual matches and a tall white candle from her basket.

The three of them separated. Mercy went to the right and Hunter to the left, with their mother going forward to the great apple tree. Abigail reached the tree and then turned to watch her daughters place two candles each atop the smooth boulders that marked the other four points of their imagined pentagram. She lifted her candle and struck the match, saying, "First, I set the white candle in its place at the top of the pentagram. White symbolizes spirit. And with it I invoke the presence of my goddess, Athena, whose path I follow on my journey. This lifetime, that path has led me to be a Wise Woman and Kitchen Witch." She lit the white candle and held it before her, as if offering it to the tree.

Mercy loved it when her mom did ritual work. She always looked so powerful and beautiful—and more than a little mysterious when she invoked Athena and opened the sacred pentagram with the spirit candle. Nerves roiled Mercy's stomach. She could hardly believe that the night had finally come when she and her sister were joining their mother in Ritual—just like so many Goodes had done for so, so many generations. The night felt special—different. There was a listening quality to the earth and plants around her that tingled through her body. She wanted to ask Hunter if she felt it, too, and when she looked across the pentagram at her sister she saw that she was gazing up at the full moon with a rapturous expression. *Hunter feels it, too! I know she does.*

Abigail carefully placed the candle in front of the tree between thick fingers of roots. Then she traced the line of the pentagram to where Mercy was standing. She was holding the first of her two candles, which she lifted. Presenting it to her mother she said, "I set the green candle in its place on the pentagram. It symbolizes the path I have chosen to follow and the goddess whose service I am in."

Her mother lit the candle and Mercy set it on top of the rock at her feet before she and Abigail together walked to her second candle, tracing more of the pentagram. Mercy liked the feel of the cool grass against her feet, but as they took their first steps her foot landed on something that was hard enough to make her ankle twist before it squished against her foot, like she'd just stepped on a raw egg that had broken and its goo leaked between her toes. Abigail instantly steadied Mercy by catching her arm while she righted herself.

"Did you hurt your ankle?" Abigail asked.

Mercy looked down. "No, I just slid on something—" She lifted her foot and under it was an immature green apple that had broken open—and was completely filled with worms. "Ugh!" She wiped her foot quickly on the clean grass, shuddering as the worms writhed in the rotten apple meat.

Her mother peered down, and then straightened abruptly. "It's fine. Reset your intention. All is well."

But Mercy noticed that her mother's face had gone so pale that in the moonlight her skin looked like milk.

Abigail continued to the rock that marked the next point of the pentagram. Mercy shook herself mentally and followed her mother. She took several breaths to re-ground herself and then she lifted the candle that waited there and proclaimed, "And I set the brown candle in its place on the pentagram. It symbolizes the path I have chosen to follow and the goddess whose service I am in."

Before Abigail lit the candle she asked, "Speak, daughter, and name your goddess."

"Freya, the great Goddess of Love, Fertility, and Divination."

"And which path will you walk with Freya?"

Mercy's voice was strong and sure. "I am a Green Witch."

Abigail lit the brown candle and bowed her head. "Welcome to The Path, Mercy Anne Goode, Green Witch and daughter of Freya."

Mercy bowed, too, and placed the brown candle on the rock that marked that tip of their pentagram. Then her mother walked through the center of the pentagram to where Hunter stood with the first of her candles across from where Mercy's first candle, the green one, cheerily burned.

Hunter presented a yellow candle to her mother. When she spoke her voice was louder than normal, and Mercy felt a little prickle of anticipation follow the line up her spine.

"I set the yellow candle in its place on the pentagram. It symbolizes the path I have chosen to follow and the god whose service I am in."

Abigail lit the yellow candle, which Hunter placed on the boulder before walking toward Mercy as they completed the final line of their five-pointed star. She picked up the blue candle that waited there and turned to face their mother.

"And I set the blue candle in its place on the pentagram. It symbolizes the path I have chosen to follow and the god whose service I am in."

Just as with Mercy, Abigail spoke the formal words before she lit the candle. "Speak, daughter, and name your god."

"Tyr, the God of the Sky."

"And which path will you walk with Tyr?"

Hunter's voice was strong and sure. "I am a Cosmic Witch."

Abigail lit the blue candle and bowed her head. "Welcome to The Path, Hunter Jayne Goode, Cosmic Witch and daughter of Tyr."

Hunter grinned when she placed the final candle on the rock by her bare feet. She and Mercy exchanged excited looks, and then they focused on their mother, who had returned to the center of the pentagram and the baskets waiting there. She shook out three quilts, made two generations ago by their great grandmother. When the girls joined their mother, Xena padded into the pentagram, purring loudly. The three women, with Abigail's familiar, sat in the center of the pentagram, marked by brightly burning candles, and wrapped the quilts around their shoulders.

From her basket, Abigail took out a stone bowl, carved with the triple moon symbol, and lit a charcoal cube, which she placed in the bowl and then sprinkled a mixture of herbs over. Instantly the smoldering herbs began filling the grassy area with fragrant smoke. She lit a piece of palo santo wood and wafted it over the three of them saying, "Incense and wood are purifiers. They change the energy around us and keep negativity at bay."

The girls used their hands to move the smoke over and around them. Their mother placed the still-smoking stick in the burner with the herbal incense.

"And now we protect ourselves. I want you each to imagine a shield—a great, glowing shield. Close your eyes. Picture it."

Mercy closed her eyes and imagined a huge round shield with a strong apple tree, much like the one in front of her, carved in the middle of it.

"Imagine it strapped to your back, so that nothing may harm you from behind."

Mercy imagined that it wasn't a quilt covering her back, but her shining shield.

"In your mind draw a circle around you, in which you are the center," Abigail continued. "Repeat after me: *This is my space.*"

"This is my space," the girls repeated together.

"I own this space," Abigail intoned.

"I own this space," they said.

"Good. Now we ready ourselves to be vessels through which the energy of the earth will flow and into the gatekeeper, strengthening our tree and keeping the gate to the Norse Underworld closed.

"Breathe with me, deeply, in and out, on a four count."

Their mother led them in several deep, cleansing breaths.

"Clear your mind of thoughts. Then *acknowledge* your feelings, and as you do don't question *why* you're feeling something. Simply breathe in with acceptance of the feeling and on your next breath out, release that feeling."

Mercy cleared her mind and then drew in a deep breath and immediately was filled with nervousness. She didn't try to decipher her nerves. Instead she thought, *hello nerves—I feel you—I acknowledge you—and now I release you!* She let out a long breath and felt the tension between her shoulder blades relax.

With her next breath in Mercy was filled with fear—fear of not being good enough, smart enough, brave enough—or worse, being too self-centered to truly walk Freya's path. Again, she acknowledged—*I get it. Fear is here. That's fine and normal and natural. Fear can be healthy. It reminds me to be smart and brave and selfless instead of selfish. And now I release you, fear.* As she breathed fear out Mercy felt the sick knot in her stomach unravel and calm.

"And we begin. We are vessels, cleansed and protected, ready to be conduits for energy. Remember, we do not keep that energy. We only guide it. Visualize the gate before you, deep within the trunk of this ancient tree who has stood guardian for hundreds of years."

Mercy kept her eyes tightly closed. She knew that Hunter's eyes were open because every Feast Day of their lives until that night they'd practiced the ritual together from *outside* the pentagram while they watched their magical mother harness the energy of the earth and direct it to close the gate. Hunter always kept her eyes open to stare at the tree, but Mercy preferred to imagine the gate in her mind's eye.

"When your image of the gate is set, reach through your bodies down into the earth—find the ley lines there—see them. What color is your ley line, Mercy?"

"Green!" Mercy said, eyes still shut.

"What color is your ley line, Hunter?"

"Deep blue!" Hunter said.

"And mine is silver gray, like the eyes of Athena. Draw your ley line up through your body and push it from the center of your forehead, like a beacon, to shine against the gate hidden within your tree. If the gate seems open at all, it will be closed. If the gate seems weary, it will be strengthened. If the gate seems small, it will grow and grow and grow until it is so powerful that nothing could possibly escape through it."

Mercy imagined that when she breathed in she drew the beam of radiant green light up and into her body—along her spine—to blaze out of her third eye in the center of her forehead.

But nothing happened.

Mercy felt the pulsing power of the ley line, just like she always could. She could even feel it lifting to her, but instead of it filling her body with luminous energy, it was like a garden hose with a kink in it, and only trickles of power sluggishly moved up to her spine and hovered there with a little warmth, like someone pressed their hand to the small of her back.

She squeezed her eyelids more firmly together and focused, concentrating on the energy that was tantalizingly close. Drew a deep breath in as she called to her goddess. *Freya, my goddess, help me. Strengthen me. Allow me to guide the energy of your earth.*

Mercy felt the warmth along her spine expand a little, but there was no infilling of energy—there was no inrush of power. The pulse of the ley line had been replaced with something cold and strange and wrong.

Suddenly Xena hissed and began growling, a guttural, dangerous sound that wasn't even recognizable as coming from the sweet, nosy feline Mercy had known her entire life.

Hunter gasped and cried, "Oh! Tyr! No!"

Mercy opened her eyes. Hunter sat beside her. They faced the tree, while their mother sat cross-legged in front of them with her back to the tree. Beside Abigail, Xena had turned to face the tree as well. The huge cat's back was fully arched and her tufted ears flattened against her skull as she continued to growl menacingly.

The thick trunk of the mighty tree dripped with something disgusting—black and foul and thick. The center of the trunk quivered, like a horse trying to shake off a swarm of biting flies, but this was no horse. A snout pushed through the darkness and took form, melted wax becoming solid as it entered this world. Red eyes broke through the shuddering bark. The thing was huge—all sinew, matted fur, and claws. Its breath came in rapid pants as it pulled its body through the corrupted center of the tree. The fetid stench of it reached Mercy—thick with sulfur and rot. Mercy tasted bile as she gagged in revulsion and fear.

The creature looked directly at them and snarled, gnashing long, pointed teeth.

Five

Abigail surged to her feet. "Run!" she screamed and pushed her daughters back toward the darkness of the open field.

Hunter's feet cemented to the ground. Her mother's shoves only jarred her enough to make her dizzy. This wasn't real. None of it.

Sealskin black liquid gushed from the tree, and spurted around the slick and matted fur of the giant wolf clawing its way into their world. It flashed in and out of focus, unstable as it tried to gain hold in this new realm. Its talons dug trenches in the grass and it bared its teeth and growled, wet nose sniffing the air. This was a nightmare, sixteen years of anxiety spilling out of Hunter's subconscious and raining down on this made-up version of things to come.

Hunter reached out for Mercy. In any nightmare, she could grab hold of her sister and will herself awake. Emptiness met her fingers. Nothing but spring air and the guttural moans of the fanged beast. Hunter whirled around. The breeze tugged at the skirt of Mercy's ivory dress as she followed their mother's instructions and ran. But Mercy wouldn't leave her. That's never how it happened. Not in Hunter's dreams and especially not her nightmares.

Mercy glanced backward and skidded to a halt. "Hunter!" she shrieked and focused her wide-eyed terror past her sister.

This was all too real. Hunter felt the monster behind her. Felt the rank air tighten and heard the otherworldly liquid slosh as the creature spilled into their realm. She couldn't turn around, couldn't force herself to move. This was supposed to be peaceful, magical, the beginning of years and years of happiness and light. What had she done to deserve this?

"Stay back, vile beast!" her mother roared over the steady crackle of the charged night air.

Hunter heard the beast's heavy footsteps crack rotting apples and beat against the earth. She whirled around as her pulse battered her eardrums.

Abigail had gathered the white candle and held it in the air. "Athena, I call to you!" The wolf cowered and its ears pressed back against its wet coat. "Give me strength in battle!" Against the crackling wind Abigail scraped a match. It left behind a trail of sparking orange that ripped through the black sky like a tear in a page and doused the scene in orange light. Magic heard Abigail's cry, but Athena hadn't shown.

The beast's image flickered as its gaze swung from the tree to the flaming arc and back to Abigail. It bared its wet teeth and stalked forward as the Goode witch pressed the flaming match against the candle's wick. She gripped the wax pillar with both hands and held it in front of her. "Athena! I call to you, my goddess, my protector!" The flame shot skyward, illuminating their small space on earth.

The wolf's top lip rippled with a growl as it sprang toward Abigail. It flashed in and out of focus as its giant paw struck out and swatted her aside. She slammed into the ground and crumpled like a rag doll.

Hunter reached out, her cries for her mother strangled by the cords of fear lining her neck. "Get away!" she finally managed as the creature prodded Abigail with his enormous muzzle.

Its ears flicked in her direction. It raised his massive head and blew out a burst of mucus-specked air. Hunter's mouth went dry, her tongue turning to paste behind her teeth. The wolf's lip curled. The magical light painted its teeth a shiny orange as he stepped over Abigail and charged at Hunter.

Mercy's bare feet slapped the earth behind Hunter as she scrambled away. Hunter stumbled over fallen apples. Her arms flailed as her feet slid out from under her and she crashed onto the ground. As the beast lunged forward, Mercy wrapped her arm around Hunter's chest and tucked herself behind her sister. Hunter squeezed her eyelids shut and held up her arms. This was the end for them both. A sob tore from her throat as hot, foul breath blew back the hair that had fallen against her cheeks.

Fangs pierced Hunter's forearm. A deep, searing ache twisted around her lungs and squeezed. Blood oozed hot and wet around sharp teeth as they sunk into her flesh. Mercy's chest shook against Hunter's back as she shouted words Hunter's pulse drowned into a whisper.

Xena was there in an instant. A streak of yowling fur, the cat hurled herself at the beast. Her howls pierced the night as she wrapped herself around the wolf's snout and dug her claws into its leathery muzzle. With a roar that rattled Hunter's bones, the creature released her arm and clamored back. It whipped its head from side to side. With a shriek, Xena flew off its face. She tumbled through the air and struck a tree limb, landing in the grass with a sickly thud.

The wolf stalked back toward Hunter and her sister. Back to finish the job and end the Goode line before the new generation could step into their power.

A screech tore through the night. The wolf cocked his head and turned toward the magical rip burning against the black sky. Hunter squeezed Mercy's hand as the cool spring air turned hot and thick. Another piercing shriek rang out as the gash opened wide. An owl burst through the tear, its feathers the same jack-o'-lantern orange as the otherworldly rip in space. Massive wings beat the air as it dove at the wolf. Blood spurted from the beast's back as the owl's talons ripped its flesh.

The owl circled Hunter and Mercy and let out another scream before landing on the ground beside their mother.

Blood oozed down the wolf's back as it spun to pursue the bird. The owl hopped closer to Abigail, tipped its beak to the sky, and shrieked. A fiery bolt flashed from the tear in the night and struck Abigail's chest. In an instant, her body was aglow in orange flames. The wolf stilled as Abigail rose to her feet and the owl took perch on her shoulder. *"Fenrir!"* Another voice coated Abigail's and a glowing spear flickered to life by her side. *"This realm is not your own!"*

With a growl, Fenrir shook the blood from his coat and stalked toward Abigail, ignoring the twins. Abigail, alight with the fiery and otherworldly powers of her goddess, pressed forward toward the ancient apple tree that grew from the magic of the Norse Underworld.

Mercy pulled Hunter to her feet and clenched Hunter's hand in her own as they crept toward Xena. The cat wound around their ankles, herding them away from their mother and the wolf who'd spilled out of its realm and flickered, unstable, into their own.

Mercy dropped Hunter's hand, scooped up Xena, and ran. This time, Hunter matched her sister's stride. Her lungs burned as she sucked in gulps of magic-charged air.

"I banish you back to your Underworld!" Abigail's voice was thunder. It clapped against Hunter's back and she whirled around in time to see her mother hurl the spear. It caught the wolf's shoulder and knocked it back into the tree. Fenrir's image flickered as it fought to break free. It howled and bucked and clawed the air, but the point of the spear had pierced through the wolf, into the tree's trunk.

Foreboding gnawed at Hunter's stomach. She left Mercy and Xena and charged back to the tree. Air fled her lungs as she slowed to a stop near her mother. She could see it now. The gash in Abigail's temple. The skin hung like wet clothes pinned to a line. Athena fueled her, kept her on her feet, but Hunter's mother was not long for this world.

"Hunter!" Athena's voice shadowed Abigail's, making goose bumps flash across the back of Hunter's neck. "Something's wrong with the gates! Don't wait until Solstice to fix them. Promise me!"

Hunter blinked through a flood of tears. "I promise!"

Abigail looked at the wolf pinned to the apple tree, its form flickering under the promise of death. Then she turned and looked past Hunter to Mercy, who tripped over Xena as the cat struggled to keep the girl at a safe distance. "Take care of your sister," Abigail said. "You'll need each other now, more than ever."

Hunter wailed as Fenrir caught the billowing skirt of Abigail's dress and pulled her to him. The beast tore through Abigail's clothes. Its teeth shredded her back and stained the fabric scarlet.

The owl shrieked as Abigail faced Fenrir and pressed her palms against the beast's matted coat. It lit like dry kindling.

Athena's war cry muted Abigail's screams as flames consumed Hunter's mother and the beast.

Hunter's knees slammed into the earth as the blaze flashed out and the rip in the sky vanished as quickly as it'd come. Tears burned down Hunter's cheeks and blood seeped from her torn forearm. She had been tapped, and now she would simply pour into the earth until her time in this realm was over.

Hunter couldn't make a sound as Xena mewled and circled the charred remains of the woman who'd once brought so much light into the world. Of Fenrir, never fully in this realm, there was not a trace. Mercy threw herself against the tree, which now showed no evidence of their loss. Hunter's chin quivered as she watched her sister slide down the trunk into the grass next to their mother's body.

Maybe they'd all stay in the field at the foot of the apple tree and let the gentle Illinois breeze sweep them away.

Six

Sheriff Dearborn lifted his Chicago Bears travel mug to his lips and blew into the round O cut into the burnt orange lid before he took a drink. Hazelnut. Dearborn's favorite. He smacked his lips, puffed a cooling breath into the navy blue tumbler, and took another sip. Trish had added an extra sugar packet even though she knew he was trying to cut out the sweet stuff.

He set his coffee mug down as he approached Goodeville's last traffic signal. The red light painted the hood of his white-and-gold cruiser a pale Christmas crimson. His thick, calloused fingers drummed against the steering wheel as he waited for the light to turn green. Dearborn had only seen a few cars on his final patrol of the night. The passenger and rear seats had all been full of teenagers who'd rolled down their windows and given the sheriff big, goofy, and if he was being honest, fairly tipsy grins and waves as they passed by. The designated drivers had remained focused on the road, and that's really all he needed to see. The sheriff wasn't in the habit of busting kids for being kids. He'd leave that to their parents.

The light turned green and Dearborn left the vibrant Main Street in his rearview and slipped under the blanket of darkness that covered cornfields and country houses. He took another sip of coffee and craned his neck to peer up at the sky. Clouds had rolled in while he'd been in his office completing the day's paperwork. Another sip. That's when Trish had made his coffee. Sweet, sweet coffee. Sweet, sweet Trish. He reached up to the transceiver attached to the shoulder of his uniform and squeezed the talk button. "Two sugars?"

Trish answered immediately. "I figured it wasn't really cheating if you didn't add the sugar in yourself." The dispatcher's voice rang back clear and smooth as if the new Alexa his nephew had set up for him at home had followed him into his car.

Dearborn fumbled with the buttons on his walkie-talkie. The darned device had always been too small for his hands. "You're too good to me, Trish."

"Don't count your chickens just yet, Sheriff. I just got off the horn with old Earl Thompson. He's been snooping around the field out by Quaker Road. Said he'll meet you out there. He also said—oh dagnabit, I had it right here . . ." Papers rustled as Trish dug through her notes.

Trish's dispatch station was a mess of Post-its, origami farm animals, and photos of her Yorkie, Pepper. Over the years, Dearborn had learned that a good leader doesn't force his team to fit into a certain mold. He allows them to be themselves. He rubbed the burnt orange and navy BE YOU sticker stuck to the center of his steering wheel. He and Matt Nagy couldn't both be wrong.

"If it was a snake, it would've bitten me." Trish's laughter tinkled through the cruiser like wind chimes. "Old Earl said that *'there's a ruckus out there at that old olive tree.'*" She'd lowered her voice and made it tremble with age. "*'Not that I'm surprised. Who plants one olive tree? A twisted, mangled one, no less. Been giving me the heebie-jeebies my whole life.'* All one million years of it." She paused. "I added that last part myself."

Dearborn's barrel chest shook with a chuckle. Trish always made him laugh. "I was hoping to end my shift on time tonight, er"—he glanced down at his watch: 02:36—"this *morning,* but I'm only a couple minutes away. I'll head over and check out the ruckus."

The sheriff flipped on his high beams as he drove deeper into the dark.

"What do you make of them planting just one olive tree all those hundreds of years ago?" Papers continued to rustle as Trish spoke, and Dearborn could picture her folding the small squares into another barnyard animal for her desktop menagerie.

He took another drink and let the sweet hazelnut drift across his taste buds as he considered Trish's question. He had never much thought about it. As a high schooler, he'd go to parties out by the aging olive tree or the lone apple tree on the other side of town or the single cherry or palm that encircle Goodeville. He'd always felt strong and protected while he was out near one of the trees. But get any teenage boy liquored up and he'd be liable to feel like Superman. Now, many years older and much, much wiser, Dearborn felt a bit like one of those lone trees—waiting, guarding, aging.

A flutter of pages. "I think it's pretty neat." Trish clucked. "Adds a bit of flavor none of the other towns have. Not sure that's what the founders were aiming for when they planted them . . ."

"I tend to agree with you, Trish." It wasn't the most honest thing he could've said. Dearborn *tended to agree* with folks a lot more than he actually agreed with them, but sometimes little white lies kept the peace and helped build trust. And a team was nothing without trust.

Sheriff Dearborn's blinker lit up the night air with a Halloween glow as he turned off the main road onto the craterous drive that passed by the ancient olive. The first-aid kit he kept in his passenger seat rattled as the cruiser bounced along the gravel. Dearborn grimaced while he did his best to pass more potholes than he hit. He closed in on Earl's parked shiny red truck as the beams from his headlights bobbed against the olive tree's gnarled trunk like he was a boat at sea and it, a buoy.

He rubbed at the pain sprouting in his neck. His old U of I football injury always acted up whenever he was out on these unpaved roads. He'd have to sit down with the mayor again. Outside city limits needed just as much care as inside.

"I'm not sure why you bother checking up on everything old Earl calls in," Trish said, bringing him back to the matter at hand. "Especially with your neck the way it is. By my count, this is ruckus number thirty-two, and that's just this year. Old Earl might beat last year's Ruckus Record."

The Ruckus Record. Dearborn's clean-shaven cheeks plumped with a grin. That was another thing that cluttered Trish's desk. She'd decorated a small piece of poster board in fancy hand-drawn calligraphy she'd learned in one of the art classes down at the fancy new craft store, Glitter and Glue. After Dearborn returned from checking out the latest call from Earl, he would come back to the precinct and watch Trish light up as she chose which of her many stickers to add to the poster board. It was a small thing, childish even, but it was a thing they shared only with each other.

He pulled behind Earl's pickup and put his car in park. "It'll give us a reason to open up that new pack of stickers you bought. Big, silver disco ball–looking stars, weren't they?"

Trish's laughter made his chest tighten.

"Oh, you caught me." She giggled. "I can't hide anything from your sharp investigative skills. And I just *cannot* stay out of that darned craft store."

Dearborn dug through the first-aid kit for the aspirin and popped a couple before he unbuckled his seat belt and threw open his door. "If Earl's going to beat last year's record, we'll need all the stickers we can get."

He unclipped the flashlight from the belt fastened around his waist and shined the light through the back window of the truck. Empty.

A faint acrid, smoky scent wafted toward him on the crisp night breeze. He took a deep inhale and followed the smell into the grass away from the tree and the truck and the suspected ruckus.

Dearborn winced as he craned his neck to talk into the transceiver. "Someone's been out here smoking—probably kids. I'll take a closer look and make sure they didn't leave any cigarette butts behind. Don't want this whole field going up."

"Ten-four." Trish was silent for a moment before she came back on the radio, her voice light and airy in that hen-like way it got when she came across a juicy bit of town gossip. "You know, old Earl hasn't been the same since Debbie left him for that spin instructor over in Chicago."

Raindrops splatted against Dearborn's back and the grass swayed around his shins. Each burst of wind through the fields brought with it the steady *whoosh* of waves on a coastal shoreline. Dearborn paused and savored the moment before resuming his march through the grass.

"That was back a year or so after the town put in the train," he said as he cast his beam back and forth over the blades' puffy tops. "What was that, five years ago now?"

A whole world of changes had happened on the heels, or maybe *on the tracks* was a more fitting description, of the new commuter train that ran in a loop from Chicago through Joliet, Bloomington, Champaign-Urbana, Rantoul, and Kankakee before bisecting Goodeville. It had saved the town from a fate too many small Midwestern municipalities had succumbed to and brought with it thriving shops and train cars packed with weary city folk desperate for the sappy slow pace of picturesque Goodeville. The commuter train had also brought Trish to Goodeville. Dearborn didn't have one complaint.

Papers rustled as Trish came back over the radio. "Five whole years this August. You know, old Earl was a member of the board that decided to bring the train into Goodeville. Without it, Debbie would be home and you wouldn't have to deal with the old coot calling every other day and sending you out on wild-goose chases. If that's not old Earl's bad luck, I don't know what is."

Dearborn paused and sniffed the air. The scent had died. He took a few steps to the right, back toward Earl's empty truck and the road and the olive tree, and sniffed again. There it was. He wiggled his nose and followed the scent like a basset hound.

"Yeah, poor Earl," he murmured into his walkie-talkie as he left the grass and crossed the road.

"*Poor Earl?* If you don't mind me saying, you should really be thinking, *poor you.*" She sighed. "In as long as I've known you, you've never even come close to finding your Debbie."

Gravel crunched under his boots as he passed through the white cones of light from his high beams. "I don't need a Debbie, Trish. I have you." Through the steady hum of the radio, he could practically hear her plump cheeks flush with heat. He scratched the back of his neck as warmth pricked his own.

Dearborn cleared his throat and pressed the talk button. "I'll check in after I've sussed out the situation. I'm headed right toward the olive tree." Another sniff. "Maybe Earl stumbled onto something real this time."

"He would love that." Trish clucked. "Be safe out there."

The line went quiet as Dearborn headed into the stretch of grass. He wiped the spits of rain from his face and rubbed the tip of his square nose. The closer he got to the tree, the thicker the stench. It bit at his nose and made his eyes water.

"Earl," he called as he swept the beam from his flashlight over the grass. "Where'd you get off to?"

The gravel crunched behind him and he spun around. He squinted through his tear-swirled vision. "Earl?" he hollered once again as he shined his flashlight along his car, Earl's truck, and then the road's shoulder. The white light struck something shiny. The hairs on the back of Dearborn's neck bristled. His mouth went dry as his fingers found his gun holster. His eyes burned and tears and rain and snot leaked down his face as he quickly, expertly closed in on the glinting metal.

Sheriff Dearborn's stomach hollowed as the scene came into view. The buckles of Earl's suspenders twinkled in the flashlight beam like trapped lightning bugs. The old man's fingers threaded through the tall grass as if he laid there, peacefully staring up at the stormy night's sky. Bile burned the back of Dearborn's throat as he shined his light on Earl's face. Blood streaked the man's wrinkled brow and cheeks, and rain pooled in the raw red hollows where his eyes had been.

Hazelnut and sick coated Sheriff Dearborn's tongue and he pressed the back of his hand against his mouth. He was a leader, and with a death like this—a *murder* like this—his town would need him to lead, need him to be strong.

The sheriff leaned into his radio. "Trish, send an ambulance to Quaker Road and wake up Carter. Wake up the coroner. Everyone! We need to—" Dearborn's eyelids slammed shut as the smoky scent intensified.

Footsteps slid across the gravel behind him.

Dearborn unbuckled his holster and drew his sidearm. "Who's out there?" Tears welled and blurred his vision. *"Who's out there?!"*

A shadow crossed his beam of light and grass mashed under heavy feet.

The acrid, burning scent was palpable, stringy sizzles of electricity biting at his eyes and nostrils. Dearborn opened his mouth to bark a command and the snapping jolts surged past his parted lips. His gun and flashlight thumped against the ground as he dropped to his knees and gripped his throat.

"Sheriff, you okay?" Trish called out into the dark and rainy night. "Sheriff?" Her voice tightened with panic. *"Frank?!"*

Seven

With each blink, Hunter's lids scraped against her eyes like sandpaper. She was out of tears. She hadn't known that was possible. Not until last night. Or had it been this morning? She shielded her eyes and squinted up at the gray, cloud-filled sky. It had rained sometime in the wee hours of the morning—the only evidence that the world knew it had lost the great soul of Abigail Goode.

The screen door creaked open as Mercy emerged from the house. She shuffled across the porch and clomped down the steps. She let out a sound, somewhere between a moan and a sigh and plopped next to Hunter on the bottom step.

Hunter grimaced as she ran her fingers along the scabbing wounds on her arm. So, she *was* still able to feel.

Mercy set her phone down on the walkway between their feet and rested her head on Hunter's shoulder. Mercy was heavy, a steel anvil where the feather-light young woman had once been. That was one of the strange things about grief. How it turned some into weights and reduced others to the molted skin of the person they'd been.

Hunter rubbed her cheek against Mercy's sable hair. Good thing her sister was there to keep her from blowing away.

Mercy's phone chimed and she plucked it up off the concrete.

Hunter averted her eyes from the screen. She couldn't bear to see any words about her mother. They were too powerful, too permanent.

"Kirk?" Hunter asked as Mercy's thumbs flew across the keyboard.

Her sister nodded and her phone chimed again.

"And Emily?"

Another nod.

Hunter twirled the end of her ponytail. "They'll be over soon." It wasn't a question. It didn't need to be. Whenever the sisters needed their friends, they were always there. Hunter's phone buzzed in her pocket. It was Jax. She knew Mercy had told him what happened. Even in mourning, her sister was at the top of the phone tree.

A white-and-gold sheriff's cruiser turned off Main Street and onto their drive. Hunter stood as the car parked and Deputy Carter climbed out of the driver's side and straightened the tan cowboy hat he was never without. Mercy hefted herself off the bottom step and mirrored Hunter as the deputy motioned for Sheriff Dearborn to join him outside of the car.

Deputy Carter's boots squeaked in the wet grass as he and the sheriff approached the twins and the bull's blood red porch that had failed to protect their mother.

The deputy removed his hat and rubbed his thumb against the brim as he blinked down at Hunter and her sister. Emily often mentioned Deputy Chase Carter and how adorable and puppylike he looked with his round gray eyes and his lips locked in a perpetual half smile. But there was nothing to smile about today. Every bit of Deputy Carter's puppylike appeal had washed away with the rain. "Girls, I am so terribly sorry. We all loved your mother." He paused before he cleared his throat and nudged the sheriff with his elbow.

The sheriff grunted and removed his sunglasses. "Yes, your mother.

We loved her. She was a, uh, a woman." Dearborn's brown eyes scraped against Hunter and the corner of his mouth twitched. "A now deceased woman."

The deputy let out a strained barking cough as he settled his hat against his closely cropped hair. "I hate to do this, but we have to go through the events one final time before we close up Abigail's file." He removed a pen and a small notepad from his chest pocket and flipped through a few pages before coming to the right one. "Mercy, you're the one who called 911."

Mercy's hair slipped from her shoulders as she nodded. She pushed it back behind her ear and mouthed a word, but no sound came out. She hadn't spoken since they'd gotten home. There weren't words to describe what they each felt. And if there had been, Hunter wouldn't have wanted to hear them.

Carter's Adam's apple bobbed with a tight swallow. "I'm sorry to ask you to go back through this." He tapped the point of his pen against the pad.

Hunter twined her fingers around Mercy's. They were stronger together, and Hunter needed strength now more than ever.

"The three of you were out picnicking." He glanced back down at his notes. "Is that right?"

"That's right." Hunter and her sister spoke in unison.

Hunter ignored the sheriff, who shifted restlessly in her periphery, and spoke directly to Deputy Carter. "Midnight picnics are a birthday tradition. We do them every year with Mom."

A tear rolled down Mercy's pale cheek and she let out a broken sob. "We *did* them every year."

Hunter squeezed her sister's hand. She'd be strong enough for both of them. "That's why we had the candles and incense . . . They were part of the celebration." Goose bumps peaked along her arms and she shivered. That wolf had assured that the Goode sisters would never have a true celebration ever again.

The deputy's brow creased as he scribbled something onto the paper. "Those were the same candles that started the fire? The blaze that—"

Mercy's sob cracked the space between them. "She's dead!"

Hunter tensed as she steadied the sinking weight of her sister. Mercy wasn't built for grief or trauma. Until now, those had always been Hunter's burden.

The sheriff fogged his glasses, wiped the lenses with the end of his untucked shirt, and fogged them again. "She won't have died in vain if you get money out of the whole debacle." He peered up at the clouds through his lenses before sliding the glasses onto his broad nose. "You could sue. That's what people do, isn't it?"

Hunter's stomach knotted as she stared at her reflection in Sheriff Dearborn's mirrored aviators. She'd never wished for the kind of evil dark magic so many people outside of Goodeville believed was part of the Practice. But she wished for it now. Her pendant heated against her chest. It didn't matter that the sheriff was wrong about how her mother met her end. Hunter wished she could call down the cosmos and send an entire galaxy of stars ripping through him. She didn't want money. She wanted her mom.

Deputy Carter clapped the senior officer on the back. "You'll have to excuse the sheriff. He's been up a long time. Everything's got him a little rattled."

The sheriff slid his glasses to the end of his nose. "You'd be rattled if you'd seen what I saw. That dead man out there—old man Thompson—with no eyes." With his middle and pointer fingers he mimed stabbing his eyeballs.

Hunter tightened her grip on Mercy's hand as the sheriff wiggled the imaginary eyes in front of them.

"Ripped right out of his head and then, poof, disappeared." He threw up his hand. "Swallowed up by who knows what."

With a strangled laugh, Deputy Carter tugged on the tip of his hat. "As I said, he's shaken up by the scene that happened last night out off Quaker Road by the old olive tree."

"Not *at* the olive tree. The tree had nothing to do with it!" Sheriff Dearborn swiped at the beads of sweat popping along his brow. "You girls got anything to drink?"

Hunter released Mercy's hand. "I'll get you a glass."

Deputy Carter's puppy-dog face was firmly affixed as he mouthed an apology in Hunter's direction. She couldn't even muster the ghost of a polite smile in return as she leaned into her sister and whispered, "You'll be okay." It wasn't a question. It was a reminder.

The deputy's words caught Hunter as she shakily headed up the steps toward the front door. "We, uh, we also have to discuss the matter of guardianship." He took a breath. "You girls don't happen to have any family close by, do you?"

Hunter couldn't look back at her sister who remained silent as Deputy Carter continued softly prodding the details of their family tree.

Xena meowed and slapped the screen door with her furry paw, refocusing Hunter's attention.

"You want out?" Hunter asked as she opened the door. The Maine coon circled Hunter's ankles and pressed her long body against Hunter's calves, forcing her inside. Hunter closed the screen and stumbled in. She caught herself on the bannister and crouched down near the foot of the staircase that led up to Mercy's and her rooms.

Hunter combed her fingers through Xena's fur. "I know it's hard. I miss her, too." The tears came then. Their well replenished, they rushed from her eyes like strands of pearls.

Xena chittered and wove figure eights between Hunter's feet.

"And now we'll have to leave our home." Hunter sagged onto the wood floor and hugged her knees against her chest. "I wish Mom was here." She pressed her swollen lids against her knees and wept onto her ceremony dress. The dress that she'd hand dyed and chosen to wear to begin her new life, her happier life.

Xena yowled and pressed her massive front paws against Hunter's shins. With a sniffle, Hunter raised her head and rested her chin on her damp knees. Xena's whiskers dusted Hunter's cheeks as the cat leaned in. Only a sliver of Xena's amber irises encircled her dilated pupils as she let out a string of clipped meows and sneezed right in Hunter's face.

"Gah, Xena . . ." Hunter grumbled as she blindly wiped her face with the collar of her dress.

"Sorry about that. The incantation always makes me sneeze."

Hunter dropped her dress and stared at the spot in front of her where the cat had been. Now there were feet—human feet attached to human legs attached to a human torso. Hunter scrambled backward and winced when her back struck the staircase.

The naked woman before her brushed her hand through her mane of wild black, white, and brown–streaked hair. "It's like you've never seen a cat before."

"Xena?"

The woman ran her clawlike nails down her bare form and smiled. "In the flesh."

Eight

The silence stretched to an unending, uncomfortable frozen length after Hunter went inside. Usually, in a situation where adults were hanging around looking lost and awkward Mercy would've easily alleviated the tension by engaging both officers in cheerful conversation.

But Mercy did not care about their awkwardness and she didn't think she'd ever be cheerful again.

So the silence continued.

"Um, Mercy? It is Mercy and not Hunter, right?"

Mercy looked up from her phone to meet the deputy's gaze. She cleared her throat and started to say yes, but decided nodding would be fine.

"Okay, well, Mercy—as I was asking your sister, do you have family close or—"

"Thirsty!" the sheriff interrupted. "Really need that drink." He cleared his throat several times and wiped his mouth on the back of his tan sleeve. Mercy cringed at the white crusty crap that rained from the creases of his lips.

Anger bubbled strong in Mercy's chest and the words that had been dammed within her broke loose. "Sorry, but we don't have the fresh-squeezed lemonade we'd usually offer you—with a plate of cookies or a sweet little spell or two. You see, our *mom,* the Kitchen Witch everyone loved, *died.* Horribly. Last night. We're a little off our social game at the moment. But, hey, come on in. Hunter's probably curled up in a fetal position in the kitchen crying. I'm sure she won't mind being rushed by someone who is—*gasp!*—thirsty."

Mercy brushed off the butt of her dress and turned to stomp up the stairs. Anger felt good—better than despair. Better than grief that was a chasm so deep her words got lost in it. She glanced back over her shoulder from the wide double doors. The sheriff was already following her, but the deputy was shifting from foot to foot, picking at the brim of his hat.

"You gonna stay out here?" Mercy shot the words at him. Now that she'd found them again they seemed to be firing out of her.

"Well. Um. No. Ma'am. I'll come in and—"

She didn't wait for the rest of his annoying and predictable reply. She marched into the house *not* holding the door open behind her—and ran smack into a tall woman about her mom's age who was wearing Abigail's fluffy flowered bathrobe. Her brown, black, and white hair was thick and fell in a mass down her back. Her unusual amber eyes narrowed.

"Excuse you, Mercy!" The woman moved back gracefully instead of staggering.

"What the bloody hell—"

"Sheriff! Deputy! Sorry it took me so long." Hunter rushed from the kitchen carrying two beading glasses of iced tea. "I was distracted by our Aunt Xena."

"Our who?" Mercy felt like her head was going to explode.

Hunter stared into her eyes giving Mercy the *look.* The one the twins had been sharing since they could formulate complete sentences. The *look* meant *just go with it and ask questions later.*

"Aunt Xena," Hunter said briskly, pushing past Mercy and the stranger to hand the two men the tea. "You were asleep when she arrived a few hours ago. I thought I told you she was here. So much has happened." Hunter rubbed her temples and winced like she had a headache before continuing. "Sheriff, Deputy, would you like to sit?" She gestured to the couch.

The sheriff was gulping the tea so the deputy said, "No. Thank you. We won't stay long. We know you have a lot of plans to make. So, um, Xena? You came to take guardianship of the girls?"

With sinuous grace Xena made her way to the empty couch and perched on the arm, carefully covering her bare legs with the bathrobe. With the back of her hand she smoothed her hair before she spoke. "Yes. Of course. No one else is suitable to be guardian of our girls."

Mercy stared at the woman—at the multicolored riot of hair and those distinctive amber eyes—and her stomach flip-flopped.

The deputy wrote a note in his little book. "I didn't realize Abigail had a sister."

"Oh, she didn't," Hunter said quickly. "Xena is really Mom's second cousin from back East. It's just that we've always called her auntie."

"Okay. Got it. And you're planning on remaining here, in Goodeville, with the girls?" asked the deputy.

"I will always be here for the Goode girls," said Xena. She looked at her hand and frowned before licking a speck of something off one of her long, sharp fingernails.

"We should go," said the sheriff as he handed Hunter his empty glass. "Lots to do with this murder happening and all . . ."

Deputy Carter wiped his brow with his sleeve. "Girls, we're here if you need us. And, again, please let me offer my deepest condolences on the loss of your mother. She was a wonderful woman." He placed his untouched glass of tea on the coffee table, nodded respectfully to the girls and Xena, and then followed the sheriff, who was already on the porch, out the door.

Mercy put her hands on her hips and faced the woman balancing delicately on the arm of the couch. "Who. Is. This?"

"Well, believe it or not it's—"

"Mercy Anne Goode, you've known me since that stormy night you were born three minutes before your sister. Now, I know you're not the Kitchen Witch your mother was, but could you be a darling and brew me a large cup of Abigail's analgesic tea with a heavy dose of honey? I'm terribly sore from what that horrid Fenrir did to me last night." She had to pause then and press her hand to her bow-shaped lips to stifle a sob before she continued in a broken whisper. "I do miss my sweet Abigail so very, very much."

Mercy walked over to stand directly in front of Xena. She stared into her eyes and then slowly reached out to touch her voluminous hair. "Ohmygoddess, Xena?"

"Oh, by Bast's spectacular nipples! Of course it's me. I know you aren't stupid, so I shall blame your shock on grief."

Mercy looked at Hunter. "How?"

Hunter shrugged. "Not sure, but the incantation made her sneeze all over me."

"Did you know she was a person inside a cat suit?"

"Oh, please! *I am a cat.* More specifically, I am a familiar who has been attached to the Goode family for generations. It is accurate to say that currently I am a cat wearing a person suit." She licked the back of her hand and brushed it through her spectacularly messy hair.

"I need to sit down." Mercy fell heavily onto the couch.

"Oh, no no no." Lithely, Xena stood, grabbed Mercy's wrist, and propelled her toward the kitchen with Hunter following closely. "That beast bruised me badly. First, I need healing tea. And while I'm stuck wearing this human skin I might as well eat some of the cannabis truffles your mother keeps in the freezer." When the girls stared at her without speaking she added, "What? They're medicinal. And then we need to make plans. There is much you girls must do."

Numbly, Mercy disappeared into Abigail's deep pantry, easily finding the clearly marked pain relief tea. She paused there for a moment and breathed in the scent of her mother, squeezing her eyes shut tightly to keep the tears from escaping down her cheeks. *Just do one thing at a time. Get through one moment and then the next. It will get easier—not better—but easier. It has to.*

She emerged from the pantry to find Hunter sitting at the bar staring at Xena, who was sitting *on* the bar—her long bare legs swinging over the side as she inspected her fingernails.

"Did Abigail know you could change form like this?" Mercy blurted as she filled her mother's fancy electric teapot and pressed the button to heat water for herbal tea.

"Yes, of course. My Abigail knew everything. She was a splendid witch."

Mercy felt as if she were unraveling inside. She drew a deep breath to steady herself as she held the old wood honey dipper over a mug and dripped thick golden liquid into it. She was trying to sort through her many questions when Hunter found the one that touched them all the deepest.

"Then Mom knew that you'd be here to take care of us—to be sure we wouldn't have to leave our home. She—she died knowing we'd be okay." Hunter choked out the last of the words and wiped her cheeks quickly.

Xena leaned forward and gently stroked Hunter's dark ponytail. "Yes, kitten. Abigail would never have wished to leave her girls, but last night when she realized she had to sacrifice herself to save you—to save us all—she died in peace and must have gone to the arms of Athena knowing I would watch over both of you and help you with what is to come." She brushed a tear from her own cheek. "My Abigail was a fierce protectoress."

The electric pot chimed at the same moment the front doorbell rang, making the three of them jump. Xena sniffed the air.

"It's the boy. The one whose scent was all over Mercy last night."

"Kirk! I'll, um—"

Hunter got up and took the teapot from her. "Let him in. I'll get Xena her tea."

Xena slid sinuously from the countertop. "Emily and Jax shall be here soon. We will greet them, accept their condolences, and then be rid of them. Your mother's last words told you what you must do; you have trees to check on and no time to waste in tending them."

Mercy and Hunter stared at her.

"But our friends—" Hunter began.

She fluttered her sharp-tipped fingers about dismissively. "Are not as important as the trees. As the adult in the household I shall tell them—"

"Xena, they can't know you're a cat," said Mercy.

"Seriously," agreed Hunter.

"Of course not!" Xena scoffed, batting her hands at them. "I am your auntie."

The front door echoed with vigorous knocking. "We have no choice," Mercy told Hunter, and she hurried from the kitchen. Her body felt strange—numb and ultrasensitive at the same time. If she didn't have to answer the door—to talk to people—she would just sit. And stare. And wish with everything inside her that she could go back twenty-four hours and wrap her arms around her mom and never let her go.

She opened the door to see her quarterback boyfriend, hair wet and disheveled, like he'd just gotten out of the shower, fist raised to knock again.

"Oh, babe! Come here." Kirk moved into the house and lifted her up in a hug. Mercy pressed her face to his chest and closed her eyes, hoping the scent and feel of him would erase the rest of the world, if only for a few beats of her broken heart. Then his arms unwrapped from around her and he stepped forward—toward Hunter, who was just coming into the living room. "Hunter, I don't know what else to say except I am so sorry." He scooped Mercy's twin into a gentle hug and patted her back. "Really. I'm here for you—for both of you. Anything. Anything at all I can do I will."

"Boy, you embrace the wrong twin."

Kirk released Hunter and took a step back as Xena, carrying a steaming mug of tea and a truffle, slunk past him and into the living room, where she resumed her perch on the arm of the couch.

"I—I know," he stammered. "I was just telling Hunter sorry, too. Who are you?"

Mercy took Kirk's arm and led him to the far end of the couch—away from Xena—as she said, "This is our Aunt Xena—from the East Coast." She sat beside him and Kirk put his arm around her, pulling her comfortingly close to him.

Hunter nodded and sat in one of the several chairs adjacent to the couch in their big, comfortable living room where everything faced an enormous fireplace framed by a mantel ornately carved with triple moons. "We called Aunt Xena last night and she caught the red-eye to Chicago. She just got here."

Kirk's shoulders sagged. "So, you're moving to the East Coast?" There was no way Hunter, or anyone, could miss the genuine distress on his face.

"No!" the three women said together.

There were two quick knocks on the door and then it burst open as Emily and Jax spilled into the room.

"Ohmygod! I just—I just can't. I can't!" Emily flew across the room and collapsed on the couch on the other side of Mercy as she took her best friend's hand. Her eyes were puffy and red and mascara was smeared down her tearstained cheeks. "What can I do? How can I help?"

Mercy clung to her hand. "You being here helps."

Jax went to Hunter and pulled her up out of the chair. Wordlessly, he took her place and then cradled her on his lap so that her head rested on his shoulder, childlike. His voice was gravelly and his eyes bright with unshed tears. "I don't understand. What happened?"

Mercy forced herself to sit up straight. She wiped her face on her shoulder. Kirk held one of her hands and Emily the other. She tried to pull strength from them—tried to form the right words. *What was it she and Hunter had decided to tell everyone?* Her anger at the sheriff's callousness and then the shock about Xena turning into a person had moved her forward earlier and allowed her to think normally, but it had drained away the second Kirk pulled her into his arms. Now her brain felt wrong—like she was trying to think through mud.

"There was a fire. Dear Abigail got the girls to safety, but it caught her and killed her."

Everyone turned to face Xena.

"Hello," said the human cat. "Emily and Jax, it is lovely to formally meet you." She looked down her nose briefly at Kirk. "I am the twins' Aunt Xena."

Kirk peered up at Xena, his brow furrowed. "You mean like their cat?"

"Yes. Exactly like their lovely feline."

"Abigail has a sister?" asked Jax.

Hunter slid off his lap and moved to the thick arm of the chair, keeping his hand in hers. "No, Xena is Mom's cousin. We've mentioned her before."

"Sorry, I didn't remember." Jax nodded at Xena. "It's nice to meet you, Ms. . . ."

"Call me Auntie or simply Xena."

"Oh, wait. Are you who Abigail used to visit on her trips back to Salem?" Emily asked.

"Yes," the three women lied together.

"I will be staying here—in Goodeville—with our girls," said Xena. She finished the truffle and then began delicately licking her fingers clean.

"So, that means you won't have to leave?" Kirk asked, as Emily wiped a tear from her cheek.

"We're not going anywhere," said Hunter. "Mom would never have wanted that."

Xena nodded, causing her mane of hair to bob around her shoulders. "Goode women belong here." She stood, put the half-empty mug of tea on the end table, and then stretched languidly, arching her back and lifting her hands high over her head like she was in yoga class saluting the sun. Then she shook herself, smoothed her hair with the back of her hands, and finally faced the staring group. "Now, kittens, you must leave. You may return later—perhaps tonight. The girls will use the phone devices to tell you when it is a more appropriate time to visit."

Jax, Emily, and Kirk looked from Xena to the twins, who shrugged and nodded.

"Uh, okay. We understand," said Kirk.

Emily spoke slowly. "But Dad told me to tell you that he would help you take care of, you know, *things* for Abigail." She paused and had to press one of her hands to her chest and blink rapidly. Her other hand squeezed Mercy's like a vise grip.

"Thanks, Em," said Mercy. "Hunter and I will come over. Later. Tell your dad that, 'kay?"

"Text us when he's ready," Hunter said.

Emily nodded, biting her bottom lip. "Yeah, of course." Then she wrapped her arms around Mercy and whispered, "I just don't know what else to do."

"I know, Em. Me, too. Me, too," she murmured.

Emily stood, wiping her face again with her sleeve. "I painted a special sumi-e to honor your mom." She reached into the Kate Spade glitter clutch slung over her shoulder on its long, metal-linked strap and pulled out an original watercolor the size of a postcard. It was a beautiful silver-gray owl in flight with the full moon over its wing. "I know how much Abigail loved owls."

Mercy took the painting and through tears looked up at her friend, who was a talented young artist. "Abigail would appreciate that. She loves—um, I mean *loved* your work." Mercy paused, her voice hitching on a sob. "It's so hard to talk about her in the past tense. I just—" Her words stopped then, dammed again by unimaginable grief. With a shaking hand she put the owl on the coffee table, propping it up against one of Abigail's many statuettes of Athena so that it seemed to soar.

"Oh, babe. Come here." Kirk slid his arm around her and pulled her against him.

Jax stood, still holding Hunter's hand. "My parents wanted me to tell you that they're here for you. Mom's already cooking you one of her famous casseroles—but vegetarian because I reminded her you don't eat meat. She said, *'Abigail's daughters are not going to have to worry about food,'* and then got on the phone and started calling the other moms from church."

"I will be here and will accept the offerings for the girls so that they may grieve," said Xena as she gestured at the door.

"Thanks, Jax." Hunter spoke softly, like it hurt to talk.

"And now you must go," said Xena.

Kirk stood and helped Mercy to her feet. With his arm wrapped around her, they followed Jax and Hunter and Emily to the door.

"Em, we'll see you a little later," said Mercy. She stepped out of Kirk's arm to embrace her friend again.

Emily sniffed and nodded. "'Kay. See ya. Text if you need me before then. I'll be here super fast." She hugged Hunter quickly and then went out the door.

Jax squeezed Hunter's hand. "Same with me. I'm here. So are my parents. Whatever you need. Whenever."

Hunter nodded and wiped at her face as he joined Emily who was walking slowly, dejectedly, down the sidewalk to where they'd parked their cars.

"Are you sure you want me to leave?" Kirk asked, pulling her close to him again.

"Yes," said Xena.

Mercy nodded against his chest. "I'll text you later."

He kissed her softly before turning to Hunter. "Anything you need—either of you. Just tell me. Promise?"

Hunter nodded. "Thanks, Kirk. We appreciate it."

Kirk went out the door, but paused and turned back, opening his mouth to say something. Xena slickly stepped in front of Mercy, lifted one arched eyebrow, and hissed.

Kirk took a few steps back. "Oh, um, shit! Sorry."

"As you should be, boy. It is only polite that when one is asked to depart—one *goes.*" Xena closed the door firmly. "Now." She turned to the girls, smoothing her hair with the back of her hand. "Which tree will you visit first?" But before they could respond a moth fluttered from the door, up the stairs, and past Xena who, with catlike reflexes stalked after it.

Mercy met Hunter's gaze. "It's weird."

For a moment it looked like Hunter might almost smile. "Sadly, I think *Aunt* Xena is one of the least weird things we're going to have to deal with."

Mercy felt her shoulders slump. "So, the trees?"

Hunter nodded. "The trees. Didn't the sheriff say he found old man Thompson's body not too far from the olive tree?"

"Yeah, I think so."

"Then we might as well start there," said Hunter firmly.

Mercy concentrated, trying to sift her thoughts through the fog of grief that blanketed her mind. "You—you don't think Mr. Thompson's death had anything to do with the tree, do you?"

"Mag, I don't know. That's part of what we have to figure out." She moved closer to her sister and forced Mercy to meet her gaze. "I need you to try to pull yourself together. If the gates are messed up we have got to figure out how to fix them—and I can't do that by myself."

Mercy struggled to make her mind work. "Okay. I'll help. Promise."

"So, you agree that we should check out the Greek tree first?"

Mercy fought against gravity to lift one shoulder. "Sure. Whatever you and Xena think is best. I'll wait down here while you get dressed."

Her legs gave out and she sat on the couch, staring at the cold fireplace.

Hunter put her hand on her twin's shoulder. "I'll be down in a sec and I'll bring you a change of clothes, too."

Words stopped coming again, so Mercy nodded wearily as she picked listlessly at the embroidery that decorated her grass-stained, torn dress and continued to stare at the ashes of what used to be a warm, brightly burning hearth fire.

Nine

"I think I better drive," said Hunter as she studied her sister.

Mercy shrugged. "Okay with me."

"Girls, remember, what you do today is gather information. Study the trees. Bring back details about everything—how they look, smell, and feel—sense the space around them. Reach out with your minds and your hearts, as well as your senses. We need details so that we can accurately consult the grimoires for what must be done next." Xena had changed into a pair of their mom's jeans and her sweatshirt that said KALE in bold letters across the breast. The cat person had hastily grabbed the clothes from Abigail's room while Hunter and Mercy dressed. They still smelled vaguely of cinnamon and spice. Mercy had to force herself not to hug Xena and breathe in deeply. "Do you understand?"

Hunter nodded. "Yeah, we've got it. Right, Mag?"

Mercy was staring at the fireplace wishing she'd had the energy to build a fire. Maybe it would chase away the cold that had settled deep in her soul.

"Mercy, did you hear me?"

She blinked and looked up at her sister and Xena. "Sorry. What?"

"I was telling Xena we understand what we have to do at the trees."

"Yeah that. We'll check them out."

"Good," Xena said, though she sent Mercy a dubious, slit-eyed look. "Be careful. Do not let people see you. Neither of you have car papers yet."

"You mean a license," said Hunter.

"Yes. As I said, car papers. Girls, be wise. And safe. And do not be gone long. Are you sure I shouldn't go with you?"

"No, stay here," said Hunter. "People are going to start bringing by food. They should see you so they know we're not alone. An adult will keep them from being too nosy."

"You are correct, of course. I will reassure the townsfolk. I shall also bring out the grimoires and have them ready for when you return. Now, do you have any questions?" Xena licked her finger and then smoothed back a section of Hunter's hair that had escaped from her ponytail.

"Eww, Xena. Stop. No, we've got it. Really. Right, Mercy?"

Mercy managed to nod. Even though she felt almost too heavy to move she followed Hunter to the garage and climbed into the passenger side of her mom's silver Camry. The key fob was in the cup holder where Abigail always left it, and for a moment the twins just sat. Hunter's hands rested on the steering wheel—Mercy's were lifeless in her lap.

Hunter leaned forward and pressed her forehead against the steering wheel. "It smells like Mom." Her voice was strangled.

"Everything does." Mercy wiped a hand across her face, which felt numb again. Actually her life felt numb, wrong—so drastically altered that it was unrecognizable. She tilted her head and looked at her sister. "H, I don't think I can do this."

Hunter lifted her head and wiped almost violently at her damp cheeks. Then she took her sister's hand and squeezed it—hard. "I know, but you have to—*we* have to."

"Do we?"

"Of course we do. We have to make sure the trees are okay and the gates are closed. It's what Mom wanted. It's what she'd want if she were still here. That's important, Mag. More important than how sad we are."

"Okay. I know you're right. Sorry. I'll try harder to get it together." Hunter squeezed her hand again before she let it loose. It flopped down on the console that separated the front bucket seats before Mercy put it lifelessly back in her lap. She blinked fast. First, to try to keep more tears from spilling out and, second, because if she closed her eyes for even a moment more she might never open them. The truth was all Mercy wanted to do was close her eyes and sleep and sleep and sleep—and hope when she woke, *if* she woke, everything that had happened since the creature had broken through the Norse gate would be a nightmare from which she'd finally awakened.

Hunter backed the car out of the garage, but instead of turning left to take Main Street through the heart of Goodeville, she turned right, heading for the one-lane country roads that snaked around the fields that surrounded the town—roads the twins knew as well as they knew their own names.

They drove in silence. Mercy stared out the open window. It was one of those spring days in Illinois where the sun seemed to highlight every tree's bright emerald leaves like they were dressed in jewels. Everything *looked* normal, just as it had yesterday before her life had stopped, but today everything *felt* wrong. The trees that used to call to her were mute. She couldn't even hear them breathe, something she'd been able to sense since she was in kindergarten. As Hunter followed the curvy blacktop from town and snaked through the verdant fields that made up the country surrounding Goodeville, Mercy realized she also couldn't hear the whispers the corn made as the breeze rustled through it, or the chattering of the soy plants, their pods heavy with growing beans. She heard nothing. She felt nothing—nothing at all except exhaustion and grief—not even when her sister slowed as they neared the section of brilliant green fields that framed the mighty olive tree. So, Mercy stared and let her mind be completely empty like her heart and the unimaginable future.

"Oh, crap. Is that a cop car?"

Mercy forced her gaze to focus. "It looks like the sheriff's car *and* a cop car. And I think I see yellow caution tape, too."

"Roll your window up! I can't turn around. It'd be too obvious. If someone recognizes Mom's car, let's hope they think Xena's driving."

Mercy kept her face pointed forward as they drove past, but glanced to the side. "Yeah, there's that yellow crime scene tape and I think I saw the outline of a body."

Hunter shivered. "No way we can check out the tree with the sheriff here. We'll have to come back." At the next stop sign Hunter turned to her sister. "I can cut across town super fast and swing by the Hindu tree. It's on the way home. Want to go there?"

Mercy lifted a shoulder. "Yeah, okay."

Hunter sighed, but didn't comment. Instead she took a right, crossed Main Street, and wove through a quiet neighborhood and past the high school as they silently made their way to the tree that guarded the gate to the Hindu Underworld.

"I'm gonna pull into the easement so the car can't be seen from the road," Hunter said as she braked and turned off the road and onto a grassy area that was flanked by a wall of willows on one side and a bean field on the other. Mercy jumped and rubbed a hand over her face as she realized she'd almost fallen asleep. Hunter put the car in park and touched her sister's arm. "Hey, are you okay?"

It was difficult to summon enough energy to turn her head to look at her twin, but slowly Mercy did. "No," she made herself speak. "I am not okay."

"I know, Mag. Me, either. But let's get this done—for Mom. Maybe we won't find anything wrong at all. Maybe it was just the Norse tree that was messed up, and Mom fixed it, so we won't have to do anything until Solstice. But I can't do this alone. I need you."

Mercy forced herself to sit up straighter. She nodded. "I'm with you, H. Like always. We can do this." The words sounded right, but felt wrong—like everything else.

"Let's take the deer path. The one that winds away from the road and runs along the creek. I can't deal with talking to anyone right now and there's no way we can be seen from the road if we go that way." Hunter pointed to a slim ribbon of a path that led from the cleared easement area through a wall of gently swaying weeping willows.

Their joined hands anchored each other as the twins followed the path that would lead to the point of the pentagram where generations ago Sarah Goode had conjured a banyan tree to guard the gate to the Underworld of the ancient Hindus.

Sugar Creek was only a few yards to their right. The scent and sound of it drifted through the tendrils of the willows. Usually Mercy would have inhaled the rich smell of the crystal water passing over rocks and soaked in the music it made as it cascaded toward Goode Lake, but that day she walked in a bubble of grief that was so thick it didn't allow the world to touch her. She would've stopped and slumped to the ground, unmovable, had her sister's hand not propelled her forward, so when Hunter abruptly halted, Mercy stumbled and did almost fall.

"There it is. I've always thought it's the coolest looking of all of them." Hunter jerked her chin at the enormous tree that filled the area between the tall bank of the creek and the bean field that stretched up a gradual incline to meet the blacktop road. "It looks fine from here, don't you think?"

Mercy wanted to say that she was having a problem thinking about anything except their mom, but Hunter was counting on her—and she tried to never let Hunter down. She cleared her throat and swallowed the dryness in her mouth. "It seems normal."

"Right? Maybe everything *will* be okay. Let's get closer."

Hunter dropped her hand and Mercy followed directly behind her as she left the little path. No one was in sight. Mercy thought even the birdsong was subdued. They approached the enormous tree that was so out of place in the American Midwest, and could never have existed—let alone thrived—without the magic of generations of Goode witches. The trunk of the tree was really strange looking. From a distance it appeared to be one big, thick base, but closer it became clear that it was actually a whole bunch of smaller trunks butted right up against each other, like the banyan was trying to be its own forest. Vines dripped from the mushroom-shaped green canopy. Even through her grief Mercy acknowledged that her sister was right. The tree was uniquely awesome. As they entered the area under the canopy the calf-high grass became sparse and short, which was good because the banyan's roots had broken through the fertile earth and they had to pick their way over them carefully. Mercy stopped and stared up. The banyan's leaves were small for such a huge tree, and shaped like little grass-green hearts.

Her sister's voice, hushed like she was afraid of disturbing the tree, pulled at her attention. "Do you feel anything? Anything weird?"

"Not yet." Mercy stopped staring up and walked closer to the trunk. Hunter sat cross-legged facing the banyan—situated between thick fingers of roots. She closed her eyes and lifted her face to the sky as her lips moved as if in a whispering prayer.

Mercy walked slowly around the tree. She turned so that her back rested against the gnarled bark and faced the distant creek. She tried to concentrate—to open herself so she could glean information from her usually astute senses. But the fog of grief refused to thin enough to let anything through. She shook her head.

"I don't know, H. I can't seem to—" Mercy paused and sneezed. She rubbed her nose and sneezed again.

"Shh!" Hunter said. "I'm trying to pick up on any bad energy."

"Sorry, but this smell is getting to me." Then her mind caught up with her words and she craned her neck around to meet her sister's gaze. *"It stinks!"*

Hunter frowned. "Stinks?"

Mercy nodded vigorously. "Get closer."

Quickly, her sister stood and moved to within touching distance of the tree. She breathed deeply before screwing up her face and backing off several feet. "Eesh! That reeks!"

"Sulphur," Mercy said. "It smells like rotten eggs."

Hunter's face paled. "That can't be good," she whispered.

Bile burned Mercy's throat as her stomach revolted. "I don't remember any of the trees smelling bad. Ever. Do you?"

"No. Never. Well, except for last night." Hunter circled the tree with Mercy as they studied the intricate trunk.

A shiver fingered down Mercy's spine as she remembered. "Fenrir—it reeked."

Hunter nodded. "Like this, only worse." She continued to study the tree. "But it looks okay."

"Yeah, nothing *looks* wrong, but that smell is definitely coming from the tree."

"Mag, I know it's really hard for you right now, but you're the Green Witch. You usually just *know* things about plants. Can't you see if the tree will tell you anything?"

The terrible lethargy that clouded Mercy's mind also numbed her senses, but she nodded and, ignoring the rotten egg smell, faced the tree. She leaned forward and braced her hands on the rough bark. Mercy closed her eyes and pressed her palms firmly against the banyan, attempting to feel its energy—something that was usually as easy for her as drawing breath.

Today she felt nothing. She sighed and wanted to drop to her butt and sob. Everything was wrong. *Their mom was dead!* In a burst of anger she pushed against the tree, like she could shove it—and her grief—away, and a section of the bark gave way, like a scab tearing loose, to expose a nest of worms beneath that were boring into the skin of the tree.

Sick filled Mercy's mouth and she gagged.

"What is it?" Hunter rushed to her.

Mercy wiped her hands over and over against her jeans and pointed at the writhing parasites.

"Oh, Tyr! What are they?"

"I don't know, but they were at the apple tree, too."

"Wait, you saw them in the bark last night?" Hunter asked as she stared up at the branches of the deceptively healthy-looking banyan.

"No. I stepped on a green apple and it broke open. It was infested with those things. Hunter, Mom said it was okay—acted like it was nothing—but I saw her face go pale." She whispered the next sentence. "Like it scared her."

"We have to tell Xena about this, and we have to see if the other three trees are sick, too."

"Hang on." Mercy's hand trembled as she reached up and grabbed a low-hanging branch. She used her weight, dangling from it so that it shook up and down. Heart-shaped leaves rained around her. They were shriveled and dead.

Hunter crouched and gathered some of the leaves. "This just keeps getting worse." She shoved a handful of leaves into her pocket. "Let's get out of here. We need to go to the other trees."

With leaden feet Mercy retraced their path to the car. She couldn't shake the feeling that worms were crawling over her skin, but she was too exhausted to say anything or do much more than occasionally brush a hand down her arms.

Hunter put the car in reverse. "Should we go to the Egyptian or Japanese gate next?"

Mercy was saved from having to care enough to respond when her phone chimed with a text message. She read the message and felt another wave of sick grief wash through her. "It's Em. She says her dad's ready to see us."

Hunter blew out a long, sad breath. She put the car back into park and picked at her thumbnail. "You think we have time to check out just one of the other trees?"

Mercy met her sister's gaze. "I think we need to take care of Mom first."

Hunter nodded, wiped her bloody thumbnail on her jeans, backed onto the gravel road, and headed toward downtown Goodeville.

Mercy let grief overwhelm her as she closed her eyes and rested her head against the cool window—and tried not to think about what was going to happen next.

Ten

Hunter had never been in a funeral home before. She'd never had any reason to. When her grandmother had passed, the service had been held at their house. Hunter and Mercy were barely out of diapers. Her great-grandmother had died before she and her sister had been born. It seemed all Goode women were destined to an early end.

The heavy wooden door of Parrott Family Funeral Home creaked open in ominous, horror movie fashion. Hunter slipped inside to the foyer. Wood paneling, forest green walls, and black-and-white photos of woodland scenes greeted her. It smelled like flowers and cedar with a hint of cinnamon. Hunter didn't know what she'd expected, but she hadn't prepared herself for normalcy.

Hunter cleared her throat. "Mr. Parrott?"

It was silent for a moment before another creaky door opened. "Be right there, girls," Emily's dad and Goodeville's only funeral director called from down the hall.

Hunter took a deep breath. She felt lighter. Maybe it was the fact that the bright Illinois sun no longer burned her tender eyes. Or maybe it was because she and her sister were taking steps forward. This wouldn't be the new, happier life Hunter had envisioned, but there was something to be said for putting the past in the past.

"You ready for this?" Hunter groped the empty air beside her as she searched for Mercy's hand. She turned. No Mercy, only the ornately carved door and more black-and-white forest photos.

The old wood floors creaked under Hunter's feet as she moved toward the door and hefted it open. Mercy was waiting just on the other side. She sniffled and brushed her pink-tipped nose on her sleeve. "I can't do it." Her chin quivered and Hunter fought the urge to scoop her sister up into her arms and rush back to the car. They had to do this. Anyone who had ever lost someone they loved had to do this. It was as much a part of life as living.

Hunter propped the door open with her foot and slid the long sleeve of her shirt down over her bandaged arm. "I'll do it alone," she whispered as she reached out and took Mercy's hand in hers. The weight was back. It hadn't been the dark colors and warm light of the funeral home or the fact that she was there to move forward, begin her new life. It had been the absence of her sister.

Hunter swallowed the thought along with the knot forming in the back of her throat. "Really, Mag, you can go home. I'll have Jax—"

"Abigail wouldn't want that." Mercy dropped Hunter's hand and slipped past her into the funeral home.

Hunter sagged against the door as it shut. She wanted to say something that would make everything better, that would fix her sister, but grief wouldn't exist without love. And Mercy had loved their mother so, so much. Hunter rubbed her finger along the raw flesh that rimmed her thumbnail as she studied Mercy's slumped shoulders and the way she hugged her arms against her middle as if her insides would spill onto the floor if she didn't hold them in. Was despair a testament to love? Hunter bit down on her fingernail. It couldn't be.

She loved her mother just as much as her sister. But Hunter *had* been through more than Mercy. The teasing, the name-calling, the bullying. In eighth grade, Rachel Leech had cut off her ponytail because *dykes don't have long hair.* A jagged piece of Hunter's nail tore free and she clenched it between her teeth. Her life had been a series of devastating events, one stacked on top of the other in a perverted game of Jenga until this—the pièce de résistance. But Hunter wouldn't let her mother's death topple her. As Mercy would say, Abigail wouldn't want that.

Footsteps creaked down the hallway as Mr. Parrott neared the foyer. "Sorry to keep you two waiting, had an unexpected call that I couldn't get away from . . ." He stilled as he caught sight of Mercy. "I can't begin to tell you how sorry I am."

Mercy hiccupped and tightened her grip around her core.

Mr. Parrott dipped his fingers into his collar and pulled gently. "I've known Abigail my whole life. She introduced me to Helene . . ." He continued to tug at his collar as he spoke. "Abigail actually gave me a special cookie recipe. She said that it would make Helene's true feelings known. We were married three months later."

The floor groaned under Hunter's weight as she scooted closer to her sister. Did hearing stories like this help? Is that what Mercy needed, to relive all the good times? Or did she need to pack away her anguish and shove it in a forgotten corner of her mind? Either way, Hunter would carry on. She'd watch pieces of herself flake off and float away like she'd been doing her entire life.

Mr. Parrott rubbed his hands together and took a deep breath. "You'll have to excuse me, girls. I was shocked to get the news this morning. Haven't quite processed it yet."

"We understand how you feel, Mr. Parrott." Hunter had meant for her words to sound comforting, uniting even. Instead they fell out of her mouth bland and dry and flat.

He moved aside and motioned for the twins to step down into the sitting room. "Dominic. You both know you can call me Dominic."

Hunter did know she could call him by his first name. He'd been saying the same thing since they'd entered high school. She'd always seen it as a prize they'd been given for going through puberty. But Hunter didn't believe in being given prizes. She believed in earning respect.

Mercy let out a strained sigh and descended the stairs. Hunter followed her sister as she dragged her feet across the maroon-and-gold Turkish rug until she reached the edge of the closest settee and plopped down. The sunset yellow glow from the overhead chandelier sparkled off the round glass coffee table that separated the girls from the funeral director.

"What happens next?" The dry leaves stuffed in Hunter's pocket crunched as she sat down next to Mercy. "We've never had to do anything like this before."

Mr. Parrott straightened a stack of brochures before he removed the top folder from a pile of folders neatly arranged in the center of the coffee table. "I need both of you to sign a few documents that will allow me to proceed with funeral preparations. Then, we'll need to go by the sheriff's department to identify and claim your mother."

Mercy's sob was cut short as she clapped her hands over her mouth.

"But I have a good relationship with Sheriff Dearborn." Mr. Parrott removed a few papers from the folder and slid them across the table. "With your signatures and Goodeville being the tight-knit community that it is, I'm sure I'll be able to claim Abigail on my own and make sure everything is taken care of before I head out of town. Then, when I return, we can proceed with the funeral."

Hunter nodded and flattened her palm against Mercy's back. With each inhale, her sister trembled like the wind-battered surface of Sugar Creek.

"If you'll both sign and date the bottom of each of these pages, we can move on to the death certificate and necessary burial permit." He plucked a pen from the table and offered it to Hunter.

"Mercy." The creases of his forehead deepened as he went on, all the while speaking to the wrong twin. "Take your time. We're in no rush."

Hunter snatched the pen from the funeral director's outstretched hand. "I'm Hunter, not Mercy." Without reading the pages, she pressed the tip of the pen against the first paper and drew the loops and swishes of her practiced signature so hard the letters imprinted across the other four sheets.

"Apologies, Hunter." Mr. Parrott cleared his throat and rubbed his palms against his thighs. "You girls wouldn't happen to have your mother's birth certificate or know if she created a will, would you?"

Mercy scooted to the edge of the settee and snatched the pen off of the table. "We want Abigail buried at home. Does it say that somewhere in these?" She picked up the pages and shook them. "I won't sign anything if we can't have *our* mother buried at *our* home." Mercy's wide-eyed, panicked gaze swung to Hunter. "I won't sign these, H. I won't!" She threw the papers down and they drifted to the floor.

Hunter gripped her sister's knee. Mercy was sinking, pulled under by the anvil of grief she'd pressed into her heart.

Mr. Parrott swept up the papers and returned them to the table with an undisturbed grace that spoke to his years of handling the bereaved. "I will list the burial location when I file the permit. If there's an issue, the city will get back to me quickly."

"There won't be an issue." Tears splatted against Mercy's shirt, darkening the heather gray fabric. "Our family members have been buried at our home for hundreds of years."

The funeral director clasped his hands and nodded. "They have been, and Abigail will be, too. I'll make sure of it."

Hunter picked the pen up off the floor and handed it to Mercy. She met her twin's eyes and telegraphed *the look* to her—sending her strength and understanding through their unbreakable bond. "Here, Mag. Let's sign these and go home."

Mercy nodded, a short, jerky movement, and wiped her face on her sleeve before taking the pen and signing each of the papers. When she was finished, Hunter wrapped her arm around her sister and helped her to her feet. Hunter needed to do something for Mercy. But the one person she would have gone to for advice was now waiting at the sheriff's office to be claimed.

Eleven

The entire drive back toward their house from the Parrott Family Funeral Home, Hunter thought about how she could help Mercy and what her mother would have said. Every thought that occurred to her eventually led nowhere. She was alone and in the dark like she'd always been. By now, the stillness was a comfort, something to hold on to when the world turned inside out and true darkness fell. And it didn't get darker than the death of Abigail Goode.

Mercy said nothing, *did* nothing as Hunter flipped on the turn signal and headed down Sycamore Street to take the long way home. A part of Hunter dreaded going back to their house, the hollow skeleton that had once been the most comforting place on earth. Her mother had been the marrow, the lifeblood, the heart. But what did that make her? What did that make Mercy? Were the sisters walking shadows that took up space without giving anything back in return? Hunter rubbed her tight, dry lips together. Her mother hadn't felt that way about her daughters. And neither should Hunter. Perhaps the Goode sisters each held a piece of marrow and blood and heart. And if Hunter could bring their home back to life, she could definitely figure out a way to revive her sister.

With a sigh, Mercy blew Hunter's thoughts right out the window. She strained against her seat belt, turned to face Hunter, and folded her legs up under her before stilling again and resuming her listless stare out the window as Hunter guided the car through the quaint neighborhood that framed Main Street. Each house was a cupcake, fatter than they were tall and each decorated in a different shade of pastel. If Hunter had more experience driving, she could get them home blindfolded and without GPS.

Mercy let out another sigh and rested the back of her head on the passenger window. "How are you so okay with everything? I feel like I'm dying."

The trench in Hunter's stomach deepened. It wasn't an accusation, but it stung nonetheless. "I'm not okay with everything." Hunter kept her eyes fixed on the road like it was the only thing preventing the car from careening into one of the cupcake houses.

"You don't seem upset."

This time Hunter did look at her sister. She opened her mouth to speak but wasn't sure what to say. She wanted to slam on the brakes and throw open the door and rush out into the middle of the street and curse the sky, the earth, the gods, whichever was responsible for taking her mother. But that would do her no good. And that would leave Mercy alone in her own darkness, her *new* darkness, and she wasn't sure if Mercy could find her way out. Hunter closed her mouth and tightened her grip on the steering wheel.

"It's just . . ." Mercy sagged deeper into the seat. "Business as usual for Hunter Goode."

Hunter bit the tip of her tongue. It wasn't her fault she was better at dealing with problems than Mercy, or that Mercy had the luxury of only having to face one devastating thing. It didn't matter how many times Mercy had been there to comfort Hunter while she cried about her latest bullying tragedy, or how many times Mercy brewed Hunter a pot of healing tea and talked about problems as simple things, shimmering bubbles of pain that would eventually pop and leave no trace. Mercy had never fully understood Hunter's pain because she'd had so little of her own.

But maybe now she would.

Hunter stopped at a stop sign as Mercy popped open the glovebox and removed the pack of travel tissues their mother kept next to the car's manual and a satchel stuffed full of dried sage. Mercy pulled out a tissue and dabbed the rounded tip of her pink nose. "I wish I was more like you."

Lint clung to the beams of light shining in through the windows. A chuckle hardened in the back of Hunter's throat. She'd been wishing the exact same thing about herself for the past sixteen years. But that wish had been a compliment to Mercy and, somehow, this didn't feel the same.

Mercy balled up the tissue and dropped her hands into her lap. "It's a charm or a tincture or something, isn't it? Something that just took away all of your feelings."

Hunter's knuckles whitened as she tightened her grip on the steering wheel. "It's nothing magical, Mag," she said, pressing a bit too firmly on the gas. The car lurched forward before she let off and resumed her twenty mile per hour cruise through the innards of Goodeville. "You know that's not—" She pressed the brakes. The car jerked to a stop in front of a pale pink house guarded by plastic flamingos. "Oh my god." Hunter's fingertips flew to her pendant.

Mercy frowned and crossed her arms over her chest. "*Ess,* H. Oh my god*dess.*"

Ignoring her sister, Hunter pulled her phone out of her pocket. She *could* help Mercy, but to do so, she'd need their friends.

Twelve

Hunter tiptoed across the kitchen and peered out into the living room. Mercy remained on the couch. The same place she'd been since they'd gotten home. The grief-stricken twin picked at the gold fringe that rimmed one of the many decorative pillows that propped her up and kept her from lying with her face smashed against the sofa cushions.

Good. Hunter nodded to herself and hurried back to the sink. Well, it wasn't necessarily *good* that Mercy was back to being nearly catatonic. But it was good that her witchy twin senses weren't tingling. Hunter preferred to spring her plan on her sister intervention style.

Hunter gathered five moonstones from the kitchen's east-facing window and exchanged them for her pocketful of crunchy, shriveled leaves. They would deal with the trees as soon as she fixed her sister.

She patted her pocket and absentmindedly glossed her fingertips over her T-shaped pendant as she set her intention on her way to the pantry.

Heal Mercy. Heal Mercy. Heal—

Hunter's hand stilled on the pantry's doorknob. Her mother's basket of Kitchen Witchery was just behind the door. Her hand fell to her side. She should return the stones to the windowsill, slink upstairs, and pour her feelings onto the pages of her book, *When Darkness Rises.* It might turn a little Poe-esque, but at least the manuscript would distract her from the memories of her mother.

She clutched her pendant: her constant reminder of her god. It warmed her palm and she let out a slow breath. She had to do this. To honor herself, to honor her sister, and, most of all, to honor her mother.

Hunter restarted her mantra and opened the pantry. She squeezed her opal and stared at the wicker basket of Kitchen Witch accoutrements sitting on the bottom shelf. One day, she would celebrate that basket and all of the funny-smelling herbs and pages of handwritten recipes it contained. A grin tugged her cheeks as she refocused and took the rusted metal step stool out of its place behind the door. Her stomach fluttered with each creak and groan of the mini-ladder as she unfolded it and climbed the three steps to reach the top shelf. This was Hunter's shelf, where she kept all of her supplies. Her favorite cauldron, her astrology charts, and most importantly, her moon water. When she and Mercy turned twelve, their mother had led them, hand in hand, into the kitchen. The trio had stood before the open pantry as their mother explained to them the importance of keeping a fully stocked and impeccably organized inventory of tools for whichever type of magic the girls chose to adopt.

Hunter inhaled. Her mother's cinnamon and spice scents hung in the air like dust, nearly bringing the memory to life.

"A witch is only as effective as she is organized. Think of what would happen if you were casting and meant to grab rosemary but instead grabbed poppy because your supplies were scattered hither and yon." Abigail's shiver tickled Hunter's hand as she mirrored her mother's pinched brow and shook her head.

Hunter still wasn't quite sure where hither and yon were, but, from that moment, she'd lived her life according to her mother's advice.

Hunter's heartbeat quickened as she pulled her large copper cauldron off the shelf and ran her fingers along her jars of moon water. She'd felt this way since that very first time, four years ago, when magic brought her to the pantry. Then, she had been excited, had wanted to jump up and down and squeal with glee that her mother thought she was old enough, responsible enough, to have her own shelf and spellwork tools, but Mercy had seized the brief moment Hunter took to savor the gift. Her sister had screamed and cried and run in circles and sucked up all of the exhilaration until the space around them seemed to crack and pop like the last bits of milkshake being slurped through a straw. Now, Hunter would give anything to have that Mercy back.

Heal Mercy. Heal Mercy. Heal Mercy.

Energy pricked Hunter's fingertips, sending a jolt down her arm that morphed the gentle butterflies flitting in her stomach into a swirling cyclone of swifts. She turned the large Mason jar and read what she'd written on her custom crescent-shaped label: APACHE TEARS. She picked up the jar and studied the stone resting in the bottom. The night Hunter had filled the glass with water and set it in the grass under the light of the full moon, the single speck of white in the center of the obsidian stone had flamed to life so bright that she'd had to shield her eyes. The power of the moon had released into the water the ancient healing properties of the Apache Tears stone. It was just the thing she'd need to heal her sister.

Hunter set the jar in the empty cauldron and resumed her scan of the few remaining jugs of moon water. Again, the tips of her fingers heated as she glossed them over the final Mason jar labeled: MANGANO CALCITE. Hunter couldn't quite remember when she'd prepared this batch of moon water, but she was no stranger to its loving, compassionate, forgiving energy. It was one of her go-tos.

She placed the second Mason jar into the cauldron and balanced the heavy bowl as she descended the stepladder and shuffled to the kitchen island.

The moment she placed the cauldron on the counter, her phone vibrated. It was funny how little coincidences like that happened. Like the universe was speaking directly to her, telling her she was doing the right thing, on the right path. Hunter suppressed the smile lifting the corners of her lips and tapped the notification. Emily's latest message in the group text lit up the screen in all caps. They were here.

Hunter blew out a calming breath and brushed her ponytail off her shoulder. She could do this. She had to. She ran her hands over the bumpy outline of the moonstones in her pocket, picked up her cauldron, and hurried to the front door.

Mercy continued to tug on the pillow fringe and blankly stare at the floor while Hunter balanced her cauldron in one hand and opened the door with the other. The jars clanked as she pulled open the door, rushed out, and nearly collided with Jax.

Jax's black brows knitted and he held out his hands. "Need some help with that?"

"Yeah, definitely." Hunter's cheeks heated as Emily and Kirk stepped onto the porch and the trio swarmed her. "Thanks for coming over so quickly."

Jax took one jar of moon water and the black-and-white stone clinked against the glass. "We came the second you sounded the alarm."

Emily crossed her arms over her chest and blew a bright pink bubble. "Yep," she said as the gum popped without leaving a trace of sticky pink on her glossed lips. "*All* of us." She rolled her eyes and tilted her head in Kirk's direction.

The quarterback reached for the second jar and hiked his broad shoulders. "What? You guys came and got me because I was included in the group text, too."

Hunter rubbed her fingers over the rough outlines of the moon phases etched in the side of her cauldron. "Well, I need all of you to make this spell work, so—"

Kirk held up the jar. "Wait, wait, wait. *Spell?* Like actual witch stuff?" He handed the jar to Jax and brushed his hands on his pants.

"Duh. They're *actual* witches." If Emily kept rolling her eyes she'd puke before the sun finished setting.

Kirk ran his hand through his hair, further spiking the gelled tips. "So, what? Are we going to do a séance or something?"

"No, moron." Emily shoved the confused football star. "Hunter's text said we're here to *help* Mercy, not make everything worse."

Kirk's thin nose and round eyes scrunched as he rubbed his shoulder. "Talking to her mom's ghost could make things better."

Hunter's pendant heated against her chest. "Stop!" She clenched her jaw and flattened her palms against the cool brass cauldron. "We're doing a spell to cleanse Mercy of her grief. She—" Hunter swallowed and tucked back a strand of hair that had fallen from her ponytail. "She goes through these periods where she won't even talk. She just sits there crying, or worse, doing nothing at all." She motioned toward the large window that looked in on the couch and part of the living room. Sunlight continued to drain into the horizon, giving the group a better view of the bereaved twin. She'd remained on the couch, awash in the gentle golden glow of the setting sun and the antique chandelier.

Emily's fingertips flew to her lips. "Oh, Mercy."

Jax's smoked topaz skin smoothed as he set his jaw. "We'll do whatever you need." Rocks clanked against glass as he lifted the jars. "I'm assuming we're using these?"

Hunter nodded. "They're moon water. If I do the spell right, they'll wash away her pain."

Kirk shoved his hands into the pouch of his hoodie and took a nearly imperceptible step back.

"Kirk, I don't have time to hold your hand through this. You're either in or out. Make a decision." Hunter's pendant remained hot against her skin as she narrowed her eyes at Mercy's boyfriend.

He stiffened and lifted his chin toward the darkening sky. "We're helping Mercy, so I'm in. No question."

The moon was brighter now, its glow no longer paled by the harsh brilliance of its sister sun. Hunter's fingers itched to draw down its powers. "Good. Just don't make a big deal about it." She swept her gaze along her three friends. "Mercy has to be an active participant, but she doesn't know that yet," Hunter said as she adjusted her grip on her cauldron and turned to open the door.

Emily rushed forward and propped open the screen with her foot. "Then how do you know she *will* be an active participant?"

Jax and Kirk had followed and mirrored Emily's furrowed brow concern.

Hunter shrugged and gripped the doorknob. "There isn't a spell Mag has met that she hasn't wanted to be a part of."

"Wait." Kirk cleared his throat and scrubbed his hand down his cheek. "Your aunt isn't here, is she? I don't think she likes me very much."

Hunter bit the inside of her cheeks. She'd laugh again someday, but not today. "She's napping. She naps a lot. Very . . . catlike." She turned the handle and leaned against the heavy wood. "If it helps, she doesn't really like anyone."

Like she'd read Hunter's mind, Mercy popped up off the couch the second her twin pushed open the door. "We're doing a spell? To talk to Mom? To see her?"

For a moment, Mercy was herself again. But it faded as quickly as it came. She knew just as well as Hunter that the magic needed to lift the veil was its own form of evil.

The quarterback shoved past Jax and Emily into the house. "What'd I tell ya? My girl and I are on the same page."

Mercy dropped the tassel-rimmed pillow and stepped forward. "Kirk, what are you—"

"Hey, numb nuts," Emily began before squeezing past Hunter and extinguishing another pink bubble. "Hunter already said that's not what we're doing."

Hunter stepped aside as Jax entered and held up the jars of moon water and gave each a little shake. "We *are* doing a spell, though."

Kirk's long legs quickly carried him to Mercy's side. "Dude." He draped his arm around her shoulders and pulled her into him. "Hunter said not to make a big deal about it."

Hunter carried her cauldron to the middle of the room and set it on the floor. "Yes, Mag, we're doing a spell." She rubbed the bumpy moonstone outlines in her pocket. "All five of us. To help you."

Emily hooked her arm around Hunter's. "Because we love you."

Jax set the jars down next to the cauldron and twined his calloused fingers around his best friend's. "And care about you."

Kirk kissed the top of Mercy's head. "And want you to be okay," he said and buried his cheek in her dark waves.

Mercy chewed her lip in that dramatic way she did when she wanted to impulsively shout *yes* but instead added a few moments of silence for effect. Even in the clutches of grief Mercy knew how to command an audience. "I'll do it."

The moonstones vibrated in Hunter's pocket. They'd heard the promise of a spell, sensed Hunter's energy and the fuel from the rising moon, and were ready to get to work. Hunter dug them out and motioned for her sister and friends to gather around the cauldron.

"Mag, you're next to me. The rest of you will sit here, here, and here." She pointed to the floor in three specific areas that surrounded the copper bowl. She used her free hand to gather the jars of moon water as Jax claimed the remaining spot next to her and Emily shuffled to the open space between Jax and Kirk. If Hunter ever got a girlfriend, she hoped Jax wouldn't be as sullen about it as Emily was about Kirk. Although, none of them, Mercy excluded, were completely convinced that Kirk wasn't a cloudy bag of old douche. But none of that really mattered. If Hunter was being honest, there was zero reason for her to think that she'd have a girlfriend any time before graduation. At Goodeville High, if anyone else's sexuality landed outside of the hetero portion of the spectrum, Hunter and company definitely didn't know about it.

The moonstones thrummed and sizzled against Hunter's palms as she cupped them and held her hands over the empty cauldron. "Pick whichever stone calls to you."

Jax, Emily, and Kirk blinked at one another before each shrugged and nodded like they shared a hive mind.

Emily tucked a stray curl behind her ear, leaned forward, and plucked a stone from the pile. "Whoa. It's warm, like, *really* warm."

Jax went next. He wrapped his fingers around the pearlescent orb and smiled. "It's magic. *Real* magic."

Kirk's eyes widened as he picked up a stone and inspected it. "Have you ever seen *Sabrina*?"

Hunter ignored him as Mercy carefully stared at the final two stones. "I can't feel anything, H. I'm all blocked."

Hunter chose for her sister, handing her a lovely pink-tinted moonstone that was the smallest of the bunch. "You'll be good as new after this."

Jax rolled the charged rock between his palms. "What exactly is *this*?"

Mercy clutched the little stone against her chest and cocked her head. "You're going to scry, aren't you?"

Hunter didn't want to share with the group. What if she failed? It was quite possible she'd bitten off way more than she could chew, and they'd all end up holding warm and aggravated moonstones while staring at a basin of room temperature water. No, she wouldn't tell. She'd pull a Mercy and leave it up to her friends' imaginations.

The wood floor made a hollow clank as Kirk set his rock in front of him. "Scry? Is that what it's called when you take out an emotion, kill it, and bury it in a hole?"

Emily sucked the air from a bubble and placed her stone on the back of her hand. She spoke as she balanced the moonstone and studied her perfectly manicured nails. "It's the act of using a crystal ball or something reflective, in this case I'm assuming it's the jars of water, to see, like, the future and stuff."

Hunter clenched her teeth to keep her mouth from flopping open. Emily was right. Unfortunately, Hunter wasn't gifted enough to see into the future (at least, she wasn't gifted enough *yet*), but she could perform small spells—or, in this case, a medium-sized one.

The stone rolled off Emily's outstretched hand and she caught it before looking up. "Gawk much?" She fisted the moonstone and crossed her arms over her chest. "What? The pretty girl can't also know things?" She cocked her head and squinted at Kirk. "Try reading a book instead of streaming. There's no way H would remove an entire emotion from Mag. That's insane."

Hunter opened her mouth to agree, but Mercy's sniffle pulled her back to what mattered most. "We should begin." Hunter set her stone in her lap and picked up the first jumbo-sized Mason jar and unscrewed the lid. "So, I'm going to say a few things while I pour the water." Her mouth went dry as she spoke and she dragged her tongue across her lips. She didn't have a script or any words prepared or a book to quote. She'd only read about spells *like* this one, but they weren't exactly this one. She'd have to trust herself and her abilities, which was a lot easier to do *before* the moment as opposed to *in* it. But Hunter did know one thing they'd need to do for sure.

"It's important that we set and maintain our intention throughout the entire spell." Her voice caught. In that moment, she reminded herself of her mother, of last night. Had that only been yesterday?

Mercy folded her legs against her chest and buried her face in her knees. She felt it, too.

Hunter cleared her throat and continued, "We're here to cleanse Mercy of her grief. That is our intention. That is our focus."

The three friends nodded and leaned closer to the cauldron as Hunter set the lid on the ground and lifted the jar over the basin. "At this time and at this place we meet before Mother Moon and Father Tyr to call for the cleansing of grief from our friend and sister, Mercy Anne Goode."

She lifted the moon water toward the sky and closed her eyes as the Apache Tear clanked in the bottom of the jar. "We humbly thank the Apache Women who shed enough tears for their lifetimes and ours." Hunter opened her eyes and poured the water into the cauldron. Emily, Jax, and Kirk gasped as the moon etchings flickered to life, then went out.

Hunter repeated the same gestures and uncapped the second jar and hefted it skyward. "We thank the sweet vibrations of mangano calcite as they free us to love and let go." Again, the etchings sputtered with magical light as the water splashed into the cauldron.

Hunter looked up and was met with a wide-eyed excitement that fed her hammering pulse. "When I say, we'll all drop in our moonstones at the same time."

She pressed her fingertips against her pendant and continued, "At this time and at this place we come together, strengthened by friendship and love, to ask for the purification of heart and mind and soul and the return of peace and hope and light."

The others joined Hunter as she reached out and held her moonstone over the brimming cauldron. "Now." She nodded, and the five stones released as one.

They fell through the water with the slow, magical syrupiness of honey through a sieve. Jagged lines of power cut through the water in electric white currents. Their intention had been granted by the moon and by Tyr and by the power that had stitched Hunter back together time and time again. The frosty white charges connected the glowing moonstones in a sacred symbol, a powerful symbol.

"Is that a star?" The reflection blazed brilliant white in Kirk's eyes.

Mercy unfurled and leaned forward. "It's a pentagram." She took

Kirk's hand in hers and sat up straight and tall. "Join hands," she instructed and clasped her fingers around Hunter's. "It'll make the incantation stronger." No, there was no spell that would keep Mercy Anne Goode away.

A geyser erupted from the center of the cauldron when the five joined hands. Enchanted moon water rained into their circle like glitter.

Hunter unclasped her hand from Mercy's and placed her palm against the back of her sister's head. As Mercy closed her eyes, a single tear washed down her cheek. Hunter squeezed Jax's hand as she began the final part of the spell. "Be rid of this despair, Mercy, and come back to me." She'd intended the last words to be a beacon of strength, a clarion call through the magical haze that filled their quaint living room. Instead, they'd been a whisper, a prayer. The words had rushed from her heart and flew out of her mouth with the ease of an exhale. Hunter released Jax's hand and rolled Tyr's pendant between her fingers. She needed her sister back. Her world was unbalanced without her.

Again, Hunter took Jax's hand in hers as she guided Mercy's head down to the cauldron. The water didn't ripple as her sister's face broke the surface. It was like glass, like ice, like Goode Lake in the dead of winter—still and peaceful. Mercy's hair fell into the cauldron, raven wings beneath the calm surface. Hunter's fingers numbed as she felt her sister take one breath and then another and another.

Kirk reached out to grab Mercy but was deflected by a magical shield of glowing white light. "Get her out of there!"

Hunter had been waiting for this. She knew Kirk wasn't the type of guy to sit back if something went wrong. Not because he was a protector but because he believed he knew what was best. Plus, she *had* seen *Sabrina.* If that's what he thought of her, of them, he'd pull out his pitchfork in no time. "Maintain your focus! Breaking it will—"

Mercy sat up. Her hair arched through the air with the perfected drama and grace of a TV starlet. Hunter couldn't move, couldn't speak, couldn't force her eyes away from the glowing cauldron and the image of her sister still caught in the skin of the water.

Jax's hand went clammy. "Hunter?" He squeezed her fingers once, twice, three times before Hunter brought herself back to the present.

Mercy's face and hair dried before any water dripped onto her shirt. "Is that me?" she asked, blinking down at the cauldron.

It worked. Hunter's heartbeat hammered between her ears. It worked. It actually worked! Hunter Jayne Goode accomplished an advanced spell using only her natural gifts and the strength of the moon and her chosen god, Tyr. If Jax didn't have hold of her hand, she'd probably float away.

"No way!" Emily pointed at the Mercy trapped in the basin of water. "She blinked!"

Kirk pressed his palms against the floor and scooted back a few inches. "*She?* That's an *it*! A water creature that we're supposed to, what? Just ignore?"

Hunter's nostrils flared and she bit down on the meaty sides of her tongue before allowing herself to react. "It's not a creature. It's Mercy. A very small part of her, anyway." She sat up a little straighter. This was her spell, her *successful* spell, and she would own it. "We asked to have her grief washed away. Not the whole thing but a tiny piece of it. Enough that she could be herself again." She gestured to the image of her sister staring up at them from the cauldron. "And that's exactly what happened."

Mercy clapped and managed to sit up a tad straighter. "It *is* me! I knew it."

Kirk scooted back toward the circle and leaned into his girlfriend. "You're okay with all of this?"

Mercy cocked her head and shrugged. "Nothing we do is evil or bad. It's all based in love and light. And, like Hunter said, it was just a small piece of my grief." She turned and took Kirk's hands in hers. "Those same two things brought you here tonight to help me, and they did. You were so powerful tonight, Kirk. So perfect. This couldn't have happened without you."

Hunter's cheeks flamed. Love and light hadn't brought Kirk there; she had. She had been the beacon of peace and hope. She had wielded the power. Hunter tightened her free hand into a fist. If Kirk had left, and he almost had, she would have figured out how to make the spell work without him. He was unnecessary, trivial. A small blip in both of their lives. A high school fling. Hunter's jagged nails bit into her palm. In ten years, neither one of them would be able to remember his name. They'd call him "the quarterback" or "that guy" or maybe they wouldn't call him anything at all. Maybe Hunter *would* become a *Sabrina* witch and erase all trace of Kirk Whitfield from her sister's memory and they'd never have to speak of him again.

Warm liquid pooled in Hunter's palm and trickled down the side of her hand. She unclenched her fingers and stared down at the blood sprouting from the crescent-shaped wounds her fingernails had carved into her flesh.

Hunter let go of Jax's hand and clutched her pendant. She needed to refocus, reground herself. She would never erase Mercy's memory. She should never even think such a thing. Wielding the power, being a conduit, it was all getting to her. It had to be.

"I'm closing the spell," Hunter blurted as she clenched her hand and hid her bleeding fist behind her back. She felt four sets of eyes press against her as she closed her own and searched for the right words. The spell no longer flowed from her. Hunter was clogged up. A big, fatty, hairy clog. She'd name it *Kirk*.

"At this time and at this place we thank Mother Moon and Father Tyr for cleansing our friend and sister and purifying her heart and mind and soul. We know you will remain near, as will we." Energy pricked Hunter's fingertips and she followed her urge, her intuition, and plunged her bleeding hand into the water. The icy cold liquid shocked her and sent her eyelids fluttering open. "This rite is ended," she continued as she watched her blood eat away the blinking image of her sister before sinking down, down, down. Hunter wet her lips and shouted the final closing line she'd heard her mother use time and time again. "Merry meet and merry part and merry meet again!"

Scarlet ribbons snaked around the glowing moonstones, turning each a petal pink. Emily sucked in a breath as the rocks lifted from the cauldron's bottom, reeled into Hunter's palm by the power of her blood.

Thirteen

It was hot inside the Goodeville precinct. Too hot. The kind of hot that made every inch sweat and stick and itch. Frank Dearborn twisted the faucet knobs and let cool water splash against his swollen knuckles. How could anyone live like this? Inside all hours of the day, fake breeze blowing down from dusty vents in the ceiling. People had come so far only to imprison themselves.

He leaned over the sink and peered into the small rectangular mirror that hung from the pristine bathroom wall. "Dearborn." He ran his tongue along his teeth and smiled. "*Sheriff* Dearborn."

It was more than convincing. It was a fact.

Pain jabbed his left eye. He clapped his hand over the spikes of heat that blurred his vision and lurched forward. His forehead crashed into the mirror. *"Mother—"* He stifled a roar and pushed himself away from the reflective glass. Shards rained onto the porcelain as he ran his fingers over the tender knot forming in the center of his forehead. It'd been like this since last night, since the olive tree. Sudden shocks of increasingly devastating pain. It would be over soon. No matter where he was, he could never escape his fate.

Eye still covered, he leaned toward his splintered reflection. He sucked in a breath through clenched teeth and forced his hand away from his eye. He affixed his gaze to the faucet. He didn't want to look.

"Damn mirrors." He flinched as he gently patted his swollen eyelid.

He shouldn't blame the mirrors. It wasn't their fault they reflected the truth. He should blame that woman. The one who'd made him love her. The one who'd turned him into a monster.

He swept his gaze back up to his reflection. If he couldn't find a cure this time, he would be like this forever. Threads of milky white swirled across his dark iris. Air hissed between his clenched teeth as he rubbed at his eye, clearing away the gunk. As quickly as the clouds of white vanished, they were back again.

He sighed. There was no use fighting it. He hadn't escaped the curse. Maybe he never would.

He unhooked his aviators from the collar of his uniform and pushed them up the bridge of his nose. Seeing through the shadows was better than revealing a problem. A *difference.* People weren't good with *different.*

His stomach roiled and saliva flooded his mouth. He was going to be sick. Not from the sight of his disgusting visage. No, this was something else. Something familiar yet out of reach. His stomach seized and a wave of vomit rolled up his throat. Chunks slipped off his tongue and squelched against the empty sink. He stared at the towel dispenser, turned on the faucet, and washed the mess away. He didn't want to look at it, either.

The bathroom door creaked open and he stepped in front of the broken mirror and the freshly cleaned sink. Deputy Carter rushed in, his hands already unbuckling his belt. "Oh, Sheriff." He stiffened. "Sorry, I, uh, I didn't know anyone was in here." He let out an awkward chuckle, took off his hat, and ran his hand through his flattened hair. "Too much coffee and not enough bathroom visits." Another bleat of laughter as he shuffled to the nearest urinal.

Dearborn's lip curled as the deputy turned his back and sighed with relief when his stream hit the porcelain. At their base, they were all animals. Caged animals. The sheriff threw open the door and charged into the bullpen.

Across the open room of desks, a woman waved at him like her arms were on fire. She was the only woman in the building without a uniform, her hair tied back tight and a row of weapons around her hips.

His teeth ground together as she waddled toward him, so eager for connection, for love. But love was weakness, downfall, the beginning of everything evil or bad. He wanted no part of it.

Her name tag glinted in the harsh overhead lighting. *Trish.* That's right. If he dug down deep enough, he could uncover the sun-bleached memory of her. But the memories were fading, and fast.

A dimple made a nest in her cheek as she smiled. "There you are. I've been looking all over for you. I was worried." Stickers, sparkling hearts and fat bears framed the capital letters on her name tag. Dearborn squinted and blinked through the haziness blurring his left eye. Maybe they were beavers. All those hairy woodland creatures looked the same. "You haven't returned any of my calls and I haven't seen you since last night before . . ." She clenched and unclenched the notepad and glittery pen between her soft hands. "Well, you know." A forced grin cracked her bleak, smooth features.

All he could do was wipe the sweat from his brow and nod. He couldn't quite remember how he should respond. The Trish memories were fading away.

"It was awful." She parted the uncomfortable silence and waded closer to him. Warmth rolled off her like she was freshly baked bread. "Old Earl Thompson finally stumbled onto something real and it killed him." She shook her head. Her red curls bounced, tossing a spicy sweetness into the air.

Pie? Was that it?

His heart clamored and the tips of his fingers tingled. His body remembered something his mind no longer knew.

"I threw out the Ruckus Report." She leaned in. Her breath fogged the gold star pinned to his chest. "Didn't think it was right to keep it since he's no longer with us. Maybe it wasn't the right thing to do to begin with."

Another shake of her head. Another swirl of sugar and spice.

He brushed the tip of his nose against her curls. "Cinnamon," he murmured as a crumb of memory rolled into focus. "You bake when you're upset."

Dearborn's memories faded in and out and would soon leave his mind altogether. But some memories stayed with the body. Things like driving, shooting, not to turn his head too quickly to the left. In a lifetime long before Dearborn, he'd been a brilliant painter. But that had ended in blood and tears and more stains on his immortal soul.

Trish pressed her notepad against her chest and took a wobbly step back. "Frank, I—" She fanned herself with her free hand and fluffed the round tips of her chin-length curls. "Well, I'm not quite sure what to say." Her cheeks flamed strawberry red as she cast a glance around the bullpen.

He followed her attention, eyes narrowed and fists clenched while he took in all the darting glances and quick returns to computer monitors, stacks of paperwork, and phone calls. There had been something between Sheriff Dearborn and this Trish woman, but that was a different person, a different life. Frank Dearborn had never learned the truth about love and happiness and the pain they both brought. Now he wouldn't allow this body or these fleeting memories to betray him again.

Trish held out the notepad and tapped at the list of names and phone numbers she'd written under two column headings: *ASAP* and *After Lunch*. "I know you'd rather not fiddle with that computer program to read your call-back list, but they're in there, too, if you're so inclined."

Although she couldn't see through his mirrored sunglasses, he kept his eyes narrowed as he snatched the notepad from her hand. He wouldn't pine after Trish. Whatever Dearborn had had with her was over, dead.

Trish fiddled with the cap of her glittery pen. "Need another cup of coffee, Sheriff? I have a sneaking suspicion you're hiding some pretty dark circles under those glasses."

A dry tickle tightened the back of his throat and his stomach seized again. Only one thing could ease his pain and quiet this restless body. He had to get away from this woman, all of these people, the hot, circulated air, and the overhead lights.

Trish rested her warm hand against his bicep. "Frank, are you feeling okay?"

"I'm fine," he croaked. He'd done nothing but lie since he'd arrived. This body knew it, and it wanted him gone.

Wet coughs tore from his lungs, a thousand molten nails searing the inside of his ribs. *Frank Dearborn isn't here!* he shouted at the battle lines carved inside his chest, his gut. *He's never coming back!*

Trish steadied him as another barking explosion ripped through him. More hands were on him, different voices shouting concerns, solutions, all guiding him toward his office door. He planted his feet and sucked in a haggard breath. "I'm fine," he repeated and jerked his arms away from the horde. "Just need—" His chest quaked as he swallowed back another coughing fit. "Just need some air." He rubbed his sweaty palms against his shirt and searched for an escape. He spotted the nearest illuminated EXIT sign, fisted his hands, and blinked past the water swirling across his good eye.

"I'll go get you that coffee, Sheriff." Trish's shoes clicked as she turned and clapped her hands at the crowd. "Back to work, everyone. Back to work."

He didn't look back as he marched to the precinct's rear exit. Their concern would do him no good. Bodies like this yearned to be reattached to their soul or given back to the earth. Bodies like Frank Dearborn's made his curse that much more unbearable. This body couldn't be fixed. It had to be fed.

Ancient words from lifetimes ago swept through his thoughts.

How delicious life would be
If only it could make you see
The hunger for what it truly is,
A way to set you free.
Now carry on with your cursed life,
And cut their eyes out, these orbs are so rife
With magic, but only one pair of these
Has what it takes to end your strife.

The memory squeezed the tattered remnants of his broken heart. Tears welled as the door slammed shut behind him. He sagged against the side of the department's dumpster. Every ounce of him ached. He wasn't a killer. And yet . . .

Cones of light bobbed against the garbage bin. He sniffled and squinted through his lenses at the headlights as they crept through the alley, closer and closer. Brakes squeaked as the car stopped short of the dumpster. The lights turned off and the car door groaned open.

He blinked the spots of light from his sight as dress shoes clicked against the pavement. "Didn't you quit smoking years ago, Frank?"

Sheriff Dearborn's stomach growled. "Stay back."

The man's cheeks lifted with a grin. "Don't worry. I won't tell anyone. Especially not Trish." He winked his right eye. His *perfect* right eye. A sparkling drop of charcoal black swimming in an endless pearl white sea.

Get away! The words wouldn't leave the sheriff's lips. They clung to the hunger tightening his throat and drenching his mouth.

The man motioned to Dearborn's mirrored shades. "Wish I could get away with wearing sunglasses. Emily's always saying that crying makes your eyes puffy." His chuckle was dry and forced. "But you know how Em gets."

"Tears make them moist," he whispered. *Heavy and juicy and—* He wiped away the saliva at the corners of his lips.

The man stepped on a soggy clump of paper. It flattened under the toe of his shiny leather shoe. "In a small town, this job is always hard. I always know who I'm preparing. If I wasn't friends with them, I was with some of their kin. Men in our positions have to stay strong. They depend on us for that."

The sheriff pushed away from the dumpster and crept closer to the man with the flawless eye. "Can I be honest with you? *Truly* honest?"

"Of course, Frank." The man's feathery lashes waved at Dearborn with each blink.

"I'm the weakest man you know." He lunged forward, caught the man by the neck, and slammed him into the pavement. Stumpy, manicured fingers clawed at the sides of Frank Dearborn's face. The wild pawing caught Frank's sunglasses and hurled them onto the concrete. Dearborn's insides thrummed. He could see more clearly now. He could watch the fight melt from those perfect eyes like the last bits of snow from the grass.

This could be it. The pair of eyes that would free him from his curse.

Blood marred the perfect white with cherry red dots and zigzags. The man's hands fell to his sides and his legs twitched in his body's last attempts to run. Finally, his jaw slackened and his pupils widened and he stilled.

Dearborn released the man's throat and slid off him. He sat on the pavement next to the body and traced the dead man's flaccid eyelids.

He leaned in and pressed his lips against the sweat streaked forehead. *"Σας τιμώ."*

I honor you.

Dearborn plunged his fingers into the eye sockets and scooped out the gems. His stomach trembled as the first warm and gooey orb touched his tongue. He stared up at the dark sky and punctured the first eyeball with his sharp canine.

Please be those I've been seeking. Please be them. Please be them. He prayed over and over as wet paste filled his mouth and washed down his throat. He dropped the second viscous ball into his mouth and quickly chewed the slippery mass.

Nothing happened.

He rubbed his cloudy eye and blinked down at the eyeless corpse.

He had done this for nothing. Frank's stomach settled as he swallowed the last bits. He'd taken a man from his family and his community for an unfulfilled dream. But he'd had to take the chance. It was the only way he could stay in this body and the only way his curse would one day come to an end.

He looked down at his wet and bloody hands and up at the back door to the sheriff's department. He wiped his hands on his pants, plucked his sunglasses from the ground, and hooked his arms under the dead man's, whose fancy shoes bounced along the pavement as Dearborn dragged him back to his car and shoved him into the driver's seat. Frank dragged his aviators along his sleeve before he slid them on over his clouded eye. He walked to the back exit, wiped his mouth, and threw open the door.

"I need help out here!"

Deputies wasted no time springing into action. He heard them scramble to their feet and rush toward the exit. He charged back to the car and he kneeled next to the open driver's side door with his head in his hands. He would sell this performance. He would dig deep and uncover each scrap of a memory. He squinted and studied the dead man's bloodied features.

Dominic Parrott.

He would use them to rebuild Frank Dearborn's friendship with Dominic. Friendship, love, created a well of excuses he could use to drown each procedural question. After all, this wasn't the first time he'd nearly been caught.

Fourteen

Babe, you already look *lots* more like yourself!" Kirk's hand slid from the hollow of the small of Mercy's back to gently cup her butt.

She sidestepped and caught his hand in hers and squelched a sigh, reminding herself to have another talk with him about how he needed to read the room better. Mercy could feel the frowns Emily and Hunter were skewering Kirk with—not that, this time, she blamed them. It'd only been an hour ago that Hunter's spell had washed the debilitating grief from her and everyone—except Kirk—was still subdued and still in awe of Hunter's magic. "Yeah, I am feeling a lot more like me. Thanks to you guys." Mercy's smile included Jax, Emily, and Hunter—along with Kirk. "But don't you and Jax have to get home? Didn't you tell me you have a chemistry test you have to study for?"

At that moment the huge pendulum clock that had been in the Goode family for generations chimed ten times.

"Oh, crap!" Jax sprang up from the couch. "Mom made me promise to be home by ten. Kirk, we gotta go."

"You can be a little late," scoffed Kirk.

Hunter narrowed her eyes and Emily manically cracked her gum. Before they could declare war on Kirk, Mercy said, "Hey, I'm super tired. This has all been a lot. I really do need to sleep."

"Of course. Sorry." Kirk put his arm around her as she led him out the front doors and onto the porch. "You know I like spending every second with you."

"Stalker much?" Emily murmured from behind them.

"Huh?" Kirk asked cluelessly.

Mercy turned Kirk so that he was on the second step facing her while she stood on the porch, which made her almost at his eye level. "Em was just calling you a big talker. But she doesn't know you as well as I do." Mercy rested her arms across his shoulders and kissed him softly. "Thanks for coming tonight. See ya tomorrow." Before he could pull her in for a more intimate kiss, Mercy squeezed his shoulders and then walked quickly to Jax, giving him a hug. "You're a good friend. Thanks for being here, Jax."

He patted her back. "No problem. Anything for Hunter and you."

She was going to hug Emily, too, but her friend had already plopped her butt down on their wide porch swing. She looked up from her phone. "I texted Dad. He said he had some stuff to do downtown and then he'll be by to get me."

"Well, hey, I could wait for Emily's dad and get a ride with him. Right, Em?" Kirk sent her friend a hopeful look, which Emily completely ignored.

Mercy sighed. She really liked Kirk, and he was being a sweetheart, but his persistence could be exhausting. She'd opened her mouth to repeat herself when Xena, in cat form, padded through the open door and across the porch. She arched her long, sleek back, slitted her eyes at Kirk, and let loose a terrifying group of sounds.

"Hiiiiiisss, mEEEwr, hiiiiiisss!"

"Shit! That cat is huge!" Kirk backed down the porch stairs after Jax. "Okay, I'm going."

"Sorry, Xena doesn't really like many people," Mercy said while Hunter covered a laugh with a cough.

"I thought that was your aunt's name," said Kirk, still backing down the sidewalk.

"She doesn't like many people, either," said Hunter.

Kirk's forehead wrinkled in confusion.

"Dude, come on! I'm not getting grounded because of you," Jax called as he opened his car door.

Kirk waved and grinned at Mercy before rounding on Jax. "You're such a wuss sometimes . . ." His words faded away as he climbed into the passenger side of Jax's car, which took off before he'd completely closed the door.

"Don't say it," Mercy said as she sat beside Emily.

Em put her phone down and shrugged. "Hey, I'm just happy you feel better."

"Yeah, me too," said Hunter. "I'm gonna go get my grimoire. I want to document that grief spell." She started to walk past Mercy and into the house, but Mercy reached out and snagged her wrist.

"Hey. Thank you. What you did tonight—it was . . ." She had to pause and swallow back her tears before continuing in a small, soft voice. "Mom would be so proud of you."

Hunter's smile was like the stars. "You really think so?"

"I know so. Thanks, H. You're the best."

Emily sneezed violently as Xena wound around her legs. "OMG, your cat is trying to kill me again!"

Mercy shared a knowing look with her sister as she said, "Xena, give Em a break. We know you really do like her."

Emily sniffed and wiped her nose on the back of her hand. "Likes me dead!" Then she cocked her head and studied the big Maine coon as if seeing her for the first time. "Hey, I just noticed she and your Aunt Xena have, like, the same hair."

"Impossible," Hunter said as she headed into the house. "Xena has fur. Our aunt has hair. But come on, Xena. There's a bowl of cream with your name on it in the kitchen. Good watchcat—good watchcat." Chattering happily, Xena trotted after Hunter, who paused in the doorway and looked back at Mercy. "You're the best, too. I'm glad you're back." Xena yowled and Hunter rolled her eyes. "*Okay,* I said I'd get you some cream. Sheesh. You're so demanding . . ." Her voice trailed off as she marched inside and headed to the kitchen.

"Aww, twin love gives me a big, warm feeling in my cold, dead heart," said Emily. Then her eyes went huge. "Oh. Shit. Sorry. I—"

Mercy bumped her shoulder. "Stop. You can't tiptoe around me and worry about everything you say. If you do—if everyone does—we'll never find our new normal."

Emily sighed in relief and brushed a strand of her hair behind her ear as she cocked her head and studied Mercy. "You *are* better, aren't you?"

She hadn't phrased it like a question, but Mercy nodded. "Yeah. I'm still sad. I miss Abigail so much that my heart feels weird and heavy, but before the spell I couldn't make my mind work. It was like I was trying to think through mud. No, not mud. Fog. My brain was all foggy. I couldn't concentrate. All I wanted to do was cry or sleep—or both. What you guys did made the fog lift."

"And now you can start feeling better?" Emily asked tentatively.

Mercy let out a long breath. "Yeah. Before I couldn't see through my grief to any future. Now I know Hunter and I *will* have a future. It'll be different than we ever imagined it would be, but at least now I can start imagining it."

Mercy pushed against the porch with her feet and the swing glided back and forth gently, soothingly, as they gazed up at the starry night sky. They didn't speak, but Emily reached over and covered Mercy's hand with her own and Mercy felt her friend's love and support flow into her.

Hunter reappeared holding a tray laden with one of their mom's many tea sets, her thick grimoire tucked under her arm. "Thought we could all use some lavender and chamomile tea."

"Great idea, H!" Mercy took the tray from her sister and put it on the wicker table that sat between the swing and the wooden rockers that were often filled with friends or Abigail's customers. Mercy spooned honey into three delicate cups before pouring the fragrant tea and passing the cups to her sister and her best friend.

Between careful sips Emily said, "Hey, um, I wanted to tell you two how cool that was."

"That?" Hunter peered up from writing in her book of spells.

Emily jerked her chin at the grimoire. "*That.* The spell thing you did tonight."

Hunter lifted one shoulder. "*We* did it. The five of us."

"But you were the witch that led us," said Mercy. "And you made the spell up yourself, didn't you?"

Hunter's cheeks flushed pink. "I didn't have time to go through all the spell books to find exactly what we needed, so I had to."

"It was perfect, H. Really," said Mercy.

Hunter met her twin's gaze. "You can be you again now."

"I can be me again now," Mercy repeated.

"You know, I forget that you two can do actual magic," said Emily.

"Well, it's not like we go around bippity-boppity-booing all the time," said Mercy.

"But you could, right? I mean, it'd be super cool if you did." Emily peered, owllike, from one twin to the other.

"An ye harm none, do what ye will." Hunter spoke the words reverently.

Mercy shared a knowing look with her sister. "Which means, Em, that what you think is super cool would make a lot of people really uncomfortable, so we don't do it."

"Like Kirk was tonight," Hunter added.

Mercy felt a jolt of surprise. "Kirk? What do you mean? He seemed fine."

Emily snorted.

"Okay, what happened?" Mercy insisted as she looked from her best friend to her sister.

Emily stirred her tea, letting the spoon clink against the porcelain cup. "He kinda freaked. Before, when Hunter was getting us ready. Setting our intention. Is that the right word?"

Mercy and Hunter nodded together. "Yeah, that's what it's called," said Mercy. "Setting the intention of a spell or a ritual is one of the most important aspects of magic." She met her twin's gaze. "What'd he do?"

"He didn't really *do* anything. He was just weird about the whole *real magic-ness* of it all. I needed him to be one hundred percent, and I wasn't sure he'd commit." Hunter shrugged nonchalantly and shifted her gaze to her spell book.

Mercy looked at her sister, who was writing in her grimoire and wouldn't meet her eyes. She sighed. "I'm sorry about that, H."

Still not looking up from her spell book, Hunter said, "The important part is that he *didn't* mess up the spell."

"No, the important part is that you included him," Mercy said, and Hunter finally met her gaze. "Thanks. Even though Kirk can be a pain in the ass—thanks."

"No problem," her sister said.

Emily pushed her feet against the porch so that the swing continued to glide back and forth. "I guess it's actually not too surprising Kirk was uncomfortable."

"How so?" asked Mercy, draping an arm over the back of the swing as she blew across the amber colored surface of her steaming tea.

"Well, Kirk hasn't been hanging around you two for long. I mean, I've known you guys since we were practically in diapers. I'm used to the fact that you're witches, but even I was shocked by how *for real magical* that spell was."

"Oh, please." Hunter's face was turned down to her grimoire again. "Practically everyone who lives in Goodeville knows we're witches."

"Knowing and seeing are two way different things," said Emily.

"I'll talk to Kirk, but he seemed okay when he left," said Mercy.

"Yeah, be sure he doesn't get the pitchforks and torches out," muttered Hunter.

Mercy frowned at her sister. "Why wasn't Jax freaked out? His parents are uber-religious."

Hunter shook her head. "His mother is. She's super Protestant. Her family has lived here since the beginning of Goodeville. He's a lot cooler, plus, we've known Jax for a million years; he accepts us. You don't need to worry about him freaking." Hunter brushed her ponytail off her shoulder. "But Kirk was never fully into the spell or okay with it, and we don't need the stress he could cause by telling people our business."

"Don't worry about Kirk. I'll take care of him," said Mercy.

Emily cleared her throat loudly, causing both girls to shift their attention to her.

"I just want to officially let you know that if you need any other help with spell stuff or ritual whatchamacallit, I'm your girl. I wasn't freaked. I thought it was amazing."

"Your energy is really good," Hunter said.

Mercy nodded. "That helped the spell's success."

Emily grinned. "Can I pretend to almost be a witch?"

From just inside the open door Xena yowled.

Emily's grin faded. "Never mind. She already wants to kill me. I'll just leave it as I'll be a substitute witch whenever you need one."

"Deal," said the twins together.

Hunter caught her sister's gaze and smiled—really smiled—at her for the first time since the night before and a little more of the grief that had cocooned around Mercy's heart loosened.

"I'm hungry!" Mercy said. "Em, do you think we have time to order pizza before your dad gets here?"

"How 'bout I text him and tell him I'm staying the night? Mom's still home until midweek and since Dad's leaving for his conference tomorrow they're spending every second getting their fight on." She paused and shuddered. "I'd way rather stay here. Can I borrow something to wear to school tomorrow?" Em froze mid-text. "Wait, are you going to school tomorrow?"

Mercy met Hunter's gaze. "What do you think, H?"

"I think people will probably treat us like freaks whenever we go back."

Mercy nodded. "Then let's do it like a Band-Aid, just get it over with." She turned to her bestie. "Yeah, we're going to school tomorrow. Text your dad and then we'll order that pizza and—"

The sheriff's car pulled into their driveway, cutting off Mercy's words. She sighed and her shoulders slumped. "Not again. Do we have to keep going over and over this with them?"

Hunter sat straight up. She snapped her grimoire shut and put it aside. "No. No, we do not. They need to leave us alone."

"Maybe you should wake up your aunt," said Emily. "She can tell them to get lost."

"Good idea," said Hunter as she stood. "Mag, I'll go get Auntie. Tell them that she'll be out in a sec."

The car door closed and Deputy Carter slowly headed up the driveway, gravel crunching under his steel-toed boots.

"At least it's just the deputy." Mercy kept her voice low. "The sheriff was kinda creepy this morning."

"Seriously," said Hunter as she hurried inside the house.

Mercy thought Deputy Carter looked unusually pale as he climbed the porch steps and took off his hat. Dark circles made his otherwise puppyish eyes look bruised and old.

"Evening, Miss Goode." He nodded at Mercy.

"I'm Mercy." She was used to supplying her name to people who couldn't seem to ever tell the two of them apart.

But the deputy had already turned his attention to Emily. "Emily, I'm going to need you to come with me."

Emily put her teacup down on the table, but she didn't move to get off the swing. "Why? Dad's supposed to be here in a little while. Actually, I was just texting him. I'm gonna stay the night with Mercy and Hunter." Then she paused and shook her head. "Wait, I don't get it. Dad sent you here? He said he had stuff to do in town. Was he at the police station? But why would he send *you* here?"

The deputy swallowed so hard that his Adam's apple bobbed. "Your father didn't send me, but you need to come with me."

As Emily started to stand Mercy covered her hand and kept her in place on the swing. "Why? What's going on?" she asked the deputy.

His eyes flicked between Mercy and Emily, coming to rest on Em. He cleared his throat again and picked at the brim of his hat with nervous fingers. "There's been an accident. Sorry, this is . . ." He paused, swallowed again, and started over. "Emily, your father is dead."

Through their joined hands Mercy felt the jolt that rocked her friend. Emily's breath rushed from her body in a terrible gasp and she began shaking her head back and forth, back and forth.

"Dead? What are you talking about? How? It has to be some kind of mix-up or mistake." Mercy gripped Em's hand.

The deputy turned his somber gray eyes to her. "There was an accident."

"No. No. That's impossible." Em spoke softly.

Mercy squeezed her hand tightly. "Like a car accident?"

Deputy Carter's gaze flitted away as he said, "Um. Not exactly.

Emily, let's get you home to your mom. She'll explain everything to you."

"No!" The word burst from Emily.

"If it wasn't a car accident, what kind of accident was it?" Mercy felt like her brain was on fire. *First Abigail and now Em's dad? How? Why?*

"Emily, let's get you home," he repeated as he shifted from foot to foot, not meeting the gaze of either girl.

"No." Emily stood, abruptly letting go of Mercy's hand. She faced the deputy and wrapped her arms around herself. "No! *No! NO!*" Her voice grew louder and more hysterical as she continued.

Mercy stood and put her arm around her friend. Emily's body was trembling like she might fly apart into a million little pieces—a feeling Mercy understood all too well. She held on to Em tightly as she shouted into the house. "Hunter! Xena! We need you!"

The deputy started forward, like he was going to help Emily from the porch. Em cringed back.

"Get away!" she screamed between soul-wracking sobs. "Don't—touch—me!"

Hunter and Xena spilled from the doorway. "What is happening out here?" Xena asked.

"There's been an, um, accident," the deputy said quickly. "Emily's father has been killed. I came to take her home to her mother."

Xena gasped. "Oh, kitten!" She brushed past the deputy imperiously to enfold Emily within her arms as the girl clung to her and wept.

Hunter joined Mercy. They faced the deputy—blocking Emily with a wall of their love. Mercy and Hunter joined hands.

"You said, *'um, accident,'* and then used the word *killed,*" said Hunter. "Which was it—an accident or a murder?"

Mercy's stomach roiled and she swallowed down bile. She knew what the deputy was going to say before he spoke.

"It, um, was a murder. Look, I am truly sorry, but Emily's mother needs her, and I have to get her home."

Emily suddenly sneezed—once, twice, three times. From the deep pocket of Abigail Goode's soft bathrobe Xena pulled out a handful of old tissues, which Em took and tried to wipe her face, but her hands were shaking too hard.

Carefully, Xena took the tissues from her and dabbed at her cheeks, though it was impossible to stop Emily's tide of tears. "Oh, kitten . . . poor little kitten," Xena murmured as she smoothed back the girl's hair.

"Is it really true?" Emily stared at the deputy, and then she looked from him to the twins. "How can it be true?" Before anyone answered, Emily's legs wobbled and she collapsed.

Xena caught her first, and then Mercy and Hunter were there, too. They lifted her, steadied her—loved her.

"We're here, Em. We're here," Mercy said as she hooked her arm around her best friend's slim waist.

The deputy picked at his hat helplessly and repeated, "I really am sorry."

Emily was sandwiched between Mercy and Hunter—while Xena stood behind her, stroking her back and murmuring softly.

"What can we do, Em? What do you need?" Mercy asked as she wiped at her face.

Emily turned her head slowly to meet Mercy's gaze. She was no longer sobbing, but silent tears poured down her smooth, fawn cheeks to soak her shirt. "I need my daddy." Then her face broke and she leaned heavily against Mercy as waves of shudders cascaded through her body.

"Emily—Miss Parrott," the deputy stuttered. "Sh-should I call your mother? Should I go get her and bring her here?"

His words seemed to give Emily strength. She looked up at him. "Mom needs me."

The deputy nodded urgently. "Yes, yes, she does."

Emily drew a deep breath and stood up straight, like her spine had turned to steel. "I'll go. Mom does need me."

"Em, do you want us to—" Mercy began.

Emily turned to her and hugged her tightly. "I have to go to Mom."

"Kittens, help our Emily to the car," Xena told the girls.

Slowly, with Mercy on one side of her and Hunter on the other, the twins guided Emily to the deputy's car and gently helped her into the passenger's seat. The deputy slid behind the wheel and silently handed a box of tissues to Emily. When she made no move to take them, even though tears still washed her face, he put them in her lap. Emily looked up at the twins.

"I don't know what to do." Her voice was strange, listless and so soft Mercy had to lean forward to hear her.

Mercy touched her tear-ravaged cheek. "Just try to breathe."

"Take it one step at a time," Hunter added from beside Mercy. "Don't think too far into the future."

Emily nodded jerkily. "Okay. Okay."

The deputy reached across Emily and closed the door. Mercy raised her hand. "We love you, Em. We're here. Remember—we're here for you!" She watched the streetlight illuminate Emily's pale, stricken face as the deputy backed down the driveway. "She looks like a ghost." Mercy whispered her thoughts as she and Hunter returned slowly to the porch.

"She's in shock," said Hunter. "We all are."

"Oh, kittens! It's just so awful." Xena put her arms around the girls and held them close.

"How could he be dead? Murdered?" Pain throbbed in Mercy's temple with her heartbeat.

"Something is wrong. Very wrong," said Xena. "First Abigail. Then Mr. Thompson, and now Mr. Parrott."

Hunter was the first to pull from Xena's embrace. "We need to go to the other trees."

"Do you really think this has something to do with the gates?" Mercy asked.

Hunter's face looked colorless in the porch light as she stared over Mercy's shoulder out into the night. "I'm beginning to believe it does."

Fifteen

"Why are people still out there? I mean, it's almost midnight!" Mercy felt like she wanted to hit something, but settled for stomping a foot against the floor of their mom's Camry as she and Hunter stared at the cluster of palm trees that guarded the gate to the Egyptian Underworld. The trees were actually one tree, which had, over the generations, sprouted into five. They were squatty with big, handlike fans of leaves that were sharp-tipped—and the palm was awash in light from the baseball diamonds that surrounded it, which were currently filled with teams and too damn many cheering spectators.

"Crap!" Hunter mirrored her annoyance. "I totally forgot about the SBA."

"SBA? What the hell is that?"

"Small Business Association—Mom was on the team for Siren's Call Art Gallery. Every spring the SBA has a tournament. The winning team gets a weekend trip to the Four Seasons in Chicago with spa services and a special dinner included, remember?"

"That's right. Abigail thought they'd win this year." Mercy sighed. "Now what? Should we just go out there anyway?"

"No way! The whole town is there. If the trees really are dying and something terrifying is happening because of it the last thing we need is to call the town's attention to the trees—any of the trees—and to us. Let's just go on to the Japanese gate. No one will be out there." Hunter shifted the car into reverse so she could back out of the lot.

"Hang on. We may not need to go all the way to the tree. Look." Mercy pointed at a group of women, all wearing pink uniforms with KINGPIN LANES blazed across their ample bosoms. They'd just passed the big clump of out-of-place-looking doum palm trees.

"They're wearing black armbands." Hunter's voice was soft.

Mercy's gaze took in the other teams who were all wearing black armbands. She felt tears clog her throat, but she rasped out, "Every team is."

"They're honoring Mom." Blindly, Hunter's right hand reached out, searching, and Mercy grabbed it.

"Abigail would like that," Mercy said. "But that's not what I wanted you to look at. Check out what the Kingpin Lanes team is doing."

"They're sneezing," said Hunter.

"And covering their mouths like something stinks," Mercy agreed.

"Oh, no—sulfur. It's here, too."

Mercy nodded. "And check out the palm leaves. The ones on the top are still green like always. But look at the lower ones."

Hunter squinted and held her hand above her eyes to shield them from the bright field lights. "They're brown!"

"The palms are sick, too." Mercy didn't think her stomach would ever feel normal again. "Let's go on to the cherry tree."

"Okay, yeah, going." Hunter backed out and headed across town.

It was late enough that there was almost no traffic, but Mercy breathed a relieved sigh when Hunter turned off Main Street and cut through the quiet neighborhood until finally coming to the one-lane blacktop that skirted that side of town. They crossed the railroad tracks and then Hunter took a hard left onto a dirt farm access road that paralleled the tracks and the corn and bean fields that bordered them. They bumped along the dark stretch of packed ground until the car's headlights illuminated a substantial tree that loomed like a phantom between the tracks and the maturing cornfield to their left.

Hunter put the car into park and left the lights on, shifting them to bright as she said, "I've always liked this tree, especially when it's blooming."

The weeping cherry tree had bloomed several weeks ago so tonight, instead of a curtain of delicate pink the long, slender boughs looked weirdly like skeletal fingers.

Mercy shivered and didn't move to leave the car. "Remember when we were super little and would come here with Abigail when she fertilized it in the spring?"

"Yeah, we'd pretend that the boughs made a curtain."

Mercy nodded. "Inside, near the trunk, was our stage."

Hunter continued the memory. "And we'd make up dances to Gaga's songs."

"'Bad Romance' is still my fav," said Mercy.

"Of course it is." Hunter turned to face Mercy. "My fav was when we performed songs from *The Sound of Music.*"

The edges of Mercy's lips tilted up. "'Sixteen Going on Seventeen'—you used to love that one."

"I had a giant crush on Liesl."

"Good times." Mercy tried to sound light and carefree, but instead her voice broke and she had to blink hard to stop the tears pooling in her eyes from escaping down her cheeks.

Hunter tugged on her hand. "Hey, we'll have good times again."

"Doesn't feel like it right now."

"I know. But we will. I'm sure of it," Hunter said firmly. "Ready to go out there?"

"No, but we have to."

"Yep."

"Yep." Mercy sighed and let loose her sister's hand. "Okay, let's go check it out. Maybe it'll be okay."

"It looks fine from here," Hunter said as they got out of the car.

Mercy didn't say anything. She was the Green Witch, and her earth-attuned senses had been tingling since the car's headlights had captured the tree. She approached more slowly than Hunter. Mercy drew several deep breaths and stretched her senses. Now that her grief fog had lifted, she was relieved that she could hear the corn whispering with the soft spring breeze. The corn felt fine—young and strong and growing.

She turned her face into the wind, which was sweeping over the bean field to her right, on the other side of the railroad tracks. The air was perfumed with green, growing things. She could sense the pods that were already beginning to swell with soybeans. All was well there, too.

Farther away, Mercy caught the scent of the eastern branch of Sugar Creek. She could smell the distant damp earth. It was normal and soothing. She drew another deep breath to steady herself. Then, resolutely, Mercy focused straight ahead at the weeping cherry that guarded the gate to the Japanese Underworld.

"I don't smell anything bad yet," Hunter called over her shoulder.

"That's good." Mercy picked up her pace so that the sisters reached the veil of boughs together. Mercy gently lifted the drape of willow strands with her hand as she listened with her sixth sense.

At first everything felt fine. The pink flowers that would've perfumed the night just a few weeks ago had already been replaced with small, lime-colored leaves that, when fully grown, reminded her of arrowheads. The leaves were there, filling the long, graceful boughs.

"It looks okay, right?" Hunter stared at the long, graceful branches.

Mercy opened her mouth to agree, and to breathe a huge sigh of relief, when the wind picked up. It caught the dripping boughs so that they swayed as if to a waltz only they could hear—and as they moved together leaves rained all around them. Mercy bent and scooped up a handful. She turned so that the car's headlights shined on her palm and the leaves curling there.

"Shit."

"What?" Hunter peered at the leaves. "I don't see any worms."

"There aren't any. Well, there aren't any in this handful of leaves. Who knows what we'll find when we look at the trunk. But this is so damn weird."

"Tell me."

"You see these leaves that are curled and yellowish?" She touched a couple with her finger.

"Yeah."

"That usually means that the tree is not getting enough water," Mercy explained.

Hunter's forehead furrowed. "But we've had normal rain this spring. That's why the corn and beans look so good."

"Yep. Now check out these other leaves." She pointed to another cluster in her palm.

"They're green. They look okay."

"That's how they seem, but touch one." She lifted her hand so Hunter could press her finger to one of the green leaves, which made it fall apart and turn to moss-colored dust.

"It's like it's autumn and it should be brown and brittle and falling off for the winter. Why's it doing that?" said Hunter.

"Cherry tree leaves stay green but get all brittle like that when the tree gets way too much water."

Hunter shook her head. "How's that possible? First, it's like it's thirsty, and then it's flooded. What the hell?"

Mercy shook her head. "I have no clue. It's wrong. It's all wrong. Come on." Mercy squared her shoulders and lifted her chin as she tried to bolster herself against what else they might find. She fished her cell phone from the boho bag she always slung over her shoulder and flipped on its flashlight.

Hunter also pulled her phone from her pocket and turned on its light.

Mercy parted the curtain-like boughs and the girls stepped inside the embrace of the tree.

"I don't smell anything, do you?" Hunter sounded breathless.

"Nope. Not yet."

Mercy led her sister to the trunk of the tree. The bark of the cherry tree wasn't rough like the other four sentinels. Mercy had always loved its smooth, almost velvety texture. She went to the tree and pressed her palm against it, closed her eyes, and concentrated.

The first thing she felt was completely normal—it was the breathing of the tree. Mercy felt the inhale and exhale against her skin in the stirring of air and a slight change of temperature. She was beginning to relax when nausea consumed her. It cramped her stomach and made her legs go weak—so weak that she suddenly dropped to her knees.

"Mag! What is it?" Hunter crouched beside her.

"She's sick. She feels awful—like that time we went to Mexico with Abigail and we got the pukes from the water. Ugh, it's terrible." Mercy took her hand from the ailing tree and leaned forward, pressing her palms against the dirt at the base of the trunk, afraid she was going to actually throw up.

And worms writhed under her hands.

"Freya! Bloody buggering hell! That's so disgusting." She wiped her hands against her jeans as she frantically skittered backward on her knees.

Hunter shined her light down and shuddered. "They're everywhere!"

Mercy stood and kept backing away. "I'm sorry. I can't stay here. It's sick. It feels—it feels. H, I'm gonna puke!" She rushed through the dangling boughs and staggered until she bent at the waist and heaved bile and tea all over the dirt road.

"Hey, it's okay. It's not you. It's the tree." Hunter soothed as she held

Mercy's hair back. "Tell yourself that. Remember? Mom always said you had to remain separate from the plants and the earth and your green stuff, even as you listened to them."

Mercy spat into the dirt and nodded, wiping her mouth with the back of her sleeve. She handed Hunter her purse. "C-could you find the bottle of w-water in there for me?" Her voice trembled with her body and her mouth filled with bile as she tried not to puke again.

"Here, Mag." Her sister broke the seal on the bottle and handed it to her. "Rinse out your mouth before you take a drink."

Mercy did as she was told and then unbent slowly. "Sod it! I hate to puke!"

"Breathe with me, okay?"

She nodded and matched her sister's breathing until the horrible sick feeling left her. "Thanks," Mercy said. "I'm okay now."

The two of them turned to stare back at the tree.

"They're all sick, aren't they?" Hunter spoke softly, almost as if she didn't want the tree to hear.

Mercy took another drink of water and then nodded. "Yeah. I don't think we need to cross the caution tape by the olive tree to be sure. The others are sick. That one has to be, too."

Hunter began to pace. "But why? They've been healthy for generations—*literally.* Why now? What's made this happen? What's different?" Before Mercy could say anything Hunter continued, "Do you have a baggie or anything like that in that giant purse of yours?"

"Uh, yeah. I keep one of those compostable green baggies in there for when I wear those dangly turquoise earrings that get too heavy. Why?"

Hunter searched through Mercy's purse until she found the baggie. "Got it! I'm going to go gather more of those dead leaves. You stay here. I don't want you to get sick again. Hang on. BRB." She hurried to the cherry tree and ducked inside its weeping boughs.

Mercy stared after Hunter, her mind whirring as it circled around and around, echoing her sister's words. *Why now? What's changed? How could trees that have been healthy and thrived for generations suddenly sicken? Why now? What's changed?*

"Oh, Tyr! This is so damn gross!"

Hunter's words drifted to her on the wind like a gift. Her sister reappeared as she rubbed her forefinger and thumb across the amulet that symbolized her god, Tyr, and Mercy felt a jolt of electric understanding.

He's what's different! Tyr, thought Mercy. *No Goode witch in our history has ever chosen a god to follow—never until now—and now the trees are infested with parasites and dying.*

The thought made Mercy dizzy. She wanted to shout down the words that whispered through her mind.

"Hey, are you still feeling sick?" Hunter hurried to her side.

Mercy nodded.

Hunter hooked her arm through Mercy's. "Let's get in the car." Hunter opened the passenger's door for her sister and helped her inside before climbing in behind the wheel. Then she turned in her seat to face Mercy. "We have to do something. Now. Like, tonight. A spell—maybe something protective? I dunno. Xena will help us figure it out." Hunter's words kept rolling from her, not giving Mercy a chance to speak. "Wait, no. How about a ritual? Like a repeat of the Beltane Ritual. You know, to make them all stronger. We could start here, and then—"

"You mean redo the ritual that killed Mom? Bloody hell, Hunter, think! It's not like you to be so impulsive—so blind."

"The world might be dissolving around us!" Hunter picked frantically at her nonexistent thumbnail, making it bleed. "Nothing is *like* me anymore. Nothing is *like* you anymore, either. This nightmare is our new norm, and we have to stop it."

"Which is why we have to be extra careful," Mercy insisted. "H, we have to figure out what's *really* gone wrong. We can't just throw spells and rituals at the trees. What if we choose wrong? What if we make it worse *or even let another monster loose*?"

Hunter breathed out a long sigh that sounded like a sob. "Okay. Okay. I hear you." She shook herself like a cat coming in out of the rain. "But we can't just sit around talking and researching. Mag, *we have to act*."

"I know. I'm not saying we do nothing. All I'm saying is that we have to be smart and careful."

Hunter sat up straighter. "I have an idea! Tomorrow I'll go to that big nursery in Champaign."

Mercy nodded. "World of Blooms."

"Yeah, that's it. I'll take leaves from the trees and even a sample of those worms." She shuddered. "Maybe there's something mundane we can do to make them better."

"And while you're doing that Xena and I will be going through the old grimoires to research what kind of magic we need to use," Mercy said.

"Yes. That's our plan. Okay?"

"Okay. That means no school tomorrow for us." She chewed her lip and then added, "And we have to be there for Em."

"I wonder what happened to her dad?" Hunter mused as she started the car and began backing carefully to the blacktop.

"I don't know, H. Everything feels so wrong. I can't even."

"I know, Mag. I know." Hunter's bloody thumb rubbed Tyr's amulet.

Silently, they drove through town—each girl lost in her own thoughts. Mercy stared out the window, overwhelmed by a terrible foreboding that had her feeling like she might puke again. *Could Hunter's devotion to a god and not a goddess be the match that will light the fire that will burn down the gates?* She didn't want to believe it, but the more the idea circled around her mind, the more it made sense in a world that had suddenly turned dark and chaotic and strange.

Sixteen

Mercy hovered between awake and asleep—and for a few precious moments her world felt normal. Birdsong and a gentle, corn silk–scented breeze wafted in through her open window. From the crack under her closed door the rich aromas of coffee and toast slathered with homemade strawberry jam teased her, and she imagined she heard Abigail's Pandora station—perpetually set to her favorite singer, Tina Malia—drift up the wide stairway as the songstress's sweet voice told tales of this world's magic and beyond.

"Mag! Psst! Mag! Are you awake?"

Mercy rubbed sleep from her eyes as she came fully awake, and with consciousness also came reality. Abigail Goode was dead. The trees that kept this world safe from ancient evils were sick. Emily's father had been killed. The world was upside down.

And Hunter's face was peeking into her room.

"Are you awake?" her twin repeated.

"I am now," she grumbled, rubbing sleep from her eyes. "What time is it?"

"Late. Seriously. Like, past noon. You've been sleeping forever. FYI, Jax is here. He's going to take me to the nursery. Xena has about a zillion old grimoires put out for you to go through. She just discovered coffee—heavy with cream and sugar—but apparently caffeine works on a cat person the opposite of how it works on people persons. She was practically falling asleep on her feet and had to excuse herself to Mom's room to nap."

Mercy yawned. "Then why are you waking me up?"

Hunter leaned against the doorframe and crossed her arms. "Because Jax just told me your boyfriend got permission from his parents, with his coach's okay, to skip a couple of his afternoon classes and come over here to 'check on his witchy woman,'" she air quoted as she rolled her eyes. "So, he'll be here in a while. Thought you'd want to brush your teeth or whatever."

Mercy sat up and stretched like Xena—in cat *or* human form. "Aww, that's sweet of him. And as Abigail would say, if you keep rolling your eyes, someday they're going to freeze like that."

"Oh, please. Just don't let him distract you for long. I'll be back with whatever stuff the tree person—"

"Arborist," Mercy supplied.

"Yeah, that. I'll have what the *arborist* recommends as mundane help for the trees when I get back. You, Miss Green Witch, need to have the magic part ready. Tonight, we fix this mess with a double-whammy—muggle stuff and witchy power."

"Stop stressing. I already have a few ideas. Why do you think I'm so tired?" Mercy jerked her chin at the pile of old grimoires on her bedside table. They had colorful sticky notes protruding from their closed pages like paper fringe. Then her eyes widened and she reached for her phone. "Oh, bloody buggering hell! Have you heard from Em?"

"I texted her and called her. Twice. I didn't get any answer until I told her you were sleeping and that I was checking on her for you. She only answered with two words: I'm okay."

Mercy ran one hand through her hair as she squinted at her phone and read through the six texts she'd sent Emily last night and early this morning while she'd been going through the grimoires. No response. Em hadn't answered her even once. "She's not okay. No damn way. I'm texting her right now. Again."

"Hey, Mag?"

Mercy looked up from her phone. "Huh?"

"Remember that we all grieve differently. Be there for her, but don't be surprised if this changes her. Mom's death has changed us."

"You're right. I'll remember. Thanks. And good luck today."

Hunter smiled. "You, too. Later gator."

Mercy's response was automatic. "After 'while crocodile!" Then she returned her attention to her phone, texting:

EM! SORRY. I JUST GOT UP. U OK? CALL ME!

While she waited for a response Mercy brushed her teeth, piled her hair up in a loose knot, and took a quick shower before putting on her most comfy Free People boho dress. It was the color of moss with blue flowers embroidered down the bodice of it and an adorable high-low ruffle that made it sexy and cute in the front, but long enough in the back not to cause stress whenever she had to bend over.

Her phone rang as she was sliding her feet into her favorite moccasin slippers.

"Em!"

Emily's voice was muffled, like she had a cold that had completely clogged her nose. "I can only talk for a sec."

"It is awful?" Mercy asked.

There was a long pause—so long that Mercy frantically wondered if she'd asked the wrong question—when Em's shrouded voice finally replied. "Mag, his eyes are gone."

Mercy's stomach rolled in rebellion. "Your dad? *His* eyes?"

"Yes," Emily whispered. "The sheriff told Mom."

"Oh, Freya!" Mercy's legs stopped working and she sat hard on the end of her bed as bits and pieces of the sheriff's creepy words about Mr. Thompson, the dead guy he'd found by the olive tree, lifted from her memory: . . . *dead man . . . with no eyes . . . Ripped right out of his head . . .*

"It's so terrible I don't want to think about it, but I can't stop thinking about it," said Emily.

"Is *that* how he died?"

"No. He—he was strangled and then the murderer took his eyes. Mag, I just—" Emily's words ran out as she sobbed.

"Come over, Em. Just get in your car and come over here right now."

Emily took several deep breaths before she answered, and when she did she sounded broken. "I can't. Mom's not okay." She paused and then added in a whisper, "They let her see him. I wouldn't—couldn't. But I *should have.* I *shouldn't* have let her go in there by herself."

"*They* shouldn't have let her see him! Bloody hell, Em! What's wrong with the sheriff?"

There was a sharp sound in the background and Emily spoke quickly. "Gotta go. I think Mom just dropped another cup. She's, uh, *medicated*. Heavily. I'll text you later."

Before Mercy could say anything else the phone disconnected. Mercy finished putting on her slippers and slowly went downstairs. She hadn't imagined Abigail's music. Hunter must have flipped on the Pandora station. Mercy was glad. She stood in the kitchen and let the beautiful lyrics of "Shores of Avalon" soothe her shattered nerves as she brewed another pot of her mom's special dark roast coffee. Mercy didn't love coffee like Abigail had, but she did like the way it smelled—and if she added enough coconut milk and sugar it didn't taste too bad. But, more importantly, it was part of her usual morning ritual, and even though it was past noon Mercy craved whatever might help her feel normal, if only for a little while.

She put two slices of thick sourdough bread in the toaster and got

Abigail's homemade strawberry jam from the pantry. As she slathered sticky-sweet goo on the warm bread her thoughts spun. *Horrible things are happening in Goodeville and it all started the night Mom was killed. What if the sick trees have something to do with it?*

Mercy sat at the table in the breakfast nook, which Xena had piled high with old grimoires the night before. She moved them out of the way and texted Em again:

CALL ME WHEN U CAN! I'M HERE. LOVE U!

Then Mercy stared out the back window as her coffee went cold as she faced the thoughts she'd pushed aside the night before.

What if Hunter's choice to swear into the service of a god instead of a goddess is causing the trees to be sick? All of it—every bad thing—started that terrible night. The night Hunter officially claimed Tyr as her god. It was the only thing Mercy could think of that differed from their Beltane Ritual and the Beltane Rituals that had been successfully performed by Goode witches for hundreds of years.

But wouldn't Mom have known that Tyr was a mistake? Mercy clearly remembered the day young Hunter had first mentioned to Abigail that she was drawn to Tyr. Their mom's response had been that it was Hunter's choice, and there was no wrong answer when a witch chose her deity. *Okay, maybe Abigail hadn't known it was a problem that H had chosen a god back then, but during the three years between that day and their dedication night she definitely would've said something if it could cause problems.* From her memory Mercy replayed her mom's words to Hunter as they walked to the Beltane Ritual: *It's about time a Goode chose a god instead of a goddess.*

She shook her head and sighed as she nibbled on her toast. "No, Abigail would've known. She was an amazing witch. She would never have let Hunter make such a big mistake. It must be something else and I'm going to figure it out and fix it. I have to." Resolutely, Mercy pulled the closest grimoire to her, grabbed a stack of pink sticky notes and her favorite purple pen, and got to work.

Mercy was deep into her great-great-grandmother Janet Goode's summer 1927 entry entitled *Healing Trees from the Drought* when she pumped her fist and shouted, "Yes! That's it!" Then she wrote quickly on the sticky notes as she muttered to herself. "This will work with just a little addition from the spell Gertrude Goode cast in 1859 after the entire state of Illinois flooded and damaged all the trees big-time." She paused for a moment, chewing the end of the pen before lifting it triumphantly and proclaiming, "Plus, I'll make a big dose of my Awake and Alive Oil! That'll be my own Green Witch contribution. This is going to be perfect!"

One problem solved, Mercy picked up her phone and clicked into the texts.

EM, HOW U DOING?
YOU OK?
EMILY, I'M WORRIED ABOUT YOU.

Zero response from her bestie. Mercy got it—of course she did. She completely understood about how grief could suffocate every other emotion. But H hadn't left her alone in her despair, and she wasn't going to leave Em alone, either. She tapped out another text.

EMILY PARROTT IF YOU DO NOT ANSWER ME I AM COMING OVER THERE. NOW!

Three dots appeared almost immediately.

CAN'T TALK RIGHT NOW. GRANDPARENTS R HERE. I'LL CALL LATER. PROMISE.

Mercy sighed and chewed her lip. "Okay." She spoke to the phone like Em could hear her. "But if you don't I *will* come get you. Seriously."

She drummed her fingers against the table as she turned her attention back to the grimoires and the spells she needed to combine. It was easy—comfortable—to focus on spellwork. It was something she could *do* to make at least part of the chaos around her right again.

Mercy was listing the ingredients she'd need for her oil and realizing she should go upstairs and get her own grimoire so she could record this new protective and healing spell when several loud knocks on the front door made her jump. Momentarily confused, she glanced at the old clock in the foyer as she headed to the door and was surprised to see almost two hours had passed while she'd been researching. She didn't have to peek out the front window to see him standing there. She could feel that it was Kirk. Mercy smoothed back her long, dark hair and opened the door.

"Babe! Man, it's good to see you!" He stepped inside and engulfed her in a hug and his familiar scent of sweat mixed with Abercrombie & Fitch's cologne, Fierce.

Mercy pressed her cheek against his chest. He was so solid and strong and *normal*. He was the guy she'd crushed on since eighth grade, when he'd seemed completely out of her league. He was the guy who made her feel special *and* needed *and* wanted. He was there, with her instead of in school preparing for finals, because he cared about her as much as she cared about him. When she looked up at him she was flooded with emotions and tears filled her eyes.

He cupped her face with his hands. "Hey, don't cry. I'm here. Everything's gonna be okay now." Kirk dipped down and pressed his lips gently to hers. He didn't deepen the kiss. Instead he looked up, checking out the rooms behind them. "Is Emily here?"

"No. I wish she was here but her mom needs her. So, everyone knows about her dad?" Mercy took Kirk's hand and led him to the couch. She curled up there beside him, with her feet tucked under her. His presence and the fact that she'd figured out the spell they needed to cast to strengthen and protect the trees had her feeling lighter than she had in days.

He nodded and kissed her hand. "Yeah, the whole school's talking about it. He was murdered, which is *really* crazy."

Mercy leaned into him. "That's what Em said."

"Did she say anything else?" Kirk asked. "There're rumors about something really nasty happening to him, but no one knows what for sure."

Mercy straightened and pulled her hand from his. "Well, I haven't had a chance to talk to Emily much. She's pretty upset." The lie came out before Mercy planned it. She just wouldn't, *couldn't* gossip with Kirk about Mr. Parrott. It was already bad enough that everyone was talking about it, which Em would hate. She couldn't add to her best friend's misery.

Kirk was instantly contrite. He slid his arm around her shoulder and pulled her close to him again. "Sorry, that wasn't cool of me. So, what have you been up to?" He glanced over his shoulder at the edge of the breakfast nook table, filled with old books and notes. "Are you actually studying in there?"

"Oh. Um. No. That's Xena's stuff," she lied again and then chewed her lip. Mercy usually hated lies—and was pretty bad at them.

Thankfully, Kirk didn't notice. All he said, with a little laugh, was, "Your aunt or your cat?"

She smacked his shoulder. "The one that can read, silly."

"Speaking of—where is she?"

"The aunt or the cat?" Mercy teased.

He grinned. "The one who hates me."

"Oh, well, that would be both. They're upstairs napping."

"Whew." He pretended to wipe sweat from his forehead. "It's weird to be hissed at."

"Sorry about that. The Xenas are protective, but they'll learn that you're one of the good guys soon, and then you'll hear nothing but purrs."

His eyes widened. "From the aunt, too?"

"It's possible."

"I'm gonna have to record that for the Cats of Insta. Talk about going viral."

"Weirdly enough I'll bet Xena would like that."

"You're obviously talking about the cat now," he said.

"Obviously!" She grinned.

He touched her cheek gently. "It's good to see you smile again."

Mercy pressed her cheek into his warm palm. "I'm better after Hunter's spell. Plus, you're another kind of magic that's good for me."

His hand dropped from her face. "That spell. It was kinda uncomfortable to see you—"

She waved her hand dismissively. "Hey, forget about that spell. Or if you want to remember it think of it as homeopathic healing."

"What do you mean?"

"Well, does acupuncture make you uncomfortable?" Mercy shifted so that instead of leaning into him she faced him as she reclined across his lap.

"It did before Coach made me go last year for my shoulder injury. It didn't hurt. Actually, it helped."

"That's what Hunter's spell was—acupuncture for my emotions. I can see that it might have been strange and even kinda freaky, but it was really just a movement of energy that helped me be able to deal with my grief in a healthier way."

His brow furrowed as he considered her words, then he let out a long breath. "I guess that makes sense."

"Of course it does. And how could I be your witchy woman without actually being witchy?"

Kirk's face cleared and he pulled her closer. "Hey, I'm here for you, not me. What happened to Emily's dad must be really hard for you after your mom."

Mercy let her head rest on his shoulder. "Yeah. It feels like my world is totally falling apart."

Kirk lifted her chin with his finger. "Then hang on to me. I won't let you fall apart." He kissed her again.

Mercy sank into him. She parted her lips and met his questing tongue. He tasted like the Big Red gum he liked to chew. His strong arms held her tightly and his mouth and touch were hot and insistent. At first she returned the kiss to keep him from saying anything more about death or spellwork, but soon she realized that his desire was a roadblock to the terrible things that had happened the past several days. When Kirk's mouth was on hers all she could think about was his need. When Kirk's hands found the ruffled edge of her dress and slipped beneath to caress her thighs and her butt, his heat burned away the misery she'd been living and breathing. She pressed herself closer to him and deepened the kiss, chasing his tongue, catching it, and then sucking softly on it. His moan drove away the sounds of the sobs that came from Hunter's room every night when she pretended to be asleep.

Abruptly Kirk broke the kiss. Breathing hard, he whispered, "It wouldn't be cool if Xena—either of them—came down here to find us like this."

And Mercy suddenly knew what she wanted—what she *needed*. She took his hand and stood, pulling him up from the couch with her. "Then let's go where we can't be interrupted—by either of them."

His answering smile was as hot and sweet as his kisses.

She led him upstairs to her room and the bed she'd never, in sixteen years, let any boy so much as sit on. That wasn't because Abigail had been uptight about sex—her mom had definitely *not* been like that. Mercy had never had a guy in her room before because until Kirk she'd never been in love.

Mercy guided Kirk to the bed and then playfully pushed him down on it. Laughing, she fell on top of him as they resumed their passionate kisses. Kirk's hands quickly went under her dress again, and she was glad that she hadn't bothered with a bra as he squeezed her breasts. She let her hands roam his body. His PROPERTY OF GOODE ATHLETIC DEPARTMENT tee was easy to untuck and she loved the way his hard, smooth muscles felt under it.

Kirk broke their kiss long enough to pull off his shirt and toss it to the floor. Then he raised a brow at her. "Your turn."

Mercy hesitated.

"Hey." He touched her cheek gently again. "We won't do anything you don't wanna do. No matter what, you say stop and I stop. Promise."

She bit her lip and then spoke softly. "I—I want to, but I don't think I'm ready for more than just, you know, making out and stuff right now."

"That's okay. Seriously. You have to be into it, too. I can wait." Kirk met her gaze and said simply, "I love you, Mercy Goode. You're worth the wait." He started to reach for his T-shirt.

Mercy's hand stopped him. "I love you, too, Kirk."

"Babe, that means so much. You're the only woman I've said that to except my mom." He looked away, blinking fast. "And then she left me."

Mercy pulled him into her arms. "I won't leave you. Ever."

His kiss was deep and hot, but he broke it off, reaching for his shirt again.

Again, she stopped him, only this time she said, "Don't put that on. I want to be close to you and your skin feels so good."

Kirk dropped the tee and then plucked at the ruffled hem of her dress. He gave her a cute, cocky smile. "It would feel even better against *your* skin."

And that did it. Mercy wanted to feel something besides sadness and worry and fear. She wanted to feel warmth and happiness—she wanted to feel safe again. Kirk made her feel safe, and *he loved her.* Mercy reached down and peeled her dress over her head so that all she wore were her panties and a tentative smile.

Kirk sucked in a sharp breath as he stared at her. Slowly, he reached out and lifted one of her breasts. "Do you know how beautiful you are?"

"No," she whispered. "Tell me."

Tenderly, his thumb caressed her nipple, causing it to harden as Mercy's back arched and a jolt of pleasure sizzled through her body. "You're not a witch. You're a goddess." His breath was ragged as his lips replaced his thumb.

Mercy wrapped her arms around his bare shoulders as she straddled him. He was right. The sensation of his hot, sweat-slick flesh against her naked skin felt so incredibly good that her world narrowed and she could think of nothing except the pleasure that pulsed through her body. She moved her hips so that the warm wetness between her legs found the hardness that pressed against his jeans, and he moaned again.

"You're *so sexy.* You feel amazing."

Mercy's hands found his nipples—smaller and tighter than hers—but his sharp intake of breath as she gently teased them made her believe that they were as sensitive. Emboldened, her hands explored downward. Her fingers traveled to the six-pack that all the girls drooled over whenever he took off his shirt after football practice.

His moan was deeper. "Ah, god! You're killing me," he said as her searching fingers found his belt buckle.

"Do you want me to stop?" she whispered.

"Hell no!"

She smiled and felt unbelievably powerful as she pushed him back on the bed. Mercy moved off his lap as she unbuckled his belt and then slowly opened his jeans. As she reached inside them to touch him Kirk shifted so that his hand could explore her bare thighs.

"Do whatever you want." He sounded breathless.

Mercy did whatever she wanted. She'd seen penises before. The internet was full of them. But she'd never touched one, and the hardness of it surprised her. She ran her hand up and down the thick length of him as his hips lifted and jerked in response. Mercy was surprised by how much she liked touching him, stroking him. It was incredible and powerful and sexy how just a small touch, a soft stroke, had him moaning and sounding like he'd just run several lengths of the football field.

She was intrigued by the drops of clear liquid that dewed the head of his penis. Mercy rubbed them gently around as Kirk gasped and whispered how good it felt and how much he loved her. And when her head dipped and her tongue replaced her fingers he groaned like she really was killing him.

"Don't stop! Oh, you fucking gorgeous goddess, *do not stop*!"

So, Mercy didn't. As her mouth covered him and she experimented by sucking and licking the thick, hard length of him, Kirk's hand slipped inside her panties. She knew how to touch herself—she knew what made her orgasm—and she rocked against his searching fingers until he found the right spot and then she moved her hips in time with her mouth.

Kirk came first, surprising Mercy with the heat and force of it, but then she sank into the waves of pleasure that cascaded through her body, making her hips buck against his hand as her orgasm engulfed her. She kept sucking and licking as another orgasm and then another rippled through her until finally she was breathing so hard she had to fall limply back on the bed. She crawled up so that she lay in the crook of his sweaty arm while their breathing slowed together.

"You are a goddess. *My* goddess," he said.

Mercy's head found his shoulder. He pulled her closer to him while she stared up at the ceiling and tried to slow her breathing and sift through her tumultuous thoughts.

Kirk kissed her damp forehead. "You were amazing."

"Um, thanks." Mercy spoke softly. Her body was still humming with the aftermath of pleasure, but as passion faded the real world rushed in to take its place. *Freya, what did I just do?*

"Seriously. A-maz-ing." Kirk laughed joyously. "Like, you blew my mind!" His fingers traced up and down the side of her neck.

Mercy had no idea why, but she had a sudden urge to pull away from him. Instead, she forced herself to be calm and turned her head to stare at Kirk's handsome profile. His face was still flushed. His full lips were lifted at the corners in a satisfied smile. He obviously didn't have a worry in the world. But Mercy's world, full of sadness and worry and loss, had come flooding back. Reality washed away the last of her pleasure and she felt utterly empty, numb—like *she* hadn't just given Kirk a blowjob and had several earth-shattering orgasms herself. Someone else had done that—someone who had tried to hide from reality, to exchange grief for lust.

It hadn't worked.

Mercy lifted herself up on her elbow. She needed to talk to Kirk—to explain to him how confused she felt—that what had just happened between them had more to do with loneliness and confusion than sex. But before she could speak she heard through her open bedroom window a car's tires on their gravel driveway and then voices floated up with the breeze. "Oh, bloody, buggering hell!!" Mercy rushed to the window. "Sodding wanker! It's Jax and Hunter!"

When she turned back to Kirk he was still lying on the bed smiling at her. She hurried back to him, throwing his shirt at him before she yanked on her dress.

"Hey, what's the big deal? Hunter's not your mom."

Mercy just stared at him until he wiped a hand across his face as he realized what he'd just said. "Oh, shit. I'm sorry. That was stupid of me."

Mercy grabbed a brush from her vanity and attacked her hair. "It's okay. I know what you meant. Kirk, I don't want Hunter to know about this. Not right now."

Kirk looked up at her as he tucked in his shirt and zipped his jeans. "Are you sorry about what we just did?"

Mercy went to him and touched his shoulder as she avoided the honest answer there wasn't time for her to give. "Now isn't a good time. Mom died. Things are not normal. I—I don't know how Hunter would take this. I don't want her to think that I've forgotten about Mom—that I don't really care she's gone."

"Okay, yeah, I get it. Hey, she already doesn't like me much and this isn't gonna help that."

"H appreciates that you've been here for me—for us. The more you're around the more she'll like you." She draped her arms over his shoulders and attempted to sound normal. "I mean, how could she *not* like you?"

He waggled his eyebrows. "Seriously." He cupped her butt cheek and squeezed. "Hey, if your sister and Jax are back that means I gotta get to practice. Crap! I didn't realize it was that late. Being with a goddess definitely messed with my sense of time. Good thing Jax is here. Mom dropped me off, and I can bum a ride from him." But Kirk didn't move except to bend and kiss her passionately.

Mercy let herself relax into his arms. *Kirk loves me,* she reminded herself.

Hand in hand they hurried down the stairs. Mercy stepped into his arms one more time as they kissed slowly again. She did feel closer to him than she'd ever felt to any guy. *And I love that closeness—that specialness that only the two of us share,* Mercy told herself sternly. *Then why do I feel so empty?* The question hovered in her mind and Mercy shoved it aside.

Kirk was still kissing her when the sound of a car door slamming made her break the embrace and push him playfully out the door.

He backed onto the porch and mouthed *I love you, goddess!* before he turned to leap down the stairs.

Mercy closed the door and sighed as she leaned against it. *What is wrong with me? If Abigail were here she'd understand. Mom would help me figure this out. If Abigail were here it wouldn't have happened,* Mercy thought, though she didn't speak the words. She felt strange, like a rubber band that had been stretched too far. Mercy shook herself and spoke the rest of her thoughts to the quiet house. "I need to eat something to ground myself. That's all. And I have to believe it's all going to be okay. Hunter and I can save the trees, Emily is going to be herself again, and Kirk Whitfield finally said he loves me." Resolutely, Mercy headed to the kitchen as she repeated, "That's right. My Kirk loves me!"

Seventeen

At this time of year, when the sun camped out in the sky and gentle rains spilled from the clouds, it was easy for World of Blooms, Champaign's largest nursery, to live up to its name. The candied scents of honeysuckle and lavender reached Hunter before she and Jax had even made it to the entrance. She inhaled and let the summertime smells pull her from the nearly empty parking lot, through the nursery's sliding double doors, past the array of pots and seed packs, garden sculptures and indoor plants to the information booth set up outside the main building's back entrance. The Qs INTO As hut looked like it belonged on the beach, complete with thatched straw roof, colorful orchid-shaped lights tacked up around the bar, and sun-streaked blond attendant.

Jax ran his hand through his earth brown hair, turning his textured fringe into a messy pompadour before he smoothed down the front of his T-shirt and flicked a speck of lint from his shorts.

Was he . . . *primping*?

Hunter trailed her best friend as he glided up to the hut and rang the small bell that sat in the middle of the bar.

The attendant's soft curls bounced around her shoulders as she turned to face them. "Heya, what can I help you find?" Her voice was starshine, bright and clear and enchanting.

Hunter's mouth went dry and she wished she, too, had combed her hand through her hair, turned it into anything other than the plain ponytail that hung down her back like the densely packed flowers of a cattail.

Jax leaned against the bar and glanced over his shoulder at Hunter. "What'd you say the name of that stuff is?"

Hunter's tongue was a ball bearing pressing against her teeth. There was no point in crushing on anyone back home in Goodeville. The one time she had, Chelsea Parham had run around school screaming that Hunter was trying to turn her into a lesbian. Since that backward day in middle school, Hunter had decided that no Goodeville girl would ever be attractive.

They're all warty toads, she'd said as her mother cupped her face and pressed their foreheads together.

There's a whole world outside of Goodeville, Abigail had whispered before she'd kissed the tip of Hunter's nose.

"It's an insecticide." Hunter cleared her throat and joined Jax in front of the hut. "For tree worms."

The attendant's eyes, robin's eggs pressed into her soft, round face, shimmered when she met Hunter's gaze. "Let me get you a map. When the trees start to bloom, it can turn into a bit of a maze." She brushed a curl from her cheek and pulled a map from beneath the bar. "We're here," she said as she took a red marker from the cup next to the bell and drew a star over the info desk. "And you want to go all the way back here." She drew a line from the hut, through the bonsai tent and the section of full sun flowering plants to the back section of the property where she marked the CONTROL THOSE PESTS! hut with another star. "And this is where I usually work." She circled the EDIBLE ORGANICS section twice and looked up at Hunter. The corners of her pink lips quirked as she spoke. "If you make it back in, ask for Grace."

Hunter's legs were bags of pudding as she collected the map and wobbled away from the information booth.

Gravel crunched as Jax followed his best friend. "That's Hunter. She's *amazing,*" he called back to the hut. "And she'll definitely be back!"

Hunter's cheeks sizzled and her palms were slick with sweat. There *was* a whole world outside of Goodeville and Hunter hadn't had to go far to find it.

"Dude." Jax bumped Hunter's shoulder. "Why are you running away? Go back and talk to her. She's clearly interested."

Hunter paused to unfold the map she'd scrunched up in her hand. Red marker stamped the scabbed-over slivers she'd accidentally dug into her palm the night before. "I don't even know what I would say. It's not like I ever get to practice any of that stuff."

"I'll be your wingman," he said as he dodged a pollen-coated bee. "I already have my pitch down: 'This is Hunter Goode. The best, smartest, kindest, most talented girl you've ever met.'" His forehead wrinkled and he scratched his chin. "There's more, but I'll proceed on a case-by-case basis."

Hunter folded the map and crammed it into her front pocket. "What's wrong with you? I'm not a prized pig, Jax. You can't dress me up and sell me to the highest bidder." The gravel walkway smoothed into round river rocks as they entered the bonsai tent and wove around tables covered with miniature trees and shrubs.

"H!" Jax stood in the entrance of the tent, hands shoved into his pockets. "A lot's going on. I get that and I'm here for you. But I'm not an ass." The slim lines of worry sprouting from the sharp corners of his eyes vanished when his brows lifted. "I don't think you're a piece of meat I can toss out to lady-lovin' hyenas. I just want to help."

Hunter picked at the edge of her thumbnail. "I'm not ready. For flirting or a girlfriend or making out or sex. I just—" Her eyes burned, and each blink sent tears down her cheeks. She'd never admitted any of that before. Never felt the reality of it until now. It had been easier to think that she was the victim of circumstance. That, if she lived in Chicago or New York or LA, she'd have a serious girlfriend or maybe even a revolving door of torrid love affairs. Goodeville kept Hunter protected. Kept her from seeing her truth.

Jax wrapped his arms around her. He blocked out the light and the saccharine scents of flowers and the pulsing buzz of nearby bees. "Take your time." His breath tickled her ear. "I love you, Hunter Goode. When you're ready, some badass gal will be, too."

She pressed her face against his shoulder. Her best friend always smelled like clean sheets and peppermint. "I liked your line about lady-lovin' hyenas."

Jax's chest shook with a laugh. "Really painted a good picture, didn't it?"

Hunter pressed away from him and wiped her face with the back of her hand.

"Hey, H, you got any mucus removal spells up your sleeve?" Jax pulled his shirt away from his shoulder and pointed at the slimy wet spot she'd left behind.

Hunter's eyebrow rose as she smiled. "Someday, when I'm a famous witch, that snot shirt will be worth a lot of money."

Jax followed Hunter out of the tent and back into the sunny spring afternoon. "So, we're eventually posting your witchy-ness for all to see?" He jutted his chin toward a bench of bright pink flowers. "You'll be able to tell the photogs that your entourage started next to a cockscomb."

"You just wanted to say *cock,* didn't you?"

His shoulders hunched and he hid his laugh behind his hand. "I did, but only because I don't remember the name of what we're actually looking for."

Hunter pulled her phone out of her back pocket and brought up the article she'd read to Jax in the car on the way over and scrolled until she saw the name in bold. *"Bacillus thur-ing-ein-sis."* She broke down the last word the same way she did each time they discussed abiogenesis in her biology class. Something about the *sis* really tripped her up.

Jax's chuckle was interrupted by a snort as he ran his fingertips along the starlike blooms of a row of daffodils. "I'm positive you're still not saying it right."

"Well, at least I don't snort when I laugh."

Jax wrapped his arm around Hunter's shoulders and pulled her into him. "You love my laugh snorts," he teased and rubbed his knuckles against the top of her head.

Hunter couldn't help but laugh as she pushed and twisted in an attempt to wriggle free. "You're like the brother I never wanted." She grunted and reached around to Jax's right side.

"Not the Claw! Not the Claw!" He erupted into a cacophony of snorts and giggles as Hunter snapped her fingers open and shut along his ribs.

Jax released her, wrapped his arms around his middle, and stumbled backward into a table of budding hydrangeas.

"Works every time." Hunter smoothed her hand over the mess of puffy bumps Jax had inflicted on her hair and sighed. "Remember when *I* was the one who would hold you down and give you noogies?" She pulled her tie from her disheveled ponytail and shook out her hair. "Oh, that was the life . . ."

Jax lifted the bottom of his shirt and wiped his eyes. Dark hair ran in a furry track down the middle of his flat stomach and disappeared behind the waistband of his shorts. Gone was the little boy who used to stand between the swings at recess, arms stretched as wide as they could go, hands gripping the metal chains in order to save her one, or the little boy who used to climb onto a kitchen chair to help her get her ponytail just right. Her best friend had turned into a man and she hadn't even noticed.

"That was back when I sounded like Mickey Mouse and Mercy said that I'd be shorter than Kevin Hart." Jax shoved his hands into his pockets and joined Hunter back on the path that wound through the sun-drenched plants to the small hut labeled Control Those Pests! "You should leave your hair down more often." He nodded toward the lengths of inky black that brushed Hunter's shoulder blades. "It's really pretty."

She gathered her hair and positioned it back into her signature ponytail. "I was just wondering what a straight guy thought about my hair choices. Tell me, should I also smile more?"

"Ah, yes, you read my mind." Jax tapped his temple and nodded dramatically. "And while you're at it, you should go back to the kitchen and make me a sammich, extra mayo, no crusts."

It felt good to laugh again. To be away from her house and the ghost of her mother. It felt good to be twin-less, free from her sister and the weight of Mercy's broken pieces that Hunter kept picking up but couldn't quite fit back together.

"Holy hell!" Jax grabbed Hunter's shoulders and ducked behind her. "It's Barbara Ritter!" he said and peered up over her shoulder before hunkering down again.

"Mrs. Ritter, your neighbor?" Hunter cocked her head at the two women who were too busy looking at plants to notice the spectacle that was currently Jax Ashley. She chewed on the tip of her pinky nail and took in the suburbanites in their nearly matching tennis outfits, one pastel yellow with sensible white tennis shoes, the other a much louder neon yellow with bright, sparkling gold shoes. Barbara was the giant, glittery highlighter, which made sense since, although her oldest child wouldn't be in high school for at least another five years, she demanded to chaperone all school dances while using a bullhorn to mortify horny teens. Maybe Barbara had given the school's principal her secret to the perfect ponytail. If Mrs. Ritter gave Hunter the recipe for a long, shiny ponytail that curled at the end like an upside-down question mark, Hunter would let her do pretty much anything.

"Yes!" Jax hissed like a stuck balloon and crawled between two large pots of flowering shrubs before he disappeared under a table covered in ivy.

Hunter bent over and parted palm-sized leaves and scarlet blooms that waterfalled like spilled cranberry juice over the lip of the pot to look down at Jax. "Why are you hiding?" She looked back at Mrs. Ritter and her friend who, aside from the neon-ness of one and the spray tanned–ness of them both, were two completely normal women.

Jax pressed his finger against his lips and frantically waved for her to join him. With a groan, Hunter obliged. Ivy stems brushed against her back and her palms smashed fresh earth as she crawled under the table and squatted next to him. "This is ridiculous," she whispered and wiped the dirt from her hands. "Why are we hiding?"

Jax blew out a puff of air, leaned forward and drew the curtain of ivy closed, and settled back against the ground. "I kind of saw her . . ." He moved his hands in front of him like he was juggling invisible balls. "Chest?" He winced and shook his head. "Her boobs, okay. I saw Mrs. Ritter's boobs."

Hunter clapped her hand over her mouth and nearly toppled onto her butt.

Again, Jax pressed his finger to his lips. "My dad made me fix that rotted spot in the fence. I had a few boards down and she just, you know . . ."

Hunter's jaw flopped open. "What? Took off her shirt and said, *'Here Jax, please gaze upon my heaving bosoms'*?"

"No!" Another hiss. "She was tanning, *topless,* and I saw her and didn't exactly look away."

Hunter dropped her head into her hands. "Jesus, Jax!"

"I know!" he said as he ran his hands down his cheeks. "I've apologized and said I'd mow her yard this summer for free. She declined, so I decided that my best course of action is to avoid her until I move away for college."

Hunter shook her head. Her ponytail slipped off her neck and hung limply in front of her shoulder. "That's in two years."

"Exactly why we're hiding."

Barbara Ritter's sparkly tennis shoes threw white spots across

Hunter's vision as she and her friend approached the table. Jax's eyes widened and he pressed his finger against his lips so hard that the pink flesh around his nail whitened.

Plain white Keds stood directly in front of Hunter. A ring of dirt encircled the sole like chocolate meringue. "Oh, Barbara, what about these? The . . ." There was a short pause and a ruffling of leaves before the woman continued. "Bleeding amaranthus. It says they get pretty big. If you plant them right along your fence line, they should block out your neighbors."

Jax's face lit up like a stoplight.

Barbara's sparkles inched closer to the large pots just on the other side of the ivy shield. "But the name, Susan. *Bleeding* amaranthus. I couldn't bear to have anything planted on my property with the word *bleeding* in the name. Not after what I overheard this morning."

The Keds spun to face the garish sparkles. "I knew there was something you weren't telling me. You may have re-upped your Botox, but I can still see it written all over your face. Spill!"

The gold-sparkled toes wiggled like two puppy butts. "Deputy Carter was pulled up outside of the Coffee Spot this morning. Windows down, practically yelling into his phone about Dominic Parrott."

Hunter's breath caught in her throat.

Susan sighed and her Keds relaxed and parted slightly. "I've always felt so sorry for Dominic." Another sigh. "That depressing job and practically raising his daughter alone while his wife is off on all of those *business* trips doing God knows what. Although I did see him at the IGA just a few days ago. He's leaving soon for some *funeral services convention.*" She paused. "I suspect that's code for *getting the H-E double hockey sticks away from my terrible wife.*" Susan sucked in a breath and her heels lifted and settled back against the gravel. "Maybe I should bring him a plate of my hot sticky buns."

"Well, don't get too excited." Barbara's right foot angled outward as she settled into her story. "You know I don't like to speak ill of the dead. Or, in this case, the family of the dead, but—"

Susan took a step back. "Dominic Parrott is dead?"

Jax squeezed Hunter's arm. She wanted to cover her ears with both hands and dig into the ground like a mole, but it wouldn't have helped. Death had stitched itself to Hunter's back and rode her like wings.

"Hush now, Susan." Barbara slid closer to her friend. "It's not common knowledge, just a fact I overheard the deputy discussing. Along with another . . ."

The dramatic pause made Hunter's stomach lurch.

The sparkle-encrusted shoes wriggled as Barbara continued, "Dominic Parrott was *murdered in his own car.* Right outside the sheriff's department. If you're not safe there, I just don't know where you can be."

Susan sucked in another breath and the toes of her shoes pressed together. "It's like in one of those *CSI* shows."

The golden sparkles halted their dance and resumed their stroll along the gravel path. "Well, I wouldn't know about that. I try to stay away from graphic television dramas . . ." Barbara's voice faded and her shoes blurred into two bright blotches as she and Susan turned and made their way back to the main building.

Hunter pressed her hands into the ground. But the killings were about her, about Mercy, about the gates, weren't they? She lifted her hands and stared down at the starlike imprints in the dirt. The sheriff's department was nowhere near any of the trees. What did that mean? What did any of it mean? She crawled out from under the table and stood. She needed answers.

Eighteen

Hunter's journal lay open in her lap and she clicked and unclicked her pen as she and Jax neared her driveway. She scrawled a note next to the name of the insecticide they had picked up from World of Blooms and let out a defeated sigh. This was her writing journal no more. It was now destined to be filled with to-do lists and random similes and metaphors she thought of throughout the day. At least, random similes and metaphors *used to* pop into her head throughout the day. But that was back when she was going to be a famous author and pen the thrilling and romantic novel, *When Darkness Rises.* Now, she was trying to stop murders, heal sick gates, survive without her mother, and keep her only remaining human family member from falling apart.

Jax slowed to a stop in the driveway and Hunter closed her journal and dropped her head back against the headrest. On the porch, Kirk closed the front door to her house and paused at the top of the steps to stretch.

Jax bumped Hunter's elbow with the side of his sweating Big Gulp cup. "Slushies fix everything." His crooked teeth poked out from between blue-stained lips.

She looked away and chewed the end of the straw. "Can we just sit for a minute? See if I can get a sugar rush before I have to entertain Kirk." Hunter pushed the switch and the window slid down a few inches before she rolled it back up. "Maybe he's leaving," she grumbled as she rolled the window down an inch and then up again.

Jax wiped his mouth on the back of his hand and shrugged at the blue smudge it left behind. "You do what you want." He unbuckled his seat belt. "I've got to pee before I head to practice." He left the car running as he got out and headed toward Hunter's front porch.

She cracked her window again as Jax intercepted Kirk on the front steps.

"Yo, Jaxie!" Kirk held up his hand for a high five. Their hands met with a loud *slap* that seemed to further invigorate the quarterback. "Today is going *so* good!"

Jax brushed his hair back and cocked his head. Hunter craned her neck, but still couldn't hear Jax's reply.

"Lookin' light and feelin' right, my man. Finally got some of Mercy's goodies, if you know what I mean." With a laugh, Kirk stuck out his tongue and held up his hand for another celebratory high five.

Jax crossed his arms over his chest.

"What?" Kirk rocked back on his heels and flicked his chin in the air. "You jealous? You'd be swimming in it, too, if you didn't spend all your time with Hunter. You do know she's never going to switch teams, right? All she is is a cockblock. Girls don't want to see you hanging with other girls. Makes them jealous and the last thing you want is some crazy jealous chick."

Jax ran his fingers along his temple. "Do you hear yourself when you talk?"

"I hear it. But I don't think you recognize that I'm spittin' gold." Kirk draped his arm around Jax and led him down the stairs. "Let me bum a ride to practice. I'll probably play like garbage. My energy is shot." Kirk unhooked himself from Jax as they neared the car. "Hey, you got a protein shake?"

The plastic Big Gulp dented under Hunter's grip as she rolled the passenger window all the way down.

"Jesus, H!" Kirk clutched his chest. "You almost gave me a heart attack." He shoved his hands into his pockets and offered a boyish half smile. "Been there long?"

"Long enough to know you're famished." She held the blue slushie out the window. "Here." It lapped against the sides of the cup as she shook it. "Have some of this." A grin stretched her lips as he walked closer, his nervousness melting back into arrogance. He underestimated the twins. He underestimated Hunter.

"Thanks. If you knew what I'd just—" he began as Jax came around the front of the car.

Blue liquid splattered against Kirk's pristine white shoes.

"What the hell, Hunter? My trainers!" Kirk lifted one foot and then the other until the large clumps of slush had splatted onto the ground.

Hunter slid out of the car and stared down at Kirk's *trainers*. "Oops." She hiked her shoulders and tipped her smile into a frown. "Slipped. My bad." She dropped the cup in the driveway next to Kirk's blue-stained shoes, waved to Jax, and skipped up the stairs.

Hunter would not feel bad about what she'd done to Kirk. He'd deserved it, hadn't he? She chewed the inside of her cheek and sagged against the heavy front door. She didn't have excess power to blame this time. That had all been her. And, if she was being honest, she'd wanted to do worse. Hunter squeezed her eyes shut. She wouldn't feel guilty. *She wouldn't.* Kirk embodied everything wrong with guys. Of course Mercy didn't see Kirk for what he was, having never had to deal with a bully herself. Yes, he'd totally deserved what Hunter had just done after saying all those things about her and boasting about "Mercy's goodies."

Mercy.

Hunter's eyelids flew open and she rushed through the living room and into the kitchen. Mercy sat at the breakfast nook on the cushy bench she and their mother had reupholstered in a swirling sixties-style lime green patterned velvet. Stacks of grimoires littered the table, pink sticky notes sprouting from the pages like petals.

Hunter set the bottle of insecticide on the counter and leaned against the kitchen island, feigning nonchalance, although she couldn't keep from picking at the jagged points of her nails. "You okay?" The casualness she'd stapled to her tone came out brassy and flat. Hunter clenched her teeth. The last thing she wanted to do was push her sister back over the edge and watch her fall into another vast, unending ocean of grief. She wasn't sure if she could do the spell again. She wasn't sure if she should.

Mercy cupped her steaming coffee mug with both hands and lifted it to her lips. "Yep. I'm good." Her gaze never quite settled on Hunter as Mercy took a sip and set her mug back down on the table.

Hunter's stomach hardened. "Are you sure? You seem—"

"Excited?" Mercy stared right at her this time, her moss-colored eyes challenging and forceful.

Guilty. Hunter's swallow was thick, a stone sliding through her chest and thudding into the hollow of her stomach.

"Hey, come here." Mercy patted the empty space at the head of the table and took another drink.

Hunter's footsteps were silent. She wouldn't ask for the truth and her sister wouldn't offer. Mercy had won, and they both knew it.

"I've figured out the spell we need to fix the trees." Mercy plucked a weathered grimoire from one of the stacks, shoved another pile to the side, and placed the manual of magic between them on the table. "The whole drought *and* flood cherry tree business gave me an idea." She drummed her fingers against the cracked cover and continued, "We need to mix together two health-boosting spells and add a little of our own magic for protection."

Hunter's face heated as she eyed the spray bottle. Mercy had done real research, magical research. All Hunter had done was google *kill tree worms.* She hid her hands under the table and resumed picking at her nails. But it could be as simple as applying the unpronounceable insecticide to the trees. Things didn't always have to be super complicated, and just because they were witches didn't mean they had to use magic to solve their problems. Magic couldn't fix everything. Abigail Goode was still gone.

Mercy opened the book to one of the marked pages and ran her fingers over the old, loopy cursive. "It says here that Janet Goode cut a stang and used it to channel healing energy into the trees when they were damaged by drought."

"Stang?" Hunter leaned forward and studied the illustration their ancestor had drawn at the bottom of the page. The ink had smeared, but Hunter could still make out the long, thin branch forked at the end like a snake's tongue. The note scrawled next to the knotted branch read, *Most powerful when cut and carved from a living being. Remember to thank the tree, for we do not understand their sacrifice and we cannot feel their pain.*

"Janet was a Green Witch, too." Mercy said it as if she and their great-great-grandmother had just exchanged texts and were now best friends and new members of an elite social club.

Hunter had yet to read the grimoire of a cosmic witch or one who had chosen a god instead of a goddess. She smoothed her pendant between her fingers and continued to study the drawing. This wasn't the first thing that made her different, and it definitely wouldn't be the last. She slipped her hand back under the table and pulled on a hangnail. She winced when she tore into fresh skin.

Mercy filled the space with the sweet scent of lilacs as she brushed her hair over her shoulders and glanced back down at the illustration. "I thought I'd use the oak that shades our cemetery."

Hunter balled her hands to hide her raw nailbeds and set her fists on the table. "If age plays into it, then that should make the stang even more powerful."

"That's what I figured." Mercy pulled another sticky note–filled grimoire from a different pile and set it open on top of her bff Janet's. "And this is the spell Gertrude Goode did after the entire state flooded in the 1800s."

Hunter read the passage and nodded. "It's really just a blessing ritual. Like what Mom does—" She squeezed her fists, rejoicing in the flash of pain that shot out from her scabbed palm. *"Did* every spring for the garden."

"It feels like a good omen, you know? Like it's what she would want us to do." A smile plumped Mercy's cheeks and her eyelids hung heavy. She was gone for a moment, lost in the silent breath of a memory. "So, yeah." Mercy licked her lips and flashed that childlike smile at her sister before refocusing on the book. "Then I'll add my Awake and Alive Oil and you can add your charged moonstones, and we'll douse the trees with it."

Hunter's attention was pulled back to the white-and-green bottle waiting on the counter. "How do you feel about *really* mixing science and magic?" Her chair groaned as she got up and hurried to the counter. "We're twenty-first-century witches, let's make twenty-first-century magic." She set the bottle in the only space between Mercy and the grimoires. "I know insecticide is, well, *killing,* and our magic is, you know, *not,* but—"

"H! You're totally right. We're modern witches and can use modern science to help us." Then she paused, chewing her bottom lip. "But which tree do we go to first?"

Hunter's fingers tingled as she and Mercy watched the pantry door creak open. It was their mom! It had to be. She was there, showing them the way. Hunter sprinted to the pantry, pulled out her rusted stepladder, and climbed to the top. Her palms heated as she gathered her tarot deck and jumped from the step stool. She untied the velvet azure satchel she kept her most prized witchy possession in and nearly bumped into Mercy on the way to the kitchen island.

"It was Abigail, wasn't it?" Mercy asked as she bounced in place next to Hunter. "I knew she would never leave us."

Hunter spread her deck out on the counter. The pearlescent silver backs of the cards showed the current waxing gibbous phase of the moon and would change each day, becoming most powerful and accurate on the day of the full moon. "We love you, Mom." Hunter breathed and flipped over the first card.

Nineteen

Hunter studied the card she'd turned over. "Huh, that's interesting. Not where I would guess we'd start, but the cards don't lie." On it was an illustration of a wide river, muddy with rich, brown silt framed by lush green banks. The vibrant colors stood out next to the moonshine silver of the backs of the rest of the deck like a Waterhouse painting hanging in the middle of a Jackson Pollock exhibit.

Mercy squinted at the card, trying to figure out what was wrong with the logs that bobbed in clumps in the river. "Um, H, what tree does that mean?"

"Easy. The hippo-filled river is the Nile, which means we need to start at the Egyptian tree, of course."

"Oh, yeah, *of course.*"

Hunter raised a brow at her sister.

Mercy lifted her hands in surrender. "I didn't mean anything except that I'm glad you're the Cosmic Witch 'cause I'm hopeless at tarot." She looked over her shoulder at the big clock in the foyer. "So, it's just a little after three thirty. I'm pretty sure I can cut and carve a stang and, with your help, get all the stuff we need for the spells together by dusk."

From the stairway they heard a long, drawn-out yawn. Xena turned the corner into the kitchen area as she stretched and yawned again. She was still wearing their mom's fluffy bathrobe. Her hair stood out around her face like the mane of an electrocuted lion.

"Good morning, kittens," she said between yawns.

"Xena, it's afternoon," said Mercy.

Xena shrugged as she headed to the fridge. "That's human time. In cat time it's morning whenever we awaken. Hunter, love, did you get me more of that extra-thick cream and delectable tuna?"

"Yeah. Cream's in the fridge. Tuna's in the pantry."

Xena's head swiveled around and her eyes skewered Hunter's. "You remembered to get me albacore, didn't you? You know I won't eat common tuna."

"Xena, we *all* know that. You're the only carnivore living in a house of vegetarian witches," Mercy said, then went on, as she continued to list what she and her sister would need to collect for the tree spell.

Xena sighed as she made her way languidly to the pantry and began pawing—literally—through the canned goods. "Yes, I am aware of your strange dietary predilections. It is the only thing my Abigail and I ever crossed words about. Ah! Here it is! Delicious albacore." She carried the can to Hunter and plopped it down in front of her. "Do be a dear and open it for me."

"How about I show you how to open it yourself. It's really easy." Hunter stood and started for the electric can opener that sat in the corner of the kitchen counter between the coffee maker and the blender.

"Oh, no, thank you, kitten. I loathe electric appliances. What if I broke a nail?" Xena batted a hand at Hunter dismissively while she peered down at the cards. Her gaze shifted from the one face-up. "Oh, excellent! You've decided on a spell *and* you'll be beginning at the Egyptian tree."

Mercy glanced up at her. "Am I the only one confused by tarot?"

"Yes!" Xena and Hunter said together.

Xena slid onto the bench seat and licked the back of her hands, then smoothed them through her crazy hair as she leaned into Mercy and read her notes. "A stang! That's a rather good idea. Very powerful in the hands of the right witch."

Mercy paused in her list making. "Am I the right witch?"

"Of course, kitten." Xena licked the back of her hand again and tried to smooth a strand of Mercy's hair.

Mercy backed out of her reach. "Xena, it's not cool when you do that."

"I'm just trying to help you look your best. You're rather disheveled." Xena hesitated and sniffed in Mercy's direction. Her yellow eyes widened. "Mercy Anne Goode, you smell like—"

"Nothing that's your business!" Mercy said quickly, super grateful that the whirring of the can opener kept her sister from hearing their exchange. She gathered her sticky notes so that when Hunter turned with the open can of tuna Mercy held them out to her. "Could you gather these things for me while I cut the stang? Then we'll meet in my greenhouse and put everything together."

"Sure, Mag," Hunter said, and took the open can of tuna to Xena.

"You do not think I'm going to eat from a *can,* do you, Hunter? Your mother is no longer with us, but we have not yet deteriorated into barbarism."

This time Mercy and Hunter shared their eye roll. "Perish the thought," Hunter murmured, detouring to the cabinet that held Abigail's collection of bone china.

"I suppose you want us to pour the cream for you, too?" Mercy asked, though she'd already taken a wine goblet from another cabinet.

"I do so love it when my kittens take care of me," said Xena, smiling and making a humming sound that was eerily purr-like.

Mercy had to smile, too, when she and her sister put the bowl of tuna—albacore with a small silver fork—and the crystal goblet of cream in front of Xena, who forked through the tuna delicately, still purr-humming with pleasure.

"Now, shoo, kittens!" Xena said, "Get ready for your spell. And remember, as you gather the items, hold your intention. That was one of the reasons my Abigail was such a powerful witch. She was wonderful at setting intentions."

Hunter read the list Mercy had given her. "These things are all in Mom's pantry, right?"

Mercy nodded. "Yeah, but I think we should add fresh herbs along with the oils made from them. The rosemary, mint, and thyme are in the garden. Want me to get them?"

"Nah, I'll harvest them for you and wash them. I need to cleanse the moonstones while I add intention to them anyway. Plus, you'll be busy carving the stangs," said Hunter.

"Stangs? As in more than one?" Mercy's fingers drummed against the old grimoire she held. "You really think we can't use the same one for each tree?"

Hunter opened her mouth to answer, but Xena interceded before she could speak. "You must have unique spellwork items for each tree. The power needs to be fresh and focused—not shared. Think of the Egyptian tree only as you prepare. Once you are successful with healing that tree, then you shift your intent to the next."

"But shouldn't we be moving quicker?" Hunter asked. "The trees are getting worse and worse."

"Which is why you must concentrate on one at a time. Do not fragment your powers. Be clear. Be strong. Be decisive. That is the advice your mother would give you. If you're in a hurry stop complaining and get to work." Xena poured the cream from the wine goblet over the tuna, dipped her head, and began to lap delicately at it.

"Gross, Xena!" Hunter disappeared into the pantry.

"Oh, bloody hell that's disgusting." Mercy gagged as she hurried out the back door and headed for the pretty little greenhouse that had been an early birthday gift from Abigail.

Mercy stood the ladder against the wide trunk of the ancient oak that had watched over the Goode Cemetery for more than two centuries.

She'd fashioned a strap around the well-sharpened hedge trimmers, which she slung over her shoulder, much like her giant boho purse. Before she began to climb the ladder Mercy went to the tree and pressed both of her hands against her trunk. She breathed deeply, catching the scent of the newly blooming lilac bushes, big as trees, that framed the little wrought-iron fence enclosing the cemetery. She listened carefully, hearing the cardinals that loved the oak so much, as well as the whirring of dragonfly wings as the helicopter-like insects darted from the water feature that decorated the other side of their spacious backyard. And then Mercy felt it—the inhale and exhale of the mighty tree that vibrated softly against her palms.

"Hi there, Mother Oak." Mercy spoke with familiarity to the tree because she knew the tree well. She'd grown up in her shade and spent uncounted hours in the deep V where the massive boughs first split from the trunk, reading and hiding from weekend chores. Mercy's lips lifted in remembrance. "It's me again. Mercy. I need your help today. I'm going to cast a heal-and-protect spell over the Egyptian palms, and a stang will channel the energy of the spell. So I need your permission to harvest a living bough. I brought wax to seal the wound." She paused and patted one of the deep pockets in her dress that held a small candle and a box of matches. "And I'll be very careful. I wouldn't ask if it wasn't important. May I have your permission, Mother Oak?" Mercy pressed her palms more firmly against the skin of the oak, closed her eyes, and opened herself.

She didn't have to wait long for the tree's response. Almost immediately the bark against her palms warmed and Mercy was flooded with a wave of affection. She imagined it was a lot like being engulfed in a hug by a grandma.

"Thank you, Mother Oak. I promise to use your energy only for good and will tend to the wound I cause you." She decided not to mention that if the spell was successful she'd be back four more times. The faithful old tree probably wouldn't mind, but still . . .

Carefully, Mercy climbed the ladder, thinking of their childhood when Hunter used to boost her up to the lowest branches. She'd swing her legs hard and scramble into the arms of the oak, where she'd spend hours reading or just absorbing the warmth and strength and love of the tree. As her thoughts turned to Hunter, the breeze, which had been gentle and warm, changed—cooled—and brushed insistently against Mercy's skin. She shivered suddenly—like a dark god had walked over her grave.

God, not goddess . . .

The feeling of foreboding was so thick—so real—that Mercy paused partway up the ladder as thoughts she'd repressed for days flooded free. "Oh, Freya," she whispered. "Are you telling me that I've been right to worry about Hunter's choice of a god instead of a goddess? Is Tyr the reason our powers aren't strong enough to keep the trees healthy? Could you show me a sign—something I can understand better than symbols from a tarot deck? Something a Green Witch would get?" Mercy drew a deep breath and opened her mind to her beloved goddess, Freya.

Nothing.

Absolutely nothing came to her except the familiar sounds and scents of Grandma Oak.

Mercy sighed. "Okay, well, I promise to pay attention in case you want to send me an omen."

The warm breeze returned and Mercy shook herself, wondering if she'd imagined the cold and the foreboding. She chewed her lip contemplatively as she continued climbing.

When she got to the familiar fork in the tree, Mercy rested a moment. She centered herself again by breathing deeply. Then she focused on her intention.

I am here to harvest a bough for a magical stang that will channel healing and protective energy into the Egyptian palm trees.

Mercy recited the sentence over and over to herself as she pressed her back against the oak and let her gaze search the branches around her. Soon, her attention was captured by a thin branch growing, straight and strong, from one of the central boughs of the tree. It was forked and about an inch in diameter—and at the end, in the early spring leaves, was a circle of tangled mistletoe. Mercy grinned and nodded as she patted the skin of the bark affectionately. Mistletoe was a powerful magnifier of magic, and would be a great addition to her spell.

"That's perfect, Mother Oak! Thank you."

Mercy climbed out, straddling the thick arm like a horse, and used the shears to slice through the much smaller branch, letting it drop to the ground. Then she pulled out the candle, lit it, and dripped wax on the cut, sealing it to keep out insects and disease. She retraced her way back down the ladder and embraced the tree one last time, whispering her appreciation before she grabbed the branch with one hand and the ladder with the other. She hurried back to the greenhouse where she opened her well-organized tool chest and brought out the little folding knife she used to trim plants. Mercy kept it razor sharp so that it wouldn't cause the plant any more damage than necessary. With a sigh, she sat in the open doorway of the greenhouse and began to trim leaves as she thought about strengthening and healing the palms that guarded the gate to the Egyptian Underworld. She whittled the finishing strokes to create a spike on the bottom of the stang, and concentrated on her intention so fully that Hunter's voice made her jump.

"Hey, that looks really good!"

"Oh, bloody hell, you scared me," Mercy said.

"Sorry." Hunter sat beside her. She carried one of their mom's handwoven baskets, which she set by their feet. "Wow, you even got mistletoe."

"Yeah, Mother Oak was super generous today." Mercy touched the glossy, pointed leaves of the circle of mistletoe.

"I'm not a Green Witch," said Hunter, "but that seems like a good omen."

Mercy met her sister's gaze and nodded agreement. "A *really* good omen." She cleared her throat and added, "Hey, H, did you ever consider any other god, or goddess, to follow except for Tyr?"

Hunter's arched brows lifted in surprise. "No. Never. And that's a weird question. What makes you ask?"

Mercy shrugged. "I dunno. As I was climbing I was thinking about when we were little girls, before we thought about anything much except toys and tea parties and whatever."

Hunter snorted. "I never thought about tea parties. That was you. I always thought about books, but now you're totally the research queen."

Mercy smiled at her sister. "Sorry. That was a weird question. We shouldn't be thinking about the past right now. We should be concentrating on our spell. Speaking of—did you get all the items for my Awake and Alive Oil?"

"Yep!" Hunter opened the basket and pulled out the bottle of insecticide she'd purchased from the nursery and five vials of homemade oils, as well as the herbs she'd just harvested. Inside the basket there was also a handful of milky stones that glowed softly against the square of black velvet Hunter had lined the basket with and the sapphire-colored pouch that held her tarot.

"Awesome! Let's mix them together and then add the insecticide." Mercy frowned as she stared at the insecticide. "Hang on. This is organic, right?"

"Of course. Mag, I'm not a Green Witch, but I'm also not stupid."

"Yeah, yeah, sorry. I'm just being super careful because I want everything to be perfect. Speaking of, I have the perfect glass bottle for our oil."

Hunter followed Mercy through the glass door of the greenhouse. Abigail had built her this incredibly awesome gift several weeks ago for Mercy to fill with young plants to transplant to their vast gardens. It was already alive with hanging ferns, a tray of thriving herbs, baby tomato sprouts, and an entire shelf of happily blooming orchids.

"It smells really good in here." Hunter gently touched a wide frond of one of the hanging plants.

"Thanks, it's mostly the honeysuckle over there. I coaxed them to bloom early. Here it is!" Mercy held up a glass bottle that was the color of the ocean, like a luminous ball sealed with a tan atomizer bulb just waiting to be squeezed.

"That's pretty," Hunter said.

"Yeah, I found it in the back of Abigail's pantry. It makes me think of old-timey perfume bottles." Mercy took the top off the bottle before she placed it on the worktable. "Okay, let's do this together to make it stronger."

"Sounds good to me," agreed Hunter. "If you tell me what you need I'll hand the oils and herbs to you."

"And then you can add your insecticide at the end to fill up the bottle. Let's set our intention."

Somberly, the girls grounded themselves with three deep breaths—in and out.

"My intention is to heal the palm trees," said Mercy. "Please hand me rosemary oil."

Hunter passed her the vial of greenish-amber oil. "My intention is to protect the palm trees."

The girls worked efficiently, sharing that special bond with which they'd been born. They mixed rosemary, mint, orange, lemon, and thyme oils—and added fresh herbs to the bottle. Then Mercy passed the bottle to her sister, who poured the organic insecticide into it until it was completely full. She handed the bottle back to Mercy, who securely screwed the top on before tucking it safely within their basket. Mercy gathered the stang and the circle of mistletoe.

"Okay, I think we're ready," said Mercy.

"Me, too, but I feel like we're forgetting something," said Hunter.

Which was when Xena, still wearing the fluffy bathrobe, hair cascading in chaos around her shoulders, hurried out the back door of the house.

"Kittens! Oh, good, I caught you before you left. You need to do one more thing—ouch!" Xena lifted one of her bare feet and frowned at it as she brushed a rock from between her toes. "If I have to wear shoes I will *die.* Simply *die*!" She sat on the back porch steps and raised her foot to her mouth.

"Freya's cloak!" Mercy gasped. "Is she going to lick her foot?"

"Not while we're watching she's not. Xena! What was the one more thing?"

The cat person froze, blinked several times, and then dropped her foot. "Sorry, kittens. Being a human is very distracting. You need to make it rain."

"What?" The twins spoke together.

Xena sighed. "The Egyptian palms are in the middle of the park, correct?"

"Yeah," said Hunter.

"People will be there—even after dark. They have those horrid lights that do not allow cats to hunt at night at all. It's really very upsetting." She shook herself. "But that is not important tonight. What's important tonight is that you cast your spell without prying eyes. So—make it rain."

"Huh. She's right," Mercy said.

"Well, of course I am. Do you need me to remind you of a rain spell or—"

"No, we've got it," said Mercy. "All we need is dried heather."

"And fern leaves," finished Hunter.

"Exactly," said Xena. "I shall leave you to it." She stood and picked her way carefully to the door. "Blessed be, kittens."

"Blessed be," Mercy and Hunter responded automatically.

"I'll get the fern fronds from the greenhouse," said Mercy.

"And I just saw the dried heather hanging in the back of the pantry," Hunter said. "I'll get that and the matches and meet you in the garage. It'll be easier to call the rain to the park if we do the spell there."

"Okay. See you in a sec."

"Hey, Mag?"

Mercy hesitated at the door to the greenhouse and glanced over her shoulder at her sister.

"She was going to lick her foot!" Hunter said with a giggle.

"Right?! That cat!" Mercy shook her head, but grinned and felt a lot lighter as her sister's laughter drifted through the evening air after her.

Twenty

Hunter parked in a corner of the lot that was made shadowy by several tall, stately white oaks. The girls briskly went to the largest of the trees, whose trunk was broad enough to conceal them both from the people who were jogging around the track and playing kickball on one of the softball diamonds.

The spell was simple, but effective—and one of the first spells Abigail had taught her daughters. Mercy could hear her mom's voice lifting from her memory as Hunter struck the match against the rough side of the box. *Girls, a witch always needs a good make-it-rain spell. We must keep our Earth Mother verdant and fertile—and without rain that is impossible.*

In the car on the way there Mercy had braided the dry heather with the lush fronds of the maidenhair fern. As Hunter lifted the long, ceremonial match, she took the braid from her bottomless purse and held it to the flame. Together the twins invoked.

"Make it rain—make it rain—make it rain!" Three times, just as Abigail had taught them.

The entwined heather and fern began smoking and Mercy traced a pentagram in the air as they repeated thrice again, "Make it rain—make it rain—make it rain!"

All along Mercy's arms her tiny hairs lifted as power billowed with the smoke. The air felt noticeably thicker as it filled with magically induced humidity. The scent of spring rain tickled Mercy's nose until she sneezed.

"It's working!" Hunter fist-pumped.

Above them, the white oak swayed in a new breeze that carried the scent of heather and fern and rain. Thunder rumbled and the girls smiled at each other as they put out the smoking brand in the dirt at the base of the tree and then went back to the car and waited.

It only took fifteen minutes for the sky to open and rain to begin leaking from the billowing clouds.

"And there they go!" Hunter pointed at the last of the people who were running for their cars as thunder rumbled overhead.

"Abigail would be very pleased at how quickly that happened," said Mercy.

"Another good omen?"

Mercy nodded thoughtfully. "H, I hope so. Okay, ready to get wet?"

"Absolutely."

Alone in the parking lot, the twins gathered their spellwork supplies and headed to the center of the park where, unbeknownst to the residents of Goodeville, the clump of doum palms had protected the town from ancient Egyptian monsters for generations. Close up Mercy saw that the damage they'd glimpsed from afar the night before was worse than she'd thought. Only the uppermost palm fronds were still green and healthy. The rest were dried husks that looked like brown knife blades jutting out from thick-armed boughs. The trunks were odd, and nothing like any other Illinois tree. Mercy had long thought they looked like someone had woven together gray corn husks to form the skin of the trees. *Well, tree,* she automatically corrected herself. Though it looked like there were five big palms placed in a close circle around one another, they were actually one tree with five shoots growing from it. Abigail had told the girls that when she was a child there had only been four shoots—that the smaller of the five had sprung up when she was in elementary school. *I hope you feel healthy enough after this to sprout another tree,* Mercy silently told the doum as she pressed her hand against its rough bark. Then she turned and got to work.

The rain drizzled lazily as Mercy wiped her face with the back of her sleeve and unslung her bag from across her shoulder to drop it beside Hunter's basket. "I'm going to put the stang here." She carried the forked bough directly in front of the clump of trees. "Then I'll drape some of the mistletoe over it."

"Okay, while you're doing that I'll set a protective circle with my moonstones."

"Sounds perfect," said Mercy as she pressed the pointed tip of the stang against the hard-packed ground.

"And remember our intention—to heal and protect," said Hunter as she began to circle the palm, dropping a moonstone every three steps.

"To heal and protect," Mercy murmured. She pushed the stang against the dirt until it stood straight and strong, forked end up. Then she went to the basket and gathered the mistletoe circle and returned to the stang. There she carefully unwound the prickly ivy so that she could form three separate circles of green. Two of the circles she rested at the base of the stang. The third Mercy draped around the stang's fork so that it looked like a slender crown atop a very skinny stick drawing of a person.

Hunter rejoined her then and Mercy took the bottle of potent ancient herbs and modern insecticide from the basket. She swirled the bottle, mixing the oils. Inside the blue bottle the potion took on a moss-colored cast that appeared to be lit from within.

"It looks good," said Hunter.

"It *is* good. A mixture of us."

"And a mixture of tradition and today," added Hunter.

"Let's do this." Mercy bent and picked up both of the mistletoe wreaths. She handed one to her sister. The other she lifted and said, "I crown you with the strength and wisdom of sacred mistletoe." Hunter bowed her head so that Mercy could place the living wreath on it.

Then Hunter invoked, "I crown you with the protection and guidance of sacred mistletoe." Mercy bowed her head and Hunter placed the green circlet there.

Mercy held the bottle aloft. "I'll make the first circle, spraying as high as I can with the atomizer."

Hunter nodded. "I'll channel our intention through the stang and take the second circle."

"Perfect," said Mercy. "Just mimic what I say in your own words. Let your intuition guide you."

"Got it. I'll let Tyr guide me. He'll give me the right words."

Mercy felt a jolt at her sister's confidence in her god—the being who could be responsible for all of this—but forced the doubts from her mind and made herself refocus. *Protection and healing . . . healing and protection . . .*

The twins faced each other and breathed together—in and out—three times. Grounded to the earth, Mercy was filled with calm. Then, Hunter walked to the stang. She turned to the trees and grasped the forked ends of the green bough with her hands, and raised her head as if she spoke directly to the cosmos—a channel between earth and sky.

"Heal and protect . . . protect and heal . . . heal and protect . . . protect and heal."

With Hunter's prayer litany as background magic, Mercy began to circle the trees. She talked to the palms and her voice, amplified by her connection with the earth and the ley lines that pulsed deep beneath her feet, sounded so powerful that Mercy was reminded of her amazing mother. *"I call on the Powers of Wind and Earth—of Sun and Rain. By tree and bough, leaf and shoot, with all my heart and the workings of my hands, I bless this palm with life and love—health and growth—protection and strength."*

Mercy felt the magic swirl around her. With a feather-like caress, it shivered across her skin. Heat from the mistletoe crown flowed from her third eye and cascaded throughout her body. With every step—every word of the spell—she squeezed the atomizer bulb and misted the Awake and Alive Oil onto the dying leaves of the suffering tree. And as she did the scent of sulfur billowed with the rain-touched breeze. It burned her throat, but Mercy ignored it and joined Hunter at the stang.

Reverently, Hunter took the bottle and Mercy placed her hands on the forked ends of the stang just below the sacred mistletoe, and focused on being a channel for healing energy to flow through her body and into the earth all the way down to the roots of the ancient palms. Her hands warmed and a soft, moss-colored light illuminated the newly cut oak bough. Excitement fluttered through Mercy—*it was working!*

"Protect and heal . . . heal and protect . . . protect and heal . . . heal and protect," Mercy invoked while Hunter began her circle around the trees, spraying the potion onto its gray bark and browned leaves while she spoke her own invocation in a voice filled with power and confidence.

"I call on the Powers of Moon and Stars—of Sky and Earth. By tree and bough, leaf and shoot, with all my heart and the workings of this modern world we love so well, I bless this palm with strength and healing—growth and health—life and love."

Hunter rejoined Mercy at the stang and placed the empty bottle at their feet. Then Mercy pulled the staff from the ground. Holding it in her right hand she grasped Hunter's hand in her left and together they strode to the tree until they stood within touching distance of it. The rain had slowed to mist. The sulfuric smell was still there, but fainter. It had been diluted by the sweetness of herbs and citrus—and the sharp scent of modern magic.

Mercy lifted the stang.

"I honor you, earth's child. I honor your growth—your boughs and leaves

and thick, mighty trunk. I thank you for your protection and your energy and your spirit—may whatever ails you be gone, and never return. And may you thrive always. Blessed be!"

"Blessed be!" Hunter shouted joyfully.

The green glow intensified, and with magically enhanced power, Mercy drove the stang into the ground at the base of the tree.

There was a terrible sound like the ripping of a curtain, and all five trunks began to shiver. The ground quaked under their feet, causing the girls to stagger backward. And then the air quivered, and a veil that had until then been invisible, lifted from the center of the clump of trees to reveal a figure. His back was to them, but he whirled around, raising a spear, ready to throw.

"Foul demons! Vile monsters!" The creature lifted a shield and took a wide stance. The air before him rippled and glistened as if he were inside a fishbowl looking out, but that semipermeable barrier didn't make him appear less menacing as the power he exuded blasted at them. Then, like a bizarre version of Gandalf the Grey, he shouted, "You shall not pass!"

Together Mercy and Hunter lurched back another step, clinging to each other's hand like they needed an anchor to reality—which they definitely did because the creature in front of them defied any sense of the real that they had ever known.

His body appeared human and male. He was powerfully built. The short, woven leather skirt he wore wrapped low around his waist, and the golden protective plates that adorned his shins and forearms left most of that body exposed. He looked like a bronze statue—except for his head and neck, which were terrifying. He glared at them from behind the veil that separated his world and theirs and though the barrier between them caused his image to come in and out of focus, almost like it was pixilated, his raised spear and shield were a palpable threat.

"Tyr! What in all the hells is that?" Hunter pressed closer to Mercy.

"I don't bloody know, but I'm not going to let it get us!" Mercy closed the few feet between them and her bag that rested on the wet ground beside her sister's basket. Never taking her eyes from the creature, she frantically felt around inside her purse until her hand closed on the pepper-spray gun she always carried with her. Mercy broke the trigger seal. She held it in a two-handed grip in front of her, just like she'd seen Mariska Hargitay do a million times on *SVU.* She swallowed back the bile of her fear and began walking toward the creature that stood in the center of the glistening trees.

"Stay back! This is our world! You do not belong here!" Mercy's voice was fierce with the adrenaline that surged through her body.

Then Hunter was there beside her, so close their shoulders pressed together. Her sister was holding part of a fallen tree branch over her head, like a club.

"We guard this gate! And we are not going to let you come into our world!" Hunter sounded powerful and confident and Mercy felt a rush of pride in her sister.

The creature tilted its monstrous head. His image wavered as he appeared to study the girls with large, almond-shaped eyes that were the color of fertile earth. They were the only things in that unbelievable face recognizably human. The rest of it was definitely reptilian—like a crocodile and a dragon had been mixed together. Small, onyx scales glistened smoothly up a long, sinuous, hooded neck to a crest of crimson horns that sprouted from his head down his back. His mouth was a muzzle lined with rows of dangerous fangs that he had suddenly stopped baring at them.

"You—you are Gatekeepers?" His voice was bizarrely human—deep and masculine—and even though the barrier between worlds made their view of him go in and out of focus, his words came to them clear and strong.

Mercy kept the pepper-spray gun pointed at him. "We are. Who are you?"

The creature put the spear down, so that its flattened edge rested by his feet, which Mercy noted, were dressed in golden sandals. "I am Khenti Amenti, son of the immortal warrior Upuaut, Gate Guardian of the Realm of Osiris. And you?"

Mercy lowered the pepper-spray gun, sent a silent prayer to her goddess, *please give me the right words,* cleared her throat, and said, "I am the Green Witch, Mercy, daughter of the mighty Kitchen Witch, Abigail, Keeper of the Five Gates of Goodeville."

Beside her Hunter also lowered her club-like weapon and spoke with calm surety, like introducing herself to a half-man, half-dragon was something she did all the time. "And I am the Cosmic Witch, Hunter, also daughter of the magnificent Kitchen Witch, Abigail, and like my sister I am Keeper of the Five Gates of Goodeville."

"So we three are demi-gods, Gate Guardians between the realms of the worlds," said the creature. He took a small step back so that when he bowed his massive head it didn't cross the flickering barrier before him. "Well met, Witches."

Mercy was standing there, mouth flopped open, but Hunter recovered more quickly. She nudged her with an elbow before executing something that looked like a bow and a curtsey had had a baby. "Merry meet," said Hunter.

Mercy quickly follow suit as she, too, dipped her head and her knees and murmured, "Merry meet."

The creature put his shield down beside him. His body language instantly appeared more relaxed with the ease of his wide shoulders and the way he clasped his hands loosely in front of him.

"Forgive me for threatening you. This gate has been problematic, and when it called to me I assumed it had continued to deteriorate, perhaps allowing a beast from another realm to enter."

"Wait, the gate called you?" Mercy asked.

"And what does problematic mean?" added Hunter.

He was looking back and forth between the girls, and his eyes suddenly widened. "You are twins!"

Mercy squelched the urge to roll her eyes. "Yeah, we are." Then she added impulsively, "What are you?"

The creature's head swiveled to her and through the glowing barrier it looked as if he were a bizarre deep-sea monster moving through water. "As I said, I am Khenti Amenti, son of the immortal warrior Upuaut, Gate Guardian of the Realm of Osiris."

"No, she means *what* are you." Hunter spoke up. "Not *who*. In our world there are no people who have the heads of, um, not people."

"How odd," said Khenti.

He raised his hand and waved it in front of his reptilian face. The air before him swirled with mist, dark as his onyx scales. Mercy squinted to try to see what he was doing, but her vision of him was just too unstable, though when the mist finally cleared she blinked rapidly and her eyes managed to focus well enough through the fishbowl-like glimpse into his world to see that in place of the dragon was the head and neck of a man—*actually, not a man,* Mercy thought. *He doesn't look much older than us.* Even though his body was football-star strong and tall and muscular, his face was young and smooth. Now that the dragon head was gone, Mercy decided his skin wasn't bronze like a statue, but more acorn-colored with a golden tint like it'd been kissed, a lot, by the summer sun.

"Thanks," Hunter said. "That face is easier for us to understand."

His dark brows lifted. "You truly have no demi-gods *or* gods who use the visage of beasts in your world?"

"We truly do not," said Mercy.

"Seriously," said Hunter. "Now, what about the gate calling you and disintegrating?"

As he spoke the air between them continued to pulse and glowed, bubble-like, in the center of the trees. Even though Mercy tried to see what was behind him, it was too obscured by the strange barrier to allow her to make out more than darkness highlighted with splotches of colors. "I heard voices. I understand now they were yours,

Gatekeepers. I could not catch the words, but I felt drawn to the gate. Though I will admit I have recently remained nearby as I could tell it was weakening."

"How could you tell?" asked Mercy.

"In my world it is an orb—a glowing sphere—in a far corner of Osiris's realm, the Underworld. It is usually colored brilliantly with violets and silvers, turquoise, sapphire, and the pink of a perfect lotus bloom, but over the past several phases of the moon the colors have changed, darkened and muddied. And the scent." He wrinkled his straight nose. "It reeks of decay. So, I have remained near, standing guard so that none of those contained here can escape—and no creatures from other realms enter."

Mercy felt a shiver of fear finger down the nape of her neck. "That can happen? I mean, our gate is sick, too, but it's still standing." She gestured at the cluster of trees he'd materialized within. "These palms keep our side of the gate closed. They're not doing great, but they're still alive. Can things go back and forth even now?"

"Yes, but only if a Gatekeeper is not strong enough to stop them." He stood taller. "I am strong enough."

"That's what you heard," said Hunter. "We were casting a spell to strengthen and heal the palms."

Mercy nodded. "Yeah, we thought if we could heal the trees, the gate would be better, too. Does your side of the gate look any different since we cast the healing spell?"

The young Egyptian sighed and ran a hand through his thick, dark hair. "No, it does not."

"You called us demons and monsters," said Mercy. "Why did you assume we were enemies?"

The warrior shrugged his broad shoulders as their view of him continued to shift and pixilate. "The only beings who wish to escape from Osiris's realm are evil, those who are being punished for the wrongs they committed on earth. I assumed it was the same in your world."

"This isn't our Underworld. This is just the regular mortal realm," explained Mercy. "There are lots of different kinds of people here. Most of them aren't monsters at all."

"But you have more Gatekeepers like yourselves who protect your world, do you not?"

Hunter picked at her thumb. "Um. No. We're pretty much it."

His smooth brow wrinkled in confusion. "Did you not say you are guardians of *five* gates?"

"Yeah," said Mercy. "There're all here—in our town."

"But your mother goddess, the mighty, magnificent Abigail—she must aid you in your guardianship."

Mercy shifted from foot to foot. "She did. She died. Not long ago."

"The other gates—do they also lead to Underworlds like Osiris's realm, or do they open to mortal realms as does this one to yours?" He fired the question at them, his powerful voice in direct contrast to his wavering image.

"No," Hunter answered. "They also lead to Underworld realms like yours."

His eyes widened and he shook his head quickly, causing the barrier in front of him to shiver, like a stone dropped into a glowing pool of water. "No, that is *not* good."

"Why? What's wrong?" Mercy fisted her hands to stop them from shaking.

"It will be the same in the other Underworld realms as it is in mine. If the gates sicken there will be creatures—vile, evil things—that wish to escape their punishment. If they enter your world they will devastate your realm and spread death and chaos with them."

"Ohmygod." Hunter turned to Mercy. "The Fenrir! I looked it up after it killed Mom. He tried to devour the sun and swallowed Odin. One of Odin's sons killed him, sending him to the Norse Underworld for punishment."

Mercy's lips felt numb. "He was trying to escape. That's why he killed Abigail."

"Gatekeepers! Did he take on her form?"

"No, our mother killed him, and with her death she sealed the gate again. What do you mean, take on her form?" asked Mercy.

"That is the only way a creature can have a physical presence in the mortal realm after crossing through the barrier that divides worlds." He gestured at the bizarre veil that glowed and swirled in front of him. "We must possess the body of a being of that realm," said Khenti.

"Bloody hell! You mean wear them like a skin suit?"

He nodded. "Yes, exactly. The mortal's skin becomes a living disguise, even though the body will eventually deteriorate and they will have to choose another. That is why I remain close to our gate. Creatures must kill immediately upon entry to the other realm or they cannot remain."

Mercy grabbed Hunter's hand. "What if we cast a spell to block off the other trees and somehow keep everyone away until we figure this out?"

Hunter turned to Khenti. "Would that work? Would that give us some time?"

"Only if you can keep *all* living beings from the gates."

"You mean the creatures can take over a body that's not human?" Mercy's stomach felt sick. Again.

Khenti crossed his arms over his chest and nodded. "As you saw when first we met, many of us who exist in other realms are not fully human. It would not be difficult for an escapee to kill and then wear the body of a bird or mouse—snake or dog—or perhaps even an insect."

"Oh, shit. That's so, so bad," said Hunter.

Mercy thought she might puke. "Mr. Thompson—he was killed near the Greek tree."

"But Mr. Parrott wasn't," said Hunter. Mercy thought she looked super pale.

"He wouldn't have to be—not if whatever came out of that tree took someone else's body and is a murderer walking around in a good guy skin suit." Mercy met the Egyptian warrior's flickering gaze. "We think something from the Greek Underworld is loose in our town, killing our people. Can you help us?"

His shoulders slumped and he shook his head slowly. "I cannot, though I wish I could. Were I to cross the barrier between our worlds I would have to take on the form of someone in your realm. I, too, would have to kill to remain."

"We need to get to the Greek tree—and I mean *really* go to it this time." Hunter spoke quickly, breathlessly. "We have to figure out if something came through that gate."

"And if so, what," added Mercy. "And then we need to find out whose skin suit it's hiding in."

"Go! I give you my oath to stand guard at Osiris's gate. Nothing shall enter your world through here." Even through the shimmering divide his strength and commitment heartened Mercy.

"Thank you," Hunter said.

"I wish I could aid you more."

"Actually, you've helped us a lot," said Mercy.

Khenti smiled at her. *He's the most beautiful guy I've ever seen in my whole life.* The thought came to Mercy unbidden and she instantly pushed it aside as she felt her cheeks blaze with heat. *What in the bloody hell is wrong with me? Get it together, Mag! This isn't a time-travel rom-com!*

"That pleases me greatly." Khenti lifted his hand, passing it before his face again, which instantly shifted back to a ferocious dragon. He lifted his spear and shield. "I shall remain by the gate. Call if you have need of me again, Witches."

The air in front of him rippled, like heat rising from a boiling pot, and Khenti Amenti, Son of Upuant, Guardian of Osiris's Realm, disappeared along with the bubble that had contained him.

"That was the weirdest thing I've ever seen," said Hunter.

"I wish Abigail could've been here. She would've loved every second of it," Mercy said. "Well, except the whole creatures escaping and spreading death and destruction and chaos part."

Hunter was already picking up the basket. "Do we leave or take the stang?"

"Leave it. It might still work, right? And let's add our mistletoe crowns to the other one." Mercy went to the stang and draped her circle of mistletoe over it. "How long did they say it would take for the insecticide to kill the worms?"

"A week to ten days," said Hunter, mirroring her sister's actions.

"We might get lucky. Even though Khenti didn't see a change yet, it could still happen." Mercy said the words, but they sounded hollow even to her own ears.

Hunter nodded grimly. "Yeah, I hope so. But right now we need to get to the Greek tree."

As they hurried back to the car Mercy kept hearing the Egyptian warrior's words playing around and around in her memory. *The mortal's skin becomes a living disguise . . . The mortal's skin becomes a living disguise . . . The mortal's skin becomes a living disguise . . .*

Twenty-one

Petrichor, the earthy scent released when rain nourishes dry land, floated on the back of the cool breeze as Hunter parked the car on the gravel road near the olive tree. Hunter didn't follow Mercy as her sister charged from their mother's car into the tall grass, headed straight for the old tree. There was something in the breeze. Something more than the sweet smell. It was prickly and magical and it pulled her and her tarot in a different direction. Hunter kicked loose gravel as she walked along the side of the road, following her witchy senses.

Halfway to the tree, Mercy stopped. "H, where are you going?" she shouted, her hands in the air.

Hunter wanted to reply but thought better of it. The explanation would bring more questions than answers.

Hunter paused at the edge of the road near tire tracks from the sheriff's department vehicles that had been on the scene. Her breath caught as she raised her hand and pointed. "Over here," she called out to her sister and waded into the grass. The tall blades swayed around

Hunter's thighs and beads of water fell on her boots as the field shook free of the magical rainstorm.

Her mouth went dry and her fingers trembled as she walked through the tall, lush grasses that arched and bowed with the wind. Ahead, the grasses were crushed, flattened down long enough and by something heavy enough that the rich crimson imprint had remained even after its absence.

A wooden stake had been left behind, nestled in the ground, a scrap of yellow-and-black crime scene tape still stuck to it. When Hunter and Mercy had driven by two nights ago, the tape had been stretched around Earl Thompson's shiny red truck and extended out toward this spot. Had it not been so morbid, the whole thing would've made Hunter laugh. Silly non-magic folk trying to solve a problem that seemed more and more likely to be caused by an issue they couldn't understand much less know how to fix. But that's why Hunter and Mercy had come here: to find out if the failing gate had let something loose.

The tarot deck sizzled in her pocket as Hunter stood at the edge of the flattened red-stained grass. Earl Thompson had drawn his last breath here, had his last thought . . . What had it been? All Hunter could think about was this uneven outline his body had left. But that wasn't what he'd thought about, what kind of temporary destruction he'd leave behind. Maybe he'd thought about fear or fury or fate.

What had Hunter's mother thought when she'd lit herself on fire and left her daughters to face the world alone?

Mercy approached, her signature lilac scent catching Hunter's attention. "Don't we need to be closer to the gate?" Mercy pointed over her shoulder at the olive tree, its gnarled limbs reaching toward the last traces of clouds.

Hunter pressed the toe of her boot into the marred grass. "We have to do it here." Deep burgundy stained the earth like spilled wine. It was blood. *Human* blood. Earl Thompson's blood. Being here, this close to the scene of a crime, should make her feel *different*. Should make her feel *something*. The only things she felt were the power of the moon, the strength of Tyr, and the tarot cards burning a hole in her pocket. But those weren't emotions.

Hunter crouched down and held her hand over the bloodstain. Her palm prickled with energy. There was power in blood. That was obvious. Countries rose and fell by it. The empowered blood of kings and queens chose the heirs to the throne. But more important, more *powerful,* was the blood of their people. Shed enough of it and any tide would turn.

Their mother had never mentioned this power or the deliciously sweet way its energy lapped against each of Hunter's nerves with the steady seduction of waves on a beach. Hunter could be comfortable here, adding blood magic to her box of tools. After all, humans were made of stardust, so what was blood if not a liquid form of the cosmos?

Hunter slid her fingers along her smooth pendant and took her tarot deck out of the pocket of her oversized cardigan. The cards weren't actually hot, but their energy felt fiery, felt ready. She pulled them from their velvet pouch the same deep blue as the sky abandoned by the sun. She shielded her eyes and looked up at the azure blanket above. The moon had settled against the sun-bleached heavens like a water stain. Mother Moon was always watching, the caretaker as the sun slipped from existence each night.

Hunter ran her hand over the silver back of her deck. She felt Mercy behind her, stuffed full of questions and opinions. But this was Hunter's time to shine, and her Green Witch sister was so far out of her element that she'd sink without the safety raft of Hunter's spellwork.

"This is gross, H. Can't you work your magic anywhere else?" Mercy tented her arms and settled her hands on her hips. "Preferably at the tree since it's the actual root of the problem." Her smooth brow furrowed. "Pun not intended."

"This is a stronger site." How could Mercy not feel the energy rising from the stained earth? Hunter gripped her opal pendant. Maybe the earth hadn't called her to this spot. Maybe this was the guidance of her god. "Tyr led me here," she said and let the pendant fall back into place.

Mercy bit her lip. "Well . . ." There was that guilty look again. It wrinkled her round nose and pinched the corners of her eyes.

"You have to trust me, Mag."

"I do!" The words rushed out too quickly.

Hunter bit the inside of her cheek and turned back to the matter at hand. She'd figure out what was going on with Mercy later. Right now, magic called to her and she wouldn't keep it waiting. She situated her knees against the edge of the ring of blood and set the deck in the middle of the crushed and stained grass. Hunter didn't follow any specific tarot spreads, and neither did her cards. She did what felt right, what the deck asked her.

Reveal yourself, reveal yourself, reveal yourself. The intention chanted between her ears as she cut the deck with her right hand, rolled her amulet between the fingers of her left, and stacked the halves back together on the grass. A new set of cards was on top. The *right* set of cards.

Hunter released a measured exhale. One breath per action, one breath per question. It's what felt right, what the cards demanded. She turned over the first card and set it face-up next to the deck. She couldn't release the rest of her breath. The deck still called to her. She turned over another card and placed it face-up on the blood-stained grass. Her palm still itched, the tarot calling out for another turn, and Hunter flipped a third card. The feeling ceased and Hunter let loose the breath stored in her chest. The face of each card was milky white, held in blank suspense as they awaited further instruction. The cards would get their questions. And soon.

Another inhale and exhale to place the remaining cards on top of the velvet satchel Hunter had left on the ground outside the circle of blood.

Mercy squatted down next to Hunter. "There's nothing there," she whispered as if the cards would be offended by her comment.

Hunter's cheeks lifted with a grin. Knowing her tarot cards, they just might.

"They're waiting for questions." Hunter rubbed her palms together and exhaled as she held her hands over the three blank cards. This moment she took to double-check the readiness of her magic usually felt like warming her hands over a fire, comforting and soothing. But this time was different. This time was *more*—a fierce, blazing excitement that sent waves of need rippling from her fingertips to her toes and back again.

"We want to know if anything came through." Mercy continued to whisper. "That's what you're going to ask, right? Will all three cards tell you or—"

"Mag!" Hunter curled her hands into fists and rubbed them against her thighs. "I know what I'm doing. Let me do it in my own time."

Mercy chewed her bottom lip and nodded. "I'm just excited."

Hunter understood. Excitement dripped from her pores like sweat. She passed the back of her hand along her forehead. She needed to finish this spell and close the channels of power that lit her from the inside out.

Inhale. She pressed the fingertips of her right hand against the first card. *Exhale.* "Did a creature, a demi-god, come through this gate?"

A sound like splintering wood and the card's white face dissolved into the ghostly image of a creature hunched over, blurry fists pressed against the ground like a gorilla. Around it, each half of the split olive tree.

Mercy's brows lifted. "I'm taking that as a *yes.*"

Inhale. Hunter moved to the next card. *Exhale.* "This *thing* that came through, did it hurt anyone?"

Hunter already knew the answer. Whatever it was had killed Earl Thompson. Tyr wouldn't have led her to his blood if it hadn't.

Smoke rose from the ground beneath the cards, beneath the blood, beneath the flattened grasses. The earth sizzled and the crushed grass turned black and formed a perfect imprint of where the life had gone out of old Earl Thompson.

Mercy shrieked and hurled herself backward. She landed in the tall grass with a muffled *thud.* She held out a trembling hand and pointed at the space where she'd squatted only moments before, her jaw bobbing open and closed—the words just out of reach.

A fresh wave of smoke snaked under Hunter's nose as she followed her sister's outstretched hand. Hunter blinked once, twice, three times, her brain unwilling to process the image it received. A set of shoe prints were burned into the ground next to Hunter—*next to* the seared memory of Mr. Thompson's corpse.

Panic tightened Hunter's chest and she coughed into the magical smoke that dissipated with each gust of spring air. "Mag—" Hunter stared at the cards. The second face had changed. The image of a gnarled branch bisected the card. Above the limb, a skull nested under the smooth arch of a sickle. Below it, a puddle of skin, its face and arms slack and empty like it'd been stripped from its frame and dropped amidst the grass.

The mortal's skin becomes a living disguise.

"It wasn't just Mr. Thompson. Someone else was here." Hunter motioned to the footprints scorched into the earth. "Someone else was taken."

Ecru grass dusted Mercy's cheeks as she crawled around to Hunter's other side where the grass was unmarred by the tarot and whatever creature had slipped through the crumbling gate. "Will your cards tell you what did this?"

That's what the last card was for. It had to be. It would tell them exactly who to look for and then they could begin to put this whole mess behind them.

Inhale. Hunter's fingers found the third card. *Exhale.* "The creature, who is it?"

Mercy gripped Hunter's arm as the sisters waited for the truth.

A gurgling sound like a growl through wet paint while images slowly flicked along the card's surface as if it were scrolling through a digital contacts list: a woman with snakes piled atop her head like hair; a three-headed beast; a female rising from ocean waves, her hands cupped around her mouth; and a drooling beast with a single bulging eye and sparse hairs that stuck up from its lumpy head like question marks. The final image froze upon the face of the card.

"Oh, Freya!" Mercy pulled Hunter against her. "*His eyes are gone.* That's what Em said about her dad."

"And the sheriff said about Mr. Thompson." Hunter glossed her fingers over the image. "It's collecting eyes."

Mercy's breath left her lips in short quakes. "H-how do we stop him?"

Hunter lifted the card and squinted at the single eye glaring at her from the middle of the creature's broad forehead. *That* was the new question.

How on earth would Hunter and Mercy catch a Cyclops?

Twenty-two

Hunter passed the card to Mercy who flipped it over and examined its silver back. "So, that's it? I mean, your cards told us that it's the Cyclops, which is great, but he's not exactly walking around like this." She pointed to the strings of saliva dripping from the creature's chin and the lone eye it was best known for. "Can you do your, you know"—she waved her hand in front of Hunter as if polishing glass—"tarot thing again and ask the cards to be more specific this time?"

Hunter picked at a tender piece of skin hanging from her index finger. "That's not really how it works." She held her palm over the charred grass. "And I used up all the magic from this site." She plucked the card from Mercy's grasp. "Sometimes the tarot gives veiled answers. It would sort of be cheating if the cards just came out with a big arrow that pointed directly to what we need to know. Half of the magic is how the images are interpreted."

Mercy groaned and collapsed onto the tall grass. "It wouldn't be cheating. It would be answering the question you asked in a clear and direct manner." As she spoke, she held up her fawn hands. Her slender forearms had begun to freckle under the persistence of the spring sun. "When *I* do spellwork, I know whether it's been successful or not. If it has, I get results. If it hasn't . . . well, nothing usually happens. But that *nothing* always tells me *something.* This isn't a nothing or a something. It's just—"

"A star!"

"I guess it's a start, but my point is that it could be a better one."

"Not a *start.* A *star.*"

Mercy sat up as Hunter flipped the card around to face her. "I didn't notice it at first, but there's a star around his eye and another in his, um . . ."

Mercy squinted and tapped the Cyclops's left pec. "Scraggly chest hair?"

"Gross, but yes." Hunter looked at the card. "This is the answer. This is who the Cyclops is wearing."

"A star?" Mercy's brow remained pinched as she untangled a seedpod from her hair. "You think the Cyclops is parading around town in the skin suit of a star? No one famous has ever come to Goodeville."

"Sure, but there *are* famous people here." Hunter bit down on the rugged tip of her fingernail. *Locally* famous was super close to *famous* famous. She snapped off the point of her nail and rolled it along the tip of her tongue.

A star.

A star.

A star.

"Oh!" Mercy clapped, her green eyes widening. "What about that retired Bulls basketball guy?"

Hunter nodded, flooding with ideas of her own. "Or the news anchor who was a former Miss Illinois? Or the deejay at Em's birthday who performs at all those clubs in Chicago? Or that eighth grader who plays those games on Twitch?"

Mercy rested her chin against her steepled fingers. "Any ideas how we figure out which person is no longer a person?"

Hunter clenched the jagged piece of nail between her teeth and ran her tongue along it. She was missing something. But what? "Let's go home and look at the grimoires."

"So, you're giving in to good ol'-fashioned research?" Mercy stood and offered Hunter her hand. "Welcome to the team, H."

Hunter gathered the cards and slipped them back into her pocket before taking her sister's hand and hefting to her feet. "I was on the book team *way* before you, Mag."

Mercy shrugged and skipped off toward the car, kicking chunks of dirt as she bubbled over about what information the grimoires possibly held.

Hunter paused at the black footprints burned into the grass. She and Mercy had gotten enough information to focus their hunt and start them down the right path, but Hunter had hoped for a bit more. She so desperately wanted to impress her sister and be the one to solve their problems.

"Oh, well." She sighed and spit the jagged nail onto the blackened earth before jogging to catch up to Mercy.

As Hunter's boots carried her away, a line of smoke rose from the ground, from the charred blood and dead grass and torn fingernail. The nail flamed for an instant, the same white as the full moon, before the gentle spring breeze snuffed it out and carried away the black from the burnt earth.

Twenty-three

Polyphemus sat in Sheriff Dearborn's car on a dirt road that dead ended at Goode Lake. The body he'd unzipped and removed from Dearborn's spirit had guided him here, though he wasn't sure why. His only guess was that the skin he wore still searched for its true owner like a lost lamb searched for its shepherd.

He removed his sunglasses and squinted out at the water through his one good eye. "Back to this, now." He wiggled his calloused fingers in front of his other eye. Nothing. Not even a shadow. It had completely clouded over, gone blind. "Always back to this . . . *Cyclops.*" Self-pity hardened in his stomach like a pound of gold. It was a useless, ineffective emotion, but he couldn't break free of its chains.

Goode Lake's crystal blue skin shivered with each gust of wind. He rolled his window down and hung his arm out. He knew the sun was warm just as he knew the water was wet, but he couldn't feel its pleasant rays. He only felt the sticky heat of his true form inside, pressed against the slopes and ridges of this human skin.

He flipped his hand over and cupped the sunlight in his palm. He couldn't stay in this world without nesting inside of a human form, but oh how sweet it would be to feel the sun against his own skin. Tartarus, the Greek Underworld from which he escaped, had no sun. It had no aquamarine lakes or sandy beaches. Tartarus was dark, cold, barren.

Polyphemus ran his tongue along his bottom lip and pressed his teeth against the wet flesh.

He had promised himself that this would be his last escape. Curse or not, he couldn't live as the monster these killings were turning him into. When Sheriff Dearborn's body failed and its time in this world ended, so would Polyphemus's. If this small town didn't hold the cure, this was it for him, his last hurrah before he was sucked back into darkness. He might as well live a little.

He turned off the car and opened the door. It swung open without a sound and he closed it just as quietly. He squinted back toward the road and the trees that encircled the lake as he crept toward the shoreline. He didn't want to be seen, or rather, he didn't want *Frank Dearborn* to be spotted. The townspeople liked Dearborn, *needed* him. But no one had ever needed Polyphemus. He paused and frowned at the thought. There it was again. The self-pity that kept him jailed just as well as Tartarus had. But he had escaped the hell of Tartarus, and he had done it more than once.

Polyphemus untied his boots and struggled to kick them off as he fumbled with the buttons of Dearborn's long-sleeved khaki shirt. The last time he'd felt this level of excitement, he'd been traveling to meet *her.* But that had been before she'd broken his heart and before she'd doomed him with this curse. His hands fell by his sides as a gust tented the open shirt. That was also the last time he'd been in the water.

"Nomia." He twirled the name around his tongue before it slid past his lips. Only briefly had he wondered why such a beautiful creature wanted him. He had assuaged his fears and padded his ego by saying that she was attracted to his greatness and the power that came with

being a son of Poseidon. After all, Nomia was a water nymph and he had been a prince of the seas.

His jaw ticked and he stared down at his bare feet slowly sinking into the sand.

No, he *wasn't* a prince of the seas. Nomia had reminded him of that.

"You thought I *could love* you*?" She crouched atop the large boulder that jutted from the center of the lagoon like a tooth. Her waves of moss green hair lapped against her bare breasts as she threw back her head and laughed. One by one, Nomia's sisters rose from the depths of the lagoon. They encircled Polyphemus, their blue eyes sparkling as they fed from his anguish. "You are a bastard, Polyphemus. Denied by your father and unloved by his wife." She brushed back her hair and her iridescent skin glimmered in the sunlight. "I would never love you. As Amphitrite has proven, no woman could."*

"Curse him, sister!" the nymphs chanted as one as they tightened their circle around him.

"He dared to make you his!" Their webbed hands and feet churned the cobalt depths and pinned Polyphemus in place.

"Now make him ours!" Water sloshed against his shoulders as the nymphs wrung out the space separating them from him.

Polyphemus blinked the water from the single eye pressed into the center of his forehead. His eye was the same deep brown as Nomia's, the only difference between her and her sisters. "Nomia, we're alike, you and I." He tore his hand free from the current pressing against him and patted his eyelid. "We match, remember?" His chin trembled as he stared up at the woman he loved more than he loved himself.

Nomia's talons snapped as she dug her fingers into the rock. "When I look into your eye, I see everything I hate about myself."

A howl of laughter erupted around Polyphemus. Had he not been held up by the nymphs' power, he would have sunk to the bottom of the lagoon.

"Sisters!" Nomia shouted. "Make him yours!"

Claws sliced his flesh as the nymphs pulled him beneath the water. Ribbons of blood twisted around him as he thrashed and reached for the surface. It was no use. This was their domain. And Nomia was right about his father. The great king Poseidon would never come to Polyphemus's aid.

His chest burned as he reached for the sunlight that splintered against the water's surface. His fingers broke through, then his palm, his wrist. He was almost there, almost out, almost free to take another breath—

A nymph caught his foot. She stabbed his leg with broken talons as she climbed him like a rock. Brown eyes met his when the top of his head split the water's surface.

"Nomia . . ." Her name escaped his lips on bubbles of air.

A smile lifted her full cheeks and she pressed her lips against his. She cupped his face in her hands and pressed her warm tongue between his lips.

Polyphemus welcomed the kiss. It was proof that she loved him. That she was sorry.

More webbed hands were on his feet, his legs, yanking him back down. Pain flashed against his cheeks as Nomia dug in her nails. A grin stretched her lips taut against his as she sucked air from his lungs. She pulled her mouth from his and water filled his chest. Nomia pressed against him as he convulsed. The lagoon darkened around him as Nomia whispered a curse against his ear.

How delicious life would be
If only it could make you see
The hunger for what it truly is,
A way to set you free.
Now carry on with your cursed life,
And cut their eyes out, these orbs are so rife
With magic, but only one pair of these
Has what it takes to end your strife.

One of the buttons smacked him in the face when a sharp gust pulled up his shirt. He smoothed down the fabric and took a deep breath. He wasn't drowning. He was here, at the edge of Goode Lake, sunk to his ankles in the sand. He shook his feet free, shrugged off the button-down, and stripped out of the undershirt and his pants. It was time to make new memories to take back with him to Tartarus. He shook his head. No, this time he would find a way to break free from his curse.

Polyphemus waded into the lake. He couldn't feel the cool water against his skin, not in the same way he could in his true skin, but the sound was enough to make goose bumps rise from Dearborn's arms. His heartbeat sped up and he dug his toes into the silt to keep from running back to shore. He wouldn't let Nomia continue to control him. He balled his hands and fell back. Goode Lake enveloped him. His chest shuddered as he sank deeper and watched the sunlight blur against the water's surface.

He couldn't end the curse by dying in another realm. He'd learned that time and time again. There was no quicker path back to the torment of Tartarus. And the number of humans kept growing. He couldn't kill them all. Nor did he want to. What he needed was an oracle, a vessel through which he could speak to the gods.

He tucked his feet under him and pushed himself back above water. He took a breath and ran his hands down his cheeks, pausing where he knew the scars lingered just beneath Frank Dearborn's skin.

"This world doesn't have an oracle." He shook water from his ear. Droplets rained into the lake as he set his hands on his hips and stared out at the water. "But it does have magic. The gate to Tartarus proves that."

He stiffened with realization. "This world would be overrun by vengeful, evil creatures if it wasn't being protected." He ran his hands through his hair as excitement crackled beneath his skin. He'd been so busy following the curse's instruction, he'd never stopped to look at this world.

He ran to his clothes. Water splashed with each hurried step.

No, the humans didn't have an oracle, but to protect this world, to protect this town, they must have a *witch*.

Polyphemus's hands shook as he tugged on his pants and brushed the sand from his undershirt. He could find Goodeville's witch. Like he'd watched death darken a person's eyes, he could also see within them the fire of life, and magic's flame blazed bright. He threw his shirt over his head and stuffed his sandy feet into his boots. He covered his mouth as a wet cough shook his barrel chest. He stilled and swallowed against the tickle building in his throat. It was starting again. His stomach lurched as he suppressed another cough.

Polyphemus needed to find the witch and he needed to find her fast.

Twenty-four

"A Cyclops?" Xena's heart-shaped face screwed up in a grimace of disgust. She shook herself as if she could rid her body of the memory of the name. "*That* is why the eyes of the victims were missing. Polyphemus is compelled to gather them." The cat person had been sitting on the arm of the couch, but she slid off it to curl up on the cushions as she wrapped a chenille throw around herself like she suddenly felt a chill. "It's really rather horrible."

"Wait, *compelled*? Why?" Hunter asked as she sat beside Xena, redoing her ponytail.

"And who's Polyphemus?" Mercy said as she rejoined her family in the living room. She carried a tray that held three mugs of steaming hot chocolate and her cell phone. Em hadn't called or responded to the last four texts she'd sent, but Mercy wanted to be sure her phone stayed close to her for when her best friend was finally able to reach out.

"Polyphemus is a Cyclops," Xena answered matter-of-factly and then said no more while she batted at the fringed edge of the throw.

"Xena, we need more information than that," said Hunter.

The cat person looked up at the twins and sighed. "I forget how inadequate the modern public education system has become. The Cyclopes were a race of barbaric giants who terrorized ancient Greece. Polyphemus was the most human of them. I do not recall exactly how his heart was broken, but it had something to do with a nymph." Xena smoothed back her hair. "Such flighty little things. Anyway, his heart was broken and I believe he did something stupid—he was, after all, a male."

The girls nodded in mutual female understanding.

Xena finished, "And he was cursed to seek that which he was lacking until he found that which could not be discovered—meaning the second eye he was born without." She shrugged. "Or something like that. But you need not pity him. Even though he was the most human of the Cyclopes he was still a hideous, barbaric beast, and I do believe Polyphemus eats the eyeballs after he, well, *harvests* them."

"Huh. That's interesting," said Hunter.

"Interesting? It's disgusting and creepy, but less creepy than what happened out there by that tree today. Xena, you should've been there." Mercy offered the mugs of steaming cocoa to Hunter and Xena, who took them gratefully. "It made my skin crawl when the cards revealed the footprints of the killer." She shivered. "They appeared *exactly* where I was standing!"

"Thank you, kitten." Xena blew quickly across the steaming top of the cocoa. "Being able to eat, or drink, chocolate is one of my favorite things about being a person," she said.

In spite of the seriousness of everything they'd discovered that evening, Mercy couldn't help asking, "What else do you like about being a person?"

The tip of Xena's pink tongue touched the creamy cocoa. She frowned at it and blew a few breaths across it again before answering. "Well, I like my hair. It is spectacular, though that is no surprise. I have always had a lush, magnificent coat. I also do enjoy a little cannabis, especially at bedtime."

"Isn't your bedtime anytime you want to nap?" Hunter asked as she peeked up at Xena over the top of her mug of liquid chocolate and coconut cream.

"Well, yes, of course, kitten. I also am surprised by how very much I like to take a lovely bath. It almost makes up for how very much I *dislike* clothes. They are so restrictive, so binding, so *not* like fur. Well, except for my Abigail's bathrobe." Xena lifted her arm and sniffed at the fluffy, well-worn robe. "It makes me feel as if my dear girl is hugging me."

"That's really nice, Xena." Mercy curled her feet up under her and made herself comfortable in the space between her sister and Xena before she carefully blew on her own steaming chocolate.

The three of them sipped their drinks silently for a few minutes, each lost in her own thoughts, until Hunter spoke up.

"So, how do we kill the Cyclops?"

Xena tossed back her magnificent hair and said, "Killing the body it is inhabiting will be easy."

Mercy's throat closed and she put her half-empty mug down on the grimoire-laden coffee table. "I don't think killing anyone will be easy—not even someone possessed by an eyeball-eating monster."

"Kitten, as the guardian of the Egyptian gate told you, the human is already dead. What you will be killing is a reanimated body a Cyclops is using as a disguise. You must get over this foolish human squeamishness if you are to have a chance at vanquishing it."

"I agree with you, Xena," said Hunter. "But you have to understand that Mercy and I will see a human—and maybe even a friend or at least an acquaintance—when we track him down."

"Him?" Mercy asked.

Hunter nodded. "You were too freaked to notice, but those were really big boot prints—like someone who worked outside a lot would wear. It's probably a large man."

"Great . . ." Mercy muttered.

"It is great, kittens! You already know three things about the

Cyclops's skin suit." She lifted her long, slender fingers that were tipped by sharp, perfectly kept nails, and ticked off, "First, the person will be a star—symbolically not literally. Second, the person is a male. And third, he probably works, or spends a lot of time, out of doors."

"That *is* a lot more than we knew this morning." Hunter spoke firmly, confidently.

Mercy nodded and tried to sound more positive. "Yeah, that's true. I'll quit being such a downer about it. It's just really intimidating to think about needing to kill a person and a monster. Together."

Xena shook a finger in front of Mercy's face. "No, no, no. You probably will not kill them together. Well, unless you push them through the Greek gate and seal it behind them. Then the body will crumble and continue to decompose, and the Cyclops will be banished back to Tartarus."

Hunter blew out a long, sighing breath. "So, that's the best way to get rid of it?"

"Indeed," said Xena. She paused and lapped delicately at the cocoa before continuing, "Otherwise you take the risk of the Cyclops killing someone else and hiding inside his or her body."

"But before we even think about how we're gonna do all of that, don't we need to strengthen the gates?" said Mercy. "I mean, it's already super awful. The Fenrir caused Mom's death. Then the Cyclops has caused the deaths of at least three people—including whomever he's hiding inside. Think of how bad it would be if even just one more monster broke through another gate."

"It would be terrible," said Hunter.

"And very inconvenient." Xena dabbed her mouth with the back of her hand and then licked the drops of liquid chocolate from her skin. "As Goode witches you can open the gates anytime you wish by simply commanding them, so being rid of the Cyclops—once you figure out who he is and somehow get him to the Greek tree—should not be difficult. But it *will* be *extremely* difficult if you have to battle several murderous monsters at the same time."

"So, do either of you have a clue how to fix the trees? What Hunter and I did today obviously didn't work—or at least it's not working fast enough."

Hunter frowned into her hot chocolate. "The directions on the insecticide said it could take a week to ten days for the worms to die."

Xena leaned across Mercy and stroked Hunter's arm gently before she said, "Oh, kitten, I believe if the mundane part of your spell was going to work the magical part would have been effective today, if even just a little."

"Khenti said he noticed no difference on his side of the gate." Mercy picked at her lip. "And, truthfully, I didn't notice anything being any better on our side, either."

Hunter shook her head. "No, neither did I."

Mercy squared her shoulders and looked from Xena to her sister. "Do either of you have any idea at all about why the trees got sick to begin with?"

Hunter shrugged. "I'm as clueless as you are about that."

Mercy chewed the inside of her cheek to keep from blurting the thought that had been swirling around and around in her mind. *It could be because you chose a god and brought a guy to a girl party!*

"Forgive me, kittens. I am only a familiar and not the witch our Abigail was. I wish I knew what was sickening the trees, but I do not."

"It's so frustrating that none of us knows what's wrong with them," said Hunter.

"Well, what that means is that you need to look deeper and create a stronger spell to heal them," said Xena.

"That sounds logical and even like it should be easy, but Mercy's been going through those old grimoires like she's cramming for finals and what we did today was all she came up—"

"Wait! I have an idea." Mercy leaned forward, digging through the piles of grimoires. "Xena, did you pull the copies of Sarah's grimoire?"

"You mean the original Sarah Goode?" Xena asked, perking up, too.

"Yeah, that's exactly who I mean."

"Actually, I did." Xena pointed one long-tipped finger at a book that rested behind the others. It looked more like a fat folder than the other leather-bound journals. "It's good to see that my feline intuition has not left me—even while I'm in human form. It told me you might need copies of the most ancient grimoires."

Mercy grabbed the folder and sat back against the couch's cushions. She opened it carefully out of habit, even though the pages within were Xeroxed copies of the fragile originals, which remained in a temperature-controlled lockbox in a Chicago bank. Generations ago the Goode witches began copying the oldest grimoires so that the knowledge of their ancestresses would never be lost, and then sealed away the originals.

"I like to think about the fact that someday Goode witches, our great-great-granddaughters, will copy my grimoires," said Mercy as she searched for the right entry. "It makes me feel like I'm gonna live forever."

Hunter snorted softly. "It makes me stress about my handwriting."

Mercy looked up and grinned at her sister. "Well, that, too." She turned a few more pages and then pumped her fist in victory. "Yes! Here it is."

Hunter leaned closer, reading along with her. "Hey, that's the original spell that Sarah used to close the gates in the spring of 1693."

"Yep. Xena made me think of it when she said that we needed to look deeper and come up with a stronger spell. What could be stronger and deeper magic than the *first* spell?"

Hunter sat straight up. "Mag, you could be onto something!"

"Right?!" Mercy's finger traced the words as she read Sarah's loopy cursive writing. She glanced up at Xena. "Did you know Sarah had help with the first spell?"

"No. I am old, but not *that* old. I don't believe I have ever read the original spell. Like you kittens, I learned the history by listening to the Goode witches retelling it."

"Sheesh, Xena, exactly how old are you?" Mercy asked.

"One never asks a lady her age." Xena sniffed haughtily and then continued, "I assumed the original spell was almost exactly like the one the Goode witches perform during every Feast Day Ritual." She peered down at the copy of the ancient grimoire. "How interesting! Sarah had four people who aided her."

"Seriously?" Hunter scooted nearer to Mercy so she could follow along.

"Yeah, look at this," said Mercy. "Sarah was at the Norse gate, just like we were. She positioned two medicine women from the Illinois tribe at the Greek and Hindu gates, and—" Mercy paused and squinted as she struggled to make out the smudged scrawl. "I think that says Gertrude Smythe, pioneer woman and Goodeville resident, at the Japanese gate and Oceanus Martin, Pioneer Woman and Goodeville resident, at the Egyptian gate. Using smoke to signal the others, Sarah led them to begin the spell, which was almost identical to the one Abigail led us through except—" She paused and felt a jolt of surprise.

"They sealed the spell and the gates with their blood!" Hunter finished for her.

"And we need to repeat this spell as close to the original as possible." Mercy chewed her lip. "But there are no members of the Illinois tribes left here anymore. There aren't even any reservation lands in Illinois."

"Such a tragedy—such a horror what happened to the indigenous peoples," said Xena softly, sadly.

"We should add something during the ritual in remembrance of the Illinois tribe," said Hunter.

"That's a really good idea," Mercy agreed.

"Hey!" Hunter's face lit with a smile. "We do have someone very close to us who has ties to the settlers of Goodeville!"

"Ohmygoddess! Jax!" Mercy and Hunter high-fived.

"Jax would be an excellent addition, but I am in agreement with both of you that it would be wise and respectful to say a prayer for the wise women and make an offering to them during the spellwork," said Xena as she finished her chocolate, placed it on the table, and settled back to groom herself.

"We'll do that for sure, Xena," said Hunter as Mercy nodded.

"Okay, so, we have Jax who is a descendant of Goodeville's founding ancestors—and *we* can represent Sarah—all three of us. You"—Mercy jerked her chin at Hunter—"Xena, and me. But we still need one more person."

"That person should live within the Goodeville city limits," said Xena as she paused in her grooming. "She or he will also represent the pioneers who came here with Sarah."

"Em is perfect. She loved being part of the grief spell and her dad's family has run the funeral home downtown for more than a hundred years. Her grandparents *and* great-grandma just moved from here to that retirement place in Florida last year." Mercy sighed deeply. "But I don't know if she's up to it."

"If she is not, you cannot wait until her time of grief is over," said Xena. "The gates must be sealed immediately."

"You're right. I'll call her and see how she's doing."

"Has she talked to you at all today?" asked Hunter.

Mercy shrugged. "Sorta. I've been texting her. A lot. She said nothing feels right and her mom is totally not okay. Other than that she's only sent crying emoji faces."

"Do not expect her to be able to help you," said Xena.

Mercy got up and headed for her purse. She fished around inside for her phone. "Well, if she can't it'll have to be Kirk."

"Oh, hell no!" said Hunter.

Xena growled softly.

Mercy frowned and looked up from her phone. "Hey, he helped with the grief spell."

"He was *freaked out* by the grief spell and almost screwed it all up," said Hunter.

"Well, of course he was. Like Em said, he was totally inexperienced about witchy things. I talked to him and explained spellwork. He's better now. And if we have to use him I'll take full responsibility for prepping him."

Hunter rolled her eyes and Xena growled again.

Mercy put a hand on her hip. "Do either of you have a better idea?" When neither said anything Mercy continued, "Then it's settled. Emily is our first choice, but if she can't do it we'll use Kirk."

"Grandma and Grandpa are like zombies." Emily's voice sounded so, so far away as she spoke softly into the phone. "Well, scratch that. Grandpa is like a zombie—if a zombie did nothing but drink whisky and watch ESPN. Grandma is a cooking zombie. She walked in—hugged me—starting crying—ignored Mom—and went straight to the kitchen. She's been there ever since. Literally the only time she leaves is to refresh Grandpa's glass, visit the 'powder room' as she calls it, and get a new box of Kleenex. She hasn't stopped crying."

"Em, I'm so sorry. Is your mom any better?" Mercy balanced the phone on her shoulder while she rinsed the pot she'd used to make the cocoa.

"Absolutely not. Meemaw and Peepaw can't make it to the funeral, even though it won't be for four more days. They're on a Greek island cruise and said something about not being able to get a flight out from any of their ports of call. Mom thinks that's bullshit, and I have to agree. But, Mag, the truth is they never liked Dad, and they *hate* his parents. Plus, you know my parents' marriage hasn't exactly been good—not that that matters to Mom right now. She's, like, totally broken, Mag. She keeps talking about everything she should've and shouldn't have said to Dad. And then she cries so hard I swear I think she's going to puke. It's awful." Emily paused to sob softly and then blew her nose. "Sorry."

"Hey, take your time. I'm totally here for you."

"Thanks." Emily sighed deeply. "So, Mom only left her bed when

Grandma got here, and when Grandma ignored her and started cooking Mom retreated back to her bedroom and the bottle of pills the doc gave her."

"Can I please come get you? Even for just an hour or so? I made hot chocolate. I could add some witchy herbs to it to help you relax." Mercy put the pot in the dishwasher and cringed as it clanked noisily against a plate—though Em didn't seem to notice.

"Relax?" Emily's laughter was filled with sarcasm. "I can't relax. I'm the only one holding it together. I had to answer, like, a zillion funeral questions today—including stuff about Dad's casket. Jesus."

"Bloody hell, Em, can't the adults do that? You have a house full of them."

"Oh hell no. My house is filled with old people who are barely functioning. I swear if I wasn't here Dad would be on a slab in the morgue for fucking ever." She sobbed brokenly into the phone. "Wilson keeps asking me what Dad would want."

"Wilson? Isn't he just a first-year apprentice?" Mercy was sure she remembered that he was fresh out of college. Em liked to say he still looked like a very gawky, zitty teenager. "How's it okay that he's running the funeral home?"

"Oh, he's not really. Mr. Burton, from Sunset Funeral Home in Champaign, is really in charge, but Wilson keeps calling me and asking me details about Dad's service. How do I know what my father, who was murdered when he was thirty-nine years old, wanted when he died? It's not like he chatted with his sixteen-year-old daughter about his fucking funeral arrangements!"

Mercy wiped her hand on a dish towel and felt sad and sick and angry all at the same time for her friend. "Em, just tell Wilson to figure it out by himself!"

"I c-can't." Emily sniffled. "Someone has to at least *try* to do what Dad would want, and I seem to be the only somebody who cares." She started sobbing again.

"Oh, Em. I'm so sorry. I love you so much. I wish I could do something—anything."

"You can." Emily blew her nose. "Keep texting me. Even if I don't answer. Just being here for me is everything."

Mercy heard a woman's voice calling Emily's name.

"I gotta go. Grandma wants me to taste something. Again. It's disgusting, Mag. Everything she cooks has way too much salt in it—like it was made with tears."

Mercy didn't know what else to say except, "I love you, Emily Parrott."

"You, too, Mag." And the cell went dead.

Mercy walked around the corner from the kitchen. Hunter and Xena raised mirrored brows at her.

"No way she can do it." Mercy sat between them as she let out a long, disgusted exhalation. "I knew Em's mom was a flake. Not just because she's from that super rich family from New York and she always seemed to be looking down her nose at the rest of us, but because she was never here. I liked her dad a lot better. I mean, he forgot things—like school stuff."

"And her birthday," Hunter added.

Xena hissed sharply and said, "There is never any excuse for forgetting a kitten's date of birth."

"Yeah, all of that, but he was a nice man. And he told Em he was proud of her—a lot. But her mom's family isn't even coming back for the funeral—wankers."

"That's awful," said Hunter.

"Her dad's parents are here now, but they won't speak to her mom and they're so wrapped up in their own grief that they're not helping Em at all. You guys, she's having to make all the decisions for her dad's funeral."

"Oh! Poor kitten! Will she not escape to us?"

Mercy shook her head. "No. She feels like she's the only adult in the house." Mercy met her sister's turquoise gaze. "H, it's going to have to be Kirk."

Xena growled.

"Bloody hell, Xena, stop!" Mercy told the cat person, who cringed back like she was afraid Mercy would swat at her. Mercy rubbed a hand across her face. "I'm sorry, Xena. I shouldn't have yelled at you like that." Then she turned to her sister. "Seriously, H, if you can think of anyone else who already knows we're witches—and I mean *real* witches—and who we can trust, I'll totally go with you to talk to her, or him. Do you?"

"I've already thought about it. I considered Heather."

"Heather? As in the president of the drama club?"

Hunter nodded. "Yeah. Remember a few Samhains ago she came by and asked Mom for some Wiccan tips because she wanted to write a modern version of *Macbeth* and make the witches draw down the moon?"

"I remember," Mercy said. "I also remember she kept talking over Abigail the whole time she was explaining the points of a pentagram to her. Heather is one of the most arrogant people I know."

"Actually that would be Kirk," muttered Xena between licks of the last of the cocoa in her empty mug.

Mercy ignored her.

"Heather's arrogance is why I thought she might work. I figured she'd love 'playing witch,'" Hunter air-quoted. "But her family's farm is ten miles outside Goodeville city limits, and I think we really do need people to stand in for the original settlers. So it has to be someone who lives within the limits of the town."

"That's Kirk."

Her sister picked at her nonexistent thumbnail. "Okay, but you're going to have to have a serious talk with him before the spell."

"I will. And he'll be cool with it. Promise." Mercy was glad her voice sounded so sure, because her intuition wasn't nearly as convinced. She shook off the feeling—*really, we don't have a choice.* "How about you and I tell Jax and Kirk we'll meet them after football practice tomorrow? We can explain what we need the two of them to do—together. You know Kirk hates to look like any kind of a sissy in front of another guy. It should at least make him receptive enough to listen to what we have to say."

Hunter opened her mouth to speak, but Xena interrupted. "I want you to be very careful about what you disclose to those boys. Tell them only enough to set the intention to strengthen and heal the trees. They do *not* need to know the true history of Goodeville. They should *not* know about the gates."

"But, Xena, won't it be better to clue them in on—"

"No!" The cat person's eyes flashed yellow and her hair lifted as she met their gazes—all lightness gone from her expression. "I have been guardian of Goode witches for generations. Modern townspeople will not understand. Sarah Goode fled as a result of ignorance and hysteria once. That tragedy must not be repeated. Do you understand me?"

"Yes, Xena," the girls spoke together.

Xena sighed and reached out to stroke each of their cheeks. "I am sorry to be so stern with my kittens, but you must heed me on this. The less they know, the better."

"We'll only tell them enough to set their intention," said Mercy.

"Don't worry, Xena. We'll be careful," added Hunter.

"Excellent. Now, I am rather sleepy. I need a bath and my cannabis truffle or three." Xena stood and shook back her hair. "I shall see you in the morning, my lovely kittens." She leaned over and licked each of them on their foreheads before padding gracefully up the stairs.

The girls exchanged a glance. "She's a lot sometimes," whispered Mercy.

"Sometimes?" Hunter quipped with a smile. "I'll text Jax and let him know we'll be there after practice."

"Okay, I'll text Kirk, too, in a sec. I just want to be sure I've read every part of Sarah's ritual." Mercy scanned the rest of the page, making quick notes on her phone of the supplies they'd need: an offering for each and a tool for each of them to use to draw a little of their blood. Mercy chewed her lip. *Little tiny ritual knives? Where the bloody hell am I going to get some of them?*

She turned the page to the end of the spell, which was also the end of the grimoire. As she closed it, her fingernail caught on a corner of a blank page glued to the inside rear cover of the book. Mercy picked at the corner, and carefully peeled the copied sheet from the cardstock cover. It was a poem, which wasn't very shocking. Sarah's grimoires were littered with poems, though most of them were written in the margins beside spells. Their ancestress had definitely been an aspiring poet. Not a big fan of poetry, Mercy had quickly scanned Sarah's other poems as she'd concentrated on the witch's actual spellwork. But something about this particular poem pulled at her attention. It was written in bold cursive that appeared to be in Sarah's hand, but the letters had been smudged by whatever had stuck the page. Mercy smoothed her fingers over the page and squinted to make out the words.

There shall come a day
when they will sicken
with sulfur and rot
fierce and deadly
the Goode witches sworn
cannot prevent it
cannot protect them
and so the gates shall fall open
until a chosen god is forsaken

*then by parting they are mended
together again*

Mercy's breath left her in a gasp as her eyes traced the lines over and over. *How long had this poem—this prophecy—been stuck to the back cover of this old copy and ignored? And even before, in the other copies that had been made of the ancient grimoire, had anyone noticed that one of Sarah's poems was foretelling the destruction of the gates?* In the sick pit of her stomach Mercy Anne Goode knew the truth, and it made her want to puke.

"What is it, Mag?"

Still staring at the words written by their long-dead ancestress, Mercy said the first thing that came to her mind. "I don't want you to be mad at me."

Sitting beside her on the couch, Hunter turned to fully face Mercy. "Mad at you? What are you talking about? We can tell each other anything. And if this is about Kirk, I promise not to be mean. I'll just listen."

"It's not about Kirk." Mercy cleared her throat. "It's about the sick trees and the gates. I've, um, been thinking really hard about what could have started their sickness—about what's different today than in the generations before us."

Hunter nodded. "Yeah, me, too."

"Well, there's one thing that I keep circling back to. I haven't said anything because I knew it'd upset you—and I could be wrong. I *wanted* to be wrong. But what I just found at the end of Sarah's ritual makes me believe I've been on to something." Mercy chewed the inside of her cheek before blurting, "H, what if all of this is happening because you chose Tyr instead of a goddess?"

Hunter's expressive turquoise eyes narrowed and her hand automatically lifted to clutch her talisman. "If Tyr was the problem Mom would've known—would've stopped me from choosing him."

"I keep telling myself that, but what if Abigail didn't know? What if *no* Goode witch could've known because *it's never happened before*?"

"No." Hunter spoke firmly. "That's not it."

"H, just read this. I just found it on a page that was stuck to the back of the copy of Sarah's grimoire—for who knows how long. It's a poem, but it reads like more. Like it could be a warning, or even a prophecy—one that's coming true right now. And it's pretty clear that a *god,* not a *goddess,* is the problem." Mercy lifted the copy of the ancient grimoire and held it up so Hunter could see it, but her sister stood as she pushed the book away, refusing to even look at it.

"I'm not reading the old crap you found to justify whatever you've made up. Tyr's my god. We're close, unlike you and Freya."

Mercy jerked back as if Hunter had slapped her.

"Don't pretend to be shocked. It's obvious. You don't even wear Freya's talisman."

"That's not fair! I love Freya. It's different for a Green Witch. I don't need a talisman to be close to my goddess. Freya is in every tree, every flower and bush—in the earth herself. Freya is all around me." Mercy shook her head. "I can't believe you'd say something so awful to me."

"It feels shitty to have your sister question your choice of gods, doesn't it?"

Mercy stared into Hunter's eyes and within their blue-green depths she saw an unexpected anger—so fierce that it was like gazing into a tsunami.

Mercy felt her own anger stir. "Yeah, it feels shitty. But the difference is I didn't say it to hurt you."

"No, *of course* you didn't mean to hurt me. You said it without thinking about me at all—as usual, it's all about Mag."

"You're wrong. You're wrong about me and you're wrong about the poem." Mercy held up the open book again. "Just read it and *then* tell me that something written back in 1693 isn't saying that choosing a god started all of this. And it also says that you're going to have to—"

"No!" Hunter slapped the book out of Mercy's hands. "Stop talking.

I am more than done listening. Tomorrow we'll get Jax and Kirk, complete the ritual, and fix the gates. And then I *never* want to hear you say *one more word* to me about Tyr." Hunter stalked up the stairs.

"Fine!" Mercy called after her. "But when it doesn't work—again—it's going to be your fault!"

Hunter said nothing.

Mercy picked up the copy of the grimoire from where Hunter had knocked it out of her hands and onto the floor. She smoothed the page and read it again.

and so the gates shall fall open
until a chosen god is forsaken

What else could it mean? Mercy gnawed at her lip. She stared at the page, wondering what the bloody hell she should do.

And then she knew. Mercy quickly stacked all the grimoires together, even the piles that had been on the kitchen table. She carried them into the library that long ago had been built as a formal dining room, but for generations had held books and comfortable, overstuffed reading chairs instead of fine china and a gleaming wood table. She didn't bother putting them away, but piled them on a coffee table.

Then she returned to the kitchen. First, she grabbed her laptop and quickly copied the ancient ritual—translating the more difficult thee's and thou's and the other language that was confusingly archaic. She figured they'd all be on their cells together—on speaker—and one of them, *probably me 'cause I'm good at this stuff,* would lead everyone through the ritual, but with novices participating they'd need extra guidelines, especially if something happened. When she was done, Mercy printed out five copies of the ritual, as well as one of the poem or prophecy or whatever it was. She stacked the ritual instructions beside the copy of the old grimoire, folded the Xeroxed page that held the poem, and put it in her bottomless purse.

"And now one more thing that will take care of the Hunter problem," she muttered.

On the table, exactly at the spot Xena liked to perch in the morning—or whenever was morning in cat time—Mercy opened Sarah's spell book to the newly unstuck page that held the prophecy and then placed a wine goblet, the kind the cat person liked to fill with cream, on top of it.

She wouldn't have to say anything. Xena would get the message, and if she was mistaken—if she'd misunderstood the poem—if it wasn't actually a prophecy—nothing would come of it. But if she was right . . .

Mercy's feet felt weirdly heavy as she trudged up the stairs while she texted Kirk.

> How bout I meet u at school tmrw after practice?

He responded right away.

> k! see u then sexy!!!

Mercy texted back, *Kay!* But in her mind she knew it wasn't going to be okay. Not until they faced the truth about what was making the trees sick, whether her sister wanted to or not.

Twenty-five

The Goodeville High parking lot was full even though school had been out for a couple hours. The town never missed the Mustangs' practice. Well, they never missed a football practice or a football game as long as the Mustangs were winning and, with Kirk Whitfield as quarterback, the Mustangs always won.

Hunter hunched, her shoulders lifted to her ears, as she hid behind Mercy while they walked through the spectators slowly spilling from the bleachers now that practice was near its end. Mercy waved and bounced through the crowd, the perfect example of an up-and-coming Goodeville homecoming queen—tenacious, girlfriend of a football star, and filled with enough school spirit to kill a horse. Hunter fanned the end of her ponytail and dusted it against her lips as she dodged *hey*'s and *sorry to hear*'s. She couldn't talk to people here. She couldn't talk to people anywhere. This town thought they knew all about her because they knew her sister and her mother. These townspeople would run screaming if they learned what she'd done at the murder scene only hours before.

The memory sent pinpricks of energy across Hunter's palms. She dropped her ponytail and clenched her fists by her sides. She knew blood magic was important. She'd felt it during Mercy's grief spell and again near the old olive tree and the imprint of Earl Thompson's body. Sarah Goode's grimoire had been exactly what she'd needed to feel at ease with her new predilection. Blood magic *had* been used before, so it wouldn't be the worst thing if Hunter used it again.

Mercy grabbed Hunter's clenched fist and dragged her toward the emptying bleachers, pulling Hunter and her thoughts from the want that radiated through her fingertips to her fluttering heart.

"Are you excited?" Mercy nearly squealed. "I mean, I know this spell and everything is really serious, but I can't help but be a smidge excited. I've always wanted to be able to share my spellwork with friends."

They stopped near the metal stands. Hunter rubbed her palms together. She didn't mind keeping her spellwork to herself. However, she *did* mind that she'd have to share more of their family secret with Kirkles.

A loud *"Mustangs!"* roared from the football field followed by whoops and cheers from the crowd. Hunter blew out a puff of air. Even though she'd dodged Mercy's question and had no interest in including Kirk in their upcoming spell, she knew her sister had been correct. No matter how much Hunter disliked Kirk, he was the only other person they trusted enough to ask to participate. Hunter scrunched her nose. *Trusted* was such a strong word.

Hunter shook away the shell she'd gotten so adept at hiding in whenever she was forced to be around a crowd, and searched the throng of people for her own Hail Mary pass. She shielded her eyes against the starbursts of sunlight shooting off the players' scuffed red helmets as, one by one, the varsity players removed them and shuffled off the field. "Jax!" She lifted onto her tiptoes and waved.

"I don't see Kirk." Mercy chewed her bottom lip and searched the crowd of stinky white practice jerseys for her beloved.

Jax returned Hunter's wave and flashed her a cute, crooked-toothed grin before he slapped his teammate on his bulky shoulder pads and jogged over, his helmet in his hand.

"H! You came to a practice!" Jax's brows lifted and he enveloped her in a sweaty hug, his helmet bumping against her back with each gentle squeeze. "Hell must've finally frozen over."

"Where's Kirk?" Mercy asked before Hunter had even taken a breath to speak.

Jax scratched the back of his neck and swallowed. "He's, uh . . ." His gaze flicked across Mercy and settled on the dusty, worn gravel between his cleats. "Talking to Coach, I think."

Mercy's cheeks plumped with a smile. "I see him," she said and practically skipped over to meet the sweaty quarterback.

Hunter crossed her arms over her chest and squinted up at her best friend. "Did you pull another Mrs. Ritter and see my sister's boobs, too?"

Jax stiffened. "What? No!"

"Then what's with the weirdness? I can practically feel it pouring off you."

He picked at a clump of dirt stuck to the back of his helmet. "You're not going to like it."

She shrugged. "I don't like a lot of things."

Jax took a breath, held it for a moment, and let the words rush out with his exhale. "Yeah, but this is about your sister."

Hunter's stomach squeezed and her fingertips went cold. Someone was talking about Mercy? Hunter's attention snapped to her sister, to the people who waved and smiled at her as they passed. This didn't make sense. Everyone loved Mercy. Hunter's throat tightened. And worse, they were saying something so bad that Jax, the guy who used to pull spaghetti noodles through his nostrils like slimy dental floss, was uncomfortable?

Mercy caught Hunter's gaze, waved, and bounded back over with Kirk on her heels.

"Tell me later," Hunter said before pinning a casual smile to her lips.

Mercy wriggled into the space next to Hunter as she positioned Kirk across from her and next to Jax. "We have something mega important to ask you two!" Mercy punctuated the statement with a short series of claps. "It's serious." She dropped her hands to her sides. The words seemed to be more a reminder to herself than an explanation. "But I'm pretty sure you're both going to say yes."

"Babe, you don't even have to ask. The answer is yes. I'd do anything for you." With his sweat-soaked hair, pinched brow, the occasional *attaboy Whitfield* that came from the passersby coupled with the way he tilted his chin slightly to the side as if to say, *yeah, I'm hot, but I'm also approachable,* Kirk *attaboy* Whitfield looked like every hunky teen heartthrob in every sappy teen romance movie Hunter had ever seen. She could fault producers for being so heteronormative, but she couldn't fault them for the jock stereotype.

Mercy shuffled forward, lifted onto her tiptoes, and kissed his cheek. Hunter's lips forgot their fake smile and tugged down with a frown. She couldn't imagine liking anyone enough to kiss them through all of that sweat.

Jax set his helmet on the gravel and took Hunter's hand in his. "And, babe, I'd do anything for you. No asking. No questions. Not one. Ever." He sealed the breathy vow with a smattering of noisy kisses against the back of Hunter's hand.

Kirk bristled. "Piss off!" He wrapped his arm around Mercy's shoulders and squeezed her against his side. "You know how much I care about my little witch."

Jax rolled his eyes and steadied himself. "Sure you do," he grumbled.

Hunter would have to find out more about that, too.

Mercy hopped away from Kirk and back to her spot next to Hunter. "Actually, speaking of witches, there's this spell—"

"I knew it!" Jax snapped his fingers and shoved Kirk's shoulder. "I frickin' knew you two were going to ask us to do another spell. What is it this time? Something for Em? Oh! What about a way to ace finals? Can you do that?"

Kirk adjusted his pads and jutted his broad chin in Jax's direction. "Calm down, butterfingers."

Jax threw his hands into the air. "Dude, I dropped *one* ball."

"But it could have been *the* ball, Ashley."

"Guys!" Hunter clapped. "We're trying to ask you to participate in a spell to keep the town safe."

Jax's forehead wrinkled. "But our town is super safe," he said. "Most of the time, my dad doesn't even lock the front door." He gripped his collar with both hands and rested his forearms against his chest. "Is that because of you? Have the Goodes been, like, spell-casting vigilantes?"

Mercy dug the toe of her sneaker into the gravel. "Not exactly."

"I was gonna say, if you are, you've been doing a terrible job. Emily's dad was just murdered and so was that old guy . . ." Kirk's temples pulsed as he searched for the completion of his thought. "Oh, you know." He jabbed Jax with his elbow. "That old guy who wouldn't ever let us use his truck in the Rooster Days Parade even though it's one hundred percent Mustang red."

"Mr. Thompson?" Mercy supplied.

"Yeah, that's it." Sweat leapt from Kirk's scalp as he brushed his hand through his hair. "Wonder if we can use his truck now?"

"Anyway." Hunter didn't keep the disdain from twisting her features. "What we need you guys to do is simple."

"You'll each go to a tree and wait for our signal and then light a candle and say a few words and do some other simple, witchy stuff." Mercy continued Hunter's thought in a way only her twin sister could. "Piece of cake," she said with another clap. "Oh, this has to happen tonight. At about sunset. And you'll need to bring a gift."

Jax wrinkled his freckled nose. "For the tree?"

Mercy tugged on the hem of her pink T-shirt. "Kind of."

Kirk rubbed his hand against his barely there chin fuzz. "So, you want us to pick a tree and bring it, like, some earrings or something? And that'll keep the town safe?"

Mercy chewed her bottom lip. "Well, uh, yeah. I mean—"

Kirk shook his head. "Sorry, but you're gonna have to be more specific."

"Yeah, I'm not even sure what I'd buy a tree. Lights, maybe?" Jax rubbed the back of his neck and shrugged.

Hunter and Mercy hadn't thought this through. They were supposed to get Jax and Kirk to agree to participate in a spell by saying it would protect the town. Sure, that was a valid reason, but if she and Mercy had slowed down and really thought about it, they would have realized *help the town and get trees presents* made them sound crazy. And not *witchy* crazy, *crazy* crazy.

Hunter took a deep breath. If Mercy could get people to do almost anything, so could she. "There are five gates in Goodeville. Each is represented by a different type of super old tree that's definitely not native to Illinois. In order to keep the town safe, we have to make sure these gates stay closed. The gift we need you to bring is just a representation of the original place the tree came from. It all stems from a lot of ancient witchy magic stuff that's been going on for centuries." Hunter clasped her hands behind her back to keep from picking at her fingernails.

Jax tilted his head. "Real gates or symbolic gates?" he asked.

Hunter's fingers betrayed her, found a hangnail, and tugged. "Real gates." She winced.

Jax shared a look with Kirk before turning back to Hunter. "To actual places?"

Mercy sucked in a breath. "Well, not—"

"Yes," Hunter interrupted. At this point, it didn't matter if Jax and Kirk drove through the whole town with a bullhorn yelling about Goodeville being full of weird old trees and witchy gates. Everyone would think they were crazy crazy, too.

Jax dragged his crooked teeth along his bottom lip. "Bad places?"

Hunter rolled her answer across her tongue, smoothing out the rough edges. "Just different. What's over there doesn't belong here, and what's over here doesn't belong there."

Jax nodded. "Cool."

"Cool?" Kirk took a step back the same way he had that night on the porch before the grief spell. But that hadn't been in front of his precious *babe,* the girl he'd do anything for.

Jax hiked a shoulder. "I'm not going to pretend like I totally understand, but I know H. If she needs my help, I'm there."

Hunter crammed her hands into her pockets. She'd lied to her best friend. Her sweet, trusting, perfect best friend. It was for a good cause. She and Mercy had decided not to tell the boys the complete truth, but Hunter hadn't expected that to make lying so easy. She swallowed as guilt flooded her stomach with the same prickly swiftness as her first and only drink of vodka. But this guilt wasn't for the half-truths, the lies. This guilt that lapped hot against her stomach was for its absence. Hunter hadn't felt bad for lying. She hadn't felt anything.

Kirk shuffled back toward the group, twitching like a fly. "Yeah, of course. I mean, I'm always there for Hunter *and* Mercy."

"Whitfield!" Coach Jamison's holler made Hunter flinch.

Kirk turned and waved an acknowledgment to the stout, balding man before turning back to Mercy. "Coach needs me, but I won't be long. He'll make the JV squad stay and practice, but the A Team is done." He pressed against her like a shadow.

"You're so sweaty." Mercy giggled and made a show of pushing her hands against her boyfriend's padded chest in disgust just to lean in closer.

Hunter rolled her eyes in her best friend's direction. She'd expected Jax to return the exacerbated expression. Instead, his temples pulsed and his gaze narrowed at Kirk. The last time she'd seen him like that, he'd reached across the cafeteria table and punched Spencer Burke in the face for calling her a dykey poon bag. Jax had gotten detention and, to this day, neither he nor Hunter knew exactly what a poon bag was.

"Don't leave yet. I'll be done in a few," Kirk mumbled against the top of Mercy's head before backing away and jogging toward the field.

Mercy let out a tiny squeal as she took Hunter's hand in hers and swung it back and forth. "I told you he'd be cool with the spell. He really is awesome, right?" She sighed and watched Kirk wave at the group before he turned his attention to Coach Jamison.

Jax crossed his arms over his chest. "He really is a dick."

Hunter hiccupped back a laugh as Mercy sucked in a breath and halted her excited arm swinging.

Jax's mouth opened and closed like a suffocating fish's.

"*You're* a dick!" Mercy fired back.

Hunter squeezed Mercy's hand and bit her cheeks to stifle another chuckle.

Mercy dropped Hunter's hand and clamped her own to her waist. "Your *friend* is being an asshole because Kirk called him out about dropping those balls in practice."

With a huff, Jax threw up his hands. "It was *one* ball. And that's not why your boyfriend is a—"

"You're just jealous," Mercy spat.

"I wouldn't be jealous of Kirk Whitfield if he got drafted to the Bears."

Hunter's hand flew to her pendant. This was it. Whatever Jax had heard about Mercy had something to do with Kirk. It had to. Jax would give almost anything to play for the Bears and would be salty for years if one of his friends got to live out his dream.

Mercy leaned forward. Her hair slipped from her shoulders. "Then what is it, Jax? What's your problem with my boyfriend?"

Jax sucked in his bottom lip. His Adam's apple bobbed just above the padded collar of his practice jersey.

"Jax." Hunter bit the tip of her fingernail. "You can't clam up now."

"He told everyone, Mercy." Jax clasped his hands together. Color drained from his knuckles with each passing second. "The whole team. He told them everything."

Now Hunter was the fish. Her mouth bobbed open and closed as she struggled to put the pieces together.

Mercy took a step back. "I don't know what you're talking about." She shook her hair away from her face and dug her teeth into her bottom lip.

Jax's gaze fell to his feet. "The blowjob and the . . ." He brushed the pegs of his cleats against the gravel. "Other stuff." His dark eyes lifted. "Everyone knows, Mercy."

Mercy wrapped her arms around her core. She squeezed her stomach as if she could keep it all in, keep herself together, if she only applied enough pressure. "No," she whispered.

"I'm sorry." Jax reached out. His hand hung in the air for a moment before dropping to his side.

Mercy cleared her throat. "If he told, there had to be a reason."

Jax shook his head. "He was bragging, Mag. I swear. Big, detailed, douchebag bragging."

"You don't know him. Neither of you. Not the way I do." Mercy straightened, stiffened, and held her fists down by her sides. "I'll be at the car. Come when you're finished with . . ." She narrowed her eyes and waved a hand in front of Jax. *"This."* And stormed off.

Hunter started to go after her but Jax caught her hand. "I didn't want to tell her. Not like this."

"You did the right thing. We all know Kirk is terrible. Now she does, too."

Jax squeezed her hand before he let go and bent to pick up his helmet.

"Mercy!" Hunter called as she jogged into the parking lot after her sister. "Wait!"

Mercy whirled around, her black hair cutting the air like a scythe. "For what, Hunter? So you can tell me more lies about my boyfriend?"

"Jax wasn't lying."

Mercy slumped against the nearest car, Coach Jamison's puke green El Camino. "Kirk wouldn't do that. Not the Kirk that I know."

Hunter couldn't stop picking at her fingernails. "But the Kirk you know is the same Kirk Jax knows."

"He's just gone through so much with his mom leaving and his dad being such an awful misogynist." Mercy pressed her palm against her chest. "He thinks that the only way people will like him is if he pretends to be mister jock."

"Or maybe he *is* mister jock and he thinks the only way *you* will like him is if he pretends to be someone he's not."

Mercy's hand fell to her side. "There's no way you could ever understand. You've never even dated anyone. You're jealous! You and Jax and Em. You're jealous that someone loves me and no one loves you."

Hunter's heart squeezed. Didn't Mercy love her? Didn't that count for something?

"I'm right! Kirk is sweet and loving and kind and respectful." Mercy's left brow lifted, and she sprang away from the car. "And I know a way to prove it," she shouted and stormed back to the practice field.

Twenty-six

Mercy had to get her anger under control. Spellwork could be volatile—unpredictable—if the witch doing it wasn't calm and focused, so she forced her steps to slow and shifted her concentration from how pissed off she was to how much she loved the way the fringe that hung around the hem of her short jeans skirt felt brushing against her thighs. She shook back her hair and her lips actually lifted in a small half smile as the beads on her hoop earrings jingled musically with her movements. Mercy drew a deep breath and let it out slowly. She was still pissed, but her mind had calmed enough to work through the angry haze that colored her thoughts.

Jax was full of shit.

But her sister's best friend's words haunted her. *The blowjob and the . . . other stuff.* Her cheeks went hot. Okay, so, Kirk had said *something* to them—or at least to Jax. But it couldn't have been like Jax was making it out to be. It couldn't have been bad.

Kirk's voice seeped seductively from her memory, overpowering Jax's stupid words. *You are a goddess. My goddess. I love you.* Kirk had probably just wanted to tell Jax about the amazing thing that had happened between them—had been trying to be actual, *real* friends with him—and Jax was making a big deal out of it. Sure, Kirk could've sounded kinda douchey. No big surprise. It's not like he had any kind of a decent role model at home to show him how to treat a girlfriend. That's why Mercy had to practically teach him how to be a boyfriend—not that she minded. When they were alone Kirk was the sweetest guy ever. He just didn't know how to make that guy public.

Well, she sure as hell did. And he'd thank her later, after everyone saw the *real* Kirk Whitfield. The Kirk she knew and loved so much.

Mercy slowed as she approached the spot at the very end of the practice field where the varsity cheerleaders had set up a big table that held a giant cooler full of sports drinks and ice. It was tradition that the cheer squad practiced along with the football team, breaking at about the same time so that everyone could share the cold drinks before the boys jogged into their locker room and the cheerleaders flitted off to theirs. Mercy tended to agree with Hunter's ongoing assessment that the whole thing was a misogynistic ritual that needed to end, but the football and cheer coaches thought it was good for morale.

Giggles mixed with deep voices drifted to her on the breeze. Mercy thought what almost everyone else did—that the morale it built by the cheerleaders basically playing the role of glorified water boys caused more touchdowns in the backseat of cars than on the football field, but whatever. Today the archaic ritual was perfect for what she wanted to, *needed* to do.

She saw Hunter walking slowly to Jax, who—along with the rest of the varsity team, minus their quarterback—was downing a bottle of something that looked like it had way too much red food coloring in it to be healthy. Hunter glanced at her and Mercy motioned sharply for Hunter to join the group. Even from that distance she could see that Hunter's shoulders were bowed and her face looked pale and drawn. Mercy's stomach tightened. She hated to see Hunter upset. For years she'd been messing up anyone who hurt her sister.

And look how she paid me back today—by siding with Jax against me. She was a bitch last night when I tried to reason with her about Tyr, and she's still pissed. That's all it is.

Mercy lifted her chin. She'd show Hunter. She'd show all of them.

The fence that ringed that end of the field and the track surrounding it was lined with Thuja trees that grew side by side in pyramids of concealing evergreens, easily ten feet tall. Several yards beyond the trees and the fence the cheerleaders clustered with the football team—and her sister, who was standing beside Jax, silent and uncomfortable.

Mercy approached the wall of trees. From where she stood she could hear the sounds of voices, but was too far away and too shielded by the living wall to make out actual words.

Kirk would think anything he said to her would be private. In the shadowy protection of the evergreen hedge they couldn't even be seen, let alone heard.

But Kirk didn't actually know anything about her witchy powers, so he had zero clue what she could coax the trees to do. Well, Hunter had just decided—all on her own and against what Xena had said—to spill a bunch of stuff about them and the gates.

Now it was Mercy's turn.

She knew the perfect spell. It was simple—one of the first Green Witch spells her mom had taught her before she was even a teenager and had first shown an affinity for plants and trees and the earth. Abigail had taken her to the huge grandmother oak in their backyard and explained to her that each tree was a living being, and because of that the right witch, using the right kind of power, could ask trees for aid.

It had been a super easy spell for her to learn. She'd already been able to feel the big oak's inhalations and exhalations against her hands, and she'd been listening to the sweet whispers of the crops that surrounded their home for as long as she could remember. So, when Abigail had shown her how to focus, how to pull energy from the ley lines and be the conduit that sent that energy into the oak so that she could beseech the tree for the help she needed—it felt as natural as breathing to young Mercy.

She looked up at the wall of evergreens. They loomed above her and made her feel safe, strong, powerful even. Mercy smiled and lifted her hands, stroking the spiky, sticky upside-down Vs that were the Thuja's leaves. It was then that her mother's voice tickled across her memory. *Well done, Mag!* Abigail had said when Mercy had executed the spell so easily. *But remember, sweetheart, never use your powers for vanity or any self-serving reason. Always keep in mind the words we live by: An ye harm none, do what ye will.*

Mercy ignored the spark of intuition that all of a sudden made her palms sweaty and her stomach sick. *I'm not harming anyone. I'm showing everyone they're wrong about Kirk. I'm doing a good thing!*

She wiped her damp palms against her jeans skirt, closed her eyes, and centered herself—and found that her anger worked for her as she easily found the potent ley line that bisected the football field and ran directly under where she stood. Mercy reached down and tapped into that vein of power as she pressed her hands against the trees—ignoring the fact that their sticky leaves scratched her palms.

"I greet you, gentle giants," she murmured to them.

Instantly she felt their combined inhale and exhalation against her hands.

"I ask a favor of you, and for that favor I will draw the power beneath you up into your roots, your branches, your beautiful, lime green leaves. You will swell with health and grow taller, ever taller. Will you grant me a favor?"

From the trees rushed excitement that teased her palms and made her smile.

"Good. Here is what I ask of you . . ." Mercy bowed her head and pressed her forehead against the Thuja as she whispered her request to the line of trees.

Again, her palms tingled with excitement that was so real it reminded her of wriggling puppies. She didn't speak her thanks. Instead, she pulled the pulsing power up through the earth. The heat of it rushed into her body and through her hands to cascade into the wall of trees. They swayed as they accepted her offering like ballerinas tethered to the earth.

She stroked the thick, leafy Thuja branches and murmured, "Thank you, my friends," exactly as Abigail had trained her to do. The wall of trees swayed once more in response.

Satisfied the spell was set, Mercy rubbed her hands on her jeans skirt and headed to the break in the fence and tree line, just in time to see Kirk jogging away from the coach and the JV team, as he headed for the refreshment stand. Mercy lifted a hand and waved at him.

As soon as he saw her he grinned and changed direction, running straight to her.

"Babe! You stayed! Damn, you look good." He bent to kiss her, but she pushed against his chest with both hands—this time actually keeping him from getting close to her.

"We need to talk," she said firmly.

Jarod Frazier, the Mustangs' senior linebacker, leered at them as he crushed a Gatorade bottle in his meaty hand. "Oooh, damn! Trouble in paradise? You need some help handling her, bro?"

Mercy didn't wait for Kirk to respond. She spun on her heels and marched back through the break in the fence, leaving Kirk to jog after her—much to the jeering delight of the rest of the team.

Mercy turned to face Kirk when she reached the exact spot she'd stood earlier, hidden by the wall of trees from the view of anyone on the football field.

"Mercy, what's—"

She lifted her hand, stopping his words.

"You told Jax about what we did yesterday!"

Kirk frowned. "What the hell did he say?"

Mercy put her fists on her hips. "How about you tell me what you said instead?"

"Nothin'. Really. Just locker room talk. You know." He reached for her and she sidestepped him.

"You talked about me—about *us*—in the damn locker room? You mean the whole team knows our business?" Mercy felt her cheeks flame. Her anger was so intense she felt dizzy.

"Mercy. Babe. All us bros talk about our girlfriends. It's, like, a compliment."

"A *compliment*? Telling the 'bros,'" Mercy air-quoted, "*personal* and *private* things about our relationship is only a compliment to douche-bag misogynistic pigs like your father! To normal guys—decent guys—it's a betrayal—an invasion of privacy." She shook her head, super pissed that tears had started to leak from her eyes down her cheeks. This really wasn't going the way she'd planned. To herself more than Kirk she said, "I'm such a fool. I thought you were different." She cried brokenly. "I can't believe I was so stupid." She wiped at her eyes and started to storm past him, intent on touching the trees and ending the spell, but Kirk surprised her by grabbing her wrist. As he stopped her he dropped to his knees and stared up at her.

"You gotta believe me," he begged from his knees. "I didn't mean nothing. I promise. Just—just tell me how to do better and I will."

Mercy looked down at him. His blue eyes were huge. His face had paled and he was truly upset. Had she overreacted? Kirk seemed genuinely sorry. She wiped her eyes and shook her head. "Kirk. What you did was *really* bad." She crossed her arms over her chest and waited for him to make it right—for him to be the guy she believed he was.

"Babe! Like I said, I just didn't know. But I totally get it. I'm not gonna say shit about us again. Seriously." He reached out for her and Mercy let him take her hand. He kissed it and smiled up at her. "You know I'm an idiot about this kind of stuff. Sorry, my witchy woman."

Relieved, Mercy pulled her hand from his as she started toward the line of trees. All she needed to do was to touch them to close the spell and then she and Kirk could—

But before she could reach the trees Kirk had snagged her wrist and pulled her around to face him. "No, please, don't walk away!"

Mercy meant to shake off his vise grip and touch the trees, but when she looked down at him what she saw had her frozen with shock.

He was on his knees again.

Oh, shit! He totally misunderstood!

And he was crying.

Really sobbing.

"Kirk." She spoke as softly as possible. "It's okay. We can talk about it." Her eyes darted from him to the trees as she tried to shift her body to bring herself within reaching distance of one of their sticky branches.

"Mercy, I mean it! I didn't get what I was doing. I was just happy! I wanted to tell everyone so they'd know how much you love me, and how much I love you." On his knees, he lurched forward and wrapped his arms around her waist. He pressed his cheek against the softness of her stomach as his sobs made his voice hitch. "Y-you know h-how much I n-need you."

Mercy felt the beginnings of panic. She'd expected him to apologize—to have a good excuse for what he'd done—to reassure her and react like a sweet guy who'd made one stupid mistake.

She hadn't expected him to be so clueless, and then to fall apart and cry.

Mercy tried to break the hold he had on her waist so she could get around him and be close enough to the trees so that she could close the spell, but Kirk was too big, too strong. The harder she tried to pry away from him—the tighter he clung to her.

"Okay, okay," Mercy tried to soothe. She stopped pulling at his arms and instead stroked his sweaty hair. "I—I overreacted." Her eyes darted from him to the trees as she tried to shift her body closer.

Through streaming tears he looked up at her. His eyes widened as he misread her worried expression.

His arms tightened around her.

"No, you can't do this!" Tears flooded his voice with desperation. "You know how much I love you."

"Kirk! It's okay. I forgive you!"

"I need you! You can't leave me."

"Kirk, shh." Mercy pressed her fingers against his lips, physically trying to dam the tide of his words. "It's hard for me to listen to you if you won't let me go."

Abruptly, he released her. She staggered backward until she touched the trees and surreptitiously stroked their sharp leaves. They quivered once more in response, and then stilled. Breathing a sigh of relief, she turned to Kirk.

He'd remained on his knees, hands held out as if he beseeched her blessing while he continued to snot cry. "H-how do I fix this? Want me to kick Jax's ass?"

Mercy shook her head, ready to tell him—not for the first time—that he couldn't blame other people for his bad choices, when Jarod's sarcastic voice came from behind Kirk.

"Dude! Are you *seriously* crying?"

"Right?!" Derek, the varsity center, a big, meaty kid who looked like a chubby Hitler youth, mimicked Kirk as he scrunched up his fat pink face and pretended to cry. "Babe! Don't leave me! Babe, I love you!"

Kirk rocketed to his feet and whirled around. The entire varsity football squad, and cheerleaders, had poured through the break in the fence and were *laughing* at Kirk. Jax and Hunter stood a little apart from the group, speechlessly staring from Mercy to Kirk.

Mercy narrowed her eyes and glared at the gawking group. She knew her words were hypocritical. It was because of her spell that the trees had amplified everything she and Kirk had said and broadcasted it to the varsity football team and the cheerleading squad, but she was too panicked to think of anything else to say—anything else to do.

"Oh, shut up! This is between Kirk and me, and none of your damn business."

"Uh, if it wasn't our business the two of you shouldn't have been yelling like that," quipped Jarod.

"Yeah, you were super loud. We heard everything," added Derek.

Kirk wiped violently at his face. His shoulders were slumped. He fisted his hands by his sides and for a moment Mercy thought he was going to stand up for her—stand up for them—and take on the mocking team. But his body language changed before he faced her. He put a hand on his hip and slouched like he was oh, so cool. Then he turned to look at her and his cute, full lips—the lips she'd kissed so, so many times—twisted in a sneer.

"Well, shit. I guess the cat's outta the bag now—or I should say the *pussy's* out of the bag." His laughter was cruel, and this time Jarod and Derek joined in, laughing *with* not *at* him. His voice was hard and cold with sarcasm. "Can't blame a guy for tryin' to get more than a bj, though, right?"

Mercy felt frozen. She swallowed hard before she could form words. "Kirk? What are you saying?"

Hunter took a step toward Mercy. Her blue/green eyes looked old and tired as she spoke low in a tight voice. "Come on, Mag. Let's go home."

Kirk sneered at Hunter. "For once I agree with the dyke. Go home, *Mag.*" He made her nickname sound like an insult.

Mercy couldn't move. The coldness inside had frozen her to the earth. "But you love me." Even to her ears she sounded like a stupid little girl.

Kirk laughed. "Love you? It was fun for a while, but you're too damn much work." He jerked his chin at the gleefully watching team. "Ask any of them. After what they just heard they know it's true, too." Then his brows lifted into his hairline. "Wait, they *shouldn't* have been able to hear us. It was you, wasn't it? You did some witch shit—like your sister did at your house the other night. You set me up, you bitch!"

Mercy stared at Kirk—at the cruel stranger he'd become. *No, he's always been this person. I just chose not to see it.*

Hunter ignored Kirk. She gestured at her sister and repeated, "Come on. Let's go."

Thawed by her twin's voice, Mercy nodded jerkily, and started to make a wide circle around Kirk. But he stepped up to block her.

"What's wrong? Don't want your *precious* freak of a twin to hear the truth?" He shot Hunter a mean look over his shoulder before he continued. "Too late. She already knows about the bj. But her bff probably didn't tell her the rest—how you humped my hand like the bitch in heat you are. You came all over me, you slut."

Shocked gasps erupted from the cheerleaders to mix with uncomfortable chuckles from the football players.

Mercy couldn't move again. Her entire body was flushed with heat and even though her whole being was screaming *run* she kept staring at Kirk like she'd never seen him before.

Then Hunter was there, stepping between them. She seemed to grow in height as she faced down the quarterback.

Twenty-seven

Rage surged through Hunter so hot and deep that her breath sloshed out in soupy gasps. Part of her yearned to relax into the warm embrace her anger promised. In its arms, there were no consequences, no remorse, no sad sisters made even more depressed by betrayal. In fury's grasp, there was nothing but revenge. Hunter clenched her fists. Her jagged nails dug into her scabbed palm. Kirk Whitfield was over, canceled. She'd take away everything he cared about.

Beside her, Mercy slapped her palm over her mouth and whimpered.

Hunter sucked in a breath and fought through the heat clawing up her throat ready to fork her tongue, weaponize it, use it to tear the star quarterback apart. Had it not been for her sister and the despair that squeaked past her lips, Hunter would have let the rage consume her.

Her hands relaxed as each inhale of cool spring air quelled her roiling insides. The corner of Hunter's lips quirked and a chuckle scratched at the back of her throat as she stared at the blustering windbag. All machismo, no substance. She would have pitied him had he not just trampled her sister.

Kirk lifted his chin and the shocked murmurs of their peers ceased. "What are you laughing at, *dyke*?"

Hunter held out her hand and motioned for Jax to stay back as he surged forward and Mercy stiffened.

Most people went their whole lives without a good showdown, with only the fantasy of burning their ex or quitting their job to fuel them from one unsatisfying moment to the next. Hunter had only had to wait sixteen years.

"You're not worth the trouble it would take to hit you." She untethered her smile and let it roll across her lips as she recited the Yates quote from memory. *"You're not worth the powder it would take to blow you up. You're an empty, empty, hollow shell of a man."*

Right now, her library card and every book she'd ever checked out were worth their weight in gold.

Kirk rushed forward and Jax charged out in front of Hunter. This time, she didn't stop him from intervening. She wrapped her arm around her sister and guided her from the wall of trees and the uniformed spectators chanting for a fight. Jax could hold his own and, with the number of parents and coaches off in the parking lot starting the traditional after-practice tailgating extravaganza, a fight wouldn't get very far.

As they neared the bleachers, Mercy pushed away from Hunter. "I just"—she hiccupped between cries—"want to—be alone."

Hunter twisted the hem of her shirt between her fingers. "I don't think you did anything wrong, if that's what you're worried about."

"It's not about what you think, Hunter." Mercy's lip quivered as she swiped the back of her hand across her tear-streaked cheeks. "You couldn't possibly understand what this feels like. I need to be alone right now." She slipped into the shadows under the bleachers, her feet making sharp *scuff scuff* noises as she jogged the length of the metal steps.

Choked sobs echoed through the shadows and filled the space between the sisters. Like caustic fumes, they twisted Hunter's insides. After everything they'd been through, could Mercy handle another blow?

Hunter ran under the bleachers. "Mag! Wait!" she called as Mercy plunged into the sunlight on the other side. The last time she'd given Mercy space to process her grief, her sister had been nearly catatonic. Hunter charged forward, faster. "This isn't your fault!" she shouted into the shadows. This was all Kirk. Mercy had done nothing wrong. If only Kirk had been better, had actually been the guy Mercy thought he was.

Hunter's shoelace had come untied. With each rushed step, the plastic ends of the ties struck her shin.

But Hunter *had* warned her. So had Emily and Jax. Even Xena had made her disapproval known. Why hadn't Mercy listened? Did she not trust her friends and family? Did she not care for them more than she cared for Kirk? The questions stoked the graying coals in Hunter's belly.

Since the beginning of their relationship, Mercy had put Kirk first. *You were so powerful tonight, Kirk. So perfect. This couldn't have happened without you.* The words Mercy had spoken after the grief spell spit fuel on Hunter's anger. She coughed as heat surged through her chest, up her throat.

You're jealous that someone loves me and no one loves you.

Hunter shielded her eyes as she emerged from the bleachers. Until Mercy apologized for placing Kirk above everyone else, she could run off alone.

Hunter stepped on her untied shoelace. She tripped forward and caught herself before she faceplanted in the gravel. She shuffled over to the shade of the now-closed snack hut and crouched down to tie her shoe. Her stomach churned as she crossed one shoelace over the other and tugged so hard she nearly ripped them from their holes.

Maybe this time Hunter would let her rage swallow her. A dying star spitting fire into the cosmos. She'd go back to Kirk and wouldn't choose the high road. She'd choose the low road, the same road he'd just torn down, slamming into everything he could on his way to feeling like a big man. Hunter double knotted her laces and brushed her hands on her shorts as she stood. Yes, that's what she'd do. She'd find Kirk and—

A man's wracking cough pulled Hunter's attention from the molten lava pooling in her gut. Sheriff Dearborn buried his face into the crook of his arm and leaned against the lamppost on the other side of the snack hut, a plate of nachos scattered in the gravel around his feet.

Hunter chewed the inside of her cheek. She wanted to leave, wanted to let the volcano of anger burbling in her stomach erupt all over Kirk and his jock friends.

Another bout of wet coughs. Sheriff Dearborn spit a phlegm ball onto his nachos, wiped his mouth, and sagged against the metal post. Hunter wrinkled her nose. The sheriff wasn't the youngest guy, but it wasn't her responsibility to help someone who had a cold. She squinted back at the packed parking lot. She didn't think she had it in her to fix *another* situation. Hunter exhaled and half expected smoke to billow from her parted lips.

He gripped his chest and lurched forward. His sunglasses slipped from his ears as he sucked in breaths between more throat-shredding coughs.

Concern doused the anger roiling within Hunter. She ran over to the sheriff and caught him as he pitched farther forward. Spittle dangled from his chin and she averted her eyes and helped him up. "You . . . okay . . . Sheriff?" she asked between grunts as he used her shoulders as crutches and righted himself.

"Fine. Fine." His voice had the same dry coarseness as the gravel beneath her feet. "Damn chips must've gotten me."

Hunter plucked his sunglasses from the gravel and wiped the dusty lenses with the bottom of her shirt. "Mercy nearly choked on a tortilla chip once. Now she'll only eat Lay's." She handed him the sunglasses. Her breath caught in her throat.

His left eye was completely clouded over. A fresh page in a new notebook.

"Your eye . . ."

He snatched the glasses from her hand and thrust them back onto his face. "Allergies is all," he said with a sniffle.

Hunter's fingertips itched. She slid her hand into the pocket of her slouchy knit cardigan and pressed her hand against her tarot deck. Power sizzled through her palm.

A star around his eye . . .

Sunlight glinted off the points of Sheriff Dearborn's star-shaped badge.

. . . and on his chest.

Hunter's throat tightened. She clutched her amulet and fed off the strength from the symbol of her god. Her insides warmed. But not with the hungry fire of rage or the slow burn of anger. Her fingertips found the smooth moonstone pressed into her symbol of Tyr. Her god was with her now, drawing down the magic of the moon and whispering affirmations to the powerful gift entangled in the blood of the Goode women.

Sheriff Dearborn slipped his fingers under his sunglasses and rubbed his clouded eye. "Give the other one of you my regards, Bright Eyes," he said and rushed off in the direction of the parking lot.

Hunter's hands shook as she pulled out her phone and dialed her sister's number.

Bright Eyes?

Hunter pushed away the question when Mercy answered on the second ring. "Meet me at the car, Mag. I found him," Hunter blurted before her sister had a chance to speak. "I found Polyphemus."

Mercy sucked in a breath. "Are you safe? Who is it?"

A cold pang of guilt flashed through Hunter's chest as she ran to meet Mercy. Mag did care about her. Hunter needed to stop being such a bad sister, such a bad friend. Her ponytail brushed her shoulder blades as she shook her head and with it, shook away the conscience threatening to derail her focus.

Hunter hid her mouth behind her hand as she wove through hot dog–eating townspeople milling about the parking lot. "It's the sheriff! And now that we know, we can put a stop to all of this and send him back where he belongs."

Power flared within her veins and the scabs crusted against Hunter's palm ached. She didn't know how this would end, but she knew it would be bloody.

Twenty-eight

And Jax is meeting us at poor Emily kitten's house?" Xena's question broke the silent ride across town.

"Yeah, Xena." Hunter glanced in the rearview mirror at the cat person, who kept looking nervously out the windows. "He took a shower while we were getting the ritual stuff together. He's bringing his offering, a dove feather from his father's collection."

"That will make an appropriate gift in honor of the indigenous women." Xena shifted and tugged at the neck of the oversized blue peasant blouse she'd borrowed from their mom's closet before she smoothed, then pulled at, and smoothed again the long, silver broom skirt that had been one of Abigail's favorites.

From the passenger seat Mercy turned to look at her. "Are you okay back there?"

"No. I very much am not. I despise these horrible, soulless things." Her long fingers fluttered at the interior of the car. "And though my Abigail was a lovely woman I do not understand how she, or any of you, ever wear clothing." Xena plucked at the sleeve of her blouse.

"Xena, you're not even wearing anything under that," Mercy said. "Bras and panties are *way* more uncomfortable than real clothes."

Xena shuddered. "I do not know how you bear it. It's already quite awful." Then she leaned forward and peered from twin to twin. "But what is even more awful is whatever is going on between the two of you."

Mercy blew out a long, frustrated breath. "There's nothing going on other than Kirk is an even bigger douchebag than you two thought. We broke up. In front of the entire sodding school. And I don't want to talk about it."

Hunter's knuckles whitened on the steering wheel. Her lips pressed into a tight line and she said nothing.

"Fine, kittens. Don't talk about it. But you two need to focus. Tonight is too important for you to bring anger and resentment into the ritual."

Mercy bowed her head. She knew Xena was right. She needed to get her shit together so that if or *when* the ritual failed there would be no doubt about why. So there, in the car with her sister's silent presence beside her, Mercy closed her eyes and concentrated on her shattered heart. On one raw, bleeding piece of it she envisioned carving the name ABIGAIL into her frayed flesh. On another wounded spot she carved HUNTER. And on the last, the newest, the most jagged piece of her somehow still beating heart she carved KIRK. Then she imagined taking a roll of gauze, like the sterile one in Abigail's emergency kit that rested in a bottom shelf of the pantry, and she wrapped it around and around the lacerations until the names could no longer be seen—until all that was left was a heart-shaped organ completely cocooned, which somehow still pulsed with stubborn life.

She turned her face to her half-open window and inhaled deeply the scents of the evening—of trees and grasses, crops and spring flowers. As she drank in the soothing earth, Mercy channeled its magic within and held it tightly to her damaged heart. The ache inside her subsided and in its place there was a nothingness that was almost equally as frightening, but a lot easier to think through.

She opened her eyes as Hunter pulled up in front of Emily's meticulously landscaped corner lot. People always oohed and aahed about the huge, brick edifice, but Mercy had never liked it. She knew the coldness of the outside and the façade of perfection were all too perfectly mimicked inside.

"There's Jax." Hunter waved and Jax got quickly out of his car and jogged across the street to them.

He put one hand on the roof and ducked down to peer inside. His left eye was swollen and black and there was a dark scab on his bottom lip. "Hi, Xena."

"Hello, Jax kitten," said Xena. She cocked her head and studied him. "Were you victorious in your battle?"

He started to grin and then grimaced as his lip began to bleed again. "Yeah, actually. I was."

"Good," Hunter said firmly.

Jax's gaze shifted to Mercy. Instead of turning away, Mercy met his kind brown eyes. "Hey, Mag. You okay?"

"Yep. Fine."

His brow lifted, but he didn't say anything else to her.

Mercy wanted to ask him if he'd really kicked Kirk's ass. Somewhere deep inside she hoped he had—hoped he'd made Kirk feel just a little of the hurt she was left suffering, but the words got trapped in the gauze that held her heart together.

Jax touched Hunter's shoulder through the open window. "How you doin'?"

Hunter covered his hand for a moment with her own. "Fine," she echoed Mercy's empty word.

Xena cleared her throat. "All right then. Shall we go get our other kitten?"

"Yeah, let's go." Without waiting for any of them, Mercy got out of the car and climbed the big stone stairs that led to a small but elaborately carved entryway. No wide, comfortable porch for the Parrotts—just lots of show that was totally devoid of warmth. As Hunter, Xena, and Jax came up to stand, fortresslike, behind her, she pressed the doorbell.

Nothing happened for so long that Mercy had raised her hand to press the button again when the door finally opened.

Emily blinked and then squinted as if the light from the setting sun was too bright for her amber eyes. Her chestnut skin looked dull; her beautiful eyes were framed with circles so dark they appeared bruised. And her hair—the gorgeous mahogany mass she was so proud of—that she liked to wear in a wild curl that fell well past her shoulders—was pulled back in a severe scrunchie. She was wearing what Mercy knew she called her *watch-TV clothes*—an old yellow sweat suit and scuffed sneakers.

Emily looked awful.

"Mag?" She sounded dazed, like she'd been awakened in the middle of sleepwalking. Then her gaze caught on the small group behind Mercy and her eyes widened. "Um, hi, guys. Do you want to come in?"

"Yes, we do." Xena pushed past her to pull Emily into her arms. "Oh, kitten! I have been so, so worried about you!"

"Uh, thanks." Emily's voice was muffled by Xena's mane of hair, but she returned the cat person's hug until a sneeze rocked her body.

"I am so sorry." Xena released Emily and took a step back. "I always forget how allergic you are."

"Allergic?" Emily's forehead wrinkled.

Mercy spoke up quickly. "Em, I know this is not a good time, but we need you."

Emily shook her head a little, like she wasn't sure she'd heard her friend correctly. "But, I—"

"Emily!" A wobbly old voice drifted from the direction of the kitchen. "If that's my delivery from the IGA, have them bring the things into the kitchen."

"No, Grandma, it's not—"

"Emily Michelle, if that's my delivery from the pharmacy, tip the boy well." Her mother's voice, which Mercy had always thought sounded shrill, splintered the air from the opposite side of the house. "They're doing me a special favor."

"It's not the deliver guy, Mom, it's—"

"It's the liquor store. Tip him well, too. Good help is hard to get." Her grandfather slurred his words from a closer room.

Emily sighed and stared at the floor.

No one came out of their respective hidey-holes to actually see who was at the door. Mercy studied her best friend, who looked completely defeated. She took Emily's hand. Her friend looked up at her.

"We need you," she repeated firmly. "Please come with us. It won't take long, and I'll explain in the car, but I promise it's important. Really important."

Emily stared at her, shoulders bowed in defeat. "I can't leave."

"Yes, kitten, you can," said Xena firmly.

"We wouldn't be here if we didn't need you," said Hunter.

Jax nodded. "Yeah, what they said. And I haven't seen you since . . . since, well, you know. But I'm really sorry, Em."

"Thanks." She cleared her throat and continued, "I wanna help you guys." Emily kept her words soft as if speaking too loudly would awaken ghosts. "I really do, but I can't leave. They're a mess. Like, my mom can barely make it to the bathroom. Grandpa's drunk. Grandma's lost her mind. Someone has to take care of them."

"Oh, kitten . . ." Xena whispered.

"Emily!" Her mother's voice made them all jump. "I need those pills!"

"I thought it was the liquor store," yelled her grandpa.

"No, I told you, it's the IGA," blared from the kitchen.

With each voice—each shout—Emily seemed to shrink more and more inside herself. *They're going to make her completely disappear and the Em I know won't exist anymore.* And Mercy Anne Goode couldn't bear to lose anyone else.

"No!" Mercy shouted, splitting the air with her anger-fueled words. "No!" she repeated. "This is bullshit!" Emily opened and closed her mouth as she stared at her friend. Mercy continued to grip her hand and kept going—kept letting the truth rush from her wounded heart and fall from her lips. "Why can't anyone be who they're supposed to be? Your mom's supposed to be a *mother,* not a drugged-out, self-indulgent brat." The words spilled around Mercy, sloshing against the immaculately decorated shell of a home. "Your grandparents are supposed to be your support system—the people *you* count on for strength and love—not the people you have to prop up."

"Mag—" Hunter began softly, but Mercy spoke over her.

"And *you're* supposed to be a girl—a teenager—a daughter who gets to be sad about losing her dad without having to play grown-up for the grown-ups!" she finished, breathing hard. Her friends stared at her as the heat of her anger drained away, leaving her heart cold and broken again. "Oh. Oh, no. Em, I'm sorry. Really I shouldn't have said all of that. I—"

"Hello, Mercy. Hello, children." Emily's mother stepped into the foyer behind them. "What is it you just said?"

Emily drew a deep breath and turned to face her mom. "Mercy said that I need to get out of the house, and she's right. Mom, I need a break. I have to have a break." She blinked hard, obviously trying to keep the tears pooling in her eyes from spilling over.

Emily's mom looked from her daughter to her friends. Her eyes were glassy, but her voice didn't waver when she spoke. "Emily, you're right. Go ahead. Be with your friends."

"Emily?" Her grandma joined Emily's mother.

"Grandma, these are my friends," said Emily.

Grandma walked stiffly to Emily and rested one hand on her shoulder. "Yes, I can see that they are."

"Beatrice, Emily was just going out," said Em's mother.

The older woman looked back at her daughter-in-law. "I think that's an excellent idea. Helene, would you join me in the kitchen?"

Emily's mom's eyes filled with tears. She nodded. "Yes. I would like that. Very much."

"What's happening out there?" slurred her grandfather.

"Nothing!" The two older women yelled together, and then they shared a real smile.

"Go. Be with your friends," repeated Em's mom after kissing her daughter on the forehead. "We'll be just fine."

Emily seemed unable to speak, so Mercy tugged on her hand as Jax opened the door and they all filed out.

They all piled into the Camry Hunter had parked across the street from the Parrotts' house, and as Mercy—with occasional help from Hunter and Xena—unfolded the truth behind the settling of Goodeville and the tragic events of the past four days, the shadows under Emily's eyes lifted. From her place between Jax and Xena in the center of the backseat, she sat up straighter, her expression growing more animated until she held up a hand and stopped Mercy.

"You're *real* witches." She looked from Hunter to Mercy. "I mean, I kinda knew it before, and that grief spell made me think that there was more to your powers than just herbs to fix cramps and an occasional love potion."

"Love potions are not actually what you think they are," said Xena. "It isn't ethical to play with someone's desires. Goode witches would never—"

"Xena, I don't think that's an important point right now," interrupted Mercy. She met her friend's gaze. "What is important is that you understand the truth. Since 1693, Goode witches have been guardians of those five gates—"

"Which are really the five weird trees?" Jax broke in.

"Yes," continued Mercy, nodding at him. "And we have to close and strengthen those gates tonight—at sunset." She glanced outside at the waning light. "Which will be pretty soon. Will you help us?"

Emily didn't hesitate. "Yes. That's what friends do, right? But it's more than that. This is why your mom and my dad were killed. So, we're getting rid of the Cyclops tonight?"

Hunter spoke firmly. "I promise."

"I'm totally in."

"Jax?" Mercy asked.

"Just tell me what I need to do."

The band of tension began to release from around Mercy's chest. She dug into her purse and pulled out the six sheets of paper she'd prepared the night before. Mercy handed out four of them, keeping two for herself—leaving the sixth sheet facedown on her lap. "Okay, ask any questions you have—anything at all. It starts with setting your intention. That means that as soon as we're on our way to our trees each of us must focus. Read my instructions carefully. Hunter and I are going to be channeling powerful energy through you tonight. You have to be prepared for it."

"How are we going to—" Emily began and then had to stop as three sneezes shook her body. "OMG, bless me!" She wiped her nose on the back of her sleeve. "Gross. Sorry. I don't know what's wrong with me. I usually only sneeze like this around . . ." Her words trailed off as her head swiveled to stare at Xena, who was licking the back of her hand and smoothing her hair.

"What?" Xena stopped mid-lick.

"We might as well tell them," said Hunter. "They know everything else."

Mercy shrugged. "Fine with me. Xena?"

The cat person shook herself, which sent her hair flying madly around her shoulders and made Emily sneeze again. "Emily, kitten." Xena took her hand gently between hers. "I *am* a cat. Their cat. And by theirs I mean I've been a Goode familiar for generations. Please don't ask for how many years—it's impolite." While Emily and Jax stared slack-mouthed at her, Xena nodded. "Oh, and Emily, I am truly sorry I make you sneeze. I give you my word I do not do it on purpose. I've always liked you, kitten." She dimpled at Jax and made a little purring noise. "You, too."

Emily and Jax turned their wide-eyed gazes from Xena, who went back to grooming herself, to the twins.

"It's true," answered Hunter and Mercy together—though they didn't share the intimate smile that usually accompanied their twin-speak.

Emily went back to staring at Xena. "In a completely bizarre way that makes perfect sense."

"Yup," said Jax, who shot Xena sideways glances.

"Kittens." She paused in her grooming. "Refocus on your intention. We can discuss how spectacularly magical I am another time."

"I'm gonna have to get some Benadryl. A *lot* of Benadryl," muttered Emily as her attention returned to the spell.

"Okay, so, to answer the question I think Em was starting to ask," Mercy said. "We're going to communicate through our speaker phones."

"Except for me," Hunter broke in. "There's no way to know if I'll be able to be on my phone. Mercy will use our connection to know when I'm in place. And then you'll have to trust me to keep up."

Mercy nodded. She didn't look at Hunter. *Good. She won't try to take over. I'm better at this part anyway,* Mercy told herself. "So, I'm going to lead you through the ritual, and I'll be sure I don't waste time on flowery words and such. We light candles, then seal the gates with—"

"Blood!" Emily squeaked, her eyes on the cheat sheet.

Xena patted her knee. "Yes, kitten, but not very much."

Mercy barreled on quickly. "Then you thank your tree and blow out your candle—and we're done!"

Emily raised her hand. "You said we each need an offering, but I don't have anything."

"Em, you'll be at the cherry tree that guards the Japanese gate," explained Mercy. "I brought your offering." She reached into her purse and brought out the beautiful little Japanese sumi-e Emily had painted in remembrance of Abigail Goode.

Emily took it, holding it carefully, gazing at the soaring owl. "It seems like a million years ago that I painted this."

"It is a perfect offering," Xena assured her. "Something precious created with love."

Jax waved his hand, getting their attention. "What's my offering?"

"The dove feather you got from your dad, remember?" answered Hunter.

"Oh, right! Got it in my pocket." Jax patted his jean's pocket.

Mercy turned to look at her sister. "I didn't see what offering you brought."

Her twin's emotionless eyes met hers. Her voice had a hard edge to it that bordered on anger. "I'm going to get it on my way to the tree, but you already knew that, so why did you need to ask?"

Mercy just stared at her, unable to arrange the right words to reply.

Into the sudden silence Emily spoke up. "My other question is about the, um, blood."

"Oh, I can answer that." Xena bent and brought out a small, rectangular box from below the seat in front of her. She opened it to expose five tiny daggers, each about the size of a pinky finger. They nestled on faded red velvet.

"I've never seen those before," Hunter said, peering over the front seat.

"They were in the attic," Xena said, "in Gertrude Goode's hope chest."

"What are they?" asked Mercy, intrigued by the perfection of their carved bone handles and their razor-like blades.

"Miniature athames." When Emily and Jax sent her confused

looks Xena fluttered her fingers at them and clarified. "Sorry, kittens. I keep forgetting how new all of this is to you. An athame is a witch's dagger—used only for rituals and spells. In the past, witches used a lot more bloodletting in their spellwork." She sighed nostalgically. "That seems to have gone out of style. Well, go on, each of you, take one." She passed the box around and everyone chose their athame.

"Cut yourself beneath your thumb, on that meaty part of your palm," Hunter said. She moved her shoulders uncomfortably when everyone's gaze turned to her. "What? It's not super sensitive there, and it'll be easy to just prick yourself and then squeeze it to make the blood drip."

"I already sanitized the blades," added Xena.

Emily sneezed and then thanked her.

"Okay, does anyone have any more questions?" Mercy asked. "Sunset will be in about thirty minutes."

"I think I get it," said Emily as she held her athame carefully.

"All I need to know is which one is my tree," said Jax.

"Your tree is the banyan. It guards the Hindu gate," said Mercy. "Em, you already know that yours is the Japanese gate."

"I've always liked that tree," said Emily.

"Xena, I thought you should go to the Egyptian tree—what with Bast being an Egyptian goddess and all."

Xena nodded. "Yes, kitten, I agree. And I have the perfect offering. I shall leave a lock of my luxurious hair. I know Bast will appreciate that."

"Hunter," said Mercy, "you'll need to go to—"

"I know what I need to do."

Mercy thought she'd never seen Hunter's eyes look so blue or so cold—like someone had frozen the Caribbean Sea. She squared her shoulders and faced Hunter. It was time.

"Do you *really* know what to do?"

"I'm taking care of the Cyclops. Cleaning up the real mess. As usual."

"As usual?" Mercy frowned at Hunter.

"And you don't need to tell me what to do."

"What's going on between them?" Emily whispered from the backseat, but Xena gently shushed her.

Mercy felt one of the wounds in her heart begin to bleed, but she ignored it. *It was time.* "Whatever, Hunter. You're still not getting it." She lifted the sheet of paper that had been waiting on her lap. "You have to put aside Tyr and choose a *goddess.* It's your *god* that caused this. Your god that made the trees sick." Mercy struck twice with her words, drew a breath, and then slashed the third and most devastating wound. *"Your god caused the Fenrir to escape."* Hunter's shoulders jerked in pain, but Mercy forced herself to go on. "Being a lesbian doesn't mean you had to choose a *god* instead of a *goddess*." Mercy turned the page and held it so Hunter could read it.

Hunter's eyes blazed with rage as she ripped the page from Mercy's hands. "My sexuality has nothing to do with choosing Tyr. So, do you also believe that Jax is my best friend because he's a guy? Did you ever think that I'm more interested in the person, or *god*, and less concerned with their gender?" Mercy opened her mouth to speak, but Hunter didn't give her the opportunity. "And, if you'd bothered to do any real research, you'd know that they didn't see queerness as an identity back when this prophecy was written, so there's no possible way great aunt *whoever* could have been referring to me." Then she balled up the paper and threw it onto the floorboard. She jerked open her car door and grabbed her backpack from where it rested on the seat between them. Before she got out of the car, she hurled her words at Mercy.

"I'll do it," she said. "I'll betray my god and choose a goddess. I'll make this sacrifice and fix everything, not because there's something wrong with me, but because you're too weak to help yourself."

Hunter surged from the car. "Jax, I'm riding with you. Drop me off at the sheriff's." She stomped away, leaving Jax to scramble after her.

"Kitten! Do be careful!" Xena called through the window at Hunter's back.

Mercy had to swallow several times before she could speak and when she did her voice sounded hollow, like something had just gouged through her. "Em, would you drive?"

As Emily silently went to the driver's seat, Xena's soft hand stroked the back of Mercy's hair as she murmured, "Oh, my poor kittens . . ."

Twenty-nine

Goose bumps peaked along Hunter's arms as she opened the heavy glass door of the sheriff's department. It was cold. *Really* cold. Arctic tundra cold. She pulled the sleeves of her holey cardigan over her hands and rubbed them against her arms. Her boots squeaked across the shiny linoleum floor as she headed to the long, beige counter that separated the townspeople from those tasked with keeping them safe.

Trish McAlister poked up from behind the counter. Her curly red hair bounced against her pink cheeks as she hefted up a box labeled DONATE and set it on top of the Formica-covered ledge. An aluminum can spilled over the top of the box and landed on the floor with a thud.

"I got it!" Hunter welcomed the excuse to jog over and supply more heat to her body. "Only a tiny dent." She pointed to the dimple and set the can of green beans back in the box.

"They're for the elementary school's food drive." Trish brushed a few perfectly spiraled locks away from her green eyes and smiled. "I don't much think they'll care about a little dent." She shivered and zipped her puffy winter jacket up to her throat.

Hunter bounced in place and flexed her stiffening fingers. "I think your a/c has gone insane."

Trish clasped her hands in front of her and buried her chin in the collar of her coat. "The sheriff is having quite the time staying cool." Her glossed lips smoothed into a thin line. "With his hot flashes and mood swings, you'd think he was going through some type of male menopause." She grumbled before glancing up at Hunter. The color in her cheeks deepened cherry red. "But you didn't come to hear about that." She waved away the comment and lifted herself onto the stool behind the counter. "Now, what can I do for you . . . ?"

"Hunter," she supplied.

"Thank you, Hunter. It's just that you girls are so darn hard to tell apart." Trish's shoulders shook with a chuckle. "So, what can I do for you, *Hunter*?"

Hunter clenched her toes. "I need to speak with the sheriff. It's an emergency."

"Oh?" Trish pressed her hand against her chest and tilted her chin, birdlike. "I hope it's nothing serious."

"Not too serious." She cleared her throat. "Well, it *is* an emergency. Can an emergency be *un*serious?" Her toes ached and she blew out a puff of air. "I just need to see the big man in charge." Hunter bit the inside of her cheeks to keep from spouting more nonsense. If her plan was going to work, she'd have to keep from saying asinine things like *unserious emergency* and *big man in charge.*

Trish slid off her stool and straightened her puffy jacket. "I'll go see if he is taking visitors."

Hunter fought off another a/c-induced shiver. "I'm not really a visitor. I have a serious emergency."

Trish stuffed her hands into her pockets. "Hunter, dear, you are preaching to the choir." Her tennis shoes squeaked on the linoleum as she spun around and marched toward the only office with its door closed.

Except for the occasional ringing phone or *whoosh* of the printer, the sheriff's department was silent. Every few weeks, when Hunter followed Mercy in and out of the businesses along Main Street to hang flyers for the bake sales and club activities the more outgoing twin participated in, the sheriff's department pulsed with energy. Deputy Carter seemed to always be up and around, flashing a straight-toothed grin and those puppy-dog eyes at the women who stopped by to hand out sweets and innocent flirtations. There was laughter from the coffee station, somber meetings in the glass-front conference rooms, and at least one very drunk, very loud townsperson. Hunter rubbed her palms against her bare thighs and shivered. Everything was different now, colder, and it wasn't just the air conditioning. But that's what happened when the easygoing sheriff was body snatched and replaced with a murderous monster.

Hunter flinched with each of Trish's sharp knocks on the sheriff's closed wooden door. Hunter strained to hear what they were saying, but her witchy powers didn't extend to super hearing. She picked at her thumbnail and waited.

Everything rested on her. Everything always rested on her, so that wasn't really a shock, but this was so much different than pulling her sister out of her despair or making sure their mother's funeral arrangements were in order. This was huge—life ending. And then there was Tyr. Hunter swallowed.

Sheriff Dearborn yanked his door open. It slammed against the stopper with a sharp crack. Tension washed over the bullpen. Even the trilling phones quieted in Sheriff Dearborn's wake.

Hunter stiffened. She could do this. She had no choice.

She lifted onto her toes and shouted, "Sheriff!"

His head jerked from Trish to Hunter. Under the fluorescent lights, the lenses of his mirrored sunglasses looked like two starbursts.

Showtime.

Hunter knitted her brow and frowned. "Out by that old olive tree, there's a—a—" She pressed her cold fingers against her lips and sucked in a jagged breath.

The sheriff brushed past Trish and stalked toward Hunter.

Deputy Carter stood and picked up his cowboy hat off his desk. "If you take Miss Goode's statement, I'll drive out there and take a look."

"No!" Dearborn's temples flexed with each sharp clench of his jaw. "What I mean is, I need you"—he swung his gaze around the bullpen—"*all* of you, to stay here. Finish your work. Protect the town. I'll use this . . ." With another clench of his jaw, he flicked the radio attached to his shoulder. "And let you know if I need backup."

Deputy Carter's puppy face disappeared as he dropped his hat back onto his desk and sagged into his chair.

Hunter kept her damsel-in-distress mask firmly in place as she surveyed the office. None of these people had gotten to say goodbye to the real Frank Dearborn. After tonight, if everything went well for Hunter, each person's memory would be stained by the final seventy-two hours they'd spent with Polyphemus, the creature who'd stuffed himself into Frank Dearborn's skin and ruined him in more ways than one.

"Come with me, twin."

Hunter didn't flinch, didn't recoil when Polyphemus pressed his meaty paw against her back and hurried her down the hall. Instead, she surrendered, turned toward him and let him push her outside. In that moment, she needed him, needed to be rescued.

"What's out at the olive tree?" he barked as soon as the door had closed behind them.

"Sheriff, I don't know if you'd believe me if I told you." She wrung her hands. "You'd think I was crazy!" She bit the inside of her cheek until her eyes watered. "I'll have to show you." She swallowed the warm pool of copper sliding across her tongue.

He adjusted the sunglasses on the bridge of his broad nose and sniffled. "Well then, Hunter, I'll drive us on out there." He fished the keys from his pocket, pointed the fob at the cruiser, and pressed a button.

Hunter followed Polyphemus to the car as it unlocked and yellow signal lights lit up the parking lot. "Good guess with the whole *which twin* thing." Hunter could only muster a slight twitch of her lips to accompany her attempt at normalcy.

Polyphemus opened the cruiser door and paused before climbing in. He leaned forward and rested his arm on the roof of the car. "Oh, Hunter." He slid his tongue across his teeth and blew out a quaking breath. "I could never forget that spark behind those blue eyes."

Thirty

Mercy bent to look into the car through the open passenger's side window at Emily and Xena. "Okay, Em, drop Xena off at the park, and then get right to the cherry tree. You two have candles and matches, right?"

"Yes," said Emily. "Don't worry. We've got this."

"Kitten, you must focus on your intention. It is your will that holds all of us together in Ritual."

Mercy ran her hand through her long hair and shoved it back behind her ears. "That's hard to do knowing she hates me."

Xena touched her arm. "No. Hunter hates what she must do tonight. And I hate it for her, don't you? How would you feel if you knew that you must reject Freya?"

Mercy sighed. "I'd feel awful."

"Then understand her instead of judging her. Now, go." Xena paused. "And as you walk to the Norse gate, gain control over your feelings. Blessed be, my kitten."

"Blessed be, Xena," Mercy said. "Good luck, Em."

"Break a leg!" Emily said as she drove off, waving out the window.

With a sigh Mercy hefted her big purse across her shoulder and headed to their backyard and through the little gate to the fields beyond—tracing the steps she and Hunter and Abigail had taken four short nights, but an eternity, ago.

Dusk settled around the cornfields. The evening had been warm, and a soft breeze caressed the growing crops that brought to Mercy the scent of fertile earth and corn silk. The thick stalks whispered secrets she could almost hear. She relaxed into the familiarity of her world and let the earth comfort her internal wounds.

My intention is to lead this ritual to heal the trees and seal the gates with the blood of witches mixed with the representatives of those who once walked this very path—and the unique power that fills this land.

Mercy repeated her intention over and over until it became like the lyrics of a song that wouldn't leave her mind. It blocked everything else and consumed her attention.

She closed her eyes tightly before she was able to approach the mighty apple tree that guarded the Norse gate, and readied herself. She knew what she would see, though as she drew closer and closer to the wide trunk and the umbrella of ancient boughs, Mercy was surprised at how little evidence there remained of the horrible battle and their heartbreaking loss.

Only a few of the gnarled roots that pushed up from the ground like arthritic fingers showed signs of the goddess's inferno that had immolated her mother, though a dark scorch marked the skin of the tree's trunk. Mercy stared at it as her internal mantra faltered.

"Oh, thank you, Athena." Awestruck, Mercy bowed her head and pressed her hand against the blackened bark. At the place where Abigail Goode had died to save her daughters—and her town—the outline of a perfect heart had been burned into the tree.

Then she lifted her head, wiped away her tears, kicked off her shoes, and got to work—and as she prepared to open the ritual, Mercy breathed deeply, evenly, until she felt so grounded that the bare soles of her feet tingled. Then she began allowing emotions to bubble up and release—bubble and release.

Feeling invigorated, Mercy reached into her boho bag and extracted a thick white candle exactly like the ones her four impromptu coven members were, hopefully, also readying. She placed her candle at the base of the apple tree, beneath the point of the heart the goddess had scorched into its bark. She returned to her bag for matches, her phone, and the little jar filled with the last apple butter she and Abigail would ever make together. Mercy's smile was bittersweet as her finger traced the pentagram she'd painted on the side of the Mason jar last fall to mark the final batch of that season's harvest.

"I'll think of you every fall—every time I make jam or apple butter or homemade bread. I'll think of you always, Mama." Mercy placed the jar beside the white candle at the base of the tree, then she waited, repeating her intention mantra over and over.

She didn't wait long. Her phone bleeped with the first text message, a smiling cat emoji from Xena—followed by Emily's READY! And then Jax's LOCKED & LOADED!

Quickly, she joined the four of them in a group call and hit the speaker button as she tucked the phone into a niche in the tree's bark.

"All right, you have placed your candles at the base of your trees?"

"Yes!" Three voices echoed back to her, like ghosts lifting from a grave.

No! No negative imagery! Mercy pushed the thought from her mind and continued.

"Your offerings are ready?"

"Yes!" they replied.

"Okay," Mercy said. "Get your matches out and give me a second. Let me find Hunter."

Mercy faced her tree and centered herself, breathing deeply once, twice, thrice, and then sent her sixth sense—that magical spark that flowed rich and thick through every sister of Salem, each daughter who carried Sarah Goode's legacy—down, down, down to find the vein of power that hummed beneath her bare feet and formed the potent pentagram that surrounded Goodeville. As she tapped into the thrumming ley lines she thought of Hunter—of everything she loved about her sister. Her generosity and kindness—her strength and wit—and above all the thing that was always there, no matter what else was happening in their world, the connection that bound them irrevocably together. The bond that had begun at their conception, forged by blood and sealed by nine months of a shared womb.

Mercy gasped as she connected with her sister. Against her closed lids Hunter swirled as a glowing sapphire orb with silver glitter as if a piece of the cosmos had come to earth, and glistened like a spot on the map of her soul.

"She's there! She's at the olive tree!" Mercy's eyes opened and she crouched before the white pillar candle. As she picked up the match she turned to the glowing face of her phone. "Okay, light your matches while I open the ritual." Mercy struck the match and lit her candle. "And so we begin. We are vessels, cleansed and protected, ready to be conduits for energy. Remember, we do not keep that energy. We only guide it. Visualize the gate before you, deep within the trunk of this ancient tree who has stood guardian for hundreds of years."

She paused to be sure the others were with her, and as she did she thought of Hunter, sending her sister an image of a brightly burning flame. *Please see me, too, Hunter! Please understand! Light your candle!* The sapphire orb in her internal map sparked suddenly brighter. *Is that it? Did you light your candle?*

Mercy's intuition demanded she continue and set the spell. All she could do was move forward and believe Hunter came with them.

"Now, place your offering near your tree. Let your intuition guide you as to where, and as you place it tell your tree that this offering is in honor of the gate it guards and the ancient world beyond. Jax, release your dove feather and thank the peoples who came before us—whose land we now call our own."

Mercy lifted the jar of apple butter. She kissed it, and then reached up and, on her tiptoes, placed it in a niche where two low-hanging limbs joined. "Thank you, mighty apple tree. I make this offering in honor of the Underworld you guard and the Norse land from which you come."

"Holy crap!" Jax's awed voice sparked through the phone. "The feather! It just lifted way, way up with the wind and then disappeared—only there isn't any wind!"

Mercy smiled. "Good. That's really good, Jax." She didn't wait for a sign from Hunter. She knew her sister's offering would be different—dangerous. The offerings at the other trees set the stage for Hunter's, heightening her power—and Mercy fervently hoped it would be enough. She drew another deep breath and continued.

"Okay, here we go. Face your trees. Ready?"

"Ready!" they chorused.

"Imagine that beneath your feet is a thick stream of power," Mercy said. "Something that runs deep and fast within the earth. Xena, what color is yours?"

Xena responded immediately. "It is the yellow of cat eyes. Rich with power."

"Jax, what color is yours?"

Jax's voice was filled with excitement. "Mine is red! Mercy! My eyes are closed, but I see it! I really see it!"

"Emily, what color is yours?"

Emily gasped and shouted, "It's pink! Just like springtime cherry blossoms! Oh, Mag, it's beautiful!"

Mercy smiled. "And mine is green, like new apples." She waited for a moment, hoping Hunter could see her sapphire blue ley line—but she had to keep going. "Think about your ley line while you take out your athames." Mercy heard the rustling as her three coven members did as she told them. "Prick your palms, just below your thumb."

Mercy didn't hesitate. She pulled the athame from the pocket of her embroidered jeans and pressed the razor-sharp blade against her flesh.

It hurt less than she thought it would—mostly it just stung—and then she squeezed the meaty part of her palm until her blood welled in fat drops. "Now, pull your ley line up through your body and push it from the center of your forehead, like a blazing star, to shine against the gate hidden within your tree." Mercy concentrated, pulling her stream of emerald power up, up, up through her body. It wasn't quite as sluggish as it had been that terrible night when Abigail had died, but it didn't fill her body with the glowing energy that always blazed from their mom during Ritual.

Mercy fisted her hands and concentrated harder. It felt like running a marathon. Sweat beaded on her face as she forced the slim stream of power up and out her third eye so that it washed the hidden gate within the tree with a pale light the color of unripe apples.

She stared at the gate, expecting it to be powerful and whole, just as it was every time their mother had shown them this ritual. It was there. It was standing. But instead of a bright, glowing gate, it had turned black, like charcoal. Mercy swallowed bile. "Are any of your gates open?"

"Yes! Mine is! It's kinda hard to see 'cause there isn't a lot of light, but it's pink, like the ley line. It looks terrible—all crumbly—and it smells bad!" Emily panted, like she'd just climbed a wall of stairs.

"Mine looks weird! Like it's made of old blood, and it reeks!" Jax, too, gasped with effort.

Xena's hiss was followed by a low, deep yowl that lifted the hair on the back of Mercy's neck.

"Xena! What's happening?" she shouted into the phone.

"Oh! That must be your Egyptian friend," Xena said. "I can see him beyond the gate. Oh, my. He does have the face of—"

"Xena, is the gate open or closed?" Mercy interrupted.

"Closed, but not well. It—it was once golden." The cat person panted. "But now it flakes like cheap jewelry and the smell is truly vile."

"All three of you—focus on your ley line! Make it shine as bright as possible from your forehead directly onto the spot where your blood dripped on your tree. The ley line power mixed with your blood will close the gate—believe it, know it, make it happen now! And then repeat after me: *By blood and offering—*"

"By blood and offering—" they repeated.

Mercy continued as she channeled her ley line into the tree. *"Through the power of olde—"*

"Through the power of olde—"

Mercy's voice rose, amplified by the energy passing through her and the generations of Goode witches that filled her DNA with magic. *"Bind this spell with our intent, set well and block this hell, block this hell—BLOCK THIS HELL!"*

The three followed her, shouting the conclusion of the spell. The power sizzled, sputtered, and finally faded as Mercy's black gate disappeared. "Now, lift your candle, ground yourselves again, thank your tree, and blow out the candle as you say, *'So I have spoken; so mote it be.'*"

Mercy completed the spell with the others.

"So mote it be!" chorused through the phone.

"Mag! The smell is gone!" Emily's voice trilled through the phone.

"Mine doesn't stink anymore, either!" said Jax.

"The vile odor is gone from my tree as well," said Xena. "Oh, kitten, it must have worked!"

Emily and Jax cheered and Xena's musical laughter lifted with the wind.

Mercy didn't feel triumphant. Not yet. She needed to reach Hunter. She closed her eyes and, wearily, found her ley line so that she could connect with her sister. She focused on her sister, seeking . . . seeking . . .

But found nothing.

Mercy tried again.

Nothing. No sapphire orb—no swirling stars and moons—not even the strange, psychic tickle she had *always* been able to feel, *always* been able to find.

"Emily!" she shouted into the phone. "Pick up Xena and get back here for me! Jax, meet us at the olive tree." Her voice faltered. "Hunter's gone!"

Thirty-one

Hunter's hands shook. She balled them into fists and stuffed them into her lap. She had a plan, had worked it out on the way to Emily's and finalized it in the stiff and bloated silence that now filled the inside of Sheriff Dearborn's car. All she had to do was ground and protect herself, forsake her god, and get Polyphemus before he got her. No biggie.

She blew out a puff of air. First things first. She planted her feet in the car's footwell. Grounding herself while on the move wasn't difficult. Hunter wasn't one for holding still. Unless she was writing, too much stillness meant too much thought, too much opportunity for her demons to catch up with her, and she preferred to keep them chasing.

Hunter closed her eyes and reached up, up, up, until she was nowhere. Until she was nothing. Just black and cold and stardust. Grounding didn't always mean reaching down into the soul of the earth. For Hunter, it meant grasping the heart of the cosmos.

"Can't fall asleep on me now, Hunter," he said. "I need those bright eyes of yours to lead me to this . . . what did you say it was again?"

Hunter flinched and her eyelids fluttered open. "By the olive tree. There's, uh . . ." She blinked through the haze clouding her vision. She'd let him pull her back too soon. She wasn't yet grounded or protected. She floated somewhere between the earth and the heavens, sinking through quicksand to get back to her body. "Burn mark. Of a person. Weird stuff. You have to see it to believe it."

He turned down the unpaved road that led to the tree and the gate and Hunter's future. He adjusted the sheriff's sunglasses and said, "I've seen some pretty weird things." His meaty paw clamped onto her thigh. "Maybe I'll tell you about them before the night is over." Moist heat seeped from his fingers and drowned every pore of her bare thigh.

"It—it's just up ahead." Hunter cursed her voice for trembling.

"I know." Polyphemus released her leg and Hunter fought the urge to wipe the ghost of his grip from her skin. His knuckles popped on the steering wheel as he guided Dearborn's cruiser onto the shoulder.

She unbuckled the seat belt and threw open her door before he'd put the car in park. "It's off the road, here," she said, tapping her phone to activate the flashlight.

His hand was back on her thigh. "Leave your phone in the car." He squeezed her flesh and a wave of nausea rippled through her stomach. "Wouldn't want to drain your battery." He let go and pulled a Maglite from his belt. "Plus, I've got this covered." He clicked it on, then off, then on again.

Hunter's throat went dry as she placed her phone on the dashboard and stepped out of the cruiser. Gravel crunched beneath her shoes as she backed away from the car, from *him*.

Polyphemus shined the cone of light across Hunter. "Where exactly is the weirdness you've been going on about?"

Hunter blinked the spots of light from her eyes and pointed at the stake the sheriff's department had left behind. He cast the light onto the field and stopped when the beam flashed on the stake and the strip of yellow caution tape fluttering in the breeze.

"You wanted to show me that they left behind some trash?"

Hunter charged into the tall grass. Polyphemus was right behind her. The flashlight's glow spilled across her left side and a half shadow stretched along the grass. Hunter looked at the sky and the sliver of moon that peeked out from behind the clouds. Mother Moon would always be with her. She couldn't say the same about Tyr. Her fingers found the pendant hanging from her neck.

She reached the stake and froze. The scorched earth was gone, vanished. "It was here." She crouched next to the grass, unstained but still crushed in the shape of Earl Thompson's body.

With a snort, Polyphemus shined the light onto the ground.

"It was right here," Hunter repeated. "I had my tarot." She mimed shuffling her deck. "I took out the cards." She drew three invisible cards and set them in the grass. "I asked each card a question and they each gave an answer. One of them burned the earth. Here." She passed her hand over Earl Thompson's imprint. "And—" Her voice caught as she turned to where the footsteps had been burned into the earth. Now, Polyphemus filled that space in the grass, the sheriff's large boots the same size as the vanished scorch marks. Hunter brushed her hands on her shorts and stood. This didn't derail her plan, it just changed it a bit.

Polyphemus stepped closer. The toe of his boot touched hers. His coppery breath warmed her face. "I'd almost lost hope, but then I found you, Bright Eyes." His palm melted against her cheek. "I've searched for you for centuries." His thumb grazed her bottom lashes, slid down the slope of her nose and pressed against her lips.

Hunter parted her lips. "I'm here now," she whispered and let her mouth graze his thumb. She watched her reflection in Sheriff Dearborn's sunglasses as she bit into his flesh.

Her teeth sunk into skin. Blood hit her tongue as Polyphemus howled. He yanked his hand free. Pain fireworked against Hunter's cheek. She hadn't heard the slap or seen it coming, but the shape of his hand now burned against her face.

Hunter scrambled backward and tripped over the flashlight he'd dropped. She caught herself as the light settled across the forest of grass. She moved backward, closer to the tree as Polyphemus stalked toward her. But this wasn't a retreat. This was a preparation.

"I am a Goode witch!" she shouted. Mangled roots jutted from the ground as Hunter neared the ancient olive. "My blood carries magic. So does yours, Polyphemus. I can feel it prick my throat like shards of glass." She spit Polyphemus's blood into her hand. "Your blood!" She pulled the athame from her pocket and sliced her blood-splattered palm. "My blood!" Scarlet gushed from the wound and swirled across Polyphemus's blood like a whirlpool against her skin. "I draw down the power of the moon and the heat of the stars!" She thrust her red palm to the sky and, for a moment, the heavens flickered.

Polyphemus roared. Hunter's pulse surged through her ears as she widened her stance and let him shorten the distance between them. With the demi-god only steps away, Hunter rushed forward. A scream scraped against the back of her throat as their bodies collided. Polyphemus grabbed her ponytail and snapped her head back.

Her hands found his shoulders, his neck, his ears. She yanked off his sunglasses and clapped her bloody palm against his good eye. "Release!" she commanded the cosmic energy she'd stored in the crimson pool that swirled against her palm. Heat shot from Hunter's palm.

With a screech, Polyphemus wrenched away. He slapped his hands over his eye and folded as he tripped backward.

Hunter ran to the base of the tree. Her hand trembled as she grabbed Tyr's pendant and yanked. The rope cord resisted. It burned the back of her neck as she pulled harder—then it snapped. Her eyes filled with tears, turning Polyphemus into a writhing blur of dark colors. She held the symbol of Tyr to her lips and whispered, "I'm sorry."

She threw the pendant to the ground and swiped the back of her hand across her eyes. "Amphitrite!" The tree's wide trunk pressed against Hunter's back as she called on a new deity—a goddess to set things right. "Wife of Poseidon and goddess of the sea, I come bearing a gift!"

Polyphemus's screams turned to growls and he charged Hunter, arms blindly thrashing the air. The flesh around his once good eye was raw, the edges charred. Hunter had blinded him, but she hadn't stopped him.

Her throat turned to barbed wire and she choked on the fear caught in the back of her mouth. "Amphitrite," she barked, her voice nearly drowned out by her thundering pulse. "I offer you Polyphemus, proof of your husband's adultery! Take him back to Tartarus and I'll submit my will to yours!"

The air cooled and the hairs along Hunter's arms bristled. Light poured from the tree, from the gate, the same cerulean as a blue giant. Polyphemus's boots beat the ground as he sped toward the brilliant glow.

Hunter pulled the athame from her pocket as the demi-god tripped on the olive tree's roots and slammed into her. Air shot out of her lungs and she lost her grip on the knife. It fell to the ground, its sharp point glinting in the blue light. Bark tore into Hunter's back as Polyphemus's weight crushed her to the ground. He roared. Spittle flew from his lips and sprayed Hunter's forehead. His hands clawed up her chest and snaked around her neck. She pawed the earth for the blade as Polyphemus squeezed her throat. The tips of her fingers brushed something cool, something metal. She gripped the hilt, raised the blade, and drove the point into his temple.

Spit showered Hunter's face as Polyphemus howled and his grip tightened on her throat.

Hunter swiped her wounded hand through the blood that leaked from his head. "We are all stardust." The words barely passed from her lips as she focused the last of her energy through her blood and into his.

Polyphemus's blood, charged with her power, sizzled against his skin. It bubbled and popped and ate through to bone. He yanked one hand from Hunter's neck and pawed at the flesh on his face that burned away into nothing.

Bursts of light flashed across Hunter's vision as Polyphemus pressed his weight against the hand still clutching her throat. The blue air coated Hunter's skin as she clawed his thick wrist. A chill tickled her spine and a woman's laughter slipped through Hunter's ears like the tongue of a snake.

Merry meet, Hunter Goode. Amphitrite's voice was like smoke, everywhere and nowhere. *I accept your offering, my child.*

Ice speared Hunter's chest. She looked down at the blue light shining through her. Amphitrite's slender arm reached out from Hunter's sternum like a spear. The goddess's laughter was a shrieking train as she grabbed Polyphemus. She sank her pointed nails into his forearm. The same blue light that shone from her skin and coated the air seeped up Polyphemus's arm. He ceased his screams and blindly blinked at Hunter. His skull, slick with blood and melted flesh, glowed as the blue light spread from one side of his body to the other.

Tartarus hath no fury like a goddess scorned. Amphitrite yanked Polyphemus's arm, and he passed through Hunter's chest as the goddess ripped him from Goodeville and cast him back into the Greek Underworld.

They vanished. Hunter fell to her knees in a fit of coughs. She sucked in air as the blue light receded back into the gate.

You are mine, now, Hunter Goode. Amphitrite's voice faded as the warm dark night retook the field.

Soft blades poked Hunter's sliced palm as she crawled through the trampled grass toward the flashlight. Her chest quaked with the memory of the otherworldly magic that had cut through her. She fumbled with the heavy flashlight and forced her legs underneath her. Her hand shook and the beam of light wavered as she guided it down the street until it landed on Sheriff Dearborn's car. She stumbled into a run. The dome lights clicked on as she opened the passenger door.

Amber light poured onto her, dirt-streaked and blood-crusted, as she swiped her phone off the dash.

With trembling hands, she dialed her sister's number. Hunter barely heard Mercy's voice over the echo of Amphitrite's words.

You are mine, now, Hunter Goode.

Epilogue

Hunter sat in the cool shadows that the palm fronds cast onto the grass. When they'd all decided to spend the afternoon at the park, she'd silently cheered. Writing outside was so much better than writing inside. But in the rush to get out of the house, she'd forgotten her journal. The worst part was that she knew exactly where it was. She closed her eyes and glided through her front door, past the living room, and into the kitchen. There it was. On top of the forgotten cooler full of seltzer and the pee-yellow tea Mag brewed and insisted tasted just like green gummy bears.

Jax's foot bumped Hunter's as he maneuvered out of the tree's shadows and back into the sun. Beside her, he closed his eyes, his lashes nearly dusting his round cheeks, and resumed tossing the football from one hand to the other while Emily and Mercy shook with girlish giggles. From now on, every day would be like this. Every day would be simple.

With an eruption of laughter, Emily threw her head back. She nearly toppled over onto the red-and-white-checkered blanket she had brought from home. She fanned her face and insisted Mercy, "Stop playing."

Hunter plucked a white clover flower and rolled the stem between the thumb and forefinger of her bandaged hand. Clover dotted the grass like patches of green fog. When the rains left and the summer sun arrived, the clover would be the only lush green in the entire park. She dusted her chin with the puffy flowers. That's what this field should be. Clover. A big, fluffy, green mattress of clover that stretched from the palm tree all the way to the playground. Hunter's neck ached as she leaned over and dropped the flower on Jax's stomach while children's laughter drifted on the breeze like faraway church bells. The scene was postcard perfect.

Hunter instinctively ran her fingertips along her sternum where Tyr's pendant had once been. Where Amphitrite had reached through her. She swallowed and dropped her hand into her lap. Well, the scene was *almost* perfect.

Mercy leapt to her feet and bounded over to Jax. "Go long!" she shouted as she stole the football and ran toward the playground. Mercy had finally gotten rid of Kirk, but no one could get rid of football.

Jax popped up. The clover flew off his shirt and landed next to Hunter's wounded hand.

Mercy jumped up and down and triumphantly waved the ball overhead. "You, too, H!" she called and added a butt wiggle to her victory dance.

Jax tapped Hunter's foot with his own. "Up and at 'em . . . or is it *Adam*?" He jutted his chin and scratched his sideburn.

Emily leaned back onto her elbows and cocked her head. "But who's *Adam*?"

"Hey!" Hunter practically heard her sister stomp her foot as Mercy cupped her hand around the side of her mouth. "You guys are taking a million years!"

With a groan, Hunter picked up the flower and got to her feet. "Doesn't Em have to play?" She tried to hide how much her muscles still ached and how much tension now hung in the air between her and her sister.

Emily scooped Mercy's giant bag onto her lap and fished out a pair of paisley-rimmed sunglasses. "I'll be the referee." She slid on the glasses and set Mercy's purse back on the blanket. "Or the cheerleader." She crossed one ankle over the other and pointed and flexed her toes. "Whichever one makes it so that I don't have to get up."

Hunter yipped as Jax launched into the air and his hip smashed into her. The sudden *thwack* of the ball against the tree was the perfect sound effect to Hunter's crash onto the grass. This time, she couldn't hide her pain.

Mercy rushed to her. "Sorry!" she squeaked, her shadow merging with the one the palms cast across the grass.

Jax offered Hunter his hand and pulled her to her feet. "H, I am so sorry!"

"I just can't stop getting beat up." She offered a heartless half smile as she glanced down at the crushed flower and brushed her hands off on her shorts.

Emily was the only one who chuckled.

Mercy clapped her hands and lifted onto her toes. "I didn't know I had such a great arm. *I* should be the Mustangs' QB."

"Yeah." Jax snorted and headed toward the ball. "Kirk wouldn't lose his mind about that."

Hunter rolled her eyes and trailed after Jax and Mercy. "Isn't most of it gone already, anyway?"

Emily pushed the borrowed sunglasses onto her head as she entered the palm's wide shadows. "It'd be really sad if what we've seen so far is him operating at one hundred percent."

Mercy stuffed her hands into the pockets of her dress. "I used to think he was smart, but when I look back, I'm like, *goddess, he was a total oaf.*"

Emily lifted her hands into the air. "Finally, she sees the light!"

Hunter draped her arm over Mercy's shoulders and pulled her in close. Mercy had not only seen the light—she'd taken a piece of it and pressed it into her heart. She glowed from the inside out. Hunter was glad to have her sister back, though Mercy's nearness no longer filled Hunter with warm fuzzies.

Jax bent over to pick up the ball and jerked to a halt before his fingers grazed the pigskin. He craned his neck and looked up, up, up. "Uh, Mag . . . ?"

Hunter stiffened. She slid her arm from Mercy's back and followed Jax's attention up one of the palm's five trunks. Cracks spiderwebbed the bark like antique porcelain.

Jax stepped back as Mercy crouched down at the base of the trunk. The football had made a divot in the tree, like a fist through drywall. Mercy sucked in a breath, pressed her fingertips against her lips, and shook her head back and forth.

Hunter's heart clicked against her ribs as her swallow lodged within her throat. "What—" She cleared her throat and started again. "What's wrong?"

"Oh, Freya!" Mercy closed her eyes and tilted her chin toward the crown of the tall palm stem. "I can barely feel it breathing."

"But we fixed them." Hunter groped at her chest for the pendant, but she'd discarded it when she threw away her god. It wasn't bad enough she'd lost her mother. She'd forsaken her god as well. But at least . . . "We healed the trees. We healed the gates. *We fixed everything.*"

Mercy's dark hair slipped from her shoulders as she reached out and pressed her hand to the trunk.

The elephant-gray bark cracked like dry earth. Hunter shielded her face as the long stem of the doum palm turned to ash and snowed down around them.

Screams ripped through the ashen air, a loud wailing that shook Hunter's bones and made her heart beat hummingbird fast. Emily gripped Jax's hand as Mercy wrapped her arms around her sister. Hunter pressed her face against Mercy's shoulder, and her spit spackled the light green fabric of Mercy's dress. It was then that Hunter realized she was the one screaming.

"It was for *nothing*!" Hunter tore away from her sister. "I betrayed

Tyr for nothing!" Her knees quaked, but she forced herself to stand. "You made me do it. You fell apart when Mom died because you've never had to face anything in your life. You dropped all of it on me. You said *I* was wrong." The rage returned. It slid through her veins like magma and cooled around her beating heart. "You're just like the rest of them." Hunter swiped the back of her hand against her cheeks. "You think if I'm not *just like* you, there's something *wrong* with me."

Tears glossed Mercy's green eyes. "But Sarah's poem said . . ." She moved closer to Hunter. Ash billowed with each step. "I thought—"

"It doesn't matter what you thought." Hunter shook her head. Papery tree bark fell around them. "What's done is done." Her gaze slid from Mercy to Jax. "Get me out of here." Hunter pressed her fingers against her chest. She wanted her pendant. She wanted her god.

Jax wrapped his arm around Hunter's shoulders and led her to the parking lot.

She ran her teeth along her bottom lip. It had all been for nothing. *She'd nearly died* for nothing. She ignored the parents and children gawking and pointing at the cloud of dust where the palm tree had been. She didn't even look back as Mercy shouted her name. Rock now encased Hunter's heart. It was better that way, safer. Hunter pressed her teeth into her lip. If she had only been stronger, maybe this would be different. Maybe this would never have happened. Maybe Hunter would have cast off the shadow of her sister and healed the gates herself.

She winced. She'd dug her teeth in too deep and bit through raw flesh. She snaked her tongue along her bottom lip. A copper tang heated the inside of her mouth and ran down her throat in a fiery blaze. A shooting star. She looked up at the blanket of sunlight overhead and pictured the stars just beyond. She hadn't known her full power before, but she knew it now. Hunter Goode held the cosmos within her blood.

She'd fix the mess that Mercy had made. And this time, nothing would stand in her way. Not even her sister.

Acknowledgments

We owe a debt of gratitude to our agents, Ginger Clark (PC) and Steven Salpeter (KC) for helping us turn an idea and a few sentences into an amazing series. Thank you!

Profound thanks to our Macmillan family. To Jennifer Enderlin, Anne Marie Tallberg, Monique Patterson, Mara Delgado-Sanchez, Sarah Bonamino, and Michelle Cashman—thank you for your support and encouragement.

Our personal publicist, Deb Shapiro, deserves accolades and applause for her imagination, innovation, patience, and hard work. You are the best!

Extra special thank-you to Sabine Stangenberg, who not only keeps my (PC) life running, but is also the talented artist who created the Goodeville map! XXXOOO

To our readers, those who have followed us for more than a decade and our lovely new fans—always remember, you are strong and smart and worthy of happiness and respect and love, always love.

OMENS BITE

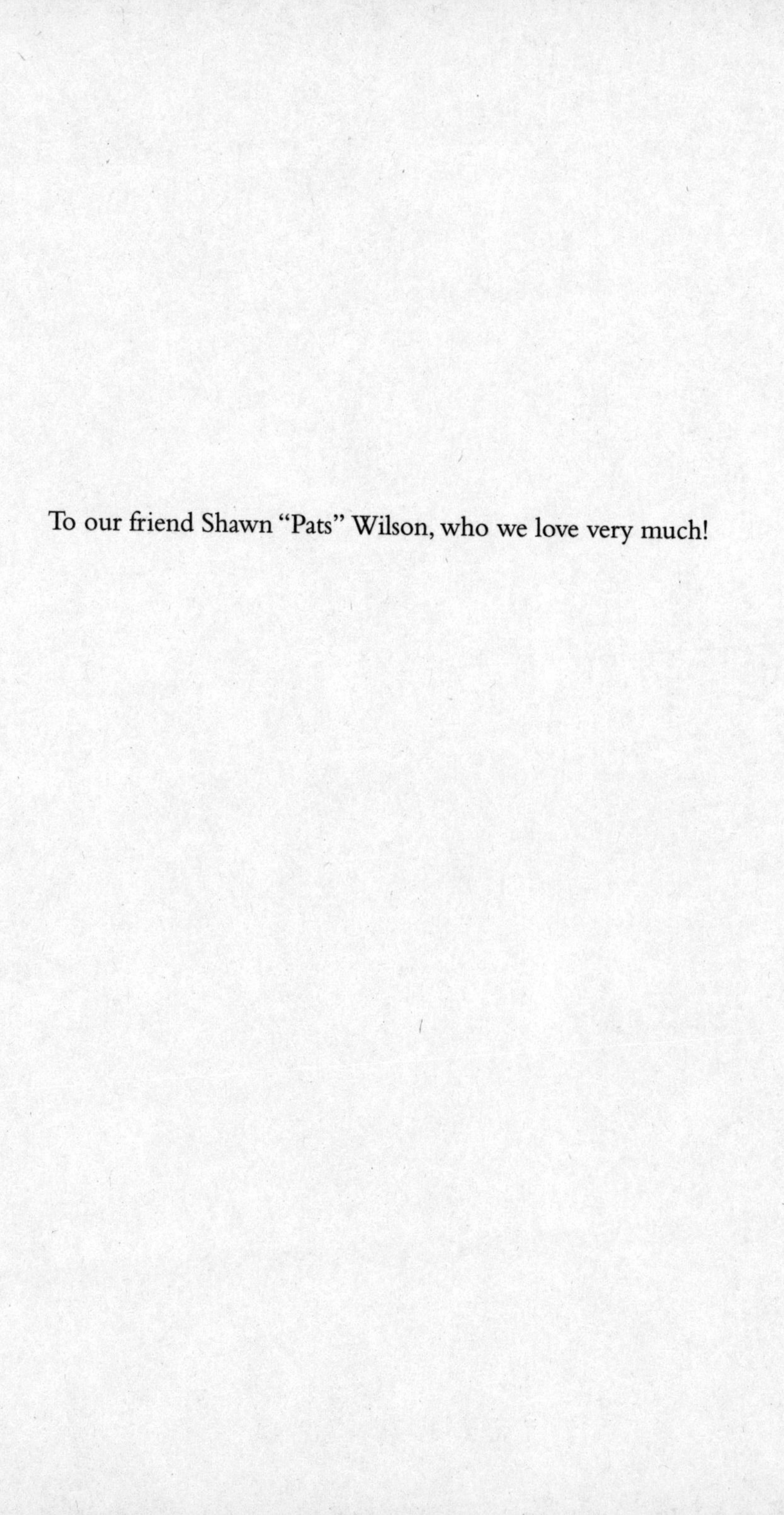

To our friend Shawn "Pats" Wilson, who we love very much!

Prologue

Hunter's shriek matched the crack of lightning that lit Goodeville's night sky. Each flash of white spotlighted her frenzied movements—chopping, shoveling, and screaming and crying—until she threw the ax onto the grass and the final log down beside it. Mud splattered against her face. She tilted her chin toward the sky, closed her eyes, and let the rain wash away the dirt. It was almost finished.

Hunter took a deep breath and wiped her cool, rain-soaked sleeve against her hot cheeks before she bent down and picked up the shovel she'd cast aside when digging had become too much and she'd chosen the ax instead. Chopping the skinny logs had felt good. The way the blade glinted in the flashes of lightning and made that chest-rattling *thwack* as it split the wood had momentarily dried Hunter's tears. But then she had remembered the doum palm and how its tall stem had turned to ash under her sister's touch. Mercy had made Hunter forsake her god in the name of a poem she had called *prophecy.* Hunter had always followed her twin sister's lead. She had always wadded up her feelings and stuffed them down her throat so no words could escape. So her *truth* could not escape.

She'd lost her mother, her god, and soon she'd lose her sister, too.

Letting go of Mercy was necessary. Letting go of Mercy would set Hunter free. Never again would she be forced to choke down her feelings. She'd let them loose, and she'd start now.

Hunter's throat burned as she screamed and flung another shovel of dirt over her shoulder. She didn't care where the mud went as long as it wasn't here, in this space she made for her mother. The shovel's wooden handle bit into the tear in Hunter's palm. She spat out a curse and threw the shovel to the ground. She jumped into the pit and her bare feet sank into the mud. It squelched as she pulled out each foot and shook off the clumps of wet earth. She dropped to her knees and dug her fingers into the ground. Mud scraped against her bleeding palm and pressed into her nailbeds as she tore at the dirt and threw fistfuls out of the fresh grave. But the pain in her body was nothing compared to that of her broken heart.

Rain pooled around her toes and sloshed against her shins. Every muscle ached. Heat pricked her chest, and her vision swam in unshed tears—for her mother, for herself. Hunter's fingers hit rock and what was left of her jagged nails bent and snapped against the unforgiving boulders. She reached out and grabbed the grassy lip of the grave and pushed herself to standing.

Hunter leaned forward and shoveled the split oak logs and snapped pine branches into the hole in the earth. She arranged the wood to cover the bottom of the grave as muddy water splashed against her knees and twigs scraped her calves. Pain splintered her body. It was almost too much, but was what she deserved for hiding in her twin sister's shadow. It would hurt worse tomorrow, but the hurt would be a reminder. That's always how it went for Hunter. Every scar, a lesson learned.

Hunter crawled out of the pit. She collapsed onto the grass next to the grave she'd dug for her mother, closed her eyes, and let sleep overtake her.

One

Hunter smoothed the hem of her white linen dress against her legs. She'd dug the dress out of the back of her closet and hadn't bothered to iron it. A fact she knew would drive Mercy insane. Hunter also hadn't bothered to mop up the dirty footprints she'd left behind as she'd dragged herself from the backyard, through the house, and up the stairs to her bathroom. She'd come in sometime after the rain had stopped and the crickets had swarmed, chirping and hopping as if they'd gotten drunk off the storm. Hunter collected her journal and pen from the kitchen counter and retraced her crusted mud footprints into the living room, parting from them to collapse onto the couch. Her gaze lingered on the muddy footprints. Her sister would hate them, too.

Hunter grinned and unclasped the lock on her journal as she stared out the living room window. The night sky had pierced the rising sun, which bled egg yolk yellow against the clouds. She set her journal on the side table and capped her pen before rubbing her eyes. Hunter had cried so much that her tears had dried up, along with any sense of compassion she'd had for her sister. Perhaps it hadn't been compassion that she'd felt for Mercy, but pity. Hunter bit down on the tip of her worn fingernail. It didn't matter now. She'd lost her mother and forsaken her god and Hunter didn't have anything left to give the one person in her life who did nothing but take.

The screen door creaked open and Hunter loosed another smile as Jax balanced four paper cups in his hands and closed the door with his foot. His head-to-toe white was less wrinkled than Hunter's, but was the same loose, cruise ship style. His crooked teeth poked out from the bottom of his sheepish half grin as he made a beeline for the side table.

Hunter dragged her fingernail along the mounds and bumps of her full pocket. Not wearing the traditional funeral black was understandable—this wasn't a traditional funeral—but why white? It wasn't the color of celebration. Heteronormative weddings had taught the entire country that white was the color of purity, virginity. And who wanted to think about sex at a funeral? But the Goode witches had worn white for mourning for ages, and it wasn't a custom Hunter was interested in breaking.

Jax handed Hunter a cup and plopped down next to her on the couch. Hunter held the cup beneath her lips and blew into the open circle. Air whooshed like a muffled foghorn as Jax draped his arm across Hunter's shoulders.

"You doing okay, H?" he asked, shaking his inky black hair away from his forehead.

NO. Hunter swallowed the word. It stuck inside her chest like a cocklebur. She took a drink. The tea scorched her mouth and burned all the way down to her belly.

There.

She leaned her head against Jax's forearm.

That's better.

The stairs announced Mercy's arrival with a groan. She walked down two steps, stopped, adjusted the crown of white flowers braided into her hair, and ran her hands along the lacy bodice of her floor-length dress before she continued her descent. The gown pooled against the stairs, and with each step, the fabric slid behind her like a shadow.

A door closed upstairs, and hurried footsteps tapped against the wood floor. Emily stopped at the top of the stairs, clutching a bundle of dried herbs in her hands like a bridal bouquet. "Mag, you forgot this." She waved the herbs in the air as she clicked down the steps and followed Mercy to the bottom of the staircase.

Jax slid his arm out from behind Hunter and reached for the side table and the two remaining drinks. He stood and walked to Emily and Mercy, his brow pinched as he watched the lids of the cups. "Two oat milk vanilla lattes." The corners of his lips quirked. "I wasn't sure what you'd want so I googled *most popular coffee drinks.*" He handed the girls their beverages and took a drink of his own.

"Thanks, Jax." Mercy wrapped her arms around him and closed her eyes as she squeezed him against her.

Hunter's grip dented the flimsy cup. If she wasn't careful, Mercy would steal Jax, too.

Mercy released Hunter's best friend and looped her arm through Emily's. "I'm so glad both of you are here." She took a step. Dirt crunched beneath her feet. She paused and stared at the muddy footprints that trailed through the living room and disappeared into the kitchen. Her temples pulsed as she jerked her head up and narrowed her eyes at Hunter. "*The wake.* What will everyone think if the floor is so—" Another pulse of her dark temples. *"Filthy?"*

Hunter bit the tip of her tongue to keep from laughing. Mercy had always been predictable.

Emily's mouth tightened into a small O. Her gaze went from the footprints, to Mercy, to Hunter and back again. "We need to cleanse ourselves, right? That's what happens before, you know, everything else." She let out an awkward bleat of laughter as she shook the bouquet of herbs under Mercy's chin. "Wave around a smoky bunch of herbs first. Sweep up second."

Hunter set her cup down and pushed herself off the couch. She fished the lighter out of her pocket and flicked her thumb against the spark wheel. A flame shot up a few inches before settling down and wiggling like a dog's stumpy tail. "Let's get started."

Mercy marched over and jerked the lighter out of Hunter's hand. "Abigail would want matches!" Coffee sloshed out of her paper cup and splattered against the floor. Her temples pulsed once, twice, three times. Mercy set the cup and the lighter on the side table and fluffed the ends of her curled hair. "*Matches* are the *right way* to begin any cleansing ceremony." She turned on her heels and marched into the kitchen.

Emily mouthed the words *I'm sorry* and scampered after her bestie. She should be sorry. There were clearly sides, factions, warring clans. Unfortunately for Emily, she had chosen poorly.

With a sigh, Jax slung his arm back around Hunter's shoulders. "So, there's no chance of any olive branching anytime soon?" He blew into the lid of his cup before he took a drink. "I mean," he said with a smack of his lips, "it *is* your mom's funeral. Wouldn't she want you and Mag to stay together?"

Again, Hunter bit her tongue. This time, to keep from screaming. "You and I are together. That's all that matters."

"Always and forever, H." He took another drink. "Always and forever."

Hunter stared into the kitchen as Mercy took the homegrown herbs from Emily. She'd cut a piece of twine and busied herself wrapping it around the bouquet until she was satisfied with the tightly bound bundle. She motioned for Emily to pick up the box of matches off the kitchen island. Together, the friends lit the match and held the flame under the dehydrated plants. Mercy hadn't bothered to wait for Hunter, hadn't even looked back to see if her sister was coming. She'd just gone on as if Hunter didn't exist. And soon, she wouldn't. At least, not to Mercy.

Jax jerked his arm from Hunter's shoulders and swiped at the brown droplets that rolled down the front of his white shirt. "Shit!" He hissed as he tried unsuccessfully to rid himself of the stain.

The woody, earthy scent of burning herbs reached Hunter as she turned to inspect Jax's shirt. Her mouth went dry as she traced her fingers along the damp streaks. It was a T. A perfect T. *It was Tyr.* It had to be. Hunter's former god was trying to reach her.

Jax frowned at his shirt. "Should I change?"

Hunter pressed her wet fingertips against her lips and shook her head.

"You two coming?" Mercy's voice held the same shrill tightness as a substitute teacher on the brink of a meltdown.

Hunter wiped her fingers on her arm and strolled into the kitchen. Mercy held out the cleansing bundle. Smoke coiled and twisted between the sisters. Hunter reached for it and Mercy jerked away at the last second.

"This has all been planned, Hunter." Mercy's green eyes narrowed in warning. "We all have our parts to play. It's going to be beautiful."

For Hunter, looking at her twin had never been like looking in a mirror. Sure, they had the same corn-silk white skin that dusted with freckles at the first sign of summer; long, coal-black hair that spilled in natural waves against their shoulders; and full round cheeks that burned cherry red at the slightest hint of embarrassment. Yes, most people couldn't tell the Goode twins apart, but most people didn't pay close enough attention.

A perfectly curled lock of hair slid from Mercy's shoulder. Hunter cocked her head, shocked that Mercy hadn't admonished it for slipping out of place. *That* was the huge difference between the Goode sisters. Not that Mercy's hair was always down and Hunter's always secured in a ponytail, but the fact that Mercy tried *so hard.* She wrangled life, strangled it. Mercy Anne Goode controlled everything.

Until now.

Hunter took the burning herb stick and brushed past Mercy, who frowned the moment she noticed Jax's shirt. Hunter waved the bundle in front of herself, letting the twisting smoke brush against her skin before she passed the burning herbs in front of Jax. She paused near his chest and squinted through the haze at the T stained into the fabric.

Tyr . . .

The back door opened and Xena sneezed as she stepped into the smoke-filled kitchen. The fragrant white fog lapped against Xena's wild black, brown, and white mane and twirled around the wicker picnic basket that hung from her arm. "Mercy, Hunter, if you have your items for our dear Abigail, we may begin." She ran her fingers through her hair. The bell sleeves of the flowing white robe she'd taken from Abigail's closet slid back past her elbow. Her pale skin was not unlike the soft peachy tan that striped her fur when she was in her true Maine coon form.

Hunter swept her palm against the chunky outline in her pocket and nodded.

"I have mine!" Mercy said. Because Mercy *always* had to say something.

The contents of the picnic basket clanked as Xena clapped her slender hands together and smiled. "Come with me, kittens."

Hunter didn't bother to slip on her shoes as she led Jax out of the house. Mud squished between her toes. A reminder that everything died and returned to the earth.

Jax leaned into Hunter as they trailed the others. "I didn't know I was supposed to bring something for your mom."

"You weren't." Hunter grinned as the heels of Mercy's pointed shoes sank into the ground with each wobbly step. "Just those closest to her."

Xena opened the wrought-iron gate to the Goode family cemetery and waved the group into the headstone-dotted plot of land. "Form a circle around Abigail's grave, kittens."

The muddy rectangle was a toothless gap against the spring grass that carpeted the rest of the cemetery. Hunter stared down at her feet, the mud between her toes, the scrapes and scratches on her shins. Her mother's ashes were in that hole. The one Hunter had dug with her bare hands and filled with split logs and broken branches. Last night, she'd emptied herself into that pit. The pieces of herself she'd left in there were far more precious than any ceremony.

Mercy took a deep breath and clasped her hands in front of her. "Wow, Xena, it looks beautiful. Abigail would love it."

Hunter's gaze slid along the grass in front of her feet and finally fell into the grave. Xena had placed a box, *the* box, in the center of the hole atop a pine branch. Its needles encircled the box like a crown.

I did it. But Hunter couldn't get the words past the lump in her throat.

Xena set the basket on the grass next to Hunter and squatted down to flip open the lid. She took out four white pillar candles and handed them to Hunter one by one, motioning for Hunter to pass them to the rest of the circle. "As we begin this Rite for the Dead, I would like each of you think of a memory of our Abigail. One that makes you smile." She paused before handing Hunter the final candle. A grin plumped her cheeks. "Soon, you'll share the memory with the circle." She turned her attention back to the picnic basket and removed a long box of wooden matches, a small bottle of red wine, and five ritual chalices, which she set on the grass next to the basket.

Hunter clutched the candle against her chest and dug the craggy tips of her nails into the wax. She had tons of happy memories of her mother, but she didn't want to share any of them. She wanted to keep them inside, like birthday wishes that would spoil if spoken aloud.

The matchsticks rattled as Xena opened the box. "And now we begin." She drew out one long, slender match. "O elements of air, fire, water, and earth, we call you to us today to aid us in our farewell of our beloved Abigail Goode—mother, friend, and most excellent witch." She struck the match against the side of the box and continued. "O Athena, lovely Goddess of Wisdom and War, we do call on thee. Be with us here at this time of great loss. We of the Olde Ways know that when a person dies, it is only their body that is lost. Their immortal soul shall return to life again and again."

Hunter held out her candle as Xena stepped in front of her. Fire chewed down the long stick as the cat person spoke. "Air, grant us release from pain. Flow through those of us who remain in this lonelier world and carry our sadness away." Xena touched the flame to the wick of Hunter's white candle. Tree branches creaked and swayed, and Hunter's ponytail lifted as air entered their circle. Xena nodded and moved to Jax, her silk sleeves billowing in the gusts.

Hunter studied her best friend as Xena called upon fire to warm them with memories and release them from pain. Jax's dark eyes widened as invisible flames warmed the circle and the steady crackles and pops of a campfire magically surrounded them. Through everything, he'd been absolutely perfect. Even now as Xena moved on to Emily and the sounds of the campfire morphed into a trickling brook and briny waves swept away the mystical heat, Jax was poised and calm. So was Emily. And, of course, so was Mercy. No one else had marred their cloud-white candle or dug their toes so deep into the grass their toenails were brown with mud or bit down on their bottom lip so hard imprints flashed against the flesh. They were perfect. Every one of them. Everyone except for Hunter.

Jax returned Xena's nod and scooted closer to Hunter as the Maine-coon-turned-legal-guardian spoke to him, Emily, and Mercy. The coffee stain on his shirt had lightened as it dried and now looked more like an unfinished game of hangman than the bold T Hunter had seen before. Tyr hadn't been sending her a sign. It had been her imagination, her wild hope.

"Hunter? What memory will you share of our Abigail?" Xena had made it back to her place at the head of the circle and was now staring at Hunter. They all were.

Hunter's breath hitched. Too many eyes, too many expectations. Why couldn't she mourn her mother in peace? Why did it have to be a show? She didn't want to *play her part.* She wanted her mother back.

Mercy let out an annoyed rumble that sent one hand to her hip. "Come on, H. You *have* to say something."

Hunter's toes bit into the earth. She didn't *have* to do anything. This whole thing was more for Mercy than it had ever been for their mother. If it was up to Hunter, if anything was ever actually up to Hunter, it would have been different. It would have been real. Not full of virgin white and circle casting and catering.

Mercy tapped the muddy point of her high heel against the grass. "I knew I should have stood on that side of Xena so I could start everything off."

The familiar heat was back. Rage ate through Hunter's stomach, her chest, her limbs. It swallowed her heart and left teeth in its place.

"This isn't for Mom." Hunter thrust her finger at the hole in the ground and the box nestled in the grave. "She's already gone. This is for everyone else. But this part, specifically, is for *me.* I don't care about the rest. You do."

Xena clasped her hands together, her white sleeves waving like flags of surrender in the tense space between the sisters. "That's perfectly understandable, kitten. We can—"

"You're seriously going to ruin this whole day?" Mercy glared at Hunter the same way she had in the house. If Hunter thought back, Mercy had been glaring at her like that for as long as she could remember. Anytime Mercy felt Hunter slipping, straying from the path, she was there with her narrowed eyes and silent threats so loud they drowned out Hunter's own desires. But that had been the past, and Hunter wouldn't go back.

Emily rested her hand on Mercy's arm, interrupting the spray of venom shooting between the sisters. "No one is ruining—"

But Mercy had sunk her fangs in too far and she wouldn't let her prey go without a fight. A pebble fell into the grave as she stepped forward. "You're seriously still mad at me for doing my best to seal the gates and protect Goodeville?"

This was Hunter's twin. This snake. Not the young woman who'd floated down the stairs like Scarlett O'Hara or who could unite every clique at school under the umbrella of love and togetherness. No, that girl didn't really exist.

Hunter's eyes burned and her pulse battered her eardrums. "I betrayed Tyr because *you* thought it would fix everything. I did it for you!" Spittle flew from Hunter's mouth and she wiped the back of her hand against her lips. "I do everything for you and you've never been worth it!" Hot wax rolled down the side of the candle and waterfalled across Hunter's fingers. "I'm leaving after this. I'm moving in with Jax."

Mercy stiffened. The flame of her candle flickered in the wake of her measured exhale. "Why don't you leave right now? You're clearly not interested in participating."

Hunter reached into her pocket and clutched the moonstone owl. She'd keep it hidden, too, along with all her happy memories. "You're right." Mercy opened her mouth to speak, but Hunter filled the space before her sister had the chance. "I'm not interested in putting on a show." Another glob of wax sloshed over the side of the candle and coated her fingers as she blew out the flame and set the pillar next to the picnic basket. "Good-bye, Xena." Hunter turned and sprinted back to the house.

She burst through the back door and left a fresh trail of muddy footprints through the main floor, up the stairs, and into her bedroom. She threw open her closet door and parted the few remaining clothes and wrestled her heavy suitcase out from between the boxes of books she wanted to donate but could never bring herself to part with. She glanced around her room at the bare spots on the walls where her favorite pictures and posters had been and the empty spaces, like missing teeth, where she'd pulled her most loved books from their places in her alphabetized library.

Everything that was important to her had ended up in the suitcase she'd packed days ago. Hunter knew then that she had to get away from her sister and into a space where she was allowed to be herself, *think* for herself. She'd only stuck around because she held a sliver of hope that Mercy would apologize and fix what she had broken. But each day that had passed while Hunter and Mercy stayed tucked away in their separate rooms, had chipped away at that small piece in Hunter that believed her sister would change.

The dried flower crowns Mercy had made along with clothes Hunter had borrowed were in a pile on the bed like the sloughed skin of a snake. The things in this house no longer served Hunter. She was an orphan. She belonged nowhere. The sooner she accepted that and got on with her life, the better.

Hunter checked the contents of the suitcase one last time. Her writing journal was tucked inside, along with her favorite pens. She would be without a permanent home, living out of a suitcase like so many famous writers had before her. She zipped up the bag and tossed it into the hall. She didn't pick it up as she approached the stairs. Instead, she dragged the duffle down each wooden step.

Boom. Boom. Boom.

Hunter's lips curled. No more padding through life on soft footsteps with a soft voice trying not to be seen. She would be remembered—by this house, by her sister, by all the people she would no longer let use her as their punching bag. She would be seen.

And Hunter Goode would be missed.

Two

I cannot believe she did that!" Mercy slammed the back door and fisted her hands at her waist as she stared at the muddy footprints Hunter had tracked into the house.

Beside her Emily brushed her dark curls back from her face and shifted uncomfortably from one foot to the other. "It is a lot of mud."

"Mud?" Mercy shook herself like a cat coming in out of the rain. "It's not just the mud, although that's pretty damn annoying. She ruined Mom's funeral—her *funeral,* Em! How the bloody hell could she be so selfish?" Mercy barreled on without waiting for her bestie to respond. "I hope Xena is telling her off. And where's Jax?" She stepped delicately over the mud prints as she headed into the living room to look through the front picture window. "I mean, seriously! She couldn't even pretend to act right? Instead she stomps off leaving me to be the adult—as usual."

At her shoulder Em peeked through the lacy sheers. "Uh, Mag, his car isn't out there."

Xena's bare feet padded down the stairs.

Mercy whirled around to face the cat person. "What? Is she feeling too ashamed to come down? Too damn bad. She needs to clean up the muddy mess she left." Mercy sucked in a breath and shouted, "Hunter Jayne Goode! Get your ass down here!"

"Kitten, she's gone." Xena sat on the corner of the couch and pulled the chenille throw up around her bowed shoulders.

Mercy's mouth closed, then opened. Then closed again. She cleared her throat. "So she ran away with Jax and left us to clean up her mess." Mercy snorted. "That's ironic since she's *so* good at whining about how *she's* always cleaning up *my* messes." Mercy plopped down on the couch and Emily sat in one of the comfy chairs close by. "What does that mean, anyway? Sometimes I just don't get her at all. Well, I'm not touching that!" She pointed at the mud her twin had tracked through the house and up the stairs. "And when our guests for Abigail's wake give the mud WTF looks I'll tell them it's Hunter's mess—not mine. It'll be here when she's done pouting and slinks home tonight."

Xena licked the back of her hands and smoothed her hair with short, frantic strokes. "I do not believe Hunter will come home. Not tonight. Perhaps not for many nights."

Emily leaned forward in her chair. "What do you mean?"

Xena sighed and stilled her hands by clutching them together. "Her things are gone. Her favorite things."

"Wait, what?" Mercy felt like she'd been gut punched. "You mean she's *gone* gone?"

Xena nodded sadly. "Yes, kitten."

"Holy shit," said Emily.

Heat lifted from Mercy's heart to flush her face. Her stomach felt twisted and for a second she thought she was going to be sick. "H-how could she leave me?"

"People grieve in different ways," said Xena.

"You mean like some choose to be a bitch?" Mercy shot back.

"Mercy, perhaps our Hunter just needs time to herself. Perhaps that is how she will work through her grief and then—"

"That's not grieving." Mercy stood and paced. "Actually, maybe that *is* grieving. How the bloody hell would I know? Hunter took my grief from me before I could work through it."

Xena frowned. "That's not fair, kitten."

"Yeah, hey, I'm on your side," Em spoke up, "but you gotta remember that you were seriously not functioning. I'm not a witch, but I did just lose a parent, too. So I understand, believe me. You needed that spell, Mag."

Mercy wiped her hands down her face. "I'm sorry, Em. You do understand."

"As do I," Xena said. "And, kitten, you need to understand as well. Your sister *took* nothing from you. She only washed the worst of your grief away so that you could move forward."

Mercy knew they were right, but being pissed at Hunter made her absence bearable. "Whatever. Hunter made up the sodding spell. We don't know what it was she actually did."

"But, Mag, she's *Hunter.*" Emily rubbed her arms as if she was cold. "You know her better than anyone. She'd never do anything to hurt you."

Mercy met her best friend's gaze. "Bullshit. She hurt me today. She hurt Xena today. If Abigail had been here she would've hurt her, too."

"Your sister has also been wounded." Xena's voice was soft, but her words felt like sledgehammers battering Mercy's wounded heart. "She forsook her beloved god."

Mercy wanted to close in on herself and let tears of heartbreak drown her feelings. She hated that her sister had betrayed her god for nothing. *I just don't get it. Everything had pointed to Tyr being the cause of the sickness killing the trees and weakening the gates to the Underworlds—the fact that no Goode witch had ever chosen to follow a god before, as well as the prophetic-like poem I found in Sarah Goode's grimoire—everything pointed to Tyr.* Mercy swallowed the guilt that flooded her mouth like bile. "It was the right thing to do. We all agreed."

"Kitten, *Hunter* didn't agree. She did it for you, and when—"

Mercy's raised hand stopped her words. "No. I don't want to hear it. I didn't force her to forsake Tyr."

Emily's phone bleeped and she pulled it from the deep pocket of her white lacy peasant skirt and frowned. "That's Mom. She and my grandparents are on their way here for the wake."

Mercy pressed her fingers to her temples as the sound of a car crunching up their driveway signaled the beginning of the people who would come by to show their respect to their mother's memory. *I wish I could run away, too!* But Mercy couldn't—wouldn't—run. Instead she stood and straightened her shoulders. "Xena and Em, if you get the door I'll put out the lemonade and be sure there's coffee." Mercy ignored her shaking hands and the fact that her sister's absence was a wound so deep it felt as if misery pumped throughout her body with each beat of her battered heart and went to handle things.

"That is the last of them." Xena closed the thick front door and clicked the lock before she collapsed onto the couch. "How do people bear so many other people? There is so very *much* talking."

"Tell me about it." Mercy emerged from the kitchen. She carried a wicker basket in the crook of one arm. Over her other shoulder she'd slung her big boho bag. It bounced against her hip as she walked to Xena. "As soon as Em left with her mom and grandparents I was ready to shoo everyone out." She handed the cat person a cup of hot cocoa with a truffled cannabis treat balanced on the saucer under it. "Here. This'll help you relax while I'm gone."

Xena took the cup and saucer and sat up straighter. "Gone? You're going out?"

Mercy nodded grimly and patted the wicker basket. "I'm going to practice some green witchery. Alone. At one of the trees. Hunter gave up and left us, so it's up to me to heal the trees and fix the gates."

Xena studied Mercy as she blew across the top of her cocoa. "Did you think of something new?"

Mercy moved her shoulders. "Yes and no. I mean, we've only tried a couple different spells on the trees." She hurried on when Xena opened her mouth to speak. "Yeah, I know one was a powerful major ritual that shoulda worked. But it didn't. So I'm gonna keep trying." Mercy paused and chewed at her lip before she blew out a long breath and continued. "I've chosen a simple heal-and-protect spell. One I've done over and over. It's always worked. Every time. Maybe uncomplicated is best."

Xena nodded and her mane of hair bounced around her shoulders. "That is a valid idea."

"And maybe I will focus better alone—stay truer to my intent. Today Hunter freaked out and ran away. How long has she been feeling like running?" *How long has she hated me?* The question echoed through her mind. "It seemed like the trees were sick because Hunter chose a god and not a goddess to follow, but what if that was only one part of what's wrong?"

"What do you mean?"

"I mean maybe it's *Hunter* and not Hunter's god who's the problem!"

"Oh, kitten, you don't really believe that."

"I don't know what to believe anymore. But I do know that for generations—*hundreds of years*—solitary Goode witches have guarded the gates and kept the trees healthy. I'm a solitary Goode witch. I'm going to do my job. Period."

Xena put the cup and saucer on the coffee table, stood, and enfolded Mercy in her arms. "Do not ever forget that you are not alone. I am here and I will always be here for you."

Unshed tears made the back of Mercy's throat burn. She clung to Xena and whispered, "I'll remember."

Xena finally sat back on the couch and smiled up at Mercy through watery eyes. "Blessed be, my kitten."

"Blessed be, Xena." Mercy responded as she headed for the front door. Xena's voice made her pause with her hand on the knob.

"Abigail would have been proud of you today."

Mercy couldn't turn and look at Xena. If she did she'd dissolve into tears and never make it out of the house. Instead, she spoke over her shoulder. "That's the nicest thing you could've said to me."

In the car she put her basket and purse on the passenger's seat where she usually sat because Hunter always drove. Mercy couldn't remember exactly *why* Hunter always drove. It wasn't like either of them had their licenses yet. Mercy had been meaning to schedule a driving test for weeks, but, well, a lot could happen in a few weeks. "It doesn't matter. It's not like I don't know how to drive. Sheesh." She turned the key and backed out—and then took a right. It wasn't the fastest way to the weeping cherry tree she'd chosen to begin with, but it was midafternoon on a bright, beautiful spring day, and Goodeville's version of heavy traffic would be meandering up and down Main Street, visiting the cute boutiques, cafés, and coffee shops. Like Xena, Mercy had had her fill of people for the day, which is why she chose the cherry tree. It was the most secluded of the five guardians.

It was also the tree she and Hunter used to pretend was a curtained stage. They'd put on more plays and concerts for their stuffed toys and dolls than she could count. Mag and H—*we're gonna be stars!* Is what they used to tell each other as they skipped to the tree, hand in hand, to perform their version of *The Sound of Music* or *Moana* or whichever pop star's current hit they loved the most.

Mercy clenched her teeth. No. She wouldn't think about that. She'd only think about the fact that the cherry tree represented happiness and love and not the shattered and battered remains of what used to be. And anyway, she shouldn't think about the past when she had to set her intention. Mercy relaxed her grip on the steering wheel and let the tension in her neck and shoulders loosen.

My intention is simple—with Freya's help and the power of the ley lines that run deep within the earth I will heal the cherry tree.

Mercy cleared her mind of all else and repeated her intention over and over as she crossed the railroad tracks and turned onto the easement that stretched green and grassy between the raised track on her right and the verdant bean field that reached to the horizon on her left. The silver Camry bumped along to the weeping cherry tree, guardian of the gate to the Japanese Underworld, which Abigail said long ago was formally called the World of Darkness.

She parked on the familiar tire tracks made just a couple days ago by the Camry. Had it only been two days? It felt like a century ago. *Focus!* Mercy mentally shook herself and deepened her breathing as she slowly approached the tree.

A warm breeze rustled through the soybeans on either side of the railroad tracks, making them sway gracefully. Still several yards from the tree Mercy stopped and breathed in the scent of growing things and the Illinois spring. The undulating crops made a sea of green and Mercy was suddenly reminded of her eighth-grade field trip to a big horse ranch a couple hours south of Goodeville. The ranch owner had asked if any of the students would like to ride a horse. Mercy had been the first to volunteer. She was trotting the mare sedately in the pasture when a yellow jacket stung the horse on the butt—and the mare had taken off. Mercy remembered clearly that as she'd clung to the panicked mare's back the long pasture grass had rippled past and looked exactly like a green sea. So, she'd jumped off—expecting to be caught gently by the grass ocean. Instead, she'd been shocked when the wind was knocked out of her and her arm broken. The memory was so vivid that Mercy's right forearm momentarily throbbed. She clutched it to her chest and rubbed it as a cotton-ball cloud covered the sun and the day temporarily darkened. Mercy shivered.

Was it an omen? Freya, my goddess, am I making a mistake? Missing something?

The soft breeze blew the cloud away and, along with Mercy, the world breathed again. Aloud, she repeated her intention while she approached the cherry tree.

"My intention is simple—with Freya's help and the power of the ley lines that run deep below me I will heal the cherry tree."

At the tree she stopped just outside the curtain of branches. It looked deceptively healthy, though even from there she could see that every time the breeze sighed through the boughs leaves rained to the ground. *Just like when Hunter and I visited two days ago and the tree was so sick it made me puke.* Mercy's body tensed. She was ready. She could take it.

From somewhere nearby a bird croaked—a sound so weird that it made Mercy pause, shield her eyes with her hand, and stare up at the pristine spring sky.

She sucked in a breath as she identified the pair of dark birds that circled the Japanese tree. "Ravens!" Mercy's body relaxed as the call of Odin's favorite birds soothed her. "Talk about an excellent omen! We never see ravens in Illinois!" She bowed her head. "Thank you All-Father." It was time to stop allowing the past to get in her way. Mercy Anne Goode had a job to do. With the chatter of the magical ravens making beautiful background music, she parted the weeping boughs and stepped within the embrace of the tree.

Her ballet flats squished sickeningly against dead leaves and writhing worms. Mercy swallowed down her revulsion and ignored it. She also ignored the fetid scent that hovered like invisible fog around the trunk of the tree.

She'd cast this spell more times than she could count. It was purposefully simple, direct, and effective.

"Past time to return to my roots," she spoke to the tree. "Pun intended. So, here we go!"

From the basket she took a checkered tablecloth—one of the many Abigail had folded neatly in their pantry always ready for an impromptu picnic. Mercy spread it on the ground in front of the tree. She placed the basket and her purse on the tablecloth, along with her shoes. Then she carefully took out five short, fat, pillar candles the color of milk, a velvet pouch filled with sea salt, a long box of wooden matches, her bronze mini cauldron that was decorated with painted ivy, a Sharpie, a small cone of juniper incense, a bottle of water that had been charged by the full moon, a stack of bay leaves, and lastly, a thick dried herb stick—it, like all of the herbs and plants Mercy used, had been respectfully harvested from her garden.

The first thing Mercy did was light the herb stick. The earthy tang of sage and rosemary and cedar filled the space around her, so thick and strong that it even blocked the stink that leaked from the tree.

Abigail's words lifted from her memory with the smoke. *When you cleanse with herbs if there is little smoke know that there is little to cleanse, but if the sage billows thick and pungent—that means the need for purifying and healing is great.*

As if she headed into battle, Mercy cleansed herself thoroughly, bathing in the thick, cloud-colored smoke. Then she held the smoldering herb stick up with her right hand and used her left hand to waft the smoke to the suffering tree. Slowly, carefully, Mercy walked clockwise, or deosil, around the tree. She forced herself not to shiver and gag as her bare feet squished on worms and dead leaves. Instead Mercy focused completely on the tree. As she cleansed the guardian of the Japanese Underworld Mercy spoke the same words her mother had taught her so long ago that she had no memory of ever *not* knowing them.

> *"Sacred sage, strong cedar, fragrant rosemary I beseech thee three*
> *by three by magical three,*
> *maiden, mother and wise woman—thy sacred trilogy*
> *protect, purify and strengthen, three by three by magical three."*

When she returned to the blanket and the rest of her spellwork supplies she propped the thick, still-smoking stick up against one of the tree's exposed roots so that it could continue to fill the area under the canopy with cleansing smoke.

To begin the spell Mercy needed to set a pentagram and cast a circle—two things that she'd done so many times that they were like breathing in and out. She placed the five white pillar candles so that they formed the points on a pentagram, with the cherry tree at its center. The velvet pouch filled with salt and the box of matches were next. Mercy went to the candle she'd placed on the far side of the tree at the top point of the pentagram. She lit a long, wooden match, and touched it to the white candle as she invoked, "Freya, Goddess of Love, Fertility, and Magic, I ask your blessing on my circle and my spellwork." The flame blazed high and hot as her goddess responded to her invitation.

She loosened the lip of the pouch, turned to her right, and strode to the second point of the pentagram. As she walked Mercy poured a thin line of salt on the ground. She paused before the second candle and lit it, calling, "Air, I welcome you to my spellwork circle." She moved clockwise to the third candle while she poured salt with every step. "Fire, I welcome you to my spellwork circle." As Mercy moved to the fourth white pillar she released more salt and paused only long enough to touch the match to the wick and invite, "Water, I welcome you to my spellwork circle." At the fifth candle Mercy called, "Earth, I welcome you to my spellwork circle." She lit the final candle before completing the salt circle by returning to the top of the pentagram, then spoke solemnly. "And now my circle is complete—cleansed by sage, cedar, and rosemary and protected by salt."

Staying within the salt circle, Mercy turned to go back to her blanket and the rest of the supplies waiting there. The ribbon of white that bound the pentagram together glowed softly. Every few seconds there was a muted hiss and she realized that the worms and dead leaves beneath the sacred granules writhed and shriveled.

Good! That's a good sign!

Her bold steps flattened more of the disgusting, writhing worms as she returned to the blanket and sat, crossed-legged, facing the tree. Mercy placed the mini cauldron in front of her. With a grace that spoke of experience, she took the slim stack of bay leaves she'd harvested from their garden the year before and carefully dried on her shelf of the pantry. Mercy drew in and out three deep breaths and then spoke the words to the ancient Green Witch spell with confidence.

"Powers of earth and wind, sun and rain
by the strength of flower and leaf, stone and tree

with my spirit and heart, I ask your aid again, again, again.
Through bay's protection and fidelity
Hear my plea to heal this tree, heal this tree, heal this tree!"

Completely immersed in the familiar spell, Mercy took the Sharpie and wrote **CLEANSE** in bold, capital letters on the first leaf. Mercy lit the match and held it to the bay leaf. It sizzled and popped as it caught fire and when she dropped it into her cauldron a delicate line of green smoke with a slight floral scent lifted lazily.

Mercy wrote a different word on each leaf—**HEAL, PROTECT, STRENGTHEN, PROSPER**—until all five smoldered in the little cauldron. Around her the fragrant smoke curled and danced as somewhere close the ravens continued to call, as if in encouragement. Mercy felt the power of the unfurling spell. It brushed against her bare arms and lifted the soft hairs on the back of her neck as she reveled in the connection to the earth that had helped her choose the path of a Green Witch.

Mercy upturned the salt pouch. She took the pinch that was left between her fingers and sprinkled it into the cauldron over the burning bay leaves.

"By earth I strengthen you."

She lit one last match.

"By fire I purify you."

Mercy touched the match to the cone of juniper incense.

"By air I protect you."

She opened the bottle that held the moon-blessed water, poured a little into her palm, and with her other hand dipped her fingers into the small puddle and then flicked it into the cauldron.

"By water I cleanse you."

Waves of smoke billowed from the cauldron and Mercy held it carefully as she stood. But instead of being hot the cauldron felt like ice cupped in her hands. She lifted it above her head and spoke to the tree in a voice magnified by the elements that filled her pentagram.

"I ask Freya's blessing from me to thee."

Power like static electricity sizzled from her bare feet up through her body to pour from her hands. The cauldron went from ice to radiate warmth—a warmth that should, with her final words, spread with the smoke and incense into the boughs of the tree to bless, heal, and protect.

"So I have spoken; so mote it be!"

Mercy readied herself for the familiar feeling of release that came with being a conduit for earth energy, but instead of the sizzle of loosed power lifting up into the tree, electric heat sparked from her cauldron through her palms. The bay smoke sputtered and died. The magic that had brushed against her skin faded. Around Mercy the curtain of long, slender boughs swayed and the cloud of smoke leaked away.

Mercy blinked back tears of frustration. *What had happened? Everything had been perfect!*

As Mercy retraced her steps and blew out and retrieved each candle she saw that the salt had disappeared, leaving only the dark outline of a circle made of dead worms and scalded leaves.

That's good, right? Mercy couldn't speak the words aloud. She'd done versions of the spell over and over, blessing and healing sick plants or cleansing negative energy or welcoming seedlings to their spring garden. She'd never felt the power this spell had invoked—and no salt circle she'd cast had ever turned black. But she'd also never had the spell seem to sputter out as this one had at the very end. It made zero sense.

Mercy wiped her feet off and then slid on her shoes and shook out the blanket, repacking it last into her basket. Then she drew a deep breath and went to the tree. She rubbed her hands together and steeled herself. *If I puke—I puke. I can handle it.* She pressed her palms against the rough bark.

"I hope that helped. I hope you're okay," Mercy murmured.

In response she felt the warmth of the tree and her gentle inhale and exhale. She didn't exactly feel sick. Mercy didn't think she felt anything.

She patted the tree's skin. "Well, that's an improvement. I'll be back to check on you. Blessed be." Mercy turned to pick up her basket and hefted her boho bag over her shoulder—and the earth below her seemed to pitch and roll, like she was trying to balance on the deck of a boat during a storm. Her vision blurred and pain spiked through her temples as she tried not to hyperventilate. Mercy staggered and automatically reached out—her hand searching for her twin, her strength, her sister who would never, ever leave her.

But Hunter wasn't there. She didn't grip her sister's hand and borrow her strength. Hunter had left her. Mercy swallowed a sob and lurched away from the tree to walk unsteadily through the veil of boughs. She kept her gaze on the silver car. *Just a few feet more—then I can sit down and rest. I just need to ground myself, that's all. This is okay. I am okay.*

Inside the Camry, Mercy tossed her purse and the spellwork basket onto the passenger's seat and then she sat heavily, her forehead pressed against the steering wheel. There was a strange, almost listening silence that surrounded Mercy. No more ravens called. There was no birdsong at all. Mercy steadied her breath, repeating to herself, *this is okay . . . I am okay.*

Mercy kept repeating those words to herself as she slowly drove home. She didn't park in the garage, but stopped beside the porch, barely able to drag herself from the car.

Xena was alone on the porch swing. Mercy didn't have to ask if Hunter had come home. She knew she hadn't. Mercy could feel it.

Xena stood as soon as Mercy was out of the car.

"Oh, kitten! You look wretched!" The cat person hurried down the porch steps to put her arm around Mercy and guide her up the sidewalk.

"I—I need to ground myself. I feel wrong. Empty. Dizzy."

"Did it work, kitten? Is the tree better?"

"Yes. No. Maybe. I don't know. I'm not sure what just—"

Xena halted and tugged at Mercy's arm to pull her off the sidewalk. "Oh, dear! I didn't see that before. Careful, kitten. Don't step on it."

"Xena, what the—?" Mercy blinked in confusion, but followed Xena's gaze down—and dread washed through her body.

On the sidewalk was a dead bird. Its head was twisted and its wings were tucked against its body so that it looked like one half of a heart. The wind ruffled its night-colored breast feathers.

"Oh no, no, no. That is a raven. A dead raven on our doorstep." She met Mercy's gaze. "Kitten, this is very, *very* bad."

"I know. There were two of them watching me at the Japanese tree. I thought they were a good omen sent by Odin. I was wrong." The words were almost too heavy for Mercy to speak. "Xena, my spell did not work."

Then she leaned on the cat person and let Xena guide her around the poor, dead creature and into their silent house.

Three

Hunter had spent the past two nights sleeping somewhere other than her bed. The first she'd spent outside, on the muddy grass next to her mother's freshly dug grave. The second, she'd passed out on the couch next to Jax's mother sometime between after-dinner tea and the second recorded episode of *Chicago Fire.* Now, *her bed* was no longer the antique wood frame and fluffy duvet with the sparkly pink and purple Orion nebula spilled against the black background like unicorn blood. Now *her bed* waited behind the black front door that got too hot in the summer. Now *her bed* would be buried under the stiff white sheets and scratchy camel-colored blankets Jana Ashley had left out on the coffee table.

Hunter balled the lengths of the plaid nightshirt Mrs. Ashley had lent her and guided the back door to Jax's house shut and leaned against it until the latch clicked. She'd never had to sneak out of Jax's house before. Technically, she didn't have to sneak out of it now, but she didn't want to catch his mom first thing in the morning. Sitting through one round of questions from Mrs. Ashley who only had Hunter's *best interests at heart* was enough. She didn't have the space in her brain or heart to deal with a substitute mom. Hunter could figure out her own life, and it started with unpacking.

Jax's dad had converted their detached garage into the perfect apartment. It was supposed to provide the Ashleys with extra income they could put aside for Jax's college fund, but Jana had shut that down three days after their first tenant moved in. Jax's mom was under the impression that the strict curfew she imposed upon her son should be shared by the forty-year-old, free-spirited Chicagoan who had signed the lease. Hunter and Jax had shared a sweating glass of sun tea on the back porch while the man, with his long beard and longer braid, ripped up the contract and threw it at Jana Ashley's feet. Neither Jax nor Hunter had laughed. They hadn't wanted to draw his mom's attention. If she wasn't praising a person in Jesus's name, she was cursing them in Satan's.

The outside of the garage apartment was identical to the main house from its bright white siding, black trim, and casement windows down to the crucifix door knocker. Hunter ran her fingers over the heavy bronze cross. In first grade, she and Jax had tied his Ben Grimm action figure to the main house's knocker along with a piece of construction paper that said *ouch* in overly practiced elementary school lettering. Jax's mom hadn't thought it was funny. Instead, she'd punished the duo with the first and longest bible study Hunter had ever been a part of. Actually, it was still the *only* bible study Hunter had ever been a part of.

Hunter twisted the knob and the door opened with a soft *whoosh*. Not a loud creak of old hinges or rough smack of too many layers of sticky paint. It was the soft exhale of starting over, beginning again, shiny and new. Hunter wheeled her heavy duffle into the tiny living room, tossed her bedsheets onto the floor, and collapsed against the couch.

For as much as the two houses looked the same from the outside, the inside of the garage apartment was nothing like the floral-patterned, crucifix-laden innards of the main house. No, this space was filled with the denim blue and move-in-ready beige of the clearance section of Champaign Urbana's TJ Maxx. Not thrilling, but it was Hunter's, a place to start over and be herself for the first time. Away from her sister, she finally had the chance to be recognized as an individual instead of Mercy's other half.

Hunter slid her flip-flops off and wiggled her toes against the stiff fibers of the unblemished rug. Her pale skin nearly blended in with the cream-colored carpet, her chipped red toenail polish standing out like torn flower petals.

Hunter unzipped her suitcase. A mound of socks and underwear exploded out of the opening and slid down the duffle like soap bubbles. She pushed them into a pile and dumped a handful of leggings and jeans on top when a silver glimmer caught her eye. She pressed her fingers to her lips as she picked up the piece of jewelry and inspected it. The ring's band had turned from crisp silver to dull gray from all the times she'd mindlessly twisted it around her finger, but the small crescent moon that decorated the top was as shiny as the day her mother had given it to her. She slid it onto her middle finger and ran her hand over the metal points of the crescent. It was a sign from her mom that she was doing the right thing, on the right path. *It had to be.*

The morning sun shone in through the blinds and painted the cover of Moira Goode's grimoire in orange tiger stripes. She tugged the heavy book free from hoodie sleeves and boot laces. Its leather binding flaked with each movement. Hunter brushed away the pieces and ignored the simile they brought to mind. If this last week had taught her anything (well, beside the fact that she shouldn't trust her sister), it was that she needed to spend less time thinking and more time doing. It was time for Hunter to take charge and change things for the better.

The book flopped open in her lap. The pages rustled like dry leaves as she flipped through one after the other. Her phone vibrated from somewhere deep in her luggage, and she ignored it. She didn't need the alarm that told her to get ready for school. This was her school now.

The front door *whoosh*ed and Hunter inhaled the rush of clean sheets and peppermint. Jax closed the door and kicked off his shoes before walking from the tiled entryway onto the laminate wood of the living room/dining room/kitchen combo. He shoved his hands into his pockets and leaned against the white wall next to a framed poster that read *leave your worries and your shoes at the door.* "You should've moved in here forever ago."

Hunter rested her finger on the page beneath the last line she'd read before she responded. "Yeah, like your mom would have let me live here before mine died."

Jax's Adam's apple bobbed. It was interesting how other people were more uncomfortable with the mention of Abigail's death than Hunter. It hadn't even happened to them.

"Well, you're here now. An honorary Ashley in all of your plaid glory." Jax wandered the few feet into the kitchen and opened the small white refrigerator. "Mom's making breakfast. Good thing, too." He wrinkled his nose as he took in the empty shelves and an open box of baking soda. "This is pitiful. We'll have to go by IGA after school and stock up for tonight's festivities."

Hunter's hand reached for her amulet before her mind had the chance to remember Tyr's symbol was gone along with her god. She swallowed and traced the nightshirt's soft collar. "Tonight's festivities?"

Jax shrugged and batted the refrigerator door between his palms like a cat toy. "Figured we'd christen the place. There's a whole group thread if you'd ever take your phone off silent."

Hunter's phone vibrated in agreement.

She kept her finger pressed against the page. In her haste to pack up and get out of her house, she hadn't remembered a single bookmark and there was no way she was going to dog-ear the pages of a centuries-old magical text. "Tonight's no good. I have to study." She motioned to the open grimoire in her lap. "Plus, *christen* implies that we'll be doing something untoward, and your mother would smite us before that happened. She probably has this whole place nanny cammed."

Her phone vibrated again, and Hunter imagined the numerous notification bubbles filling the screen.

Jax paused his playtime with the fridge door and squinted up at each corner of the room. "My mom can't even program the DVR." The refrigerator door inched closed as Jax bounded the few feet from the kitchen to the living room. He leapt over the arm of the couch and landed on the stiff cushion with an *oof!*

"I wouldn't be so sure." Hunter tapped his ribs with her elbow. He jerked away and scrunched into a tickle-proof ball. "There's probably an antique bureau in your parents' room that turns into some kind of Bat Cave when your mom waves a bible in front of it."

"Oh yes." Jax unfurled and leaned against Hunter. He stroked his chin in the way that every poorly written bad guy from every poorly written book did. "The Christ Cave where we keep watch over the entire town. Make sure our flock never strays . . ." He stiffened and whipped his head in Hunter's direction, the combed and styled lengths of his dark hair unmoved by the dramatic reaction. "Wait! I've said too much!"

"You are such a nerd." Hunter's cheeks warmed. She *should have* done this sooner.

Jax pressed his hand to his chest and rested against the stiff couch cushions. "That's the nicest thing you've ever said to me, H."

They sat in silence, the occasional vibration of Hunter's phone or chime of Jax's reminding them that they'd soon have to rejoin the world.

"I don't know how you read that." Jax squinted down at the grimoire. "The words are so small."

Hunter moved her finger and scanned the rest of the page before turning it to resume her search on the next. At this rate, it would take her until the end of the week before she found something useful. If there was even anything useful to find. "Wear your glasses, Jax Ashley."

His phone chimed again, and he dug it out of his pocket. "You sound like my mom."

Hunter shrugged. Being compared to the overly perky, overly caring Jana Ashley wasn't the worst thing that could happen.

As Jax spoke, his thumbs tapped against the keypad. This was Hunter's least favorite part of texting—being two places at once. "Found anything on how to heal the trees and fix the gates?" He finished both conversations at the same time and set his phone on his stomach as he waited for replies.

Hunter's heart fluttered. She might never get used to her best friend discussing the secret Goode women had once guarded with their lives. Especially since she was the one who'd given it away so easily. That day at the football field, it had rushed from her lips like water. And water could lay waste to anything it wanted.

"Not yet." Hunter closed the grimoire and sagged against Jax. "It would be so much easier if Tyr would talk to me, but Mercy ruined any chance of that happening."

Jax sat up a little straighter and his phone slid down his shirt and into his lap. "Tyr? Like, your former god, Tyr? You two actually spoke?"

Hunter picked at the grimoire's flaking cover. "Not how the two of us are talking now. It was more like, a feeling . . . Or a sudden surge of power." She peeled a piece of the cover back to the spine and ran her finger over the curling leather strip. "It's hard to explain."

"Burning bush style." Jax nodded and pushed himself off the couch. "I get it." His phone chimed and he plucked it off his lap. "Mom says the *fakeon* isn't going to eat itself?"

"Fake bacon," Hunter clarified and slid the grimoire onto the cushion. "You go ahead. I have to change out of this giant shirt before I go out into the world."

"No." Jax's crooked smile lifted the corners of his eyes. "You look

great!" He hid a chuckle behind his hand as he stuffed his feet into his shoes.

"Ha. Ha." If he'd been closer to her, Hunter would have pinched his sides until he squealed.

Jax opened the front door and sunlight bleached the tile. "I'll be sure to leave some fakeon for you, roomie." He tossed a wink over his shoulder and disappeared into the blinding morning light.

The moment the door closed Hunter slipped out of the oversized, plaid nightshirt. She should have taken it off the second she'd come inside her new home, but the enormity of setting a new routine had taken over and she'd forgotten she was being swallowed by a tangible example of Mrs. Ashley's desire to become her surrogate mother. Hunter tossed the pajamas over the back of the couch and sank down next to her duffle. She could do this. School was easy, a place where she'd learned to hide in plain sight. But she'd always hidden behind her sister, and now she was alone . . .

Hunter pressed her hand against her chest, where her pendant of Tyr used to be, and blinked back the tears that stung her eyes. "Tyr, I need you. Talk to me. Please . . ."

A cool gust lifted her ponytail and blew across the goose bumps sprouting from her flesh. Hunter pressed the back of her hand against her mouth and choked back a sob. Tyr had answered her! He hadn't abandoned Hunter the same way she'd abandoned him. He was there in her time of need. He was—

Laughter like cracking ice made Hunter spin around and trip over her open luggage.

A glowing blue figure leaned against the back of the couch, eyeing the plaid nightshirt. *You should light this on fire.* Her vibrant cobalt arm reached out and long fingers pinched the cotton pajamas off the back of the couch. *Put the poor thing out of its misery.*

Hunter's gaze slid up the rippling azure forearm to the slender shoulders and up the lithe neck to the goddess's delicate features.

Hunter rubbed the center of her chest where the same glimmering blue arm had stabbed through her middle like an icy pick.

"Amphitrite?"

The goddess nodded slightly, her crown of starfish and seashells unmoving with the gesture.

Hunter swiped the first T-shirt she saw off the floor and tugged it on, not caring about how the base of her ponytail got caught up in the collar and loosened into a floppy tail. She deepened her bow as she plucked a pair of jeans from the pile. What was the proper etiquette when meeting a goddess? She'd never met her former god and there was nothing she'd read in any Goode grimoire or magical text that even hinted at the possibility of seeing a chosen deity in the flesh. Much less one who had already stabbed you.

Amphitrite dropped the pajamas on the floor and brushed her hands off on the skirt of her dress, shimmering like scales in the scattered sunlight.

"Tyr does *hear you."* Her long pinkish eyelashes rippled like anemone tentacles with every blink. *"But* I *chose to come."* She glided around the back of the couch, each step a subtle, wavelike push forward. *"Twice now, that I've come to your aid, Witch."* She dragged a long finger along the arm of the couch and left behind a trail of water that darkened the blue fabric. *"Twice to Tyr's zero."*

Hunter buttoned her jeans and smoothed down her black T-shirt. "Thank you." She swallowed, her throat tightening the same way it did when she was called on in class.

Amphitrite's algae-green gaze slid down Hunter and back up again. *"I can help you, Hunter Goode. Together, we can restore order to this realm."* Her attention drifted around the room and settled on Moira's grimoire. *"But you need the right kind of magic. The right kind of guide."*

Hunter tugged on the jagged edge of her thumbnail. "Yeah, I haven't really been able to find anything that will help me fix the gates."

Amphitrite's crown didn't budge as she swept her kelp-brown curls off her shoulders. *"That's because there hasn't been a problem like this before . . . or a witch like you. You're special, Hunter Goode, and I can help you be everything you desire."*

The lump in Hunter's throat solidified. The same surge of power she had felt when she'd first used blood magic brushed against her senses now.

Amphitrite held out her blue hands. Turquoise waves rippled up from her palms, and a white rectangle shimmered beneath the surface like a mirage.

Hunter's palms tingled and her blood pulsed inside her veins with the ebb and flow of Amphitrite's magical waters. The waves stilled and sank beneath the surface of the book until each drop had emptied back into the goddess. She stepped closer to Hunter. Cool spray lifted from Amphitrite's skirts and dusted Hunter's arms.

Hunter's hands flew to the book, her body sensing its power before her mind had time to process it. A gasp slipped past her lips as her fingertips grazed the ivory cover. It was puppy-ear soft and vibrated with a magic so fierce Hunter wanted to sink her teeth into it and drink every last drop.

A smile slid across the goddess's lips with the fluidity of a serpent starfish. *"Feed it and it will grow, and the stronger you'll both become."*

Hunter couldn't take her eyes from the book or her hands from its cover. "What does it eat?" The question rushed out of her as if it was normal. Like taking a magical book that felt like flesh and hummed with energy from a sea goddess was what every sixteen-year-old did before school. "I mean . . ." she stammered.

What *did* she mean? The only thing Hunter knew was that she'd never give the book back. Not after touching it and feeling its power. The power she needed.

Hunter's knuckles whitened as she clutched the fleshy grimoire. Her heart clicked against her ribs. She sucked in air, slowed her breathing, and lifted her gaze to her goddess's cerulean cheeks and sparkling green eyes. The lump in Hunter's throat was back and she tried to force it down with a tight swallow. She would take care of the book. Feed it, like a houseplant.

Amphitrite brushed back the stray hairs that had fallen from Hunter's ponytail and slid her fingertips down Hunter's neck. *"Witch, you know that I can't tell you everything. Think of this as a heroine's journey. It'll be your most exciting story yet, and you deserve it."* She pinched the sleeve of Hunter's T-shirt and rubbed it between her thumb and forefinger the same way she had Mrs. Ashley's nightshirt. A frown ticked the corners of her lips.

"It's No Doubt," Hunter looked down at her T-shirt, shifting her weight from one foot to the other. "Gwen Stefani's band from forever ago." She pointed to the slender blonde posed in her bright red latex mini dress and matching boots. "I found it at the thrift store."

Amphitrite tilted her head to the side and swiped her finger across the bottom of the oversized tee. The shirt sizzled and a black O of fabric pooled around Hunter's feet.

Hunter pressed the book against her bare stomach. "Oh, I don't think—"

Before she could finish, Amphitrite slid her glowing azure finger from the collar of the T-shirt to the middle of Hunter's sternum. The two sides frayed and flapped open like lapels.

Hunter stared down at her own cleavage. She knew she had boobs, but no one ever saw them. Especially once she put her clothes on. "I can't go to school like this. It's not me. It's—"

Amphitrite pursed her lips and her chest rose with a full inhale. She flicked her wrist at the bathroom door. It flew open and *thwacked* against the door stopper. She grabbed Hunter's hand and pulled her into the bathroom. *"Witch, if you're going to be different, you have to* be different.*"*

Hunter lifted onto her tiptoes and slid her hand down her bare waist and the gentle slope of her hips. Somehow Amphitrite knew—knew how desperately Hunter wanted to be different, to not stand behind Mercy as the silent, obedient twin. Amphitrite had seen Hunter, *understood* her without her having to bare the soft and delicate pieces of her life. The goddess was right. Hunter deserved the kind of life she'd been held back from living.

Amphitrite looped her finger around Hunter's hair tie and pulled. *"Isn't that better?"*

Hunter's stomach squeezed. She looked like her sister. And like Mercy, Hunter would take center stage and be the heroine of her own story.

Amphitrite's hair slid in front of her narrow shoulders as she leaned down and pressed her cold lips to Hunter's cheek. *"Feed it, Witch, and it will show you things not of this world."* She whispered, her cool breath sticky with salt. The goddess's glowing skin rippled, replaced with the same pulsing waves that had delivered the magical book still clutched in Hunter's hand.

"I have questions!" Hunter shouted at the glowing current quickly dissolving into sea spray. "How do I reach you?"

"You are mine now, Hunter Goode." Amphitrite's words echoed between Hunter's ears. *"And I am always watching."*

Four

Hey there, Mrs. Laughlin, do I spot a new hairdo under that net?" Kirk Whitfield flashed his perfect white smile charmingly at the gray-haired lunch lady. "Be careful, people will think you're a student here!"

Mrs. Laughlin's cheeks pinkened. "Oh, Kirk, you're such a pill!"

"Just keepin' it real!" Kirk winked at her as the lunch lady predictably piled his plate with extra tater tots.

"Take this apple, too. You need to eat healthy so we can keep winning those Friday-night games."

Kirk executed a little bow. "Thank you, Mrs. Laughlin, and you have a nice day." He paid and balanced his tray with one hand as he tossed the bright crimson apple up and down with his other hand while he scanned the lunchroom.

"Whitfield! Over here!" A meaty fist raised in the middle of the crowded cafeteria and Kirk headed toward it and the table packed with most of the starting lineup and several of the varsity cheerleaders. The group scrunched together to make room for their quarterback and captain.

Derek Burke, the team's starting center, reached across the table and tried to grab one of his tater tots, but Kirk's excellent reflexes smacked his hand with a spoon before he could snag it.

Derek rubbed the back of his hand. "Dude, how do you always get so damn many tots?"

"He pays double," said Heather Johnson.

Kirk frowned down the table at the cheerleader. *Why did females always have to butt in and say crap like that?* "I pay the same as you do. I can't help it if the lunch ladies crush on me."

Jarod Frazier, Kirk's favorite linebacker, grinned. "That's right. *All* the ladies want Whitfield."

Heather snorted a little laugh that grated on Kirk's nerves like fingernails down a chalkboard.

"What the hell's funny about that?" he asked her.

She flipped back her long, dark hair and wiggled her fingers in the direction of a cluster of tables to their right. Kirk followed her gaze to see Mercy sitting beside Emily. The two had their heads together, as usual. Mercy was wearing a short mint-green dress the color of her eyes. Her long legs were crossed and bare and too damn sexy. He glared at her, but she didn't so much as glance his way—all damn morning every time he'd passed her in the hall she hadn't looked at him. Not once. Kirk felt anger bubble up from his stomach as the tots he'd shoved in his mouth turned to sawdust. He swallowed, shrugged, and ran a hand through his sandy blond hair with a nonchalance he definitely didn't feel.

"Whatever. I broke up with her."

"Yeah, right. We all heard." Heather's knowing smile was starting to piss him off.

Kirk glanced up and down the newly silent table at his crew—his players and the cheerleaders who shadowed them. No one met his eyes. The anger that festered in his stomach boiled. It was time to deal with this Mercy crap. Now. Before it got worse and fucked up everything he'd worked his seventeen years for. He leaned forward and pressed his hands against the table on either side of his lunch tray so that his biceps and the thick muscles of his chest bulged against his favorite red and white GOODEVILLE MUSTANGS tee.

"What you *heard* was me trying to deal with a bitch who's too high maintenance to be worth the trouble. And you wouldn't have heard anything at all if she hadn't zapped me with some kinda spell." Their gazes snapped to him. The disbelief there was super easy to read. "I'm not making that shit up. Think about it. Did I sound like me? Act like me? And how the hell *did* you hear us? It wasn't like we were yelling. I'm telling you—Mercy Goode and her sister are witches. *Real* witches."

There was a long, silent pause. Kirk's hands fisted against the table. Why the hell hadn't he thought to try to record some of that bizarre witch shit Hunter had done the night he helped those freaks take some sadness, or whatever, from Mercy? Then everyone would see that he was telling the truth.

Derek, who always had his back, cleared his throat and said, "It's true. That stuff you were saying, and the, uh, crying part—definitely wasn't you."

"Right? That's what I've been trying to tell you guys." Kirk tossed him a tater tot, which he caught and shoved in his mouth.

Jarod nodded and spoke through a mouthful of pizza. "The Goode twins are weird. That's for sure. I mean, hot, but weird."

Dillon Sanders, who weighed in at an even three-fifty and was the top 2A linebacker in the state added, "Hunter isn't that hot 'cause she dresses like a dude. Should be, like, against the law for a girl with a body like that to be a lesbo."

Tiffany Wilson, the cheer captain they called Blow-Up Doll behind her back, smirked. "She doesn't look like a dude today. Actually, she looks kinda skank-a-licious." She jerked her perfect chin to their left.

Kirk glanced over to see a girl who had to be Hunter sitting across from pussy Jax Ashley—only this version of Hunter had her long, silky hair free. Her back was to him, but he could definitely see that her vintage tee was short enough to expose a nice length of flawless skin. As if she felt his gaze she swiveled around. She was holding a book that almost seemed to glow white against her black shirt, but he didn't spend much time looking at *just a book*. His gaze focused on the deep V of the shirt and the perky globes of her partially exposed boobs. His hands twitched and he felt himself get semi-hard. He knew those boobs. They looked exactly like Mercy's.

"Daaaaamn." Derek breathed the word. "Think she changed teams?"

Even from a distance Hunter's sneer of disgust was obvious before she turned back around. Kirk's jaw set. He really hated that little bitch.

Jarod rubbed his hands together. "I say we send Tiffany over there to see for sure—and we all get to watch if she *hasn't* changed teams."

"That'd be a mistake," Kirk said. "I'm telling you. The dyke is a witch, too. A major witch." A sudden thought had him sitting up straighter. "You know those five weird trees around the town?"

All eyes returned to him. Derek shrugged. "You mean like the palms in the middle of the park?"

"And there's that super strange tree that's kinda by the school? The one that looks like it should be on an island or down South somewhere?" added Tiffany.

"Yeah, I mean those and three more. The trees are here because the Goodes are witches. They're gates to someplace, or something like that." Kirk paused, trying to remember exactly what Hunter had said that day at the football field when she tried to get him to be part of another freaky spell. "The point is—they're real witches and they have real powers."

"Powers?" Derek asked.

"Yeah, dude. How do you think they made me say that cornball shit to Mercy?" His voice turned mocking, *"I love you—I need you—whaa, whaa!"*

Derek slowly nodded his head. "I thought somethin' was wrong. Like I said, no way are you gonna cry over a chick."

"It's not right," agreed Jarod. "They can't just randomly put spells on people. We should tell someone."

Derek cracked his beefy knuckles. "Or *do* something."

The anger that roiled in Kirk's gut reduced to a simmer. It was working. His crew would listen to him—they always did.

"Hey, why don't we leave it alone right now?" Heather's voice grated against Kirk's ears. "Their mom just died. Plus, have you ever seen them *not* eat lunch together? Well, I mean before you two started dating and she ate at our table for a while."

"No, they're joined at the fucking hip," Kirk grumbled.

"Not now they aren't," Tiffany said as she dabbed a napkin against her glossy pink lips. "I saw them in the library earlier, and they didn't even look at each other. So something is going down between them."

"Could have something to do with the fact that Mercy's bff's dad just died," said Heather.

An idea had Kirk's lips tilting up in a satisfied smile that he quickly squelched. "Don't you think that's a bizarre coincidence? The fact that the freaks' mom died—and then a night later Mr. Parrott was killed along with that old dude with the truck?"

Heather sipped her Coke as she shook her head. "Mr. Thompson died the same night as their mom."

Kirk had to stop himself from telling her to shut the hell up. Instead he loosened his jaw just enough to grind out, "That pretty much makes my point. The deaths have something to do with the Goodes."

The table went silent again, but this time it was an electric silence—like they were waiting for Kirk's next pronouncement—as they shot glances from one twin to the other.

"Come to think of it—that is pretty crazy," said Derek, whose perpetually flushed face had gone pale.

"Still, guys, their mom just died. I—I don't feel great talking about them like this," insisted Heather.

Kirk decided he'd pushed enough—for right then. He held his

hands up innocently. "Hey, you're right. It's real bad about their mom—and Emily's dad." Kirk picked up another tot and tossed it at Derek. He was still staring at Mercy, so it hit him square on the forehead, which made the table laugh. "Dude, where are we partying after practice?" He smoothly changed the subject. It didn't matter. He'd seen the fear begin to spark in his friends' eyes and Kirk knew all he needed to do was wait, bide his time, and what he'd begun today would eventually blaze and burn.

After all, the twins deserved it. They were witches.

Five

The bleachers glinted in the late-afternoon sun as Hunter unzipped her backpack and pulled out her new goddess-given book. She flipped past the initial blank page to the fourth. The first three were simple: home protection, strengthening a lunar bond, and a spell to aid in restful sleep. She'd performed versions of each of these the first month she was allowed to practice magic on her own. By now, they weren't only simple, but boring with a capital B. But the fourth spell . . . Hunter's blue eyes traced its simple instructions and the spoken words written in an unfamiliar language for the millionth time since Amphitrite had gifted her with the deliciously otherworldly book destined to change her life. It had to. She was a witch. She must be fated for something more than afternoons spent watching football practice.

A gust of wind blew Hunter's hair into her eyes and tickled her exposed middle. She sighed and tucked the charcoal-black waves into the collar of her ripped T-shirt. Being different was a lot harder than she'd expected. She snorted. The irony wasn't lost on her. This was the only time in her life she had *chosen* to be different, yet she was now more like her peers than she'd ever been before.

Hunter opened her spellbook across her lap and ran her fingers along the title written in bold cursive on the top of the page. *WANT.* She blew out a puff of air and twisted her ring around her finger as she stared out at the football field. She didn't really know what she wanted. Being on her own was a start, but it's not like that and a new look immediately changed the world. A few days ago, she would have used her tarot to guide her and to help her heal the gates, but she'd left her cards behind the same way she had Tyr. The two felt intertwined. How could she use one without the help of the other?

Jax and the rest of the Mustang wide receivers ran drills down half the football field while the cheerleaders practiced a multitude of terrifying stunts on the other. Hunter winced as her best friend jumped seconds too late and missed another ball. He was never this off. Not that Hunter had ever watched him practice before, but she did make it to every game. Supporting Jax was way more important than her dislike of football, crowds, and cheering. She shielded her eyes and squinted at Jax.

"You're kidding." She breathed as she locked onto his crooked smile and followed his attention to the gaggle of cheerleaders taking a water break. Jax Ashley couldn't stop grinning at Kylie York.

A high-pitched *boo* came from the cluster of girls huddled together a few rows below Hunter. The *murder.* At least, that's what Hunter called the group of football player girlfriends who flitted through Goodeville High ready to peck the eyes out of anyone they deemed a threat.

Hunter clamped her mouth shut and rubbed her sweating palms together. There was a chance the murder hadn't noticed her. She was traveling down a new path and didn't want to be derailed by the girls who'd tormented her in middle school.

Hunter's breaths were shallow, shoulders tensed as she studied the group's perfectly curled hair and polished nails and—

One of the girls whipped around to face Hunter. Shayla's long strands of beachy blond waves caught in her mauve lip gloss. "You *really* need to take control of your man."

Hunter couldn't swallow past the ball of nerves tightening her throat. She hadn't gone unnoticed. She'd gotten caught in the murder's territory.

"I mean, if Jax plays like this all summer, we'll get slaughtered next year for sure." Shayla tilted her head from side to side and examined Hunter with the beady-eyed intensity of a crow as she swept her hair free from her lips. "You don't want him to be the reason another perfect season is ruined, do you?"

Two other girls turned, and then two more, and then three more, until they all stared at Hunter through their expertly lined eyes, ready to attack.

Hunter's tongue stuck to the back of her teeth as she shook her head. "Jax's isn't *my man.*" She cleared her throat. "There's nothing I can do about how he plays."

Isabel swept up her brown curls and tied them into a perfect messy bun on her first try. "But you've, you know"—she waved her hand in Hunter's direction—"*changed* and everything."

Shayla adjusted the lacy straps of her Mustang-red tank top and giggled. "I mean, you'll always be the same loser doormat person you've been since middle school, but at least you look half-decent now."

Hunter pressed the fleshy cover of her book against her bare stomach.

Cara cocked her head and fiddled with the large gold hoop that dangled from her earlobe. "We figured you updated your style because you and Jax finally hooked up." She tapped her long fingernail against her earring and shrugged. "But why he'd want to stick any part of his body even remotely close to yours is a mystery to me."

Hunter stiffened. "You all think that I changed my hair and my clothes because I'm suddenly straight and with Jax?" Her cheeks burned as if the murder had clawed her face with their talons. "You have to know that's not how sexuality works."

Shayla pursed her mauve lips. "But you could, like, switch to bi or whatever to at least try to make yourself more interesting."

Hunter's fingertips tingled and the book heated against her belly. *"Yeah, totally."* She snatched her backpack off the bleacher and stood. "I'm going to go, like, rub my vag all over Jax so he doesn't fumble any more balls. *Goooo Mustangs!*"

The murder sucked in a collective breath and Hunter felt their gaze press against her back as she stuffed her book into her bag and stomped down the bleachers. Tears burned her eyes and the cold rock encasing her heart heated. Why did everyone have to test her? Sure, Goodeville wasn't completely filled with people as ignorant as the murder, but anyone birdbrained or with hate to spew always seemed to be the loudest and always seemed to target her. Hunter was *tired* of being laughed at and bullied. It was time for things to change.

She yanked her backpack over her shoulders and clutched the railing that protected shouting fans from faceplanting onto the gravel track that bordered the field. If only they'd seen how she'd conquered Polyphemus. How she'd drawn down the power of the stars and melted the skin from his bones. Metal groaned under her grip. She hopped backward and shook out her hands as she stared down at the railing. Indentations the same fiery orange as the blood moon remained where her hands had been.

Footsteps clanged against the bleachers behind her, and Hunter whirled around, hiding the railing with her backpack.

"I know you think you're royalty because some man named this town after your dirty dishwater family." Shayla spat, her finger inches from Hunter's face. "But you're *nothing.*"

Fire raged inside Hunter's belly. "Sarah Goode named this town Goodeville because of everything she did to—" Hunter grasped the metal railing and steadied herself. No more telling of family secrets.

Salt filled the air and a cold spray dusted Hunter's arms. *You don't deserve this, Witch.* Amphitrite's voice snaked like a river between Hunter's ears. *You have the power to stop it.*

Hunter's gaze searched the stands for the brilliant blue goddess, but Amphitrite was nowhere.

"Are you finally realizing how pathetic you are?" A grin stretched Shayla's lips as she crossed her arms over her chest and cemented her place between Hunter and the only set of stairs. "I don't know which is more depressing, being a slut like your sister or an ugly dyke no one wants."

Harness your power and use it, Witch.

Metal melted under Hunter's grasp, molten pieces sizzling when they hit the ground. "Leave me alone, or else . . ."

"Or else what?" She scoffed.

You'll show her why you should be revered and not reviled.

Hunter's heart thrummed in her throat. Amphitrite was right. Hunter deserved better. But even if she knew how, she couldn't harness her power here in front of everyone.

Another sharp *boo* from the stands, and Shayla's attention snapped up to the murder who disapprovingly shook their heads at Jax and his most recent failed catch. Hunter glanced over her shoulder as Coach Jamison barked commands from the sidelines and Jax jogged, shoulders slumped, to collect the lone pigskin before he joined the rest of the players in a huddle.

Practice was almost over. Shayla, the rest of the murder, and the parents, students, and faculty all watching from the stands would descend and see what Hunter had done and know that she was a true witch who couldn't control her gifts. She needed to get out of here, get under control.

She elbowed past the blonde, the sharp point of Hunter's crescent ring catching on Shayla's tank. The delicate *rip* of fabric was ice water through Hunter's veins.

Shayla screamed and covered her exposed bra with her hands. "You ripped my fucking shirt, you bitch!"

The murder stood, their feathers flapping as they rushed down the bleachers.

"You gross, desperate cow!" Shayla cawed and rushed toward her group.

Hunter's breaths were crashing ocean waves roaring through her thoughts as she hurried away from the bleachers. She would go to the parking lot and hide next to Jax's car and never come to another practice again.

Don't run, Witch. Amphitrite's voice coated Hunter's ears like oil. *They need to learn their place.*

Gravel dust billowed around Hunter's boots as she dashed to the shuttered snack hut and pressed herself into its shadow while she again searched the bleachers and the field for her new goddess.

I don't have to be in your presence to see you, Witch. Amphitrite's laughter was the metallic *shink* of sharpening knives. *As I told you, I am always watching.*

Hunter sagged against the paneled side of the snack hut and wrung her trembling hands.

"Hey!"

Hunter yipped and clapped her palm over her mouth as she spun around to face the voice.

Kylie York stood in the sun-drenched gravel. Her Mustang red sports bra and shorts beamed like rose petals. "Sorry! I didn't mean to scare you."

Hunter hooked her thumbs around the straps of her backpack and shook back her hair. "I'm not Mercy."

"I know. Although, when you didn't answer, I thought I might have messed that up." Her smile tugged at the corners of her hazel eyes. "Glad to know I was wrong." She cocked her head and her reddish blond braid slid off her shoulder. "Or *right*?" She shook her head. "Practice kicked my ass and now my brain is mush."

Hunter didn't know what to say. Had the murder sent Kylie to deliver a final blow?

"Looked like a lot of drama back there, but Shayla would probably shrivel up like a raisin if she wasn't the center of attention." The cheerleader adjusted the thick strap of her sports bra and scraped the toe of her white-and-red sneaker against the gravel. "Your backpack is unzipped, and you dropped this." She held out her hand. The bubblegum-pink Lamy fountain pen stood out like a glowstick against Kylie's sandy complexion. "That's why I followed you."

Hunter stepped into the sunlight and plucked the pen from Kylie's outstretched hand. She smoothed her thumb over the scratch that marred the cap and smiled. "Mercy found this at the pawnshop. She got it for twenty-five dollars. The owner had no idea what he had." Hunter's cheeks heated and cooled just as quickly. Who cared about Mercy or fancy pens? She certainly didn't. And neither did Kylie. Hunter folded her arms in front of her midriff, suddenly very aware of how bare it was.

"I'm more of a Montblanc girl." Kylie twirled the end of her long braid. "Glitter and Glue has one of their amazing limited-edition fountain pens in the locked case by the register. I stare at it every time I'm in there."

"Oh yeah!" Hunter lifted onto her toes. "The Moctezuma. I saw that last time I was in. It looks like an—"

"Atlatl!" they said in unison.

Kylie's laughter was morning time and chickadee calls, sweet and light and everywhere. "I thought I was the only one who even knew how to say *atlatl.*" She freed her hair from its braid, and it fell against her shoulders in reddish blond waves.

Hunter's mouth went dry. Thirty seconds ago she'd known what an atlatl was, but now she could barely remember how to pronounce her own name. She never thought she'd share the same interests with anyone so popular, so perfect.

Kylie's hazel eyes scanned Hunter's ripped tee and tight jeans. "'Just a Girl' is one of my favorites. It's crazy that Gwen wrote it forever ago and it still speaks to exactly what we're going through right now, you know?"

Hunter was supposed to respond. She was supposed to fill this space with a witty feminist rejoinder or Ruth Bader Ginsburg quote, but all she could do was twist her crescent ring around her finger while she looked down at her ripped shirt and her boobs that billowed out of her pushup bra like muffin tops.

"H! There you are!"

Hunter barely recognized Jax's voice as it jolted her from her stupor.

Sweat clung to strands of his slicked-back hair and he still had a red spot on his forehead where his practice helmet had pressed against it a little too hard.

Kylie adjusted the elastic band on her tight shorts and stood a bit straighter as Jax joined them. "H and I were just discussing the music industry and its amazing feminist icons." Kylie picked up Hunter's nickname like she'd been a part of their group her whole life.

"Yes." Hunter's voice cracked like a middle school boy's, and she cleared her throat. She bit the inside of her cheek and silently scolded herself. She had no chance with Kylie and there was no use thinking otherwise.

"You didn't tell me she was so clever." Kylie chirped as she slapped Jax's arm.

And there it was. The real reason Kylie York had chased Hunter from the bleachers to the snack hut. It wasn't to return a pen. Kylie wanted to get closer to Jax, hook him with her beauty and charm and reel him in with her ability to fit into his life without causing so much as a ripple.

Jax's tawny cheeks reddened and he swept his hand through his damp hair. "What can I say? H is a genius."

Hunter fought the urge to roll her eyes. She was in the Twilight Zone where gorgeous cheerleaders loved fancy pens and nineties music and she was a budding Albert Einstein.

"Jax, I really need to get back to the house. I have a lot of, uh, homework." A jolt of energy pricked her back and she could practically feel the spellbook wriggling with excitement.

Kylie combed her fingers through her hair as she looked up at Jax. "Did you guys still need a ride?"

"Abso-fruitly!" he emphasized with a crooked-toothed grin.

Hunter's grimace was swept away when Kylie let out another exhale of sweet chickadee laughter. "I'll get my bag and meet you in the parking lot." The mouthwateringly tart scent of grapefruit splashed against Hunter as Kylie brushed past and headed toward the locker room. "Top's down!" she called over her shoulder. "Hope that's okay!"

Gravel crunched as Jax shuffled next to Hunter and rested his arm on her shoulder. *"Fuuudge."* He pulled the word from his mouth like taffy. "Remember those porta potties the school set up when the plumbing went nuts a few months ago?"

Hunter shivered and suppressed a gag. At least Jax had given her something to think about besides Kylie's strong legs and full lips and everything Hunter wanted and would never have.

"There were so many things written in there." He continued while he leaned against Hunter like a kickstand. "Things that I thought I would *never* think about a girl, but I'm definitely thinking about—"

"Stop." Hunter shrugged away from him and held up her hand. "Your horny boyness is overwhelming."

Jax scrunched his nose as if he could suddenly smell the hormones rushing from his pores. "We should go before I say anything you might regret." He picked up his bag and paused to zip Hunter's open backpack before they headed toward the parking lot.

"What's wrong with your car?" Hunter asked as they crossed the sharp line where the gravel ended and blacktop began.

Jax shrugged. "Dad sent me a text before practice. Something about helping out a friend." He adjusted the strap of his red-and-white football bag and shook his head. "You and I will be carless for at least a week. We're supposed to bum rides from Kirk."

Hunter snorted. "Yeah, like that's gonna happen." She eyed the remaining cars in the parking lot, thankful the quarterback's red Jeep was nowhere to be found.

"My thoughts exactly," Jax said as he steered them toward Kylie's sunflower-yellow Camaro. "I saw Kylie before practice, and I've been trying to find the perfect way to talk to her, so—"

"I didn't know you were interested in Kylie York." Hunter wanted to take back the comment, carve out the jealousy and offer it casually. A simple question rather than a scathing accusation or personal admission.

With another shrug, Jax fished his phone out of his pocket and tapped a quick message. Probably to Kylie. Hunter shook her head and bit down on the raw spot inside her cheek.

"A lot's been happening in your life. It didn't seem important."

Hunter swallowed the copper painting her tongue. It was so like Jax to put her needs before his. He was an amazing friend. And she was too busy being jealous to notice.

Kylie waved to Jax and Hunter from the edge of the parking lot as she jogged over to meet them. "You live by the Gas-N-Go, right?" she asked before hefting her bag into the backseat.

"In Hollow Pines." Jax nodded so furiously, Hunter worried his head would topple off.

Kylie opened her door and tipped the driver's seat forward. "The leather's probably hot, but it'll cool down as soon as we get going," she said, motioning toward the seats.

Before Hunter could call shotgun, Jax had rounded the car and leapt over the closed passenger-side door and into the seat next to Kylie. Hunter's nostrils flared. No matter how much it felt like one, this wasn't a competition. Kylie and Jax were into each other, and Hunter was the magical third wheel.

She tossed her backpack onto the floorboard beside Kylie's and climbed into the small backseat. The leather was warm against her skin and kept her at the perfect temperature as they drove out of the parking lot and headed toward Jax's. Hunter leaned against the headrest and closed her eyes while the wind muted Jax and Kylie's conversation into a steady drone. She took a deep inhale and smiled. Her whole world smelled like grapefruit.

Six

Mercy felt old. Not sarcastically pretend old, like if she said she felt like she was thirty-five or whatever, but truly old. The day before at Abigail's wake she'd watched Emily's grandma get up from sitting on the couch—slowly, as if every joint in her body ached. The grandma had hobbled through the living room to give Mercy a dry kiss on her cheek before she'd slowly followed her daughter and granddaughter to their car.

That's just how old Mercy felt, but she'd forced herself to ignore her exhaustion. She'd had to. *Someone* had to be responsible and continue the work Goode witches had been doing for centuries, and goddess knew Hunter wouldn't help her. Mercy thought about the outfit her twin had worn to school that day—how weirdly revealing it had been and how she'd been overly animated with Jax. She'd even *giggled* at him between classes like a flirty cheerleader. The difficult truth was Hunter wasn't Hunter anymore.

As soon as school was out Mercy had known what she had to do. She'd forced herself to check the trees—by herself—even though all she'd wanted to do was go home, crawl into bed with a bag of chips and a big bowl of her favorite dip, and watch one old rom-com after another until she finally passed out. Now she was almost done. Almost able to go home and crash . . .

Wearily, she closed the door of the Camry, rested her head against the steering wheel, and forced herself not to cry. She'd been so glad when the final bell had rung that day and she'd been able to escape. Mercy usually loved school—well, the classes were mostly whatever—but she loved everything else about it. Her friends, the fashion hits and misses, the gossip, the ever-changing cliques, *everything.*

Not today.

"Maybe never again." She lifted her head and wiped at a tear. It had been exhausting to pretend not to care that everyone whispered about her or stared at her and Em like they were freaks. About half of the girls she'd been hanging with since she started dating Kirk wouldn't speak *to* her at all—though they were definitely talking *about* her.

"Kirk." She curled her lip like the name tasted foul. "At least I didn't look at him—not even once." Of course every time she passed him in the hall her stomach revolted. She'd actually had to rush into the bathroom twice because she thought she was going to be sick.

And then there was Hunter. She hadn't spoken to Mercy all day. Not even during the class they shared. Mercy couldn't figure out if she should be pissed or upset—or both. And instead of trying to figure it out she'd escaped the misery school had become and then for the next several hours she'd shoved everything from her mind except her job.

Check on the trees. Figure out how to fix them.

Mercy's sigh reverberated throughout the car. *Four down—one to go.* The windows of the Camry were cracked and the sounds of evening insects buzzed and hummed around her so that she was reminded of how late it was. Mercy lifted her head to watch the sun just begin to dip below the olive tree she'd parked just a few yards from. She hadn't cared that the car had bumped over grass and rocks. No damn way was she going to park beside the spot where Mr. Thompson's body had been—and where Hunter had used her tarot to reveal that a Cyclops had escaped the Greek gate—and walk by all of that to the tree. A chill fingered its way down Mercy's back and she started the car and carefully reversed to the blacktop road. There was also no damn way she was going to stay out here after dark. Plus, she had one more tree to check.

Slowly, she headed into town, winding through sleepy streets to Goode Park. She'd saved the doum palms for last. The park tended to be busy, but would be less so on a weeknight at dusk. People would finish up their tennis games and pack up their Frisbees to go home to dinner, which would give Mercy a chance to see what she was 99 percent sure she would see—a sick and dying clump of trees.

Mercy pulled into the nearly deserted lot that framed the street side of the park. She slouched down in the driver's seat and hid behind the steering wheel as little clusters of people meandered to their cars and bikes. It didn't take long. She checked the car's dashboard clock. It was hard to believe that it was almost eight o'clock. She was glad Xena had made her eat a quick tomato sandwich after school before she took off for the five trees. Her stomach felt empty—not hungry. Just empty.

"I shouldn't have spent so much time at the apple tree," she muttered to herself as she picked at her lip and watched the happy groups of people leave. But she hadn't been able to help herself. The Norse tree was the only one that was healthy. Abigail's sacrifice had stopped whatever caused the worms and the stench and the rot. The magnificent ancient apple tree had soothed and centered her, provided her an island of relief in a sea of shattered promises and broken hearts.

An old Mustang parked a few yards from her backfired as its engine turned over. Mercy startled like it was gunfire. She blinked and looked around at the empty, twilight park. She sighed, slung her bottomless boho bag over her shoulder, and got out of the car. The day had been warm, but the setting sun had drained away the spring heat and the grass felt cool and damp against her sandaled feet. The park lights hadn't switched on yet, and the sky's fading blues cast everything in undersea colors. Mercy's favorite time of day was dawn, but dusk had magic, too—though that was usually something Hunter was more drawn to.

Mercy shook her head. *No. Stop thinking about Hunter. Focus on your job.*

She came to the cluster of doum palms that appeared to be four trees, but was really just one and its offshoots. Mercy's gaze went to the debris made of bark and dead leaves that was all that was left of the fifth tree. What used to be a healthy offshoot of the doum crunched beneath her feet. She didn't see any worms, but the stench was there—like rotten eggs mixed with really old roadkill. As she had the other four guardians, Mercy ignored the smell and pressed both of her hands against the bark.

"Hello, Mother Palm." She spoke softly and asked the same question she'd posed to the others. "How are you?"

The tree didn't warm against her hand as the healthy Norse guardian had. The Norse apple tree had heated her skin and filled her body with the sense of rightness that healthy green and growing things always gave her. This tree's bark was dry and brittle and felt slightly cool.

"What is it?" she whispered to the ailing tree. "What's wrong?"

Nothing. Mercy felt nothing at all. At the cherry tree she'd felt its breath—though it had definitely been sick. Worms had writhed among its roots and dropped from its curtain-like branches. The banyan tree, guardian of the Hindu gate to the Underworld, had been breathing, too, though when she'd touched it Mercy had felt sick. Not puke sick, though. More like she had the flu, with aches in all of her joints. The olive tree had reeked so badly that it'd made her gag, and when she touched it she'd felt chilled and weak.

Mentally, Mercy shook herself and concentrated. She patted the palm gently, like it was a frightened bird, and then pressed her hands against the bark again, closed her eyes, and went inward.

Suddenly she couldn't breathe. Mercy cleared her throat, coughed, and tried to draw a deep breath, but it felt like someone had wrapped a rope around her chest and was slowly tightening it so that her lungs couldn't expand. Mercy stumbled back, tripped over a root, and fell to her knees as she curled in on herself while she gasped for air. She didn't realize she was sobbing until the tears plopped onto her bare legs.

Mercy swiped angrily at her cheeks and sucked in more breath. She looked up at the palm and her fear and frustration boiled over. "I don't know how to fix you! Please, help me! Please!"

Like she'd pressed a play button the base of the tree began to flicker as if it was trying to bring itself into focus. The bark shifted to become semi-translucent. The colors of an oyster's shell rippled up the trunk as an image took form *inside* the tree. Mercy held her breath as the image became the shape of a warrior who had the body of a young god and the head of a snarling reptile.

"Khenti!" His name burst from her lips as she hastily stood and brushed dead leaves and rotted bark from her dress.

The warrior's nightmarish head turned in her direction and his snarl instantly stilled. The spear he'd held up, ready to throw, lowered, and he bowed respectfully. "I greet you!" He squinted dark eyes that were disturbingly human, and then added, "Gatekeeper and Green Witch, Mercy."

"You remembered who I am!" Mercy blurted and then felt heat rise up her neck to her cheeks as she realized how silly she sounded.

He nodded his massive reptilian head. "Of course, Gatekeeper." He glanced around as the opalescent gate rippled like a rock-disturbed pool. "Is your sister, the Cosmic Witch Hunter, not with you today?"

"No, she's—" Mercy paused and searched for the right words. "No," she began again, "I'm alone." And then, to Mercy's complete mortification, she burst into tears.

Khenti raised his hand and mist, black as his onyx scales, swirled to obscure his face. When it cleared the ferocious reptilian head was gone, replaced by that of a boy about Mercy's age. His skin was golden brown, his long, dark hair was tied neatly back, and his umber eyes filled with concern as they focused on her.

"What is it? What has happened?"

Mercy shook her head and dug into her purse for a wadded-up tissue. Hastily, she wiped at her eyes and nose and gulped more air. "It's nothing. I'm—I'm just being silly."

Khenti cocked his head to the side. "Are your emotions not honest?"

She sniffled. "Yeah, I suppose they are."

"Then how can an honest emotion be silly?"

"Actually, that's a good point." Mercy brushed her hair back from her damp face and dropped the tissue into her purse. "It's just that a lot has happened lately and I have had a spectacularly bad day." She blew out a long breath. "I'm usually better at controlling my emotions."

His sigh echoed her breath. "I, too, have had a spectacularly bad day."

"Really? I, uh, don't want to get into your business, but I'm here if you want to talk about it," said Mercy.

Khenti's wide shoulders moved restlessly. "It's difficult for me to speak about." He glanced over his shoulder and lowered his voice. "Families can be difficult."

Mercy snorted. "Tell me about it. I don't know what's worse—messed-up trees or messed-up family."

Even through the shimmering barrier between them Mercy read the worry on his face. "When we spoke before you said your mother, the magnificent Kitchen Witch, Abigail, died not long ago."

Mercy nodded. "Yes, just a few days ago."

Khenti mirrored her nod. His dark eyes were shadowed. "I, too, know the loss of a mother. Your sadness should not shame you. It is a tribute to your mother and your love for her."

Mercy took a step closer to the tree. "Your mom died, too?"

"She did." He clipped out the two words.

"But you get to see her, right? I mean, you're in the Egyptian Underworld. So, isn't she there with you?"

Khenti looked down at his golden leather sandals, but even through the shimmering barrier that separated them Mercy saw his grimace of pain. "No. There are different realms of our Underworld—the Land of the Dead. In my mother's Book of the Dead she described her after-life in detail. After her heart was weighed and her life judged as just, her spirit moved on. She is beyond even the reach of her beloved son until the day that I die." His grim expression shifted and a smile lifted the corners of his lips. "That day, if I have lived a just life, I will join her, as she and I have each inscribed in our books."

Mercy squinted as she tried to see through the incandescent gate between worlds Khenti stood behind. "You write in a book, and whatever you write comes true after you die?"

His smile widened. "Yes and no. Yes, if you pass the tests of the gods. No, if you do not."

"And, um, you're not immortal?"

"No! I am a demi-god, like my father. My mother was a mortal woman—the daughter of Ka, the Pharaoh's favorite architect." His expression softened as he spoke about her. "That was how Father met her. She was taking lunch to Ka in the Valley of the Kings. Upuant, my father, visits the valley regularly to note the progress of the great tombs. He glimpsed my mother, Meryt, and became obsessed with her."

"She must have been beautiful," Mercy said as she thought of how much like a goddess her own mother had often seemed to her.

"She was—and is again."

"Your father must miss her, too," Mercy said.

Khenti's expression instantly hardened. "I am not sure that my father has the ability to miss anyone."

"Ugh, let me guess—your dad is powerful, cold, and distant."

The swirling barrier between them stilled long enough that Mercy saw Khenti's dark eyes widen in surprise. "Yes, exactly. How did you know?"

"In my world too many men believe they can't be strong unless they're shut off from their feelings."

"But you do not believe that?" Khenti asked.

"Oh, bloody hell no! That doesn't make any sense to me. Our hearts, our *feelings* are where we find strength."

Their gazes met. "I agree. I did not know Upuant well before my mother's death, and since she has been gone and I have been here, guarding the gate to the Land of the Dead, I have often wondered how such an aloof being could have earned my mother's love." He looked down again. "Or perhaps it is my father's disappointment in me that has made him so distant."

"Don't blame yourself. When Hunter and I were upset about something crappy someone said or did Abigail used to remind us that we are only responsible for our own feelings—no one else's. She'd tell us that all we can do is be the best versions of ourselves because that's all we really have control over."

Khenti's grinned. "Your mother was a wise woman—as was mine. I look forward to my reunion with her, though not too soon."

Mercy returned his smile. "I understand. My mother is with her goddess, Athena. Someday I'll see her again, too. Whether in this life or after we are reborn in the next."

"It is a comfort, even in loneliness," agreed Khenti.

"Yeah, but I wish she was here. I really need her advice." For a moment, as she'd been talking with Khenti, Mercy had forgotten the sick gates and the fight with Hunter, but now it all came rushing back. Her shoulders sagged and she sighed heavily.

"Can I help?"

Mercy's gaze met his. "I don't really know. Is the gate still sick on your side?"

"It is."

"Is it any worse?"

Khenti let out a long breath and nodded. "I'm afraid it is. I have had to burn sacred incense to cleanse the area and have remained near the gate. That is why I was close enough to hear your cries."

Mercy felt her face heat again, but she pushed aside her embarrassment. "Four of our five gates are sick, and seem to be getting worse."

"What of the fifth gate?"

"It's where my mother died. She sacrificed herself to keep a creature from coming through into our world. When she did that she healed whatever was wrong with the tree and the gate to the Norse Underworld," Mercy explained. Then she threw her hands up as her frustration boiled over. "What am I supposed to do? *Die* to save a tree? There's only one of me! My sister moved out. We aren't even speaking, but if our only answer is to die to save the trees there are just two of us and four trees, so we've already lost."

Khenti shook his head quickly. "There is no logic to requiring a Gatekeeper to die to heal a gate. It would defeat the purpose of being a Gatekeeper. What of your magic? Is that not how you maintained the trees for generations?"

Mercy paced back and forth in front of the flickering barrier between their worlds. "Yes, that's exactly how each Goode witch kept the trees and their gates healthy generation after generation, but something's happened to our magic. Well, *my* magic for sure." She stopped and faced Khenti again. "Below us are streams of power called ley lines. Five of them intersect here, in our town, to form a powerful pentagram. You know what that is, right?"

"A five-pointed star."

"Right. Okay, so, each generation the Goode witch has been able to pull power from those ley lines. We use our bodies as conduits to aim the power at the trees. The trees stay healthy and the gates remain sealed. But it's not working anymore."

His brow furrowed. "The power of the lines is gone?"

"No, which is totally frustrating. It's still there. I can feel it right now. Yesterday, I cast a simple heal-and-protect spell on one of the trees. I've cast that same spell more times than I can count. Everything seemed fine. I tapped into the power like usual, pulled it up into my body, and then when I aimed it at the tree it just . . . just . . . *fizzled*. It reminds me of seeds sprouting."

"Seeds? I do not understand."

"Not seeds—*sprouting* seeds. I do it in my greenhouse in the winter. Um, a greenhouse is a place where plants can be safe and warm, even when it's cold outside." He nodded in understanding and Mercy continued. "I'm a Green Witch, so my plants thrive. But once in a while a seed will begin to sprout—to push up through the dirt and appear just fine like the rest of them. And then, for no apparent reason, it withers and dies. It happens fast. Like, *poof!* Seedling suicide or whatever."

"And that is what your magic feels like when you aim it at a gate—a dying sprout?" Khenti asked.

She shrugged. "It's the best comparison I can make."

His brows went up. "Have you tried any other spells recently?"

"Yeah, I've tried different spells on the trees. Everything I can think of."

"No, I do not mean spells on the trees. I mean other magic."

"Hmm, now that you mention it, Hunter and I cast a rainmaking spell just a few days ago. It worked with no problem at all." *And Hunter's spell to take away my grief worked, too,* Mercy added silently.

"But you and Hunter are not casting spells together now?" Khenti asked.

Mercy fisted her hands so she wouldn't pick at her lip. "No. She's mad at me."

Khenti's brow furrowed again. "But is she not your Gatekeeper partner?"

"Yeah, but she's also my sister who is super pissed," Mercy said.

"So she betrays her duties?" Khenti shook his head. "I would not speak ill of your sister, but that is extremely irresponsible."

"Right?!" The word burst from Mercy. "She said she was going to fix the trees on her own, but I visited every sodding tree today and she was nowhere to be seen—*and* I didn't feel any of her magic." Mercy's anger felt good—righteous—and so much easier to deal with than tears and loneliness.

"It seems to me that you should cast your own spell, but not on one of the gates."

She nodded and felt a stir of hope. "That's not a bad idea. At least then I'd know for sure if it's me or—"

"If it's the trees and the gates they hold," Khenti finished for her as his sweeping gesture took in the opalescent gate between them.

Mercy straightened her spine and grinned at Khenti. "I'll do it. Tonight. I'll go home and cast a spell by myself and see what happens! Hey, thanks. I really needed someone to talk to."

"I am here for you, Gatekeeper. I will not forsake my duty to the gate, which includes my duty to you." Khenti paused and took a small step closer to the barrier between them. "And I have enjoyed our conversation." His deep voice softened. "It can get lonely here."

Mercy stepped closer to the glistening gate. "Loneliness is something that I never understood before. But, since Abigail died and Hunter—and really my whole world—changed, I'm sorry to say I understand it way too well now."

His dark eyes caught hers and the barrier stilled so that it looked like Khenti was just beneath the surface of a crystal lake. He raised his hand, palm toward her, and spoke quietly. "I am here for you," he repeated. "Call me. I will always answer. I give you my oath."

Mercy lifted her hand, palm facing him. She didn't think. Mercy just pressed her palm to the gate and it gave way. Her hand slipped within the glistening surface. It felt like nothing—only a slight pressure against her skin—and then her hand was through and she felt the warmth of Khenti's world.

The warrior stared at her hand and reached forward. Khenti pressed his palm to hers and they touched. Against her hand Mercy could feel the roughness of his palm, calluses caused by the spear by his side, or the sword strapped to his waist. Mercy's gaze went from his kind brown eyes to their joined hands. Hers was gray! And that grayness was creeping up her arm. She gasped and yanked. There was a liquid *plop* and the barrier released her arm. It was dry, but still gray. Mercy rubbed it frantically and gradually it pinkened.

"What the bloody hell was that?" Mercy kept rubbing at her wrist and forearm. "Am I okay?" *What were you thinking? That you could high-five him? Touch him? Hold his hand?*

"Yes, of course!" Khenti started to move forward, as if to take her hand again, but stopped at the barrier and instead ran a hand across his face. "You are a living being from another world, another realm. You cannot cross through the gate into my Underworld unless you have a vessel to inhabit. If you do not—you die." At her wide-eyed expression he hurriedly added. "Not immediately! What was happening to your hand and arm would eventually spread throughout your body and you would die unless your spirit found another home."

Something tugged at Mercy's mind. "Wait, you said I wouldn't die immediately. How long would it take?"

Khenti moved his broad shoulders. "From what I have observed that depends on how long you have lived in your own world."

She shook her head. "I don't understand."

"It isn't complicated. The younger a being, the sooner they die. You seem quite young."

Mercy squared her shoulders and attempted to look mature. "I'm sixteen."

"Yes." Khenti's lips tilted up at the corners. "Young. You could visit for perhaps half of a day. Those who are older can exist full days, even longer, before their bodies fade and then cease to breathe."

"The Fenrir! He was powerful enough to come close to killing all of us—my mom, my sister, even our cat, and me—and he wasn't gray *at all*."

"Do you know the creature's age?" Khenti asked.

"Super old, like from ancient Norse mythology."

Khenti nodded. "Yes, a creature who is that old would be powerful in its own body for some time before he began to fade."

"Ohmygoddess! Polyphemus, the Cyclops who came through the Greek gate the day my mom died, was really, *really* old, too. But he killed Sheriff Dearborn that night and took his body." Then she smacked herself on the forehead. "Of *course* he killed someone and took his body fast. No way could a one-eyed monster walk around Goodeville killing people without being noticed."

"Which is why most of the creatures that slip from their realms to another kill quickly, no matter their age."

"Huh. That's good to know. I'll be sure to write all of this down in my grimoire," Mercy said.

"Grimoire?"

"Every witch has a collection of grimoires. It's where she records all of her spells and notes about them. For a Goode witch they're super important because we pass them down from generation to generation," Mercy explained.

"Ah, I see. A record of how you have cared for the gates."

"Sorta. But it also has a lot of other spells in it, and random information. What you just told me could help a Goode witch centuries from now—literally."

A full smile bloomed on his handsome face and he bowed his head slightly to her. "I am pleased to know that I have aided you."

"You've also helped me." Mercy grinned back at him. "I'm going to go home and cast a spell."

"You will tell me what happens?" His gaze captured hers again.

She couldn't look away. "Yes. Promise." The park's lights chose that moment to blaze and splashes of white illuminated the parking lot and the cars that parked there. "Crap! I totally lost track of time. Lights are on. I gotta go before someone sees all of this." She gestured at the swirl of colors between them.

"Yes, of course. Fare thee well, Gatekeeper Mercy." He bowed to her.

"You, too, Gatekeeper Khenti. And thanks. I needed a friend tonight." She bent her knees in what she hoped was a cheeky curtsy.

As the barrier faded Khenti's voice echoed, "As did I, my friend."

Seven

Jax had brought his Xbox console from the main house and had connected it to the small TV in Hunter's garage apartment. He and Kylie had gone from the couch to the floor, and now sat even closer to the television (and each other) to better see each of their players in the split-screen *Call of Duty* game. The sun had also changed positions and slipped from the heavens, replaced by the cool black cloak of night as Jax and Kylie sat whooping and hollering after each kill. Normally, Hunter would have found it annoying, but there was something about Kylie that shimmered in the air and quelled Hunter's nerves.

A burst of citrus filled the small space as Kylie shook back her hair and glided her fingers through her shiny reddish blond waves. Hunter clutched her open spellbook and inhaled so deeply her shirt strained against her full chest. She was calm, focused, inspired—maybe this is what it was like to have a muse.

When their current game ended, Jax shouted a testosterone-fueled *yes* and pulled Kylie into a hug that lasted much longer than a friendly embrace. Hunter frowned. No, Kylie couldn't be her muse. Not when the cheerleader was so clearly interested in Hunter's best friend.

Kylie's phone chirped and she pulled away from Jax to answer. "It's my mom." She smiled and lifted the phone to her ear as she headed toward the front door. "Why, hello there, Momster—" The door closed behind her, reducing her words to the dull *wah wah* of a Charlie Brown adult.

Jax plopped onto the couch next to Hunter. "She's great." He sighed, his dark eyes sparkling as he stared at the door. "Really, really great."

Beneath Hunter's hand, the spellbook thrummed. Her gaze flicked from it, to Jax, and back to the spell she'd been focused on all day. *WANT.* She flattened her palm against the page. "Say that again."

Jax stretched his arm along the back of the couch as he turned to Hunter. "Kylie frickin' rocks." His crooked teeth peeked out from under his top lip. "I wish she wouldn't have put her sweats on over those tiny shorts."

You feel it, don't you, Witch? Amphitrite's voice slipped into Hunter's mind with the ease of sunlight through glass. *How the book speaks to you, calls to you?*

Hunter squeezed her eyelids closed. "Shut up," she commanded, her eyes fluttering open.

Jax sagged against the couch cushion and tossed his hands into the air. "I can't help my *horny boyness.* I *am* a horny boy."

Hunter's heartbeat quickened and her fingertips heated. "Not that." She glossed her tongue across her lips and swallowed a shaking breath. "I mean, yes, you're gross, but that's not why I said to be quiet."

Feed it, Hunter Goode, Amphitrite urged. *Feed it and it will grow, and the stronger you'll both become.*

Jax held up his finger. "You told me to *shut up,* which is way more hostile than *be quiet.*"

Heat swarmed Hunter's hand and climbed up her wrist. "Do you want to argue about my level of sass, or do you want to do a spell?"

Jax's brown eyes flew to the closed front door. "Kylie's right outside." He leaned forward and lowered his voice to a whisper. "Of this room *and* our pentagram of trust."

A grin lifted Hunter's lips. *Pentagram of trust.* Not cool enough to be the name of their coven, but definitely cute. "True, but this spell is about her."

Again, Jax's attention wandered to the door as if he had X-ray vision and could see Kylie's lithe, powerful form through the wood. "About her how?"

Hunter slid the spellbook between them. "This book sent a message straight to my witchy woman powers and told me that this spell is for you." She forced her hand away from the page and the magic that rose from it like steam. "You *want* Kylie. Let's see if Kylie wants you. It'll be like all those years ago when my mom gave Em's dad cookies that made Helene's true feelings known. They were married three months later."

Silence stained the air between the friends. Hunter's mom and Emily's dad were both dead, and neither Jax nor Hunter could do anything to fix it.

Jax opened his mouth to speak but paused, his lips working on an answer his tongue wasn't yet ready to supply. Finally, he spoke. "Before everything happened, Mr. and Mrs. Parrott were days away from getting divorced."

"Not because of my mom's spell. If you can even call it that." Anxiety pooled in Hunter's gut and she bit down to keep her teeth from clacking.

"You're *witches*! What else would you call it?"

Hunter shook her head. "That's not the point!" she hissed. "Do you want to know whether or not Kylie wants you the same way you want her? Or are you going to spend the entire summer playing video games and bumming rides hoping *she* makes the first move?"

Jax's jaw looked carved from steel as he pondered Hunter's question. "Fine. As long as the spell doesn't force her to have feelings that aren't really there."

Hunter glanced down at the open spellbook and the subtitle penned below the title, *WANT.*

Once an Empty Well. Now Your Cup Runneth Over.

She knew exactly what to do. Excitement pricked hot against her skin as she swallowed back her questions and hung a smile on her lips. "That's not even possible."

She hadn't lied. She just wasn't sure of the truth.

A rush of heat swept through Hunter as she picked up the book and moved from the couch to the floor. "We're making a pentagram out of items." She paused to listen for the muffled *wah wah wah* of Kylie's conversation before she motioned for Jax to join her. "Three of yours and two of hers."

Jax looked around as he folded his long legs and sat on the floor across from Hunter. "We don't have anything of Kylie's or mine in here."

Hunter puffed out panicked breaths as she scoured the room for something, *anything* she could use. "Shoes!" She pointed to the front wall and the poster that read LEAVE YOUR WORRIES AND YOUR SHOES AT THE DOOR.

Jax laid back, stretched his arms over his head, grabbed the shoes, and sat back up before Hunter had even gotten to her feet. He dropped the shoes next to the spellbook and grinned. "You want mine, too?"

Hunter grimaced. "Absolutely not." He still hadn't showered from practice. Kylie was the only reason Hunter couldn't smell how sweaty and gross he was. Even though she was outside, her sweet grapefruit scent still coated the air.

Jax shrugged and shoved his hands into his pockets as Hunter moved Kylie's shoes to the points at the arms of the invisible pentagram and placed the book between them.

"Will these work?" Jax held out his phone, school ID, and two protein bar wrappers.

Hunter plucked the phone and ID from his hands. "I'm pretty sure trash doesn't count, so we're still one short."

With a nod, he closed his mouth. His jaw worked like he was chewing gum before he held his hand up to his chin and spit. Clear plastic flew into his palm along with a dollop of saliva. "Number three," he chimed and placed the Invisalign tray at the head of the pentagram.

Hunter couldn't help but frown. The pentagram looked like the contents of Goodeville High's lost-and-found bin. She shook her head, pushed her doubts aside, and surrendered to the magic that increased her heart rate and plucked at her nerves.

She read the spell's next steps a final time before she sucked in a deep breath and took Jax's hand in both of hers. "Do you trust me?"

Jax nodded, his gaze never leaving hers.

And so it begins . . . Amphitrite hummed.

Hunter relaxed into the laughter that snaked between her ears and lifted the hairs on her arms. The goddess had already given her more than Tyr ever had. And now Amphitrite was assisting with a spell that would not only make Jax happy but would also fill in the empty pages of her spellbook. This is what she'd meant by *feed it.* Hunter was going to grow her power and make everything better. She knew it, just as she knew the moon would once again be full.

Another deep breath and Hunter flipped Jax's palm toward the ceiling. Blue light coated Hunter's fingers and salty spray dusted her cheeks. Her eyes flicked up to his. "Do you see that?"

He blinked back at her, his brows pinched. "See what? Is something supposed to happen?"

He is a mortal. There are many things he cannot see, Amphitrite hissed. *Hurry, Witch. Complete the spell before the girl returns.*

"We have to be quick." Hunter squeezed Jax's hand in hers to keep from trembling. "And remember your intention: *what does Kylie want?*"

His hair flopped against his forehead with another nod.

Hunter dragged her blue-tipped index finger along the end of Jax's thumb. "Τομή." *Cut.* Her voice deepened to a purr that vibrated against the back of her throat as she uttered the Greek spell word without thinking. The line she drew morphed into a thin cut, and Jax flinched as blood welled against his skin.

Hunter guided his hand to the top point of the pentagram and squeezed his thumb. Blood dripped onto the plastic and pooled in the hollows of Jax's dental imprint before sizzling and disappearing into nothing.

"θέλω." *I want.* Another low hum, and Amphitrite's laughter slithered through Hunter's veins.

Jax's breathing quickened as Hunter brought his bloody hand to Kylie's shoe. "Θέλεις." *You want.*

Sweat popped against his forehead as she squeezed his thumb and dripped crimson over his school ID, his phone, and finally Kylie's other shoe.

Amphitrite's ghostly laughter tightened Hunter's chest and squeezed her heart as the young witch cupped her hand under Jax's thumb and collected his blood. She released him and held the scarlet pool over the white pages of her spellbook.

"Θέλουμε." *We want.*

She roared and slammed her bloody palm against the pages. The pentagram ignited with electric red light that illuminated each item and connected them with fiery bolts. She and Jax shielded their eyes as the book slammed shut and the five items lifted from the floor.

It is done! Amphitrite's laughter screeched through Hunter so loud and sharp that she pressed her hands over her ears.

Power exploded from the pentagram and crashed against Hunter. She flew backward and landed on the floor with a heavy *thud.* The five items dropped onto the rug as Hunter sat up and blinked the red star from her vision.

Blood dripped from Jax's thumb as he rubbed his eyes. "What the hell was that?"

The doorknob jiggled and the door let out a breathy *whoosh* as Kylie ended her call. Hunter's stomach squeezed and her heart galloped within her chest as she tossed Kylie's shoes back to the front of the room and snatched her spellbook from the floor.

Jax shoved his braces and ID into his pocket and busied himself with his phone as Kylie stepped inside.

"Sorry about that." She brushed her hair behind her ears and smiled. "My sister's birthday is next week and my mom's trying to plan our trip to Northwestern to surprise her, but she *refuses* to hear that Reese would rather die than have us pop up at her dorm."

"Yeah, for sure," Jax stammered, wiping the sweat from his brow. "I mean, surprises . . . they're just—"

"The worst." Hunter supplied, nodding so adamantly her hair flopped in front of her face.

Kylie cocked her head and slipped her phone into her pocket. "You guys okay?"

Hunter leaned against the couch and did her best to feign nonchalance while she hid her bloody palm. "We're terrific."

"Super great." Jax swept his hand through his hair and flashed a cute, crooked-toothed grin. "How about you?"

She shoved the sleeves of her windbreaker up past her elbows and stuffed her hands into her pockets. "I'm actually starving. How do you feel about pizza?"

"You had me at *starving,*" Jax said and leapt to his feet. "Want to come to the house with me to get some pop?" he asked, leaning down to offer Kylie his arm. "With you there, my mom is less likely to yell at me about pizza not being a real meal."

With a giggle, Kylie stuffed her feet into her shoes and hooked her arm through his. "How can pizza not be a real meal?" she asked as Jax opened the door. "It has all the food groups . . ." Their conversation faded as the door closed behind them.

It was only a matter of time before they knew for sure whether or not Kylie wanted Jax. Hunter released a pent-up exhale and caught herself before she collapsed onto the floor. The spellbook spilled out of her lap and landed on the rug beside her. Her heart thrummed with another surge of adrenaline as she scooped up the book and brushed her hand along the fleshy cover. A crimson streak ran along the bottom of the book and faded into pink then milky white at the top. She flipped through the spells and stopped when she reached *WANT.* She gasped and pressed her fingers against her lips. The page was the same deep red as the blood crusted against her palm. Her hand trembled as she turned the page. Another spell. She laughed against her copper-tinged fingers as she turned one page, and then another, and another. Four new spells. She was that much closer to fixing the gates.

Hunter sprawled out on the rug and clutched the book against her bare stomach. "Thank you, Amphitrite."

Salt coated Hunter's tongue, sticky and dry, as mist dotted her lashes.

You're welcome, young witch, Amphitrite purred. *But it is far from finished feeding.*

Hunter nuzzled the creamy soft cover against her cheek and pressed down the worry that had begun to tug on her stomach. Feeding the spellbook once had been easy. It couldn't be that hard to do it once more. Plus, additional spells meant additional power. And more power meant Hunter would never again get lost in the shadows.

Eight

It was fully dark when Mercy pulled out of Goode Park. She halted at a stop sign and tried to decide whether she should chance it and cut through the neighborhood that surrounded the park to Main Street, where she'd then turn left and be home super fast—or whether she should go the opposite direction and wind around the country roads that framed the corn and bean fields outside of town to take the long way home—when her phone lit up. The screen said ABIGAIL/MOM with her familiar Aretha Franklin "Respect" ringtone.

For an instant Mercy froze and her heart felt like it was going to fly out of her chest. And then she remembered that Xena had been using Abigail's phone. With a trembling hand she hit the accept button and the cat person's voice blared throughout the Camry.

"Kitten! Are you *ever* coming home?"

"Yes! I just left the last tree—the doum at the park. Sorry it took so long, but Khenti—"

"Yes, yes, you can tell me all about the odd Egyptian reptile boy when you get home and we are eating dinner." Xena paused. "Which means we need dinner, kitten!" she shouted.

Mercy cringed. "Sheesh, Xena, you don't need to yell. I can hear you just fine."

"You know I am not good with electronics!" Xena continued to shout.

"I know." Mercy hastily turned the volume down on the phone call. "I'll be home in a few minutes and we'll decide what to eat."

"Oh, I already know what we should eat, which is why I called. On your way home please stop by that restaurant where my Abigail used to get my seafood pizza."

"Foxfire Woodstove Pizzeria?"

"That is exactly it! I would like one small pizza—with extra tuna and no vegetables except broccoli."

Mercy shuddered in disgust. "Gross, and broccoli?"

"It is the only green I can abide besides the wheatgrass you and Abigail grow for me," said the cat person.

"It still boggles my mind that they actually make a pizza with shrimp and tuna on it."

"It is quite delicious. And, of course, get your vile vegetable concoction, too."

"Um, you do remember that the seafood pizza always makes you sick, don't you? I mean, seriously, Xena, last time Abigail got it for you I had to clean your litter box. Talk about vile."

"That was because my cat body has trouble with too much cheese. My *human* body likes it. Very much. And you needn't worry; I shall use the human litter box."

"You mean the toilet?"

"Yes, of course. Will you be a dear and hurry? I am quite hungry and none of the cans of albacore tuna are opened. I tried to use that *thing* and I broke a nail."

Xena stopped talking and Mercy heard a weird wet sound echoing from the car speakers around her. "Ohmygoddess, are you licking your fingernail?"

Xena swallowed quickly and audibly. "Not now I'm not. Hurry, kitten. I think I might be faint with hunger."

Mercy rolled her eyes as she envisioned the voluptuous cat person who definitely was in no danger of passing out if she missed a meal. "Xena, if you're that hungry call the pizza place and give them our takeout order. I know Abigail has Foxfire in her contacts; you don't even need to look it up."

"Kitten, I prefer not to speak to *strangers.*" She whispered the last word so that it almost sounded like a hiss.

Mercy sighed. "Okay, well, then you'll have to wait a little longer. I'm only a few minutes away from downtown, so I'll stop by the pizza place, wait for our to-go order, and then be home." Mercy cleared her throat and then added with feigned nonchalance, "Uh, have you heard from Hunter?"

There was a stretch of silence before Xena answered in a much-subdued tone. "No. Shall I find her name in Abigail's phone and press call?"

"Oh, bloody hell no!" Mercy's response was quick and the words burst from her like a command. She sighed and licked her lips, which felt as dry and cracked as her feelings, and started over with less emotion. "What I mean is don't call her because of me. If you want to try to talk to her, go ahead, but be prepared for her to hurt your feelings. I wasn't exaggerating when I told you she barely looked at me all day at school."

Xena's sigh mirrored hers. "Perhaps our Hunter just needs some time."

"Yeah, perhaps." Mercy said the words without believing them. Something had happened to Hunter and she didn't think time would change it. "I'll get your pizza—with extra tuna. See ya soon."

"Oh, kitten, could you also bring home some of those lovely salts for my bath? I've used all of Abigail's and I do need my nightly soak. I am not as young as I once was, you know."

"Exactly how old are you, Xena?" Mercy asked mischievously—knowing the question would definitely get the cat off the phone.

Xena's gasp was Oscar-worthy. "A lady never tells her age!"

"You're not a lady."

"I most definitely am. At this moment. Now, will you get me my salts?"

"Of course. The IGA's just down the street from Foxfire. I'll get them while the pizzas are cooking."

"Thank you, kitten! I shall be waiting on the porch with the light—" Midsentence Xena accidentally hung up on her.

"That cat . . ." Mercy muttered. She was so used to Hunter being with her that she heard her twin's response of, *Right? That cat!* lift from her memory—but that's all it was. Just a memory.

Mercy shook herself mentally. "Welp, Xena made my decision for me." She spoke aloud to chase away the ghost of her absent twin. Foxfire Pizzeria was in the northern section of Main Street, not far from the IGA. Mercy glanced at the digital clock on the dash—it was almost nine o'clock on a weeknight. "Sod it!" Mercy took a left. "Hardly anyone will be downtown anyway."

It didn't take her long to navigate through the sleepy neighborhood to Main Street, where she turned left again and easily found a parking spot right in front of Foxfire Pizzeria. Feeling relieved that the heart of the town appeared to already have gone to bed, Mercy closed the car door with her hip as she shoved her hand in her bottomless purse and felt around for her violet Kate Spade wallet.

"Repent, Witch! The end is near!"

The shout was punctuated by the siren of a police car.

Mercy was so startled by the simultaneous shout-siren that she almost dropped her purse. Her head snapped up to see a tall, painfully thin man with dishwater-colored hair that hung in mats around his shoulders pointing a dirty finger at her from the middle of the sidewalk.

"Bloody hell, Chuck. You almost gave me a heart attack." Mercy glanced around, expecting to see the police cruiser speed by, but the siren seemed to be coming from the neighborhood behind Main Street—and it shut off abruptly. She turned her attention back to the shouter on the sidewalk and frowned at the man she and her sister had dubbed Creepy Chuck when they were in grade school. Goodeville's conspiracy theorist and self-proclaimed Prophet of Jesus was harmless, except for his smell and his ability to be soundless when he *wasn't* shrieking at Goodeville residents to repent and prepare for the Rapture. She started to walk past him as she shook her head. "Seriously, it's not cool to sneak up on people and yell at them like that."

He moved with fluid quickness to block her and bent down so that his face was way too close to hers. Spittle flew as he shouted, "It spreads! Infects! Poisons! From them to me, and me to us. Can you not see?" The horrible stench of gum disease wafted over her along with another, more coppery scent.

She gagged and stumbled back, as the door to the pizzeria opened and the middle-aged owner, Terry Mitchell, rushed out.

"Chuck, I've told you before—you harass people by my restaurant and I'll call the cops on you! Now leave Hunter alone and get goin'." Mr. Mitchell made a shooing motion at him.

Chuck glared. "You are blind, too! When will you see the poison? What will it take?"

Mr. Mitchell pulled a cell phone from his pocket. "Okay, then. Calling the cops it is." Before the restaurant owner could connect the call a second siren wailed from somewhere behind him, and even though its sound was different—more ambulance than police—Creepy Chuck spun around as if he could see through the block of buildings before he turned back to face Mercy.

"You'll be sorry! Repent and stop the abomination you have caused!" Chuck shouted in Mercy's face then laughed maniacally as he sprinted past her and into the street where he caused a truck to brake abruptly to avoid hitting him.

Mr. Mitchell shook his head as Chuck disappeared into the shadows. "That crazy is a nuisance. You okay there, Hunter?"

"Mercy," she corrected automatically. "Yeah, I'm fine. Sheesh, he has bad breath."

"Next time Sheriff Dearborn comes in for a pizza I'm gonna have to have words with him. Chuck's gotten worse and worse. He's setting my customers on edge. I actually had to stop a fight between two grown men right out here yesterday afternoon—broad daylight! The truth is Chuck's bad for business. Speaking of—you coming in for a pie, or you going down the street to a lesser restaurant?" Mr. Mitchell smiled good-naturedly at her—and then his brows went up as his memory kicked in and in a much more subdued voice he added, "Real sorry to hear about your mom, Hunter. Real sorry."

Mercy sighed, but didn't bother to correct him. Again. "Thank you, Mr. Mitchell. Yeah, I'm here for takeout."

"Your usual? Individual seafood pizza, extra tuna add broccoli, and a large veggie pie?"

Mercy's stomach felt sick as she corrected the order. "Well, almost. Make the large veggie an individual, too. And, um, add a Greek side salad, please."

"I can do that!" Mr. Mitchell said, his jovial self again. "Want a Coke while you wait?" He opened the door to the pizzeria and the delicious scents of bubbling cheese and roasting dough teased Mercy's nose.

"Sure, but I need to run to the IGA real quick." Mercy jerked her chin to her right at the almost deserted parking lot of the one grocery store in Goodeville.

"Better hurry. It's almost nine, and the Igga closes then," said Mr. Mitchell.

"'Kay, I'll be right back." Mercy gave him a little wave as she slung her purse over her shoulder and jogged up the concrete stairs that led from the diagonal parking spaces that lined Main Street to the wide sidewalk, then she turned right and walked briskly along the quiet street.

The shop next door to Foxfire Woodstove Pizzeria was Olde Towne Florist. Mercy had zero clue why they'd added the two *e*'s, but she'd always kinda liked the way it looked, especially because she and Hunter pronounced them and laughed and laughed . . .

"Nope. Not going there," Mercy said. She averted her eyes from the *e*-filled storefront sign. Beside the florist was J'aime le Vin, a high-end wineshop, which made Mercy feel suddenly nostalgic. She smiled sadly as she remembered Abigail's gasp of happiness when she found out Goodeville was getting the store. For the first time she was glad she wasn't twenty-one. With a quick glance inside as she hurried past she recognized Samantha Monroe, the woman behind the counter who was arranging expensive bottles of wine before closing. "Like I want to be called Hunter again and told how sorry she is about Abigail?" Mercy muttered.

The post office was next to the wineshop. It had been closed for hours, but instead of being silent and dark Mercy heard male voices coming from the alley that separated it from the IGA. Mercy slowed as the red-and-blue lights of a police cruiser reflected off the brick side of the IGA across the alley.

Mercy stepped over the curb and gawked down the alley. She wasn't sure what she expected to see—maybe a kid who got caught painting graffiti, or that the cops had pulled over someone who had run one of the two stoplights on Main Street. What she hadn't expected—hadn't even considered—was that there would be an ambulance beside the sheriff's car, yellow CRIME SCENE tape going up, and a bloody-faced body being zipped into a black bag by two EMTs.

Mercy's feet stopped moving as the red lights of the ambulance grotesquely illuminated the face of the corpse. Just before the EMT closed the body bag she clearly saw that *he was missing his eyes.*

Mercy must have made some sound, because Deputy Carter was

suddenly jogging toward her, obviously trying to block her view. "Please move along," he said. "There's nothing here you want to see."

"He's dead!" The words hurled from Mercy's mouth. "And his eyes are gone!"

"Oh, it's you, Miss Goode. Hey, I wanted to say how sorry I am that I had to give you the third degree the other day. Still no sign of Sheriff Dearborn. Really wish we'd find him, though." Gently, Deputy Carter took her elbow and guided her from the alley and back to the sidewalk. "This is a crime scene. I need to be sure it remains intact. You understand that, don't you, Hunt—"

"I'm Mercy, not Hunter," she interrupted. "Who is it? Who was killed?"

Deputy Carter tilted his hat back and wiped his forehead with his sleeve. His kind gray eyes were shadowed and he looked decades older than his twenty-five years. "I can't say. His family hasn't been notified."

Mercy caught his gaze with hers. "But the dead man's eyes are gone, right? Just like Mr. Parrott." *And Mr. Thompson, and almost Hunter . . .*

The young deputy's gaze slid from hers. "Can't really talk about the details of the case," he said. He took her elbow again and walked her a few feet back toward the pizza place. "I'm going to ask you to move on, now, Mercy."

Mercy felt like her head was going to explode. She nodded dazedly. When the deputy let loose her elbow she stumbled. He reached out to steady her, but she shook him off. "I'm fine. Really. I'm okay. Gotta, uh, get my pizza." Mercy turned her back to him and forced herself to put one foot in front of the other.

But Hunter killed Polyphemus . . . Hunter killed Polyphemus . . . Hunter killed Polyphemus!

The words circled around and around inside Mercy's mind as she numbly paid for the pizzas and salad. Later she couldn't recall anything Mr. Mitchell had said to her. She also barely remembered the short drive north to the end of Main Street. Xena was on the porch when she parked the car in their driveway without bothering with the garage. The cat person was on her feet, clapping happily as Mercy trudged up the front stairs with the boxes from the pizzeria. From the porch swing behind her Emily stood and said, "Surprise! Xena called and invited me over for dinner." Em smiled at Xena and then sneezed. "Sorry, 'scuse me. Anyway, she thought I needed something to get my mind off Dad's funeral tomorrow, and I was like, *that's really sweet Xena,* and so I—" One good look at Mercy's face and Emily's words broke off.

"Are you okay?" Em asked.

"What is it, kitten?" Xena hurried to take the to-go boxes from her.

"Th-there's been . . ." Mercy had to stop and clear the shock from her throat. She looked from Xena to her best friend, who had just lost her father to a horribly similar murder just days before. "Can we go inside? I need to brew some chamomile and lavender tea."

Xena's eyes narrowed. "Yes, of course." She handed the pizza boxes to Emily. "Darling Emily kitten, would you take these for me and put them in the oven on warm while I help our Mercy inside?"

Emily's brow furrowed in confusion, but she shrugged and took the boxes. "Yeah, sure." Ahead of them, she went inside while Xena hung back with Mercy.

"Tell me," Xena said.

"There's been another murder. Downtown in the alley beside the post office. I don't know who's dead, but I do know that his body is missing its eyes."

Xena gasped. "This is bad. This is so, so very bad . . ."

"What the bloody hell do I tell Em?" Mercy asked as she picked at her lip.

"The truth, kitten. It will come out eventually anyway. So, let us tell your friend the truth. It will be better coming from those who love her." Xena took her hand. "I shall help you and we shall both be there for our Emily kitten."

Nine

"I don't understand. Didn't Hunter kill the Cyclops and send him back to the Greek Underworld?" Emily's umber skin looked ashen. She sat on the couch between Mercy and Xena. Three untouched plates of pizza and salad rested before them on the coffee table. Each of them held a mug of steaming chamomile and lavender tea that Xena kept reminding them to sip.

"She did," Xena said firmly.

"But did she, or was she so freaked out from losing Tyr that she only *thought* she did?" Mercy asked.

Xena's eyes flashed with anger. "Hunter returned Polyphemus to Tartarus. She is not here to say it, but you know better than that. Our Hunter would *not* lie about something of such great import."

Mercy's shoulders bowed and she picked at the gold rim of the porcelain cup. "Yeah, I get that. I didn't mean that she lied. I just meant that maybe she thought she'd gotten rid of the Cyclops when she really hadn't."

"But her new goddess was involved." Emily picked up her piece of pizza, nibbled at the end of it, and then listlessly put it back on the plate. "Doesn't that mean something?"

"It does indeed," Xena said. "Amphitrite is a powerful deity. With her aid Hunter defeated the monster."

"Then why did I just see an eyeless dead guy get loaded into an ambulance?"

"I shall call my Hunter kitten," Xena said resolutely. She stood and then looked around the living room helplessly before asking, "Has anyone seen Abigail's phone?"

Emily cleared her throat and almost smiled. "Yeah, I saw you put it in the pocket of your bathrobe."

Xena's hand disappeared into one of the voluminous pockets of Abigail's robe and emerged with the phone that still wore the cover decorated with a pentagram wrapped in vines that Mercy and Hunter had made for their mom's birthday the year before. "I shall call my Hunter kitten," she repeated. "Now."

Mercy and Emily watched as the cat person pawed at the screen of the phone. Brow furrowed it took her several tries, but finally she flashed a victorious smile and pressed the call button. Then she lifted the phone to her ear. "I found her!"

"Xena, Abigail has both of us in her favorites, so you could just—"

"Shh!" Xena help up a hand tipped with sharp, perfectly manicured nails and whispered, "It is ringing!"

Mercy waited. And then waited some more. Finally Xena said, "Kitten! I wish to . . ." but her words trailed away as she realized it was only a recording of Hunter's voice. Still, the cat person straightened her back, paused, and then in one rush said, "Kitten, it is your Xena and I must speak with you urgently about the horrid Cyclops killer because there had been a death! Downtown! Tonight! Oh, kitten, Mercy says the body has no eyes and we are quite wor—" Xena's wave of words ended as she lowered the phone and blinked rapidly. "It did not allow me to finish."

Mercy put her cup and saucer on the coffee table and dug her phone out of her giant purse, which was by her feet. "I'll try." She tapped Hunter's number and looked away from the contact picture that showed a selfie Hunter had taken with the open first page of her writing journal that blazed WHEN DARKNESS RISES, the title of her perpetual book in progress, across it. Unlike Xena, she wasn't surprised when Hunter's canned voice told her to leave a message, which she did not do. "She's not answering me, either."

"Try texting her. It is late for a school night. She might have her phone on silent and she'll see your text first thing in the morning," said Emily.

"Will do." Mercy tried not to sound super negative, but she knew her sister—or rather, she *used* to know her sister—and the Hunter she knew would never have ignored back-to-back calls from her family. Still, she texted quickly, *DEAD BODY DOWNTOWN—NO EYES—COULD CYCLOPS BE BACK???? WE NEED 2 TALK!!!* "Done. But if she doesn't answer we're gonna have to make her talk to us."

"Do you, uh, think she'll be at Dad's funeral tomorrow?" Emily's voice sounded heartbreakingly young.

Mercy put her arm around her best friend and squeezed her shoulders. "Em, we'll *all* be there."

"That is right, Emily kitten." Xena leaned into her and Emily sneezed. "Oh, sorry. I do wish you weren't allergic to me."

Emily wiped her nose on the back of her hand and quickly opened the little strawberry-colored crossbody she'd slung over her shoulder. She pulled out a small plastic bottle and then popped a pill into her mouth, using the tea to wash it down. "It's okay. I gotta set a reminder to be sure I take this allergy medicine Mom got me." She smiled at Xena and zipped up her purse. "I told her that it makes me feel better when you curl up on my lap—except that you also make me sneeze my brains out—so she got me some Zyrtec or Claritin, or whatever. It's supposed to help."

"What a lovely idea!" said Xena.

"Sounds like you and your mom are getting closer," Mercy said.

Emily's smile turned sad. "Yeah, it's like she's trying to make up for Dad being gone. When I think about getting closer to her I'm glad, but when I think about *why* I feel guilty for being glad."

"Don't do that to yourself, Em. I didn't know your dad real well, but I think he'd be happy you and your mom are close."

"Yes, kitten." Xena licked her fingers and smoothed a dark curl back from Emily's face. "And your mother *is* trying."

Emily stared at Xena as the cat person licked her hand again and reached out to continue smoothing her curls—and Mercy hastily rescued her by standing and pulling her bestie up from the couch with her. "Xena! People don't think it's okay to touch each other's hair like that."

Emily snorted a laugh as she patted her dark curl back into place. "And there's a much bigger conversation we need to have about hair-touching."

Xena turned her frown from Emily to Mercy. "Then it is a rather good thing that I am *not* a people."

Mercy opened her mouth to start explaining that bigger conversation to Xena when Emily sneezed so hard that the cup and saucer she was holding rattled and almost toppled to the wood floor. Em wiped her nose and shrugged.

"Xena does have a point. She's definitely not a people."

"Exactly," said Xena before she blew across her teacup and then lapped at the golden liquid.

Mercy shook her head in defeat before she said, "Hey, I need to cast a spell. How about you come with me and be my witness?"

Emily's fawn eyes lit with excitement. "Ooooh, magic? Do you need my help?"

"Well, not with the spell itself. That's pretty simple. But it would help if you'd watch the results with me. I need to understand if the trees are sick because my magic isn't working—or whether it's something else."

"Like that the only place your magic doesn't work is the gates?" Emily said.

"Yeah, like that. Xena, you wanna come with us?"

Xena froze mid-lick of her tea. "Sorry, kitten, what did you say? I so enjoy the taste of honey that sometimes I forget myself."

"Em and I are going out to my greenhouse so I can cast a quick spell. It was Khenti's idea, and I think it's a good one. Do you want to come with us?"

"No, you kittens go ahead. I shall finish my tea and, perhaps, lick the tuna and shrimp off my lovely pizza. Do you think it would be too unhealthy of me to ignore the broccoli?"

"You do you, Xena," said Mercy as she and Em shared a grimace at the grossness of Xena's tuna, shrimp, and broccoli pizza. "We won't be long."

"And I'll say bye now." Emily bent and hugged Xena while carefully turning her face away from the cat person's mane of wild hair. "I need to get home and try to sleep. Tomorrow is going to be really hard."

Xena hugged her back. "Then good night, kitten. We will be there for you tomorrow." Then the cat person cupped Emily's face between her hands and licked her gently on her forehead before releasing her.

Emily waited until they were in the kitchen to wipe at her forehead. "That's really nasty."

"Right? But it does mean she loves you." Mercy disappeared into the voluminous pantry and gathered a white pillar candle and wooden spellwork matches, a bag of salt, and a Mason jar of water that had been charged by the full moon. Then, arms linked, the girls went out the back door and slowly walked the stepping-stone path toward Mercy's beloved greenhouse—the last birthday gift Abigail would ever give her daughter. The moon was waning, but the night was clear and the stars looked like a goddess had broken a necklace of crystal beads that then scattered across the black velvet sky. Abigail's koi pond and the fountain of Athena that poured into it were lit up so that lazy, watery shadows washed across the yard. The best friends tilted their heads together.

"You haven't said hardly anything about your Egyptian guy," Em said.

"He's not *my* anything."

Em snorted. "So, he's super fine, right?"

"His head looks like a cross between a dragon and an alligator—or maybe a crocodile. Gotta look up the difference between the two again."

Emily bumped her shoulder. "You said he also has a human head. And I remember that Hunter said he didn't wear very many clothes."

"It's hot in Egypt." Mercy felt her cheeks also get hot as her imagination sent her an image of Khenti in his almost-nothing warrior's outfit.

Emily pulled her to a stop. "You are blushing."

"Well, I just . . ." She sighed. "Yes, he's super fine."

"I knew it!"

"Em, he's from *another world,* plus I'm on the rebound and the last thing I need is a boyfriend right now."

"He doesn't have to be your boyfriend for you to spill all the deets. So, *spill.*"

They started walking again as Mercy shrugged and tried to find the right words to describe Khenti. "He's nice. I mean *really* nice and not Kirk pretend nice."

Emily gave her the side-eye.

"Seriously! Khenti actually listens to me. And, um, I didn't want to admit this when I was with him, but Kirk really isn't very smart."

"Ya think?"

Mercy rolled her eyes, but continued, "Khenti seems authentically smart. And he doesn't have mommy issues, even though his mom is dead."

"Oh shit! I'm sorry."

Mercy nodded. "Yeah, he told me that today. It sounds like they were really close. And his dad's some big, important demi-god guy who stresses Khenti out. He's lonely, and I understand that."

"Hey, you okay?" Emily touched her shoulder.

"Yeah. The Hunter stuff is hard, though." Mercy cleared her throat. "Anyway, he's nice and cute, but all we are is friends."

"For now."

Mercy's snort mimicked Em's. "Forever. Did you miss the part about him *literally* being in another world?"

"Girl, you know I'm a hopeless romantic, so I'm gonna ignore that part."

Just outside the greenhouse was a tidy compost bin. Mercy paused there to use her gardening scoop to get a little of the fertile mixture. Then she opened the door and flipped on the row of overhead grow lights. She breathed in her favorite scents—dirt and growing things.

"Holy crap, Mag! I haven't been in here since you got it all set up." Emily walked up and down the rows of raised beds, gently touching delicate leaves and baby plants. "You seriously have a green thumb."

Mercy laughed. "Em, I'm a Green Witch—it's all part of that."

"Well, I'm jelly. I can't even grow cactuses."

"I've told you like a zillion times—*stop watering them so much and give them more sun*."

Emily shrugged. "I hear the words you speak, but somehow I can't make your directions work."

Mercy took Em's shoulders in her hands and looked into her friend's face. "It's okay. You have other strengths."

"Like?"

"You're smart and funny and kind—and you have amazing hair."

"Hmm. You're right. I'll stop murdering plants and leave the green stuff to you." She gently touched the frond of a hanging fern. "So, what kinda spell are you doing and what do you want me to observe?"

"Oh, it's simple. Come on over here to the orchids." Emily followed Mercy down the length of the tidy greenhouse packed with thriving plants to the part of the center table that held rows of orchids. Some of them were blooming, but the majority had long, curving stems that dipped under the weight of as-yet unopened blossoms.

"These are so pretty. I'm almost scared to stand too close to them in case they recognize a plant murderer and shrivel up."

Mercy laughed. "Don't worry. They know they're safe with me here." She studied the grouping of orchids before picking one that had six tightly closed blossoms resting along a gracefully curving stem. "Em, could you move the rest of the orchids a little way down the table so I have room to draw a salt pentagram around this one?"

"Sure!" Emily carefully pushed the potted plants toward the end of the table so that Mercy was left with an open space between them and a tray of tomato starts that weren't quite ready to be transplanted to the Goode's massive garden yet. "Like this?"

"Perfect." Mercy placed the orchid in the center of the cleared space. "Okay, I'm going to draw my pentagram, light my candle, and then cast the spell. My intention is to coax this orchid's blossoms into full bloom."

"What do you want me to do?" Em asked eagerly.

"Well, you can help by setting the intent of the spell."

"For the orchid to bloom, right?"

"Yep, exactly. And then watch with me. I'm going to channel the energy from the ley lines. If my magic is working right at least one of those blossoms should open," Mercy explained.

"Can I ask a quick question?" Emily whispered.

"Sure." Mercy smiled at her bestie before returning her attention to the bag of salt. She reached in and began to sprinkle a white line that was the beginning of a pentagram—the center of which was the potted orchid. "This isn't a difficult spell for a Green Witch, especially because my intent is always to help things grow. Ask away." Mercy poured the second line of the pentagram.

"Well, if this is a bloom spell, why don't you use it all the time? Wouldn't that, like, speed up stuff like these little green spindly looking things?" Emily pointed at the sprouts to their left.

"Those are tomatoes. And that's a good question." She drew the third salt line as she explained. "In theory I could come out here every day and cast a spell to force everything to bloom and grow, but the key word is *force.* It wouldn't be natural, and when any witch messes with what is natural too much it's not a good thing and there will be consequences." She scattered the white salt crystals to make the fourth line of the pentagram. "Think of it as me changing from a friend who is supportive and a good listener—someone who nurtures others and gives them space to be themselves—to a bossy bully who tries to force her will on everyone."

"If you did that no one would be your friend," said Emily.

"Exactly." Mercy completed the salt pentagram with the fifth line.

"Oh, I get it! That would make you a plant bully."

Mercy brushed her hands together to wipe off the salt. "Yep, and my plants would stop thriving."

"So, does that go for all witches, or just Green Witches like you?" Emily asked.

Mercy took the white pillar candle and placed it above the top point of her salt pentagram. "It's all witches because all of our powers are tied to nature in some way, whether it's plants and growing things like I do, or cooking like Abigail."

"Or the sky and the moon and such like Hunter?"

"Yep, cosmic energy is part of the natural world." She turned to face Emily as she picked up the compost scoop and distributed the rich fertilizer equally over the dirt already in the orchid's pot. "Would you hand me the jar of moon water?"

Emily passed her friend the water. Mercy unscrewed the lid and poured some of it onto the orchid. Then she put the jar aside and took a long wooden match from the ritual box, but before she struck it she caught Emily's gaze.

"I'm going to cast the spell now and then light the candle. While I do that imagine with me that the orchid bursts into bloom."

"Okay. Wait—I want to get it right. What color are its flowers supposed to be?"

Mercy studied the plant for a moment. "This one's petals are white with just a blush of pink."

"Got it." Emily drew a deep breath and nodded. "Ready."

Mercy turned to face the table that held her salt pentagram with the orchid in its center. She breathed in and out thrice to ground herself and reached down, down, down to the luminous green ley line that ran, riverlike, within the earth beneath her. In her mind's eye she imagined that she tapped into that glowing stream of power and drew it up and into her body. Mercy felt the ley line's answer as she flushed with warmth. Channeling that energy, she struck the match to the box and spoke the words of the simple grow spell.

"Freya, my goddess, in your name I do invoke:
As the season wheel turns
As the candlewick burns
Awaken with the light I bring
I ask that you bloom this night as you would for Mother Spring!"

Mercy touched the match flame to the wick of the white candle, and as she did so she envisioned her orchid bursting into full, beautiful bloom. There was an electric crackle and the candle blazed alight. At the same moment power shimmered around Mercy so fiercely that it became visual, like waves of heat lifting from a hot sidewalk newly cooled by summer rain.

The orchid in the middle of the pentagram shivered, as if in a gentle breeze, and then with the sound of a woman's sigh, all of its tightly closed buds opened into bloom.

"Holy shit!" Emily gasped.

Mercy was staring at the orchid and felt a giant rush of relief as it blossomed. "Whew, it's not me!"

"Girl, look around. It's *definitely* not you!"

Mercy's gaze swept her greenhouse and her gasp echoed Emily's. *Every flower in the greenhouse had opened and was in brilliant, beautiful full bloom!*

"Freya! Ohmygoddess!" Mercy turned in a slow circle as she drank in the fragrance of newly opened geraniums and petunias, jasmine and freesia. She laughed in delight. "Look, Em! Even the little tomatoes are flowering!"

Emily's eyes were bright with amazement. "Mag, this is incredible."

Mercy faced her friend and grabbed her hands. "The trees aren't sick because I'm not a powerful enough Green Witch to keep them well!"

"Seriously. You're amazingly strong. There's no way that what's going on with the trees and the gates is your fault." Emily paused, and looked down. "Does—does this mean that it's Hunter's fault?"

"I don't know, Em, but I'm going to find out."

Ten

Christian funerals are so very dreary," Xena said, sotto voce, as she tugged at the neck of the amber-colored silk blouse, then almost tripped on the hem of the long black peasant skirt she'd borrowed from Abigail's closet. She hissed softly at the flats on her feet then made a sad mewing sound. "Shoes are horrible. Are you quite sure I cannot take them off?"

Mercy shifted the orchid she'd brought so it was cradled against her hip like a toddler, took Xena's arm, and guided her to one of the shadowy alcoves outside the funeral home's main viewing parlor. She kept her voice low, but spoke firmly. "No, you cannot take off your shoes. You have to act like a person. Remember? We talked about this when you refused to wear a bra."

Xena looked down at her plentiful breasts, currently covered with a spandex tank top beneath the silk blouse. "It is odd to have bosoms, but odder yet to be expected to bind and torture them."

Mercy sighed. "That is something you and Abigail would be in agreement about. But you've gotta stop fidgeting and picking at your clothes. This is the visitation. The interment service is private, so we're only here to support Em and show our respect for Mr. Parrott, then we can go home."

"I shall be naked for the rest of the day."

Mercy fervently hoped that meant Xena was going to change into her cat form versus walking around the house as a well-endowed, voluptuous naked woman—who liked to sit on the arm of the couch, but decided that was a battle she wasn't willing to fight just then. "You can be as naked as you want at home. But you can't keep messing with your clothes and hissing while we're in here." Mercy lowered her voice more and delivered the coup de grâce. *"People will think you have fleas."*

Xena hissed. "I have never!"

"Well then don't act like it. And stop hissing! Come on. The sooner we go in—the sooner we can leave." Mercy had taken a step forward when the door to the Parrott Family Funeral Home opened. A group of teenagers, somberly dressed and unusually quiet, poured inside. They blinked as their eyes adjusted from the bright sunlight of a pretty spring day to the funeral parlor's sunset interior lighting of mauve and taupe. Mercy stepped back and froze, studying the group from the shadowy alcove. Tiffany Wilson, the captain of the cheerleading squad was there with Heather Johnson—which made Mercy's stomach roil, because where there were cheerleaders Kirk and the other football douches could usually be found. With them were three underclassmen from the pom squad, and several band kids. Following hesitantly behind were only two kids from the football team, Jarod Frazier and Dillon Sanders. Mercy held her breath as she waited for Kirk and his asshole of a bestie, Derek Burke, to show up, and then breathed a long, relieved breath when the door closed without them appearing. She couldn't handle dealing with that on top of everything else right now.

"What is it, kitten?" Xena whispered.

"Nothing. It's okay. Let's go in and see Emily." Mercy squared her shoulders and smoothed a hand down her simple floor-length black lace tank dress and the little sage-colored cardigan she wore over it.

Then, arm in arm with Xena she headed to the easel that held a poster-sized portrait of Mr. Parrott and the open double doors to the viewing parlor beyond. She felt the stares of her classmates on her ramrod straight back and was glad she clutched the orchid and Xena so that she couldn't pick at her lip.

Mr. Parrott's visitation was in the biggest, most ornate of the viewing rooms. Just inside the doors to their left was a long table that held stately silver urns with placards of gold that labeled them filled with coffee, tea, and water—beside which were row after row of fine porcelain cups and saucers, as well as plastic cups and plates. Claw-footed crystal pastry trays elegantly held an impressive assortment of petit fours. The linen napkins beside the fine flatware were embroidered with elaborate cursive *P*s.

Mercy's gaze swept from the table to the gold-upholstered chairs that rested in neat rows. A few people were seated, but most were clustered in little groups around the perimeter of the room. They sipped from the delicate teacups and murmured like wind soughing through fall leaves. At the far end of the room was a raised dais filled with huge bouquets of flowers and enormous wreaths. In the center of the mass of flowers was a tall, marble pillar that held a silver urn, beside which were several more easels. Each held a different picture of Emily's dad, and standing to the right of the display at the bottom of the dais were Mrs. Parrott, Emily's grandparents, and Mercy's best friend with her hands fisted at her side. In one of those fists was a tissue and every few breaths Em mechanically wiped at the tears that leaked silently down her cheeks.

"Oh, poor little kitten," Xena said softly. "Let us go to her."

It was hard for Mercy to speak, so she nodded and was suddenly glad Xena was there, warm and alive and loving. Their linked arms propelled Mercy forward, though her feet felt as heavy as her soul.

As soon as Emily saw them she touched her mom's arm, whispered something to her, and then stepped around the visitation line and met Mercy and Xena at the edge of the room.

Xena unwound her arm from Mercy's and pulled Emily into a mom hug. "Little kitten, my kitten, I am so, so sorry."

"Th-thank you, Xena." Emily sniffled and buried her head in the cat person's shoulder. "I'm glad you're here. I took my allergy pill this morning just so that I could hug you."

"Oh, sweet kitten! I love you and I shall always be here for you." Xena released her and stepped aside so Mercy could take her place.

"Mag! Y-you brought one of your m-magic orchids." Emily's voice shook with emotion.

Mercy blinked quickly as she tried not to burst into snotty sobs. "This morning I asked Freya to bless your dad's spirit journey"—she kept her voice low—"and when I did the blooms on this orchid changed from purple to pure white. So I had to bring it to you."

Emily engulfed Mercy in a hug. "White—the mourning color for Goode witches. It's perfect. Please thank Freya for her kindness."

"Freya hears you, Em. I promise she does."

The best friends clung to one another and as they did Mercy reached down, down, down through the plush carpet and the rooms below them to the earth on which they rested. She found the thrumming ley line of power and gently, carefully, pulled it up, up, up through her body so that it could wash into Emily.

Em gasped and held tighter to Mercy. "That's so warm! Oh, Mag, thank you. I've been so, so cold all morning." When Emily finally stepped out of Mercy's embrace her cheeks had regained some of their color and the circles that bruised her eyes had faded. She linked hands with Mercy and Xena. "Come on, you can say hi to Mom and my grandparents and put the orchid by Dad's urn. It'll be beautiful there."

They bypassed the growing visitation line, which earned them narrow-eyed looks from some of the adults, but Em's grandparents hugged them and thanked them for coming, and her mom smiled tearfully as she said how beautiful and thoughtful the orchid was. While Xena spoke somberly with Mrs. Parrott, Emily led Mercy up the stairs of the dais to the marble pillar that held the remains of her dad.

"Put the orchid here, right next to the urn." Emily touched the silver container gently, reverently. "It's hard to believe everything that Dad was is in there . . ." Her voice broke on the last word and Mercy quickly placed the orchid beside the urn and then put her arm around her friend.

"That's just what remains of his body. Everything your dad was isn't in there. It's here." Mercy pressed her fingers over Emily's heart. "And here." She lifted her hand and gently touched Em's forehead. "He's not really gone as long as he's remembered. I'll always remember him with you."

Emily's face crumbled. "And I'll always remember Abigail with you. W-would you do something for me?"

"Anything."

"C-could we do a witchy ritual for Dad? Not like Abigail's funeral, but just something to—to—" A sob broke her words as she stared out at nothing and tears washed her umber cheeks.

"Of course, Em!" Mercy squeezed her shoulder. "You, Xena, and I can perform a beautiful Rite of Release. I'll check my grimoire and get the perfect—"

"Hunter," Emily interrupted.

"Um, I can ask her next time I see her, but please don't be upset if Hunter doesn't show. You know she's not acting like herself."

"No, I'll ask her. But what I meant is Hunter's here." Emily gestured surreptitiously toward the entrance of the viewing room.

Mercy followed Em's gaze to see Hunter with Jax beside her. They were by the refreshments table and Jax was pouring water into a plastic cup. She'd barely processed the fact that her twin had entered the room when Emily's mom joined them on the dais.

"Emily, honey, I hate to interrupt." Mrs. Parrott gave Mercy a watery attempt at a smile. "But your third cousins from Michigan are here. I know you don't remember them. *I* barely do, but we must be polite, especially as they've come all this way. Mercy, do you mind if . . ." She glanced over her shoulder at a group of strangers who were talking animatedly with Em's grandparents.

"Oh, of course." Mercy gave Emily another hasty hug. "Go do what you need to do."

"I'll text you later so we can plan that thing we were talking about," said Emily.

Mercy nodded and Emily followed her mom back to the visitation line as Xena joined her on the dais.

"Your orchid looks lovely there." Xena batted at one of the fleshy petals.

Mercy grabbed her hand and murmured, "Hunter is here." She jerked her chin in the direction of the refreshments table, where Hunter was choosing a petit four. Jax stood beside her, clearly uncomfortable in a dark suit that had to have belonged to his dad.

Xena squeezed her hand. "We must speak with her."

"Okay, but remember where we are. There's not much we can say here."

"I understand. Come. I shall let you do the talking so I do not rouse the villagers."

Mercy almost told the cat person not to be ridiculous—that it was the twenty-first not the seventeenth century—but then the horrible insults Kirk had hurled at her when they'd broken up replayed in her mind, along with how everyone had been staring and whispering the past few days, and she pressed her lips together and nodded. Together they walked down the dais steps and headed to the back of the room. Mercy's skin prickled and her eyes swept the room to rest on Jarod and Dillon, who were clustered in a small group with Heather and Tiffany at the perimeter of the room. They were openly staring from Mercy to Hunter. There was something about the boys' narrowed gazes that put Mercy's intuition on high alert.

"Something feels wrong," she whispered to Xena.

"It certainly feels oppressive." Xena plucked briefly at her skirt before sighing and clutching her hands together.

"No, I mean really *wrong* wrong. I think we should leave as soon as we get done talking to Hunter."

Xena met her gaze. "We shall listen to your intuition, my Green Witch."

Even through her worry about Hunter and the weirdness thrumming around them Mercy felt a rush of pride at Xena's acknowledgment of her witchy intuition. It boosted her confidence so that she ignored the stares of her classmates and the sickness in her stomach. Her steps were sure as she walked up to Hunter—though as she got closer she saw that her sister, her twin who hated to show skin and hardly ever bared her legs, was wearing a black spaghetti-strap dress with an asymmetrical hem that exposed most of her thighs. Yeah, she had an oversized tan boy-cut jacket over it, but still there was more of Hunter showing than usual. And her long, dark hair, instead of pulled severely back in a ponytail like usual, cascaded loosely past her shoulders.

Hunter's back was to them and Jax cleared his throat in obvious warning, but before Mercy could say anything Xena beat her to Hunter and pawed at her shoulder. Hunter turned and the cat person pulled her into an embrace so enthusiastic that the petit fours almost toppled off her disposable plate.

"My Hunter kitten! I have missed you so!"

Hunter returned her embrace. Her lips tilted up as she spoke in a low voice. "You're wearing clothes *and* shoes."

"I know. It is quite horrible," said Xena.

"I miss you, too, Xena." Hunter squeezed her one more time and then stepped back and faced Mercy.

Mercy started with her sister's best friend, who felt a whole lot more approachable than Hunter. "Hi, Jax."

"Hey there, Mag," he said.

Then she faced her twin. "Um, H, Xena and I called you and I texted you," blurted Mercy.

"I got the messages."

Mercy glanced around them and stepped closer to her twin. "We need to talk and figure out what's going on."

"*We* do not. I've got it handled." Hunter bit into a petit four.

"What do you mean?" Mercy paused and lowered her voice. "Could the Cyclops be back?"

Hunter's blue eyes were glacial. "Not possible."

"But then what's going—"

Hunter broke in. "I said I have it handled. Now, I'm going to pay my respects to Emily."

Before Mercy could speak again, Hunter marched around her to join the reception line.

Jax shrugged and followed Hunter. "See you in class tomorrow, Mag."

Mercy had no clue what to do. She wanted to scream and run after Hunter and shake her—or maybe grab her long, suddenly emancipated hair and pull it. Hard. Instead she moved to the table and pretended to be interested in the assortment of teas.

Xena was a warm, comfortable presence at her side. "Give her time," she said softly as she stroked her back. "Our Hunter will come back to us."

Mercy shook her head and continued to stare at the tea.

Do not cry. Do not cry. Do not cry.

Eleven

Hunter looked down at her small plastic plate and the remaining petit four sitting in the middle like a store-wrapped present. She pressed her finger against the white icing and wasn't surprised when, like the plastic cakes she'd fed her toys when she was a child, it didn't smudge. She tucked her hair behind her ear and sighed. It figured. Wearing the slinky spaghetti-strap black dress she'd borrowed from Kylie, Hunter felt like a doll.

She glanced around the room as she popped the treat into her mouth and it dissolved on her tongue in a rush of sugary lemon. She spotted Mercy milling about the beverage station, her lips puckered and brow furrowed. All her sister needed to complete the look was a neon sign that said PAY ATTENTION TO ME! I AM GOING TO CRY!

Hunter quelled the pang of guilt that squeezed her heart. Mercy had made her choices. She couldn't really expect Hunter to follow her around forever.

"Read the room, Mag," Hunter grumbled and turned her back to her sister. She wouldn't give Mercy another opportunity to make

Mr. Parrott's funeral service about her like she did with everything else. It was completely inappropriate to talk about murder and witch gates at the funeral of Mercy's best friend's dad. And Hunter wasn't even going to touch on the fact that her twin obviously didn't think she was capable of making sure Polyphemus remained in the Greek Underworld.

The line moved forward, and Hunter hooked her arm around Jax's and shuffled along. It was strange how this funeral was so different from her mother's but also resembled aspects of a wedding. A few months ago, she and Mercy had been Abigail's dates to her client's wedding. They'd stood in a line just like this, eating desserts just like these, as they'd waited to wish the couple a long and happy marriage. Shortly after, half of the couple cheated, and her mother's client filed for divorce. Lies usually ended things.

The thought of lying made Hunter pull Jax a little closer and guilt paint pink blotches across her chest. She shook her head. The spell she'd performed last night would work out fine. Not knowing wasn't the same thing as lying. She took a deep breath and her shoulders softened away from her ears. No, she definitely hadn't lied to her best friend.

Hunter's grip tightened on the empty plate and crinkled its plastic edge as a thought wormed its way between her ears. Maybe her sister didn't believe that she had fought Polyphemus *or* called upon Amphitrite to banish him back to Tartarus. Maybe Mercy thought Hunter was lying . . .

"I didn't know you could get cakes this small. I feel like a giant," Jax said and stuffed three petit fours into his mouth at once. He swallowed and brushed the back of his hand across his lips. "Think we should bring a few to Em?"

Hunter wrinkled her nose. "She might not want sweets."

They felt too celebratory. Another year alive? Cake! Graduation? Cake! Promotion? Cake! She wasn't sure what she would say if they reached Emily and offered her a plate of tiny sugar loaves. *Your dad is dead? Cake!?*

Hunter used her plate as a fan as they trailed the guest in front of them and inched closer to Em and her family. "We should bring her one of the casseroles your mom has stashed in the freezer."

Jax swished water around in his mouth before answering. "Her *rainy day* casseroles." He shook his head and took another sip. "I don't think she understands what a rainy day fund actually is."

Tiffany and Heather seemed to appear from nowhere as they stuffed themselves into the narrow space before Hunter and Jax. The captain of the cheer squad tented her hands on her narrow hips like she was about to lead the room in an enthusiastic ditty about the power of a good defense.

"Kylie said she started hanging out with you. I didn't want to believe her, but here you are, wearing her Zara." Tiffany cocked her hip, and her faux leather pants creaked with the motion. "She usually has better sense."

Hunter exchanged a confused glance with Jax. She had only been *hanging out with* Kylie by default. "Being the third wheel isn't tantamount to choosing to hang out with someone."

Tiffany's fake eyelashes swallowed her eyes as she squinted. "Isn't *tantamount,* Hunter? Really?"

Hunter couldn't tell whether or not Tiffany was confused by the word or didn't believe her. "Kylie wants to spend time with Jax. I just happen to be there."

"Oh." Tiffany and Heather blinked in unison.

The dense cheerleader stereotype was created to shame and minimize vivacious, outgoing athletes. Cheerleaders weren't unintelligent. Unfortunately, Tiffany and Heather were.

Jax's arm stiffened around Hunter's. "Why does it matter to you who Kylie's friends with, anyway?"

Heather smoothed her fingers over the small pearls that embellished her black cardigan. "Normally, it doesn't, but we want her to be safe."

The plastic plate crunched between Hunter's fingers. "Kylie's not going to turn into a lesbian because we breathe the same air."

Heather snorted and pressed her polished fingertips against her square-tipped nose. "Obviously."

Maybe Heather wasn't as ignorant as Hunter thought.

Her brown eyes narrowed. "But she might if you do a sex spell on her."

The corners of Hunter's lips twitched with a chuckle. Never mind, Heather was definitely that dense.

The cheerleader brushed the lengths of her brown hair over her shoulders and continued. "I was totally on your side, and then Kirk informed us of some *questionable behavior* that Shayla totally confirmed." Her glossed lips thinned into a straight line as she crossed her arms over her chest.

Hunter exchanged a confused look with Jax who shrugged and took another drink of his tea.

With a sigh, Heather tapped the toe of her strappy sandal against the floor. "Shayla told us what you said at practice about your magical vagina." Her gaze scraped down Hunter, paused at her crotch, and clawed its way back up again. "Doing some kind of nasty pervert spell is the only way Kylie, or anyone, would ever be interested in a freak like you."

"Your mom *literally died* to get away from you!" Tiffany's pants squeaked in punctuation.

Water sloshed over the rim of Jax's cup as he tightened his grip around the plastic.

Heat crept across Hunter's chest and tickled her neck. Her fair skin kept no secrets, and she wished for the comfort and protection of her slouchy jackets and high-neck tees.

Witch! How can you abide their slander? The screech of laughter that accompanied Amphitrite's words scorched Hunter's thoughts. *You could take them all. Burn this place to the ground with them inside.*

The gap behind Tiffany and Heather widened as the line moved forward without them.

Hunter put her hand behind her back and channeled her rage into her fist. The bent edges of the plastic plate dug into Hunter's palm. She vented her anger through each painful gouge until her chest no longer burned and the blush of hate and embarrassment faded from her skin. "What's the point in all of this? It was cute at first, but now—"

Dillon and Jarod charged into the gap in the line like two sharks who smelled blood.

Jarod slipped his arm around Heather's waist and brought his lips close to her ear. "You ask her yet?" He punctuated his fake whisper with a sneer aimed at Hunter.

"Not yet." Tiffany's pants creaked as she shuffled closer to Heather. "We were waiting for you two."

Dillon draped his meaty arm around Tiffany's narrow shoulders and pulled her against him. "Careful how you do it, baby. You don't want the witch to curse you with chlamydia or something."

Jax unwrapped his arm from Hunter's and clenched his hand into a fist at his side as Hunter's grip tightened around the ball of plastic. But the pain no longer offered relief. "I can't curse someone with something you've already given them, Dillon."

The line continued to move, and the teenaged goons continued to hold Hunter and Jax—and the stream of unaware people behind them—hostage in the middle of the funeral home. Hunter's fingers itched to take Amphitrite up on her offer. To add her goddess's gifts to the power that already slipped through Hunter's pores like smoke and stop her tormentors once and for all.

I will show you how. Just say the word, young witch.

The scent of lilacs burned Hunter's eyes. She blinked away her watery vision as Mercy rushed to her side. Hunter tipped back her head and groaned. What kind of magnet was she standing on that kept drawing people to this spot?

Mercy crossed her arms over her chest and stared down the tip of her nose at Dillon and co. "This is a *funeral.* Only Emily's real friends and family should be here."

Dillon led the group in a howl of laughter.

The hairs rose on Hunter's arms and, behind her back, her palm heated. "Mag, I've got this. I don't need—"

Mercy shook away Hunter's objection and pressed on. "What's wrong with you?"

Heather made a show of drying her eyes as she focused her attention over Hunter's shoulder to where Xena stood. "I didn't know you needed *three* bodyguards."

They make you look weak when you could end them all with a droplet of blood.

A roar flexed in Hunter's throat as Xena's hand settled on her shoulder. She didn't need them. She could fight her own battles. She shrugged Xena's hand away and leaned into her sister. "*Mag.* Stop. I have—"

Mercy's elbow jabbed Hunter's ribs as her hands flew to her hips. "Em's dad is *dead* and you decide that his funeral is the best place to bully my sister? Not only is it inappropriate, it's completely—"

"Mercy!" Fire bit at Hunter's fingertips and scorched the back of her throat. "Go away!" She spit the words from between clenched teeth.

Mercy's hands slipped from her hips and her brow pinched. "I'm helping."

The group's steady laughter popped against Hunter's skin like blisters. "I don't need or want your help. Go be someone else's hero."

Mercy's lower lip quivered as her green eyes searched Hunter's face. They looked more alike now than ever, yet Hunter could barely recognize the sadness in her sister.

Xena brushed back her tabby hair, took Mercy's hand, and led Hunter's sister toward the front doors of Parrott Family Funeral Home.

Dillon sucked his teeth and smiled. "Never thought a funeral would be such a party."

"You really are a bitch, Hunter Goode." Tiffany cackled.

Hunter tilted her head. "I suppose I am." She brushed her hand through her hair and stared at the gap between them and the rest of the line. "This has been lovely, but it's time for you to go. You're holding up the line, and we'd really like to pay our respects."

Jarod stepped closer. "Not until we get our questions answered. Can't have a witch running around town."

Jax's chest swelled, and Hunter placed her hand on his arm before he, too, swooped in to save her. She brought her hand from behind her back and held her palm in front of her. Heather gripped Dillon closer as Tiffany gasped.

Hunter eyed the melted ball of plastic in her hand before slicing her gaze over the group. "I don't think I'm the one who should be running."

The herd took a step back and bounced into each other like confused squirrels before they darted away from the line. Hunter couldn't deny that showing off her power and being her own hero felt great.

"You did a plastic melting spell in your head while confronted by piping hot douche." Jax downed the rest of his water and squashed his cup into a similar sized, but way less melted, version of Hunter's plate. "You leveled up."

Hunter looped her arm back around Jax's as they closed the gap in the line. "Guess you never know what you can do until a bunch of dipshits act like assholes at your friend's dad's funeral." Jax didn't need to know that she'd unlocked the power of the stars and now her anger rushed from her fingers like lava. She had leveled up, but he was still many locked doors behind.

Jax's voice rose an octave as he asked, "And we're *not* talking about Mercy?"

Hunter looked up at her best friend.

He nodded and tossed the crumpled cup into the air and caught it. "So, you think there's a way to fix the plastics crisis with that melting spell?"

Hunted swallowed back her fury and remained quiet as Jax mused about her potential planet-saving powers. Before she could use her power for good, she'd have to keep it from burning her alive.

Oh, Witch. I sense your worry. Do not fret.

Hunter relaxed as the gentle hum of invisible waves drowned out the crowd, and a salty, otherworldly breath pressed against her senses.

I will teach you to leash the beast of rage. But only a fool would tame it when you can use it instead.

Twelve

Xena held tightly to Mercy's hand while she sat in the Camry and sobbed. Finally, when she felt like she was at least temporarily out of tears, Mercy dug a handful of tissues from her giant purse, wiped her eyes, and blew her nose before she asked Xena, "W-what's wrong with her?"

"Hunter is grieving and angry. Until today I believed she would return to herself—and to us—on her own."

"And now?" Mercy sniffed and wiped her nose again.

"Now I am concerned that her sadness is leading her down the wrong path." Xena spoke quietly, as if the words were difficult to say. "I scented something odd—something that is *not* our Hunter—on her."

"R-really?" Mercy hiccupped. "What was it?"

"I could not tell. It was indistinct, but most definitely *wrong.*"

"What do we do?"

Xena let out a long breath. "We need more wisdom—more guidance—than I can give. Kitten, let us go to the Norse tree and invoke your goddess. Freya will know what we must do."

Mercy sat up straight and felt a rush of relief. "Freya! My goddess *will* know what to do! That's a fantastic idea, Xena." Quickly, she started the car and pulled out of the funeral home parking lot. "Bloody hell! Why didn't I think of invoking Freya's help with Hunter before now?"

"Kitten, you must remember that it would be highly unusual for Freya to materialize and speak with you. Abigail devoted herself to Athena, yet the goddess only appeared to her a very few times. It is not the role of our goddesses to tell us what to do, or to give us easy answers. Were that true we would no longer have free will. You must invoke Freya's aid, but look for her response in omens and symbols rather than words."

"Well, yeah, of course. But Freya is super wise. She'll be able to let me know what I need to do to make things better, even if it's only in a symbolic way. Xena, she must have some advice that will help."

"Let us hope so, kitten . . ."

By the time Mercy had changed out of her funeral clothes and collected the sacred items she would use to call on Freya, the morning had turned into early afternoon. Mercy was glad that so much of the day had already passed that by the time she invoked her goddess school would be out.

"It's weird not to like school anymore," Mercy told Xena as the two of them walked slowly along the well-worn path that led to the enormous old apple tree that guarded the Norse Underworld.

Xena, in cat form, trotted beside her. The feline looked up at Mercy and chattered and mewed in the distinctive way Maine coons vocalize to their humans.

"Welp." Mercy swung her wicker spellwork basket and grinned down at Xena. She'd felt so, so much better ever since they'd made the decision to invoke Freya's aid. "Unlike Abigail, I can't understand you, but I'm going to believe that you didn't just chastise me and instead said that I'm too cool for school anyway."

Xena made a very human-sounding snort, which caused Mercy to laugh.

"That feels good," Mercy said. "Laughing feels *good.* Xena, I'm so tired of being sad and worried and stressed all the time. I'm going to remember to laugh more. Sod it! I'm going to start doing things that make me happy again."

Xena chattered at her.

"Oh, I know, I know. I still have trees to save and gates to close—and a sister who has lost her mind. But does that mean I have to be Debbie Downer for the rest of my life?"

Xena's response was a rolling rrrrow.

"Right? I don't have to be screwed up just because my twin is."

Xena's answer was the feline version of a grumble.

The path emptied into the grassy clearing that surrounded the enormous apple tree. It was framed by maturing corn that had already grown as tall as Mercy. She stopped and wrapped her arms around herself as she gazed at the tree.

"It's beautiful and bittersweet." Mercy spoke more to herself than Xena. "The last time I was truly happy was here—when we were all together." Tears burned the back of her throat and Mercy swallowed quickly. *No more tears today!* "Okay, I'm going to get everything ready. Are you sure you don't want to zap yourself back to human form and help me?"

Xena hissed.

Mercy grinned cheekily at the cat. "Well, you could be naked."

The feline's slant-eyed look clearly said that she was *already* naked.

"Okay, fine. I'll do it myself." Humming a wordless tune Mercy put her basket on the ground. First, she took out the huge bouquet of happily blooming daisies—a favorite of Freya—from Abigail's garden and placed it at the base of the apple tree, just below the heart that had been seared into its bark by her mom's sacrifice. She'd tied the bouquet together with a velvet ribbon the blue of clear spring skies and Freya's eyes, taking special care to make a beautiful bow.

Mercy returned to the basket and shook out the quilt she'd folded on top of her spellwork items. She lay it on the ground a few yards in front of the tree where the roots weren't so gnarly. Then she slipped off her shoes. The sparse grass felt cool under her feet as she placed her five candles. The white candle went at the top point of the mini-pentagram just a few inches off her quilt. She placed the other four candles, brown and green to symbolize the earth, around her quilt at the points of the pentagram.

Next Mercy took out the velvet bag she'd filled with salt. She moved with confidence as she traced the shape of the pentagram to connect the five candles—with her quilt in the center. Satisfied, she pulled out the two remaining items in her basket—her small incense holder that was shaped like a miniature cauldron and her box of ritual matches. Mercy left the cauldron in the center of the blanket and strode to the white candle at the top of the pentagram.

"In the name of the Norse Goddess of Love and Beauty, my Freya, I open this pentagram!" Mercy lit the candle and then walked to the next point of the pentagram and the green candle waiting there. "I set this pentagram of power in the name of the Norse Goddess of Fertility, my Freya." She lit the green candle and moved on to the brown candle that waited its turn at another point on the pentagram. "I set this pentagram of power in the name of the Norse Goddess of War, my Freya." The brown candle blazed as she touched the flame to the wick, which made Mercy grin fiercely. She hurried to the next candle, the second green one. "I set this pentagram of power in the name of the Norse Goddess of Wealth, my Freya." The candle caught easily and Mercy completed the pentagram at the second brown candle as she said, "And now this pentagram of power is complete in the name of the Norse Goddess of Divination and Magic, my Freya!" The brown candle flamed even brighter than the others.

Mercy returned to the quilt and the cauldron in the center of her opened pentagram. Xena sat beside the cauldron watching her with knowing eyes. Mercy seated herself so that the little cauldron was in front of her and she faced the apple tree. Then she lit the small charcoal circle she'd already placed within her cauldron. It sizzled and sparked, and within a few heartbeats smoke lifted from the paste-like mixture of myrrh and dried apple blossoms Mercy had smeared on the burner when she packed the basket.

As the fragrant smoke rose around them, twining among the fruit-laden boughs of the old tree, Mercy said, "Freya, I am Mercy Anne Goode, Green Witch newly accepted into your service—though since I was a little girl I've understood that I belonged to you. I know that you are with me—that you have seen my losses and my hurts. It—it feels like my world isn't really mine anymore." Mercy paused as she searched for the right words. She'd never formally invoked Freya before, and reading the grimoires of other Goode witches gave her very little guidance about how to do it. Apparently, calling on one's goddess was so highly personal that, as Constance Goode wrote in 1911, *I shall only write that I invoked my goddess. All else must be written only on my heart*. Mercy drew a deep breath and continued. "Freya, I've lost my mom and now it feels like I'm also going to lose my sister. The gates are crumbling and I have no one to turn to for help except you. So I ask humbly, with love and respect, that you send me a sign or omen as to what I should do next. I—I'm lost, Freya." Mercy caught her breath on a sob and had to wipe an escaping tear from her cheek before she finished. "Please help me."

Mercy had intended to sit there and meditate—open to receiving any signs or omens from Freya—until the charcoal turned gray and the sweet invocation smoke dissipated. But almost immediately the smoke shifted. It poured from the little cauldron and lapped against the trunk of the apple tree. It engulfed the bouquet of daisies and wound around and around—as if Mercy was circling the tree with a thick stick of dried herbs

While she stared at the tree, almost forgetting to breathe, the bark began to shimmer like a light from within it had been suddenly switched on. And then the glistening surface rippled and Freya emerged from the tree. The goddess wore a golden helmet decorated with Valkyrie wings. Her hair, so blond it almost appeared silver, cascaded to her waist. She was dressed in a surprisingly simple robe of blue silk—the same color as her eyes, and wrapped in a cloak made of falcon feathers. She carried a sword with a pommel that glittered with jewels.

The shock of seeing her goddess in person was so overwhelming that Mercy could barely speak, but she did collect herself enough to bow so deeply her forehead brushed the quilt as she said, "Great Goddess! I greet you!"

You may rise, Mercy Anne Goode, Green Witch sworn to my service.

Mercy straightened and had to blink several times to accustom her eyes to the luminous presence of her goddess. "You came!" she blurted—and then Mercy pressed her hand against her mouth, shocked that she'd said something so obvious.

Freya's laughter made fireflies—that should only have been visible on a summer night—appear in the air around her—shining with a goddess-touched light so that they blazed like living diamonds.

Yes, daughter, I heard your heartfelt call and I came. Freya's robin's-egg-blue gaze turned to Xena, who immediately bowed her head respectfully. *Ah, Xena, it is good to see you—loyal familiar to the Goode family. You remind me of my own felines.*

Xena's purr rolled around them.

The goddess's attention shifted back to Mercy. *So, it is guidance you ask for, my young Green Witch?*

Mercy clutched her hands together in her lap to keep them from trembling. "Yes, Freya."

But I have been guiding you, Mercy Anne Goode, since the day you first heard Grandmother Oak breathe.

Mercy blinked in surprise. Being able to feel trees breathe was something she had been able to do since she was four years old. The summer day she'd touched the old oak in their backyard and felt it inhale and exhale was one of her earliest memories.

"You were there then? When I was just a little girl?"

I have always been here.

"Wow! That's so awesome!" Mercy grinned—and then quickly sobered. "But I've felt so lost recently. The trees are sick—you know, the ones that guard the gates. And Hunter, my twin sister, is changing. Or has changed, and not for the better. I don't know which and I don't know what to do about it—about any of those things. Freya, I feel like I'm drowning."

Yes, I am aware that the gates crumble and the trees sicken. And I know your sister, though she is not in my service.

"Will you help me? Will you tell me how to fix the trees? My magic works just fine unless I aim it at the trees. Then it just, I don't know, *fizzles.* And Hunter—there's something really wrong with her. I think—I think I caused it when I made her reject her god. I didn't mean to do anything wrong! I thought the fact that she chose Tyr instead of a goddess was why the trees weren't healing. Please help me, Freya."

Daughter, it is the destiny of Goode witches to guard and nurture the trees that hold the gates to the Underworlds. Not even I can alter fate for you.

"But I don't want it altered! I'm ready to fulfill my destiny. I just don't know how."

That is something I cannot tell you, as it involves choices you make freely, without the coercion of even your goddess. It is a thing the Goode sisters must discover for themselves.

"But Freya, Hunter and I aren't doing anything together!"

Exactly. It is destined that you and Hunter have your own paths to follow—and in finding those paths you shall also find the answer, which will heal the trees and save the gates.

"I don't understand. How are we supposed to fix the trees when we're not even talking?"

Find your path, daughter, and you will find the way.

Mercy resisted the urge to sigh in frustration. "Can you help me with my magic? Help make it work better on the trees—to at least make them strong enough to hold on until I figure out whatever I need to figure out?"

You have been granted ample magic to do what needs be done, daughter. I cannot gift you with more without upsetting the natural order of things. Beware! What you do in this world is far-reaching—for good and ill! Abruptly the bright spring afternoon darkened and the boughs of the tree whipped as if a storm brewed. *The Goode sisters must be careful where they seek power.*

A cold shiver of foreboding fingered its way down Mercy's spine. "I'll be careful. I promise!"

As quickly as the darkness blanketed the sky the goddess's smile chased it away. *I do not doubt your fidelity, daughter. But 'tis a warning you need to hear. I shall reward your devotion with omens. As you discover your path I shall send you signs of my approval.*

Mercy bowed her head again. "Oh, thank you, Freya! I'll watch for your omens. I—I'll try really hard to make you proud."

Daughter, I have been proud of you since the day you opened yourself to Grandmother Oak. I believe in you—and in the woman you shall become. Now, in return for your gift of my favorite flower and the sweet scent of myrrh and apple blossoms with which you so lovingly invoke me, I leave you with a gift in return. The goddess pressed her lips to her hand and then blew the kiss at Mercy.

Mercy felt a jolt of warmth, like she'd been wrapped in a blanket newly taken from the dryer. Then, before she could say anything else Freya pulled the cloak of feathers around her. Light exploded from within the cloak and a huge falcon, more magnificent than any mundane bird, appeared in the place of the goddess. It flew low over Mercy—so low that its wings made her hair lift—and then it circled and dived for the center of the scorched heart and disappeared back within the tree.

The instant the goddess was gone the charcoal in Mercy's cauldron turned gray, the fragrant smoke dissipated, and each of the five ritual candles blew out—closing the pentagram.

Mercy felt oddly light-headed. She wiped a hand across her face and looked at Xena, who was still staring at the apple tree.

"Oh. My. Goddess. That was amazing! Freya was here, Xena! My goddess actually came to me!"

Xena turned wide yellow eyes on Mercy and chattered at her—but inside Mercy's head—Xena's human voice echoed. *Oh, kitten! It was quite the honor!*

"I know, right? I didn't think she'd actually . . ." Mercy's words trailed off as she stared at the cat. "Wait, did you just say it was *quite the honor*?"

Xena blinked twice, slowly, then mewed, *Indeed I did, kitten.*

"Freya's gift! She gave me the ability to hear you! Just like Abigail did!"

Chattering with excitement Xena rubbed against Mercy. *Blessed Freya! What a lovely gift to bestow upon us.*

"It's so cool! It means Freya *will* help me! Even if the help is in the form of omens—which kinda bites because, you know, they're symbols and such and can be misinterpreted. But I guess the more I get used to them, the easier they'll be to understand."

Xena's chattering became tearful words floating through Mercy's mind. *You know what else it means, kitten? It means that I am now your familiar—connected to you until your death.*

Mercy stroked the huge Maine coon's silky fur. "Really?"

Really, my own sweet Green Witch. Xena curled up on Mercy's lap as Abigail's daughter put her arms around the cat and held her close.

As the afternoon faded into evening, the Green Witch, with her familiar close beside her, made their way home. Mercy's steps were lighter than they had been since before Abigail had died. "Xena, I vow that I *will* be worthy of Freya's love. I *will* find my path. I *will* fix the trees. I *will even* figure out what the bloody hell is wrong with Hunter." Mercy opened the back gate to their yard and the Green Witch and cat gasped together in surprise.

The entire backyard was filled with daisies in full bloom.

"Now that's an omen I do understand!" said Mercy happily.

Indeed, kitten! Xena chirped. *I find that I am famished! Shall we—meaning you—open a can of lovely albacore and pour some cream to celebrate?*

Mercy looked down at the big cat who rubbed against her legs as she purred loudly. "Are you always going to be inside my head like this?"

Of course, kitten! Is it not wonderful?

Mercy grinned cheekily down at her familiar. "Welp, it's *something,* that's for sure . . ."

Thirteen

Hunter's hangnail wouldn't stop bleeding. She'd stuck the gnawed edge of her index finger in her mouth, pressed her thumb against it, and flapped her hand under her desk, but the scarlet bubbles persisted. Each droplet slipped down her finger and splatted against the dark blue dress Kylie had insisted she borrow. Finally, she wrapped her finger in the cotton and squeezed.

Her blood was powerful. Powerful and uncontrolled. The last thing she needed was for it to drip onto the desk or the floor or anywhere else in this glorified daycare. She didn't know what would happen if she got mad. Scratch that—*when* she got mad. These days, rage was a common occurrence.

With a sigh, she squeezed the wadded-up fabric around her finger and, again, let her attention slip to the right side of the room and land on her sister who she hadn't seen since Mr. Parrott's funeral the day before. Mercy's long hair spilled over her shoulders and covered the back of the plastic desk chair. Hunter untangled her hand from her dress and combed her fingers through her own wavy black lengths. Maybe she would dye hers pink or blue or purple.

Mercy spun around in her seat. Hunter froze and her heartbeat skipped the way it had all those times she'd been caught pawing through her sister's closet. Mercy narrowed her gaze, tilted her head to the side, and flipped her hair in perfect Mag fashion. She was no doubt thinking about what a disappointment Hunter was and how she, the ultra-important and wonderfully magical Green Witch, would heal the trees *and* figure out who was copying Polyphemus's horrid murders. Hunter's teeth creaked as she clenched her jaw. It wasn't anything she hadn't already thought about herself. But *she* would be the one to fix the trees and figure out a way to bring the copycat killer to justice. Even if Mercy didn't believe her, Polyphemus was gone for good, but what if something had come through the disintegrating gate while she'd been dealing with the Cyclops? Hunter crossed her arms over her chest. She could defeat another monster. She had the perfect weapon. She had Amphitrite.

Mr. Cormican wrapped his knuckles against the whiteboard. "Hunter, you with us?"

Hunter's breath hitched as she blinked and swept her gaze around the room. Mercy wasn't the only person watching her.

She cocked her head and flipped her hair the way she'd watched her sister do only moments before. "Unfortunately."

A few stray chuckles as Mr. Cormican pursed his lips and scratched his dark, closely cropped beard. "You want to tell us how speech and silence play a role throughout the text?"

Hunter glanced down at her desk and the large tree and clear blue sky on the cover of her unopened copy of *Their Eyes Were Watching God*. Like most of their assigned readings, she had read Hurston's novel long before she knew what *themes* meant or that a book could have more than one. She'd had every intention of rereading it for class, but then her mom lit herself on fire, her sister became even more of a selfish brat, she betrayed her god, moved out, and discovered the power of blood magic. She'd left a few things out, but that just proved her point. She didn't have enough time. Not that she could tell Mr.

Cormican about her new goddess or that she'd recently cast a spell on two of her three friends.

She looked up at the clock and let out a relieved sigh. "Can I get a raincheck?" With a shrug, she pointed at the glowing red numbers. "Looks like we're out of time."

"Give me five, Miss Goode," Mr. Cormican said without looking at his watch.

"Crap." The word hissed between Hunter's teeth. Mr. Cormican had never asked her to give him five, which was the same as telling her she was going to have detention, and he'd only ever called her by her last name at the beginning of the semester when he'd had a difficult time telling her apart from her sister.

The low *ooh* of her classmates was quickly drowned out by the sharp chimes that signified the end of the school day and the beginning of freedom.

Instead of cutting through the cluster of desks that filled the center of the classroom and passing by Hunter, Mercy took the long way around. As she and their other classmates filed out of the room, Hunter sagged into her chair and rested the back of her head on the stiff plastic. She wanted to be different, but she didn't want to be different at the expense of her grades, and she definitely wasn't interested in spending mind-numbing minutes in after-school detention.

The door closed before Mr. Cormican left his position at the front of the room. He straightened the desks on his way to Hunter's and slipped into the seat in front of her.

"I'd rather do before-school detention," Hunter blurted. Every night, when the lights were off and she was left alone with nothing but her thoughts and scratchy sheets to comfort her, she couldn't keep herself from drifting back to that night at the apple tree—to the smell of burned flesh and the glow of orange flames. The scene of her mother's sacrifice and death playing over and over and over. Waking up early wouldn't be a problem.

Mr. Cormican's smooth forehead creased. "You're not in trouble,

Hunter." His gray eyes searched the concrete wall behind her and the laminated *Playbills* and Shakespearean quotes that had strands of hot glue stuck to them like spiderwebs.

"When I was a kid, I had this bunny, Wookie Wabbit. She would hop around the backyard and come when I called her. We would lie on the floor of my bedroom together and listen to CDs and stare at all of the posters I'd sticky-tacked to the wall. She was the small dog of rabbits." His grin lifted the corners of his eyes and highlighted the thin wrinkles that had begun to crease his clear skin.

"I came home one day and found her in the middle of the street in front of our house. She'd gotten out of the backyard and someone had hit her with their car." He tugged at the top button of his plaid button-down and stared out the narrow windows at the students milling about in the courtyard.

"No one could console me. I was devastated, but more than that, I was mad." He set his arm on Hunter's desk as he turned his attention back to her. "Like, pissed on a whole other level. I ran inside, smashed my stereo, tore all my posters off the walls, and ripped them to shreds. Nineties poster confetti was everywhere. And it felt good to get that rage out and to see how much I could destroy. How much power I had. But that feeling faded and was replaced by more sadness. Not only had I lost my best friend, but I had also ruined the things I cared about."

Hunter shrugged away the twinge of guilt that sputtered to life in her chest as she twisted her silver crescent ring around her middle finger. "I didn't know you were going to go all allegory on me, Mr. C. I feel like there's an inspirational montage waiting for me in the hall."

He searched her face before tapping his fingers against the desk. "I didn't think I had it in me, either. Guess it comes with the mortgage and the teaching certificate." His hand stilled and he pursed his lips, his gray eyes once again inspecting hers. "But Hunter, really, if you need someone to talk to—"

"I know. I know." Hunter swiped her binder and book from the desk as she stood. "Your door is always open."

He hiked his shoulders and resumed drumming his fingers on the desk. "I was going to say that I know a good therapist, but sure, my door is always open."

A smile broke through Hunter's gloom as she cut through a row of desks and pushed open the door. "Thanks, Mr. Cormican."

The door closed behind her and Hunter fished her phone from the dress's droopy side pocket. She had six texts. Three from Jax, two from Kylie, and one from Em. She opened Jax's first as she walked on autopilot to her locker.

Waiting for you in the plot.

Pking lot. Abbreviation fail.

The last message was a photo of Jax and Kylie with their cheeks puffed and eyes crossed.

The corner of Hunter's lips slid into a half smile. She clicked on Kylie's texts. Two more silly photos. Hunter's spell had definitely worked. If their relationship lasted, she was sure they'd be the couple sending silly holiday photo cards to everyone in their contacts. Finally, she hit the text from Em.

Talked to Mag about a Rite of Release spell for my dad. At the lake tomorrow 1p. Come! Pleaseeeeee

Without a second thought, Hunter replied.

For sure!

It didn't matter that Mercy would be there. This wasn't for Mercy. This was for Emily. And healing from her father's gruesome murder was more important than the Goode sisters' issues.

Hunter turned down the hall to her locker as three dots pulsed above the keyboard while Emily typed out her reply. She glanced up and jerked to a stop. Kirk-the-quarterback-Whitfield leaned against her locker with his ankles crossed and his hands stuffed inside the pockets of his letterman jacket. The poster boy for preppy douchery.

Hunter let out an exasperated sigh that blew strands of her wavy hair from her face. "I don't know where Mercy is."

Kirk shrugged. "I'm not here for her."

Hunter put her phone back into her pocket and cradled her book and binder against her hip. "Well, what have I done to deserve the pleasure of you blocking me from my locker?"

"I know about the body." He said the words like he'd asked her for the weather.

Hunter tightened her hold on her books and forced her breaths in and out, steady and sure. *What body?* she wanted to ask but knew the question would spur more problems than answers. How much had Mercy told him about the Cyclops?

Giggles erupted from the other end of the hall and shoes squeaked against the tile. Hunter didn't look to see who owned the now hushed voices. She kept her gaze locked with his. A silent battle that she would lose if her attention shifted. She wouldn't look away, wouldn't assuage her curiosity and give Kirk the satisfaction of thinking he'd won. Unlike her sister, she wouldn't give Kirk Whitfield anything.

Kirk's heavy gaze didn't falter as he pushed himself away from Hunter's locker. "I know about the body," he repeated, louder this time, restarting his performance now that he had a suitable audience.

The incomers' overlapping whispers fell silent, but their steady footfalls matched the quickened beat of Hunter's heart. But, from the outside, Hunter remained a fortress, her secrets locked behind her stony features.

Shoes squeaked closer this time and Hunter felt bodies surround her, Kirk's sycophants come to watch him capture his prey.

Kirk removed his hands from his pockets. "Did Abigail know about you and your sister?" He stepped toward her. "Did she know that you're both murderers?"

Hunter twisted the ring around her middle finger. She could control her anger. She *would* control it.

"Is that why you killed her?" He inched closer and the scents of sweat and leather filled Hunter's nostrils. "I should burn you at the stake . . . just like you torched your hippie whore of a mother."

Hunter tightened her hand into a fist and swung. Her fist slammed into his cheek with a low *tack.* Bolts of pain arced from her closed fingers, through her hand, and up her forearm. Gasps erupted around her as Kirk's hand flew to his face and blood oozed from the jagged trench torn across his cheek from her ring.

Hunter's breaths swirled in and out of her like swifts on the rising currents of her rage. She had to get away before she completely lost control. She spun around. Tiffany, Heather, Jarod, and Dillon closed in. They'd soon replace their slack-jawed shock with cold-eyed revenge. Hunter clutched her books to her chest, shouldered her way between Tiffany and Heather, and ran. Tears clung to her eyes. Open classroom doors and milling students were a blur as her legs carried her to the place where she'd hid and cried countless times before.

The old brass hinges creaked as Hunter pushed open the bathroom door. She dropped her books onto the ledge of the expansive mirror opposite the sinks and ran into the open middle stall. Acid washed up her throat as she puked into the toilet. Hunter sank to her knees and gripped the edge of the toilet bowl as she heaved again.

Clean yourself up, Witch.

A gentle spray of salt dusted Hunter's cheeks as she brushed the back of her trembling hand across her lips.

No mortal should bring you to your knees.

Hunter peered under the stall's partitions. Sure she was alone, she pushed herself to her feet and cleared her throat. "Where were you?"

As I have said, I am always with you.

Hunter's wobbly legs carried her to the row of sinks opposite the door and the large mirror certain girls would flock to to check their contour and reapply their gloss after lunch.

"But you usually say something." Hunter averted her gaze from her reflection in the small mirror over the sink and depressed the faucet knob. "This time, you were silent. You just—" Hunter's words caught in her throat as she stared down at the blood smeared across her knuckles. Her ring glinted scarlet in the bathroom's harsh fluorescent lights as she lifted her hand to inspect the crescent. A torn chunk of skin hung from the pointed tip of the sickle-shaped moon.

I've offered my assistance before, and you have never taken it. I know when I'm not wanted.

Behind her, the door creaked open.

Hunter's chest tightened as she stared in the mirror at Kirk's reflection. He'd lost his jacket and his smooth forehead glistened with sweat. The gash across his cheek wept a stream of blood that dotted his white T-shirt and the toes of his clean white trainers brilliant red. This was the second time she'd ruined his shoes, and the second time she'd embarrassed him in front of his friends. From the way his jaw tightened and his clenched fists trembled at his sides, Hunter knew he'd come to deliver her punishment.

"You little bitch!" he cawed, spittle flying from his lips. "Look at my face!" He pointed to the split skin and trails of blood. "Look at what you've done."

As she turned to face him, Hunter swept her hair from her shoulders and crossed her arms over her chest. "You called my dead mother a whore, and me a murderer."

He stalked closer. His shadow overlapped hers and the air between them heated with his anger.

Hunter tilted her chin to look up at him. "Sure you should get so close? I thought I was a danger."

Kirk's throat tightened with a thick swallow. "I'm sure I should stop you before you get your hands"—he peeled his lips from his teeth and bared his perfect ivories as he glowered down at her—"or *spells* on someone else."

The corners of his lips twitched with a grin as he lunged forward. His fingers pressed against her arms while he shoved her backward. Hunter's head smacked the mirror. Her vision danced and the back of her head ached as shards of glass rained onto her shoulders and cool porcelain dug into her back.

"I'll make sure people know what you are." His grip on her biceps tightened, and his fingers dug into her skin like she was a ripe peach. "You and your slut of a sister will be chased out of this town." He growled hot against her cheek.

Hunter tried to pull away from the shattered mirror and the boy who'd once been welcome in her home, but Kirk had pinned her arms and legs. He was too strong to escape.

Her swirling vision stilled, and she stared at her reflection in the mirror mounted to the opposite wall. Amphitrite was right. She looked weak, powerless. But that was far from the truth.

"Let go," Hunter hissed through clenched teeth, anger rising.

"Have you learned not to cross me?" The bitter scent of his hate hung in the air like smoke.

Rage prickled beneath Hunter's bruised skin. "Let me go." She spit each word against his ear.

He squeezed her tighter. "Have you learned your lesson?"

He expected her to be scared. More than that, Kirk *wanted* her fear. To feel it flutter against his skin like butterfly wings. No doubt he'd savor it. Wrap his hands around her terror and pull it from the inside out until it consumed her. But Kirk underestimated the powers of a woman. He underestimated the powers of a witch.

Amphitrite, I'm ready when you are. Hunter called on her goddess with a simple thought.

Oh, Witch, I thought you'd never ask.

Heat coursed through Hunter's limbs as the steady crash of waves roared against her ears. Glass slipped down the back of her shirt as she relaxed into the rage and the power mounting within her like a storm. Blue mist coated Hunter's skin. It hissed and popped against her bloody knuckles and erased all trace of scarlet from her flesh.

I accept your offering, young witch.

The back of Hunter's throat tickled. She opened her mouth and

Amphitrite's screech of laughter rang from between Hunter's lips in bursts of cerulean fireworks.

Kirk's hands snapped to his sides and he stumbled backward, the reflection of the otherworldly sparks exploding in his wide-eyed gaze.

Salt stung the tip of Hunter's tongue as she licked her lips. "Unfortunately, Kirk, I don't think *you've* learned *your* lesson." Her hair floated off her shoulders in an invisible current as she held up her right hand and spread her blue-coated fingers wide. Kirk shuffled backward as she bent her index finger. A wet *crack* echoed off the walls. Kirk let out a pained shout and clutched his hand against his chest. Hunter bent her thumb next. Another *crack,* another scream, and his thumb hung limp. One by one, she brought each of her fingers to her palm. One by one, Kirk's digits snapped. His anguished shrieks popped against her skin like dry rubber bands. As she lowered her pinky, Kirk crumpled to the floor.

Still aglow with Amphitrite's power and the surge of energy that came from finally striking backing instead of cowering, Hunter lifted the hem of her dress and stepped over him. "Looks like your football career is over." She licked the final bits of salt from her lips as the otherworldly blue drained from her skin. "Such a shame."

The bathroom door's worn hinges creaked once again.

Take his blood and end them! All *of them!* Amphitrite's roar sent a fresh surge of adrenaline through Hunter's body. *More blood, Witch!*

It was Kirk's group, his minions—they'd come to finish what he had tried to start. This time, Hunter would do what she should have done at Dominic Parrott's funeral. Her fingers twitched with the promise of more power as she reached down to press her palm against Kirk's blood-crusted cheek. She'd burn his sycophants to the ground. All she needed was *more blood*.

The refreshing sweetness of grapefruit splashed against Hunter's senses.

"Oh god! What happened?"

Hunter snatched her hand back to her side and whirled to face

Kylie. Her golden-strawberry hair fell in tangled waves around her shoulders and glowed so brightly in the harsh light that, for a moment, Hunter thought she was another goddess come to life.

The crash of ocean waves ceased, and the salt turned to vinegar on Hunter's tongue.

Kylie rushed forward, pulled Hunter to her feet, and enveloped her in soft citrus. She didn't hear the hinges creak as Kylie pushed open the door, but the rush of air brought goose bumps to her arms.

Hunter peeked over Kylie's shoulder as she squeezed Hunter against her side and ushered her down the hall toward the exit. Kirk was in the doorway hunched over his mangled hand.

"I'll burn you for this, Witch!" His shriek was a fourth person in the corridor. It tore down the hall and crashed against lockers with the force of a summer cyclone.

Kylie picked up the pace and nearly shoved Hunter out of the double doors and into the sun-soaked parking lot.

Kirk's promise burrowed into Hunter's back and wriggled, sticky and sharp, into her lungs.

What had she done?

Hunter gulped down one breath after the other, but it wasn't enough. Black speckled her vision and her feet slid across the pavement like melting butter as emotion overwhelmed her. Jax was there. His clean peppermint scent and strong arms replaced Kylie's, and Hunter's feet no longer touched the ground.

The fires of anger and revenge, stoked by Amphitrite's otherworldly magic, no longer raged within her chest. Hunter was drained, emptied. Except for the guilt that wrapped its cold hands around her throat and made it a struggle to breathe.

As Jax laid her in the back of Kylie's convertible, Hunter saw black birds circling overhead. *Great, all I need is another murder of crows.*

Fourteen

Mercy closed her locker, hefted her backpack with a sigh, and headed out the side door of the school that led to the student parking lot. She kept her gaze forward and walked quickly, like she didn't notice the side-eye looks classmates were throwing at her or the whispers. She had on her favorite pair of jeans—the ones it had taken her months to freehand embroider with flowers down the sides and around the hem. She'd paired the jeans with a simple turquoise-green crop top that matched the color of her eyes and the ivy that wound around the flowers. The outfit usually made it impossible for her to feel down.

It hadn't worked. Not even looking super cute could brighten her day.

A group of cheerleaders heading from the girls' locker room to the football field cut through the parking lot not far from where Mercy waited for Emily to meet her. Their animated chatter stopped the moment Mercy came into view. Not one of them looked directly at her, but their voices dropped so that all Mercy could hear was *witch*.

Mercy straightened her spine and focused her gaze on the group.

She didn't say anything. All she did was stare at them as she thought how ridiculous it was that just last week these same girls had pretended to be her friends—until she and Kirk broke up.

As if they were marionettes being controlled by one brain, the group turned to gawk at her.

Mercy smiled wickedly, lifted her hands, and said, "Boo!" as she flicked her fingers at them. At that same moment a cluster of big, black birds lifted from a nearby tree, croaking angrily like she'd banged a gong and disturbed them.

The marionettes became scared little hens. Hastily they turned their backs to Mercy. Throwing the retreating ravens worried looks, they scuttled the rest of the way across the parking lot.

Mercy's satisfaction at their obvious fear didn't last long. *An' ye harm none, do what ye will* played through her mind in her mother's voice. She sighed again and her shoulders slumped. It really didn't matter that she hadn't actually hexed the cheerleaders. Scaring them into thinking she did—or even would—wasn't cool.

It was just that everything felt so *wrong.* Mercy had never considered herself one of the popular girls, but until recently her classmates had seemed to honestly like her. Even before she dated Kirk, Mercy had felt included; she was laughed *with* not *at.* Being with Kirk had just solidified the fact that she was accepted. But her messy and super public breakup with Mr. Football Star had ended all of that. Mercy had been fun! She loved to dance and hang out and party a little. Now she just wanted to stay in bed with her covers over her head.

Mercy fished her phone from her purse and quickly texted Emily. *Where are u? I'm on the sidewalk by the west parking lot.*

A car's engine gunned and Mercy just caught a glimpse of Hunter in the convertible that sped past. She felt a jolt of surprise. That was Kylie York's car. She was a cheerleader who usually hung with the popular crowd. Jax was with them as they drove past her and didn't even bother to look her way like none of them had one bloody buggering care in the world—like she didn't even exist.

Mercy felt like her wounded heart might break into irreparable pieces. She couldn't decide if she should scream after them for Hunter to *be my sister again!* Or if she should just sit down right there in the middle of the sidewalk and sob. She didn't do either. Instead she took a couple steps back so that she was hidden behind a big, ugly concrete column, though they'd already left the parking lot.

How can she not miss me—miss us? I don't understand it. I don't understand her.

"Mercy! Oh good. I'm glad I ran into you."

Mercy jumped in surprise and turned to see her biology teacher, Mr. Carmody, coming around the sidewalk from the front of the school.

"Oh, uh, hi, Mr. Carmody."

"I finished grading the botany test and I am very proud to tell you that you made a perfect score." Mr. Carmody's kind face crinkled into familiar laugh lines as he beamed a proud smile at her.

"That's great." *Of course I made a one hundred. It was a plant test.*

Mr. Carmody clasped his hands in front of him as his expression became serious. "Hey, I want you to know I'm here for you if you'd like to talk. You've had a tough time recently and I've noticed you and your sister, well, you aren't spending much time together—at least not at school."

Mercy shuffled her feet. "Not anywhere, really."

His kind brown eyes looked sad. "Well, if you need to talk, know that I'm here for you, and if you'd rather speak with a counselor I can facilitate that, too. Remember, people grieve in all sorts of ways. And time does ease pain. I promise."

"OMG, Mag! Sorry I took so long to—" Emily barreled around the corner of the school and almost ran into the biology teacher. "Oops, didn't see you there, Mr. Carmody."

"No harm done, Emily. Well, see you girls tomorrow in class. Keep my offer in mind, Mercy." Mr. Carmody awkwardly patted Mercy's shoulder before he disappeared into the school.

"Bloody buggering hell, can we get out of here, please?" Mercy began marching to Emily's car without waiting for a response.

"Hey, what was that all about?" Em scrambled to keep up with her friend.

"Can we go first? I'll tell you in the car."

Emily's brow furrowed, but she nodded, unlocked the car, and turned the ignition of the old Thunderbird as Mercy slid into the passenger's seat and slammed the door. She slumped dejectedly, clutching her backpack in her arms like it was a security blanket. Em put the car into gear, took a right out of the parking lot, and then glanced at her friend.

"What's wrong?"

"What's right would be a quicker answer."

"Okay, start with Mr. Carmody. Was he being weird?" Em asked.

Mercy shrugged. "Nah, he was trying to be nice. He was telling me that I got a one hundred on the botany test and—"

"One hundred! That's awesome!"

Mercy shrugged again. "Em, plants are super easy for me, remember? A one hundred on a geometry test would be awesome and miraculous." Mercy sighed. "Right before he told me about the test, Hunter and her new cheerleader best friend and Jax zoomed out of the parking lot like they were heading for a big party or whatever. I looked so pathetic standing there, even clueless Mr. Carmody felt sorry for me. I just—" She had to pause and blink rapidly to keep tears from leaking from her eyes. "I just want my old life back."

Emily didn't say anything for several minutes, but she did reach over and squeeze Mercy's hand. At the next stop sign Em turned in her seat to face her friend. "I know. I totally get it. Nothing feels normal for me, either. But I'm here, Mag. I've got your back."

Mercy clutched her one remaining friend's hand. "Spend the night tonight, 'kay? We'll order pizza and I'll sneak us some of Abigail's strawberry wine. We can have a *Pride and Prejudice*–athon. Hell, Em, we can even get Xena to call the school tomorrow and tell them that we both have a stomach bug. We could sleep till noon and then go to Goode Lake and bask in the sun like the goddesses we are!" As Mercy spoke, her voice became more and more animated, until she was practically bouncing in her seat.

"Mag, I'd love to. Seriously. But my mom isn't doing so great. It's not like before." She hurried on when Mercy frowned. "She quit with the double Xanax and the constant crying, but interring Dad yesterday really hit her hard. I can't leave her tonight. I'm sorry."

All the excitement that had built within Mercy at the thought of a girls' night with Em and cutting school evaporated to leave her deflated and empty. "Okay. Yeah. You gotta be there for your mom." Mercy let loose Em's hand and picked at her lip instead as she stared out the passenger's side window.

"You're not mad, are you?"

Mercy shook her head. "Nah. I get it. If Abigail was alive and needed me I'd be there for her, too."

"How about I tell Mom that I'm gonna spend the night at your place tomorrow? Hey, we can even take the train to Chicago Sunday morning and go to that place you love so much for brunch."

"Native Foods Café," Mercy said.

"Yeah, that's it. And then—shoe shopping! What do ya think?"

"Okay, sure." Mercy turned from the window to attempt a smile. "Sounds good."

"Cool! I'll let Mom know. I'm sure it'll be okay to—" Behind them someone lay on their horn, which caused both girls to jump. "Oh, shit. Sorry!" Emily waved an apology and pulled forward. "Sheesh. Talk about impatient."

"Right?" Mercy said automatically. Her eyes stared sightlessly out the window as Emily talked about the pop quiz her French teacher had pulled on them that day. Mercy made the appropriate sounds and responses, but all the while felt like she was crumbling into pieces.

It didn't take long to get to the big Victorian house at the edge of town that had been home to Goode witches for more than two hundred years. Emily stopped in the driveway and waved to Xena, who was sitting in the porch swing swathed in Abigail's bathrobe as she lapped at something in a teacup.

"Do you think that's tuna juice?" Emily asked.

"I hope not." Mercy shuddered. "Hey, thanks for the ride home. I really need to get around to taking my driver's test so that I can drive myself to school without getting in massive trouble." She put her hand on the door latch, but Em's voice stopped her.

"Mag, are you okay?"

Mercy forced her lips to tilt up as she lied. "Yeah. I'm fine."

"Really?"

"Don't worry. I'm just bummed today." She met Emily's gaze and saw such worry and sadness there that her self-pity dissolved. "Em, I'm really sorry. I'm being a super crappy friend. Your dad's funeral was yesterday. I know you're hurting. I'm here for you, too."

"I know, Mag. Hey, are you still up for doing the release ritual for my dad?"

Mercy's smile was a lot less forced. "Of course I am. Whenever you're ready."

Emily's fingers worried the leather ties on her old-school steering wheel cover.

"I asked Hunter to join us." She hurried on before Mercy could say anything. "You're my bestie, but Hunter and I have always been close, and I've been thinking that if everything was normal between you two she would definitely perform the ritual with you. So, maybe if she does, things might start to get back to normal for my twins."

Mercy felt like the air had started to solidify and was pressing down on her. Finally, she cleared her throat and answered her best friend honestly. "That sounds logical, but Em, you didn't see what happened yesterday at your dad's visitation." She met Emily's gaze. "Hunter was mean. To me. In front of kids who were already being shitty to me. She's changed. It's like we're not sisters anymore."

"Oh, Mag! It won't be forever. Hunter's just trying to figure out how to stop hurting."

"She's taking it out on me," said Mercy.

"It's a cliché, but it's true—the more we love someone, the more we can hurt them. Remember that, 'kay?"

"'Kay," Mercy said. "And I can prepare everything for the release ritual for your dad. I'd be honored to."

Em smiled with relief. "Awesome! How about tomorrow afternoon about one-ish? We can go out to Goode Lake. Remember when Dad used to take all of us out there and we'd rent paddleboats?"

Mercy grinned at the memory. "Yeah, and he'd buy us so much cotton candy from the refreshments stand that we'd get super sick? Good times!"

"*Great* times!" Emily agreed. "The lake has so many awesome memories I thought that it would be nice to do the ritual out there."

"That's a good idea, Em. I'll gather the ritual things I need and have them ready to swing by and get after school tomorrow."

"Do I need to bring anything?"

Mercy nodded. "Yes, something small that reminds you of your dad—or belonged to him. You're going to burn it, though, so be sure it's not something you want to keep."

Emily's forehead furrowed for a moment, then she grinned. "I know! I'll bring some of his pipe tobacco."

"Perfect!"

"Emily, kitten, would you like to stay for dinner?" Xena called from the porch.

Em shouted through the open passenger's door. "Not tonight. I can't. But thanks, Xena!"

"We'll be eating soon!" Xena shouted back. "I am quite famished!"

"Uh-oh," said Mercy as she got out of the car.

Emily laughed softly. "She's hangry. You better go."

"See you tomorrow at the lake." Mercy turned and spoke through the open window. "Hey, sorry I was so selfish earlier."

"No problem. Love you!"

"Love you, too!"

As Em drove away Mercy's shoulders slumped again. She hefted her backpack and trudged up the stairs to plop down next to Xena on the porch swing. Thankfully, the cat person was only lapping cream from the porcelain teacup.

"Hello, kitten."

"Hey there, Xena."

The swing carried them smoothly back and forth, back and forth. Mercy tilted her head and stared at the ceiling of the porch, which Abigail had painted with delicately shaded triple moons, and thought about nothing but the warm afternoon breeze and the scent of growing crops it carried to her.

"Your spirit feels heavy today, kitten," Xena said after she'd finished licking the last drop of cream from the teacup.

"Feels?" Mercy asked without taking her gaze from the triple moons.

"Now that I have formally been awarded the gift of being your familiar I can feel things about you—just as I could about my Abigail."

"Huh," Mercy said. "That's weird and kinda cool."

"It is the calling of a familiar to support her witch," Xena said simply. "What is it, my Mercy?"

"I want my old life back!" Mercy blurted. With her head still tipped back, tears leaked onto the swing.

Xena turned to her and gently stroked her hair. "I know. But you will adapt and find a new life."

"I—I don't think that life will include Hunter," Mercy said brokenly.

"I hope it does, kitten, but if not you have the strength of generations of Goode witches in your blood. You will survive."

"What if surviving isn't good enough? I'm just so, so sad, Xena."

Xena continued to stroke her hair. "There is one good thing about your sadness."

Mercy dug into her purse for the ball of wadded tissues always there and wiped almost viciously at her nose and eyes before she sat up and looked at Xena. "What could possibly be good about sadness?"

"Your ability to feel sadness proves that your sister did not take grief from you. Her spell worked just as she intended—it allowed you to move forward and not be paralyzed by your emotions. Remember that, my Mercy, and continue to move forward as we hope that, someday, our Hunter joins us."

Mercy felt something loosen inside of her as Xena held open her arms. With a sigh she was engulfed in Abigail's bathrobe and her familiar's embrace. "I don't know how I'd do this without you, Xena."

"Hush, kitten. You shall never be without me." At the same moment thunder boomed deafeningly and the sky opened to dump cool spring rain on Goodeville.

With her head still on Xena's shoulder, Mercy said, "I really hope that isn't one of Freya's omens."

"Well, kitten, I believe you said it best yesterday—omens bite."

Fifteen

"Bloody buggering sodding hell!" The words exploded from Mercy as she dropped the needle that had just pricked her finger, pushed the pair of jeans she'd been attempting to sew lace panels into off her lap, and hurried into the kitchen to hold her bleeding finger under cold water.

Xena, who had been eating cannabis truffles and bingeing *Love Island, UK* on the couch beside Mercy followed her into the kitchen and perched on the edge of the counter. She didn't say anything, but watched as Mercy dried her finger and wrapped *another* Band-Aid around it.

"What?" Mercy asked after she threw away the bandage wrappers.

"Well, kitten, if you keep sewing whilst you're this emotional you are going to run out of bandages." She fluttered her fingers at Mercy's three swathed digits. "Or fingers. Also, choosing to work with the antique lace Hunter gave you for your birthday is really just adding to your upset."

Mercy frowned at her wounded fingers. "You're probably right about that."

"Of course I am right. Why do you not put aside the sharp objects, make some lovely cocoa, and watch the TV with me? *Love Island* is quite fascinating."

"It's brainless reality show garbage, Xena."

"Kitten, that is exactly the point." Xena sighed. "But it does not seem to work for you, so I recommend that you take a ride."

"A ride?"

"Yes, in Abigail's car. Perhaps you might like to drive to the park and take a brisk walk to get rid of your restlessness. And then on the way home you could be a dear and stop by that lovely little sandwich shop with the odd name and get me a tuna sandwich."

"You mean Goodeville Sammiches?"

"Yes, that is the odd name. Tell them they may hold the bread. And the lettuce."

"So, basically, you just want tuna?"

Xena nodded enthusiastically, which made her thick, untamed hair bounce around her shoulders. "Yes, but I also like the things they mix into it."

"Mayo, onions, and celery?"

"Oh, no. Just the mayo. I lick around the onions and celery. Vegetables are entirely too crunchy for something I didn't have to kill to eat." The cat person shuddered delicately.

Mercy ran a hand through her hair. "Okay, but I'm still confused. You want me to drive to the park and then go to the sandwich shop?"

"Kitten, you are emotional and lonely because you miss your sister. Our Emily must be with her mother, so she cannot be here, and even though I am an excellent familiar my company alone is not what you need tonight. But I believe the Egyptian boy would brighten your mood, would he not?" Xena raised her brows and looked very pleased with herself.

"Khenti?" Mercy's cheeks heated. "He's probably busy."

"Did Khenti not tell you that he was often lonely?"

"Well, yeah."

"Then perhaps you will do him a favor by calling on him tonight." Xena shrugged. "And if he is busy then you could still walk briskly around the park. Fresh air is good to clear the mind—and work up an appetite. You hardly ate anything today."

Mercy blew out a long breath. "I suppose that's not a bad idea. I did tell Khenti that I'd let him know how my magic test went. I could stop by real quick and check in with him."

"It would be doing him a kindness," Xena said with only a hint of slyness glinting in her yellow eyes.

Mercy nodded. "Okay, yeah. I'll go for a drive to the park and then stop by Goodeville Sammiches on the way home. Good idea, Xena!" She grabbed the keys from the kitchen table and hefted her purse over her shoulder, but Xena's voice halted her before she started for the door.

"Kitten, you'll need a black taper candle and ritual matches."

"Huh?"

"Or you could cast another rain spell, but that would make for a very soggy visit, especially as it already rained this afternoon—and it wouldn't ensure your privacy. Some people will still exercise in the rain—though it is a ridiculous thing to do. Why would anyone—"

"Oh, I get it! I can cast a quick cloaking spell and not worry about people seeing Khenti and me. Xena, you're a genius!" Mercy hugged Xena quickly and then disappeared into the pantry. She took a black taper from the basket of spellwork candles and grabbed a box of ritual matches. She shoved both in her boho bag and waved at Xena as she hurried out the door.

"Do not forget my tuna!" echoed after her.

Mercy checked the dashboard clock before she pulled out of their driveway. It was almost eight o'clock, which meant sunset wasn't far off. It also meant that she had about an hour before Goodeville Sammiches closed.

"Well, that should be enough time. Khenti is probably busy and I want to be his friend, not that annoying witch who keeps bothering him," Mercy muttered as she put the car in gear and took a right to circle around town. "I have got to remember to get my bloody license!"

Mercy rolled down her window and breathed deeply of the scent of the verdant fields surrounding Goodeville. The air was rich with green, growing things, which soothed Mercy's frayed nerves like a cup of honey-drenched chamomile tea. The sky had cleared from the brief afternoon shower and the setting sun blushed pink and orange and yellow watercolors. By the time she'd wound around town to the park Mercy already felt less on edge and more like herself. Not that her sadness had decreased. Hunter's absence was a wound—a raw sore that felt a little like an emotional toothache. Mercy found she had a hard time letting it alone, but kept pressing on it and causing herself more pain.

"So stop it! Stop thinking about Hunter! I'm pretty damn sure she's not thinking about me." Mercy pulled into Goode Park's paved lot and studied the green space in front of her. One of the baseball diamonds was lit up and two teams were in the middle of a softball game. The tennis courts were also busy, though they were on the other end of the park. A group of suburban moms in yoga pants were speed-walking around the track. Basically, it was a pretty busy night at Goode Park. "But my familiar is a very smart kitty." Mercy slung her purse over her shoulder and got out of the Camry. She'd parked in the far corner of the lot near the stately white oaks, and she hurried to their concealing shadows.

At the oaks Mercy retrieved the black taper from her purse and the ritual matches. The cloaking spell wasn't particularly difficult, but it did take concentration, power from the ley lines, and shadows. *Luckily for me, I have all three things right here.* Working quickly and confidently, Mercy grounded herself by drawing and releasing three deep, cleansing breaths. Then she reached down, down, down to find the thick ley line of pulsing green power beneath her feet. It was super easy to hook into the earth power in the park. The palm trees in the middle of the park had been conjured to their position atop the convergence of two strong lines of power to create one of the points of the pentagram that enclosed Goodeville.

Mercy tapped into the power and then lifted her candle. She lit the match and touched it to the dark taper. It caught fire easily and Mercy spoke the familiar words to the ancient spell.

"Come, shadows, cloak me from prying eyes
With the night I am disguised
In darkness you cover me
Neither seen nor heard shall I be!"

After she said the final words of the spell Mercy imagined pulling the power of the ley lines up through her body and into the taper she held. Then she blew out the candle. Immediately the shadows under the trees thickened, stirred, and then surrounded her. Had Mercy been a different kind of a girl, one who hadn't been raised with magic and witchcraft, it would've been creepy to be surrounded by shadows, but Mercy was the product of generations of powerful witches. She smiled at the concealing darkness and felt herself relax. The shadows were like a weighted blanket meant to quiet anxiety, not cause it.

Mercy put the snuffed candle carefully in her purse with the matches. To close the cloaking spell she would light the candle again and release the shadows. Until then Mercy Anne Goode would be indistinguishable from the gloom of dusk. She enjoyed her invisibility as she slowly made her way to the cluster of palms.

I wonder what would happen if I never released the spell. Would anyone even notice that I was gone?

Mercy shook herself mentally. That was a ridiculous way to think. Xena would freak if she was gone, and Em would be super upset.

Would Hunter care?

Mercy pushed that thought from her mind and buried it in the wound her twin's absence had left.

At the cluster of four trees that made up the doum palm, which guarded the gate to the Egyptian Underworld, Mercy went directly to the center of the group of trees where Khenti had appeared to her twice before. She was nervous, but performing a little witchy housekeeping would settle her. Mercy faced the tree and lifted both of her hands, concentrating on the shadows around her. Using a scooping motion, Mercy's hands sifted through the concealing darkness—a lot like she was finger painting—and she spread the shadows until they also engulfed that side of the trees. Mercy smiled as she surveyed her work. It seemed she stood in the middle of a dark bubble. She could see through it easily, but Mercy knew that her spell was set. Anyone who glanced at the trees wouldn't see more than lengthening shadow, or hear anything more than the soughing of the wind, even if they walked close by.

Her palms still tingled with the magic of the cloaking shadows when she pressed them to the dry bark of the center palm. Mercy closed her eyes and readied herself as she opened to the tree. Sadness engulfed her, followed by a deep, flu-like ache in her joints.

"I know," Mercy murmured to the palm. "I'm sorry. I know you're hurting. Let me see if I can help—even a little." She reached down, down, down again to tap into the powerful ley lines that converged beneath her feet and imagined pulling the earth energy up, up, up through her body. Mercy felt the rush of power as a tide of warmth. She gritted her teeth and with all of her witchy might sent the invigorating energy from herself, through her palms, and into the tree.

The power surged. Mercy felt that easily, but as every time before, it fizzled when it should have poured into the tree. She grunted with the effort, not willing to give up, and was rewarded by a slow leak of heat that dripped into the tree. She wasn't sure how long she stood there, forcing warmth and energy into the cluster of ailing doums, but when she finally broke the ley line connection she felt the tree draw a deep breath—in and out, in and out—and knew that, even if it wasn't permanent, she'd helped the tree feel a little better.

"I'll do this again, soon," she promised the palms. *And I'll also go to the other sick trees. It's not much, but it's something. Maybe I can Band-Aid the problem long enough to buy me enough time to figure out how to fix them for good.*

Mercy stepped back and wiped the sweat from her face. She stumbled and almost tripped as dead grass crunched under her shoes. Dizzy, Mercy looked down. "Ugh," she muttered. "I didn't even notice that the grass all around the trees is dead." Mercy stared at the ground. Like sludge-filled arteries pumping from a diseased heart, blackened grass extended from the doums. "Gross. It's spreading." Mercy sighed, feeling so exhausted that only then did she realize the effort it had cost her to force energy into the trees. "Worth it," she said resolutely. "It's totally worth a little tiredness." Her hands were shaking and she was glad for her giant boho bag from which she fished out a bottle of water. Mercy gulped it down and felt a little better. *Next time I'll send some healing power into the grass. Can't have any attention drawn to the palms.* She flipped back her hair, and then held the thick length off her neck and fanned herself to dry the sweat. Her hands had stopped trembling, so she took a couple steps back, smoothed her crop top—yay for her super cute outfit from school!—then she straightened her shoulders, cleared her throat and called, "Khenti? Are you there? It's me, Mercy."

Nothing happened. No luminous swirling oval of color materialized. No warrior's roar sounded from within the trees.

When Mercy tried again she decided to use his formal title—there was magic to a person's true name, no matter what world they were from.

"Khenti Amenti, son of Upuant, Guardian of Osiris's realm, it is Mercy Anne Goode, Green Witch and Guardian of the Goodeville gates. I call to you!"

A hum resonated from the center of the palms and then with the sound of a woman's sigh, the glowing gate between worlds became visible. On the other side of the barrier Mercy could just make out a figure striding quickly toward her. As he got closer she could see that it was Khenti. His reptile head looked magnificently fierce, and he held a long, sharp-tipped spear, but as soon as he caught sight of her he shifted from otherworldly guardian to boy.

"I greet you Gatekeeper and Green Witch, Mercy!" He smiled and bowed.

"And I greet you, Khenti."

Khenti squinted as he peered past Mercy. "Has another creature escaped into your realm?"

"Oh, uh, no! Nothing like that. I was just, um, passing by and I thought I'd say hi. So, hi!" Mercy lifted a hand and waved. Then she wanted to take that same hand and smack herself. *I was just passing by? Could I sound any more awkward?* She hurriedly added, "And I remembered that I promised to let you know how my magic test went."

Khenti's response made the heat in her cheeks cool. Even through the glistening barrier between them, his smile flashed. "This is a welcome surprise. I was just thinking of you."

"You were?"

He nodded. "Yes, I hoped that you were well and not as sad as last time we spoke." He cocked his head and studied her. "How are you, Mercy?"

Mercy bit her lip and didn't say anything for a moment. *Isn't it wrong to dump my problems on him? I don't even really know him . . .*

As if he could read her mind, Khenti stepped closer to the opalescent barrier. "Mercy, please, you may share your feelings with me. We are friends, are we not?"

"Yeah, we are." Mercy moved her shoulders restlessly. "So, the truth is that I wasn't passing by, and didn't just come to tell you my magic test went well. Really well. The truth is I've been sad today and Xena—um, she's my familiar. Do you know what that is?"

Khenti nodded. "A creature that is a gift from the gods."

Mercy smiled. "That's a great description. I'll have to share it with Xena when I go home. Anyway, Xena thought that it would make me less sad to say hi to you. So, here I am. I hope I haven't interrupted anything."

Khenti put the blunt end of the spear he carried against the ground and leaned on it. "Not at all. It pleases me that your familiar thought to send you to me, and I am also pleased to know your magic is well." He paused and cocked his head as if listening to a whisper. "The gate feels less ill. Not well. But not as sick as earlier today when I was forced to burn healing incense to stop the rot that spilled from it. Is that because of a spell you cast?"

"Sorta. Before I called you I tried to channel some earth power into the trees." She let out a long sigh. "It didn't work great, but I could tell that the trees felt a little relief."

"That is something," said Khenti. "So, your magic is well and good."

She nodded. "It's *really* good when I cast any spell that doesn't involve the trees, which is super frustrating because that's when I need it to work most."

"It is a puzzlement," agreed Khenti.

"I spoke to my patron goddess, Freya, and she basically told me that I have to find my path, and when I do then I'll find the way to fix the trees."

"Was your goddess no more specific than that?" Through the swirling barrier Mercy could see his brow furrowed with concern.

"No. Freya is big on free will, which means I have to figure stuff out on my own."

"Ah, yes, the complexities of free will. Father and I were just discussing that subject last night."

"Are you for or against?" asked Mercy.

"I am my mother's son and most definitely for. My father, Upuant, is a complicated demi-god." Khenti looked away as he spoke about his father. "He tends to be cynical. I champion mortals. He is of the mind that most mortals are too limited in their understanding of the world to do well with free will."

Mercy thought about how ludicrous Hunter was acting and

muttered, "I can't say he's entirely wrong. My sister is exercising her free will to be a total bitch." She sighed and mentally shook herself. "Anyway, Freya didn't give me specifics, but she did make me realize that I have to stop obsessing about what Hunter is or *isn't* doing, and focus on myself—on my path. Oh! Freya did gift me with the ability to communicate with Xena, though, so that's pretty awesome." Mercy smiled as the memory of Xena's voice echoed through her mind.

The young warrior blinked in surprise. "Xena! Is she the human who was here just a few days ago? She was part of a ritual casting, and she hissed at me."

Mercy's smile widened to laughter. "Yeah, that's Xena. Only she's not really a human. She's only taken human form since my mom died. She's really a cat."

Khenti grinned. "Now the hissing is much more understandable! Is your familiar a demi-god? The only felines in my world that can take human form are gods or demi-gods."

"Well, until recently I would've said no, bloody hell, no Xena is not a demi-god—she's just a really, *really* old cat, but now I wonder . . . Though I'm not sure I actually want to know."

Khenti nodded. "Demi-gods can be a handful."

"More proof that she's probably one." They laughed together. "Well, Xena was right. You've already made me feel better."

"And you me."

"Were you having a crappy day, too?" Mercy stepped a little closer as she struggled to get a clear view of Khenti, though looking through the shifting barrier was frustratingly like trying to watch a pixelated TV screen.

Khenti shrugged his broad, bare shoulders. "Lately it has been difficult here. The gods and goddesses are unusually restless and demanding. And there was more to my conversation with my father than just discussing the free will of mortals." Khenti sighed. "I often wonder how he could have ever been with my mother, as she is mortal and he has such disdain for them."

"I'm sorry. 'Rental problems can be tough."

Khenti cocked his head to the side. "'Rental?"

"Oh, sorry. Short for parental units. Mothers and fathers."

"Ah, indeed, very true." He squinted and looked past Mercy again. "Your world appears odd tonight. I can usually see trees and greenery behind you, but this night all I see is darkness."

"Oh, that's just my cloaking spell. It's sunset here and this gate is in the middle of a busy park. It was either cast this conceal spell or make it rain. Again. And this seemed like the better of the two choices. Plus, I didn't want to get soaked."

Khenti's dark eyes gazed up and down the length of her. "It would be a shame to soak your unusual, but beautifully adorned clothing."

"Oh, thanks! I embroidered the jeans myself." Mercy made a little flourish and bowed.

Khenti leaned forward so that his face almost touched the barrier between them. "I wish I could see the design better."

"Well, I wish I could see what's behind you better. All I can make out is a bunch of colors."

Khenti straightened. "Then cross over! I would very much like to welcome you to my world."

A wave of excitement washed over Mercy. "Really? I can just come over?"

"Yes!" Khenti shuffled his feet and looked down. "I hope you do not mind, but I made an inquiry since last we spoke. You may cross the barrier between our worlds and visit here for no longer than from one mark of the sundial to another without any ill effects."

"Seriously?"

His gaze trapped hers. "I will never lie to you, Green Witch Mercy." Khenti lifted his hand and held it out to her. "Come. It is simple. Take my hand and let me show you the colors of my world."

Mercy didn't give herself time to think. She was done thinking and overthinking and thinking again. She pushed her hand into the barrier. Like before, it didn't feel like much of anything. But this time Khenti didn't just press his palm against hers. He grasped her hand and pulled, very gently. Mercy held her breath and stepped into the glistening maelstrom of light as she allowed Khenti to guide her through the glowing barrier.

Sixteen

"You may open your eyes now."

Mercy had to blink several times—the light and color of Khenti's world was a jarring contrast to the dusk and shadows she had just left. When her vision finally cleared she gasped in delight. "Oh, Freya! This is amazing!" She realized she still held Khenti's hand, which she quickly dropped.

"Welcome to Osiris's realm, the Land of the Dead." Khenti bowed deeply to her and as he straightened his smile beamed.

Mercy stared at him. With no barrier between them she realized that, minus his dragon head, Khenti wasn't freakishly tall. He was basically normal height—just a few inches taller than her five-foot-seven. His mostly bare body was in amazing shape, but what was most striking were his dark, compassionate eyes. But not even Khenti's gorgeous eyes could keep Mercy's gaze from shifting around them. She turned in a slow circle, breathing deeply of the spicy-sweet incense, hardly able to believe the splendor that surrounded her. "What is this? A palace?"

"Yes, I suppose you could describe this part of the Land of the Dead as a palace, though *temple* is more accurate—one that stretches on infinitely. Within this temple's walls the dead arrive and are judged and sorted, according to the lives they have lived and the writings in their Books of the Dead." Khenti's gaze followed hers. "There are parts of the temple that make this chamber look rather simple, though."

"Simple? That's hard for me to believe. I mean, this place is gorgeous!" She tore her gaze from the room to find Khenti smiling at her. "Is it okay if I walk around?"

"Of course! I will note the time and be sure you do not stay overlong."

Khenti gestured to what Mercy had on first glance taken to be another piece of art in a room filled with exquisite treasures. She walked to it and realized it was a sundial made of gold that sat on top of an intricately carved pillar of luminous blue marble. Mercy reached out hesitantly to touch it, and a little yelp of shock escaped her lips as she saw that her hand and her arm had turned a pale gray color. "Bloody hell! Are you sure it's okay for me to be here? I mean, I'm definitely not usually gray."

"You need not worry. It's normal for the color of your skin to change. It will not cause your body harm unless you stay beyond the allotted time."

"Promise?" Mercy met his gaze.

"I give you my sacred oath, Green Witch Mercy Goode. You may trust me."

"Okay, I will." Mercy breathed a sigh of relief and purposefully turned her gaze up—well away from her weird-colored skin. Above the sundial, through a round opening in the distant domed ceiling, light streamed down. Mercy squinted and blinked and tried to catch a glimpse of the sky above them. "Is it daytime here?"

"It is always both day and night in the Land of the Dead."

"Sounds confusing," Mercy said as she wandered to the closest wall, which was covered with a spectacular mural of bejeweled goddesses and mighty gods accepting offerings from a long line of incredibly beautiful people.

"Only when I am trying to sleep," said Khenti.

Mercy's gaze went to him and she realized his grin said that he was joking with her. "Well, next time I visit I'll bring you what we call a sleep mask. That should fix you right up."

"A sleep mask changes day to night?" He joined her by the wall mural.

"Yep. It's mortal magic. You'll love it." On the gleaming limestone floor below the mural sat jar after jar—one more exquisite than the last—all painted with bright colors and trimmed in gold. "What are these?"

Khenti followed her as she moved from jar to jar. "These are canopic jars."

Mercy's brow furrowed as she tried to place the word. "Canopic? Does that have something to do with funerals?"

"Yes. They are part of the mummification process. Within the jars rest the viscera of the dead. They are entombed with the body. The preservation of the organs helps to ensure a flourishing afterlife."

Mercy was astounded by the artwork. The jars were huge—many reached from the floor to the middle of her chest. Lifelike carvings of the heads of animals capped each of them. Some jars had scenes depicting more gods and goddesses wrapped around them. Some depicted painted animals—beautiful and fierce—and a whole section of them were decorated with the same golden symbol over and over. "I know that one! It's an ankh." Mercy's finger delicately traced the symbol that looked a little like a cross, but was looped on top.

"That's correct. It is our symbol for life, especially sacred to the goddess Hathor. These jars are the divine originals, which are copied by mortals. In much smaller, more subdued versions, of course." Khenti reverently touched the nearest jar. "All of the jars in this chamber were created by the goddess Qebhet, who brings water to soothe

the souls of the dead as they await judgment. No mortal artist could ever be her equal."

"Right?! I've never seen anything so lovely." Mercy's gaze moved from the jars to the life-sized statue of a goddess carved from stunning lapis lazuli. On her head was a crown that looked like an exquisite column—one that could hold up the world. A black bird shaped like a hawk, but made of a glossy ebony stone, perched on her shoulder. "Who is she?"

"That is Nephthys. She is one of the goddesses who protect the souls of the dead."

Mercy studied the goddess. "Why does she have a column on her head?"

Khenti smiled. "That is the hieroglyph for house."

Her brow furrowed as she looked from the statue to Khenti.

He laughed softly. "Don't think of it as a literal house. It's symbolic of Nephthys' protective nature—just as a house protects its occupants."

"Oh, I get it. That bird—it looks like a hawk, but hawks in our world aren't black."

"Egyptian hawks are not black, either," Khenti explained. "Unless they're one of Nephthys' hawks. Then they're black to show that they belong to a goddess who watches over souls on their way to the Land of the Dead."

"She does look fierce. I believe she's a good protector," said Mercy.

"She is," Khenti assured her. "Though Nephthys is also filled with compassion—especially for the newly dead."

A sudden thought struck Mercy. Excited, she turned to Khenti. "Nephthys' hawk reminds me—lately I've noticed black birds, ravens mostly, which is weird because ravens aren't really a thing in Illinois. It's like they're following me. I thought they were positive omens, sent by Odin All-Father. He is the father god of my goddess, Freya's, pantheon, and closely tied to ravens. But then one died at my feet, which really doesn't scream *good omen*. What if the black birds are being sent as omens of death?"

Khenti drew a long breath and let it out slowly as he considered. "Black birds, especially carrion eaters, do tend to symbolize death, but perhaps your black birds are simply omens sent by your goddess to lead you here, to the Land of the Dead. Maybe here you will find something to help you solve the mystery of why the gates have sickened."

"That's a good point." Mercy glanced around and then lowered her voice. "Don't tell anyone, but I think omens are super confusing and annoying."

Khenti lowered his voice conspiratorially. "Probably because the gods and goddesses can be confusing and even annoying."

Mercy snorted a laugh. "You get to talk to goddesses a lot?"

Khenti shrugged. "And gods as well."

"You have a really cool job," she said.

He grinned. "Job? Is that what you call being a Green Witch?"

"Nah, that's more of a calling—or maybe destiny."

"Exactly." He caught her gaze and held it. "Destiny. I am glad we are both believers in destiny."

"I don't think it's possible to be much of a witch without that belief."

"Nor much of a demi-god Guardian of the Underworld," said Khenti.

They exchanged a smile that had Mercy's stomach flip-flopping. To cover the sudden blush that heated her cheeks she continued to walk around the magnificent room. She stopped before another statue—a woman with the head of a cow. The bovine head should've made the figure look bizarre and awkward, but the opposite was true. The cow's eyes were arresting with their intelligence and the goddess, because she had to be divine, had an elegant grace that was extremely attractive.

"That is Hathor. She is Goddess of Joy, Love, and Women. She guides the souls of the dead here, to this temple."

"What is that?" She pointed to a thick golden necklace the goddess wore.

"That is the sun held within Hathor's horns. All of Egypt recognizes her sacred symbol."

"She's so beautiful!" Mercy reached a hand out to touch the jewel-laden statue, but drew it back, afraid to cause offense.

"She is," said Khenti. "You may touch her image if you wish. Women often touch statues of Hathor when they leave her offerings."

"But she isn't my goddess." Mercy stared up into the wise eyes of the statue.

"That matters not at all. You are a woman. Hathor's benevolence extends to you."

Slowly, Mercy lifted her gray-tinged hand to touch the incredible jeweled collar that decorated the statue and gasped. "She's warm!"

Mercy didn't have to look at Khenti to know he was smiling. "That is a sign of her pleasure. She greets you."

"Wow, I'm honored." Mercy paused and then shifted her purse and opened it. "Wait, I have something for her. Here it is!" Her fist closed on the little crystal tube that was firmly corked and rested in the side pocket of her almost bottomless bag. She pulled it out and held it up so that the flickering light from the flaming wall sconces made the liquid within glitter.

"What is it?" Khenti asked.

As she bent to place the vial at Hathor's sandaled feet, Mercy said, "It's the perfume I make for myself. I mix oil and the essence of lilac blooms with a little pure vanilla—and, of course, I add some bippity boppity boo to it." She straightened and bowed to the statue. "I hope Hathor likes lilacs."

Around the statue the air shimmered and suddenly a shaft of brilliant yellow light illuminated Mercy.

Lovely . . . the whispered word made the beam of light glow even brighter before it disappeared.

Mercy turned quickly to Khenti, who was still smiling at her. "Did you see that? Hear that?"

"I did! Hathor accepts your offering."

"That's so cool!" Mercy grinned up at Khenti and the two of them stood there, just smiling at one another.

Khenti broke the silence first. "Might I smell the perfume you gave to Hathor?"

"Sure. I mean, if she doesn't mind I don't mind." But before Mercy could retrieve the little vial, Khenti stepped close to her, bent, pressed his face near her neck, and breathed in deeply. His breath sent ripples of electricity from her neck throughout her body.

He straightened slowly. His gaze caught hers. "It is as Hathor said—lovely."

"Thanks," Mercy whispered.

"I am very glad you called on me tonight."

She couldn't look away from the heat in his dark eyes. "Me, too."

"Is your sadness better?"

She tossed her hair back, not caring one damn bit that Em would say she was being super flirty. "Absolutely. How 'bout you?"

"Absolutely."

Mercy felt as if she could fall into his dark eyes.

"Tell your familiar that she may send you to call on me anytime," he said.

"Xena! Bloody hell! What time is it?" Mercy quickly pulled the phone from her purse. She definitely had no service, but it told her the time was eight-forty. "Oh, crap! I have to go."

Khenti's brow furrowed and he looked back at the sundial. "You still have time. You need not leave yet."

"It's not that. I promised I'd pick up dinner for Xena and me, and the sandwich place is going to close soon." Side by side, she and Khenti walked slowly toward the glowing barrier. "Sorry I have to rush off like this. I've loved being here."

"Then allow me to gift you with something to remind you of Osiris's realm." Khenti strode to the line of canopic jars that were decorated with golden ankhs. He stood before one of them, bowed his head, and as he spoke words Mercy could not understand, his fingers swept down the jar and over the ankh. When he lifted his hands and turned to face her Khenti was holding a necklace made of tiny jet beads from the center of which dangled a small golden ankh. "This is for you."

"Oh, Khenti! It's beautiful!"

"May I put it on you?" he asked.

"Yes!" Before she could turn and move her hair out of the way Khenti stepped forward and placed the necklace over her head. Gently, he lifted her hair so that the ankh settled intimately between her breasts. Mercy touched the golden symbol. "It's warm."

Khenti nodded. "It will always be warm. It carries a very small piece of the Land of the Dead within it. Now, let us return you to your world." He took her ash-colored arm and guided Mercy back to the glowing gate.

Mercy paused there and made a gesture that took in the treasure-filled chamber. "I'll never forget this."

"Then return. Soon." Khenti took her hand in his.

"I'd like that."

Khenti held her gaze as he lifted her hand to his lips and kissed it. "As would I."

At the touch of his lips against her skin electric sensations zapped through her body again, and Mercy had to force herself not to fidget. Khenti squeezed her hand and then released it. Mercy felt the absence of his touch like a cold shower.

"How, um . . ." She had to pause to get her thoughts in order. "How do I get back?"

"As easily as you arrived. Simply step through the barrier."

She looked down at herself. Her arms were completely gray—as was her skin beneath the warm golden ankh, but the little sliver of belly showing between her crop top and jeans looked almost normal. "Do I need to do anything to make my skin go back to its regular color?"

"Just cross over to your world. It will immediately flush back to cream."

Their eyes met. Mercy had to swallow several times before she found her voice. "Okay, well, bye. I'll see you again soon. And thank you for my gift." She touched the ankh lightly.

"You are most welcome. Farewell, Green Witch Mercy."

"See ya later, Khenti, Guardian of Osiris's realm." She dropped into what she hoped was a cute curtsy, and then drew a big breath, held it, and stepped through the barrier.

Seventeen

Crickets chirped and a soft breeze blew through Hunter's bedroom window. She pushed her sheets aside and opened her eyes to darkness. She sat up at the airy *whoosh* of the front door and the sudden blaze of the living room light. She draped her legs over the side of her bed and squinted through her open bedroom door and into the glow.

Kylie's pigtail braids swayed back and forth as she walked toward Hunter's room. "You're awake!" she chimed and turned on Hunter's bedroom light.

Jax jogged into the room, his flip-flops making quick *slap slap*s against his feet.

Hunter wrapped the comforter around herself and blinked. "How long was I out?"

Jax shuffled past Kylie and plopped onto the bed beside Hunter. "A few hours. Makes sense with the trauma you went through."

Hunter shivered and tightened the comforter around her. "Trauma?" This was it. Her reckoning. The one Kirk wasn't able to provide. Her friends now knew her true power and their fear would lash out and strike her down before she even had the chance to explain.

"Kyles told me everything." He leaned forward and grabbed the cheerleader's hand and pulled her onto his lap. "She also had to keep me from busting into the hospital and obliterating Kirk. Fuckin' bag of shit."

Kylie draped her arms around his broad shoulders and brought her face inches from his. "Violence is not the answer."

The words needled between Hunter's ears and sent acid washing up her throat. Violence had never been the answer before—all the Goode witches lived and swore by "An it harm none do as ye will"—but today it was. And today, it had felt *right*.

Jax shrugged. "He would've been in the ER anyway. They could've stopped the bleeding, no problem."

Kylie rested her hand on Hunter's shoulder. "I'm so relieved you got out of the way and Kirk hit that mirror. If he would've hit you, instead . . ." Brow furrowed, she squeezed Hunter's shoulder.

Jax clenched his hands into fists. "Let's just say, he got what was coming to him. Coach knows now, too. Even if Kirk heals up quick, he won't play for Goodeville."

"But enough of the negative." Kylie clapped and leapt to her feet with ease. "The new Lupita Nyong'o movie is out. We should go!"

Hunter remained silent, scared that if she spoke, this illusion would vanish and be replaced with the truth—that *she* had injured Kirk, broken every finger in his hand with magic she'd borrowed from her goddess. That she'd broken her oath to do no harm. And, although guilt pecked at her heart, she couldn't say she wouldn't do it again.

Jax cupped his hand around his ear. "I hear Sour Patch Kids and Sour Skittles calling your name." He dropped his hand and nudged Hunter with his elbow. "They'll destroy your mouth, but it's worth it."

She couldn't pretend things were normal. The comforter slid off Hunter's shoulder and she shimmied back inside the warmth of her protective cocoon. "I think I'll stay here."

Her intention was never to lie about what happened with Kirk. To be honest, she hadn't thought about what she would say, but Hunter was now in too deep. For hours, Kylie had been running with this story, this version of the truth. Who was Hunter to say that that couldn't have happened? Kirk was violent. *If Amphitrite hadn't been there to help . . .*

Another shudder and Hunter stretched the blanket taut around her. "Alone time sounds good."

Jax wrapped his arm around her shoulder and squeezed her against him. "Text me if you need me," he whispered and rubbed his knuckles against her head.

Hunter pushed him away and sat silently as he and Kylie walked, hand in hand, from the room.

"I'll bring you back some candy, H!" Kylie called from the entryway before the gentle *whoosh* of the door signaled their departure.

Hunter pulled the blanket over her head and groaned. "My life would be so much easier if you hadn't let me do that."

Invisible waves lapped against Hunter's bare feet. *He attacked you, and by extension, me. You did the right thing, Witch. Rest assured, I would never steer you wrong.*

"You don't think it got, like, a tiny bit out of control?" Hunter shrugged out of the comforter and padded to her dresser.

The mortal got exactly what he deserved.

Hunter opened the top drawer and pawed through her underwear. The white-and-red ombre spellbook wriggled with excitement and purred against her fingers as she lifted it from the dresser drawer.

He should know not to mess with a pure-blooded witch.

Hunter chewed her bottom lip. That was the second time she'd been told that Kirk had *gotten what he'd deserved.* Even though Jax didn't know the real story, he knew the real Kirk.

She set the spellbook on top of her dresser and patted its furry cover before she crouched down to open the bottom drawer. She pulled out a pair of black leggings and a faded black DARE T-shirt and tossed them onto her bed.

"Even if it was justified, it still wasn't completely right. *And ye harm none, do what ye will."* She repeated the phrase her mother had preached to her for as long Hunter could remember.

Take off their head before they take yours. The air turned thick and salty around Hunter as she slipped the dress straps from her shoulders. *It might not be as fancy as yours, but it's served me quite well.*

"We won't be removing any heads," Hunter said as she shimmied into her leggings. "But I do need your help with something else."

And I need more blood.

Hunter plucked her shirt off the bed and paused. "No, it's not like it was with Kirk. I don't want to do anything like that again."

But it felt good, didn't it? That kind of power is . . . A briny gust swirled through Hunter's hair. *It's intoxicating. I can show you how to command it. How to wield it without it burning through you as it did earlier.*

Hunter shoved aside the questions that bubbled within her. Amphitrite was a goddess. Goddesses had different rules. But Hunter wouldn't be pushed into doing something she didn't feel was right. Not after what happened with Tyr.

"Before you sent Polyphemus back to Tartarus, he murdered people and took their eyes."

Ate *their eyes. To free him from his curse.*

Hunter grimaced and tugged her shirt over her head. "Well, the Cyclops is gone, but the same thing is still happening. Minus the eating . . . I hope." She frowned and shook her head. "Anyway, I thought I could use a spell from the book to find out where to look for the killer, but it hasn't given me anything useful." She pulled her hair from the collar of her shirt and went back to her dresser for her spellbook. "I think I need my tarot. The cards told me who Polyphemus was. They'll tell me who this is."

The tarot will speak to you in symbols and riddles. I *can tell you the truth. I only need payment.*

Hunter took survey of the small room with the nearly empty dresser, twin-sized bed, and nightstand that held her journal and pink Lamy pen. "I don't really have much. Maybe if I went home—"

Blood, Amphitrite insisted. *I only need blood.*

Hunter stared down at the scabs that puckered against her palms and arm, constant reminders of internal wounds that may never heal.

Not yours, Witch. I already have plenty. The invisible waves returned, brushing over Hunter's feet and sending a chill up her spine. *I need new blood.* Fresh *blood.*

"That's not an option." Hunter shoved her feet into her boots and grabbed her spellbook off the dresser. "I don't have a problem deciphering my tarot. I've been doing it for years." Hunter switched off her bedroom light and clomped through the small living room. "I'll just sneak into my house, somehow avoid Mercy and Xena, and—"

Stop!

Waves thundered against Hunter's ears, and her feet stuck to the floor. Was it fear that kept her from moving or Amphitrite's magic?

The waves subsided and the goddess's voice mellowed into the gentle pulse of water licking the shore. *I will guide you to a place that has what I ask. Then, I can receive my payment and you can receive your answers.*

"I d-don't want to hurt anyone." Hunter ground her teeth, hating the way her voice trembled. Hurt anyone *else.* But she needed to find out who was taking people's eyes, and get enough power to heal the gates, as soon as possible.

Hunter took a deep breath and her shoulders relaxed. With Amphitrite's help, she'd bring the killer to justice and tip the karmic scales back in her favor. Then, she'd turn her attention to the trees. She didn't have the payment Amphitrite desired, but the goddess *was* helping her with this. Hunter could figure out a different form of payment, some otherworldly IOU. She glanced at the clock glowing green from the microwave. She had more than enough time to accomplish both tasks tonight. And after she fixed everything . . . Tomorrow, Mercy would come, tail tucked between her legs, and lay her white flag at Hunter's feet.

Hunter clutched her spellbook against her chest and smiled. "The crownless again shall be king."

Eighteen

Two miles didn't sound like a long way. In a car, it wouldn't have been, but Hunter only had two legs to carry her. Two stumpy short legs that would definitely benefit from a lunge or two.

Faster! Amphitrite's voice slipped between Hunter's ears and prodded her for the hundredth time.

Hunter picked up her pace as she passed the Coffee Spot's darkened widows. This section of Main Street closed down hours before the rest. It seemed no patrons were interested in visiting the coffeehouse, crêperie, bagel shop, or butcher shop late into the night, which was fine with Hunter. She preferred to be alone. She caught her reflection out of the corner of her eye and her breath hitched as she slowed. With her hair down, she looked so much like her sister.

Just there!

Amphitrite's excitement was an icy hand against Hunter's back. She shook all thoughts of her sister from her head, adjusted her grip on the spellbook, and dashed across the street to the shimmer of otherworldly blue that glistened in the alleyway between Suzette's Creperie and Main Street Meats, the butcher shop that had been a part of Goodeville for as long as Hunter could remember.

"This is going to be so gross." Hunter groaned and trudged toward the giant green dumpster that was sandwiched between a sewer drain and the butcher shop's back door. "Do you want me to open the lid so you can dive in and—" Hunter whirled around as a strangled yowl sounded from deep within the dead-end alley.

"A cat," she told her frayed nerves. "It was just a cat."

Help the creature, Amphitrite urged.

Hunter shuffled deeper into the black, her hands sweaty as she clutched the spellbook to her chest. "Here, kitty kitty." She squinted, but the alley was a cave, a maw that consumed light and left nothing but darkness.

The sharp *call* of a raven echoed overhead as Hunter inched into the dark. "Here, kitty—" She swallowed her words as another wail sounded. She stopped and looked over her shoulder at Main Street and its bright white lights that flooded the sidewalk and vanquished all shadows.

You do not wish to help the innocent? Amphitrite asked.

Hunter clenched her jaw. She'd be devastated if Xena was in need and the only person who could save her didn't because they were afraid of the dark. Gritty cries of the ravens rang out again as she charged forward. She wouldn't let something so silly keep her from doing the right thing.

Heavy breathing stole her burst of confidence, and she slowed as liquid squished beneath her boots.

"Hello?" Hunter called into the dark.

The light over Suzette's back entrance crackled and flickered to life.

The adrenaline that told Hunter to run also nailed her feet to the ground. She couldn't blink, couldn't move, as the yellow light filled in the scene before her. Two men were on the ground, one flat on his back, the other hunched over his torso.

Another gurgling yowl, and a twitch of the prone man's legs. The noises . . . they had never been from a cat. Creatures in agony all sounded alike.

"Stop." Hunter wasn't sure if she'd said the word aloud. Wasn't sure if it had gotten past the stickiness that tacked her tongue to the back of her teeth.

The squatting man tucked his long hair behind his ear and craned his neck to face her. Blood splattered his cheeks and stained the creases of his mouth. "It's you." He breathed. A knife blade glinted in the flickering light as he wiped his face with the sleeve of his dirty flannel shirt.

Hunter tightened her grip on her spellbook and forced herself to take a step back. It was Creepy Chuck. Yes, he was never groomed, always yelling about the Rapture, and a little strange, but this?

Black feathers glinted silver in the light as ravens stared down from the power line.

"Stop," she repeated, sure this time the word had left her lips.

Slowly, Chuck stood. "It's you!" He cheered and took a step away from the man on the ground. The man had stopped twitching. Stopped wailing. The stillness of his legs and the glistening pool of deep red that spread around him like ivy made Hunter's knees quake.

"A-Amphitrite." She whispered through clacking teeth.

Chuck's wrinkled forehead smoothed, and his eyes glistened with tears. "I have seen Her in my dreams glowing like the sea, and now She is here. In the flesh. Praise all that is holy!"

Chuck took another step away from the body, and Hunter choked on a scream that clung in her throat on barbed wire.

The bottom of the man's button-down shirt was ripped, and a knife wound parted the skin, leaving it like an oozing mouth, puckered and open. Bloody handprints painted his shirt and crimson streaked his neck and cheeks and shined slick and wet in the hollow pits where his eyes had once been.

The blade of the hunting knife gleamed red and silver as Chuck inched closer. "Many days She has spoken to me." His smile curled at the ends and the dried blood around his mouth cracked and flaked as he shuffled toward her. "Has She spoken to you? Has She told you that *they* cannot see?" He shook the knife at the man behind him. The man that he'd murdered. Tears carved tracks through his blood-crusted cheeks as he stared at the empty space behind Hunter. "I have followed your instructions."

Hunted jolted backward. She slammed into the building and winced as her bruised arms and the knot on the back of her head struck the brick.

"Amphitrite!" she shouted.

Bricks tugged on Hunter's shirt and scraped her arms as she scurried along the wall away from Chuck. "Amphitrite! Help me, please!" Air rushed from her lungs and the spellbook flew from her hands as she slammed into metal. With sweaty palms, she groped the garbage bin, using it to steady herself as she bolted into the center of the alley.

Chuck continued toward her. "It is your time." He wrapped his hand around the blade and held the knife out to Hunter. "She has chosen you. It's your time to make them see."

Salty spray dusted Hunter's back and wrapped around her like fog. Blue light pooled around Hunter's feet and the sound of crashing waves brought goose bumps to her skin.

"God is here! God is everywhere!" Chuck bolted forward. He prodded the air with the hilt of the knife and reached out to the darkness that pressed against Hunter's back like granite. "They were blind, and now they see. It is your turn!"

Hunter stumbled backward into Amphitrite. The goddess's cold hands gripped Hunter's shoulders and her skirts tangled around the witch's legs.

Wings flapped and a single black feather floated to the ground as the dark birds cackled and croaked overhead.

"I have done what She asked," Chuck shouted, his eyes wide and wild. "I am Her servant! Praise be to Her!"

He was inches away. Hunter pressed herself against the great queen of the sea and squeezed her eyes shut as she waited for the explosion of power that was sure to come.

The bitter heat of Chuck's copper-tinged breath spread against Hunter's cheek as he spoke. "Take it." He jabbed her clenched fist with the blunt end of the knife. "It's your turn. Your duty now. Make them see."

Tears fell from Hunter's closed eyes. "Amphitrite," she sobbed.

The goddess's cold hands slid between Hunter's shoulder blades. Hunter's head snapped back as Amphitrite shoved her forward. She slammed into Chuck. There was a sound like boots squelching into mud, and he collapsed onto Hunter, draping his arms over her shoulders. Warm liquid gushed over her hands and squished sticky hot between her fingers.

"The poison. It's spreading. Make them see," he whispered against her ear. "Praise be to Her." His body fell away from hers like an old coat as the knife clattered to the pavement between them.

The ravens screeched, their wings like thunder as they soared from the alley.

Hunter held out her trembling hands and backed away, whispering, *no, no, no* until it was nothing more than a steady pulse against her lips.

Again, Amphitrite was behind her. The goddess covered Hunter's arms with her own and gripped the witch's shaking fingers.

"You pushed me." Hunter's voice quaked as water poured from Amphitrite's palms and washed the blood from Hunter's hands. "You pushed me," she said, tears hot against her eyes.

"I tried to funnel my power into you." Amphitrite's words were a cleansing sea spray against Hunter's warm cheeks. *"It did not work as it had before."* Her wet hands fell from Hunter's as she glided to stand between the young witch and the men on the pavement as still as mannequins. With damp fingers, Amphitrite lifted Hunter's chin. *"But now you have what you need."* She nodded toward the dumpster. *"Get the book."*

Hunter wrapped her wet hands around her stomach. "We have to call someone. We have to do something." She couldn't keep her voice from hitching or her tears from streaming. "The sheriff's department." She sniffled. "I'll call the sheriff's department."

"I am your goddess, your protector. You do not need mortal aid. You need only me." Amphitrite rode invisible waves and knelt down next to Chuck. She held her glowing hands over his chest and her lips moved with a silent command. Droplets poured from the goddess's hands and spread like a liquid skin across Chuck's body. *"Get the book, Witch,"* she instructed once more as the last beads of water fell from her fingers.

Hunter tripped over her own feet as her quaking legs carried her to the spellbook. Amphitrite *was* her protector. The goddess had saved her when Kirk had pinned Hunter to the sink and nearly beaten her with his hate. Trusting Amphitrite had been a mistake. A huge mistake.

But Hunter couldn't fix the gates without a powerful spell, one she couldn't conjure on her own.

"Bring it to me," Amphitrite instructed as Hunter picked up the book and dusted bits of gravel from its cover.

Maybe this was a *necessary* evil. Chuck *was* bad and Amphitrite *had* ended his murderous spree.

Hunter hugged the book against her chest before handing it to her goddess. "What will you do with it?"

Amphitrite didn't answer. Instead, she stroked the spellbook's furry spine and pressed her moving lips against its soft cover. The book shuddered as she nuzzled her glowing blue nose against it. She placed it on the ground next to Chuck and motioned for Hunter to scoot back.

Hunter did as she was told as Amphitrite extended her pointer finger and poked the fluid layer that encased Chuck. It popped like a water balloon and Chuck spilled against the concrete. Hunter's stomach lurched. Amphitrite had turned him into liquid that lapped against Hunter's boots on its way toward the sewer drain.

Amphitrite's skirts brushed against Hunter as the goddess glided to her side.

"*Να αρχίσει*," she said and nodded at the spellbook.

The cover rippled and the book lifted from the ground and hovered above the pavement. Overlapping whispers brushed against Hunter's ears as the spellbook opened and the pages fluttered. Blood slithered like a snake from where Chuck had been and reached up from the concrete to touch the magical tome. A sound like water sucked through a straw, and the book drank in the crimson streams. The cover bulged and glowed the deep red of plum flesh as it fed. When nothing was left, it slammed shut and dropped to the ground.

Amphitrite combed her fingers through Hunter's hair. *"It will give you what you need. A spell for the gates and the realms."* She pressed her hand against Hunter's back, the same way she had minutes before, and urged Hunter forward. *"Collect the book and perform the spell at my gate tonight, Witch."*

Hunter picked up the book. She cradled it in her arms, warm and fat like a baby. "What about him?" She motioned toward the man Chuck had killed in the name of God.

"Leave him for the mortals. I have taken care of what's important. There is no longer a sign that you were here." Amphitrite lifted her slender hand and snapped her fingers. The light above Suzette's back exit flickered and went dark. The goddess was gone. Only the scents of salt and sand lingered as evidence she had intervened.

Nineteen

Kirk couldn't remember the last time he'd been this pissed. That witch bitch had sent him to the ER—where not one fucking person had believed him when he'd tried to tell them what had happened. *Not one.* They all believed the shit story that pussy Jax had told Coach—that he'd tried to punch Hunter after he'd followed her into the bathroom—she'd ducked—and he'd smashed his fist into the mirror.

Not. Fucking. True!

But no one would listen to him, including his dad, who had told him to *shut the hell up about that made-up witch garbage* then turned his back on his son and shot questions at the doctor. Nothing had gone right since then. The doc had been Mr. Doom and Gloom. He'd actually said Kirk's career as a quarterback was over—like a damn doctor could know that! His dad had blown a fuse. He'd stormed out of the ER before they'd immobilized and set Kirk's five fingers, each neatly broken at the joint, and stitched up the gash in his face the witch's ring had gouged.

The ER doc and the orthopedic dude who he'd consulted with

had explained that surgery might be needed, but he'd have to see a specialist in Chicago for that. They'd also said Kirk would never be able to grip a football and throw it with accuracy again in his life.

They were full of shit.

Kirk wasn't giving up football because there was no damn way he was going to end up like his has-been dad. It'd suck if he couldn't throw a ball. He liked being quarterback, but he could beef up and be a linebacker with no damn problem. He was tall. He already had to run his ass off to stay lean. It'd be no big thing to muscle up—especially if he took a page outta his buddy Derek's playbook and snagged himself some 'roids.

With one hand Kirk awkwardly shook a Percocet out of the pill bottle, tossed it in his mouth, and washed it down with beer. His dad had left him at the ER, but that was fine with Kirk. He'd driven himself there anyway. After they'd wrapped up his hand and sewed up his face he'd stopped by the Pink House, a bar/liquor store in a little shithole of a town named Ogden where they served anyone with a pulse, bought a sixer of PBR, and driven out to Goode Lake to do some thinking. Alone.

Being a leader was tough. Being team captain was even tougher. Everyone wanted to be Kirk Whitfield—star quarterback on his way to a Big Ten university, a fraternity where he'd make friends who would have his back for decades, and then a cushy white-collar job in Chicago where he'd get himself a wife as hot as she was brainless. But he'd lose his position as team leader, his free ride to college, his *entire future* if he listened to the assholes. No damn way was he going to let this injury stop him from the life he was entitled to. With his good hand he smashed the empty can against the side of his Jeep and then tossed it into the lake.

A little unsteadily he slid off the hood of the Jeep and got behind the wheel. The fucking Goode sisters—they were responsible for all of his problems. Hell, they were probably responsible for all of the *town's* problems.

"I shoulda never even looked at Mercy Goode." Kirk burped loud and long. He'd killed the six-pack of PBR trying to get himself together—trying to figure out what the hell he was going to do. He put the SUV in gear and threw gravel as he headed away from the lake and continued to talk to himself. "Good thing beer makes me think better—*and* drive better. Add Percocet and I'm golden!"

Kirk's one-handed grip on the steering wheel left greasy marks on the leather wrapping, and he automatically drove with his knee so he could rub his palm on his jeans. Just thinking about losing football and his future had him sweating. "Gotta stop it. I'm not some nervous pussy. Those Goode bitches caused this. The little sluts aren't gonna get away with it."

Kirk turned onto Main Street, surprised that the streetlights were on. He hadn't realized he'd spent so long at the lake, but it'd been worth it. His head was clear now. He was only a junior. The season was over and he had all summer to bulk up. When school started in the fall he'd be ready. He'd impress the hell outta those scouts and get his scholarship. Kirk braked at one of the two stoplights in town. His fingers drummed against the steering wheel as his mind worked. Jarod and Dillon had said that Hunter had basically told Mercy to fuck off at the Parrott funeral, so they weren't just pretending like they were pissed at each other. "Too damn bad they hadn't been fighting when the slut and I were dating. I definitely could've gotten more than just a bj from her without Hunter around. But it's perfect that they're fighting now. Bitches don't know about divide and conquer, but I do!"

Kirk had to stop himself from gunning the Jeep's engine as the light turned green. He definitely wasn't drunk—he was thinking way too clearly for that—but Goodeville cops weren't exactly known for their smarts and the last thing he needed was to have one pull him over and smell beer on his breath.

"Fucking small-town pigs," Kirk grumbled. "It'd be just like one of them to hassle me when they should be hauling in those witches and grilling them about the murders that just *happened* to start the day their mom burned up." He drove slowly down the heart of Main Street as he continued to talk to himself. "But the cops don't see the truth—just like Coach and my dad and the docs. Because they're not smart like me! They're clueless old assholes. I need to make them see. I gotta make them see." Kirk braked at the second stoplight on Main Street and glanced in his rearview mirror at the sound of squealing tires.

A girl was waving an apology at someone in a truck who had almost hit her as she sprinted across the street, clutching something in her arms. Kirk instantly recognized her. He kept watching in the mirror. Yeah, she was definitely alone.

"Divide and conquer, just like a general—or better, a Navy SEAL. Yeah, that's me, *a Navy SEAL,*" Kirk muttered to himself. "Mercy has no damn backbone anyway. Hunter is just a freak—a mean dyke witch. Now that I get what she can do I'm ready for her." He flexed his uninjured hand so hard his knuckles cracked. "Dad gets some things right, and one thing he's for sure right about is that bitches need to know their place."

The light changed to green and Kirk took a right so that he could go around the block and park down the street where she wouldn't be able to see him until it was too late.

Kirk pulled his Jeep into a parking space a block or so away from where he'd seen her cross the street. He grabbed his Mustangs ball cap from the backseat and pulled it down low and kept to the shadows as he made his way slowly along the sleepy stores. It was almost nine o'clock and fully dark. Most of the Main Street stores closed up at nine or before. Kirk glanced up and down the street. The wine bar at the other end of Main was pretty busy and, of course, Kingpin Lanes had the usual geriatric crowd of retired losers filing in and out with their ugly league shirts on and their bowling shoes over their shoulders. Other than that hardly anyone was around, which was very good for Kirk—and very bad for the witch.

He heard a weird sound somewhere behind him—maybe coming

from one of the alleys that held big blue trash bins and designated smoking areas for Main Street shop employees.

What the hell kinda noise was that?

Kirk stopped and listened hard for another few moments, but didn't hear anything else. "Probably a fucking cat," he said under his breath, which gave him another excellent idea. *I should take out that evil damn Goode cat—that'd show those two bitches.* The thought made Kirk grin and when he turned his attention back to the street in front of him he saw her! She was on the sidewalk and had paused to pull out her phone and text something.

Still hugging the shadows, Kirk moved with athletic quickness so that as she sprinted across the street he followed her and caught her at the door of her car. Too damn bad for the witch that she hadn't parked under a streetlight, so her car was in a pool of shadow. Kirk didn't hesitate. He shoved her from behind so that she tripped and fell heavily into the silver Camry. He put his good hand on one side of Mercy and pushed his forearm against her neck, trapping her. Then he shifted and pressed his body into her so he could push her harder against the car.

"Ouch! What the bloody hell?" Mercy regained her balance and pressed the hand that wasn't holding her to-go bag against the side of her car so she could push back against him.

"You're not going anywhere, bitch." He breathed the words into her ear. Her body felt good against him and he loved how she tensed when she realized it was him.

"Kirk? Get off me!" She shoved against him again.

"What'll you do if I don't? Zap me like your fucking sister did and break my other hand? Good thing I'm onto you two now so you won't get the chance, *you whore.*" He still spoke low and into her ear. Her long, dark hair tickled his nose, but he ignored it—though it was more difficult to ignore the hardness between his legs that pressed against her tight ass.

"Break your hand? I don't know what you're talking about. Get off me!" She struggled against him again.

"Keep wiggling that ass. Feels real good." He panted in her ear.

Mercy froze. "What do you want?"

The second she asked him the question he knew his answer—his *real* answer. The one that would solve all of his problems. "I want you to tell that fucking sister of yours if she doesn't fix what she did to me that I'm coming after both of you. I'm gonna tell *everyone* about the shit I watched Hunter do that night at your house. About the spell you did at the football field to make me look like a fool. About the freaky fucking trees that shouldn't exist in Illinois and what they do. And *especially* about the murders—the eyeless murders I know you two witches are behind."

Mercy remained frozen, but her words were filled with heat. "You've lost your bloody buggering mind—what's left of it. Hunter hasn't done shit to you. We literally want *nothing* to do with you."

"Riiiiight." He drew the whispered word out in her ear. "Your bitch of a sister did this to me!" He pressed his body even harder against her so that he could shift his arm from her neck and she could see his splinted hand. He felt the jolt of shock that went through her. "That's right! She broke all five of my fingers with that blue witch light shit!"

Mercy was completely still against his body. Then she drew a breath and hurled her words at him.

"Okay, so you are crazy. The first rule of being a witch is that we are to harm no one. Hunter wouldn't break your hand. Now, get the *fuck* off me you drunk moron!" Before Kirk knew what she was doing, Mercy stomped on one of his feet. She wore a pair of wooden wedges, which totally smashed through his Nikes.

Kirk staggered back. "You bitch! You could've broken my foot!"

Mercy didn't so much as glance back at him. She grabbed the door handle and wrenched it open, but Kirk hurled himself forward so that he body slammed the door shut before she could sneak away. He raised his good hand to knock some sense into the bitch when a car pulled up beside them.

"Everything okay here?" asked Deputy Carter as he rolled down his window.

"No!"

"Yes!"

Kirk and Mercy spoke at the same time. Then Mercy's shoulder rammed into him and she dodged past him to the deputy's car.

"He attacked me!" Mercy told Deputy Carter.

The deputy instantly got out of the car and Mercy moved so that she stood beside him. "He did what?"

Kirk slouched against the Camry and shrugged. "I didn't do shit. I was just playing. Not my fault if she can't take a joke."

Mercy turned to the deputy. Her face was flushed. Tears and snot tracked down her face, but her voice was strong and clear. "Kirk Whitfield is a liar. He pushed me against the car and threatened me. If you hadn't stopped he was going to hit me."

"Tell him why!" The words exploded from Kirk. "Because your sister did this to me!" He pointed to the ten stitches that held the gash in his cheek together as he lifted his splinted hand. "And worse than that—they have something to do with the murders. You want to figure out who's doing all the killing in town? Lock up the Goode witches and I'll bet it stops."

Deputy Carter shook his head. "What are you talking about, Whitfield? And what the hell happened to your face and hand? Football accident?"

"That's what I'm trying to tell you!" Kirk's finger pointed at Mercy like it was an aimed gun. "Her sister did this to me. She's a witch. They both are. I've *seen them* cast spells. The murders started the night their witch of a mom died. They had something to do with it—I know it!"

Deputy Carter's gaze went from the six-two, almost two-hundred-pound football player to Mercy—who was almost a foot shorter and half a person lighter. His brows lifted sardonically. "So, a girl—exactly Mercy's size—beat your face and broke your hand."

"Yes! Because she's a fucking witch!"

"He's such a liar and almost as disgusting as he is drunk," Mercy said. "I'll bet he's driving, too."

"You fucking whore!" Kirk started forward but Deputy Carter blocked him from getting to Mercy.

"You need to calm down. Now!" Carter said. He sniffed at Kirk. "You stink like a bar. Looks like I'll be giving you a Breathalyzer and calling your dad." He grabbed Kirk firmly by his arm. "Get in the cruiser."

Deputy Carter ducked Kirk into the rear of the sheriff's car and slammed the door firmly behind him. Kirk was too shocked to say anything. No cop had *ever* manhandled him before—no cop had *ever* called his dad. He was the captain of a victorious football team—Goodeville's hero! He'd never even gotten a speeding ticket! His thoughts were suddenly jumbled and his palm was sweating again. He wiped it on his jeans and listened incredulously through the open window as Mercy got away with every fucking thing she'd done.

"You okay, Miss Goode?"

Mercy nodded, wiped her nose with the back of her hand, and shifted the sandwich shop to-go bag to her other arm. "Yeah, now I am. Thank you so much, Deputy Carter."

"Can you drive home, or do you want to call your aunt?"

"Oh, no. I'm fine. Really. You saved the day." Mercy glanced at the cruiser, but didn't look at Kirk. "What's gonna happen to him?"

"Don't worry about that," said the deputy.

"Oh, I'm not worried at all. Nothing that jerk does could worry me. But I do want you to know that if Kirk Whitfield doesn't stay away from my family we're going to get a restraining order against him."

"Fuck you, you bitch!" Kirk shouted.

"That's enough from you, Whitfield!" barked the deputy before he turned back to Mercy. "There'll be a record of this, so you won't have trouble getting that restraining order, but I'll talk with his dad. I doubt Kirk will bother you again."

"Thanks, Deputy Carter. I appreciate you." Mercy got in the car, put on her seat belt, and then drove away.

Kirk stared at her from the backseat of the cruiser. *This isn't over, you witch. I promise you that. This is not over.*

Twenty

Hunter's swollen spellbook purred against her arms as she carried it down the gravel road toward the olive tree. She'd been walking for more than an hour. Her arms ached under the weight of the blood-filled book and her legs felt like bags of mashed potatoes, but she would've kept walking right out of Goodeville if it meant freedom.

"After tonight . . ." She nodded to herself. Soon, freedom. First, she had to go to each gate and perform the spell that Amphitrite had told her would seal the realms and fix things for good. It would work, and the last few hours would have been worth it.

Hunter focused on grounding herself, and channeled what was left of her energy up, up, up, until it bathed in the light of the moon.

A chorus of croaking screeches bellowed overhead—the same as the alley—as Hunter clicked on her phone's flashlight and swept the beam of light toward the sky.

Ravens. We don't have ravens in Illinois . . .

Magic had taught her many things, and one of them was that coincidence was rarely ever by chance. This was an omen. It had to be. But of what?

Bile burned the back of Hunter's throat and she forced it down with a tight swallow as she waded into the tall grass that surrounded the ancient olive tree. She was tired of seeing flames and blood when she closed her eyes, and now the hot slick of blood had branded her fingers with the memory of Chuck. Tonight, more than ever, she didn't want to feel anything. She wanted to ignore this omen and what had happened in the alley and be devoid of all emotion. She could live her life like that, hollow and empty. This world, her magic, they weren't made for people like Hunter, people who felt too much.

I sense your guilt . . . your pain. Amphitrite slipped into Hunter's thoughts with the ease of a shark through water. *It wasn't your fault, Witch. That mortal was unhinged, demented. No mortal can hear any god.* Laughter punctuated her words. But not the usual shriek that set Hunter's teeth on edge. This was a barren chortle that itched the inside of Hunter's ears.

She adjusted the book in her arms and followed the path she'd worn into the tall grass only days before. "Chuck killed that man. And now he's dead, too." She shuddered under the memory of his dying body sagging against hers. She wiped her hand over her ear, trying to scrape away the wet *pop* of liquid skin that had turned him into water that had rushed over Hunter's boots and down the drain without a sound.

Better him than you.

Hunter's hand tightened around her phone. "You pushed me!"

I tried to lend you my power!

"I killed him!" Hunter's hands shook and sent the beam of light swaying against the grass.

A hard lump cracked beneath Hunter's boot. She guided the light to the ground and set her book in the grass as the T-shaped pendant glinted in the beam. Her heart stilled inside her chest as she picked up Tyr's pendant that she'd ripped off her necklace when she forsook her god and called upon Amphitrite. It had been days since she'd last worn it or felt the presence of her former god. Hunter's knees buckled and hit the ground with a *thump.* Tyr . . .

I have guided and aided you more than Tyr ever did.

"Shut up." Hunter spat. She ran her finger over the opalescent stone that had once swirled purple and pink beneath her touch. Her throat tightened with a sob as it swirled for a moment before turning black.

Your emotions are high—

"Get out of my head, Amphitrite!" Hunter shrieked, her eyes blurry with tears.

Gather your wits and return to me. I'll be here. I'll always *be here.*

Leaves rained down as black birds restlessly hopped from branch to branch, their yaps and caws scraping against Hunter's frayed nerves.

"Go away!" she screamed.

The ravens let out a final *screech* as they fled the tree and disappeared into the night.

Hunter clutched the pendant to her chest. "Tyr!" she choked out between sobs. "I'm sorry. I made a mistake. A huge mistake. I never should have cast you aside. I never should have listened to Mercy." She wiped away her tears with the bottom of her shirt. "Amphitrite . . . she scares me. There's something wrong. I just—" She shook her head. "I don't know what it is." She pressed the pendant against her lips. "I need your guidance. Please, Tyr, talk to me."

The grass bent and swayed around her as she waited for the god's response. Silent moments passed and her feet feel asleep and her head ached from sobbing, but Tyr never gave her a sign. When her tears dried and her phone's battery flashed red, Hunter gathered her spellbook and began her trek back to her apartment. She would close the gates another day when she had more of herself to give away.

Twenty-one

"Witch."

The word was a cold, damp breath against Hunter's cheek. She swatted the air in front of her face and rolled over. Her arm draped over the side of the bed and her fingertips dusted the thin beige carpet. "It's okay." She ran her jagged nails along the rough fabric and grumbled to the dizzy space between awake and asleep. For the first time in a long time, she dreamt of nothing. "It's okay . . ." Drool slipped from her parted lips and soaked into her scratchy pillowcase as her breathing deepened and she surrendered to sleep.

"Witch!"

The comforter was snatched off and an air-conditioned gust blew across Hunter's bare legs. She sucked in a breath and snapped awake. Algae-green eyes and a crown of orange starfish and blush-pink seashells met Hunter's bleary-eyed gaze. She blinked away the sleepy haze that clouded her vision and squinted up at the glowing azure goddess.

"I turn my back for one night and you forsake me?"

Hunter's jaw bobbed, but her cloudy mind couldn't find the words to calm the enraged sea queen.

Amphitrite's nostrils flared and her skirts tangled around her ankles in an invisible current. *"You have nothing to say for yourself?"*

Hunter pushed herself up and folded her naked legs against her chest. "I'm sorry—"

"You're sorry?" Amphitrite's hair cascaded down her back in a Sargasso-brown waterfall as she tipped her chin toward the ceiling and laughed.

Hunter clapped her hands over her ears as the howl punched through the small room like a tornado siren. The goddess closed her mouth and the sound ceased, leaving behind a ringing shadow that tumbled through Hunter's ears.

"You are mine!" The unseen raging current tossed the goddess's skirts and pushed her from the dresser at one end of Hunter's small bedroom to the nightstand at the other and back again. *"I am always here for you. Always watching."* Water splashed as she smacked her blue palm against the top of the dresser.

Goose bumps exploded across Hunter's flesh and she hugged her legs tightly against her body. She'd gotten good at being small and invisible, but no amount of silence could keep her from Amphitrite's ire.

"But Tyr . . ." A sigh rushed from between Amphitrite's lips with a spray of salt as she wiped her hand along the dresser and brushed invisible specks of lint from her fingertips. *"He is nowhere to be found."*

Hunter held her breath as Amphitrite opened the top dresser drawer.

"It's clear he never cared for you the way I do. Yet you still call to him." With a flick of her slender blue wrist, Hunter's socks and underwear leapt from the drawer and landed in a pile at the goddess's feet. *"What have I done wrong? What am I lacking?"* She reached inside the nearly empty drawer and Hunter clutched her legs closer to keep from lunging forward. *"Shh, shh,"* Amphitrite whispered into the drawer and pulled out the swollen and bloated crimson spellbook. *"There, there my sweet."* She cooed and nuzzled the kitten-belly-soft cover against her cheek before taking a deep breath and narrowing her gaze on Hunter.

"I have given you everything, Witch." She stroked the book's scarlet spine as she spoke. *"And like any keeper, I can take it all away."* Water dripped from Amphitrite's hand, painting the book's soft fur a deep, brick red. *"Is that what you want?"*

Panic galloped through Hunter's chest. She'd seen the power of water, the power of her goddess. Hunter couldn't sit back and watch that book end up a puddle on the floor. It contained a way to cure the trees, to stop the next creature from entering Goodeville. It *had* to. Hunter dug her jagged nails into her skin and pressed her teeth against her bottom lip. If she'd only performed the spell last night. She could remember it and cast it again at the remaining three trees. But how could she focus after what she'd seen last night? After what she'd done.

Hunter shook her head as bile exhaled a bitter breath against her tongue. "I'm sorry," she blurted again. "I was upset. That man, he—" Acid pricked the back of her throat and she clamped her mouth shut.

"That man was a gift." Amphitrite floated to Hunter and set the book on her nightstand. *"All mortals are gifts. Like fruit."* She twirled her fingers through the air. *"To be plucked and consumed for our enjoyment and nourishment."*

Hunter's spine stiffened and she relaxed her hold on her legs. "My friends are mortals. *Jax* is mortal." Once again, she shook her head, her tangled hair brushing against her shoulders. "I don't want to hurt him. I don't want to hurt anyone."

Amphitrite sat on the edge of Hunter's bed and ran her hands over her skirts. *"With time, Witch, you will learn."*

"No. I won't." Hunter rested her legs against her sheets and forced her chest to rise and fall with slow and steady breaths. "People aren't *fruit*. What happened last night won't happen again."

Amphitrite leaned toward Hunter. *"What happened last night was a mistake."*

"Was it?!" Hunter's body shook, not with fear but with anger. She should have fought harder, and never forsaken her god. "You brought me there. You pushed me! We could have helped Chuck. We could have stopped him without more death."

Amphitrite slithered closer. *"You expect the trees to cower to the ants? You expect your precious Mother Moon to bow to the tide?"* Water leaked from her skin and dappled the sheets. *"Mortals are vessels of want and need and seduction and lies. Help them?"* Her lips twisted into a grimace as she eyed Hunter. *"Your kind has mingled with theirs for too long."*

A chuckle rolled across Hunter's tongue. "You're still mad, aren't you?"

Amphitrite's face stilled, her features wet and unreadable.

Hunter combed her hand through her hair and tilted her chin. "I mean, your anger was on full display when you snatched Polyphemus from this realm and locked him back in Tartarus, but *I* wanted to put that behind me. *I* wanted to fix the gates and heal the trees and move on with my life, but *you* . . ." Hunter brushed away droplets of water that hadn't yet soaked into the sheets. "You don't want the same thing. You *like* your pain." Water rained from Amphitrite's glowing skin and dripped off the side of the bed. "You want to keep punishing mortals because you can't punish your husband." The invisible rapids returned around Amphitrite's legs and tossed cool spray into the air around them. "He's a cheater. He's a liar. He's a horrible snake bastard, but you have to let it go. You have to—"

A frigid spike pierced Hunter's chest. The familiar cold burn sucked the air from her lungs and wrapped her heart in ice. Her eyes flew to her chest and Amphitrite's slender arm plunged through her sternum like a stake.

"Do not speak of my husband. You are the sand beneath his feet. Small. Worthless." Water sprayed Hunter's face as Amphitrite hissed the words through clenched teeth. *"No one speaks ill of Poseidon, the god of the sea!"*

Flashes of white burst across Hunter's vision as she grabbed her goddess's forearm. Hunter yanked and briny water sprayed between her fingers, but Amphitrite's grip on Hunter's heart did not loosen.

Swirls of glowing blue and spots of endless black painted Hunter's sight as she collapsed against the bed.

"You will learn, Hunter Goode." Amphitrite was a salty storm thundering overhead. *"You will learn your place and you will thank me when I'm through."*

Hunter choked and sputtered on the salt water that flooded her mouth, but the pressure in her chest kept her from coughing. This was another lesson taught with hate and fear and pain. Amphitrite, great goddess of the sea, was no different than the mortal Kirk Whitfield.

Hunter's hands and feet tingled, and her breaths twitched in and out of her lungs, sharp and short. The pain in her chest was like the burning sun. She could no longer fight it. She'd been at war since her mother died. This small apartment had been her only safe space, and Amphitrite had destroyed it.

Hunter stopped the battle. Her arms splayed at her sides, her right hand smacking her bedside table. Her ring clinked against the wood and her fingertips dusted the warm and fat cover of her spellbook. Adrenaline spiked beneath her skin as she walked her hand up the cover and dug her fingers into the bloated heat.

Amphitrite's wet hair brushed Hunter's cheeks as the goddess brought herself closer to Hunter. *"Yes, Witch. Stop your fight."* The torrential sea rain had given way to a light sprinkle as Amphitrite's voice softened to a purr. *"Give in and your pain will end, and we can start anew."*

Hunter plunged her hand deeper into the cover. Blood gushed around her fingertips, still warm from the magic of the book. It bubbled against her skin and a hot ache of power rolled through her body as she noiselessly whispered to the blur of rain and cerulean above her.

"Tell me again, Witch." Amphitrite leaned closer, her pink eyelashes dancing in an unseen current. *"Did you say* surrender*?"*

Hunter pulled the rage from the pit of her stomach where it slept like a dragon. "Inferno!" Flames erupted from her skin in a wild blaze.

Amphitrite's scream was the screech of tires as she tore her hand from Hunter's chest and flew backward. The splash of an anchor into the sea, and Amphitrite vanished, leaving behind thick clouds of white steam. Hunter clutched her chest and sucked in breath after breath before she smoothed her hands over her skin. Satisfied the roar of magic had left her undamaged, she pushed herself from the bed.

Blood dripped from her fingertips and its metallic tang clung to the steam-filled air. Hunter smeared red across her nightstand as she pawed through the white clouds. Her fingers found the Lamy pen, its smooth sides and metal nib. She followed the trail of red back to the book and sank the pen into the crimson pulsing from the cover. She lifted her wet shirt and balled the fabric in her hand as she fished the pen from the blood.

"Begone Amphitrite!" Hunter screamed and stabbed the pen's metal point into her left hip. Blood trailed down her legs as she carved a line to her sternum and down to her right hip bone. "I call upon the strength of my blood, my ancestors, to banish you!" Tears streaked her face and dotted her feet while she sliced the arm of the pentagram across her stomach. "I banish you from my body. I banish you from my mind. Begone Amphitrite!" Blood painted her flesh as she tore her skin and closed the pentagram. "You have no power over me!"

The pen fell from Hunter's trembling fingers as she reached through the steam for the book and plunged her hand into its warm depths. She cupped her hand and lifted a pool of scarlet from the fleshy cover. Blood dripped from between her fingers and soaked the carpet as she brought the handful to her stomach. "As I command it, so mote it be!" Hunter clapped her palm against her etched flesh. White light burst from the wounds. Hunter released a guttural shriek as her skin sizzled.

The white blaze ceased, and the sulfuric scent of burnt hair and flesh twisted in the steam. Hunter let out a shuddering breath and, with shaking fingers, traced the pentagram, now a painless ropy scar, bright pink against her fair skin. As much as she yearned to collapse onto the firm mattress and wet sheets and close her eyes until tomorrow, she knew she couldn't. Her body was once again safe, as it had been with Tyr, but her home . . .

The steam began to dissipate as Hunter grabbed the spellbook and stepped up onto her bed. The blood warmed the book, swirling and burbling from the cover each time Hunter dipped in her fingers. She flattened her palm against the wall and started to draw the same pentagram she'd carved into her flesh.

"Begone Amphitrite. I call upon the strength of this mortal's blood and his ancestors to banish you. I banish you from this room. I banish you from this—"

"Satan!"

Hunter whirled around. The book slid from her blood-soaked hands, bounced off the bed, and landed at Jana Ashley's feet. Blood splattered across the lace hem of Jax's mom's floral-patterned housedress and stained her fluffy yellow slippers with splotches of red.

Hunter froze. She hadn't heard Mrs. Ashley come in or thought about what the past half hour must have sounded like from outside of the small apartment.

The color drained from Jana's cheeks as she clapped her hands over her mouth and muffled another scream of *Satan!* Mrs. Ashley scrambled backward. Her back hit the wall with a dull *thud,* yet her feet kept striking the ground, kept trying to move her far, far away from the young witch who stood motionless in a room dripping with blood.

Hunter wiped her hands on her wet shirt, but only managed to spread the crimson farther up her arms. "Mrs. Ashley." She stepped off the bed and held her hands up as she approached. "I can explain—"

Jana clutched the gold crucifix around her neck. "Stay back, Satan!" She pressed her body against the wall and turned her head from Hunter and the partial pentagram painted in blood on the wall. "Please, Lord God, protect me! Fill me with Your holy presence. Protect me from this evil, O God."

Hunter stepped forward and Jana pinched her eyes tightly shut. "I am safe in Your shadow, Lord God. I am safe in this home built with Your love."

Tears slipped down her cheeks as she brought the cross to her lips and muttered against it.

Hunter's stomach tensed and a brick lodged in her throat. Jana Ashley had only wanted to comfort her. And in return, Hunter had done this. *All of this.* She stared down at the blood crusted under her fingernails and flaking against the backs of her hands. If this got out . . .

Hunter grabbed her backpack and stuffed it with clothes, her phone, and the healing spellbook before shoving her feet into the nearest pair of boots.

"I'm sorry," she whispered to Mrs. Ashley.

Hunter ran from the room, through the open front door, and into the morning sunlight.

Twenty-two

Ivy tickled Hunter's back and the sharp thorns of a rosebush scratched her thighs as she crouched, next door to Jax's, in Barbara Ritter's foliage. Hunter wiggled out of her blood-soaked clothes and into the mismatched black-and-red-checkered shorts and blue pin-striped tee she'd grabbed from her room before bolting. No, it wasn't *her* room anymore. Not after what Jax's mom had walked in on.

"Jax." Hunter breathed as she took a half-empty water bottle from her bag and poured the contents onto her still-damp sleep shirt. She'd lose her best friend for sure. He wouldn't understand what she'd had to do to keep herself safe, and she could never explain all the blood. But more than that, this was evidence. They would point to it and call it proof that Hunter wasn't a harmless kitchen witch who mixed herbs and spices and only told people what they wanted to hear. They would say Hunter was a *real* witch, a *bad* witch, a *Satanist,* and a *murderer.* The type of evildoer that altered minds and perverted hearts and would snatch babies if they got too close.

Kirk would get the chance to burn her after all. And after what she'd done . . .

Hunter swallowed past the lump in her throat as she scrubbed the dried blood from her body and peeked through a gap in the bushes at the garage apartment and its open front door. If only she could get back in there and scrub the room from baseboards to ceiling until it sparkled in all of its beige glory like it had the day she'd moved in.

An idea fluttered in Hunter's chest. She squatted down and dug through the front pocket of her backpack until she found the small silver pouch her mother placed in her backpack at the beginning of every semester. She opened it and dumped the contents into her palm. Dried cloves and calendula blossoms piled in her hand on a wave of spice.

Hunter's heart longed for her mother. She would know just what to do. Hunter brought the handful to her nose and inhaled the woodiness of the dried plants. *If her mom were here, none of this would have happened.* She closed her fingers over the cloves and calendula. But there was no use in thinking about what didn't exist. The only thing that mattered was here and now. She'd clean up her mess before Mrs. Ashley gathered her wits and tore out of the house, revitalized by the wrath of God.

With her free hand, Hunter brushed the shriveled leaves and rose petals from the ground in front of her and drew a pentagram in the soft dirt. She poured the cloves and calendula from her palm into the middle of the five-pointed star and took the warm book of blood from her backpack.

"The rest is for the trees," she promised herself before she pressed her fingers into the healed cover. Red spurted around her nails and she tipped the book over to dribble a stream of blood onto the dried plants. She dabbed her fingers into the puddle and painted her palms with crimson that sizzled and popped as it coaxed the magic from her skin. It wasn't lost on her that the very thing she'd needed to erase from her room had the potential to energize the spell. That was life—full of contradictions.

Hunter held her palms over the inactive spell and chewed on her bottom lip. Clove was for . . . *purification?* She shook her head. That wasn't right. She should have paid more attention when Mercy blathered on and on about plants and their properties. That's what she really needed—help from her sister. It was second to her mother's, but her mother was no longer here.

Again, she peeked through to the garage apartment. No change.

"Think, Hunter, think." She closed her eyes and imagined her sister. Mercy's encyclopedias of plants, the cleaning spells they used to attempt in order to get out of chores, and all the times Mag had bored Hunter to tears reciting everything she knew about—

Hunter's eyelids fluttered open and a grin lifted her cheeks.

Clean up my mess. Set the room right. Clean up my mess. Set the room right.

Her intention played on a loop in her head as she swept her hands in a counterclockwise circle over the pentagram.

"Clove, please drive away
What I did today.
Clean this hostile energy,
And take it far away from me."

As Hunter cast her spell, the small pool of blood bubbled and stretched. It slid from the center of the pentagram and flooded the lines of the star. Hunter continued. Her heartbeat quickened as her palms heated and the edges of the cloves and calendula blossoms started to smolder.

"Calendula is purity,
I beseech you, hear my plea.
Scrub this mess I've made, make it sparkle, make it free
From blood and pain and all negativity."

Smoke drifted from the burning plants. It followed her hands, swirling under them like a tornado. As she stood, the smoke thickened, and the funnel grew. It stretched from the earth to her waist. She continued to sweep her hands in a counterclockwise motion over the gray cyclone as she lifted them above her head. The smoke swelled until it eclipsed Hunter and blew away the blossoms from the nearby roses.

"As I command it, so mote it be!" With a forceful flick of her wrists, she threw the smoke in the direction of the apartment. The funnel barreled toward the converted garage and slipped noiselessly through the open door.

Jana Ashley shrieked and shouted another prayer for her lord to protect her from evil. Hunter crouched down behind the bloom-less roses as Mrs. Ashley burst through the front door. She screamed and waved her hands above her tousled hair as she raced to the main house. Her muumuu billowed behind her and her fuzzy slippers beat the pavement. But they were clean. Scrubbed free of blood.

Relief filled Hunter as she dragged her foot over the pentagram and the clump of charred plants, erasing the evidence of her spell. One problem solved. A million more to go.

She pulled out her phone and dialed Kylie's number while she stuffed her things back into her bag. She needed to get her thoughts together before she talked to Mercy. Luckily, she had time to do so before they met at Goode Lake to help Em.

Kylie answered on the third ring. After a few muffled words and a deep sigh, she sleepily mumbled, "Jax?"

Hunter tossed her backpack over her shoulder and peered out around the rosebushes before jogging to the sidewalk and speed-walking toward the neighborhood's main entrance. "It's Hunter."

"Hey, H." She yawned. "Is Jax okay?"

"Unless he's having a nightmare . . ." Hunter pinned a cheerful smile to her lips and waved at an early-morning jogger before she turned down one of the neighborhood's winding streets.

"I should call him," Kylie said, a little more alert.

"I need your help first." Hunter adjusted her backpack strap and peered over her shoulder to make sure she wasn't followed. "Can you pick me up from the Gas-N-Go down the street from Jax's neighborhood? I just got kicked out of the apartment."

Blankets rustled, and a few seconds later Hunter heard the click of a light switch.

"Kirk, that shriveled little prick." Kylie seethed. "I knew it was only a matter of time until his puckered asshole of a father convinced Jax's mom to throw you out. Tiffany and Heather were group texting about it yesterday. I told Jax, but he said his mom would never listen to Michael Whitfield. Bunch of dicks."

The sick feeling was back. It kneaded Hunter's stomach and coated her throat in sick. "Yeah, bunch of dicks," she repeated, the words like BBs in her mouth, chipping her teeth as she shot them out.

A muffled rush of water and Kylie was back on task. "I'll be there in ten. We can go by Sunnyside Up and get some eggs, or whatever you vegetarians eat for breakfast." The water stopped and she spoke with her mouth full. "And you can stay with me, if you want. Be there soon."

The phone went silent, and Hunter slipped it into her back pocket as she neared the bed of purple-and-yellow pansies that framed the stone entrance to Jax's neighborhood. She hadn't really lied to Kylie. She also hadn't lied the time before when Kylie shoved words into her mouth about Kirk's hand. It wasn't Hunter's fault that she kept tripping and falling face-first into a decent, albeit incorrect, version of the truth.

Hunter looked up and down the sleepy two-lane street before she jogged across and headed down the sidewalk that passed the Gas-N-Go. This was part of her problem. These half-truths and veiled lies had to end. She needed to stop trying to be so different and go back to what worked, what she trusted, and what had never hurt her. In her haste to flee her sister, she'd left behind her tarot—the tool she'd once thought of as an extension of herself. Like Tyr, she'd cast her deck aside in the name of a more powerful magic. But power came at a price.

Hunter hissed in a breath and pressed her hand against her fresh scar as a salty breeze brushed over her. She spun around, but the goddess was nowhere to be seen. Hunter picked up her pace and jogged down the sidewalk. Before she could come clean to her friends, she needed to heal the gates, and with the help of her sister, banish Amphitrite for good.

Twenty-three

Kitten! Did you remember the boughs of evergreen for the release ritual?" Xena's voice drifted from the kitchen up the stairs to Mercy's room.

"Yes! I cut them a couple days ago so they could dry a little and make it easier to light them." Mercy hurried down the stairs, her giant bag slung over her shoulder as she headed to the kitchen to collect her spellwork basket. She was wearing a long, cream-colored tank dress that had ivory vines embroidered along the bodice. She usually paired it with her bright pink fringed vest, but that would've been super inappropriate for a release ritual—so that day her pink ballet flats were her only splash of color.

Xena studied Mercy closely from her perch at the kitchen counter. "That white dress is quite fetching on you."

"Fetching? Exactly how old are you, Xena?" Mercy teased.

"Let's just say I'm old enough to be very wise," said the cat person. "Are you quite sure you're up to this ritual? I am still appalled at what that horrible boy did to you last night!" Xena wrapped Abigail's fluffy bathrobe more securely around her as if it was a defense against the Kirk Whitfields of the world.

Mercy went to the pantry and brought out the spellwork basket she'd already loaded with a ritual robe, white candles and long, wooden matches, ritual goblets, and a bottle of rich red wine. She looked up from the items to smile at her familiar. "I'm okay. Really. Though I'm still super confused about what that ass was talking about. He seriously accused Hunter of breaking his fingers and cutting his face. That's just crazy." She paused before adding, "Isn't it?"

Xena licked the back of her hand and smoothed her hair. "I would be shocked if our Hunter did harm to him, though . . ." Her words trailed away and she moved her shoulders in a small shrug. "She has not really been our Hunter since my Abigail left us."

Trepidation fingered its way down Mercy's spine and she shuddered. "I know she hasn't been herself. Actually, Hunter has been a real bitch, but I just can't believe she'd break anyone's fingers—not even Kirk's. Or, if Hunter did have something to do with Kirk's injuries I'll bet they were in self-defense."

Xena nodded slowly. "Well, self-defense is a gray area in the Witches' Rede. The old words say, 'Live and let live. Fairly take and fairly give.' Which some interpret as—if someone hurts us we may retaliate in kind."

"So, you think Hunter did it?" Mercy remembered Kirk's five splinted fingers and the stitched-up gash on his face. Her stomach felt sick as she thought about it. Not because she was upset—Kirk had looked like he'd totally lost a fight. She felt sick because Abigail had lived by the one true law that had ruled Goode witches for centuries: *An' it harm none, do as ye will.* She'd raised her daughters to live by that law of compassion and fair play, too.

"I think that is a question for Hunter to answer," said Xena. "Has she responded to you at all?"

Mercy sighed. "I texted her last night and told her I needed to talk to her. That it was real important. She hasn't said shit back to me."

"Kitten, did you not tell her that Kirk accosted you?"

Mercy tucked a strand of long, dark hair behind her ear. "No! If she can't bother to even text me, then why should I tell her anything?"

Xena shook her head sadly. "Do not let stubborn pride come between you and your sister."

"It's not pride! I'm just—I'm just pissed. It's like Hunter doesn't care about us anymore. I guess I figured she wouldn't care that Kirk pushed me around."

"Perhaps after you finish with the ritual for Emily's father you and I should go to Jax's home and insist Hunter speak with us." Xena gnawed on the side of one perfectly pointed fingernail before adding, "Though I do not want to make her any more defensive than she already is. I worry, though, about leaving her alone too long. It is not good for a witch to suffer alone."

Mercy snorted. "She's not alone. She has Jax and her new bestie, Kylie. They sped out of the school parking lot yesterday like they were heading to a party or something." *One I wasn't invited to,* she added to herself silently. Just the thought was like fingernails on a chalkboard to Mercy's nerves. "No. You know what? I'm going to focus my intention on the ritual for Em's dad and stop worrying about Hunter. It's super clear she's not worried about me." Mercy ducked out the back door quickly where she'd hung the fluffy green pine boughs to dry.

"Well, kitten, I shall worry about the two of you."

Mercy circled the boughs around the candles in her basket and smiled at Xena. "Thanks. You're an awesome familiar."

"I am, indeed, my Mercy kitten. Is Emily on her way to get you to drive you to the lake?"

"No, she had to go with her mom and grandparents to that little restaurant in Ogden, Sunnyside Up, for brunch. She did manage to get out of going shopping with them in Champaign, though. She said she'll meet me at Goode Lake, over by the cabins on the far side of the lake at one o'clock." She fished her phone out of her purse. "It's twelve-thirty. Perfect timing!"

"Those cabins are lovely little homes. Slightly too rustic for my liking in my human form, but still—passably nice."

"Yeah, Em's dad loved to take her out there when she was in grade school. Remember when Hunter and I would go with them?"

Xena smiled. "You kittens called it camping, which always made Abigail laugh." The cat person nodded appreciatively. "That is a good spot for Emily kitten's release ritual for her father. There are many good memories there imprinted into the earth."

"That's what I thought, too. Okay, I'm ready. Hey, don't be surprised if I'm not home until late—or if Em comes over for the weekend. That is okay, right?"

"Oh, kitten, of course. As I said, being solitary and sad is not good for us. I shall not worry if you and your friend wish to stay out, nor if she would like to come to our home for however long—or you hers for that matter." Xena studied her pointed fingernails. "Actually, kitten, I shall slip back into my feline skin and do some lovely hunting. I have missed the stalk and kill."

Mercy shuddered. "Xena, seriously. Please do not bring any dead birds into the house. Again. It's super gross."

"Oh, kitten, not to worry. I shall eat any bird I kill outside." Xena hugged Mercy tightly. "Blessed be, my sweet Green Witch."

Mercy hugged her tightly back. "Blessed be, my awesome familiar."

The morning clouds had cleared, and it was a gorgeous Saturday afternoon in Illinois. The sky was bright, birthday cake frosting–blue with giant, puffy clouds drifting lazily around to create *Winnie-the-Pooh* images. Mercy breathed deeply, loving the springtime scent of green, growing things. She put her spellwork basket on the passenger's seat with her giant purse, and quickly texted Em as they'd already planned. *OMW to the lake!*

She put on her seat belt and started the Camry, and her phone bleeped with Em's text reply. *Me 2! See u soon!* Mercy smiled at the phone, put it in the cup holder beside her, and began to meander along the old state road that took her around town to Goode Lake.

Her phone synced automatically with the Camry and began to play a TLC song—one of Hunter's favorite oldies.

Mercy frowned. *Why couldn't Hunter just text her back?* Up until just last week the twins had barely spent a weekend apart for their entire lives, and now Hunter wouldn't even speak to her. The sharp pain of missing her twin made Mercy's shoulders bow and the fragrant, springtime air no longer seemed so blissful. She felt the humidity that promised a hot day that would bring out the mosquitoes and maybe even a storm later. Mercy chewed her lip. *Hunter was being such a bitch!*

"No!" The word exploded from Mercy. "Hunter is *not* going to mess up today like she messed up Mr. Parrott's funeral. No, no, *no!*" She grabbed her phone and changed the song. The sweet voice of her mom's favorite singer, Tina Malia, replaced TLC and instantly Mercy's mood shifted as Malia sang of Avalon and the beauty that awaited in the Summerlands of the goddess. "Thanks for sending me an omen that doesn't bite, Abigail," she whispered to the listening air—and put Hunter out of her mind.

Emily's T-Bird was a cherry red beacon that easily drew Mercy to the sleepy cabin her dad had always preferred to rent. Em sat on one of the four wooden rocking chairs that dotted the porch of the unoccupied cabin. She stood and waved as Mercy parked beside the T-Bird.

"Hey, look! The rocks are already all set up for a campfire." Emily grinned as she skipped down the porch steps. She was wearing a white maxi dress trimmed in pretty yellow daisies.

Mercy grabbed the spellwork basket and met Emily in front of the cabin. Her bestie hugged her. "Did you have any trouble getting away?"

"Nah, Mom and Grandma are getting along really well. They were headed to the opening of some boutique called Sundance in Champaign. Grandpa said he'd go with them, but wanted to wait somewhere he could get a beer. I have no clue what Sundance is, but they seemed super excited."

"I know what it is—boho clothes for old people."

"Oh shit. They'll probably buy me something." Em sighed.

"Yep, but you can say it doesn't fit and then we'll take a trip to Champaign to 'exchange'"—Mercy air quoted—"whatever broom skirt and cardigan set they buy you. It's a pretty pricey store—Abigail used to love their catalogue—which means we'll have money to treat ourselves to an awesome lunch."

"Girl, it's a plan. So, what's in your magic witchy basket and what do you need me to do?" Em peered at the pine boughs that curled over the white candles.

"Well, you did the first thing perfectly. Your dress is great—white symbolizes the new beginning of crossing over to the Summerlands, and as a Green Witch in the service of Freya I can say the daisies are a great choice. And you're right. The campfire that's already set up will definitely work." Mercy and Em headed to the soot-marked ring of stones a few yards from the front of the cabin. "Okay, make a nest of these evergreens inside the stones and sprinkle your dad's pipe tobacco over them. Place the fattest of the white candles in the center of it, and then put the other four smaller white pillars around the stone circle about equal distance apart." Mercy paused to quickly get her bearings. "The lake is right over there, to the south, so place the first of the four candles there," she pointed to the correct spot, "on the northernmost point of the circle. While you do that I'll open the wine."

"Oooh! There's wine? Pagan funerals are way better than regular funerals."

"Well, yeah, but this is really just a release ritual, not a full funeral like we did for Abigail, but I promise it'll work, and it'll be nice."

"Hey." Em touched her best friend's arm gently. "I know. I trust you. Totally."

Unexpectedly, tears filled Mercy's eyes and she had to wipe at her cheeks.

"Mag, what's wrong?"

Mercy shook her head. "No, now is not for me—it's for you and your dad."

"It's Hunter, right? And the rumors about Kirk."

"What do you know?" Mercy shot the question at her.

"I didn't want to say anything to you 'cause it's just gossip," Em said.

"Kirk's saying Hunter hit him and broke his fingers." Mercy's voice was flat.

"You know?" Emily's hands stilled as she reached for the fifth candle to place around the circle.

Mercy blew out a long breath. "I was gonna tell you later because right now we're supposed to focus on your dad."

Em put the last candle in place and fisted her hands on her waist. "We can multitask and set our intention in a sec."

Mercy couldn't help but smile through her tears at her friend. "You're starting to sound like a Goode witch."

"If only! Tell me."

"Last night I was getting sandwiches for Xena and me late, just before Goodeville Sammiches closed, and Kirk snuck up on me." As Mercy quickly recapped what the douche had done, Em's fawn eyes got huge.

"Oh. My. God! That ass! He fucking attacked you!"

"Well, he tried. Deputy Carter stopped him and hauled him away. Good riddance."

"Yeah, Whitfield has lost his damn mind. It's all over Insta that he said something awful to Hunter at school—she punched him, lots of people saw that—and then she ran into the bathroom. Apparently, he followed her and then the story gets super cray. He says she used magic to break his fingers. Kylie and Jax are saying that he tried to punch her, she ducked, and he smashed his hand against the bathroom mirror."

"Oh, Freya!" Mercy's stomach heaved. "That's what he was babbling about when he held me against the car. He was super drunk and not making any sense. Is Hunter okay?"

Em nodded. "Yeah. She's totally fine. Or that's what Jax and Kylie have been saying. Hunter hasn't posted anything."

Mercy flushed hot. "So, she's hanging with Jax and her new friend and can't bother to tell her twin, *who Kirk attacked,* that's she's okay—or even give me a damn heads-up that I might need to look out for a rampaging ex-football star ex-boyfriend out for revenge. Great. She just left me out there clueless—the perfect target."

Em shook her head sadly. "I'm sorry Mag."

"Yeah, me, too." Mercy drew in a long breath and let it out slowly. "Well, okay. Now I know what happened and I can quit thinking about it. So, let's set our intention and create a lovely ritual of release."

"Are you sure you're up to it?" Emily asked softly.

Mercy forced herself to smile. "Absolutely. I'm going to open this bottle of wine and fill our goblets, and while I do that you stand there, in front of the southern candle facing the fire pit." Emily took her position. "Think about your dad and a super happy memory of him, and I'll do the same."

Mercy pushed Hunter—and all the swirling emotions surrounding what had or had not happened with Kirk—from her mind. At the very bottom of her spellwork basket was Abigail's favorite white silk ritual cloak, the same one Xena had worn as she presided over the Kitchen Witch's funeral. Mercy slipped it on. She loved the way it slid over her bare arms, and her mother's faint scent of cinnamon and spice still lifted from the silk. The robe helped Mercy ground herself and be present. She felt much more prepared as she filled the two goblets from one of Abigail's favorite bottles of red wine, then picked up the long box of wooden ritual matches and positioned herself before the northern candle, facing Emily.

"All set?" she asked Emily, who nodded solemnly. "Okay. Now we begin." Mercy drew one long, slender match from the box.

The sounds of gravel crunching under tires followed by a car door slamming made Mercy pause before she lit the match to begin the ritual.

"I checked. No one rented this cabin this weekend." Emily's voice sounded very young, and filled with disappointment.

"Hey, don't worry. We haven't started yet." Mercy looked around, trying to see where the car noises had come from, but the old willows that surrounded the cabin made for excellent cover, one reason Em's dad had liked the privacy they offered so much. Then there were more tires-crunching-gravel noise, which quickly faded. Mercy smiled in relief at Em across the campfire circle. "See—it was probably just someone who took a wrong turn. Okay, so, we'll begin again now by—"

"Oh, good! I got here in time." Hunter stepped through the wall of trees as she spoke. She batted at a spiderweb, readjusted the backpack she carried over her shoulder, and rolled her eyes. "I forgot how stuck back in the trees this cabin is. Sorry I'm late, but you would not believe all the crap that's happened."

Twenty-four

Emily recovered her voice before Mercy could make a sound. "Oh, hi, Hunter. You're actually not too late. We were just starting."

"Why are you here?" Mercy shot the question at her twin.

"Uh, because Emily asked me to be here. I thought you knew."

"I told you I invited her, remember?" Em said softly.

Mercy lifted her chin and squared her shoulders before she faced Hunter. "Yeah, I remember, but I didn't figure you'd show. You're not even wearing white."

Hunter looked down at the maxi dress she was wearing that was emerald green decorated with tiny pink flowers. "Well, this isn't mine. I didn't exactly have access to my clothes this morning and had to borrow this from Kylie. Mag, we need to talk. Like, now. Some really crazy shit has gone down, and I need—"

"*You* need?" Mercy kept herself from yelling at her sister, but she couldn't keep the sarcasm from filling her voice. "This isn't about *you*. This is about Emily's dad."

Hunter nodded. "Right. I know." She approached the circle of rock and candles.

"Have you even set your intention?" Mercy frowned at Hunter.

"I've been pretty busy," said Hunter. "Hi, Em. Sorry, again, for being late. I had to—"

"Whatever you *had to* do isn't important right now unless it involves Mr. Parrott," snapped Mercy. "Step away from the ritual circle, ground yourself, and set your intention. If you can do that quickly we'll wait for you. If not, go sit on the porch or whatever until we're done."

Hunter shook her head. "Mag, you don't understand. If you'd just let me tell you—"

"And you call *me* selfish?" Mercy rolled her eyes. "I've been trying to get you to talk to me for *days.* You can't even bother to text me—or Xena—and let us know you're okay. *Or* that Kirk is on the fucking rampage. Thanks for nothing, H. I found that out myself."

"Wait, what?" Hunter took a step toward Mercy.

Mercy held out her hand like a stop sign. "No. Don't even pretend you give a shit."

Hunter narrowed her turquoise eyes. "I have been dealing with things you can't even imagine *by myself.*"

Mercy snorted. "You mean *by yourself by your own choice,* don't you?"

"Mag—Hunter, come on. You're sisters. Twins. This stuff that's going on between you isn't right."

"What isn't right is that our issues are getting in the way of your dad's release ritual," said Mercy. "Hunter, ground yourself and then join us, or not. Choose. Now."

"You're so fucking wrong and you're too self-absorbed to see it," said Hunter.

"Then leave! Go away! I don't need your help!" Mercy repeated the words that Hunter had struck her with at Mr. Parrott's first funeral.

"No problem. I'm better on my own anyway. Sorry, Em." Hunter turned and disappeared back through the wall of willows.

The little clearing was unusually quiet after Hunter left. There wasn't even the sound of her sister's shoes on gravel. The wound in Mercy's heart was raw and felt like Hunter had stabbed it with her words and her latest abandonment.

Emily cleared her throat. "Maybe you should go after her."

Mercy shook her head. "No. I'm not going to let her mess this up. Let's ground ourselves together and then we'll do the ritual."

"But . . ." Em began and then she moved her shoulders. "Well, okay. If that's what you want."

"Absolutely. Breathe with me in and out three times to a three count and let's both think about your dad. Okay?"

"Okay."

Mercy led Emily in the breathing exercise that would ground them, and as she did she closed her eyes and closed out the pain and anger her sister seemed to carry around with her like an extra backpack. Mercy reached down, down, down to the ley lines that pulsed deep in the earth. They weren't as strong here as near any of the five gatekeeper trees, but she could still tap into their emerald power. She pulled it up into her body and—temporarily—let its warmth wash away Hunter and the hurt she caused. When she opened her eyes she was invigorated. She smiled at Emily and repeated, "And now we begin."

Mercy drew one long, slender match from the box. "O elements of air, fire, water, and earth, my friend, Emily Parrott, and I call you to us today to aid us in our farewell of Dominic Parrott, beloved father to Emily." She struck the match, touched it to the white candle on the eastern side of the stone circle, and invoked, "Air, grant Emily release from pain. Flow through her in this more lonely world and carry her sadness away."

Mercy lit the candles working clockwise, ending with the candle in front of her. "Earth, grant Emily release from pain. Ground her in your nurturing lap. Let her know strength in remembrance without the winter of grief."

Then Mercy blew out the match and took two new matches from

the box. She kept one and handed the other across the circle to Emily, who watched her closely. Mercy raised her arms. The silk sleeves of Abigail's white ritual robe moved gently, soothingly, in the soft morning breeze.

"O Freya, Goddess of Love and War, I do call on thee.
Be with us here at this time of great loss.
We of the Olde Ways know that when a person dies
it is only their body that is lost—never their soul
their immortal soul
For we know the soul shall return to earth.
That is a tenet of loving faith
Taught since long before history began.
Our lore tells us another mother shall give birth
And the soul—dressed in new flesh
With sturdier limbs and brighter brain
The old soul shall return to life again . . . again."

Mercy met Emily's watchful gaze.

"O daughter of beloved Dominic Parrott, I do call on thee
to speak before us and the goddess.
To show honor and love for he whom you have known
Who has passed beyond.
Tell me, Emily Parrott, what memory will you share of he?"

Emily cleared her throat. When she began to speak her voice was hesitant, but as she relaxed into the memory her words became as bright as the afternoon sunlight. "I'll always remember how Dad took me camping here. It was our special place. Just for Dad and me—and lots of times you, too. We toasted marshmallows here. We swam in the lake. We laughed and sang songs. We made memories I will never, ever forget and someday when I have kids I'll bring them here and tell them about their grandpa." Emily's gaze left Mercy's and lifted to the sky. "We'll make memories that include you, Dad. And a whole new generation of kids will remember you and know you. I promise." When her eyes found Mercy again they were filled with tears, but she was smiling.

"That was perfect, Em," Mercy said. "And now we'll light Freya's candle together." They touched their long matches to the candles in front of them, and then as one they leaned forward and their two matches lit the thick white pillar of the goddess.

Mercy lifted her arms and spoke to the sky. "O gracious Freya, we do thank thee for releasing Emily's grief and for guiding her father to your beauteous Summerlands. We ask that you convey to her father the love and good wishes sent to him by his daughter, Emily, and her friend—your servant—Mercy Goode. And we ask that he will blessed be."

"Blessed be," murmured Emily.

"Now we'll light your dad's symbolic pyre." Together Emily and Mercy crouched. Mercy tilted the center goddess candle so that it caught the pine boughs, and soon the candle began melting with the greenery and the flames crackled cheerfully as they burned.

Mercy picked up the two goblets of wine she'd already poured and passed one to Emily. They stood and lifted the goblets. "I propose a toast," Mercy said. "To Emily's dad, who has been freed of this world!"

"To Dad!" Emily lifted her goblet, clinked it against Mercy's, and then the girls drank deeply as the flames grew. And as they drank the sweet, tobacco-scented smoke rising from the burning pyre turned the purest of white, swirled, and took the form of a beautiful dove, one that lifted up and up to meet the sun in the Caribbean blue sky.

"Hey, thanks again. That was a really great ritual." Emily leaned against her T-Bird while Mercy put the repacked spellwork basket in the passenger's seat of the Camry. "I do feel better. A lot better, actually. Somehow, I don't really know how to describe it except that I'm *lighter.*"

"That's a perfect description and I'm glad, Em. Also, I'm really sorry Hunter almost messed everything up."

"She didn't, though. Hey, maybe you should go find her. I mean, we heard a car drive away, so someone dropped her off. She must be walking and she did seem upset. Hunter said she needed to talk to you, and it musta been important for her to come to you, Mag, especially right now," said Emily.

"If what Hunter had to say was important enough to interrupt your dad's ritual—then she knows where I live and *she* can come find *me.*" Mercy slammed the passenger's door.

Emily moved her shoulders and looked down. "I really hate that you two are fighting."

"I really hate that everything has to revolve around Hunter."

Emily nudged a rock with her foot and sighed. "Yeah, I get that you're upset. So, you want to have a mini-vacay at my house this weekend? We can order pizza, watch one of *The Real Housewives,* and judge them for being so damn crazy. And I promise—not one word about Hunter all weekend."

Mercy made herself smile. "That sounds really good. Let me drop off my spellwork basket at home and tell Xena where I'll be—or leave a note for her. I think she's hunting."

Emily wrinkled her nose. "Like for real? With a gun?"

"Oh, goddess, no! With her paws and claws."

"Is that better or worse?" Em said with a little laugh.

"I'm actually not sure. But I did tell her she'd need to leave the dead bird outside the house this time." Mercy shuddered.

"Oh, gross! What'd she say?"

"That she'd be sure to *eat it outside.*" Mercy's laugh was almost authentic.

"Okay, now I'm super grossed out. That cat person licks her hand

and my face *and* puts her dead bird spit on me!" Emily slid into the driver's seat of her T-Bird.

"Yeah, but she does it with love," said Mercy.

"I think I could do with a little less cat love," said Em. "Okay, so, I'll see you pretty soon?"

"Yep, as soon as I put away my spellwork things, change, and tell Xena what's up."

"Awesome! And bring the rest of that bottle of wine. Mom won't care if we drink it as long as we don't go anywhere." Emily put the car in gear and waved.

Before Mercy left she checked the fire pit one more time to be sure the dirt they'd covered their mini-pyre with had extinguished everything. Satisfied she wouldn't be responsible for burning up Em's favorite cabin, she got in the car and drove slowly around the lake. She didn't actively think about looking for Hunter—but she did do a lot of gawking out her open window.

But there was no sign of her twin. Not that Mercy expected there to be. She wasn't driving the most direct route home, and the truth was chances were whoever had dropped Hunter off had probably stuck around to give her a ride back. No, Mercy was *not* going to worry about her sister. Like she'd told Emily—Hunter knew where she lived.

Mercy parked in the driveway of her beloved Victorian house. Xena wasn't on the porch swing, and as she opened the door and plopped her spellwork basket down on the kitchen counter she called, "Xena! You here?"

No feline padded into the room and no cat in a human suit answered her, so Mercy jogged up the stairs, changed her white dress for a short T-shirt dress covered in happy sunflowers, though she kept on her pink flats. The ankh Khenti had given her rested warmly between her breasts. With a smile Mercy pulled it out from under her dress so that the gold of the symbol complemented the sunny yellow flowers. She'd been wearing the necklace since Khenti had given it to her, but she'd hidden it under her dress during Mr. Parrott's ritual, and was looking forward to seeing Em's face when she finally showed it to her and told her the amazing story about her quick visit to the Egyptian Underworld. Even Xena had been impressed by the golden ankh. Emily was going to flip out!

Mercy put PJs, a pair of jeans and a tee, and her toothbrush in her backpack and skipped down the stairs. She hurried to the kitchen and had just finished putting away her spellwork items—and stashing the bottle of wine in her backpack—when the back door opened and Xena, completely naked, walked into the house.

"Oh, hi kitt—" she began and then coughed violently, twice, before she pulled a small feather from her mouth. The cat person licked her lips and grinned at Mercy. "Sparrow! My favorite." She tossed the feather in the air and batted playfully at it. Then she wrapped herself in Abigail's robe, which she'd left on the back of one of the breakfast nook chairs.

"So, I'm assuming your hunt went well?" Mercy tried not to sound as completely grossed out as she actually was.

"Oh, yes, kitten! Superbly. You should have seen me stalk the silly bird—so clueless—and my pounce! It was sublime and appropriately deadly." She coughed again and another tiny feather floated from her mouth. "How was your ritual?"

"Great—no thanks to Hunter who showed up and tried to ruin everything."

Xena's brow furrowed as she took her usual perch on the corner of the kitchen bar. "Hunter came to the ritual?"

"Yeah." Mercy grabbed a crystal wineglass and quickly filled it with heavy coconut cream from the fridge. She placed it in front of Xena and then slouched against the opposite counter. "She marched in all entitled and mouthy, saying how she just *had* to talk to me about something oh, so important. She wasn't even dressed for the ritual."

"What was it she wanted to talk with you about?"

Mercy shrugged. "No idea. She kept trying to make everything all about her and whatever *she* wanted. When I wouldn't let her mess up Em's ritual she had the nerve to call me selfish and say *I* didn't understand. So I told her what she'd said to me at the funeral. Go away—I don't need you. Then she did what she seems to do best—she left."

Xena said nothing. She watched Mercy with wise yellow eyes.

Mercy picked at the strap of her backpack. "What?"

"Kitten, I am your familiar. I love you. You know that, do you not?"

"Well, yeah, of course."

"Then know I say this with love. Shame on you, Mercy Anne Goode." Xena didn't raise her voice, but the disappointment that filled her words weighed heavily on Mercy. "For the past several days—no, since your mother's untimely death—you have been asking your sister to talk to you. To share with you. To not shut you out. And now, today, Hunter finally comes to you. She reaches out in front of your best friend, which I am quite sure was difficult for our proud Hunter, and instead of showing her the compassion you've wished so desperately she would treat you with, you did what?" Xena didn't pause, but answered herself. "You threw her ill-considered words back at her and rejected her—your sister—your twin." The cat person shook her head. "I am disheartened by this, my Green Witch. Worse, Abigail would be ashamed of you."

Mercy's stomach felt awful—hollow, but hot and sick at once. She blinked hard to keep from crying. Instead of allowing the wound Xena's words had caused to hemorrhage and destroy her, Mercy got mad—really mad. She straightened and hefted her backpack over her shoulder. Her voice was cold, like she didn't even know Xena. "You should be on my side."

"I shall always be on your side, but that does not mean that I will not speak out when you are wrong, and you are wrong about this, my kitten." Xena spoke slowly, as if she measured each word. "You need your sister. Your sister needs you. It is past time the two of you end this estrangement."

"I'm gonna spend the weekend at Emily's house. If Hunter shows up don't call me. I'm turning off my phone. I'm sick of everything being about *poor, grieving, misunderstood Hunter.* Have a good weekend, Xena. Maybe by Monday you'll be over your disappointment in me and remember you're my familiar—not Hunter's!" Mercy strode past the cat person, grabbed her purse from the table, stomped out of the room, and slammed the front door behind her.

Fighting back tears, Mercy sat in the car as she tried to collect herself. She expected Xena to rush out after her, say she was sorry, and wrap Mercy in a hug that smelled like Abigail and home—she more than half wanted her to. But when no one followed her—no one in cat or human form—Mercy's anger bubbled in her sick stomach. She started the car and was just putting it in gear when her phone chimed. Instantly, Mercy felt a rush of cool relief. Xena was probably texting her to please come back. She lifted the phone eagerly to see that the text was from Emily.

Mom called. She heard about another murder in town last night! What if that's what H was trying 2 tell u??? We should find her Mag!

"Bloody buggering hell!" Mercy hurled the words out into the empty car. "Hunter! Hunter! Hunter! I'm so damn sick of my familiar, my best friend—*everyone* freaking out about Hunter! She left! I stayed! She's off doing goddess knows what while *I'm* the witch stressing about the trees. All by myself—without Abigail *or* Hunter *I'm still trying to do my best!*"

Anger made Mercy's hands shake so hard that she had to try several times before she wrote the reply to Emily.

X and I had a fight. I'm staying home. Talk at school Monday.

And then Mercy did what she'd told her familiar she was going to do. She turned off her phone and dropped it onto her lap. Without thinking about where she'd go, Mercy drove away from her home.

Twenty-five

Mercy hadn't intended to drive to Goode Park. It was like the Camry had a mind of its own, because all of a sudden there she was—pulling into the parking lot. It was way less busy than usual on a sunny Saturday afternoon, but then she remembered that the Mustangs were having a late-spring scrimmage—varsity versus junior varsity—which meant the entire football-worshipping town would be paying homage to douchebags like Kirk Whitfield at the stadium.

Thinking of Kirk fueled the fire inside Mercy. At least that asshole would be benched. For a moment she considered driving to school to witness his humiliation firsthand, but then she remembered the nasty looks and the whispers that had followed her around school all week. *No, bloody hell, no!* She didn't want anything to do with Kirk *or* the football-obsessed who would no doubt blame her for whatever had happened to their star quarterback's hand.

"It's not like they can ever tell Hunter and me apart anyway," she grumbled to herself as she put the car in park. "As usual, Hunter did whatever she wanted to do without bothering to think about how it would affect anyone else." Mercy's anger continued to build. "I don't need this shit. I'm tired of trying to do the right thing—to make up for Mom's death—heal the sodding trees—worry about Hunter. Fuck that! When will someone worry about me?"

Mercy got out of the car and slammed the door—and her phone clattered against the asphalt parking lot. "Shit! That's all I need. A broken phone." She frowned at it as she bent to pick it up, brushed off the undamaged screen, and slid it into the pocket of her sunflower dress. Then she tromped through the spongy grass. Mercy headed straight to the clump of doum palms without even telling her feet to take her there, but as she got nearer to the trees her feet slowed. Beneath her the grass, which was a vibrant green carpet in the rest of the park, was shriveled and blackened.

"It's worse," Mercy murmured as her gaze followed the veins of dying grass that fingered their way out from the clump of doums. Mercy glanced around her. No one was close to her—no one would notice. She went to her knees and breathed in and out several grounding breaths. Then Mercy closed her eyes and searched for the ley lines far below. She found the emerald rivers of power easily—and just as easily reached down as she whispered, "Come to me—use me as conduit for your healing. Banish all sickness and restore the grass to health. So I have spoken; so mote it be."

Mercy felt a stirring beneath her knees as she released the earth energy into the sod. She opened her eyes in time to watch dead, blackened grass being replaced by new growth that shot up eagerly.

"Thank you." Mercy patted the ground affectionately before she stood and brushed dead grass off her knees as she continued on to the palms. She reached up. Her fingers traced the ankh. It radiated comfortable warmth that reminded her of sand and sun and the brilliant colors of Khenti's world.

He said I could come back. He invited me. We're friends.

"And I am absolutely sick of *my* bloody buggering world," she muttered.

Instead of stopping in front of the group of palms, Mercy walked the circumference of the trees—slowly, absently, as if she'd just been out for a stroll. When actually, walking the circle allowed her to look all around Goode Park. There were some grade school–aged kids playing a game of softball on a distant diamond. Two men were batting a tennis ball back and forth on the only court that was occupied. But no one jogged the track that framed the park—those people were probably at the scrimmage. By the time Mercy had completed her circle of the trees, she felt confident that no one was paying any attention to one teenager standing in the shadow of the palms.

Mercy went to the center tree and pressed her hand against its bark. It felt dry, like the skin of a really old person. She closed her eyes and whispered, "I greet you, doum. How are you today?"

Under her hand the tree shivered, and Mercy felt the cold that chilled the doum pass through it to her skin. She shivered in response. "I know. I feel it. I'm sorry. Let me see if I can help again." Mercy closed her eyes and reached down, down, down. She barely had to concentrate. The converging ley lines thrummed with power and glowed like a stream of liquid emeralds. Mercy tapped into that stream and pulled it up into her body. She was flooded with warmth that instantly chased away the ailing chill of the trees. Then Mercy gritted her teeth, put both hands firmly against the bark, and then whispered, "From me to thee, warmth, power, strength. From me to thee, from me to thee—three by three by magical, mystical three—send from the earth to the trees warmth, power, strength. So mote it be!"

Though it was more than the quick healing she'd done for the grass it wasn't really a spell—wasn't really a full casting—but sluggishly the power oozed from her body into the trees. It was like pouring molasses on a cold day, and too soon Mercy had to break the contact so she could gasp for breath and wipe the sweat from her brow. Then she patted the skin of the bark affectionately. "I hope that helped."

The bark did feel warmer. As she smiled in relief two men's voices drifted to her. Not wanting to be seen, Mercy pressed herself closer to the concealing clump of palms.

"There's nothing like a total sweep!" one of the men said. His voice was filled with good humor.

The other man said nothing. Mercy peeked around the doum to see that the two middle-aged men who had been on the tennis court had finished their game and were taking the path past the palms to the parking lot.

The first man gave the second a friendly shoulder shove. "Come on, man. You usually win every game. No reason to be a sore loser the one time I get lucky."

The men were close to the palm—so close that Mercy could see the anger in the silent man's eyes as he rounded on his friend.

"I'm no sore loser, but I fucking hate a cheater."

The first man's eyes narrowed. "Stan, are you seriously calling me a cheater?"

"If the shoe fucking fits!" said Stan.

"Yeah, well, if the fist fucking fits, too!" The first man, who had been smiling and happy, reached back and *punched Stan in his face.*

Mercy had to cover her mouth to stop her gasp of shock. She'd never seen grown men fight, but here were two totally grown men—just a few yards away from her—throwing punches like teenagers. She was thinking that she should probably call 911, but before she had a chance to punch the numbers, the men had gotten farther from her and closer to the parking lot—and it looked like they were actually laughing together. She shook her head and turned her back to them in disgust. *I do not think I will ever understand men. Why the bloody hell do they have to hit each other to bond?*

Then the center of the group of trees began to shimmer and an oval, as luminous as a fire opal, appeared. Behind it stood a warrior with the head of a dragon and the body of a god.

"Khenti!"

"It is you! When I felt the gate strengthen I had hoped it was my friend, the magnificent Green Witch Mercy. Have you found a way to heal the trees and fix the gates?" As he spoke he lifted his hand and as it passed in front of the ferocious reptilian visage that was his face, his skin shivered and shifted into the familiar lines of her young Egyptian warrior friend.

Mercy sighed. "No, I didn't heal anything. I didn't figure out anything. All I did was just channel some warmth into the palms. I'm a failure."

"What has happened? You look as if your world rests on your shoulders." The oval that separated them swirled and changed from opal to mother of pearl.

"I had a crappy day. *Another* crappy day. Sorry. I probably sound like a crybaby." She shook back her hair and lifted her chin as she tried to hold on to some of the anger that had fueled her thus far.

"Is it your sister again? The Cosmic Witch Hunter?"

"Yeah, she and my familiar and my best friend. I'd say it feels like my whole world's against me right now, but I get that that sounds pretty pathetic and self-pitying." Her fingers found the ankh and she absently traced the cross-like shape.

"Well, then, perhaps you would like to hear some good news." Khenti flashed a smile at her that even the barrier between them couldn't dim.

"Good news would be awesome!"

"I spoke with Hathor. The goddess was pleased with the offering of your perfume—so pleased that she granted me a boon." His grin widened.

"A boon? Like what?" Mercy wished that ever-present barrier wasn't between them.

"The great goddess Hathor has gifted me with a spell that will allow you to visit our realm and remain in your true form!"

"What? Ohmygoddess!" Then she added, "You mean without me turning gray and having to come back here within an hour?"

"Exactly! Hathor gifted me with a life-giving spell. When I cast it on you, you will be marked by her sign in henna."

"Her sign? The moon and the horns?"

"Exactly! You may remain here, in your own body, without any side effects until the henna disappears."

"That sounds fantastic!" Mercy bounced up on her toes. "Any clue how long it'll last?"

Khenti shrugged his broad shoulders. "It is difficult to say as time moves here in a different stream than in the mortal world."

Mercy chewed her lip and then grinned as she realized what she could do. "I know! I can bring my phone." She pulled it out of her pocket and flipped it on, though she made sure it was muted. It was almost fully charged. Mercy held it up so Khenti could see it. "The one part of this thing—it's called a phone—that will definitely work in your world is the clock. I can set it to tell me when a certain amount of time has passed."

His dark brows went up. "Time according to your world!"

"Exactly."

"Well." Khenti cleared his throat and suddenly looked adorably shy. "Mercy Goode, Green Witch and Gate Guardian, would you do me the honor of visiting my realm again?"

Mercy felt a thrill of excitement. "Would I? Hell yes! A vacay is exactly what I need."

"Now? Would you come now?"

"Absolutely. Everyone here is so busy chasing after my sister that they won't even notice I'm gone—and if they do wonder where I am it serves them right. They *should* worry about me for a change, instead of me always trying to make sure everyone else is okay."

Khenti nodded in understanding. "You do need a break, and I would appreciate the company. My day hasn't been pleasant, either."

"Problems with the gods?" Mercy asked.

Khenti moved his broad shoulders. "Demi-god, actually. My father is still visiting Osiris. I mentioned before that our relationship is rather difficult."

Mercy snorted. "I totally understand. *Rather difficult* also describes my family."

Khenti lifted his hand and offered it to the swirl of color that separated them. "Then take my hand, Mercy, and let us leave the troubles of both of our worlds to others for at least a short time."

Before she raised her hand to press through the barrier she said, "Hey, we don't know how long Hathor's magic will let me stay, but I really can't be gone too long. I gotta be back at school Monday. I'm pissed, but I don't want people to think I ran away." *Like Hunter,* she added silently.

"How long does that give you?" Khenti asked.

"The rest of today and all of tomorrow. As long as I'm back early the following day I'll make it to school just fine."

"Then two days it shall be. Join me, Mercy." He extended his hand.

"Gladly, Khenti." Mercy stepped forward, reached through the barrier between them, grasped his warm, calloused hand—and stepped through the glowing divide.

She drew a deep breath the moment she was completely in Khenti's world. The fragrance of exotic incense already seemed familiar, as did the vibrant colors that filled the beautiful chamber.

"Welcome to the Land of the Dead." Khenti smiled and bowed to her.

"Why, thank you ever so much!" Mercy tipped her head in her impression of a queenly nod. Then she caught sight of her arm, which was already beginning to turn gray. "What do you need for the spell that'll make this"—she pointed to her ashen skin—"go away?"

"That's easy. I have everything here that we need. Come to Hathor's statue."

Mercy walked with him to the statue of the kind-eyed, graceful goddess. She bowed, this time deeply and respectfully, before Hathor. "Hello, Goddess," she said. "Thank you so much for your gift. It's exactly what I needed today." The air around the statue swirled and the fragrance of lilacs and vanilla filled the room. Mercy gasped. "That's my perfume!"

"Hathor wears your fragrance. It pleases her greatly," said Khenti.

"Well, I'll definitely give her more. I always have some in my purse."

Mercy automatically reached for the big fringed boho bag that was usually slung over her shoulder. "Uh-oh. I left it in my world."

"Do you need to return for it?" Khenti asked.

"No! I'll be fine without it." She internally cringed at the thought of someone stealing her precious purse filled with everything, but she was in the ancient Egyptian Land of the Dead, and didn't want to waste one moment of her impromptu vacay. "What do we do now?"

"All you need do is to face Hathor's statue. I will conjure the spell. As soon as the henna appears the spell is set," said Khenti.

"Okay." Mercy turned from Khenti to face Hathor's statue. "Um, is it gonna hurt?"

Khenti stepped into the space behind her. He rested his hands gently on her shoulders. He was close enough to her for his breath to rustle her hair and make her shiver. "Have you never been hennaed, Green Witch?"

"No. There's not much of that going on in central Illinois. Ask me about beans and corn and football and I'm a pro."

"I will have many questions for you, but right now you should just look into the goddess's eyes," said Khenti.

Mercy pressed her lips together and nodded. She lifted her gaze to Hathor's eyes. They rested in the head of a cream-colored cow. Mercy was struck anew by the grace and intelligence of this image of the Egyptian goddess. As she stared, Khenti spoke the simple words of the spell.

"Lovely Hathor, Goddess of the Sky, of Women, of Fertility and Love
I collect the boon you granted me
From your domain—below and above
Allow Green Witch Mercy to truly be
Here with me, here with thee, here to see
The Realm of Osiris as you so decree!"

Khenti lifted his hands and brought them together in a deafening clap above her head. A shockwave of fragrant air flowed down against

Mercy's body. Her vision, still trained on Hathor's eyes, was suddenly obscured. She thought it was a little like being caught in a spiderweb, or maybe a giant funnel of cotton candy, but it wasn't painful or unpleasant. The air shivered over her body. It made her skin tingle with warmth.

And then the gossamer threads of magic that had swirled around her evaporated. Mercy blinked quickly as she tried to clear her vision. "Did it work?" she asked Khenti.

From behind her he laughed joyously. "Yes! Absolutely! Look at yourself, Mercy."

Mercy blinked several more times before she was able to focus. Her gaze shifted from the goddess to herself and she gasped. "Oh, Freya! This is beautiful!" Somehow in the middle of the magical threads, Hathor had changed Mercy's clothes. Instead of her sunflower dress she was wearing a brilliant turquoise blue linen gown. It was floor length and felt so soft against her skin it could have been made of water. A jeweled belt wrapped around her waist, highlighting her curves. The bodice was sleeveless and was cut deeply to show off her golden ankh—as well as another symbol—one that was newly drawn in rust-colored henna. It decorated her chest, with the curved tip of each of the goddess's horns reaching up to her neck. The large, center sun disc perfectly framed Mercy's ankh. Golden bracelets stamped with images of the bovine goddess clattered musically together as Mercy's fingers traced the pattern of the sign of Hathor's magic. "It's incredible! This is so, so much more than I expected."

Mercy stepped forward. She kissed her fingers and then touched them to the statue of Hathor. She bowed again, deeply. "Thank you, Goddess. I'll never forget your kindness. When I return to my world I'll burn incense to honor you, and I know my goddess, Freya, will be grateful for your kindness to her servant, as well." Then she straightened and turned to face Khenti—whose eyes widened as his mouth flopped open. "What?" She glanced down at her gorgeous goddess-given outfit to be sure her boob hadn't slipped out or anything. "Is something wrong?"

"No! There are many things that are right. Come, observe the rest of Hathor's gifts."

Khenti motioned for her to follow him to a golden plate that hung on one of the walls of the chamber. It was obviously supposed to represent the sun shining over a mural of a wide river. Khenti moved aside so Mercy could stand in front of the plate. She stared, not recognizing herself for a moment. And then she laughed with joy.

"Ohmygoddess! She did my makeup!" Heavy kohl framed her eyes and made them look bigger, highlighting their color, which the goddess had matched perfectly with the dress. Her lips were stained the blush of her cheeks. Golden scarab beetles dangled from her ears. "I feel kinda like Cinderella at the ball."

"Is that a good thing to be?" asked Khenti.

She grinned at him. "I'll tell you at midnight. Oh, crap! My phone!" Mercy looked around frantically and then felt a thump against her thigh. Her magnificent linen dress just happened to have a deep pocket, inside which was her phone. "Whew! Hathor doesn't miss anything, does she?"

"Not usually," said Khenti. "Now, I have only one thing left to do, and then we may leave this chamber."

Khenti returned to the rear area of the room where the glowing orb still swirled opal and mother of pearl. Resting against the wall beside it was his long, razor-tipped spear, which he retrieved. He lifted the spear high and then spoke a single word, *"PROTECT!,"* that battered Mercy's ears so that she cringed and stepped back as he brought the spear down on the marble floor. There was a thunderous *boom!* Khenti stepped back beside Mercy. His spear was stuck in the floor. It shuddered and then a sound like the wings of a flock of birds filled the chamber as the spear multiplied until it formed an intimidating wall that stood between them and the entry to Mercy's world.

"Now we may go." Khenti paused and added, "I apologize, Green Witch. I did not ask if you needed to perform a protective spell to watch the gates while you are not in your world."

Mercy's face flushed hot. She hadn't even thought about the gates! Then she mentally shook herself and met Khenti's dark eyes. "I don't need to worry about the gates. My sister keeps telling me that she can take care of them by herself—so this weekend they're all hers."

Khenti smiled. "Then, come. Allow me to show you my world." He offered her his arm.

Mercy took his arm. "I'm all yours! At least until Monday."

Twenty-six

"Why the hell are you going to the Booster Club's BBQ? You're not even on the team." Kirk's dad's sarcastic words echoed in his mind as he parked his Jeep at Goode Lake.

It hadn't mattered that Kirk had corrected him. He was definitely still on the team. Sure, he couldn't play. Yet. And of course that bitch had gotten him in so much trouble that he had fucking detention until school was out at the end of the month. But Coach hadn't said shit to him about not being on the team. Kirk Whitfield was still a Mustang.

"Dad, I'm going to the BBQ. I'm the team captain. I gotta be there."

His dad, already well into what he liked to call his Sunday case of beer, slurred a laugh. *"Whether Coach Jamison has given you the bad news yet or not, boy, you're no damn captain. But go ahead. Go out there. Just stop with that witch crap you keep trying to shovel on everyone. You already look like a big enough fool. When you gonna learn that if you have to teach a broad a lesson you do it without leaving any marks and you sure as hell don't break your hand in the process?"*

Kirk hadn't said anything. There wasn't a damn thing he could say.

He hadn't really expected his dad to believe him. The only thing his dad believed in was touchdowns and applause—and reliving through his son what he and Springsteen liked to call their glory days.

Kirk stepped on the emergency brake, opened the glove box, took out the bottle of pills he'd stashed there, and popped a quick Percocet. He swallowed it dry, ran his good hand through his hair, and then got out of the Jeep and followed the sounds of laughter and shouts to the picnic area—the same place they'd had the birthday party not long ago for the Goode bitches. Kirk's teeth ground together. He'd give anything to be able to go back to that night and break up with Mercy then and there.

"Whitfield! Get over here!" His buddy Derek's voice boomed across the picnic grounds and heads turned to gawk at Kirk as he headed to the volleyball net where the team and the varsity cheerleaders were dividing up to play.

Kirk pretended that the stares were what they used to be—envy and adoration from his town, his fans. He smiled and nodded at the parents who watched him with narrowed eyes. He was going to show them all that he wasn't, as his drunk of a dad had said, shoveling *that witch crap* on people. He was telling the truth. All he had to do was to get someone to listen to him. Then he'd figure out how to prove it.

Coach Jamison stepped into his path. "Mr. Whitfield, glad you showed."

Kirk stopped and forced an amiable smile on his face. "I wouldn't miss it, Coach. Anything for my team."

"Which means you're going to go to that anger management class I recommended."

Kirk pushed his uninjured hand into his jeans pocket to keep from balling it into a fist. "Sure, Coach," he lied. "Soon as school's out for the summer. Like I said—anything for my team."

The coach stepped closer to Kirk and lowered his voice. "I'm glad, son. Hitting a woman is unacceptable behavior. How's the hand feeling?"

Kirk lifted his splinted, bandage-swathed hand. "Doing just fine. Hardly hurts at all. Hey, Coach, I wanted to talk to you about an idea I have. I've been thinking that I should bulk up this summer. Really focus on lifting. I can come back in the fall a lot bigger, and could kick some serious butt on the line."

The coach wouldn't meet his eyes. "We'll see, Whitfield. You just focus on healing that hand and those anger management classes. You know, son, there are a lot of things more important than football—your integrity for one."

"I know, Coach. I totally agree with you."

"Excellent, Whitfield, good talk. I gotta go get ready for the big cake auction. We need all the cash we can get if the team's going to have new uniforms next season." Jamison patted Kirk on the shoulder and walked away.

Kirk was damn glad he'd popped that Percocet. Not only did it help the throbbing, unending pain in his hand, but it took the edge off of his anger enough that he didn't feel like he needed to grab the nearest picnic table and throw it at the coach's clueless head.

"Whitfield! Come get in this game!" Derek shouted.

How the fuck am I supposed to play volleyball with my left hand? Kirk waved his one good hand at Derek and motioned at the table of refreshments. "Go ahead and start. Gotta get something to drink!" Without hanging around to hear Derek whine at him any more, Kirk turned his back to his friend and headed for the table where moms were pouring lemonade and handing out burgers and hot dogs. *Too damn bad there's no beer.*

"Well, hello there, Kirk." Jarod Frazier's mom gave him a tight smile. "Would you like some lemonade and maybe something to eat? Good idea to keep your strength up so your hand can heal."

"Yeah, thanks, Mrs. Frazier. Got any dogs left?" Kirk took the plastic cup of lemonade she offered him and made himself take a big swig of the sour crap.

Mrs. Frazier looked over her shoulder at the grill, where members of the Booster Club were flipping burgers and dogs. "Fred, are more dogs ready yet?"

A man with a gut that swallowed his belt lifted long grill tongs. "Be just a few more minutes, Evelyn!"

"I'll get you that dog soon, Kirk."

"Thanks, Mrs. Frazier. I'll wait over here in the shade and drink your delicious lemonade." He flashed his signature smile at the frumpy, middle-aged woman. But unlike usual, she didn't respond with a blush and a giggle.

"I'll give you a shout when it's done" was all she said.

Kirk saluted her with his plastic cup before he backed into the shadows between two big oaks not far from the grills. He poured the disgusting lemonade on the ground and dropped the cup behind him. *What the fuck is wrong with everyone? It's like they actually think I did something wrong!*

The breeze shifted and brought grill smoke to him. Kirk coughed and ducked back behind one of the oaks, out of the hot dog–smelling cloud, and gossipy mom voices drifted to him.

"He was going to hit her! The principal's secretary, Mrs. Anthony, told me she saw the mirror. It was completely shattered."

"It's just awful. Well, you know his father is an abuser. It's hardly a surprise. The apple doesn't fall far from the tree."

"But it's crazy, isn't it? My Sarah told me she saw him chase that poor girl into the bathroom. And those twins just lost their mom."

"You want to know what's really crazy? Jana Ashley. Have you heard the insane stories she's telling?"

"No! What?"

"Well, I heard from Doris Sanders that she's saying that Satan has possessed her garage apartment."

Kirk held his breath, straining to hear their whispery voices.

"Is she serious?"

"As a heart attack. She went on and on about blood being everywhere. Apparently, she was hysterical."

"Well, I've always said she has those crazy eyes. Where is she?"

"Over there by the dock. Poor Jana. Cathy, her eyes are not crazy. We shouldn't judge her. Or at least not until we get the full story. I know. Let's invite her over for girls' night."

"Oh, good idea! We do need to hear the truth from her and then . . ."

Their voices faded as the wind died, but Kirk had heard everything he needed to hear. He quickly circumvented the refreshment table and headed to the dock where a lone woman was sitting in a director's chair that had MUSTANG FOOTBALL blazed on the back of it.

Kirk walked a little past Jax's mom before he stopped and stared out at the lake. He sighed loudly, bowed his shoulders, and swiped at his eyes.

"Kirk? Are you okay?"

Kirk jumped and turned quickly. "Oh, Mrs. Ashley! Sorry. I—uh—I didn't see you there."

"That's okay. I didn't mean to startle you." Mrs. Ashley rubbed the large gold crucifix she wore around her neck nervously between her thumb and forefinger.

"No problem. Actually, it's funny. I was just thinking about you."

"Me? Are you sure you don't mean my son?"

"No, I mean you, Mrs. Ashley. I was wondering about something, but I don't want to seem disrespectful, so I'm not real sure I can talk to you about it."

Mrs. Ashley sat up straighter. Her dark hair was cut in a graying mom bob and she was wearing khaki capris and a GOODEVILLE MUSTANGS T-shirt, which she tugged at with the hand that wasn't worrying her cross. "What is it, Kirk?"

"Well, I guess I'm just kinda shocked that a good Christian woman like you would let a witch live in your garage apartment."

Mrs. Ashley's muddy brown eyes widened. She leaned forward and lowered her voice. "Hunter Goode is no longer welcome in my garage *or* my home."

"Whew." Kirk blew out a long, exaggerated breath. "That's a relief.

I really don't want you—or Jax, of course—mixed up with her. Mrs. Ashley, I just found out some stuff that freaked me out pretty badly." He looked around to be sure no one was close to them before he continued. "I think she worships Satan."

"Oh, Kirk! I believe you are so right. Please! Tell me everything."

Kirk squatted next to her. "Okay, so, you know what everyone's saying about me punching the mirror and breaking my hand? Well, that's not what happened at all . . ."

Twenty-seven

The Land of the Dead was the most beautiful place Mercy had ever been—and so far they hadn't even gone outside the never-ending temple. Just when she thought there couldn't be anything more gorgeous than the room they'd just left, Mercy would turn a corner with Khenti and they'd come to another chamber, like the huge, domed room dedicated to the queens of Egypt, and she'd be blown away by its magnificence. Mercy felt as if she could've stayed in the temple forever, wandering around and gazing at wonders. Khenti even allowed her to peek into the incredible chamber where the newly dead waited to be judged. An endless line of people, who looked totally alive, stretched in a long, somber queue that snaked around a room where Mercy actually got to see the lovely ostrich goddess, Qebhet, as she tenderly brought the dead fresh water and kind words.

As she and Khenti were crossing a wide hallway made of polished golden stone a woman draped in see-through white linen whose skin was completely covered in golden scales stopped them. She nodded to

Mercy before she asked Khenti, "Gate Guardian, are you not going to attend the Beautiful Feast of the Valley Festival this season?"

"Thank you for the reminder, Hatmehit. That is one of my favorite festivals. My guest, the Green Witch Mercy and I will attend." He bowed to her.

The fish woman nodded magnanimously and turned to Mercy. "Well met, Green Witch Mercy."

"Hello," Mercy said. She followed Khenti's lead and bowed. "It's nice to meet you."

The woman's pouty, fishlike lips tilted up and she continued past them to disappear into one of the decorative chambers.

"Is that a fish goddess?" Mercy whispered.

"Yes." Khenti smiled. "She is widely worshipped in the Mendes Delta. I rarely see her here, but of course she would be attending the festival—the river does play an important part in it. Are you hungry?"

"Now that you mention it, I'm starving." Mercy took the phone out of her pocket and was shocked to see that it was Sunday afternoon. "Wait, I've been here for an entire day?" Quickly, she looked down at the henna sun disc and horns on her chest. None of it had faded, which made Mercy breathe a long sigh of relief.

"Time does pass differently here," said Khenti as he led her toward an opening in the golden hallway from which warm air fragranced with jasmine caused floor-to-ceiling curtains to billow. "Sometimes slower—sometimes faster—than in the mortal worlds."

"Worlds? Have you been to other worlds than Egypt?" Mercy breathed deeply of the perfumed breeze as they parted the curtains and left the temple to enter a courtyard filled with a riot of blooming jasmine that covered the walls, as well as an exquisite water feature that held purple lotus blooms the size of dinner plates.

"No, though I would love to."

"It'd be great if you could visit my world, although it's really nothing like . . ." Her words ran out as they moved from the fragrant courtyard to the landing at the top of a wide staircase made of creamy limestone. "Wow!" Mercy had to remind herself to close her mouth. The view that stretched before them was every bit as incredible as the endless temple. In Mercy's mind she'd imagined ancient Egypt, or at least Khenti's Underworld, to be sandy and hot—basically a desert. She'd been absolutely wrong.

To their right a wide river meandered lazily past the enormous temple. Both banks were lined with greenery—palms (doum!) and grasses and trees that were less familiar than the doum. Across the water colorful linen streamers waved like the wings of enormous, exotic birds. Framing the mighty river were homes built of clay stained sunset colors that ranged from sandy yellow to burnt orange. The homes all had rooftop gardens filled with flowers and more greenery. At the foot of the temple a wide limestone street was lined with open-air shops that were a cacophony of color. Flowers were everywhere! Mercy felt like a frustrated butterfly because she longed to flit between jasmine and chrysanthemum, poppy and rose, lotus and daisy—as well as many flowers she couldn't name.

Even from their perch above it all delicious scents of baking bread lifted to mingle with spices and the sweetness of blooming flowers. Among everything were people! The women were dressed in diaphanous dresses in the same style as Mercy's goddess-gifted clothes. Their jewelry caught the light of the brilliant sun and twinkled and winked enticingly. Their eyes were heavily lined like Mercy's, too, though many had additional swirls and symbols painted all the way to their temples. The men wore either long, pleated skirts or shorter, more military versions in leather like Khenti. Also like her companion, they were mostly bare chested or wore open, linen vests. They, too, often lined their eyes with kohl and many wore heavily bejeweled neck collars.

When Mercy finally tore her gaze from the wonders she found Khenti watching her with a knowing smile. "It's beautiful, isn't it?"

"I don't have enough words to describe how wonderful it all is. I want to go everywhere at once—look at everything at once!"

He laughed. "And you're hungry?"

She grinned at him. "Starving! What's for dinner?" She paused and added, "Um, I don't eat meat. I hope that's okay here."

"Absolutely!" They made their way down the stairs as Khenti continued, "How does flatbread stuffed with dates, raisins, honey, and goat cheese sound to you?"

"Super yummy!"

"Then come, my favorite bakery is just down the street." Khenti offered her his arm again. She threaded hers through his. She liked touching him. His arm was strong and warm, and even though he'd offered it to her frequently during her tour of the temple, he hadn't tried to slip his arm around her, or stared at her boobs, or done any of the number of invasive, annoying things someone like Kirk Whitfield would continually try.

Mercy felt safe and relaxed with Khenti—and she liked both feelings.

She also liked how the people of this realm interacted with him. Everywhere they went, men and women greeted him with respectful bows, but they also smiled at Khenti and called his name. If Khenti paused to speak more than a simple hello to anyone, he introduced her like he had to the fish goddess, as Green Witch Mercy—or sometimes as my friend, the Green Witch Mercy.

She could tell by the smiles and warm hellos they turned on her that Khenti was well liked and that they were comfortable around her demi-god friend.

"Khenti." She lowered her voice and he tilted his head to her so that he could hear her. "Are all of these people, um, *dead*?"

Khenti's laughter had the people within hearing distance smiling in response. "Yes." He kept his voice low, though it was filled with good humor. "That is why this is called the Land of the Dead."

Mercy stared around them. No one looked dead. No one. There were even children playing in a fountain from which a jeweled phoenix looked as if it could take flight at any moment, but instead of flames shooting around it water danced musically against the blue basin from which it perched.

"Well, I know that, but everyone looks so alive," she whispered.

"That is because the Underworld is alive. It is simply a different realm than the mortal one. These people you see around us—they wrote in detail in each of their Books of the Dead exactly how they wanted to spend their eternities. That is why you see such color and joy and vibrancy. They asked for this, for their city by the Nile, and were judged worthy. The result is an infinite mixture of beauty, which can only be echoed in the mortal world, though never matched."

"That's lovely," said Mercy. "But, um, what happens if they aren't judged worthy? Is there, like, a bad part of the Land of the Dead?"

His dark eyes stopped sparkling with humor. "There is. You will never see Duat. It is a place of chaos, inhabited by demons who torment those who lived evil mortal lives."

Mercy shivered at his intensity. "Sounds like Hell."

"Yes." His expression relaxed into his familiar smile. "But you shall never know it. Ah! Here we are. I believe you will love this stuffed bread. And beer? You must try our beer!"

"Definitely! I want to try everything. Well, except exploring Duat, of course."

"Of course," Khenti agreed. He quickly got two thick, warm pastries that reminded Mercy of hand pies, and two big, clay mugs filled with cloudy beer that tasted rich and tart and went perfectly with the pies. As they nibbled on the food and sipped beer they made their way down a winding limestone path that led to a large patio that looked out over the amazingly decorated river. There, with a dozen or so other people, they sat on a trestle table and ate as they gazed out at the water.

"Is that really a copy of the Nile?" Mercy asked.

"Yes. Well, it would be more accurate to say that the river that exists in the mortal world is a copy of this one. Everything in mortal Egypt originated here—the food, the art, the rivers, even the temples. They are all just lesser versions of that which the gods created and passed on to mortals through dreams and omens that inspired them to attempt to mimic what flourishes in the Land of the Dead," Khenti explained. "For instance, that jeweled belt you're wearing cannot be found in mortal Egypt. What could be found is a dyed or beaded version inspired by it."

"That's amazing. Does it go both ways? Do things that happen in mortal Egypt influence anything here?"

"Yes, but not always in such a positive manner." He glanced to their right where a beautiful barge was just coming into view. On it there was a raised platform where a tall, muscular man stood. His skin was russet and gleamed in the sun. His head wasn't human—it was a ram, with alabaster fur and golden horns that curled majestically. Beautiful women, clothed only from their waists down, waved wide, feathered fans. More bare-breasted women played a kind of instrument that looked like decorative rattles and sounded like wind blowing through water reeds. All along the river people cheered and tossed chrysanthemum petals into the water. "That is Amun, God of the Sun. This is his festival. He will ride down the river to the Valley of the Dead, where he will feast with his subjects until sunrise tomorrow, then he will return to this temple. In the mortal realm they mimic this festival—and sometimes Amun joins them—in disguise, of course. But should mortals forget Amun's Beautiful Feast of the Valley Festival, and not honor the god properly, Amun would know. It would displease him, and the consequences of his displeasure would be felt throughout the land."

Mercy washed down her last bite of pie with beer before asking, "Two questions. First, you mean if Amun is pissed he'd do something awful to mortal Egypt?"

Khenti nodded somberly. "Yes, he could hide the sun and make crops fail."

"That'd definitely be awful. Second question, you said sometimes Amun joins the mortals during his festival, but he disguises himself.

Why? I thought Egyptians were used to people who have the heads of animals and such."

"Oh, his visage is not why he disguises himself. It is often not wise for mortals to mix with the gods." His grin turned sardonic. "Believe me—I am the product of a demi-god mixing with a mortal."

"But you seem to have turned out okay," said Mercy.

Khenti shrugged. "You should tell my father that."

Mercy spoke automatically. "I totally would!"

Khenti's expression lost all lightness and humor. "No, Mercy. If you ever meet Upuant, which you will not, it would be best to bow and say nothing."

Mercy touched his arm. "Is he really that bad?"

"He is." Khenti spoke softly. "Upuant is unhappy, so he makes those around him unhappy. I believe it is because he has never accepted the fact that his mother was mortal."

"But your mom's mortal, and he married her, right?"

"He bedded her and conceived me. He did not marry her." His voice was tight and his jaw clenched and unclenched. "He expected my mother to give me up at birth—to surrender me to the gods as his mortal mother did him—but Meryt refused." His voice changed and filled with warmth. "She loved me and insisted on raising me. It was only after she died that I was presented to the gods and came to be Gate Guardian in the Land of the Dead. Even now that my mother and I both reside in this world, he forbids me from seeing her. He will not even allow me to know where she is."

"I'm sorry," Mercy said softly. "My dad has never been in my life, but like you, my mom made up for it. She was everything."

Khenti's hand covered hers. "I understand that completely."

"Thanks for explaining all of that to me." Mercy paused and took another sip of her beer. "It's so amazing that what happens here is more or less echoed in your mortal realm—and vice versa. It's cool that everything is so connected that—" Mercy's words cut off as realization flooded her with images—the ravens, Creepy Chuck getting worse and worse, Kirk's out-of-control anger, the dead grass expanding from the doums, and finally the two grown men who were suddenly so angry that they had a fistfight, but only when they were close to the palms *that she had just tried to heal.* "Oh, Goddess! All the changes—all the bad stuff that's been happening since Mom was killed and the gates have started to crumble . . ."

"What is it, Mercy? What are you saying?" Khenti's dark eyes were filled with concern.

As the words exploded from Mercy she felt the rightness of them, like a puzzle piece finally falling into place. "I think whatever is wrong with the trees and the gates is seeping out into town! So, so much bad stuff has happened and keeps happening. Shit! It's like you just said—the influence goes both ways. This might even be the reason Hunter and I have been so pissed at each other. Khenti, I have to go back. Now! I have to tell Xena and Hunter. This is so, so bad!"

Suddenly there was a commotion around them as the people who had been sitting rushed to stand. They quickly turned from the river, and bowed low. Those who were standing hastily joined them. Until that moment the atmosphere had been celebratory. Men and women, like Mercy and Khenti, ate and drank, laughed and cheered on the approaching barge. But as the crowd bowed and went silent, the air became charged with tension—like how it feels just before an ominous sky releases thunder and lightning and rain. Mercy looked around the crowded patio, trying to see what had caused the change.

A man, several heads taller than anyone else in the crowd, strode onto the patio. He was wearing golden armor and carried a wicked-looking spear that had razor-tipped points on both ends. He was massive—thick muscles bunched under terra-cotta brown skin. Between his shoulders was the ferocious head of a jackal in shades of tan and rust and red. His eyes were dark, with red pupils. He was followed by two rows of warriors who were heavily armed. They appeared human, but each of them wore the mask of a red jackal.

Beside her she felt Khenti's body tense. "Stand. Bow. Say nothing," he whispered urgently as he stood. "I shall get you back to the palace as soon as he is gone."

Reluctantly, Mercy stood beside him as the jackal-headed god's ruby eyes searched the crowd, landing on Khenti, who bowed low. Mercy joined him, holding the bow as long as Khenti. When he finally straightened, she did as well—and found herself looking up into the bestial face of the demi-god.

"Khenti! I went to the gate chamber to speak with you and found your post abandoned. And here you are, reveling with commoners and—" The creature leaned forward toward Mercy. His nostrils flared as he breathed in her scent. "What is a living mortal doing at the side of my son in the Land of the Dead?"

Khenti stepped protectively closer to Mercy. "Upuant, Right Hand of Osiris, I present to you the magnificent Green Witch Mercy, of the mortal realm called Goodeville."

Mercy bowed deeply again. When she straightened she forced a friendly expression on her face, even though Upuant was terrifyingly close—and huge—and clearly super pissed. "It is an honor to meet Khenti's father."

The jackal's lip lifted in a sneer. He said nothing in response, but skewered his son with his red gaze. "Khenti, explain yourself!"

Twenty-eight

Hunter had spent the weekend being smothered by Jax and Kylie when the only thing she'd wanted to do was go, *alone,* to each of the trees and cast the REALMS spell from her spellbook. She could have snuck out of Kylie's at night, and she almost had, but fear strangled that idea the moment it took root. Amphitrite was still near, still watching, and darkness provided the perfect cover for the unhinged goddess. Hunter was afraid she wouldn't be able to fight off the queen of the sea again.

So, Hunter let her friends hold her hostage in the basement of Kylie's McMansion surrounded by the IGA's entire junk food aisle. They *kept her mind off things* with board games and movies and a vintage Nintendo that Kylie's mom had had since she was a kid.

Jax opened a bag of Cheetos and plopped down onto the sectional next to Kylie. "H, I have to tell you something." He and Kylie shared a look Hunter couldn't quite place before he continued. "It's about my mom, and, uh, what she says happened the other day."

Hunter's insides went cold and the beanbag made a loud *shh shh* as she shifted her weight.

Kylie tugged on the zipper of the blue onesie she'd insisted she and Hunter each wear. "Just know that we don't believe any of it. Not a word."

The tips of Hunter's fingers were ice as she rested her hands against her legs. "What did she say?" she asked, gritting her teeth to keep them from chattering.

Jax looked down at the open bag of Cheetos. "I'm just going to say it and then it'll be out there, and we can all move on."

Kylie wrapped her fingers around his and squeezed.

"My mom said that she heard noises coming from your place and, when she went out to check, you were standing on the bed, covered in blood and drawing satanic figures on your body and the walls." He finished recounting his mother's tale and looked up. "I'm so sorry, Hunter. I don't know why she'd make up such a twisted lie."

Hunter pressed her palm against the scar that rested just beneath her onesie. "Oh." She breathed, unsure of what to say or how to get her tongue to form the truth.

Kylie smoothed her braid between her fingers. "We definitely don't have to talk about it."

"It's okay." Hunter wasn't sure if she'd spoken, but Jax's grip tightened on the bag of snacks.

"It's not okay." The bag crinkled under his hand. "If she didn't want you there, she could've said no when I asked her. She didn't need to make up something so crazy."

Kylie absentmindedly picked at the fuzzy pillow next to her as she spoke. "I'm telling you, it's all Mike Whitfield's fault. He and Kirk are so desperate to blame someone for Kirk's ridiculousness, and they've set their sights on Hunter." She crossed her arms over her chest and shook her head. "This town is full of sheeple." She bit her lip and frowned. "No offense, Jax."

"No, I agree with you." He hung his head and stuffed a Cheeto into his mouth. "My mother is a sheeple."

Hunter couldn't move. She was a cold spot, the prelude to a ghost.

Footsteps pounded the stairs behind her, and Hunter craned her neck and offered a polite smile to the woman who'd saved her.

Kylie's mom's round cheeks dimpled as she returned the grin. Then, her dark brown eyes focused on her daughter. "Time for Jax to leave." The air conditioner switched on and the ruffled hem of her shorts fluttered around her full legs. "And, girls, you have school in the morning. Try not to stay up too late."

"Thanks, Ms. York." Hunter waved as Kylie's mom padded up the stairs. She hadn't hesitated when Kylie had told her that Hunter would be staying with them for a while. She'd simply looked up from the mountains of paper that covered her desk and asked what they wanted to order for dinner. According to Kylie, when her hotshot lawyer mother left her skeezy personal injury attorney father and moved her two daughters from Chicago to Goodeville, she'd built this giant house for her kids and their friends. Having Hunter stay with them wasn't odd. To Ms. York, it was expected.

Hunter rested her head against the beanbag chair and stared at the planked wood ceiling while Kylie and Jax exchanged giggles and saliva. Moments later, a shadow fell over her, and Hunter refocused on Jax as he kicked the side of the beanbag.

"I really am sorry, H." He stuffed his hands into his pockets and dug the toe of his shoe into the side of the beanbag chair. "I'll make this right. Promise."

"Yeah," Hunter whispered to his back as he headed for the stairs. "Me too."

Eventually, Hunter and Kylie made their way upstairs and into Kylie's bedroom that was filled with cheer awards and the pale-yellow glitter paint she'd chosen when she was nine. The redhead had stuffed herself under her fluffy down comforter and Hunter crawled onto the air mattress and under the soft blankets they'd carried in from the guest room, *true sleepover style* as Kylie had put it. Hunter spent the next hour lying on the air mattress on the floor next to Kylie's bed listening to her new friend go on and on about Jax and how perfect he was and how she'd never imagined she could feel so strongly about someone so quickly. It didn't bother Hunter. Her spell was partially to blame. It had found Kylie's desire to make Hunter's best friend her beau and pulled it to the surface like a sunken treasure chest.

As Kylie's excitement blurred into the slow, deep breath of sleep, Hunter rolled to her side and nuzzled the soft blankets under her chin. Tomorrow was school, and right now, school was freedom.

Twenty-nine

Hunter had nearly made it through her first day back at school since she'd magically broken Kirk's hand and splashed blood all over herself and her room like something out of *Carrie* without anything horrible taking place. Well, that wasn't completely true. Whispers flew around her as she drifted like a wraith from class to class, itching to get through her final period and to the freedom that football and cheer practice provided. She would have skipped, but with the Goodeville High School policy being as terrible as it was, she and Mercy were quickly running out of absences that wouldn't force them into summer school. Like anyone should be punished for exceeding the predetermined number of absences related to a family member's death. But sure enough, that line was in the Goodeville High handbook and enforced by a principal as empathetic as a pencil sharpener.

Shuffling down the hall on the way to her English class, Hunter slid her hand into the faux leather crossbody bag she'd borrowed from Kylie. She stroked the soft fur cover of her spellbook. Its swollenness had gone down after she'd banished Amphitrite, and the cover had faded from beet red to a light cardinal, but there was still more than enough blood to perform the spell at each gate.

As she walked into her English class, Hunter kept her eyes fixed on the gray scuff mark on the toe of her boot and tried her best to ignore the hushed comments that bit at her ears like fleas. She plopped the purse onto her desk and only looked up after her legs had disappeared under the wood. Her gaze swept over Mr. Cormican, who sat at his desk mindlessly scratching his dark beard with one hand while he tapped at his keyboard with the other. Her sister's seat was empty. Hunter looked over her shoulder at the open classroom door. A few students hurried past in their rush to beat the bell, but not Mercy.

Hunter pulled her phone from the pocket of her shorts and checked her notifications. The group text with Jax and Kylie had blown up toward the end of last period. Hunter ignored the alerts and opened the chain of messages she shared with her sister. She wasn't sure what she expected to find. At the lake, Mercy had made it clear that she didn't want anything to do with Hunter's problems. But it was odd for her twin to miss school. Not only did they have few remaining no-show days, but Mercy was also the queen of Goodeville High social hour. Maybe not so much now since Kirk had poisoned the waters against the Goode twins, but she still had friends and a need to socialize that Hunter would never understand. At the very least, she expected Mercy to send her some self-involved text about needing a mental health day. Hunter could almost hear her sister's long-winded explanation for ditching school.

You have put me through so much, Hunter. I just need a day alone to sort through my feelings. Self-care doesn't just benefit me, you know. It helps heal all of my relationships.

"Whatever," Hunter grumbled to the imaginary version of her sister and slipped her phone back into her pocket. Mercy could pout all she wanted. Hunter didn't have time to baby her sister's ego. She was the one in actual danger. She was also the one who would seal the gates and fix the trees. Now *those* were real reasons to skip school.

Thirty

The last school period felt like years. Hunter's legs bounced under her desk and she chewed on what was left of her nails as she stared at the clock and ignored the lively debate around her on the responsibilities of literature in the twenty-first century. Hunter had enough responsibilities for this century and the next combined. Thankfully, she'd cross a big one off her list as soon as she made it to her house and collected the tarot cards she never should have left behind.

Finally, the clock flashed 3:15. Hunter was out of her seat before the bell rang. Her classmates gave her a wide berth as she leapt from her desk and raced to the door, her footsteps punctuated by the shrill *ding ding ding ding* of the final school bell. She jogged toward her locker as she sent a quick message to Jax and Kylie.

Have to stop by the house. See you after practice.

Luckily, she didn't need to wait for a ride to her house. The sparks of adrenaline that zapped every inch of her legs could carry her for miles. Plus, the Goode's ancestral home wasn't a long walk from the school.

She turned down the hall to her locker and exhaled the anxiety that had hardened her lungs. Kirk and his gang were nowhere to be found. Even if they didn't believe Kirk's account of what had happened, maybe they'd all learned to leave her alone.

Hunter brushed past her locker neighbors and spun the dial on the narrow metal box. She'd had the same locker combination, the date she and Mercy were born, and the same locker since eighth grade when she'd finally been assigned a locker on the top row instead of the bottom. Hunter dug through the purse for the papers and pens she could dump back into her locker as the metal door groaned open. She froze, a handful of highlighters poised for deposit. The highlighters clattered against the floor as she sucked in a breath and slammed her locker shut.

Alex Feretto, who'd had the locker next to hers since freshman year, tapped Hunter's elbow. "Dropped these," she said, shaking out her blond bangs as she held up the highlighters.

Hunter cleared her throat and offered a smile that was more a slight twitch of her lips as she grabbed the neon writing utensils and stuffed them back into her purse. Alex said a few more words that Hunter couldn't hear over her own hammering pulse before Alex tossed her backpack over her shoulder and disappeared around the corner.

Hunter's breath stored in her chest as she waited for the last person to abandon the wide hallway and the steady *squeak squeak* of shoes against the tile to vanish behind the loud *clink* of the school's heavy metal doors. She let it out in a slow hiss as she faced her locker. With trembling fingers, she pulled the latch and winced at the door's ominous groan. Hunter bit down on the inside of her cheek as the contents of her locker met the harsh hallway light. A naked Barbie stood in the center, its feet melted and affixed to a small square of wood. Red and orange construction paper flames twisted around its partially melted, ash-streaked legs. Hunter pressed her fingers against her lips as she read the words scrawled in black Sharpie across its bare torso.

Thou shalt not suffer a witch to live. And you're next.

Hunter's eyes stopped on the doll's face. Its long black hair was hacked off and singed around its pointed chin, and its expression melted into an unreadable blur of soot.

She closed her locker and took a step away from the wall of metal and the threat that someone had hidden inside. No, not *someone.*

"Kirk." Hunter breathed.

I'll burn you for this, Witch.

Once again, his words echoed through her mind as she raced down the hall and away from campus. Hunter's chest burned and her shins ached with each hard *thump thump* of her boots against the pavement. She'd made it all the way to the alley behind Main Street before she slowed to a stop. She covered her face with both hands and screamed into her palms.

Pain needled against her fresh scar as sea breeze dusted her neck and raised the hairs on the backs of her arms. *"Looks like you're in a bit of a tight spot."*

Hunter clutched her purse to her chest and whirled around. Amphitrite leaned against Glitter and Glue's painted brick, her cerulean skin aglow in the afternoon sun.

Hunter took a step back. "You can't be here."

"I can be wherever I'd like," she said with a flourish of her thin hands.

Hunter's fingers found the thick scar beneath her shirt as she chewed on unspoken words.

"Don't worry, Witch. The mortals cannot see me." Amphitrite flicked droplets of water at a fly buzzing near her head. *"I won't allow it."*

"You and me in an alley behind Main Street." Hunter nearly choked on a laugh. "Other people seeing you is the last thing I'm worried about."

"It shouldn't be. With everything you've been up to, truly the last thing *you need is to be seen with a creature as dazzling and otherworldly as I."* The goddess pressed herself away from the white brick and walked past Hunter as if they were friends out for a stroll. *"I suppose it wouldn't be great if you were spotted talking to yourself, either."*

Hunter whipped her head from side to side and stared up and down the length of the street. No employees were outside, but Hunter took out her phone and pressed it against her ear for safe measure.

"We were getting too close." Amphitrite continued as she glided down the sidewalk. *"I see that now."* She paused and glanced over her shoulder at Hunter. *"You taught me a valuable lesson, Witch. I only hope that I can return the favor."*

Hunter kept her distance from the goddess while she spoke into her phone. "I've experienced how you teach lessons. Not interested."

"I suppose I was a bit harsh."

Hunter stopped in front of a dumpster and gawked at Amphitrite and the magical waves that propelled her into the middle of the narrow street. "*Harsh?* You could have killed me."

A car sped down the alleyway and through the invisible goddess who stood in the middle of it. Water burst against the windshield. Hunter clapped her hand over her mouth. Amphitrite was gone. Red brake lights illuminated, and the car screeched to a stop. The door opened, and the car rocked as a man Hunter didn't recognize climbed out of the driver's seat.

"You think throwing water balloons at cars is funny?"

With her phone gripped in one hand, she held both of them out as evidence. "I didn't throw anything."

His cowboy boots knocked against the concrete as he walked to the back of his car. "What are you hiding in there?" He hooked his thumbs around his belt loops and jerked his stubbled chin toward Hunter's purse.

Hunter crossed her arms over her chest. "That's none of your business."

He removed his hat, wiped the sweat from his bald scalp, and tugged it back on. "Well, I do see how that would be an invasion of your personal space. My apologies." He waggled his finger in her direction and added, "Try not to be a menace, there, young lady. You have your whole life—" He coughed, and water dribbled from between his lips.

It splatted against the pavement as another round of wet coughs sent his hands around his throat. Water spurted from his mouth like a fire-hose.

Amphitrite slid out of the open car door. Her laughter was trains crashing as she drifted over to the man. His knees slammed against the wet pavement and water continued to spew from his open mouth.

"Stop!" Hunter screamed. "Let him go!"

"I want something in return."

Hunter shook her head.

Amphitrite looked down at the man and hiked her narrow shoulders. *"Then he dies."*

"What?" Hunter bit out.

Amphitrite cupped her hand around her ear and leaned forward as the man's hands splashed into the growing puddle.

Heat built within Hunter and her palms itched for the power of the blood that waited in the purse pressed against her side. But she needed that blood for the trees. Without it, she didn't have a hope of sealing the gates.

"What do you want, Amphitrite?" Hunter shouted.

"A nicer tone, to start." She adjusted her crown and brushed her hair over her shoulders. *"And you, Hunter Goode, my young witch."*

"You have me."

Amphitrite lifted her skirts and stepped over the man, kicking his ball cap as she passed. *"Yes, but there's a distance now."* She motioned toward Hunter's stomach. *"I know I can't be allowed back* in *as this type of banishment spell is nearly impossible to undo, but I want to be included. Let me help you with the realms."* She pressed her palms together as if praying. *"Please, Witch. I will use my power to assist. The only payment I require is you. Don't turn your back on me, Hunter."*

Hunter's heart pounded in her throat and her gaze rested on the man behind Amphitrite. His lips had begun to turn blue and the color had drained from his cheeks.

"Yes!" The word tore from her dry throat as a harsh bark. "Just let him go!"

Amphitrite snapped her fingers and the rush of water ceased. *"Meet you at the cherry tree. Go back on your word again and I won't be so forgiving."* Another snap of her fingers and the puddle vanished.

The man stood. He pressed his hands against his chest and slid them down the front of his body.

"Are you okay?" Hunter rushed forward, but he jerked away.

Tied to Amphitrite, this was now her fate. She'd forever walk this earth alone, destruction and fear in her wake.

He said nothing as he ran to his car and skidded away. Hunter picked up his ball cap and set it on top of the dumpster. Whether he knew it or not, she had saved him. She should feel good about that. Instead, a piercing ache sat in her stomach like broken glass.

This didn't change Hunter's plan. Until she found a way to banish Amphitrite for good, the vengeful goddess would always be watching. No, this didn't change her tactic one bit. She quickened her pace and rounded Honey Bees Children's Boutique, the final Main Street business, and started through the small field of wildflowers that separated her house from the bustling section of the street.

Hunter brushed her fingers along the delicate petals of white and purple daisies as she finalized what she would say once she got to her house. She paused as a grasshopper leapt from one side of the path to the other. Actually, Amphitrite *had* changed her plan. The goddess had made it *better.* How anything Amphitrite touched could come out improved was a mystery to Hunter, but somehow it had.

"Double trouble," Hunter whispered to the wind and ran toward her driveway.

Thirty-one

"Father, as you are aware, I have never abandoned my post," Khenti said. "You were there, so you saw that my spear shields the gate in my absence. I would know should any being try to breach it and I would return immediately." He gestured at their table. "Come, join us. I'm sure Mercy would like to hear stories of Amun from the mighty Upuant, who has known him for uncounted generations."

Mercy wasn't as sure. Though she was surprised—and horrified—by how expressive the jackal face was. The demi-god's disgust was undeniable in the glance he gave her before he turned his massive body so that she looked at his broad back.

"I have no time for such frivolities. How is she here, in our realm?" Upuant shot the question at his son.

"Mercy is here as a guest of Hathor. You see she is clearly marked by the goddess's divine symbol."

Mercy had to resist the urge to shrink behind Khenti as his father's eye raked over her body, stopping to focus on her chest and the sun disc between mighty horns that rested there.

"Hathor." Upuant growled the name. "That goddess meddles too much."

"Hathor does not meddle," Khenti corrected. "She is Goddess of Women—Mercy is a woman, and a powerful witch in her world. That she has found Hathor's favor is not surprising."

"I suppose it is no more surprising than my son simpering after a goddess when he should worship a god like the divine Amun or the powerful Osiris."

Around them the people pretended to return to their food and merriment, but the more Upuant spoke of Hathor, the more Mercy noticed that the women began to whisper to one another, and though the men didn't look directly at the demi-god they frowned and were stonily silent.

"I must protest the disrespect you show Hathor." Khenti's words were clipped.

Upuant moved his hand as if brushing away something dirty. "Hathor is unimportant. What is important is that my son uphold his duty as Guardian of the Gate."

"I have never shirked my duty," Khenti said. "Nor will I ever."

Mercy stood close enough to Khenti to feel his body tense. She wanted to reach out—to touch his arm and comfort him. His dad was clearly as horrible as he'd described—and most definitely a misogynist as well as a bully, but she was not in her world. Upuant, no matter how much of a jerk, was a demi-god here and right hand to the god who ruled the entire Land of the Dead. So she chewed her lip to keep her mouth shut and silently hoped Upuant would go away. Soon.

Upuant's bark of laughter was cruel and devoid of humor. "That is what you do now. You choose revelry and dalliance with a mortal whore instead of your duty."

"Hey! I am *not* a whore!" The words spilled from Mercy before she could stop them.

Slowly, the jackal's head swiveled to pierce her with his reddened gaze. "Did I grant you leave to speak, mortal?"

Before Mercy could respond Khenti stepped between his father and her. "You insult my friend and Hathor's guest. There is no reason for your rudeness. I only attend the festival, as is my right as a citizen of the Land of the Dead."

Upuant towered over his son as he shouted at him. "I brought you here. I made you Gatekeeper, but your mother spoiled you—made you more human than god. I knew I should not have left you with her so long. *Weak!* Her emotions made you weak!"

Khenti's face drained of color. He squared his shoulders and stepped forward, which forced Upuant to shuffle back. "You will not disrespect my mother. She taught me things you are incapable of understanding—like that love and compassion aren't weakness, but an integral part of a life fully lived. Without them a person becomes cruel, shallow, bitter, and lonely—without them a person becomes *you,* Father."

The people on the patio now stared openly at Upuant. Some whispered. Some shook their heads. Other turned and walked away as they sent the demi-god disgusted looks over their shoulders. Mercy watched the jackal head. She saw his red eyes flick around at the crowd. When he'd arrived he'd been oblivious to the watching dead, but no more. Now he realized that his exchange with his son was being observed—and public sentiment was clearly on Khenti's side. Upuant's lips lifted as he bared his teeth at his son and Mercy braced herself. It did not surprise her that Upuant was a god who wouldn't tolerate being embarrassed—especially not by the son he so clearly disliked.

"You dare speak to me thus!" Upuant stepped forward, almost bumping his muscular chest into his son. "I have made you everything you are! Given you everything you have!"

"Not true!" Khenti stood his ground as he glared up at his father. "My mother made me who I am, and Osiris fulfilled my destiny by naming me Guardian of the Gate. The only thing you've ever given me is a spark of immortality and the misery of knowing no matter what I do, no matter how hard I try, I will never be the son you wish you had."

"I should have done this long ago when I first observed your mortal weakness." Upuant lifted his enormous spear and something dark blotted out the brilliant yellow sun. It was like boiling tar in the air, rolling and twisting around the demi-god's weapon. "I deny you, Khenti, son of Meryt. Henceforth you are no child of mind. I take my blood from you—and with it that spark of immortality you shun."

Mercy gasped in horror as Khenti doubled over, as if his father had punched him in his stomach.

"And because you are no longer a demi-god, I strip from you what Osiris gifted you with—henceforth, you are no longer Gatekeeper of the Land of the Dead!"

Khenti's body jerked in agony again and Mercy wrapped her arm around his waist, lending him her strength so that he didn't crumple to his knees. She looked up at the malevolent jackal-headed demi-god and was filled with rage and arrogance. She didn't pause to think—Mercy only acted. She focused and felt the warm limestone under her feet and thought of the verdant plants that filled the city and framed the immense river. She was rewarded by a zap of power she drew up through her feet. It sizzled along her spine. She lifted the hand that wasn't supporting Khenti, and in a voice filled with power she did something she'd never done and before that moment had believed she would never have to do—Mercy Anne Goode hexed someone.

"Three by three by mystical, magical number three.
Land of the Dead—hear my plea
Green Witch I am, Gate Guardian I be
Return to Upuant the harm he dispenses with such glee
Three times three return it to he
Three times three return it to he
Three times three return it to he
Upuant, hexed you shall forevermore be!"

Mercy coiled the power lent to her by the green growing things all around them. Emerald light shimmered in the palm of her hand, and like it was a magical, glowing baseball she threw it at Upuant.

Upuant roared as it struck his jackal face, and he staggered back. Then he raised his spear higher and roared, *"Witch and son no more, in the name of divine Osiris thou art banished!"* The demi-god drove his spear down so that it hit the limestone with a thunderous crack, which opened to expose a maw of darkness. With a motion so quick it blurred, Upuant leapt across the darkness, and shoved Khenti, so that his son, along with Mercy, fell into the pit.

Mercy clung to Khenti as they fell. She had never been so completely terrified in her life—not even when the Fenrir had torn from the tree and attacked them. She hadn't realized that night that she would lose her mother, hadn't understood the danger she'd been in. But then, the moment she fell with Khenti, Mercy was completely aware that her world, her entire life as she had known it, had ended.

It seemed they fell a long time—or maybe only a heartbeat—and then they hit sand and Mercy could do nothing but fight for breath and try to blink her eyes clear of tears so she could see.

"Mercy!" Khenti lifted her so that she rested half in his lap, half on warm sand. "Mercy! Are you hurt?"

She shook her head and coughed, finally able to gulp air. She wiped her eyes. Her voice shook almost as hard as her trembling body. "I—I d-don't know!"

"Breathe, just breathe with me. Look at me, Mercy. In and out . . . in and out."

Mercy focused on Khenti's dark, compassionate eyes and she breathed with him. Her vision cleared and she was able to sit by herself. She stared at a world drastically different than the land they had just left.

Nothing was green. Dunes waved around them, like the sand was water swept forward by a never-ending tide. The sky above them was bruised, as if a Midwest thunderstorm brewed, but there was no hint of rain in the hot air, though humidity pressed stickily against her skin.

"Where are we?"

Khenti took her shoulders in his hands. "Upuant has banished us."

"Well, yeah, I heard him. But to where?"

"Duat," Khenti said.

Mercy's stomach clenched and she had to swallow several times before she could be sure she wasn't going to puke. "But Duat is your Hell."

Khenti nodded somberly. "Yes."

Mercy pushed away from him and stood. "No! I can't be in Hell! I'm not even dead. Plus, I haven't been perfect, but I'm not a bad person. When I die Freya is going to welcome me to the Summerlands. My mom will be there. My sister will be there. *My damn cat will be there.* I don't belong here! Plus, I have to get home! I have to tell Hunter and Xena what's going on—that the sickness the gates have is poisoning our town!" Mercy realized she was hyperventilating when she couldn't yell anymore, when she couldn't say anything at all.

Khenti stood and took her into his arms. He held her tightly as he murmured, "I know, Mercy. I know. I will fix this. I will make this right. I will get you home. Trust me. Please, please trust me."

Mercy clung to him. He was solid and warm and strong. *This is his world. He can get us out.* Mercy's breathing slowed and became normal. Gently, Khenti released her.

"Better?" he asked.

"Are we still in Hell?" she quipped.

His lips twitched. "You are better." Khenti looked around them. "We cannot stay here. We must find shelter."

"Shelter? There's shelter in Hell?"

"Yes, so that the people condemned here may hide. It is more enjoyable for the demons if their prey are a challenge to hunt." Khenti started to climb up the closest dune. "And we must find Anubis."

"Anubis? He's a god, right?" Mercy scrambled up the dune beside Khenti.

"Yes. He is the Guardian of the entrance to Duat. I will explain to him that you do not belong here." Khenti stopped suddenly and turned to Mercy. He stared at her chest and breathed a long sigh of relief. "Hathor's mark is still there."

Mercy looked down at the henna and frowned. "The horns are fading."

"But the rest of her mark remains." They trudged up the dune. "Anubis will see that you are a living mortal. He will recognize Hathor's mark. All he need do is speak to the goddess and you will be returned to your world. My father is only a demi-god. His power rests in Osiris, but he is *not* Osiris. Anubis should be able to reverse your banishment."

"Mine? What about you?"

Khenti didn't speak for several breaths and when he did he would not look at Mercy. "My father has disowned me and banished me from the Land of the Dead. Osiris will not overturn his general's command. And I am no longer a demi-god."

"But what does that mean?" Mercy grabbed his arm as she slipped in the sand. He pulled her to her feet and they continued, hand-in-hand, to climb up.

"It means I am fully mortal. I will age normally and I can be killed here, which is the only way I will escape Duat. My heart will be weighed against the feather of judgment, and I believe I will be found worthy to enter the Land of the Dead. Then Osiris will have to grant me the afterlife promised in my Book of the Dead."

They crested the top of the dune. Mercy struggled to catch her breath as she tried to comprehend what Khenti had just told her. "Wait, you mean the only way out of Hell is for you to die?"

"Yes." He smiled at her. "It is not that terrible. Well, the death part will undoubtedly be unpleasant, but then I will be welcomed back to the Land of the Dead, and eventually rejoin my mother and spend eternity joyously."

"But you'll be dead."

His smile slid from his face. "My alternative is to remain alive, but here." Khenti gestured around them. "And I do not wish to remain here."

They'd reached the crest of the dune. Mercy stared around them at a desolate land lacking in beauty or plant life. She shuddered and felt terribly weak.

"What is it?" Khenti held tightly to her hand as if he could transmit reassurance by touch.

"I've never been anywhere without plants. Khenti, I get my magic from green, growing things. Without plants I feel worse than naked. I feel abandoned and powerless."

He touched her chin and lifted her face so that she looked into his dark eyes. "But plants are anchored to the earth, correct?"

"Well, yes."

"Then the earth is also the source of your power. Remember that beneath your feet is an ancient earth. It does hold power for those who know how to access it. I believe you accessed it when you hexed my father."

She nodded shakily. "I did, though I also pulled energy from the plants around me. Sorry, I'm usually not so whiny. I'm just—not myself right now. This is my first time in Hell."

His lips lifted. "Mine as well. Do you think it is too much for a second date?"

Mercy couldn't help smiling at him. "Yeah, you went a little overboard, but you get points for effort."

He made an exaggerated show of wiping his brow. "Whew! I was worried it was not going well."

"How about we find this Anubis guy and see what he has to say, and then you can check back in with me about how date number two is going—but fair warning, if it ends in death for either of us that's an automatic bomb."

"Noted," he said. "Anubis guards the entrance of Duat—and there is only one. So, he must be close."

"What do we look for?" Mercy put her hand over her eyes to stop the glare of the angry sky against the sand and looked around them.

"A jackal-headed god."

Mercy stared at Khenti. "But your dad's a jackal-headed god."

Khenti nodded. "Yes, because Upuant is a son of Anubis."

"Oh, shit. That can't be good."

Khenti shrugged. "It is not bad. Anubis is also my grandfather."

"Point taken. Um, does he like you?" Mercy asked.

There was a crackling beside them. Khenti whirled and pushed Mercy behind him as he lifted his hand over his head and shouted, "To me, ramah!" Instantly, his long, razor-pointed spear appeared in his hand and Khenti held it at the ready as he faced the darkness that swirled before him.

From the middle of what looked like a billowing black cloud come to earth an enormous man strode toward them. His skin was dark umber. He was dressed all in black leather and carried a huge sword. His head was similar to Upuant's, only this jackal was larger, more ferocious, and as dark as rich, newly plowed earth.

Khenti dropped to his knees and bowed so low his forehead almost touched the sand. Mercy quickly did the same, though she also peeked up, trying to see if the giant god was going to skewer them.

The god stopped and rested the point of his sword against the sand. The jackal's fierce expression softened. "Ah, grandson! There you are. Please, rise. Your companion may rise as well."

They stood as Khenti said, "Grandfather, I greet you! I would like to present to you my friend, Green Witch Mercy Goode, Gate Guardian of Goodeville."

Mercy bowed again. "It's nice to meet you, Anubis."

"Hathor told me my grandson had made a friend from a mortal

realm. I did not imagine that I would meet her. I would say I am pleased, but your situation is not, how shall I put this, *ideal.*"

"So, you know what Father has done," said Khenti.

Anubis nodded his massive head. "I am immediately aware of all banishments from the Land of the Dead. I was saddened by Upuant's decree, though not entirely surprised. His temper has always been mercurial. I went to him the moment I felt the banishment."

"Then you know how unfair this is," said Khenti. "Even had I died, I have not lived an evil life and would not be sentenced to Duat."

"And I'm not even from here," added Mercy.

"Yes, it is unfortunate," said Anubis.

"But you can fix it, right?" said Mercy. "Zap us back to where we're supposed to be?"

"I wish I could, young Green Witch. I can easily rescind any of my son's commands. He is only a petulant demi-god with limited powers. But when Upuant banished the two of you he did so in the name of Osiris. My brother and I have an agreement. I do not interfere in the Land of the Dead, and he does not tamper with Duat. I cannot reverse Upuant's banishment."

Mercy felt like she was going to puke. "Then what are we supposed to do? How do we get out of here?"

"It is quite simple. You die," said Anubis.

Thirty-two

Hunter stopped in the middle of the driveway where the Camry should have been. But the car was gone. She adjusted the thick purse strap over her shoulder and stomped to the closed garage. Mercy had to be there. She couldn't just skip school *and* go gallivanting around Goodeville in a car she wasn't legally allowed to drive. This wasn't a party. This was life or death—saving the town, the *planet,* or letting it perish at the hands of otherworldly monsters.

She grabbed the garage door's metal handle and hefted it open. The wheels squealed against the rusted track before abruptly stopping. Hunter tried to tug the door down then back up, but it was no use. The heavy door was stuck. She tipped her head back and sighed. She just wanted one thing to go her way. Apparently, that was way too much to ask.

She bent over and peered into the musty garage. No car. Only the matching pair of bicycles their mother had gotten them when they'd turned eleven, and the rickety old shelves covered in cans of paint and boxes puckered and wrinkled with age.

The purse slid down Hunter's arm and she jerked it back over her shoulder. Of course Mercy wasn't home. Anytime Hunter needed her sister, Mag made herself unavailable. Hunter had wanted to grieve at their mother's funeral in a different way than her sister had organized, and Mercy had made sure Hunter didn't feel welcome. Before arriving at Goode Lake for Mr. Parrott's Rite of Release, Hunter had practiced what she'd wanted to say to Mercy over and over again. Her sister had kicked her out then, too. And now, when Hunter was hours away from fixing the gates for good, when she needed her sister the most, Mercy was gone. Poof. Vanished.

Whatever. She didn't actually *need* her sister. Hunter could and *would* do it all on her own. She did everything on her own anyway. Double trouble had ended a long, long time ago.

Hunter's jaw pulsed as she walked around the front of the house and stormed up the porch steps. As she yanked open the screen and barged through the front door, Xena leapt off the arm of the couch and landed on the balls of her feet, hands raised in the air, and teeth bared.

"Kitten!" She relaxed onto her heels and scooped Hunter into a hug.

Xena's wild puff of hair tickled Hunter's nose and made her eyes water, but the cinnamon and spice that drifted from her mother's bathrobe made Hunter's eyes water for another reason. Hunter pushed away from Xena and swiped the back of her hand across her eyes. She wouldn't let emotions cloud her judgment or keep her from her goal. She was fixing the gates—with or without Mercy.

"Where's Mag?"

Xena's smooth brow furrowed. "School." She tapped a pointed nail against her lips.

"School's over." Hunter adjusted her purse and brushed past Xena through the living room. "She wasn't there, anyway." The scent of tuna wafted over her as she entered the kitchen. Multiple cans in different stages of being opened were spread across the counter. "Did she bail on you, too?" Hunter asked, nose wrinkled.

"We had a tiff." Xena slid onto the kitchen counter. Tuna juice sloshed onto the quartz as the cat person batted the half-open can. "She spent the weekend with Emily, but I expected her back after school."

Hunter opened the pantry and took out the rusted step stool. "Looks like she's fully into her *self-care* routine." She gritted her teeth as each step creaked and her gaze washed over her mother's basket of Kitchen Witch accouterments. This house was too full of memories, too full of comforts. She needed the turmoil of her current life. It kept her awake. It kept her alive. It kept her ahead of her feelings.

"I'm worried about her, kitten." Xena's voice was small and hushed. "She hasn't returned my messages, and I can no longer feel her."

Hunter grabbed her tarot deck from the top shelf and slipped the blue velvet satchel into her purse. "I haven't been able to feel her in weeks."

Xena jumped off the counter and met Hunter in the pantry doorway. "But I am her familiar. I should be able to—"

Hunter put her hand on Xena's arm and guided her back into the kitchen. "I get that you're worried, but I'm not. Mercy is doing what she does best, selfishly seeking out the most attention she can possibly get. It's an old, tired story, and I'm not here for it." She closed the pantry door behind her and headed back into the living room.

With a hiss, Xena stomped her foot on the ground. "There is something wrong with my Mercy kitten!"

Hunter stopped at the front door as a growl struck her back. "I can't do it again, Xena." Exhaustion coated her words as she turned to face the creature that had been looking over the Goode family for decades. "I can't let Mercy railroad me into another bad decision. I can fix the gates. For real this time." She clutched her purse against her side and pushed open the screen door. "When I'm finished, I'll help you find her."

Xena's pointed chin quivered and she wrapped the bathrobe tight around her chest. "You will never forgive yourself if you leave now and something tragic has truly befallen your sister."

"I think I can handle it," Hunter grumbled as the screen door slapped against the doorframe and she charged down the stairs and into the driveway.

If Mercy had been where she was supposed to be instead of out on a *pay attention to me* bender, Hunter wouldn't be relegated, *again,* to walking all over town to solve their problems. As soon as she fixed the gates, she was getting a job so she could pay for a Lyft whenever she needed one. Who'd ever heard of a superhero who *walked* from crime fighting gig to crime fighting gig? It's a bird! It's a plane! No, it's a *pedestrian*? Hunter groaned and shifted the purse strap when a purple glimmer pulled her attention to the half-open garage.

A smile plumped her cheeks. Yes, Hunter Goode could handle anything.

The purse thumped against her side as she ran to the garage and ducked under the door. Glittery purple and yellow tassels hung limply from the handlebars of her old bike and sparkled in a narrow beam of sunlight. She wheeled the bike out of the garage. The dirty white plastic snap-on beads that decorated the spokes clacked as the wheels turned. Hunter adjusted the purple seat and handlebars before she dropped her purse into the basket and balanced on the bike she hadn't ridden for more than three years. No, it wasn't the Batmobile or even a flying broomstick people so often associated with witches, but it was faster than her two feet alone. She pedaled down the driveway with the same fury she'd possessed as an angsty preteen and skidded onto Main Street.

A bronze-and-white sheriff's car flashed its headlights as she zoomed past, but she couldn't be bothered to stop and discuss the biking rules of the road when the safety of the town hung in the balance.

Hunter relaxed into the burning ache that spread through her legs and lungs as she pedaled away from Main Street and through neighborhoods on her way to the cherry tree. She left thoughts of her sister and Xena, Kirk and Amphitrite on the sun-soaked breeze and replaced them with focus and intention.

Close the gate. Close the gate. Close the gate.

Thirty-three

When Khenti said nothing in response to Anubis's bizarre announcement Mercy blurted, "No! That's not a thing. I'm sixteen—barely. I have lots of years left to live. I am *not* dying now."

"Yet in your world you have a patron goddess, do you not?" Anubis asked.

"Yes, Freya, Norse Goddess of Love and War," said Mercy.

"She will call your soul to her when you die. You will be returned safely to your goddess, though early for your afterlife." The god spoke nonchalantly, as if he talked about showing up early for a random appointment.

"No, no, no! I have to get home. Alive. The fate of *my* world—or at the very least my town—depends on it," said Mercy.

"That is unfortunate," said Anubis.

"There must be another way," said Khenti. "I do not mind dying, though I wish I had lived a fuller life, had a mate and children." His gaze found Mercy. His smile was sad. "But this is my fault, not Mercy's. She shouldn't have to pay for my father's anger. And more than that, her world shouldn't have to pay."

"It saddens me," said Anubis, "but I cannot cross Osiris and disrupt the balance of *our* world, though if Green Witch Mercy discovers a way to return to her world alive I give you my oath that I will do nothing to stop her."

"Even if that includes getting Khenti out of here *alive,* too?" Mercy shot the question at the god.

"I will not be an obstacle to anyone leaving Duat who has been wrongfully banished here," said Anubis.

"But you won't help us?" Mercy wanted to scream in frustration.

"I *cannot* help you leave. I *will not* force you to stay" was his evasive answer.

"Can you advise us?" Khenti asked.

"Ah, that is the correct question. My advice is to flee the storm and when the hooded figure beckons—go to her." Anubis raised his sword. It gleamed black, like ice on a dark pond. "Go with my blessing, grandson and his Green Witch companion." Then he brought the sword down once more and the swirling cloud he'd materialized from engulfed him. A gust of wind blew the darkness away and there was nothing left of the great god Anubis except his slowly filling footprints in the never-ending sand.

"I used to wish I could hang out with Freya and my mom's goddess, Athena, and even my sister's ex-god, Tyr," Mercy began.

"Ex-god?" said Khenti.

"It's a long story. Anyway, now I'm pretty sure that it's better not to be too damn friendly with immortals."

"I am beginning to agree with you."

Mercy brushed sand off her dress and as she did she noticed both of her henna horns had faded to nothing. "Oh, crap. Time passes differently here, too?"

"I imagine so, but as this is my first time in Duat I can only speculate . . ." He shrugged.

"Uh-oh!" Mercy reached into her pocket and breathed a relieved sigh when her hand closed around her phone. She lifted it out and checked the screen. "Bloody hell, now it's Monday afternoon. I missed school! Xena is gonna kill me, and my cell doesn't have much power left. Wait! Xena!"

"Your familiar?"

Mercy nodded enthusiastically. "She and I are connected. Hang on, let me see if I can feel her." Mercy closed her eyes and grounded herself with three deep breaths in and out. Then she thought about Xena—about how magnificently big she was in feline form and how motherly and kind she was in human form—how she'd been completely devoted to Abigail, and now was similarly devoted to Mercy. She also thought about how pissed she'd been that Xena had chastised her for being harsh with Hunter . . . tears leaked down Mercy's cheeks as she tried to find her connection with her mama cat who had probably been right about Hunter. *I'd give anything to go back there—to say sorry and let Xena pull me into a mom hug and surround me with love and Abigail's robe.* Mercy opened her eyes and wiped at her cheeks.

"Did you feel her?" Khenti asked.

Mercy couldn't speak. She only shook her head and looked away.

Khenti took her hand. "Do not despair. Perhaps she is asleep. She is a feline—they do sleep a lot."

Mercy sniffled. "Yeah, Xena definitely sleeps most of the day."

"You shall try again later. And we must find shelter."

"Which way do we go?" Mercy stared around them. Everything looked the same—endless wavy dune after endless wavy dune. It was like they were in a giant cat box which, ironically, her familiar would love.

"Does that sky seem darker to you over there?" Khenti pointed behind them.

Mercy studied the dreary sky. "Well, yeah, I think so. I mean, it looks muddier than the sky in front of us."

"Could be a storm, and Anubis did say to flee the storm."

"So, the opposite direction it is." Mercy put her phone back in her pocket. Her other hand rested firmly in Khenti's as they began to descend the far side of the dune. "I wonder who the hooded woman is your grandfather mentioned. Do you have any idea?"

Khenti shook his head. "The only spirits who are sent here are those who lived such terrible lives that their hearts were weighted down with the darkness of their evil deeds. It's difficult to believe anyone sentenced to Duat would grant us aid."

"You don't think Anubis would—"

"Wa-hu! Wa-hu!" A horrible barking sound echoed around them.

"Mercy! Return to the top of the dune!" Khenti surged back up the sandy hill.

Mercy tried to keep up with him, but Khenti was stronger—faster—and he practically pulled her arm out of its socket as he hauled her with him.

"Wa-hu! Wa-hu!"

The snarling bark bounced against the sands making it impossible to trace where it came from. Khenti crested the dune with Mercy, who fell as her foot tripped on the hem of her dress. She was on her hands and knees when the thing scrambled to the top of the dune just a few feet in front of them.

It was a creature of nightmares. It was the size of a baboon or monkey—and had the hunched shoulders of that kind of an animal, but it looked all wrong. Its flesh was rotten. Big hunks of brown fur were missing from its diseased coat. But beneath the hunks of putrid flesh were corded muscles and it moved with a deadly grace. Khenti raised his spear just as it bared two rows of glistening fangs and charged, racing toward them on all fours, while it barked eerily. *"Wa-hu! Wa-hu!"*

Khenti moved with blurring speed. He lunged to meet the creature, whose red eyes widened with surprise as the spear skewered it through its chest. Still the thing barked and strained and kept coming! It reached long, knifelike claws for Khenti as it impaled itself, driving the spear farther and farther through its body in its manic quest to reach him. Khenti dug his heels into the sand and leaned back, yanking the spear free from the thing's bloody body. Using the momentum of the movement he pivoted and sliced the blade across its neck. Scarlet spouted and the thing gurgled and staggered. Khenti spun and kicked the creature so that it rolled down the side of the dune where it left a rust-colored trail before it finally collapsed, motionless, and then it dissolved into the sand leaving only a red stain to show it was ever there.

Mercy struggled to her feet and ran to Khenti. "Are you hurt? Is it dead? What in all the bloody fucking hells was that?"

Khenti pulled her into his arms and they held each other tightly. "I am uninjured. I defeated it, but an In-tep demon cannot be killed by anyone but an immortal. It will return, and probably not alone. We need to move."

"It was the most disgusting thing I've ever seen." Mercy stepped out of his arms and ran a shaky hand across her face. "It looked like a monkey on crack."

"I do not know what crack is, but an In-tep is a demon who possesses and then changes into a baboon."

Mercy shuddered. "It was vile." She sniffed and then covered her nose with her hand. "And it reeks."

"In-teps cannot possess humans. The closest they can come to us is to infest a baboon, and their infestation kills the poor beast so that the demon can then reanimate it."

"Zombie baboons—it's like we've been dropped into Jumanji." Mercy gazed around them, terrified of what might come after them next. "What other kind of demon does this—" Her words broke off as she stared at the sky over Khenti's shoulder. "Shit!"

Khenti turned. "Sandstorm! Run, Mercy! Run!"

Khenti took her hand and began to sprint away from the encroaching wall behind them that looked like it was filled with mud. Mercy cursed her beautiful, goddess-gifted dress as she tripped over it again. She yanked her hand from Khenti's and quickly wrapped the diaphanous skirt up and tucked it into her jeweled belt like it was a diaper, then she scrambled after him. The two of them slid down the other side of the dune, Khenti took her hand again, and they raced along a narrow path of hard-packed dirt. Behind them the sandstorm gained on them. As it got closer and closer the air battered their backs and howled like a living being.

Everything was getting darker and darker. Khenti stopped and bent so that he could shout into her ear. "The skirt of your dress! I must cut it. If we wrap our faces and huddle together we may survive."

"May?!" Mercy shouted.

"It is the only chance we have!" Khenti changed his grip on his spear and dropped to his knees as he reached to tug her skirt out of her belt.

"Here! Come!" The voice bounced from the dunes.

Khenti and Mercy looked wildly around as they tried to follow the voice.

A cloaked figure seemed to step from the inside of a dune just yards in front of them. The person gestured for them to come.

"It's what Anubis said!" Mercy yelled against the thunder of the wind. "A hooded woman!"

Khenti nodded. Though he kept his spear raised and ready, the two of them ran to the hooded person, who turned, still beckoning, and disappeared into the dune.

Mercy didn't hesitate. She rushed into the strange entrance with Khenti close behind her. The sound of the storm was too loud for speech, so the hooded figure kept gesturing for them to follow deeper and deeper into the dune until finally they turned a corner that led to a circular chamber where a fire burned in a small hearth. The hooded figure moved behind them and loosed a thick length of linen so that it covered the entrance, then dropped to her knees as she quickly began placing rocks, the size of loaves of bread, along the bottom of the covering to secure it. As she did so, her hood fell back, exposing long, dark hair. When the rocks were all placed she stood and then turned slowly to face them.

All the air rushed from Khenti's lungs in a loud *"Oof!"* like he'd been kicked in the stomach. He swayed and would've fallen had the woman not rushed forward and wrapped him in her arms as she sobbed. "Son! My son!"

Mercy felt like an interloper as Khenti and the woman who had to be his mother wept in each other's arms. To give them some semblance of privacy she turned her gaze away and was astounded by the beauty in the simple room. Wall sconces flickered around the chamber, lighting everything in a soft, yellow glow. Though it had been miserably hot outside, Mercy realized that it was many degrees cooler in this room. Between the sconces the walls were filled with colorful hieroglyphics, murals, and tapestries that depicted scenes from a happy life—a mother on the beach of a wide river with her child—the same mother making bread as the child played with a round, leather ball—the mother and child, a son, walking through a flower-filled marketplace—Mercy looked closer and realized the son was Khenti! *These are scenes from his life. Everyday things he and his mom used to do together.* Tears blurred her eyes. Mercy understood the love and longing in the murals, and the beauty of remembering simple, daily routines. She would always remember the small things she used to do with Abigail and Hunter when they were a family—when they were happy. *I miss her so much. I miss Mom, and I miss Hunter. I have been a sodding fool.*

"Mercy!" Khenti's voice was filled with joy and tears.

She turned from studying the wall art and wiped her eyes. Khenti had his arm around his mother's slim shoulders. He made no move to hide the tears that still washed his face. He motioned for her to come closer and she was able to get a good look at his mom.

She was so pretty! Khenti had her kind, dark eyes and her high cheekbones. Her skin was lighter than her son's, but the same burnished color. Her cloak had opened to reveal how petite she was—small and delicate and graceful. Her hair was still mostly the black of a raven's wing, but it had one silver-white streak that ran from her right temple down to where the length of it waved around her slim waist.

Her smile, which she beamed first up at her son and then at Mercy, was almost identical to her son's.

"Mother, this is my friend, the Green Witch Mercy, who is a Gate Guardian from Goodeville. Mercy, this is my beloved mother, Meryt."

"It's so great to meet you!" Mercy said. "Khenti has told me a lot about you."

"Oh, my dear!" Meryt moved forward and took Mercy's hands in hers. "Blessings to you." Then she paused and looked closer at her. "You are not dead!"

"No." Mercy smiled. "And neither is your son."

Meryt turned quickly and touched her son's cheek. "Oh, Tee! I should have noticed before—you, too, are alive! Why are you here? How are you here?"

"Father banished me to Duat, and Mercy with me," Khenti said.

"Then that makes the three of us, my darling."

Thirty-four

Khenti explained quickly to her mother the events that led them to Duat. She listened carefully as she motioned for them to sit on colorful cushions that rested against the side of the circular chamber. From an urn she took from a cabinet-sized hole in the wall, Meryt poured cloudy beer much like the drink Khenti had already introduced Mercy to into wooden mugs for them. When Khenti was finished speaking, Meryt shook her head.

"That is why I kept you from him. Upuant rejected love and laughter and joy as frivolity. I was so young when I first met him that I believed my love could show him how to be happy, could erase his sadness. I was a fool, which I realized not long after I discovered I was to bear him a child. I kept him from you and refused to let him take you away to the Land of the Dead because I would not allow him to taint you with his gloom and misery." She paused and stared into her own mug of beer. "Hathor aided me. That is the only reason I managed to keep you in the mortal realm. I would have kept you there your entire life, but Upuant found a way to circumvent even the goddess."

"How? What did he do?" Khenti's eyes darkened with rage.

Meryt looked up and met her son's gaze. "He killed me, effectively ending the pact I made with Hathor at your birth. I would dedicate my son to her service as long as you were allowed to remain with me. I thought I would live long enough that Upuant would father another son and leave us in peace. I was wrong."

"Oh, Muta. I am so sorry." Instead of being filled with anger, Khenti deflated. His shoulders bowed and he bent in defeat. "I caused this. You would still be living in the Valley of the Kings surrounded by your family had I never been born."

Meryt went to her son and crouched before him. She took his face between her hands. "Listen to me, my precious Tee. You did not cause this. Upuant is responsible for my death; no one else. He is also responsible for giving me you—and I have loved you fiercely and completely since the moment you were conceived. You are the single thing I am most proud of in my life. I would spend a million lifetimes in Duat to know one as your mother." She kissed him gently on his forehead and stood. "Now, sit up straight, wipe your tears, and let us figure out how the two of you are going to get out of here."

Khenti straightened and wiped at his eyes. "We go nowhere without you."

"But we will figure out how to get out of here," added Mercy. She gestured at the comfortable, beautifully decorated room around them. "This doesn't seem very Hell-like."

Meryt returned to resting on the cushion she'd placed between her son and Mercy. She smiled at Mercy. "That is because Hathor still cares for me. She could not overturn Upuant's banishment, like you and my Tee have already discovered, what Upuant commands in Osiris's name cannot be overturned, not even by another immortal. But my goddess is loyal and merciful. Upuant burned my Book of the Dead. When Hathor realized that I was not in the Hall of Judgment she knew Upuant had to be responsible, so she slipped into his chamber and discovered he had burned my Book. Thankfully, Hathor rescued several pages from his brazier. I was never judged and sent to Duat because of the evil in my heart, so there is no immortal law against allowing me that which was listed in my Book." She gestured around her. "I am quite comfortable here, though it is rather lonely."

Khenti shook his head. "I do not understand. Why were you not judged?"

Meryt sighed wistfully. "It was my own folly. Upuant found me while I waited in line to enter the Hall of Judgment. He said he was sorry that he had killed me—that he had been too impetuous, and he regretted his anger. To prove his remorse Upuant said that if I went with him, he would take me to you, my beloved Tee, so that we could say our farewells until the time when you would join me in my after-life."

"Instead he burned your Book and banished you to Hell," Mercy said.

"Indeed," said Meryt.

"He is vile." Khenti's words were filled with sadness. "And to think of the years that I spent trying to win his approval."

"You are a good son." Meryt patted his hand. "But it is not possible to win Upuant's approval. He loathes himself too much to care about anyone else."

"Don't worry," Mercy said. "He'll get what he deserves."

"If only that were true," said Meryt. "But Osiris dotes on him and refuses to see his flaws."

"Oh, that won't matter," Mercy explained. "I hexed him."

"Yes, I do remember that clearly," said Khenti, almost smiling. "What exactly does it mean to hex someone?"

"Well, it's something that Goode witches rarely do. We don't believe in using the dark side of the Craft—ultimately it taints the witch who wields it. But every generation learns how to safely hex some-one, even though it's basically a last resort. A normal hex is never cool to cast, like say I hexed my ex-boyfriend, Kirk, because he's a total jerk. So, I get mad and hex him to get fat and bald. He would definitely get fat and bald, but that hex would return to me times three."

"Do you mean you, too, would become fat and bald?" asked Khenti's mom.

Mercy nodded. "Yeah. Three times as fat and bald as Kirk."

"Oh, I know what you did differently to Upuant," said Khenti. Mercy nodded encouragement, and he continued. "You hexed him by cursing him with his own actions. *'Return to Upuant the harm he dispenses with such glee—Three times three return it to he.'* " Khenti quoted Mercy.

"Ah, I see," said Meryt, sitting up straight with excitement. "You didn't wish outside ill upon him. You only wished his own actions returned to him."

"Yep, three times three. Which also means that I need to pay really close attention to my actions for the rest of my life, especially when something I do causes me glee." She shrugged. "The flip side of the hex is that if Upuant changed, if he somehow began to treat Khenti with kindness, then those good things would return to him multiplied by three as well."

"It is an excellent curse," said Khenti.

"I agree with Tee. You must be a wonderful witch," said his mom.

"Well, I try. I had a really good teacher. My mom was the very best." Then she grinned at Khenti. "You didn't tell me you have a nickname."

When he looked at his mom Khenti finally smiled. "She has called me that since I was a baby."

"And he has called me Muta since he first began to babble words." Meryt touched his cheek gently. "Oh, my Tee, I hate that you are here—and yet I love that you are here."

He covered her hand with his. "I am glad of it. Now I can ease your loneliness. The only thing that saddens me is that Mercy was caught up in Upuant's wrath."

"Nope, we're not doing this," Mercy said firmly. "None of us are staying in Hell. No bloody way. I have to get home and like you said, Meryt, I'm a wonderful witch. Like Khenti said earlier, even though there is nothing green living here, I can still draw power from the earth. And, like Anubis said—he won't stop us from leaving if we can figure out a way out. So, I'm going to get us some help from my world, and believe me—when my sister and my familiar find out I'm stuck in Hell, they are going to rescue me, and that means you two as well."

"I appreciate your positive attitude," said Khenti. "You make me believe we can escape."

"Did you say that green things help your powers?" asked Meryt.

"Yeah, I'm a Green Witch, and that means I have a special connection to plants."

Meryt's brilliant smile blazed as she stood. "Well, then, Green Witch Mercy, I have something to show you."

Mercy looked at Khenti. He shrugged and grinned as they stood and followed his mom to a section of the circular room that held a lovely tapestry of the goddess, Hathor. Meryt brushed aside the richly embroidered fabric to expose an arched doorway that led to an enormous room that was lit by a glowing summer sun, though as Mercy stared up at the ceiling of the chamber she saw that it wasn't open to the sky at all, but across its domed expanse was painted a sun and a perfect cerulean sky—and the sun glowed like a summer day in Illinois.

Mercy had to blink her eyes clear of sunspots before she could focus on what was in the room, and with a happy cry she rushed forward. The perfume of flowers and the scent of green, growing things engulfed Mercy, and she had the urge to burst into tears of joy and relief. In the middle of a wide expanse of new wheat, she turned in a circle with her hands caressing the tops of the growing plants gently.

"This is amazing!" Mercy stared around her. "Jasmine! It smells so wonderful! And you have avocado trees! Ohmygoddess, there are artichokes—I love artichokes! And, ooh, your lettuce looks fantastic!

And cucumbers! Holy crap! There's even a stream." Water bubbled over smooth stones through the center of the room. Mercy went to it, crouched, and touched the crystal surface, which was icy cold. She stood and met Meryt's amused gaze. "Hathor?"

"As I said, my goddess is loyal. She fashioned this cave for me. It hides me from demons. I also have an embarrassingly opulent bedroom chamber, but that was something I wrote into my Book when I was quite young. Will this do, Green Witch? Can you draw power from my garden?"

"Absolutely!" For the first time since Upuant had pushed them into the pit to Duat, Mercy felt a rush of hope.

"What do you need to send a call to your sister?" asked Khenti.

"Just this." Mercy's arm swept around her to take in the garden chamber. "I'll ground myself and see if my link to my sister can stretch from one world to another."

Khenti went to her, took her hand, and lifted it to his lips. He kissed her skin gently and then his warm, brown eyes smiled at her. "She is your twin. You shared a womb. Forget the recent strife between you. You will reach her. I believe in you and your powers, Magnificent Green Witch Mercy, Guardian of the Goodeville gates."

Meryt joined her son. "If my son believes in you, then I do as well. You cursed a demi-god. You can definitely do this, mighty Green Witch."

"I can do this." Mercy looked around and decided on a spot in the middle of the room beside the stream where it was surrounded by daisies—Freya's favorite flowers. She sat, cross-legged, and rested her hands on her thighs.

"Shall we leave you?" Khenti asked.

"No, actually you can help, if that's okay."

"I will do anything I can to help you," said Meryt firmly.

"Awesome, just sit next to me. I'm going to close my eyes and ground myself by breathing deeply three times in and out."

"We can do that with you," said Khenti as he and his mother sat on either side of her.

"Yes, good," said Mercy. "Then, after we're grounded we set our intention. That means I want you to think of nothing but getting a message to my sister." She looked at Meryt. "Her name is Hunter. She looks exactly like me. I'm also going to think of my familiar and hope she gets the message, too. Her name is Xena and she's a huge Maine coon."

Meryt's brow creased. "Maine coon?"

"It is a feline," explained Khenti.

"Oh, wonderful!" Meryt clapped her hands like a girl. "I adore felines."

"This one is really big and has lots of black and brown and white fur, with long black tufts on her ears."

"She sounds lovely," said Meryt.

"If she was here she'd tell you herself that she is a magnificent feline." Mercy grinned. "And she wouldn't be wrong. So, just concentrate on our intention. Then I'll tap into all this great green power around us and send a message back home." She looked at Meryt. "Ready?"

"Yes, I am ready."

Mercy's gaze shifted to Khenti and she lifted a questioning brow.

He grinned at her. "Ready!"

"Then let's breathe." They followed Mercy's lead and drew in, then released three long, slow breaths. "Now, set and maintain your intention."

Mercy closed her eyes. With that extra sense that each Goode witch had passed from mother to daughter for hundreds of years and generation after generation, Mercy reached around her and was instantly rewarded by eager plants, bursting with joy. Her lips tilted up as she felt the strength of their happiness, which at first baffled her. They were in Hell. How could they be so happy?

We serve Hathor! And Hathor's most favored servant! That fills us with joy!

"Well, that makes sense." Eyes still closed, Mercy murmured to the plants around her. "I need your help. Will you aid me?"

Meryt wishes it and you have been marked by Hathor, so we will happily aid you!

"Thank you. All you need do is lend me some of your growing power. I give you my word not to take so much that you'll be harmed."

As you wish, friend of Meryt—friend of Hathor.

Immediately, warmth washed through Mercy with such verdant intensity that she had to grit her teeth together to hold it within her body—though she didn't keep it for long. With everything inside her, Mercy channeled that green power to the invisible third eye that rested in the center of her forehead.

"Find Hunter!" she commanded and she shot the power from her forehead up, up, up and out, out, out while she concentrated on her twin—on how much she loved her, on how much she missed sharing her life with her—on how much she needed her sister, now and always. And, mostly, how sorry she was that she'd let anything come between them. Xena had been right. She'd been wrong to turn away from Hunter. With a jolt, Mercy felt their connection! It was stretched thin, like a rubber band about to break, but it was there and it was still intact. Mercy focused on that connection as she channeled as much energy from the plants around her, and the ancient, magical earth below her, as was safe and then she drew a deep breath and channeled the power up along her spine, to her neck, and finally she shot it out of her third eye as she called, *"Hunter Jayne Goode! I'm stuck in Egyptian Hell and I'm going to die unless you and Xena help me!"*

Her eyes were still tightly closed, but with her third, magical eye, Mercy saw her call take form and shoot along their connection like a bullet. Then the power fizzled and like a snuffed candle, it went out. She opened her eyes, blinking them into focus, to find Khenti and Meryt staring at her, wide-eyed.

"What? Did you see something?" she asked.

Khenti reached for her and took her into his arms as his mom laughed happily. "Yes, you amazing Green Witch! We saw power!"

"You did it, my dear! I believe you did it!" Meryt's arms went around them as the plants beside them swayed in response and their laughter echoed off the walls of the goddess-touched room.

Thirty-five

Hunter steered her bike from the road and over the bumpy field to the cherry tree. She hopped off and hefted her purse from the basket before she leaned the bike against its kickstand. Leaves crunched and worms squelched beneath her boots, but she didn't let it distract from her intention, her purpose.

Close the gate. Close the gate. Close the gate.

She silently chanted as she combed her fingers through her hair and swept it into a high ponytail.

Her phone rang in her bag once, twice, three times before it went silent. Hunter wouldn't check to see who called. She had more important things to do. Just because she had a phone didn't mean she had to be available all the time. They could leave a voice mail or a—

Her text tone sounded in rapid succession. A machine gun assault on her focus. She definitely wasn't going to answer now.

Cold gusts blew off the water that surged through Sugar Creek as if they'd had a weekend of heavy storms. Hunter swallowed, her intention drowning in a sudden burst of fear as pain gnawed on the scar that covered her stomach.

"Took you long enough." Amphitrite appeared in the middle of Sugar Creek, a scowl etched into her smooth features. Before Hunter could answer, the goddess waved her hands in the air. *"It's no matter. You're here now."* She floated to the shore on the back of a surging wave.

Falling leaves tickled Hunter's bare arms as she gingerly parted the boughs and slipped under the cherry tree's decaying canopy.

"Do you have the book?" Leaves rained around Amphitrite as she forced her way under the branches.

Hunter took a deep, cleansing breath and restarted her intention as she bent over and placed the book and her tarot at the base of the tree.

Close the gate. Close the gate. Close the gate.

"Witch!" Amphitrite thunderous roar shook loose more leaves from the branches.

Hunter brushed the sea spray from her neck and shivered as a gust pressed her wet shirt against her back. "I'm trying to maintain my intention," she said as she kneeled onto her empty purse and opened her spellbook. Her fingertips tingled as she thumbed through the pages to the spell entitled REALMS.

Amphitrite glided closer. Her skirts brushed Hunter's arm and left a trail of sand in their wake. *"I am here to help. Remember our agreement."*

Hunter reread the first line of the spell's instructions. She grimaced as she stood and flicked a squished worm from her knee. "I remember you almost drowning a man," she said while she dug the toe of her boot through the layer of rotted leaves and writhing worms to fresh dirt. She kicked the earth, moist under the decay, until she'd made the point of the pentagram needed to begin the spell. She needed a trowel, and could get one if she had the car, but *no,* Mercy had to go off and—

She bit the inside of her cheek. She had to focus. She wouldn't let this spell fail because she was too caught up in sister drama.

"I had no other way to get your attention. You banished *me."*

Hunter didn't answer. Instead, she continued to plow the dirt with her boot and repeat her intention until it coated her insides like peritoneum.

"Move aside, Witch." The goddess pressed her glowing blue fingers against Hunter's arm and ushered her away from the start of the pentagram. Amphitrite snatched her hand back as water popped and hissed against Hunter's skin. She spat a curse through clenched teeth and a spray of water burst from her mouth.

The corner of Hunter's lips lifted. "Hence from Verona art thou banishèd."

Amphitrite twirled her sizzling fingers between the waves of her skirts and again lifted her hand and shooed Hunter backward. She knelt next to the rut Hunter had dug and pressed her hands against the ground. Hunter strained to hear the words the goddess whispered to the earth, but the unfamiliar language only twisted against Hunter's ears.

Behind them, Sugar Creek's pulsing waves surged into a roar. Its whitecaps writhed and the water splashed onto the banks.

Amphitrite's kelp brown hair lifted around her as she buried her hands in the earth. She ushered a final command and water swelled up from the ground. It swirled around the dirt and brittle leaves and fetid worms and pulled them down into the earth.

Hunter pressed her fingers against her lips and shuffled backward. The water had carved a pentagram into the dirt.

Amphitrite washed her hands in her skirts and stood. *"Water is powerful,"* she said as she adjusted her crown and combed her fingers through her hair.

Hunter's ponytail slid off her shoulder as she tilted her head and narrowed her eyes at the goddess. "Water is dangerous."

Amphitrite pursed her lips. *"We are fated to be together, Witch. It's in the stars you hold so dear to your heart."*

Hunter stared up through the sparse leaves that clung to the branches. The sun still bleached out the sky, hiding the stars from sight. She couldn't agree or disagree with Amphitrite. It'd been too long since she'd called on Mother Moon or the power of the stars and the cosmos. She no longer knew what the universe had in store for her.

She pushed back the sadness and the loneliness that had crept in between blood spells and lies, sister fights and goddess troubles, and knelt down beside her book. She read the next line over and over but couldn't get the words to stick in her head. She'd strayed too far from her path. She was a lost sheep in need of a shepherd. She'd thought Amphitrite was that leader, that she was the luckiest witch who'd ever lived that her goddess deemed her worthy of the privilege of so many visits. But the queen of the sea wasn't a leader. She was a wolf. And if Hunter wasn't careful, the goddess would eat her alive.

Amphitrite hovered behind Hunter. She could no longer touch or slither into the young witch's thoughts, but she would never be far. She'd pin herself to Hunter's shadow before she'd let her go.

"A thank you would be nice."

"Thank you," Hunter muttered automatically as she closed the book and dug her hands into the cover before she got back to her feet. With a pool of blood in her palms, she stood at the tip of the pentagram and faced the tree.

Close the gate. Close the gate. Close the gate.

"Counterclockwise." Amphitrite's interjection was a saw through Hunter's focus. *"You started to turn to the right. You want to go in the opposite direction."* She motioned to the arm of the pentagram that pointed toward the road and Hunter's bike. *"You are trying to* close *something, not open it."*

Hunter glanced down at the blood warm in her hands, the crimson liquid swirling. "You know the spell," she said more to herself than to the goddess. "You know all the spells."

Amphitrite clasped her hands and rested them against her skirts. *"It* is *my book."*

"This whole time you knew how to stop the trees from dying—how to close the gates for good—but you let me run around *feeding* that book." Blood sloshed over her fingertips as Hunter gestured in the spellbook's direction. "Waiting for it to give me an answer you already had."

"I give no handouts in this realm or any other. You must earn your way, Witch."

Hunter thrust her hands forward. Blood spilled over her fingers and dripped onto the ground. "But you would have done it for the right payment." She tipped her hands over the point of the pentagram and walked, counterclockwise, in a circle around the five-pointed star. "The great goddess Amphitrite will do anything for a price." The blood didn't sink into the earth. Instead, it shimmered and pulsed against the ground, one end of the circle swallowing the other like an ouroboros.

"The great goddess Amphitrite is here for you, Hunter Goode. Helping *you, Hunter Goode.* Saving *you, Hunter Goode."* Cracks marred her smooth, blue skin and her skirts swelled and writhed around her feet. *"You may not like my methods, but I come from a realm of heroes. You live in a realm of manufactured empathy, performance activism, surface hope, follow for a follow."* Blue light beamed from the fissures that turned her skin into puzzle pieces. *"I have saved worlds, crushed evil with my bare hands."* Her skirts dipped and curled around new slopes as the goddess swelled in size. *"I have earned the right to name my price. You have only earned your breath."* Tentacles slid from beneath her dress. They caressed her arms and snaked around her shoulders. *"And do not fool yourself, Witch, for I can still take that away."*

"Then do it!" Hunter shouted. "Stop with the threats and kill me."

Amphitrite's tentacles carried her forward like spider's legs.

Hunter planted her feet, her toes curling in her boots. She was part of this land. Her ancestors had protected this town and their bones fed this earth long after they were gone. Yes, Amphitrite was a goddess, but this was not her realm and Goodeville was not her home.

Hunter's hands tingled and the blood coating her palms fizzed and crackled as she tapped into the power of the ley lines.

"You will regret this, Witch!" Amphitrite screeched as she lunged forward.

Hunter held up her hands. Energy sizzled through her veins as she channeled the well of power that had led Sarah Goode to this place more than three hundred years ago,

"Begone Amphitrite!"

Magic exploded from Hunter's palms and struck the goddess. Amphitrite shrieked as her skin burst apart and light flooded the field.

Hunter flew backward, air wheezing from her lungs as she hit the tree.

She blinked through the bright spots staining her vision. Amphitrite was gone.

Hunter pushed away from the tree and peered at Sugar Creek. The water had quieted back into a lazy, steady trickle.

"I know you're not gone. Not for good." She whirled around to face the pentagram. "Getting rid of you won't be that easy."

Hunter swallowed back the rush of certainty that had come from accessing a piece of her power that had gone undiscovered and wiped her hands before she plucked her spellbook from the base of the tree. It nuzzled her palms, delighted to be free of the worms and the rot that coated the earth beneath the gatekeeper of the Japanese Underworld.

Hunter stepped over the circle of shimmering blood and around the sunken point of the pentagram and into the middle of the five-pointed star. Withered leaves drifted down from the branches like ash as she settled back into the spell and refocused her intention.

Close the gate. Close the gate. Close the gate.

She faced the ancient cherry tree and held her spellbook out in front of her. "Realms," she read the title aloud. "Locked, secured, shielded." She buried her nerves in the pit of her stomach and reread the last line of directions. "Read the spell, let your declaration be known, and revel in your power."

Close the gate. Close the gate. Close the gate.

"This *will* work." Her fingers searched for the pendant she used to wear around her neck.

She inhaled a deep, cleansing breath and did her best to pronounce the Greek spell with a magical power that spawned unfaltering confidence. "Ξεκλειδώστε, εγκαταλείψτε, καταστρέψτε." Her tone deepened and an otherworldly vibration tickled the back of her throat. "Αυτό που αποφασίζει η μάγισσα, το αντίθετο θα είναι."

The waters of Sugar Creek burbled and splashed, but Hunter remained focused.

Close the gate. Close the gate. Close the gate.

Another inhale. "χάος ελευθερωμένο από σένα."

The spellbook heated and the edges of the page flapped against Hunter's palm.

"Heal, strengthen, close!

Lock, secure, shield.

What I decree, so mote it be!"

The ring of blood burbled and hissed around her and white smoke drifted up from the pentagram.

Close the gate. Close the gate. Close the gate.

"Ακούστε την εντολή της και κάντε το"

Flames shot up from the burbling scarlet as Hunter shouted the last line of the spell. She clutched the open spellbook against her chest and shielded her eyes from the roaring flames. She squinted through the fire and tried to get a look at the tree. Sweat popped against her forehead and rivulets cascaded down her back as she struggled to capture a view of the guardian of the gate. But the flames were too high, too thick, too ferocious.

The spellbook heated against her chest and red smoke drifted from the pages. She dropped the book and blew on her tender palms. The red smoke curled around the pentagram and settled in the hollow nooks of the carved star. Hunter blinked back the sweat burning her eyes and wiped her brow as the flames settled and the tree came back into view. Black feathers encircled the trunk. Hundreds of ravens soared, up, up, up through the branches, croaking and cawing as they flew around the tree.

"Close the gate. Close the gate. Close the gate," she chanted to the wind that twisted around her and swept the charred and acrid air from the pentagram.

The ravens seemed to stop midflight, gliding on an unfelt rush of air. Whispers tickled Hunter's ears as the birds sailed into the sky as one and dove down toward her. Her gaze shot to the base of the tree and the blue velvet pouch that held her tarot. She jolted forward and the unkindness of ravens flew after her. Birds swirled around her and choked out the sun. Hunter opened her mouth to speak, but only a pained wheeze escaped. She dropped to her knees as screeches and cackles tore at her ears and feathers scraped against her bare arms and legs.

This evil was wild and dark—the stuff of stories. But Hunter was stronger than any character in any storybook. Hunter Goode was a witch. A witch whose ancestors lived in her blood, and the earth beneath her feet, and the cosmos above. Hunter closed her eyes and reached up. She was a giant inhaling stardust, cradling Mother Moon, and comforted by the black that stretched on for eternity. *This* was her power—not wrath, not blood, not a goddess—but the cold, unending dark of forever and the burning fires in between.

Hunter's eyelids snapped open. She rose to her feet and stared up through the whirling black feathers. She could see *everything.*

She spread her arms wide and called on the power of the stars that blazed overhead like ignited cherry bombs. "Close the gate! Close the gate! Close the gate!"

She challenged the spell, the unkindness, the very air around her to defy her wishes.

"What I decree, so mote it be!" Lines of power shot from her fingers like lightning. They clawed through the ravens with the force of cannon fire. Feathers exploded in the wake of her power and rained against the earth as black ash.

Hunter's chest throbbed and her skin ached. She collapsed onto the scorched earth and stared up at the specks of otherworldly ash, the canopy of branches, and the last of the leaves that still clung to life.

She'd done it. She'd defeated whatever evil had broken the gate in the first place. She, Hunter Goode, Cosmic Witch, had won.

Tears pressed against her eyes and swirled her vision. It wasn't the grand surge of *rightness* she'd hoped for. This success was hollow and barren and a spotlight on her loneliness.

Hunter's back prickled with energy and the leaves overhead seemed to . . . *sparkle?* She pressed her hands against the thrumming earth and squinted up at the tree. The leaves were green. *Really* green. Lime green, frog green, sour candy green. *Living, thriving green.* She sat up and brushed away the lazy tingling that crawled on the back of her arms like ants as she continued to stare at the tree and its Technicolor foliage. Power spiked through her fingers and she stared down at her hands. Thin strips of green light floated up from her palms like dental floss. She jumped up and whirled around. Green light sprouted from the back of her body. It followed her as she spun and leapt and flapped her arms, creating emerald light trails in her wake. This was it! Proof that her spell had worked! Proof that she had vanquished the evil and—

Pain sawed through Hunter's head and blared static against her ears.

"Hunter Jayne Goode!"

Hunter cupped her hands over her ears and shook her head as her name echoed through the ache.

"I'm stuck . . ."

There was a familiarity about the voice that Hunter couldn't quite reach through the fire that scalded the backs of her eyes.

"Hunter Jayne Goode! I'm stuck!"

Green continued to shoot from her skin. The green of the ley lines. The green of her sister.

"Mercy?" Hunter breathed through clenched teeth.

"I'm stuck in Egyptian Hell and I'm going to die unless you and Xena help me!"

The pain vanished and stole with it the echo of her sister's voice and the light that coated her skin and the cherry tree.

"Mercy?!" Hunter's gaze swept over the burnt earth and the tree, Sugar Creek and the road Hunter had taken to get there. "Mercy!" she shouted again as her phone chimed. Hunter ran to her purse at the base of the tree. Her hands shook as she dug for her phone.

"Xena!" Hunter was breathless as she answered. "It was Mag. I heard her! I heard her in my head. She used the ley lines, Xena. She's trapped."

"I know, kitten." Xena's voice was rushed and frantic. "I heard it, too. I *felt it*. She's terrified, Hunter. She *will* die if we don't find her."

"We won't let that happen. Meet me at the palm." Hunter pinched the phone between her ear and shoulder as she stuffed the spellbook back into her bag. "And, Xena, *run*."

Hunter grabbed her tarot off the ground and paused. A thin loop of rope had fallen out of the satchel's opening. She tugged on it. Tears sprang to her eyes and her breath stilled inside her chest. She ran her fingers over the rope cord and choked out a sob as she grazed the symbol of Tyr. The T-shaped opalescent pendant was shiny and new and swirled purple and pink beneath the energy of her fingertips. She slipped the necklace on over her head and tucked her tarot cards into her purse. Tyr had sent this to her. He was back. *She* was back. And she would save her sister.

Thirty-six

Amphitrite had watched as the Goode witch completed the ancient spell, and had almost intervened when the chaos it had released tried to claim her as its first victim, but the goddess had thought better of stepping in to rescue Hunter from yet another mess. Too many times Amphitrite had attempted to steer the witch down the correct path, the easy path, to no avail. Youth was, indeed, wasted on the young. Plus, the goddess had no need for a witch who could fall prey to a faceless and unorganized evil such as chaos. No, Amphitrite needed a stronger witch than that, and it seemed that Hunter Goode was on the right track.

Tentacles the shiny white of a fish belly twirled around Amphitrite's arms and stroked the lengths of her hair. She smoothed her hands over the writhing appendages that made up her true legs before lifting the end of her thin skirt.

"Away with you," she commanded, and eight of her ten tentacles receded under the gauzy fabric. There, they shimmered and twitched before resettling into the glamour that they wore when outside of her realm, and resumed their appearance as layers of full and undulating

skirts. Her two longest tentacles settled against the silty bottom of Sugar Creek and morphed back into the slender, blue-tinged legs that suited the mortal realm and its narrow-minded views much better than her true form.

She left the cool creek waters and glided on the steady push of her camouflaged tentacles to the old and wilted guardian.

"You are ill." She frowned and flicked shriveled leaves from her skirts as she parted the boughs and approached the strong trunk. *"Such a shame."* She bent down and pressed her palm to the scorched pentagram. Blood pulsed just beneath the surface of the charred earth. It had waited for her. She brushed off her hand and stood in the middle of the pentagram. *"I didn't lie when I told the young witch that she and I were fated."* She faced the trunk and spoke to the guardian as she would an old friend. After all, it had once been powerful. Not as powerful as she, but strong enough to protect the mortals who scurried about this realm like roaches. *"As you know, what comes next was written in the stars. I couldn't stop it if I wanted to."*

The branches creaked and groaned in response.

"Well, maybe I could *tweak things a bit. But where's the fun in that?"* She held her arms out by her sides and shivered as energy rushed to her fingertips. "*After all, mortals are only good for one thing.*"

She let loose her power and water poured from each finger like a hose. It splattered against the earth and rushed to the blood that encircled the pentagram and waited just beneath the dirt. It bubbled and spurted as it fed from the blood, absorbing it until the cerulean waters turned scarlet.

Amphitrite grinned as she held her hand beneath her lips and exhaled a perfect orb of glittering blue liquid. She pressed her lips to the bubble and whispered a command before she tossed the sphere into the air. The crimson ring of water surged up from the ground and collided with the glittering orb. Beneath the tree limbs, the air exploded into burgundy rain.

A moan escaped Amphitrite's lips as she tilted her head back and let the water drench her face. She licked her wet lips and stared down at the current of water that rushed against the base of the tree trunk. Imbued with her magic, it carved out a hole in the once great guardian. Again, the boughs creaked and groaned with the tree's complaints.

Amphitrite pressed her finger against her cool lips. *"Shh. It won't be long now."*

The rain ceased and the last of the water snaked into the dark hole at the base of the tree.

"I'll be seeing you," she whispered to the limbs that trembled overhead before she narrowed her gaze to the tunnel her magic had carved in the trunk of the cherry tree. *"A goddess doesn't like to be kept waiting."*

A shriek of laughter tore from her lips as Amphitrite snapped her fingers and vanished.

Thirty-seven

"Mercy, my dear, how long before your sister and your familiar arrive to take us away with them?" Meryt asked as she poured Mercy and her son fresh mugs of thick, fragrant beer.

Mercy shrugged and smiled at Khenti's mom. "I don't know, but Xena and Hunter are pretty impatient—and they're really smart. I imagine they're going through grimoires, making notes, and figuring out spells right now. It won't be too long."

"But long enough for me to fix Tee's favorite meal?" Meryt smiled lovingly at her son.

Beside Mercy, Khenti had been lounging against the curved side of his mother's luxurious cave. He sat straight up. His grin lit up the homey room. "Stuffed bread with garlic and cheese?"

"Of course, sweet boy."

Khenti cut his gaze to Mercy. "I know you must leave—soon. We all must, but . . ." He looked at her beseechingly.

Mercy laughed. "Abigail, my mom, used to say that a man's heart could be found in his stomach. Until this moment I thought she was being sarcastic."

Meryt nodded. "Your Abigail was a wise woman."

"She absolutely was. Well, we might as well eat." Mercy grinned at Khenti. "And if the cavalry arrives too soon we'll just take it to go."

Meryt's brow furrowed. "And that means?"

"That I shall get my favorite meal, no matter if we—"

Khenti's words were interrupted by the terrible sound of *"Wa-hu! Wa-hu! Wa-hu! Wa-hu! Wa-hu! Wa-hu!"* which echoed eerily all around them, drawing ever closer.

Meryt's slender hand pressed against her throat. "No! Hathor bound the In-teps, as well as all other demons, from finding me!"

"What's happening?" Mercy's stomach roiled as the cries of the In-tep demons mixed with shrieks, snarls, and roars of other creatures—all growing louder, all getting closer.

Khenti stood and took his mother into his arms. "Muta, forgive me."

"My dear, there is nothing to forgive!"

"Yes, Mother, there is. *You* are protected by Hathor. Mercy and I are not."

"Oh, shit! The demons followed us here." Mercy's heart pounded so loudly in her chest she thought it would explode. She glanced down at herself, sure that she would see it thumping against her skin—and she felt the blood drain from her face, leaving her pale and terrified. "Khenti." She spoke softly, but his gaze instantly found her. Mercy pointed to her chest where Hathor's sun disc had faded so much that only a slim crescent was still visible. "I—I think I'm going to die here."

Epilogue

Nure-Onna was brought abruptly out of the stupor-like existence she had fallen into unnumbered eons before by a scent she thought at first was a cruel dream sent to torture her. She uncurled her thick, serpentine body and slithered to the murky stream she burrowed by—as she could never be far from water. Her crime demanded it. Her sentence required it.

The serpent woman's forked tongue flicked between her scarlet-stained lips to taste the brackish stream. She shuddered with distaste. No, the enticing scent wasn't coming from there. Her powerful reptilian muscles contracted as she glided along the muddy bank following the scent. Just as she was about to give up—to believe the aroma was nothing more than a fever dream—she discovered the source of it. From a hole in the bank of the fetid stream poured a luminous liquid. Nure-Onna hardly breathed as she lifted her human torso up, rested her long, white arms on either side of the weeping hole, and flicked her forked tongue out to taste.

Salt water and *blood!* Human blood—*mortal* human blood. She smacked her thin lips and rolled the liquid around in her fanged mouth like it was a fine wine she savored. The blood was not fresh, but it had been so, so long since she'd tasted of the copper succulence that it hardly mattered. She dipped her head and lapped more of it, almost drunk with ecstasy as it filled her mouth and spilled from the corners of her lips to stain the ancient kimono that was all she had left of the distant life she had once lived.

Nure-Onna's scaled body quivered with equal parts need and excitement. From the hole, that widened even as she continued to lap from it, came another odor—that of living things, greenery, fertile earth, clear skies, and *mortals* filled with fresh, delicious blood. The perfume of life beckoned as the bloody conduit before her continued to expand. Even in Jigoku, the Hell she had been sentenced to so many centuries before she had lost count, earth eventually surrendered to water.

Nure-Onna smoothed back her perpetually wet, long, dark hair. Before one of Emma-Ō's minions could stop her, she dived into the tunnel and wriggled against the delicious red tide up and up and up, until her head broke the surface. Using her human arms and hands, she pulled herself from the hole and was astounded to find herself in a world where the sky was clear and as heart-achingly blue as Lake Mashū in the summer. Behind her was a weeping cherry tree that could have grown in her family's garden, though its scent was odd and its leaves withered—but Nure-Onna had no time for trees and skies. Water drew her as surely as did blood. Her forked tongue flicked out, tasting the breeze, which was ripe with a freshwater creek. Moving in an undulating motion, she followed the breeze to the creek. She sighed in pleasure and slithered into the water, submerging herself completely to wash away the foul scent of Jigoku. Underwater, Nure-Onna allowed the creek to guide her. It flowed swiftly, musically, over rocks and sand until it emptied into a lovely lake, framed by greenery. Nure-Onna swam along the shore while she delighted in the freedom she had somehow, miraculously found.

Finally, she surfaced, flung back her long hair, and breathed deeply of the world.

"Living humans!" The perfume of mortals drifted to her on the lazy breeze. Her nose quivered and her forked tongue flicked in and out, in and out, tasting the air.

There were humans close, which is all Nure-Onna needed to know. She must quench her hunger. *She must.* Silently, she swam toward a gentle shoreline. Once there, she contracted the muscles of her massive serpent body. Her torso lifted and her sodden kimono fell to the ground giving her body the appearance of a woman. She glanced down and smoothed the kimono and frowned at the gray tint that had begun to stain her beautiful porcelain skin and blue-green scales. *I do not have long to feed. I must be swift.*

She held out her arms and whispered to the wind, *"Come to me, child."*

A bundle materialized, swaddled and weighted exactly like her son had been that day—that terrible day. Nure-Onna began to sway back and forth and weep brokenly.

"Julie, are you sure you don't want me to stay and help you clean up this mess?" The middle-aged woman paused with the driver's door to her BMW open. "I don't mind at all."

Julie waved her friend away. "No, Marge, you go on home to Frank and get dinner set out for those hungry boys of yours. We got most of this cleared up yesterday, but the Booster Club just can't leave cups and cans around the picnic site like this or the city will start making us pay a cleanup fee to use the Goode Lake grounds. I'll make one more sweep around the BBQ grills, and down to the beach, and then head home myself. My Katie just texted me and said she's making spaghetti dinner for the family tonight, so I'm in no rush to get home."

"You sure raised those kids right, Julie! See you at the PTA meeting Wednesday night!" Marge waved as she pulled out of the gravel parking lot.

Humming her favorite Backstreet Boys song, Julie meandered around the empty picnic grounds as she picked up discarded plastic cups and an occasional paper plate. Satisfied that the site was up to her standards of cleanliness, she headed to Goode Lake's sandy beach—and that's when she heard it. A woman was crying.

No, not just crying. A woman was sobbing as if her heart was broken.

Julie picked up her pace. Someone clearly needed her help—and Julie loved to help. The year before she had even been voted Goodeville's Top Volunteer, something of which she was inordinately proud. As she broke through the row of willows that lined the beach, Julie saw a solitary figure standing at the very edge of the water. She wore a long, silk robe that was tied with a wide cloth belt around her waist. The poor woman was drenched. Her dark hair dripped down her back and though she was turned toward the lake, Julie was sure she held an infant in her arms. Her head was bowed over the child and she wept with such intensity her slender shoulders quaked.

Julie didn't hesitate. She dropped her garbage bag of trash and jogged onto the beach. "Excuse me, are you okay? Do you need help?"

The woman didn't look at her, but she nodded frantically. Between sobs she said, "Yes! My child!"

Her voice broke Julie's heart. She had a terrible feeling that when she reached the woman she would discovery a tragedy. *Oh, please don't let the baby be dead!* Julie hurried to the woman's side. A strange scent came from the woman—like water had diluted meat that was rotten, but Julie shook off the foreboding prickle of warning her intuition tried to give her. "What's wrong? How may I help?"

The woman straightened and Julie could see that she did clutch what appeared to be a swaddled infant in her arms, and there was something wrong with the child. She could only glimpse the top of its little head, but the color was strange—a sickly blue-gray. Then her gaze caught the flesh of the woman's arms where her silk robe had fallen back. They, too, were the same dead gray color.

Dead . . .

Julie shivered and took a small step back. "Honey? Should I call 911?"

In answer the woman finally turned to face her. Terror froze Julie's feet. She stopped breathing. She wanted to run—wanted to scream—but her body refused to obey her as the creature captured her with its reptilian gaze. It slithered to her. Its tongue flicked out—forked and red like new blood. It licked the skin of her neck.

"Yessss, you may help me."

Gray-tinged arms that Julie had sworn had been cradling an infant wrapped around her as the creature opened its mouth to expose long, hooked fangs that dripped with saliva. The thing reared back like a cobra and then it struck Julie's neck with such force it opened an enormous gash from which the serpent began to feed—and Goodeville's Top Volunteer screamed and screamed and screamed until she knew no more.

Acknowledgments

Thank you so much to our awesome Team Cast: Our agents, Ginger Clark and Steven Salpeter, our lovely longtime editor Monique Patterson, and the rest of our very talented team at Wednesday Books/Macmillan, especially Jennifer Enderlin, Anne Marie Tallberg, and our incredible cover art team, marketing, and production staff. We heart you!

#1 *New York Times* and #1 *USA Today* bestselling author P. C. CAST was born in the Midwest, and, after her tour in the USAF, she taught high school for fifteen years before retiring to write full time. P. C. is a member of the Oklahoma Writers Hall of Fame. Her novels have been awarded the prestigious Oklahoma Book Award, YALSA Quick Picks for Reluctant Young Adult Readers, Romantic Times Reviewers' Choice Award, Booksellers' Best Award, and many, many more. Ms. Cast is an experienced teacher and talented speaker who lives in Oregon near her fabulous daughter, her adorable pack of dogs, her crazy Maine coon, and a bunch of horses.

KRISTIN CAST is a #1 *New York Times* and #1 *USA Today* bestselling author who was born in Japan and grew up in Oklahoma, where she explored everything from tattoo modeling to broadcast journalism. After battling addiction, Kristin made her way to the Pacific Northwest and landed in Portland. She rediscovered her passion for storytelling in the stacks at dusty bookstores and in rickety chairs in old coffeehouses. For as long as Kristin can remember, she's been telling stories. Thankfully, she's been writing them down since 2005.